THE MORNING STAR

Also by Karl Ove Knausgaard

A Time for Everything
A Death in the Family: My Struggle Book 1
A Man in Love: My Struggle Book 2
Boyhood Island: My Struggle Book 3
Dancing in the Dark: My Struggle Book 4
Some Rain Must Fall: My Struggle Book 5
The End: My Struggle Book 6
Home and Away: Writing the Beautiful Game (with Fredrik Ekelund)
Autumn (with illustrations by Vanessa Baird)
Winter (with illustrations by Lars Lerin)
Spring (with illustrations by Anna Bjerger)
Summer (with illustrations by Anselm Kiefer)
So Much Longing in So Little Space: The Art of Edvard Munch
In the Land of the Cyclops: Essays

THE MORNING STAR

KARL OVE KNAUSGAARD

Translated from the Norwegian by Martin Aitken

Harvill *Secker*

LONDON

1 3 5 7 9 10 8 6 4 2

Harvill Secker, an imprint of Vintage, is part of the Penguin Random House group of companies whose addresses can be found at global.penguinrandomhouse.com

Penguin
Random House
UK

Copyright © Karl Ove Knausgaard 2020
English translation copyright © Martin Aitken 2021

Karl Ove Knausgaard has asserted his right to be identified as the author of this Work in accordance with the Copyright, Designs and Patents Act 1988

First published by Harvill Secker in 2021
First published with the title *Morgenstjernen* in Norway by Forlaget Oktober, Oslo in 2020

A CIP catalogue record for this book is available from the British Library

penguin.co.uk/vintage

ISBN 9781910701713 (hardback)
ISBN 9781910701720 (trade paperback)

This book was published with the financial assistance of NORLA

NORLA
Norwegian
Literature Abroad

Typeset in 10/15pt Swift LT Std by Jouve (UK), Milton Keynes

Printed and bound in Great Britain by Clays Ltd, Elcograf S.p.A.

The authorised representative in the EEA is Penguin Random House Ireland, Morrison Chambers, 32 Nassau Street, Dublin D02 YH68

The epigraph is from Revelation 9:6

Penguin Random House is committed to a sustainable future for our business, our readers and our planet. This book is made from Forest Stewardship Council® certified paper.

MIX
Paper from
responsible sources
FSC® C018179

And in those days shall men seek death, and shall not find it; and shall desire to die, and death shall flee from them.

FIRST DAY

ARNE

The sudden thought that the boys were asleep in their beds inside the house behind me while the darkness descended on the sea was so pleasant and peaceful that I wouldn't let go of it at first, but tried instead to sustain it and pin down what was good about it.

We'd put the nets out a few hours earlier, so I imagined their hands still smelling of salt. There was no way they would have washed them without me telling them to. They liked to make the transition between being awake and asleep as brief as possible; at any rate, they would pull off their clothes, get under the covers and close their eyes without so much as switching the light off, as long as I didn't intervene with my calls for them to brush their teeth, wash their faces, fold their clothes up neatly on the chair.

Tonight I'd said nothing and they had simply slipped into their beds like some long-limbed, smooth-skinned species of animal.

But that wasn't what had felt so good about the thought.

It had been the idea of the darkness falling independently of them. That they were sleeping as the light outside their rooms retreated from the trees and the forest floor to shimmer faintly for a short while in the sky, before it too darkened and the only light left in the landscape came from the shining moon, spectral in its reflection on the surface of the bay.

Yes, that was it.

That nothing ever stopped, that everything only went on and on, day became night, night became day, summer became autumn, autumn became winter, year followed year, and they were a part of it, at that very moment, as they lay sound asleep in their beds. As if the world were a room they visited.

Across the water, the red beacons on top of the mast winked in the darkness above the trees. Beneath them lights glowed from the summer houses. I swigged a mouthful of wine, then jiggled the bottle to gauge how much was left, unable to see in the gloom. Just under half full.

When I was little, July had been my favourite month. Nothing unusual about that, it was the simplest, most carefree of months, with its long days full of light and warmth. Then, when I became a teenager, it was the autumn I'd liked, the darkness and rain, perhaps because it brought a sense of gravity to life that I found romantic and could measure up to. Childhood was a time for running around immersed in life, youth was the discovery of the peculiar sweetness of death.

Now it was August I liked best. Nothing odd about that either, I thought; I was in midlife, at that juncture in time when things come to completion, when slowly and steadily life's increasing abundance starts to stagnate, on the cusp of its beginning to wane, to tail off into quite as slow a decline.

Oh, August, your darkness and warmth, your sweet plums and scorched grass! Oh, August, your doomed butterflies and sugar-mad wasps!

The wind rose up over the sloping ground. I heard it before I felt it against my skin, and then the leaves in the treetops rustled a moment above my head before settling again. Rather like a person asleep, perhaps, turning over after lying still for a long time. And then quickly descending into deep sleep again.

On the flat rocks at the shore below, a figure came into view. Although from where I sat it was impossible to identify a person from such a shadowy outline, I knew it was Tove. She crossed over their smooth, gently inclining surface onto the jetty and from there onto the path that led up the slope. Not long after, I could hear her come up the grassy bank just below the garden.

I sat quite motionless. If she was alert, she would see me, but it had been days since she'd been alert to anything.

'Arne?' she said, and came to a halt. 'Are you there?'

'I'm here,' I said. 'By the table.'

'Are you sitting here in the dark? Can't you light the lamp?'

'I suppose,' I said, and picked up the lighter from the table. The wick lit up with a deep, clear flame, the light it produced, surprising in its strength, forming a dome of illumination in the murk.

'I could do with a sit-down,' she said.

'Be my guest,' I said. 'Do you want some wine?'

'Have I got a glass?'

'Not here.'

'In that case it doesn't matter,' she said, plonking herself down in the wicker chair opposite me. She was wearing shorts and a cropped top, her feet in a pair of wellies that reached to her knees.

Her face, always on the pudgy side, was swollen from the medication she was taking.

'I'll have some on my own then,' I said, and poured from the bottle. 'Was it a nice walk?'

'Yes. I had an idea along the way. So I hurried back.'

She got to her feet.

'I'll start straight away.'

'On what?'

'A series of pictures.'

'But it's nearly eleven o'clock,' I said. 'You need to sleep as well.'

'I can sleep when I'm dead,' she said. 'This is important. You can look after the boys tomorrow, seeing as you're on holiday. Take them fishing or something.'

When the hell are you going to care about anyone but yourself? I thought, and gazed towards the winking mast.

'Yes, I might,' I said.

'Good,' she said.

I watched her as she crossed the garden to the white annexe at the far end. She switched the light on inside and the windows shone yellow through the looming shadows the darkness had made of the trees and bushes outside.

A moment later she came out again. The shorts she was wearing, and her bare legs in her oversized wellingtons, lent her the appearance of a young girl, I thought. The stark contrast with the top that sat so tightly around her bulky frame, and her drawn and weary expression, immediately filled me with a sense of pity.

'I saw three crabs in the woods,' she said, coming over to the table once more. 'I forgot to mention it when I got back.'

'Some seagulls will have dropped them, I imagine,' I said.

'But they were alive,' she said. 'They were crawling in the under-growth.'

'Are you sure? That they were crabs, I mean? Not some other small creature?'

'Of course I'm sure,' she said. 'I thought it would interest you.'

She turned and went back to the annexe, closing the door behind her. A moment passed, then music came from inside.

I poured the rest of the wine and wondered whether to go to bed or sit for a while. I'd need a sweater if I was going to stay out.

She'd been on a high for days now. The signs were always the same. She'd start emailing and phoning, posting long reports on Facebook, obsessing about things that didn't matter, or at least didn't warrant such concern — housework, for instance — or she would immerse herself completely in some drawn-out project. Another sign was that she became so careless. She would sit on the toilet and leave the door open, or turn the radio up extremely loud, without a thought for anyone else, and if she made dinner, the kitchen would be left like a bombsite.

It annoyed me intensely, all of it. When at last she had some energy, why couldn't she channel it in a way that could benefit us all? At the same time, I often felt sorry for her. She was like a little girl who'd got lost and kept telling herself everything was all right.

But crabs in the woods? How could that be? What kind of creature could have made her mistake it for a crab? Or was it just something she'd imagined?

I smiled as I got to my feet. Standing, I drained the rest of the wine in a single gulp before taking the bottle and glass in my hand and going inside. The warmth of the day still lingered in the rooms. It felt almost like taking a dip, the way the warm air enveloped my face and the bare skin of my arms. That everything was illuminated merely intensified the feeling, as if somehow I'd stepped into a different element.

I put the bottle away with the other empties in the cupboard, consid-ering for a moment whether to bag them and take them out to the car ready to drive to the recycling station the next day, realising all of a sudden what such a number of bottles might look like to someone else's eyes. But there was no reason to do anything about it now, it was eleven o'clock at night, it could wait until tomorrow, I told myself, and rinsed the glass under the tap, rubbing the bottom and rim clean with my fingers, drying it with the tea towel and putting it back on the open shelf above the sink.

There.

A tiny spider was lowering itself from a thread underneath the shelf. It was no bigger than a breadcrumb but looked like it knew exactly what it was doing. It got to about twenty centimetres off the work surface, then stopped and dangled in the air.

At the same moment, a window somewhere in the house banged several times in succession. It sounded like it came from the bathroom, so I went to see. Sure enough, the window was open, flapping with the whims of the wind that was now picking up. It banged back once more against the outside wall, the curtain billowing out in the open space. I gathered it in and shut the window, then stood in front of the mirror and began to brush my teeth. Absently, I pulled up my T-shirt and considered my stomach, finding again that I could no longer identify it as my own; it didn't belong to the man I felt I was. I didn't have what it took to get rid of it, for while I told myself at least several times a day that I needed to lose weight, start running and swimming, it never got to the stage where I actually did anything about it. The question therefore was whether I could turn it into something positive.

The worst thing to do was try to hide it, wear big shirts and baggy trousers in the belief that no one would notice as long as no bulging fat was visible. What was visible instead was a fat man with his shame. In fact, what you saw was more than just a fat man, it was somebody real, whose most personal, intimate sphere had been embarrassingly breached.

I spat the toothpaste out in the sink, rinsed my mouth with water directly from the tap and put the toothbrush back in the glass on the shelf.

Was it not manly to be big? Was it not masculine to possess weight?

The wind rushed in the leaves outside, tugging at the branches of the trees and shrubs; now and then a gust would cause the old walls of the house to creak. It would start raining soon, I thought, and went into the living room, turning off the lights before going upstairs and looking in on the boys. The air inside their room was still warm, the sun had shone in all afternoon, and they were both lying on top of their duvets,

Asle's bunched up in the tangle of his arms and legs, the ceiling lamp throwing its light on them.

They were even more alike when they slept, for much of what set them apart from each other was a matter of behaviour, the way they did different things, the way they held and turned their heads, moved their hands, furrowed their brows, or the way they said things, the nuances of their voices, the tone in which a question would be posed. Now they were just bodies and faces, and as such almost completely alike.

I still hadn't got used to it, for although their likeness was no longer something I tended to think about that much, I would always become so keenly aware of it in moments like this, when suddenly I saw them, not as two individuals, but as two versions of the same body.

I put the light out and went into the bedroom at the other end of the house, undressed and got into bed to read. But I'd had too much to drink, and after a few sentences I closed the book and switched off the lamp. Not that I was drunk, the sentences and their meaning didn't swim about like that; it was more that the alcohol had softened my will, weakened it and made it almost impossible to mobilise even the small measure of effort required to read a novel.

It was so much better to lie with eyes closed and allow the mind to wander wherever it wanted, in softness and darkness.

In the daytime there was something hard and edgy about what I contained, something dry and barren, as if I comprised some singular realm of the negative, where so much was about desisting, declining, abstaining. The wine made up for it; the hardness, the edginess didn't go away, it was just no longer so all-consuming. Like seaweed when the tide has gone out and it's been lying there on the rocks, dried up by the sun, and then the water rises again: the way the seaweed feels then! When it senses the cold, salty water lifting it up; when it waves back and forth in that wondrous, replenishing element and all its surfaces become soft and moist once more . . .

Wavering in the zone immediately beyond conscious thought, where a person may drift in and out for several minutes before sleep eventually kicks in, I thought I could hear raindrops against the window and roof, as if foregrounded in the unremitting rush of the trees and bushes in the garden, the more distant washing of the waves down in the bay.

I was woken by Tove's voice.

'Arne!' she was shouting. 'Arne, come quick!'

I sat bolt upright. She was in the hall below, and the first thing that came to my mind was that she would wake up the boys.

'Something's happened,' she shouted. 'Come quick!'

'Yes, I'm coming,' I said, as I pulled on my shirt and hurried down the stairs.

She was standing in the doorway in her shorts and wellies. She was crying.

'What's happened?' I said.

She opened her mouth as if to say something, but not a sound came out.

'Tove,' I said. 'What's happened?'

She gestured for me to follow her. We went over to the annexe, through the passage and into the living room.

One of the kittens was lying on the floor there, fluffy and fine. But it wasn't moving, and when I went towards it I saw that it was lying in a little pool of blood.

It was still alive, I realised, for then it twitched its paw.

The other kitten was standing a bit further away, looking at it.

'I didn't see it,' Tove said. 'I trod on it. I feel so terrible.'

I looked at her, then crouched down to the kitten. Blood had run from its mouth and ears, and it lay with eyes closed, now scraping the floor with its paw.

'Can't you do something?' she said. 'Take it to the vet's in the morning?'

'We must put it out of its misery,' I said, getting to my feet. 'I'll fetch a hammer or something.'

'Not a hammer, surely?' she said.

'There's nothing else we can do,' I said, and went off to the kitchen in the main house. I'd never killed an animal before, in fact I could barely do away with a fish, and I felt vaguely sick as I opened the drawer and took out the hammer.

When I returned to the annexe, the kitten moved its head slightly, though its eyes were still closed. A kind of spasm went through its little body. I crouched down beside it again and gripped the rubber handle of the hammer tightly in my hand. I was filled with disquiet at the thought of how the skull would smash beneath its point when I struck.

Tove had stepped back and stood watching.

The kitten was quite still now.

Cautiously, I stroked an index finger over the fur on its head. It didn't react.

'Is it dead?' Tove said.

'I think so,' I said.

'What are we going to do with it?' she said. 'What are we going to tell the boys?'

'I'll bury it in the garden somewhere,' I said. 'We can tell them it's disappeared.'

I stood up and only then became aware that I was in my underpants.

'I didn't see it,' she said. 'It just got under my feet all of a sudden.'

'It's OK,' I said. 'It's not your fault.'

I went towards the door.

'Where are you going?' she said.

'To put some clothes on, then I'll go and bury it.'

'All right,' she said.

'Can't you go to bed?' I said.

'I won't be able to sleep now.'

'Can't you try?'

She shook her head.

'It's no use.'

'Maybe if you take another tablet?'

'It won't help.'

'OK,' I said, and went out into the rain, crossed the grass between the two buildings, put my trousers on in the bedroom, found my raincoat on the peg in the little extension where we kept the spade too, and went back to the annexe.

Tove was sitting at the table cutting up a sheet of red paper with a pair of scissors. Beside her was a sheet of stiffer card on which she'd already glued some red figures.

I left her to it, put the spade down on the floor, and lifted the kitten cautiously onto its blade then carried it outside like that, on the blade of the spade, held out in front of me.

The tree branches swayed like boat masts in the darkness. The air was filled with rain, heavy drops cast on the gusting wind. I stopped by a cluster of fruit bushes in a corner of the garden, laid the kitten on the ground and thrust the spade into the upper layer of bark chips and soil. When the hole was dug some minutes later, my hair was wet through, my hands freezing cold.

The kitten was still warm, I could feel it as I picked it up and put it in the hole.

How was it possible?

I began to shovel the earth on top, only then it seemed to move.

Was it alive?

No, it was a muscular spasm, I reasoned, and filled in the earth until the body was completely buried, patting it down and sprinkling some bark over the grave so as not to arouse the boys' curiosity if for some reason they happened to come near the next day.

I hung my wet coat back on the peg, watched the soil colour the water brown for a few seconds as it ran towards the drain when I washed my hands, went upstairs into the bedroom, took off my clothes and got into bed again.

The thought that the kitten had been alive when I buried it refused to let go of me. It didn't help in the slightest telling myself it was only a spasm, all I could see in my mind was it lying there under the soil with its eyes open, unable to move.

Should I go out and dig it up again?

It too was a creature of the world.

What kind of a life had it lived here?

A few weeks in a room with wooden floorboards before being consigned to the cold, dark earth where it couldn't move, only to remain there until it died, all on its own.

What was the meaning of such a life?

Oh, for crying out loud, it was just a cat. And if it hadn't been dead when I buried it, it certainly would be now.

The next morning I woke up to the sounds of the television downstairs. It was just after eight, I noted, and sat up in bed. The wind had died down, everything was quiet outside. The sky I saw through the window was grey and so heavy with moisture that the clouds seemed to hang just above the trees across the bay.

A film of perspiration covered my skin. But I wasn't in the mood for a shower, and anyway one of the pleasures of being on holiday was not having to bother about appearances.

I got dressed and went downstairs into the kitchen where I drank two glasses of water while standing at the sink. Out in the garden the trees stood motionless. Their thick, green foliage glistened green in all the grey.

'Are you hungry in there?' I called out.

There was no answer, so I went in to see what they were doing. They were lying on the big corner sofa, each under his own blanket. Asle had his feet up on the wall and had twisted his body into what looked like a very uncomfortable position in order to see the television, whereas Heming was lying on his stomach, stretched out along the backrest.

'Are you ill?' I said.

They removed their rugs without looking at me, knowing full well how much I disliked them wrapping themselves in blankets or duvets in the daytime. In fact, it amazed me that they hadn't taken them off as soon as they'd heard me coming down the stairs.

'Are you hungry?'

'Not really,' said Asle.

'A bit,' said Heming.

Well, you'll need to get some food inside you,' I said. 'We're going out to check the nets this morning.'

'Do we have to?' Asle said.

'Come on,' I said. 'You helped put them out. It's only right you should bring them in as well! Think what you might have caught!'

'The water's so cold,' said Asle.

'Can't we just do nothing today?' said Heming.

'What do you mean, the water's cold? We're not going swimming!'

They said nothing but fixed their eyes on the TV.

'Listen,' I said, 'I'll fry us some eggs and bacon and then make some cocoa, OK? After that we'll go out and bring the nets in, and then you can do what you want for the rest of the day. All right?'

'OK, then,' said Asle.

'Heming?'

'OK, OK.'

What had happened the night before seemed so oddly remote as I went back into the kitchen, as if it belonged to some other reality from the one I occupied now. The darkness, the wind, the rain. Tove's despair, the dead kitten, the blood on the floor, the spade, the soil, the grave in which, possibly, it had been buried alive.

Where was she now, anyway?

A jolt of anxiety went through me. I felt an urge to run out and see, to dash from room to room in search of her, but when I did go out into the hall and put my shoes on to cross over to the annexe, my movements were slow and measured, not wanting to alert the boys to something perhaps being wrong.

Strangely, the air outside was as warm as it had been the day before, even though the sun hadn't come out.

The door of the annexe was ajar. Usually she made a point of shutting things properly and locking up after her; it bordered on a disorder, her compulsive need to make sure she was safe, but in the state she was in at the moment everything tipped over in the opposite direction.

The living room was empty. I opened the bedroom door, but she wasn't there either. Then I went up into the loft, finding her lying motionless on one of the beds under the sloping walls.

'Tove?'

She didn't answer.

My heart thumped as if I were about to plunge from a great height.

I stepped slowly towards her.

'Tove?'

'Mm?' she said from the depths of sleep.

So everything was all right!

'It's OK, go back to sleep,' I said, and drew a blanket over her before going back down the stairs. The table was covered with sheets of card with the red figures she'd been cutting out glued on. I paused and studied them for a moment.

Some looked like the figures found in the ancient Nordic petroglyphs; there were primitive boats and men with erect penises, and some resembled Matisse's ring of dancing figures, only with the legs of animals. One of them was a human on horseback, formed as if it were a single creature; another picture showed a number of foxes, while yet another seemed simply to be red dots, and not until I picked it up did I realise they were ladybirds.

On the table underneath all this was a piece of paper on which she'd written the words *I want to fuck Egil* three times on separate lines, one below the other.

Oh, for God's sake, I thought to myself, but left it where it was, covering it with the sheet of card with the ladybirds on in case the boys happened to come in, glancing up the stairs at the same time to make sure she hadn't caught me looking.

Was it too a part of what she was working on? A strategy, perhaps, to open up the sluices of her subconscious? Was that what she was thinking?

But Egil, of all people.

Jesus Christ. Do you have to be such a bloody idiot, Tove?

The blood from the kitten was still on the floor. Best clean it up before the boys get wind, I thought. Only not now. Now there were eggs and bacon to be fried, bread to be toasted, cocoa to be made.

The lawn, a sheen of moisture, lay like a floor between the trees and flower beds.

I got the breakfast things out of the fridge and discovered there was only one egg left in the box.

I wanted to keep my promise to the boys and decided to cycle down to the shop. I could have asked them to go, only it would have allowed them to say it didn't matter and I'd have looked weak then, letting them have their way, or, if I stuck to my guns, it could have led to a situation where I'd force them to go so as not to lose face, something that could dent the mood for hours to come, perhaps even the whole day. It wasn't worth it. Especially since we were going fishing afterwards.

I went into the living room to tell them.

'Just popping down the shop,' I said.

'Where's Mum?' said Asle.

'Mum's still asleep,' I said. 'Is there anything you want from the shop? Apart from ice cream, that is?'

'Yes, ice cream!' said Heming.

'No, you're not getting ice cream,' I said. 'How about orange juice?'
They didn't answer.

'OK, back in a bit, then,' I said, and went out into the hall, put my shoes and coat on, went to the shed and wheeled the bike out.

Our house was at the end of an unpaved road; or actually, the road continued into the woods, though it dwindled there to more of a track, barely passable for a car at all. Further up was the house belonging to Kristen, a funny old sort who'd always lived on his own and made solitude an art: he'd built everything down there himself, even the boat he used for fishing.

In the other direction were several houses much like our own, most of them only used in summer or at other holiday times. I knew most of the people who owned them, though it had been a while since I'd had anything to do with them. Most had gone back home now, at least it looked that way judging by the empty parking areas outside their houses.

The many potholes were filled with rainwater, cloudy, brimming puddles that made me think of the 1980s, when they'd seemed so common in the autumn and winter, whereas now anyone would think they'd been abolished by law. The gravel, wet and soft-looking, gleamed here and there like silver between the reddish outcrops of rock and the green conifers past which the road wound its way.

I hoped it would be gone when she woke up, whatever it was that had affected her like that.

Or did I?

If it carried on, it would soon spiral out of control and eventually she'd have to be put in the hospital.

There was something definitive about it, something concrete and unyielding. And that was a good thing. For the problem was always a matter of boundaries. Hers, mine, the children's. It was impossible to say exactly when the illness took over, it was more of a slow slide along the scale, from good cheer and well-being to something that pulled her further and further away from us, and we went along with it, passively accepting a situation which from the outside wasn't acceptable at all, because we weren't on the outside, we were inside, where the boundaries became so gradually displaced that we barely noticed it was happening.

It was like that too because I covered for her, shielding her from the kids and the world outside.

And then, whenever she was admitted to hospital, everyone could suddenly see how mad she was, how much I had to do on my own.

I cycled past the two outcrops of rock that at one point flanked the road. When I was a boy they made me imagine I was sailing a boat between two islands, and when I was a young and pretentious under-graduate I'd given them names: Scylla and Charybdis. After that, there was a bend before the road fell steeply away towards the shop and the little marina. Once, I'd come off my bike on that hill and split my head open — nobody wore helmets in those days, and I hadn't really learned to ride a bike properly either — but the recollection I had of it was probably false, based on what I'd been told rather than on my own experience. It was impossible to know one way or the other.

I gently applied the rear brake as I went downhill, remembering the other kids gathered around me, the ambulance that had come, at the exact spot where I was now, only forty years earlier.

The shop at that time had gone from being a small store to a small supermarket, to what it was now, a hub with a supermarket, a fast-food outlet, a cafe and a souvenir shop. At the rear was a filling station with petrol and diesel pumps, and next to that a low building containing showers and toilets for the tourists who came in their sailing boats. Tjæreholmen Marina, it was called.

I parked my bike and went inside, picking up one of the red baskets and filling it with a bag full of freshly baked rolls, some butter and milk, and then the eggs that were the reason I'd come.

A man wearing shorts and a T-shirt, a baseball cap pushed back from his forehead, stood at the checkout putting his items onto the conveyor belt as I approached. He turned slightly as I came up behind him, then fished a credit card out of his back pocket and inserted it into the reader, before turning again.

'Arne?' he said.

I didn't know who he was.

'Yes?' I said.

'Long time, no see,' he said with a smile.

I looked at him without saying anything.

There was something about his eyes.

'Don't recognise me, eh?'

'Well . . .' I said.

'Trond Ole,' he said.

'Oh!' I blurted out. 'I'd never have guessed! What are you doing here?'

'We've bought a place over on the other side. It's our first summer here.'

He turned back and entered his PIN, waited a few seconds until the transaction was approved, then went to the end of the checkout to bag his items as I placed mine on the conveyor.

'What are you doing with yourself these days, anyway?' I said.

'Workwise, you mean?' he said without looking up.

'Yes,' I said.

'I'm off sick at the moment,' he said. 'How about you?'

'I'm at the uni.'

'Professor, is it?' he said, looking at me now.

I felt my cheeks go warm.

'Yes, as a matter of fact.'

He smiled.

'I was here with you once, do you remember?'

He stood with his bulging carrier bag in his hand as I collected my items.

'Of course,' I said. 'We'd have been what, ten?'

'Something like that.'

We went outside. He pressed his key and the lights on one of the cars in the car park flashed twice.

'Have you got much holiday left?' he said.

'Into the last week now,' I said.

'Then come over one night,' he said.

'Maybe I will,' I said. 'It'd be nice.'

We shook hands and he went over to his car while I unlocked my bike, hung the carrier bag on the handlebar and began walking up the steep hill.

'Arne?' he called after me.

I turned and saw him come half trotting towards me.

'I should give you my number. Or you could give me yours.'

'Of course, how stupid,' I said. 'Maybe I could have yours?'

That would be best. I wouldn't actually have to phone him.

I entered the number he dictated and added him to my contacts.

'OK,' I said. 'I'll be in touch!'

'If you call me now, I'll have yours too,' he said.

'Good idea,' I said, and pressed his number.

The boys were gawping at the TV when I got back. Tove was nowhere to be seen. I put the bike in the shed and went through the glistening garden, cracked an egg into the frying pan and then another, watched them advance across the surface until the heat took hold and they each solidified into a little mound, poured some milk into a saucepan, cut some slices of bread and put them in the toaster.

Trond Ole had come out here with us one weekend before school had broken up for the holidays; we were friends that year and I'd been looking forward to showing him everything there was to see in the area.

We'd stolen some of my dad's booze and gone off into the woods with it, drunk a few sips with pounding hearts and then reeled about like we were drunk.

Could we have been ten years old then?

More like twelve or so, I thought to myself, slipping the spatula underneath one of the eggs, which balanced stiffly on the metal blade as I lifted it over to the plate.

The yolk in the middle and the white all around looked like a planet with a milky atmosphere.

The whole episode had been fraught with anxiety. We'd been nervous as hell pouring the alcohol into the little plastic bananas from our bags of sweets after we'd emptied the sherbet out of them, filled with trepidation as we stood among the trees and drank it, and scared witless the rest of the evening in case we gave ourselves away.

But neither Mum nor Dad had said anything, and afterwards we could boast about it at school on the Monday.

The toast popped up with a snap, and the milk started to froth in the saucepan, swelling with little indentations. I pulled it away from the heat, mixed some cocoa and sugar with water in a glass, then poured the concentrated substance into the opaque white liquid, where for a moment it diffused, the dark brown colour thinning into the milk until the two were one.

Someone was in the room.

I wheeled round.

It was Heming. He stood there with his bare legs, arms hanging down at his sides like an ape, staring at me.

'Oh, it's you,' I said.

'Will breakfast be ready soon?' he said.

'Yes. Are you hungry?'

He nodded.

'Can you set the table, then?'

'Where's Mum?'

'Mum's asleep.'

'No, she isn't,' he said. 'I saw her. She went past the window.'

'Perhaps she just went for a walk before breakfast,' I said. 'Come on, set the table, chop-chop!'

'If I have to, then Asle has to as well.'

'Of course,' I said, snatching the toast from the toaster, then the bread basket from on top of the cupboard, dropping the hot toast into it as I peered out of the window to see if I could see her. 'You go and tell him.'

While the boys set the places, I fried the bacon, poured the cocoa into some mugs, got the butter out, the cheese and the ham, and put everything on the table.

'Aren't we going to wait for Mum?' Heming said when we sat down, then abruptly jerked his head back and opened his mouth wide three times in quick succession.

I forced myself to take a deep breath and halt the impulse to correct him.

'We should eat while the food's still hot,' I said.

'Where's she gone?' said Asle, half rising from his chair as he reached for the bread basket.

'For a walk, that's all,' I said.

'Is she coming with us to bring in the nets?' said Heming.

'I don't know,' I said.

I visualised the room as it had been that summer forty years ago: dismal, with dark walls, and dark rugs on the floor. The drinks cabinet in the corner with the bottles inside. We'd been careful and made sure to close it after us, but we'd transferred the alcohol into our little plastic receptacles without removing the bottle from the cabinet and it has been impossible to avoid spilling.

When you're a child you think you have secrets and no one knows what you're up to.

I smiled.

'What are you smiling at, Daddy?' said Asle.

'Just something I thought about,' I said.

'What was it?' said Heming, spreading butter on his toast, which broke apart as he drew the knife across.

'I was thinking about your grandfather,' I said.

And then I saw Tove come through the garden and disappear into the annexe. She was wearing the same clothes as the night before. Fortunately, both the boys were sitting with their backs turned.

I needed to clean up the blood before they went in there.

'What was it about Grandad that was so funny?' said Heming.

'Nothing in particular,' I said. 'I just thought about him, that's all. He did do a lot of stupid things in his time, though!'

'Like what?' said Asle, lifting his toast from his plate.

'Lots of things I've already told you about,' I said. 'For instance, the time he mistook the salt and the sugar and sugared the cod. Or the time he chopped the big tree down in front of the house and it fell onto the roof and smashed it to smithereens.'

'Was there anyone inside?' said Asle, his lips yellow with egg yolk.

I shook my head.

'Luckily, no!'

'Did you see it?'

'I saw it when I came home. The tree was gone by then. It looked like a giant had come and sat down on top of the house.'

'You've done lots of stupid things as well,' said Heming, looking at me with those dark eyes of his.

'Yes, I'm sure I have,' I said. 'Was there anything in particular you were thinking about?'

'That time you forgot to moor the pontoon we had and it drifted out with all the boats attached.'

'I didn't forget,' I said. 'I just didn't moor it properly, that's all.'

'And when there was no oil in the car engine, so it broke down and we had to buy a new car.'

'That wasn't me, it was the gauge that was faulty!' I said. 'As well you both know! A car's supposed to tell you when it's run out of oil.'

'That's just an excuse,' said Heming.

They looked at each other and laughed.

It made me glad.

Tove wasn't in the annexe when I opened the door and went inside after we'd eaten, the boys safely absorbed in their devices. There were more sheets of card on the table now, red with black cut-out silhouettes glued on. She wouldn't be able to concentrate much longer. Unless she levelled off and came down on her own.

The blood had congealed and hardened. I scraped it away with a palette knife before soaking what remained and scrubbing it with a stiff brush.

The other kitten lay on the floor in the corner, staring at me.

I rinsed the cloth and washed away the scrapings in the sink in her studio. The space was a clutter of paint-spattered glass jars, paintbrushes, cotton pads and empty tubes, and the air inside smelled strongly of turpentine. I went back out into the garden to see if the grave I'd dug the night before could be seen, half preparing myself for the eventuality that the kitten had scrabbled its way to the surface and left behind an empty hole, but of course everything looked the same as it had done when I'd left it, and it was impossible to tell that the soil underneath the layer of bark chips had recently been dug up.

A light drizzle filled the air. Not refreshing, the way you'd expect from a Nordic summer day, but clammy and warm. Tropical, almost. And everything around me was damp, from the grey-black trunks of the trees to the green leaves of the redcurrant and blackcurrant bushes, where the moisture had collected in tiny, unmoving droplets.

The sound of a heavy vehicle accelerating in the distance passed through the landscape.

I went back into the kitchen and cleared away the breakfast things. A wave of noise rose outside as the bus approached. On such a narrow road it was a monstrosity, I thought as it went past the window, its yellow side momentarily blotting out the view.

I dropped a tab of detergent into the little compartment in the dishwasher, closed the door and switched it on. The bus swung round in the turning space at the end of the road and came back the other way. I noticed the little spider again, now at work on some construction in the corner between the ceiling and the wall. Dad always said spiders were a good sign, it meant the house was dry, and I thought of it nearly every time I saw one.

Ingvild came along the path outside. She was looking down at the ground ahead of her and was carrying a bag slung over one shoulder.

I went out into the hall when she came in.

'Did you have a nice time?' I said.

'Yes, very,' she said, and smiled before bending down to take off her shoes.

'Do you want some breakfast?' I said.

'I had something at Gran's,' she said, and went off to her room.

'All right, then,' I said.

I stood quite still for a moment in the middle of the kitchen and looked around me before getting some plastic bags out of the drawer, putting the empty bottles in them and carrying them out to the car. I opened the boot and dumped them inside for the next time I happened to be near the recycling station, as tips were called now. Then I went back into the house, to the boys in the living room.

'Are you all ready, then?' I said.

'Do we have to?' said Heming.

He threw his head back and opened and closed his mouth in rapid succession.

'Why do you keep doing that?' I said, irritated.

'What?' he said.

I mimicked his tic, only more exaggeratedly.

'You keep going like this all the time,' I said. 'It's bad manners.'

He nodded earnestly.

'I'll try not to,' he said.

'Good!' I said.

And then he did it again.

'Come on, let's get going,' I said.

With the red fuel can in my hand, I followed the boys down the steep grassy bank to the jetty. The water that stretched out before us lay quite still beneath the low canopy of heavy cloud. The planks of the jetty, slippery with moisture, were a yellowy sheen against the water's glittering silver and the dark, near-black rock they traversed.

I got in the boat and coupled the hose to the fuel can while Heming let go of the moorings and Asle raised the oar ready to push off and propel us a few metres into deeper water.

The inside of the bay, which petered out into a little pebbled shore, was teeming with crabs. Not just little stone crabs, but big sea crabs. There seemed to be hundreds of them, creeping and crawling on top of each other.

I'd never seen anything like it.

It was like a snake pit.

I looked away so the boys wouldn't notice, and once Asle had pushed us out I started the outboard and set off without them having seen anything.

The two red floats weren't far from the shore on the other side of the bay, just off the headland. The spruce stood like a wall of green almost at the water's edge. Asle hooked the first float with the gaff and pulled it in. I killed the engine. The boys began to draw in the net, pulling and heaving on the rope, but without getting anywhere. They both looked at me.

'It's too heavy,' said Asle.

'Let me,' I said. 'Maybe we've got ourselves a shoal of mackerel or something.'

It felt like pulling up a great, sopping carpet. A few moments later, the net itself came into view below the surface, the bodies of the fish inside it like green-white lanterns in the gloom.

'Pollock,' I said as the net came over the side with the first of the fish.

'Whoa, look how many!' said Heming.

'You two take the fish out of the net as they come in, all right?' I said. 'Just throw them in the tub.'

There was no end to it, the net was thick with pollock, and when at last we headed back not only was the tub full of smooth, shimmering fish that occasionally flapped violently, the bottom of the boat too was covered with them.

It made me feel queasy. Not the fish themselves, because individually they were just creatures like any other, but the sheer number of them. All their identical eyes, all their identical gaping mouths, all their identical fins and vents.

'Are you going to gut them all?' said Asle.

'I suppose so,' I said. 'But I don't know what we're going to do with so many fish.'

'Can't we freeze them?'

'Yes, we'll have to. But we're going home in two days. I'm not sure we'll want to be eating year-old fish next summer.'

'Fish-flavoured ice cream!' said Asle.

'Mm, delicious,' said Heming.

'Did you count them?' I said.

'A hundred and eighteen,' said Asle.

We were approaching the bay when a figure came out of the garden at the top of the bank and started down the path towards the jetty.

It was Egil.

He was wearing a yellow waterproof, unbuttoned, and holding a white carrier bag in one hand.

I switched the outboard off and we slid in next to the jetty. Happily, the crabs seemed to be gone. The boys clambered up onto the decking, I handed them the fuel can and lifted the tub up to them, moored the boat and then climbed ashore myself.

'Quite a catch, I see,' said Egil, who had now reached the jetty too.

'You're telling me,' I said. 'Do you fancy some?'

He shook his head and gave a faint smile.

'Have you just got home now, or what?' I said.

'Last night. Brought you this. A token for your help.'

He handed me the carrier bag a bit sheepishly. I didn't need to open it to know what was inside; both its weight and size told me it was a bottle, and since he liked a good whisky himself, and presumably reckoned on

me offering him a glass after he'd made the effort to come and give it to
me, the only question was which brand.

'Excellent!' I said. 'Thanks, indeed!'

'Dad, can we go now?' Asle said.

I nodded and off they went, scampering up the slope.

'Time for a coffee?' I said.

'Love one, thanks,' Egil said. 'Do you want that bringing up?'

He indicated the tub.

'Afraid so,' I said. 'And the ones in the boat as well.'

'I'll give you a hand,' he said.

Between us, we lugged the tub up the hill. There was something
unpleasantly intimate about it, working together like that, it was as if
we were joined up, and I couldn't find the words that would make it
any more tolerable. And Egil wouldn't say anything.

Did he feel the same way?

It was impossible to say, Egil was a person I'd never been able to
fathom.

As we put the tub down in the cellar, I insisted on fetching the rest
of the fish myself and said he could put his feet up in my study until I
got back.

Had she had her eye on him, been thinking about him, fantasising about
him when he'd come round? Or was it just an impulse from the depths
of her tormented soul?

I went and got a fish crate from the boathouse, one of the old ones
made of polystyrene, and started putting the fish in it.

In a funny kind of way it had made sense to see what she'd written
about Egil. He was a person who'd ground to a halt in life, no longer
going anywhere, but with a firm footing where he stood. He was a capable man in many ways, but quite unable to apply himself, and now his
aptitude simply lay there with no earthly use, like a field left fallow.
Her father had been exactly the same. Just as lackadaisical and as
unpurposed. Knew everything, did nothing. When Tove and I first got
together, I'd been the antidote to all that, so I reasoned, someone with
a healthy, innocent outlook, and highly ambitious. She wanted away

from what she came from, wanted something new and normal and quite ordinary. And that's what she got: first came Ingvild, then the twins, and our early years together with them had been as ordinary and as normal as it gets.

Why else would she have fallen for me, an otherwise unexceptional student of literature? She could have had whoever she wanted.

Had she actually wanted something different all along?

Had she only been pretending, to herself and to me?

I put the crate down on the cement floor of the dim cellar. The fish ought to be gutted straight away. Still, a couple of hours wouldn't make much difference.

First Egil, then dinner. Gut the fish, and after that a quiet evening with a glass of wine and a book.

Anyway, there was nothing to be done about it now.

The best thing was not to give it another thought.

I washed my cold, gooey hands in hot water, fetched two glasses and went into the study, finding Egil standing in front of the bookshelves with a book in his hand.

'What's that you've found?' I said.

He held up the volume so I could see. *O, Death! Where is thy Sting?* it was called, from the thirties sometime, the once white dust jacket now yellowed.

'Oh, that,' I said. 'Join me?'

He nodded, I poured for us both, and we sat down. A small sound of contentment escaped him as he took the first sip.

'It's not one I bought myself,' I said. 'The book, that is. I seem to remember my dad laying his hands on it at an auction years ago, somewhere inland, a box full of books from someone's estate. Do you know the story? The Køber case?'

'Yes. Never read his books though.'

'They're fascinating. Full of progressive optimism, and they transform the idea of life after death, or contact with the dead, into something rational and scientific.'

'He lost his sons, didn't he?'

'That's right. And then he was reunited with them through his daughter, a medium.'

'Hm,' said Egil, turning the glass in his hand.

'There're some very lovely descriptions of the afterlife in there,' I said. 'The kingdom of the dead is like Fredrikstad in the 1920s.'

'Perhaps he was right,' he said, and smiled.

There was a lull. The bushes outside had grown greedily up the wall and now blocked out the window almost completely; the road and the rocky, sparsely vegetated upland beyond it were visible only through little peepholes in the foliage.

'I was in India once,' he said without looking at me. 'In one of the cities I visited they'd been burning bodies on the same pyre for three thousand years. That's what they said, anyway. A temple city, it was. I can't think of anywhere in the world that could be so different from here.'

He made a sweep of his arm to indicate that he was referring to these houses, this landscape. His gestures were sometimes grand like that, which always seemed so odd in view of his normally hesitant manner.

'So I don't think the kingdom of the dead *there* can be much like Fredrikstad, not exactly.'

He smiled again.

'I've never much wanted to go to India,' I said. 'China, yes. Japan, yes. But India? Skinny cows and diarrhoea?'

'There are so many people there,' he said. 'People everywhere. Some places look like the streets in *Blade Runner*. A concoction of animals and people and high technology.'

'You know India's overtaking China now in terms of population?' I said. 'And they're rising up the table of the world's biggest economies. Everyone talks about China, but India's where it's all happening. Or at least it's happening there too.'

'Perhaps,' he said. 'But it's the poverty that's so striking. It takes it out of you, seeing all that suffering. It's such a spiritual culture, everything's in the hands of the gods, so they accept poverty in a completely different way.'

Again, there was a lull. Egil was a big, thickly built man with next to no charisma, comfortable in conversation, attentive to what others had to say, but never stamping his mark, avoiding anything that might be difficult.

Gutless, many would say.

Too nice for his own good, I thought now. But I liked him all the same. It hardly mattered what book or film I talked about, he'd read it or seen it.

He smiled to himself and drained his drink.

'Anyway, how's the book going?' he said, still without looking at me.

'It's coming along,' I said, leaning forward to pick up the bottle, pouring him another in the glass he held out almost simultaneously, and then one for myself.

Why had I told him about my book? It was a huge, huge mistake. But I'd been drunk and it had felt as if the book was nearly finished then, and bloody good at that.

'Smoke, if you want,' I said. 'I'll get you an ashtray.'

I got to my feet and went out into the kitchen. Tove was there. She was staring out of the window, her hands flat against the work surface.

'How are you feeling?' I said.

'Is that Egil you're talking to?' she asked without turning round.

'Yes,' I said.

'Why didn't you come and get me? He's my friend too.'

'I didn't know where you were,' I said. 'Anyway, I thought you were busy.'

She turned now and looked at me, her face expressionless, before leaving the room. A moment later I heard her voice in the study.

The sky further out over the sea had cleared up and was blue with patches of thin white cloud, not grey and heavy as it was above the land. I thought I'd give them a few minutes on their own and stood looking out. A magpie flew down from the apple tree and landed on the grass, where it stalked a few steps, like a man with his hands behind his back, a man who saw something and bent down to see what it was.

Gulls cried down at the bay, while a muffled, irregular thud repeated at the rear of the house. It sounded like the boys were playing football.

I went into the empty living room and looked out of the window there. Sure enough, there they were on the lawn, kicking the ball about between them.

A feeling of satisfaction came over me and then vanished again.

I went through the house and knocked on Ingvild's door.

'Yes?' she said from inside, her voice lacklustre. I opened the door and went in. She was lying on her stomach with her laptop closed in front of her.

'What are you up to?' I said.

'Nothing,' she said.

I could have asked her why she closed her laptop the minute I came in, only then she would feel like I was accusing her of something, and I wanted to talk to her, so I didn't mention it.

'How were things with Granny?' I said.

'Good, I think,' she said, and sat up. 'She gets mixed up sometimes, but it's been like that for a while now.'

'What did she do this time?'

'Forgot the buns in the oven. And then she'll forget she's said something and say it again. She's still all there, though, apart from that.'

I sat down on the sofa.

'It's nice of you to go and see her,' I said.

'Yes,' she said.

'How are you getting on, anyway?'

She looked at me exasperatedly. It was something I asked her a lot, apparently.

'Fine!' she said, giving me a stare before looking away.

'Good,' I said. 'Anything on your mind?'

She shook her head with a smile.

'Were the plums ripe?' I said.

'Mm,' she said.

'The yellow ones?'

'Mm.'

'They're the best plums in the world,' I said. 'A really old strain, did you know that?'

'So you've said.'

I stood up.

'Egil's here,' I said. 'Thought I'd hear how you were getting on, that's all.'

'I'm getting on fine.'

'Great, then!' I said. 'Fish for dinner. OK?'

'Sure,' she said.

When I went into the study again, Tove was sitting in my chair and Egil was as before, now with a cigarette in his hand. He was using one of our old coffee cups for an ashtray. I put the ashtray down next to it, took the spindleback chair from in front of the desk and sat down.

Tove was telling one of her stories. Her face was lit up from inside, her hazel eyes gleaming, and she laughed as she spoke.

Egil was looking at her, smiling.

I took a slurp of my whisky and ran my eyes over the books on the shelves. She was telling him about a dinner party she'd been to with some artists, how everything had gone quiet at the table when a detractor of a prominent figure among them had suddenly turned up. The only thing the host could do was find him a chair. When he sat down, opposite the prominent artist, the chair had collapsed and he'd fallen on his behind.

Tove mimicked the prominent artist.

'*Beware the spells I cast,*' she said, deepening her voice.

She laughed until her eyes watered.

'Can I cadge a smoke?' I said, looking at Egil.

'Of course,' he said, and shoved the packet across the little coffee table.

Tove was still laughing.

Egil chuckled too.

I lit a cigarette, my first in six years, and inhaled cautiously.

Tove did her best to settle, breathing deeply in and out a couple of times, only then to burst out laughing again. She was in hysterics.

Egil glanced at me rather uneasily.

Tove got up and left the room. We heard her laughing as she went through the corridor, the door of the bathroom shutting, her laughter continuing, muffled then, though still clearly audible, great waves of laughter, with pauses in between.

'She's in a good mood,' I said.

Egil said nothing, but smiled tentatively.

After a bit, Tove came back in and sat down. She started laughing again, hiccuping uncontrollably.

I poured some more whisky into my glass. She pulled herself together, but only a few seconds later she was at it again.

'Ha ha ha ha! Ha ha ha ha!'

She stood up.

'I think I'd better go,' she said between hiccups. 'See you, Egil. Ha ha ha ha!'

This time she went outside, I supposed to the annexe.

'I should probably get going,' said Egil.

'No, you shouldn't,' I said. 'Here, have some more.'

I lifted the bottle towards him.

'Just the one, then,' he said.

'That's the spirit!' I said, and poured him another. 'It's rather a good one, this.'

'Good?' he said. 'It's heavenly.'

Egil lived on his own a few kilometres away in what had originally been a holiday home. He'd been born into a shipping family and had grown up in the UK, but then his parents had divorced and he'd come back to live with his mother in Norway, where he'd attended gymnasium school. He'd got into the film school in Copenhagen but ended up dropping out — he liked the idea of adventure, was loaded with money, but completely lacking in drive; that was how I tended to think of him. He'd lived abroad for a few years after that, and then, returning to southern Norway at the age of thirty, he'd set up his own production company and started making documentaries, most of them relatively obscure — but he could afford that. He was interested in subcultures, and the little esoteric enclaves that formed in all societies. One of his films was about the Brunstad Christian Church, also known as Smith's Friends, a small Norwegian church community; another was about a supported living arrangement for people with Down's syndrome; another concerned a group of young men from the radical right. When eventually he tired of it and closed the company down, he'd just spent a year following an extreme death metal band from Bergen, but while he found the material interesting enough he'd never got round to actually making a film out of it. I'd never quite understood why he'd given it up, because the work itself absorbed him and had clearly given meaning to his life. When pressed, he would say that documentarism was a lie. Not because it was always subjective and never true in any objective sense, the way I would have reasoned if it had been something to do with truth — no, his argument was more about being, and thus it was existential in nature, a matter of all events and occurrences not only belonging to their time, but how that was also their most important characteristic. Things manifested themselves, only then to be gone, never to return, and nothing could be repeated or even captured — and if anything was captured, it could only ever be something else.

But so what? I always asked him. So what, if it is something else? Whatever happens happens, regardless of whether it's captured on film or not. And people have always captured what happens by telling stories or writing about it. In fact, even remembering an event is to capture it.

He didn't care, he would say then. He wasn't a philosopher, it wasn't a theory, it was about how he wanted to live his life. And about what he believed in.

'All those images and films only pollute our lives,' he might say. 'We store up events and people to such an extent that the time we live in is forced aside.'

'Well, maybe,' I would say. I didn't doubt that he meant it, but something told me his real issue was a different one entirely, and much more straightforward: he didn't believe in anything, and he didn't love anyone. All his films, with the exception perhaps of the one about the people with Down's syndrome, were about people who possessed some burning faith, or a faith so different to what others believed in that it compelled them to live in isolation. He was drawn by what he lacked himself.

It was why he'd become interested in theology too, I supposed.

Now he was sitting with one leg crossed over the other, whisky in hand, looking down at the floor. I racked my brain for something to say that might smooth over or normalise Tove's behaviour, though only half-heartedly, the alcohol had begun to spread its warmth inside me, easing my anxiety about her as well as what Egil might be thinking.

If I searched long enough, the clear light of the drink would eventually shine on me.

I wanted that too. Only not on my own, I wanted him to stay here drinking with me.

I thought about saying the weather had cleared up, but then thought it would direct his attention outside and perhaps make him think of something he had to do, meaning that he would then get to his feet and leave.

'I'm lecturing on the epic poem this autumn,' I said instead. 'Starting with the *Iliad* and ending with the *Divine Comedy*. Then as a sort of spin-off I'm giving an elective on kingdoms of the dead in literature.'

'Oh yes?' said Egil.

'It just occurred to me that book you were looking at, *O, Death! Where is thy Sting?*, might be interesting in that respect. Perhaps I ought to include it in the reading list. I mean, it depicts the kingdom of the dead just as much as the *Draumkvedet* does.'

'Sounds interesting,' said Egil.

'Yes, I reckon I might.'

'Where do you stand yourself?' he said.

'On what?'

'Life after death.'

I gave a shrug.

'I don't think I've got much of an opinion, to be honest.'

'But do you or do you not believe there to be life after death?'

It was unlike him to force an issue, and I looked at him quizzically. He was sitting there with a smile on his face. I got the feeling he knew something about me that I didn't know myself. It was a feeling I often got when talking to Egil.

'No, I don't believe in life after death.'

'So how come you find it so interesting? What does it represent to you?'

I shrugged again.

'I'm lecturing on a literary form that just happens to give it prominence, that's all.'

'But you didn't have to pick it out as a theme. You could have talked about the body, or violence, or the Divine. The Divine has a prominent place too in those epic poems, doesn't it? In Dante, especially.'

I looked him in the eye and smiled. Clearly, this meant something to him. I leaned forward and picked up the bottle from the table, pouring some more into first his glass then my own before leaning back into my chair, taking a sip and looking at him again as the fiery, smoky taste filled my mouth.

'I don't believe in the Divine either,' I said. 'But I am interested in the relationship between reality and notions of reality.'

'You mean the kingdom of death becomes real if you think it is?'

'Not exactly. But the world and reality aren't the same thing — the world is the physical reality in which we live, whereas our reality is in addition to everything we know, think and feel about the world. The point being that the two layers are quite impossible to tease apart. The kingdom of the dead was once a part of our reality. But it's never been a part of the world.'

'Eww,' said Egil. 'All that relativism is so tedious.'

'How do you see it, then?'

'Me? I believe in the Divine.'

'You believe in God?'

He nodded.

'Yes.'

'Why?' I said.

'How do you mean?'

'I just don't understand how a rational human being can believe in God.'

'Have I gone down in your estimation now?' he said.

'No, no, not at all. I'm just surprised, that's all.'

Outside, the sun glittered in the puddles. The gravel had already taken on a lighter hue, I noticed, the warmth releasing the moisture and lifting it invisibly into the air. The leaves on the trees across the road fluttered in the breeze.

'Smith's Friends believe that Jesus was born a man,' said Egil. 'Meaning he was born with a will contrary to God's own. But he chose to follow God's will in everything he did, and eventually, in that way, he became a part of God's nature.'

'Do you believe that?' I said.

'I believe that the Divine is something we can be near to or remote from, and that a good life is a life that seeks to be as near to the Divine as possible.'

'What does that mean?'

'In India there are people who can't drink water unless they filter it first, because they don't want to take life,' he said. 'The microorganisms contained in the water.'

'Is that a good life?'

'Acknowledging that all life is sacrosanct is a start.'

'And from there you become divine?'

'Jesus did.'

'You don't believe that, surely!'

At the same moment, the front door opened, followed by a bustle of feet in the hall.

The door of the study was flung open and Asle and Heming came bursting in.

'Dad, one of the kittens has gone!' said Asle.

'We can't find it,' said Heming. 'We've looked everywhere.'

'Perhaps the door was left open and it got out,' I said. 'When did you see it last?'

'Yesterday. But we've looked outside as well.'

'A fox might have got it, or a bird of prey,' I said. 'It happens sometimes.'

'But it might be lost,' said Heming. 'Can't you help us look?'

'We've got visitors,' I said. 'I'm sure you can look on your own.'

'Please, Dad,' said Asle.

'I'll come,' said Egil. 'We'll form a search party. I'm sure we'll find it. A kitten never ventures far from its mother.'

'All right, then,' I said with a sigh. The alcohol had made me light-headed, but my body felt heavy, and when I bent down to put my shoes on I lost my balance and fell against the wall, which fortunately I was right next to, preventing me from ending in a heap on the floor.

'Whoops-a-daisy!' I said.

The boys stood watching me as I tied my laces. Egil, in his boots, opened the door and went out into the garden. The sun was shining from a clear sky now. A steady breeze from the sea swayed the branches of the trees.

'Right,' I said. 'If you two look inside, Egil and I can search the garden. OK?'

'It's not inside,' Asle said.

'We've already looked everywhere inside.'

'OK,' I said. 'We'll all look together, then.'

'Pss, pss, pss!' the boys said as they walked between us over the lawn. 'Kitty, kitty, kitty!'

Egil lifted the shrubs and peered underneath, and likewise among the flower beds we passed. I almost believed we were going to find it, curled up and frightened to death.

'I don't think it's anywhere here,' I said when we reached the wall at the other end. 'Let's go back and have another look, and if we don't find it the only thing we can do is hope it comes back on its own.'

'It's here, Daddy, I know it is,' said Asle. 'They're good at hiding.'

'Yes, they are,' I said.

Egil couldn't be persuaded to stay for another drink after we'd finished looking. He had things to do, he said, got on his bike and pedalled off home.

I poured myself one more and sat down in the chair he'd just vacated. Luckily, I'd had the presence of mind to ask him to leave me a few cigarettes.

I lit up, crossed one leg over the other, leaned back and blew smoke at the ceiling.

The boys were playing football again, Ingvild was in her room talking to someone on the phone, and Tove had shut herself away in the annexe, so I could sit where I was with a clean conscience.

One drink. Then I'd go and gut those fish.

I stood up and went over to the stereo cabinet, opened it and switched on the amplifier, flicking through the small collection of records that bore the mark of my parents' uninformed tastes which I'd been so scornful about in my teenage years. Diana Ross alongside Steve Harley alongside Pink Floyd alongside Lillebjørn Nilsen.

I'd been ashamed of them. My electrician dad and my primary school teacher mum. Hadn't I deserved better?

At least I'd got a bit wiser with age.

The Wall!

What did that sound like now?

I lowered the stylus onto the rotating record and stepped back into the middle of the room as the first gentle concertina tones welled from the speakers.

Then suddenly: DA! DA DA! DA DA DA DA DA!

I started to sing along, finding that every note had remained with me since childhood, when my parents had sat in the same room, playing the same record, while I'd lain awake, listening, in my own room.

La la la la lalalala.

La la la la lalalala.

I went over and picked up my drink, knocked it back and poured myself another. My hands beat the air with imaginary drumsticks that pounded out the rhythm, and when the song went into the crescendo, a plane engine rising and rising in intensity, I closed my eyes, holding my hands out in front of me and making them tremble as if in delirium, faster and faster, until the engine noise abruptly came to a halt and the sound of a wailing baby kicked in, and then I stood quite still, for the sound of the baby crying touched me so profoundly, and my eyes filled with tears.

I sat down and lit another cigarette, happier than I'd felt in years. The urge for that feeling to continue was powerful. But there were things in the way. I had to make the dinner, for a start, but faffing about with such minutiae didn't appeal in the slightest; what pulled on me now were the sweeping swathes of much greater things. I didn't even feel like sitting down to eat with the kids. Not that I wouldn't be able to — as long as I got myself together a bit they wouldn't notice anything — but the effort required to return to such a piddling domain seemed almost insurmountable. Couldn't I just give it a miss for once?

I could drive over to Egil's.

Or Trond Ole's!

It was just what he'd suggested.

No questions there.

Only there was something else I needed to do first.

Something important.

I got up and went over to the record player, picked up the arm and switched off the amplifier.

What was it now, that had been so important?

Outside, the door of the annexe opened and Tove emerged. She'd put on her raincoat even though the sun was out; it reached to her knees, where it met the top of her wellies.

Where was she going now?

I went out. As I opened the front door, she was already on her way over the lawn.

'Tove!' I called out.

She spun round.

'Where are you going?' I said.

'For a walk,' she said.

'Can you make dinner?'

She shook her head.

'You'll have to,' she said.

She turned round again and carried on walking towards the path that went down to the sea.

I went back inside. The elation had left me, but it wasn't far away yet, I could still feel it.

Only there was something I needed to do.

What was it?

Gut the fish. That was it.

The deflation came instantly as I realised what it was.

It had to be done, yes. No two ways about it.

But it would require some ammunition.

Supplies. Not ammunition. Supplies was the word.

I filled the glass to the brim and went out with it in my hand, pausing for a slurp on the doorstep while staring at the sea.

The sun was descending in the sky, its rays, invisible in the air, ricocheting into little shards of light on the smooth surface of the water.

A small, rasping noise came from somewhere on my left. I turned round to see what it was. A squirrel was scaling the wall of the house, defying gravity it seemed, for the wall was quite perpendicular and the little animal was scurrying about on it with ease.

It stopped. Twitched its tail a few times. Downwards, to the side, upwards. Downwards, to the side, upwards.

Was it looking at me?

'Hello, little squirrel,' I said. 'What are you looking at?'

It made a chirping, chattering kind of sound, then darted diagonally towards the roof, clambered over the gutter and ran along the ridge, its paws pattering on the roofing felt before it disappeared from view on the other side.

I took another slurp.

Maybe I should just bring the bottle? It would save me going back and forth.

I went inside again. Ingvild's door opened down the corridor and I slipped into the bathroom just before she emerged, locked the door and sat down on the edge of the bath.

How idiotic was this? Hiding from your own kids.

'Dad?' she said.

'I'm on the loo,' I said.

'I was just wondering what time dinner's going to be ready.'

'Soon,' I said.

'What are we having?'

'I'm on the bloody toilet, for God's sake!'

'OK, OK, sorry for asking,' she said.

I heard her door close again. I pulled some paper from the roll, dropped it in the toilet bowl, flushed and then rinsed my hands under the tap, went back out and got the bottle, took it with me to the cellar, put it down on the workbench and stood staring at the crate of fish for a minute before bending down and gripping the first between my fingers and thumb. With the knife that lay ready on the bench I cut off its head, not without pleasure, for the blade slipped so easily through the dry skin, the moist flesh and the hard backbone. Then I made an incision down the length of the belly, spread out the two sides and scraped out the intestines and organs, rinsed the now gutted fish, put it to one side, took a slurp from the glass, to which fish scales immediately affixed themselves, and gripped the next one.

I did five before taking a break and sitting down on the rickety old stool under the little window.

I only had one cigarette left now, as I discovered when I opened the packet.

I lit up, leaned my head back against the wall and closed my eyes.

I woke up coughing, without fully realising where I was at first. I was sitting in almost complete darkness. And then the smell kicked in, the smell of muggy cellar and fish, and it all came back to me. It was like being in a hot-air balloon, I thought, as if while I'd been asleep I'd slowly lost altitude, descending towards the ground and life down there. I needed to ascend again before it was too late.

I'd run out of cigarettes, but still had whisky, and I downed what was left in the glass.

'Brrr!' A shudder went through me and I shook my head before pouring another.

I couldn't stay here.

I pulled my phone out of my pocket and found Trond Ole's number.

If I texted him, he might say he was busy. I'd be better off just going over there.

I poured myself another drink with one hand while swiping to my messages and scrolling for Ingvild's name with the other.

I need to pop out, I typed. *There's pizzas in the freezer. Can you heat them up for you and the boys? Won't be long.*

I stood up and went outside clutching the bottle in my hand, closed the door behind me and started to walk towards the car when I realised the key was in my jacket pocket on the peg in the hall.

'Bollocks,' I said, and went back along the side of the house, opening the door as quietly as possible and stepping inside. The TV was on in the living room, so the boys were most likely in there watching it. And Ingvild would still be in her room unwinding after coming home from her grandmother's.

I found the car key and crept out again. As I pressed the button on the fob and the lights flashed briefly in the gloom, my mobile pinged.

I got in and turned the ignition before checking to see who it was.

It was Ingvild.

OK, she wrote.

Great! I typed back, with three heart emojis, threw the car into gear and pulled out onto the road. The kiosk at the marina would still be open, I reckoned. I drove slowly to be on the safe side, having only a vague sense of how drunk I was. Probably not very, if I was making sure to drive safely.

The thought was a good one and I kept it in mind all the way down to the jetty. After the bend, when the road straightened out, I twisted the top off the bottle and took a swig. The next bend came before I had time to replace it, forcing me to steer with one hand while holding the bottle in the other.

The car park in front of the kiosk was empty. But the window was lit up, and I could see the outline of a figure inside. I pulled in and opened the door to get out. Still gripping the bottle, I staggered and had to steady myself.

It occurred to me it might be best to leave the bottle behind, and so I put the top back on and put it down in the footwell in front of the passenger seat, while glancing towards the kiosk to see if whoever was in there had noticed.

Nope. He or she was sitting with their head lowered, looking down, and as I got closer I saw a face, faintly illuminated from below.

I tapped a knuckle against the pane.

He − I could see now that it was a he, a fat-looking lad of about seventeen − gave a start.

I gestured, index and middle finger dabbed against my lips, the universal sign for smoking.

He opened the hatch.

Forty Marlboro, I said.

Right you are, he said.

I stuck my card in the machine he held out to me and entered my PIN, picked up the two packets and went back to the car.

I got in and removed the wrapper from one of the packets, found a lighter in the glove compartment, lit up and took a couple of drags while staring out at the marina. If it hadn't been for the bottle being nearly empty I could have forgotten all about Trond Ole and just sat there.

On the seat beside me my phone lit up.

I picked it up. It was Ingvild, a text.

Where's Mum? she wanted to know.

Christ. Couldn't I get a moment's peace?

How should I know? I wrote back.

I turned the ignition, swung the car round and drove back onto the road, the cigarette still in my hand. There were no other cars about, and the police weren't going to be out here checking at this time, so I had nothing to worry about, I told myself, and put my foot down.

The phone lit up again. With my eyes on the road I reached for it, felt its hard surface against the palm of my hand and held the screen up in front of me.

She's not here, it said.

OK, I typed, and put it down. The road led on through an area of forest, the trees standing darkly on either side. In the daytime you could sometimes glimpse the sea between their trunks, and it was always hard to tell if the rushing sound you could hear came from the trees or the waves running against the shore further down.

I lowered the window and tossed my cigarette out, lit another, and took a swig of whisky. I put the bottle in the drink holder and couldn't believe I hadn't thought of it before. It was secure there even without the top on.

A new text message appeared. This time I left it.

There was a bend in the road, after which I emerged onto the outstretched plain that made you think you were somewhere up in the high fells.

Suddenly there was a crunching noise from under the wheels; it sounded like a series of small explosions.

I slammed on the brakes.

Was it a flat tyre?

No.

There was something on the road.

All over the road.

They looked like pebbles. But they were moving.

I opened the door and got out cautiously.

And then I saw that they were crabs. Crabs, in their hundreds.

They made a ticking sound.

Bloody hell.

What was going on?

I went back to the car and got in, and shut the door.

They kept coming, crawling out onto the road from the grass.

I gulped some more whisky and lit another cigarette.

It was like they were answering the call of some other power. As if they were drawn by a light.

But on land?

Ugh. They were steered by instinct, and why shouldn't instinct break down like everything else?

I sat for a while, hesitating to turn on the ignition, for there was no way I could carry on without running them over. Then, just when I'd got myself together and put the car into gear to slowly make my way, the sky flared over the ridge at the end of the plain.

It looked like the forest was on fire.

But it was a heavenly body, I realised, for the light ascended into the sky, separating itself from the ridge in moments.

It was a star.

And what a star.

I killed the engine and got out, leaned back against the car and gazed up at it. Behind me, on the passenger seat, the phone lit up again.

KATHRINE

I, who am always early, never late for anything — and I mean never — found myself scurrying along the platform towards the lift up to the departure hall at Gardermoen only half an hour before my flight on a Sunday evening in August, pulling my trolley case behind me, my bag dangling awkwardly from my shoulder and my heart thumping in my chest. It would be no disaster if I missed it — I could always check into the airport hotel, catch the first flight the next morning and be at the office by nine o'clock — but I simply couldn't bear the thought. There was a darkness in it that was already seeping out, and there was badness in it too. This was irrational, of course, but it didn't help at all to know this. The only thing that helped was to make it in time.

The lift was already going up when I reached the door.

Typical.

Why hadn't I taken the escalator instead?

I pressed the button, leaned forward and saw through the glass doors the bottom of the lift, halted above me. I checked my phone for any messages. There was one from Gaute asking when my flight got in, one from Camilla to say thank you for a lovely weekend, and one from SAS, unopened since the day before.

Where was that lift?

I pressed the button again.

'It doesn't matter how many times you press, it won't come any quicker,' a voice behind me said.

It made me jump and I turned to see who it was. A man in his sixties with a singularly soft, round face was standing there.

How had I not been aware of his presence?

'I know,' I said. 'I still do it, though.'

'It won't do any harm, at least,' he said with a smile.

He clearly belonged to the category of jovial men, the sort who need to be cheery all the time, and who exploit others to that end.

The lift came gliding down.

'There, you see,' I said. 'It did help.'

I pulled my case inside and stood by the door at the other end.

'Off to Bergen, are we?' the man said.

How on earth did he know?

'No,' I said. 'What makes you think so?'

'Doesn't look like you're going far,' he said. 'And the Bergen flight's one of the last domestic departures.'

'Ah,' I said, hoping he wasn't going to press the matter.

I hurried through the enormous departure hall which was rather empty at that hour, checked in and passed through security without having to queue. In fact, I may have been the only passenger there. The departure board told me the flight was already boarding, and as I set off along the wide, endless corridor I broke into a trot. I didn't care for it at all, it made me feel irresponsible with my flapping coat and dangling shoulder bag, my arms flailing back and forth like that, but the chances of anyone I knew witnessing such a loss of dignity were almost non-existent, and to anyone else I was just a woman who was late for her flight.

Apart from two airline staff behind the counter, the gate was empty.

'You're just in time,' one of them said, a young man with a dark, trimmed beard. Breathless, I handed him my boarding card. He scanned it, and as I went towards the plane I heard him give the *boarding completed* announcement over his walkie-talkie.

I was still gasping, and paused for a second to get my breathing under control. I felt slightly unwell too.

Was I really in such poor shape?

Entering the aircraft a moment later, I saw the man from the lift in one of the business-class seats. Immediately, I looked the other way, but too late.

'Changed your mind, did you?' he said, his face lighting up.

'No, just trying to keep my private life to myself,' I said, and gave him a smile of sorts before putting my case in the overhead compartment and sitting down in my seat, two rows behind him.

I leaned back and closed my eyes as my pulse began to settle. But the queasiness I felt wouldn't go away, its waves of nausea washing through my chest and stomach. I knew I ought to send Gaute a text message, but at that moment I didn't feel up to it.

I opened my eyes.

How had he got here before me?

He'd been behind me at the lift. I'd hurried, run even, and there'd been no queues anywhere.

Perhaps he'd gone another way. Perhaps he worked for one of the airlines and had used a shortcut for staff only.

Outside the window a ground-support vehicle was pushing one of the bigger aircraft back. Wherever I looked I saw flashing lights. Yellow, orange, red. Two men wearing overalls and ear protection stood idly watching. They seemed so oddly small, like the vehicles that whirred this way and that, as if they belonged to a miniature world, vastly inferior in the majestic presence of the aeroplanes.

Peter had PE the next day. I would have to remind him. Gaute almost certainly hadn't remembered to wash his sports things after training the day before, but there had to be something that was clean. And Marie had to go to the library with the books she'd borrowed.

They'd seemed cheerful enough when I'd spoken to them. Gaute had taken them to the baths at Nordnes, which both of them loved so much. Water had always done them good; all conflicts dissolved the moment they immersed themselves in a pool or swam out from a beach.

A flight attendant welcomed the passengers on board over the tannoy. I got my phone out of my bag and opened the text message Gaute had sent.

When do you land? Entrecôte and red wine await! he'd written.

Home around eleven, I typed back. *Looking forward to late dinner with you!*

Only then I deleted it and sat with the phone held forlornly in my hand as the plane began to move. The domes of light above the building we were leaving behind were etched with rain. I remembered the dark clouds I'd seen from the railway station in town, they'd been almost black.

I wished I could stay where I was, in that seat, never having to move. If only I could just sit there, taxi out to the runway, take off, and fly

away somewhere else, far above the world. I would have to get up to
leave the aircraft, of course, but in a foreign city, in a foreign land.

Anywhere but home.

Anywhere.

Abruptly, I was gripped by a sense of grief.

Was *that* how things were?

The thought was so very painful.

But it was true. I didn't want to go home.

I didn't want to go home.

On the Thursday before, I'd sat on the airport shuttle on my way out
to Flesland, relishing the feeling of being on my way somewhere,
though everything I saw out of the bus window was familiar to me
and the only reason I was going away was for work. It happened less
and less frequently that I actually looked forward to something. But
I'd been looking forward to this particular trip for quite a while. For
some years, I'd been a part of a team of translators working on a new
version of the Bible, and now that the work was coming to an end
everyone involved had been called together for an intensive three-day
seminar at the Bible Society premises in Oslo, where those travelling
from outside the capital were also being accommodated. Most of those
taking part were people I knew already — Norway's theological circles are rather small — and the thing I was looking forward to most
was seeing them again. Or at least some of them. Camilla, Helle and
Sigbjørn, whom I'd been at university with, and Torunn, whom I'd got
to know later and who was a researcher. I missed the discussions we
always had, the openness towards the world and life that had felt so
much a part of them. Perhaps that openness had been naive, but it
was certainly genuine. In those days I'd thought *that* was how life was
going to be. We squandered our time and thoughts, and only when it
was over did I understand that it had all been unique and would never
return. That is what life is like, is it not? When we're young we think
there's more to come, that this is only the beginning, whereas in fact
it's all there is, and what we have now, and barely even think
about, will soon be the only thing we ever had. There had been no
new abundance of friends, only Camilla, Helle and Sigbjørn, and no

new abundance of thoughts; the ones we'd had then were the ones we still have now.

In a way, my life was more truthful than it had been then, for the reality in which it was anchored was more absolute. I'd given birth to two children, and the love I felt for them was perhaps the only thing I had that was unconditional, the only thing I never questioned or doubted. On the other hand, I thought to myself as the bus crossed through Danmarksplass, which glistened in the rain, and I looked up in the direction of Solheimslien, life being more absolute didn't simply mean that it was more truthful, but also that there was no getting away from it. Nothing stood open any longer, the way everything had when we were in our early twenties.

But who said life had to be open?

The priest who'd supervised me when I was a student had once said to me that a person only has to step sideways for everything to look different. He'd been talking about the priest's role as a director of souls. I don't know why I remembered it so vividly, because he said all sorts of clever things, but I reasoned it was because it was true, and because it was something I'd needed to know and thus found significant. People disappeared into their own lives and conflicts, and in doing so they lost perspective, not only on where they were, but also on who they were, and who they had been or could become.

But stepping sideways in one's own life was well nigh impossible.

Just the thought of this filled me with guilt. I had Peter, I had Marie, what more could I want? What good was openness to me now?

I missed them already, even though I'd seen them that morning and would be seeing them again in three days' time.

It was pouring down as the bus swung into the bay outside the Lagunen shopping centre to pick up more passengers. People hurried past, huddling under umbrellas, cheerless faces lugging their carrier bags, pushing their kids ahead of them in their strollers. Tail lights shone red, car boots were opened and slammed shut, buses roared past.

The priest had said something else that time too, that had likewise etched itself into my memory: One must fasten one's gaze.

'Have you seen *Being There*?' Camilla had said when I told her what he'd said.

'Why, do you think it's trite?'

'Yes, I do! Can't you hear it? "Step sideways". "Fasten one's gaze"!'

What had I said in reply?

I couldn't remember. But probably something about the simplest things often being the truest.

Which also could have been said by Chance the gardener in *Being There*, I realised with a smile, and I looked out at the fields, their green sheen in the rain, their almost archaic appearance among the industrial buildings and construction sites.

Some sheep stood with their heads lowered, grazing beside an outcrop of rock a few hundred metres away.

How inconceivable it was that someone could make a sacrificial site there, pick out one of those sheep and cut open its throat, splash its blood in accordance with the ritual, and then cook the beast on an open fire in honour of God.

How different our times now.

But the sheep were the same. The grass was the same, the rocks, the clouds, the rain.

At that moment I received a text message from Gaute. I opened it and saw that it was all hearts, smileys, cars and planes. Underneath he'd written, *Marie wanted to say this to you.*

I replied with a heart of my own.

On the flatland in the distance the air traffic control tower came into view.

If I stepped sideways in my own life, I considered, there would be nothing missing. And if I fastened my gaze, I saw the children and nothing else.

I decided to close the door on my daydreaming for good.

I would fly over to Oslo, take part in the seminar with all my enthusiasm, come home on the Sunday evening and be glad of all that I had there.

And for a while it worked; I enjoyed the flight, the train ride into the main station, the taxi ride and the atmosphere of the grand building that was home to the Bible Society, to which I arrived late in the evening, the small, austerely furnished room I'd been given there. Something white that resembled semen was floating in the toilet bowl and I laughed when I saw it, entertaining the idea for a moment that I could enquire as to who had been staying in the room before me, though I quickly dismissed the notion. I went out for something to eat at a Chinese restaurant nearby, slept like a log all night, gave my talk the next day, took part in a discussion that carried on over lunch, and then in the evening met up with Torunn. The two days that followed continued in the same vein: sessions in our various groups, talks in the lecture room, fruitful discussions afterwards. Everything was conducted to such a high level, and it was a joy to listen to what the others had to say, not least because it all reminded me so much of my time as a student — many of the speakers had lectured then too.

Only now it was over.

I didn't want to go home.

It was a dreadful insight.

But it was truthful.

I stared at the phone in my hand and tried to think as clearly as I could as the plane taxied out to the runway and the rain streaked the small windows, the cabin crew going through their safety routine in the aisle.

Then, breathlessly almost, I typed a message to Gaute and sent it before I had time to change my mind:

Missed the plane. Having to stay over at Gardermoen. Catching first flight in the morning then going straight to work. Really sorry. Maybe the wine and the entrecôte will keep till tomorrow?

Immediately, three little dots rippled under the text I'd written, and I visualised him standing alone in the living room, his head lowered as he typed. The flight attendant who was standing two rows in front of me put on her life jacket, demonstrating exaggeratedly how it was to be deployed, her gestures timed to coincide with the instructions being voiced over the tannoy.

Not like you at all. What happened?

Went out with Camilla and Helle after the seminar, couldn't get a taxi and the train stood still for an age, I replied as the flight attendant began walking down the aisle, her head moving from side to side, little abrupt movements as she checked the rows of seats on both sides, and then three more dots appeared beneath my message.

I put the phone down in my lap, but she must have seen me texting, because she stopped beside me.

'Have you got your phone in flight mode?' she said.

I nodded and gave her a smile.

'It is now, yes,' I said.

She carried on down the aisle.

I had to answer him, otherwise he was bound to become suspicious. If I was at a hotel as I'd told him I was, my silence would have no plausible explanation, and I couldn't say I was running low on battery, because why wouldn't I just recharge it? And if I'd forgotten my charger, something he would find unlikely — and surely two unlikely occurrences, first missing my flight and then my battery running down, would already have him wondering — couldn't I borrow one from reception?

I turned the phone in my hand and read his new text:

A lot of misfortune all at once! All well here, kids asleep and I'm working. Miss you.

Miss you too, I typed back. *Sleep well.*

I switched the phone off, dropped it into my bag and stared out of the window. I looked at the rain as it darkened the concrete underneath us, the runway lights that close up looked as if they'd been laid out haphazardly, but which from a distance formed straight, luminous lines.

The plane halted and the engines began to roar. With a jolt, their restrained force was unleashed and the aircraft began hurtling down the runway.

I suddenly had no idea why I'd lied to Gaute, or what good it would do me to stay the night in a hotel. I hardly ever did anything rash, always thinking things through before doing anything.

But since there was no way I could go home now, at least not without dishing up another pack of lies, I should just make the best of the few hours I'd stolen.

The feeling of freedom had been overwhelming.

That's what it was.

But I hadn't done anything wrong. Stupid, perhaps, but not wrong.

Nothing more needed to happen. I could stay the night in a hotel, go to work as usual in the morning, come home in the afternoon and spend time with the children. Read to them, put them to bed, perhaps work for an hour or so . . .

Life itself was never the problem, it was the way you looked at it. Provided, of course, that it was a life without hunger, need or violence.

Gaute was a good husband and good father, considerate and unselfish; I couldn't ask for more. And the life we had together was fine too, if only I allowed that aspect of it to shine through.

What was I doing?

In the depths of the darkness outside, lights glittered from a road, twisting serpent-like around invisible hindrances. A small town shone like a chandelier a bit further away. Beyond it, darkness once more.

A soft pling sounded in the cabin and the Fasten Seat Belts sign switched off. The cabin crew at the front jumped to their feet and started getting ready to go through the aircraft with their trolley cases. The flight time was only just over half an hour, so it was no wonder they looked like they were in a hurry, I thought to myself, bending down and taking a book from my bag, one that Camilla had been talking about for years, a copy of which she'd finally given me at the seminar. *The Kingdom of God is Within You*, by Tolstoy. I put it down on the seat beside me, rummaged for my glasses without finding them, then lifted my bag onto my lap for a proper look. I couldn't have left them behind at the restaurant, surely?

I'd put them on to look at the menu.

Hadn't I put them back in my bag?

I couldn't remember.

As I put the bag down again a new wave of nausea ran through me. I leaned back and tried to breathe steadily. I felt like I could be sick at any moment.

As a matter of precaution, I took one of the little white bags from the pocket of the seat in front and held it discreetly in my hand next to my thigh.

My brow was sticky with perspiration.

Ohh.

I tried to control the wave inside me as it continued to rise, sitting completely still and allowing my thoughts to ride with it in the hope they would tame it and make it go away. And it worked. Slowly the queasiness receded and soon it had settled sufficiently for me to put the bag back in its place and start breathing normally again.

The snack trolley was coming closer and I got my purse out. I wanted a Coke and a packet of biscuits, if they had any — it was what my father had always given me whenever I'd felt sick as a child, and I'd connected the combination with getting better ever since.

It must have been the food I'd eaten. We'd all had moules-frites, perhaps the mussels had been off. A single bad one was enough.

I remembered I'd have to remind Gaute to pay the mechanic before they sent the overdue bill to a debt agency. And to bring the two dishes home that we'd left at the school after the get-together to celebrate breaking up for the holidays.

Perhaps not both things at once. He disliked it intensely if I went on at him. Still, he only had himself to blame, putting things off the way he did.

And then there was the funeral to prepare for on Tuesday.

I was rather dreading it, I sensed. The deceased was a man with no next of kin, and no friends had made themselves known either. After burying children, it was the most unpleasant of all my undertakings, to conduct someone's funeral in an empty church.

The flight attendant pushed her trolley past. I tried to catch her attention, but she was busy with the passengers across the aisle.

'Excuse me,' I said.

She gave no sign of having seen or heard me.

'Excuse me!' I said again, louder this time.

Too loud, it seemed, for when she turned towards me it was with a look of annoyance on her face.

'Yes?' she said.

'Could I have a Coke, please?'

She said nothing, but opened one of the trolley drawers and took out a can, handing it to me together with a plastic cup, though still without a word.

'Have you got any biscuits of any sort?' I said.

'Biscuits, no.'

'How about crispbread?'

She sighed and pulled out another drawer, then handed me a thin green-and-white packet with a piece of Wasa crispbread inside.

I held out my debit card.

'Payment's with my colleague,' she said with a nod in the direction of the other flight attendant, before turning her attention with a smile to the passengers in the row behind me.

I didn't see why she had to be so unfriendly. Could it have been that I used my phone when I wasn't supposed to? But surely they were used to that?

Anyway, it was no reason to act the way she did.

I opened the crispbread and took a couple of bites, washing them down with a mouthful of Coke. After that, I got my phone out again and looked at my recent photos, mostly from the holiday we'd spent in Crete a few weeks earlier. Marie had learned to swim there, all of a sudden she could just swim. Fortunately, I'd had my wits about me and managed to film her, not the first time, when she'd discovered it was something she could do, but the second, a few minutes later. We'd been at a little bay next to a busy road, and there were some industrial buildings quite close by, but none of that could be seen in the video, all you could see was little Marie with her head held high above the surface, arms and legs paddling away beneath her. Behind, the blue sea stretched away until meeting the bluish-green rock face on the other side of the bay which rose steeply towards the bright sky, dashed with sandy-coloured ruts and crevices. Her whole face exuded concentration and joy.

'Wow, Marie!' Gaute exclaimed in the background.

He'd been standing next to me as I filmed and had put his arm around me.

What would he say if I told him I was leaving him?

But I wasn't.

I wasn't.

I put the phone back in my bag. The noise of the engines changed; we must have already started our descent.

He wouldn't understand. He'd think I'd found someone else. It would be the only explanation he'd be able to comprehend.

'What have I done?' he would say. 'Is there something I can do differently?'

What was I supposed to say then?

I hadn't found anyone else, he hadn't done anything, and there was nothing he could change to make it any better.

But what is it, then?

We've nothing but the children in common any more, haven't you noticed?

No. We've got *everything* in common. We have a *life* together.

I'm sorry, Gaute. But I can't go on.

Would he cry? Would he be angry? Would he refuse to have anything to do with me after that?

No, I couldn't leave him. I had no reason to. Besides, it would be devastating for the children. Especially for Peter, who was so sensitive. Things were difficult enough for him as it was.

Was I really that selfish? So selfish that I would completely mess up our children's lives and Gaute's too, just because I felt like it?

Below, the lights of the city came into view. It wasn't often I'd seen it from that angle; usually the flights came in from the south, over the rugged fells and the small islands there, but now I could see the entire city clearly: there was Sandviken, there was Nordnes, there was Bryggen, there was Klosteret, there was Sydneshaugen.

The sky was clear, and the lights of the Vågen harbour district shimmered on the inky water.

After the long walkways of Gardermoen, it felt good to enter the small airport terminal and walk just a few metres to the staircase leading down to the baggage reclaim area and the exit.

At the bottom I paused to put my case down and pull the handle up when there was a voice behind me.

'I didn't think priests were supposed to tell lies.'

It was the man from the lift. He smiled.

I began to walk away.

'No offence,' he said, coming up alongside me. 'Only you said you weren't going to Bergen. And where are you now?'

'Do I know you?' I said without looking at him, pressing on.

'I don't think so,' he said.

I knew I shouldn't say anything, that it would only encourage him further, yet there was something about him that invited me to ask:

'How do you know I'm a priest?'

'I go to church now and then,' he said. 'I've noticed you. You're a good priest. You've got lots of interesting thoughts. Not all priests have.'

I said nothing, but carried on through the exit, and when I halted outside to get my bearings and look for the taxi rank he was gone.

Torgallmenningen lay almost deserted in front of me as I walked towards the hotel. Only the odd night owl was about. The hotel was in one of the side streets off the square. I'd booked the room from the taxi. It felt strange to be in town in such circumstances. I crossed Torgall-menningen several times a week and had done so nearly all my life – this was my city, it was where I'd grown up and spent my entire working life – but all sense of familiarity and belonging seemed sud-denly to have dissolved. I wasn't supposed to be there, I reasoned, and so I felt detached from it all.

It was as if I'd put my whole life to one side.

As if for one night I was now someone else.

A woman in her twenties was standing behind the reception desk in the lobby and glanced at me as I came in through the door, only then to continue staring at the screen in front of her. I heard the clicking of her keyboard. Her face was pale and rather full, in contrast to her slim figure, formally dressed in a blue jacket, blue skirt and white blouse. Her lips were too red, but her hair was thick and beautiful. It made me want to be her. She looked like she had no problems, and even if she did, they wouldn't have been anything I couldn't have solved.

'Kathrine Reinhardsen,' I said. 'I phoned just a short time ago and booked a room until tomorrow.'

She looked up and smiled.

'Hi, and welcome,' she said. 'I've got your key ready for you here. If you'd just like to sign your name?'

She placed a sheet of paper and a pen on the counter, and once I'd signed she handed me the key.

'So, you'll be on the third floor. The lift's over there. Breakfast between seven and ten. OK?'

'Thanks,' I said.

'You're welcome,' she said. 'Goodnight!'

'Goodnight,' I said, and pulled my case behind me to the lift. The walls inside were mirrors and I stared at the floor as we slid upwards.

There were no sounds to be heard from any of the rooms I passed along the carpeted corridor. I unlocked the door at the end and stepped inside. The room was a lot smaller than I'd envisaged when this ridiculous idea had occurred to me.

I felt stupid.

I left the case where it was, unopened in the middle of the floor, and lay down on the bed without removing my coat or shoes.

Now they would all be asleep at home. My family.

And I was lying there.

What should I do?

Go to a bar?

It would only make things worse.

Go for a walk, then?

I stood up, slipped the key card into the inside pocket of my coat and went out again. First down to the ferry terminal, then out in the direction of Nordnes, past the old city gate and up to Klosteret, the old town, the houses there incandescent in the yellow light of the street lamps. There was a chill in the air, it felt uplifting after the long, hot summer. I walked all the way to the park at the far end, sat down on a bench at the point and gazed out at the lights across the fjord.

What a lovely evening it was, I thought to myself. And then I thought of the children and started to cry.

When I stopped, I looked around, feeling suddenly unprotected.

If only I could talk to someone.

There was nothing I couldn't share with Camilla. But I couldn't phone her now, not this late. Anyway, I didn't know what to say. It *was* nothing.

Sigrid, whom I'd know all my life, was another person I could talk to about anything. Apart from Gaute and our relationship. Her husband, Martin, had become good friends with Gaute, and I didn't quite trust her not to divulge to him the things we talked about. Or rather, I trusted her, but a person's loyalty to their partner is so often greater than to their friends.

It was just the way it was.

But when had I last told Gaute anything that no one else knew?

I'd even kept my great crisis from him.

Someone came walking along the path behind me. I turned to look, but there was no danger, it was just an elderly couple with a dog.

I got my phone out and scrolled through my contacts.

Stopping at my mother's number.

I could phone her late, she wouldn't mind.

But did I want to?

I put my hands in my coat pockets, pressed my arms close to my body.

The darkness in the tall trees around me was dense and seemed almost to be a part of them as they loomed there, black against the sky.

When I was a child, I'd known every tree in the neighbourhood. In my mind they were individuals, each with their own particular characteristics, though the thought hadn't ever been so explicit. They bent down to me, and like feelings seeped into my consciousness. Birch, oak, spruce, pine, aspen, ash, rowan.

My father had been like a tree. Wasn't that what I'd thought when I'd sat on his shoulders so high above the ground with my hands holding on to his head?

I remembered his hands, they were so big. And I remembered his beard. His eyes, the gleam in them. But if I tried to think about him, those images dissolved and I was left with only the vaguest suggestion of him ever having lived.

He existed only at the edgelands of my thoughts now, the habitation of the vague. Suddenly, I saw myself surrounded by great, living creations. Silent and inscrutable, neither hostile nor friendly, and quite without opinion regarding us little people, who always scuttled and scurried about at such a speed that they themselves could not comprehend it, nor even did they care. And they *were* living creations, not just things, as people so often considered them.

As a teenager I'd read an absolutely staggering poem in *The Book of Hours* by Rilke. *My God is dark*, it said, *and like a webbing made of a hundred roots that drink in silence. I know that my trunk rose from his warmth, but that's all, because my branches hardly move at all near the ground, and just wave a little in the wind.*

It was the first time the thought of God transcended me and what was mine.

The trees were living creations, and God was their creator.

The darkness, the earth, the moisture: this was the God of the trees.

What was my God?

What was my warmth?

I'd said that I was a Christian long before I became one. Someone in my class had been a member of Ten Sing and persuaded me to go along with them one night. I knew my mother would dislike the idea intensely, and perhaps that was part of the reason I went, because it was something forbidden that wasn't actually illegal. I was thirteen years old, with a right to my own life. That was basically how I felt. When I was sixteen, I left Ten Sing and joined a church choir, with whom a year later I attended a choir festival in Kraków, Poland. We sang in a magnificent old church, and as our voices filled the room I heard them as if from without, at the same time as I was a part of them, and my soul filled with an intense joy and delight, stronger and purer than anything I had ever known, and in the same way, both from without and within. I think it had to do with being alive, the feeling of being alive, but also of belonging, of being a part of some greater connection, and it was in that connection all meaning resided.

These had been the feelings of a seventeen-year-old. But they were still valid now, more than twenty years on, they were still true, regardless of how much experience and knowledge I'd gained. Meaning wasn't in me, meaning wasn't in another, meaning arose in the encounter between us. Singing in the choir was the simplest example of that. And the teachings of Christ were about practising it. Everyone was equal, everyone was a part of something greater, and in that greater thing was God. The radicality of that idea could not be overestimated. But in order to properly understand it one had to peel away two thousand years of theological history and look at what Jesus actually did and said. He had sought those who were marginalised, those without a voice, the oppressed. In one of the few passages of the Bible where a woman is heard, namely in the Magnificat, Mary says of the Lord that He put down the mighty from their seat, and exalted the humble and meek; that He filled the hungry with good things, and sent the rich empty away. The Lord she exalted was subversive. And the child to which she gave birth, Jesus, later went among the ostracised and the unliked, the sick and the poor, lepers and whores. His message, that we are all of us equal before God, cannot live as theory, for the majority are excluded from theory, which was precisely why Jesus went among the disenfranchised rather than aspiring to join the Scribes, or the theorists, as I tended to refer to them. There was a chasm between the theorists and the ordinary run of people, and there was a chasm between the ordinary run of people and those at the bottom of society. The teachings of Christ were practical: he did not write about those he went among, did not write even for their sake, but went among them. Talked with them, listened to them, included them. All were equal, all were a part of something greater, and in that greater thing was God. And in God grace, in God forgiveness, in God the fullness of being.

That was my warmth.

But what good was it when I couldn't even sustain my relationship to the people who were closest to me in my life?

I pictured myself arriving home, pecking Gaute on the lips, bending down to hug Peter and Marie, finding their presents in my suitcase, catching Gaute's smiling look over the top of their heads as they unwrapped them, smiling myself.

It was theatre.

It wasn't me.

But who was I then?

What did I want, if things could be exactly as I wanted them?

Did I want to install myself in a little post-divorce flat, with the children every other week?

I turned the phone so the screen lit up, and saw that it was just past midnight. I found Mum's number and tapped it.

It rang for a while.

'Is there something wrong?' her voice said when at last she answered. 'Are the children all right?'

'Hi, Mum,' I said. 'Everything's fine. I'm sorry to be calling so late. Were you asleep?'

'Yes, I was asleep. What time is it? It's the middle of the night, isn't it?'

'Yes,' I said, and wished I hadn't phoned. I didn't know what to say, or if there was anything to say at all.

'What is it, then?'

'Nothing, really,' I said. 'Or rather . . .'

'Or rather what?'

I took a deep breath.

'I didn't go home tonight. I went to a hotel.'

'What for?' she said. Her voice was so objective and unsentimental that I had to resist the feeling of being rejected. It was the way she was. It had nothing to do with me.

'I don't know,' I said. 'I honestly don't know.'

'Are you crying?' she said.

I didn't answer.

'Are you and Gaute having problems?'

I wiped my tears with the sleeve of my coat.

'In a way, I suppose,' I said.

'Do you want to divorce him?'

I didn't answer.

There was a silence at the other end too.

'I don't know, Mum,' I said. 'I think so. Or no. I can't really, can I?'

I began to sob.

'Where are you now?' she said.

'Nordnes.'

'Can we meet up tomorrow and talk about it properly?' she said.

'Yes,' I said.

'How about lunch? Half past twelve at Kafé Oscar?'

'All right,' I said.

'You get yourself a good night's sleep,' she said. 'It'll all look different in the morning, and then we'll have lunch.'

'Thanks,' I said.

'That's all right,' she said. 'Goodnight.'

'Goodnight,' I said, but she'd already hung up.

As I slept, the nausea stirred and grew inside me. I sensed it in my dream, imposing itself, though without my waking. For what felt like a long time, it was a place from which I tried to escape, but it kept drawing me towards it. It had no name, and was nowhere in particular, just a place from which I wanted away. Gradually, thoughts began to interject — I feel sick, why do I feel sick? — and I drifted in and out between them, thoughts that were neither mine nor not mine, until at last I identified them as my own, and opened my eyes.

It felt as if the slightest movement would cause me to vomit.

For a while, I lay quite still in the hope that it would pass. But then suddenly it all welled up, I jumped out of bed, dashed for the bathroom, knelt in front of the toilet bowl and let everything spew out.

Afterwards, I brushed my teeth, and stood under the shower for some time before getting dressed and sitting down on the edge of the bed to text Gaute and tell him everything was all right, and to remind him about what the children needed to take with them to school, and the bill he had to remember to pay.

Mum was right: it all looked different now.

I sent her a text to say that the conflict had resolved itself, apologised for having phoned her so late, and told her we no longer needed to meet up for lunch.

I don't believe it, not for a minute, she wrote back. *Besides, what if I wanted to see you? Half past twelve.*

She was such an annoying person. Not least because when she thought she could see through a matter, it very often turned out that she was right. I'd always had to contend with it. Struggled to hold on to my illusions, even though I knew they were illusions, just because it was she who pointed her finger at them.

As you wish, I replied. *Looking forward to seeing you!*

I deleted the exclamation mark, finding it made the message come across too chirpy. Without, it was measured, ominous almost, but at least closer to the way I felt.

As you wish. Looking forward to seeing you.

She didn't reply, and I called Karin to tell her I wasn't feeling well and wouldn't be in today, but that I would try to get some work done at home. It wasn't untrue, I'd just been sick after all, and for the next two hours I sat at the little desk in my room, replying to emails, running through the funeral order for the day after, and continuing my discussion with Erlend about translating Leviticus, and my ongoing quarrel about Ezekiel with Harald, whom I so disagreed with on some points that our correspondence bordered on conflict.

At twelve o'clock I checked out and went into the street with my case trundling behind me. The sky was overcast, though thinly so, the cloud as white as milk, the air warm and muggy. The buildings, which in rain appeared so grey and drab, now stood out sharply in their every nuance. I looked up at the sky. Two birds were circling high above, their wings stretched out and unmoving. They were birds of prey, though I couldn't tell what kind. Hawks, perhaps. Eagles wouldn't be flying over the city, would they?

Emerging onto Torgallmenningen, which was busy with people, I made my way to the bookshop on the corner. I didn't want to sit and wait for her, but would rather be a few minutes late.

Outside the bookshop some workmen were standing smoking around a hole that had been cordoned off. Their orange overalls reflected the light in a way I found odd, it made them look like they were floating, as if the men wearing them were simply stuck inside.

Entering the shop, I looked first at the shelf of new publications, before going over to the small philosophy section. Sometimes, though not often, they would have something interesting there.

I pulled out a book with what I thought was a promising title. *Experience and Nature*, it was called, by John Dewey. I knew of it, but had never read it.

I opened it at a random page.

We have substituted sophistication for superstition, it said. *But the sophistication is often as irrational and as much at the mercy of words as the superstition it replaces.*

I turned the book in my hand and read the blurb on the back. The work had originally been published in 1925. Before the world began, in other words.

What did he mean by *sophistication*?

I took the book with me to the till and paid for it with my card, dropped it into my bag and went out. I still had ten minutes, and the cafe was only a five-minute walk, but it no longer felt important to be late. It was a silly reflex from my teenage years.

*

Mum appeared at the far end of the little square just as I sat down at one of the tables outside the cafe. I could pick her out in any crowd and at almost any distance. She was thin and straight-backed, which made her seem taller than she actually was, but most characteristic was the way she held her head, always slightly tipped back, which lent her an air of superiority or arrogance, but also gave a faintly birdlike impression. Her hair was red, her skin pale and freckled, and when I was a child I'd thought that everyone with red hair and freckles belonged to their own race, and more than anything else had wished that I'd been like that too, because it would have meant that she and I, and not just she and Eirik, belonged together.

As she came closer, I saw she was wearing her favourite colours. Light brown cords, white blouse, dark green jacket.

'Hello, Mum,' I said, and gave her a hug. 'You're looking good.'

'Thank you,' she said. 'Are we sitting out?'

'I thought we might. It's certainly warm enough?'

She nodded and sat down.

Yellowed leaves lay on the ground under the tree next to our table, and I looked up. It was a chestnut tree and seemed to be blighted by something, its foliage sparse, the leaves small and withered. So it wasn't that the autumn had come, it was just disease.

Mum caught the attention of a waiter who was clearing one of the tables by the wall.

'How are you?' I asked her.

She looked at me.

'I thought I was supposed to be asking you,' she said. 'But I'm fine. Everyone's back at work after the holiday. Mikael's still away at the summer house.'

Behind her, the waiter went inside with a tray full of cups and glasses.

'What's he doing there now?' I said.

'Fishing a lot, and reading.'

'Enjoying retirement?'

'He hates it. That's why he's still there, I think, so he can pretend it's just a holiday. But he likes to read. He's got the time for it now.'

She turned round.

'Where did he get to?'

'He went in with a tray. I'm sure he'll be back again in a minute.'

Mum looked out over the square that narrowed into a street with shops on both sides. She looked at the stone church, so solid and substantial in between all the white-painted wooden buildings. The grey-stone walls had a touch of green in them. As if the church stood in a forest, I thought, and imagined it among towering spruce and toppled tree trunks, overgrown boulders, a mossy rock-side, some hills in the distance.

Christ, wandering the forests.

Mum put down the bag she'd been holding in her lap on the chair beside her.

'So, Kathrine,' she said, and looked at me. 'You were in a bit of a state last night.'

'Yes, I was,' I said. 'But it's all right now. I'm sorry to have bothered you about it. I shouldn't have.'

'You stayed the night at a hotel in your own city?'

'Yes.'

'But why?'

I didn't know what to say, and looked down. I didn't want to give her anything to go on. At the same time, I wanted her to know.

I looked up at her and smiled.

'I honestly don't know,' I said. 'It was an impulse.'

The waiter appeared, wiping both hands on his apron as he came down the steps before taking two menus from an empty table and coming over to ours.

'What's the soup of the day?' Mum asked.

'French onion,' he said.

'It was French onion the last time I was here, too,' she said.

'Did you like it?' he enquired.

'Yes, as a matter of fact I did,' she replied. 'But that's beside the point. If you have the same soup every day, you can hardly call it soup of the day. Soup of the day means it's a different one every day.'

The waiter smiled without speaking.

'I'll have the quiche with feta,' I said.

'Caesar salad for me,' Mum said.

We sat for a moment in silence after he'd gone. A bit further away, two sparrows landed on a table that hadn't been cleared. They hopped about on their matchstick legs, pecking and pulling at some half-eaten pieces of bread.

'Has Gaute been unfaithful?' Mum asked.

'God, no!' I said.

'Have you?'

'Mum. You know me better than that.'

'What do I know?' she said. 'You phone me up crying in the middle of the night and say you don't know if you want to get divorced or not. The next day you're saying it was nothing and everything's fine. What am I supposed to think?'

'I don't know,' I said.

'Things aren't well between you and Gaute,' she said.

'They're not exactly bad though either,' I said. 'There's just nothing there, that's all. No excitement, no curiosity. We've got nothing in common. The only thing we can talk about is the children. Yesterday was the first time I understood I don't want to live like that. I was sitting on the plane and realised I didn't want to go home.'

'Not many marriages are exciting after twenty years.'

'I know that,' I said. 'And I'm sure I'll stick it out.'

Above us, something came sweeping through the air. I looked up in time to see it come hurtling, closer and closer, bigger and bigger. It was a large bird of prey. It swooped down on the neighbouring table and snatched one of the sparrows, beat its wings a few times and then rose above the rooftops before disappearing from view.

'*Did you see that?*' I said, astonished. 'In the middle of the city?'

Mum nodded.

'What a remarkable thing,' she said.

'What was it? A sea eagle?'

'I wouldn't know. A hawk, I should think. Mikael would know.'

'I can't believe it,' I said. 'It just came down and took that little bird.'

Mum lit one of her cigarettes, cupping her elbow in her other hand, the way she always did when she smoked.

'What if you found yourself a bit on the side?' she said.

I stared at her.

'Is that supposed to be a joke?'

'No, not at all. It would be a practical solution to what is clearly a very palpable problem. You lack excitement and someone to share the things that interest you. And you wouldn't have to leave your family. It stands to reason.'

'I can't believe you're even suggesting this,' I said.

'Yes, you can. But it's your life.'

'I'm a priest.'

'It would have to be kept secret, priest or not,' she said.

'No, you don't understand. It's not that someone could find out. It's the fact that it's immoral. *In itself*. It's the fact that it's wrong. *In itself*.'

Mum nodded.

'I hear you,' she said, and placed her hand on mine for a second.

Abruptly, tears came to my eyes and I had to look away. Fortunately, the waiter appeared at that same moment, carrying a full tray, and the seconds that followed were all about the food he placed on the table in front of us.

She'd noticed, of course. But she pretended she hadn't, and I was thankful for it.

The house was empty when I got home. I unpacked my case, put some washing in the machine and emptied the dishwasher while I waited for them to return. Peter and Marie attended the same school just down the road and went there and back on their own.

I sat down on the sofa with a cup of coffee and stared at the uniform suburban landscape outside the window.

Mum would say morals were relative rather than absolute, and socially and historically determined. Nothing was absolute to her, aside perhaps from her belief in rationalism.

There was something cold about her. Always had been.

How many times had I wondered what it was like to be her, what went on inside her mind?

And how many times had I wondered what she thought of me?

I got up and went into the study, standing in front of the window to see if the children were on their way.

Instead it was Gaute I saw, coming up the hill in his red Polo. I stepped back into the room, put my mug down and went upstairs to the bathroom to run a bath. I didn't feel like encountering him on my own, without the children there.

And yet, as I pulled my top over my head, I changed my mind. Why should I have to avoid him? I had nothing to hide. I'd done nothing wrong.

I turned the tap off, ran the brush through my hair and went downstairs to meet him.

He came into the kitchen from the hallway with his brown leather briefcase in his hand.

'Hi,' I said. 'Do you want some coffee? I just made some.'

'Are you home already?' he said. 'I thought you were at work?'

'I missed you all,' I said.

He came up and gave me a peck on the cheek.

'Coffee, then?' I said.

'Yes, please,' he said, but remained where he was. I was about to turn when he said: 'Can I ask you something?'

'Of course,' I said.

'Have you been unfaithful?'

My face immediately felt warm. But my eyes didn't move from his.

'I can't believe you're asking me that,' I said. 'Don't you trust me any more?'

'Have you?' he said.

'I won't even answer that.'

He sighed.

'So you have, then,' he said.

I didn't reply, but went over to the side, took two mugs out of the cupboard and poured us some coffee while he sat down on the sofa, leaned back and stared up at the ceiling.

'Why don't you trust me?' I said, putting his mug down on the table in front of him.

He answered without looking at me.

'You just told me you've been unfaithful,' he said.

'No, I didn't,' I said. 'I told you I wasn't going to answer you.'

'And why wouldn't you want to do that? No, I'll tell you why. Because you won't lie.'

'I want you to trust me,' I said. 'You think badly of me. That's up to you. But don't come to me expecting to have your paranoid suspicions confirmed or dispelled.'

'You blushed when I asked you.'

'I was angry.'

'So why can't you just tell me you haven't been unfaithful?'

'This is an all-time low, Gaute.'

'Is it?'

'Yes.'

'What hotel did you stay at?'

'What does it matter?'

'So you won't tell me that either?'

'No, not when you're asking like that.'

The front door opened, followed by the bustle of the children coming into the hall.

'There, I told you,' I heard Marie say. 'Mummy *is* home.'

I went out into the hall.

'Mummy!' Marie exclaimed, and threw her arms around me.

'Hello, poppet,' I said, and kissed her on the head. 'Hello, Peter, have you got a hug for me too?'

'I suppose so,' he said. Marie let go and I put my arms around him.

'Have you been all right?' I asked them.

'Yes,' said Marie, already on her way into the living room.

'And you, Peter?'

'OK,' he said.

While Gaute made dinner and Peter sat doing homework at the kitchen table, I gave Marie a bath. After the holiday in Crete she kept pestering us to take her to the pool, and when we couldn't go the bath became her alternative to quench her unstoppable desire to be immersed in water. She pulled off her clothes and climbed in before the water had even covered the bottom. I sat on the edge and handed her various toys and other things to play with. At one point she lay face down with a diving mask on, her breathing hollow and alien-sounding, then sat up and played with her plastic dogs, before putting on her goggles and pretending to swim lengths of the tub that was barely longer than herself.

She was fun to be with, and I gave not a single thought to the argument with Gaute while we were together there.

Washed and dried, and wrapped in a big towel, she marched off into her room, where with a little help she chose some clothes to put on and got dressed.

Downstairs smelled of chops and onion being fried. On any other day, I'd have asked Gaute if we could dispense with the thick gravy he liked the chops to be served in, the way his mother had always done when he'd been growing up. But just one look at him as he stood there whisking the gravy in the pan was enough for me to see that he'd retreated into himself, and when he was in that sort of mood even the most innocent of comments would be construed as a provocation.

I didn't need this, he could do as he pleased.

Peter sat reading, his head propped in his hand, elbow against the table next to his book, pen at the ready in his other hand. Gaute, who had gone over to get something from the cupboard, tousled his hair as he came back. Peter looked up and smiled at him.

'What's that you're reading?' I asked, sitting down beside him.

'Science,' he said.

'About what?'

'We've got to find information about an animal that's extinct, and then write about the way it lived.'

'That sounds interesting!' I said. 'What animal have you chosen?'

'I don't know yet. That's why I'm reading this book.'

'Dinosaurs?'

He sighed.

'Mum, that's too obvious,' he said.

'My clever boy,' I said, glancing at Gaute as I got up.

'When's dinner ready?'

'In ten minutes,' he said.

'I'll set the table, then,' I said.

'Yes, do that,' he said.

Gaute didn't speak as we sat eating. I tried to lighten the mood, asking Peter about various things, to which, bent over his food, he replied only grudgingly. Marie, on the other hand, was talkative as ever.

'Can I eat the white bit?' she said, poking her knife at the thick wedge of fat on the outside of her chop.

'You can eat it, yes,' I said. 'But I don't think you'll like it much. Do you want to taste?'

She shook her head.

'Can't you cut it off?'

I leaned across and cut away the fat.

'I don't want it on my plate,' she said. 'It looks like an animal.'

'That's because it *is* an animal,' said Peter.

'Leave it on the side,' I said.

'No!' she said.

'It's your food,' I said. 'I've got mine.'

'I'll have it,' said Gaute, and lifted it onto his own plate.

I looked at him, but he didn't return my gaze.

Fine, I thought. If you can't be bothered, I can't either.

We ate the rest of the meal in silence. Afterwards, Peter and Marie disappeared into their rooms while I took care of the washing-up and Gaute sat down on the sofa to read the paper. Then, with the dishwasher started and the saucepans and frying pan scrubbed and put away, I made myself a coffee and went into the study.

I skimmed the book I'd bought without being able to concentrate or muster much of an interest.

Once during the time we'd been married, Gaute had fallen in love with someone else. He never said anything about it, but I knew him and realised what was happening. He'd had a student teacher in his class for a few weeks. He talked about her the first few days, what she was like, what she was good at, and less good at, the things she did. Then he stopped talking about her. He started switching his phone off when he came home, and something radiated in him. It was so strong he was unable to conceal it no matter how hard he tried, all of a sudden he was bubbling with excitement even when he was with the children, with me.

I said nothing. If he wanted to give up what we had together for a twenty-five-year-old, then he wasn't worth sharing my life with, it was as simple as that.

Then, just as quickly as it had started, it was gone. And as obvious as his earlier radiance was now pain, and it too could not be concealed from me.

But he didn't know that I knew. He thought it was his own little secret.

The TV came on in the living room.

I pulled my Mac out of my bag, put it down on the desk and plugged it in at the socket.

Erlend had sent a new draft the evening before, so I noted, from the beginning of the Book of Leviticus. I knew it wouldn't engage me at that moment, but still I opened the document and glanced at what he'd done.

No, I wasn't going to sit here pretending.

Like a prisoner in my house.

I got up and left the room. As I passed the sofa where Marie sat snuggled in the crook of Gaute's arm watching TV, I told them I was going for a walk.

'At this hour?' Gaute said. 'Where are you going?'

'No idea,' I said. 'Just out.'

'As long as you're back before their bedtime,' he said.

'You're here, aren't you?' I said.

He didn't answer and I closed the hall door behind me, put my shoes on and a lightweight jacket, got in the car, started the engine and drove through the estate to the main road. I didn't know where I was going, turning right, turning left impulsively in the general direction of town. At Solheimsviken I made a left and carried on towards Laksevåg. Reaching the roundabout, where there was a choice between the tunnel and the bridge, I chose the tunnel, and as I came out the other side I decided to drive on to the sea.

The roads narrowed increasingly, the vegetation becoming more and more sparse, dwindling eventually to little more than grass and moss in an undulating landscape, until at last the sea was in front of me, dark and vast.

I parked on a pier, turning off the engine but leaving the headlights on, each beam opening a tunnel in the darkness which the rain lacerated with hundreds of scratches. The sound of the waves as they battered the shore was not a rush, but a roar. It was as if something were coming apart out there.

I folded my hands together and lowered my head.

'Lord God, I am in distress,' I said. 'Help me. Help me now.'

Gaute was asleep, or pretending to be, when I got home. I undressed as quietly as I could, shielding my phone so the light of the display wouldn't wake him as I set the alarm.

I was getting up at five.

When it rang, it felt like only a moment later. I resisted the temptation to snooze and got up, taking my clothes with me in case I woke him while I got dressed. I would have preferred to go straight to the office and begin the day's work there, but I couldn't leave the children to Gaute again, so I went to the kitchen and got some coffee on the go.

The sky was competely blue, not a cloud in sight, and sunlight flooded across the floor. The birds were singing and chirping outside the window. I opened it. An odd boot lay in the grass under the badminton net, next to it a discarded plastic bowl from the weekend before last when my mother, my brother and his family had been here and we'd sat outside with ice cream and cake.

The light seemed not to fill the garden, I thought, but rather the other way round: it emptied it — of darkness, but also of meaning.

The emptiness of the world.

But it was the wrong way of looking at it, I knew that. Meaning was something that came from us. Meaning was something we gave to the world, not something we took from it.

I put the dish that had been left in the sink in the dishwasher, wiped the work surface, draped the cloth over the tap. I poured some coffee into a mug and took it with me into the study, sat down and opened the document from Erlend again.

I read through the text as slowly as I could.

If your offering is a goat, you shall show it to the face of the Lord and lay your hand on its head; it shall be slaughtered before the tent of meeting; and the sons of Aaron shall dash its blood against all sides of the altar. You shall present as your offering from it, as an offering by fire to the Lord, the fat that covers the entrails; the two kidneys with the fat that is on them at the loins, and the appendage of the liver, which you shall remove with the kidneys. Then the priest shall turn these into smoke on the altar as a food-offering by fire for an aroma that is pleasing to the Lord. All fat is the Lord's. It shall be a perpetual statute throughout your generations, in all your set-tlements: you must not eat any fat or any blood.

I took a slurp of my coffee and read it quite as slowly again.

I didn't care for the wording 'the face of the Lord', but we'd been instructed to use it, it belonged to the modernisation, so there was nothing to be done. But 'the presence of the Lord', as it had been before, was better; 'the face of the Lord' made it so human. On the other hand, it was a reasonable interpretation of the Hebrew לִפְנֵי, or *lifney*, for while strictly that meant 'before', it came from the same root as 'face' — *panav* — and there were certainly plenty of humanising details in the rest of the text, not least the smell of the burnt offering being pleasing to the Lord. So in a way, 'face' was probably better than 'presence', precisely because it was more human, whereas 'presence' was better in a different way, being older.

But a pleasing aroma?

Wasn't that a bit too refined and cultivated?

It wasn't my job to correct the language, but the language was almost impossible to separate from the theology, so I did it all the time.

for a smell that is pleasing to the Lord, I wrote down, just to see what it looked like.

It wasn't much better, but still I noted it for Erlend's sake. He could not be reminded enough that the language of these texts was simple and concrete with barely any abstractions at all, the references were to bodies and actions, even in Leviticus with its laws and commands. Entrails, kid-neys, loins, fat and blood: this was the law.

No wonder there were Gnostic sects that had believed the Lord in these texts was in fact the Devil. That the earth was made by the Devil, and that it was he we worshipped when we worshipped God.

Imagine if I were to preach such a thing.

I smiled.

Even today it would be the stuff of headlines.

There were many other interesting matters I could not take up or discuss, of course. The church and congregation was not the place to try out thoughts and ideas, to alter existing conceptions by questioning new life into them. What was important about faith was that it was true, and what was important about truth was that it eliminated all other possibilities. Truth was absolute. And it had to be too, I often thought, with life being so brittle. At the same time, the Bible was so complex, contained so many conflicting voices and models of under-standing that theology in the main had been all about bringing them together as an expression of one and the same thing, and the only pos-sible way to do that was by suppressing and hushing up, ignoring and letting be. One of the most familiar passages in the Old Testament was the story of Abraham being commanded to offer his son Isaac to the Lord, a sacrifice Abraham was prepared to make without asking ques-tions, and indeed he would certainly have done so had the Lord not intervened and stopped him, directing him to sacrifice a lamb instead. Less familiar, but also related, was the Old Testament story of Jephthah, who swore an oath to the Lord, saying that if he succeeded in defeating the Ammonites in battle he would offer to the Lord the first person he met on his return. And Jephthah duly defeated the Ammonites, and conquered twenty cities, and when he returned home the first person he met was his own daughter, who came from the doors of his house to greet and celebrate him. She was his only child. He tore his clothes in despair and told her he had given a promise to the Lord which he could not break. And she said to him, Father, if you have given your oath to the Lord, then do with me according to its word. But allow me one thing: let me be alone for two months so that I may go up and down on the mountains and weep for my virginity, I and my companions. And when the two months expired, Jephthah offered her to the Lord, and the Lord did not intervene to stop him as He had done when Abraham had bound his son for the offering.

This was a story that could not be held up in the work of any priest. Had I been a theologist, in the employment of that university department, I could have written about it and brought it up in my teaching, but I wasn't. No one wanted a priest who would preach on the religion's female offering. I didn't want to be that kind of priest, either. If there was such a thing as feminist theology, it had to unfold itself in practice, not in theory. In encounters with people, not in the sermon, not in ideas, but in goodwill and benevolence between people. We had to listen, ask, empathise, accommodate. For it was there, in the spaces between us, that God was to be found. That was the message of Jesus. *In the eyes of God we are all equal.*

There were a lot of things I didn't believe in. But I believed in that.

That was the core.

Or rather, not the core, I thought, swallowing another mouthful of my coffee, which had now gone cold. A core is something solid and unyielding.

This was something fluid, something in constant flux.

Or rather, not in flux exactly, because it remained the same albeit in ever shifting forms, among ever shifting constellations of people.

I'd been staring out of the window for some time without looking at the view. Now, what I saw seemed to suddenly materialise and come into being. Dry lawns, white wooden fences, fruit trees, outer walls, all drenched in sunlight.

Was it really the case that colours did not exist on their own, but were constructed in the brain?

A cat appeared down by the fence. It sauntered onto the lawn, lay down and lazed in the sun.

Upstairs, the shower was turned on.

Was that the time already?

I sent my email off to Erlend, opened another document and began to type what I was going to say at the funeral. A bit later, I heard Gaute come down the stairs. I knew that he would sit on one of the bar stools at the kitchen island with a bowl of Special K while checking the news on his phone, and then have a cup of coffee. In the half-hour that followed he would prepare his day at the desk in the living room, before the children woke and took up the next hour until it was time to go to school.

I couldn't avoid him for the rest of my life, and I couldn't disappear for another evening either, so when the children had gone to bed either conflict or reconciliation was inevitable.

At eight o'clock I went upstairs to their rooms and woke them up. Marie was in good cheer from the word go, up and dressed in no time. Peter was reluctant and difficult to rouse.

Did he pick up on the ill feeling between us?

Of course he did.

But was it sufficient to get to him like that?

'Peter, my big boy, you're going to be late,' I said, returning to his room and finding him still not up. 'You've time for breakfast, but you must get up now.'

He lay with his eyes closed.

'He's asleep,' I said, as if to myself. 'I wonder how I can wake him. Or perhaps he can sleepwalk?'

'Mm,' he said.

I took hold of his hands and pulled him slowly upright.

'That's amazing,' I said.

He put his feet on the floor and stood up, still with his eyes closed, and stretched his arms out in front of him.

'Are you asleep, Peter?' I said.

'Mm,' he said.

'I wonder if he can get dressed in his sleep too?'

Five minutes later he was seated at the table eating his cornflakes with his sister. Perhaps I was too sensitive to his moods, I thought, and leaned in over him, putting my cheek to his.

'Good morning, grumpy guts,' I said. 'Are you awake now?'

'Mm,' he said, nodding.

'I want a hug as well!' said Marie.

I hugged her, and then sat down opposite them.

'Why isn't Daddy here?' said Marie.

'He's got some work to do,' I said.

'He works before working at work,' said Peter.

Marie laughed.

The little loves, I thought as they went down the drive with their school rucksacks on their backs and I stood in the doorway waving. They'll be fine.

Gaute, who I'd barely seen that morning, left shortly after. We hadn't exchanged a word, but at least he said goodbye when he went.

The only thing in my diary for that day was the funeral service beginning at eleven o'clock, which I'd already prepared, but still I drove off to the church as soon as Gaute had left. I liked being there, in the church itself, and in my little office in the adjoining building.

Another lovely day by the looks of it, I thought as I got out of the car. Everything was still and the air already so warm that in some places it was actually visible, shimmering little columns above the gravel.

But the church, with its thick white walls, looked almost wintry, even in the sunshine.

I walked past it and went into the annexe, where first I knocked on Karin's door. She looked up with a smile as I went in. She asked about the seminar, and I'd just started telling her about it when a car pulled up at the rear of the church. That will be the undertakers, I thought, glancing at the time. It was hardly even ten o'clock yet.

'I'll go out and speak to them,' I said. 'Looks like there'll be no mourners.'

'How awful,' said Karin. 'Man or woman?'

'A man.'

'Elderly, was he?'

'In his sixties,' I said.

'Ah,' she said. 'I'm not sure how you cope, surrounded by all that grief.'

'There's always a light,' I said, smiled and left her again.

The doors of the side entrance were open. Two men from the funeral directors' stood bent over the open coffin. I'd seen both of them before, a number of times, but I couldn't remember their names.

'Hello,' I said.

They straightened up and nodded in reply.

One of them was young, no more than in his early thirties. He had a beard and his hair was gathered in a ponytail, but his informal appearance was at least partly compensated for by the white shirt and black suit. The other man was around sixty, with a large head and a ponderous-looking face. In terms of age, they could have been father and son, but were of such different builds they probably weren't.

'Did you find any more information on him?' the older one said.

'I'm afraid not,' I said. 'All we have is his date and place of birth. That, and his address. How about you?'

'Nothing,' the young one said. 'Not a trace. No relatives, no friends.'

'Workmates, colleagues?'

'No luck there, either. He had his own firm, apparently, though what he actually did seems a bit of a mystery, too.'

'There's nothing sadder, is there?' I said. 'When there's no one to mourn the deceased, I mean. Will you stay for the service?'

They nodded, and I looked down into the coffin.

At once, it felt as if the blood drained from my head.

I knew that face.

It was the man from the lift. The man who had pestered me in the arrivals hall.

But it was impossible.

It was impossible.

The death had been registered ten days ago. The funeral was booked a week ago.

'Are you all right?' the young undertaker said.

'Do you know him?' the older one said.

'No,' I said. 'I don't know him.'

EMIL

The last hour was always the best. The youngest kids would just have finished their nap then and were so drowsy and lifeless all they wanted to do was sit in your lap, while the older ones were exhausted after a whole day bombing about, they too ready for a bit of peace and quiet. I normally took them all into the comfy room and put some music on for them, before reading them a story or two. They liked Americana, and that afternoon I put Father John Misty on. Other favourites were early Pink Floyd — 'Echoes' in particular they liked — and Kraftwerk.

After a year working there, it still amazed me how they bought into even the most sophisticated music, as opposed to the stories, which had to be almost impossibly simple to hold their interest. The stories they liked best were ones that mirrored some aspect of their own lives, so there was a lot of Molly and Polly going to nursery school, or eating their dinner or going to see Nana and Nanda, Peppa Pig splashing about in paddling pools, and that cute crocodile.

How weird was that? They could actually *enjoy* a violin concerto by Bach, sit there spellbound and listen, while everything else in their lives had to be simpler than simple.

I switched the fan off, put the music on and sat down against the wall with Aksel on my lap and Liam and Frida snuggled up to me on either side. The others lay on their backs looking at the ceiling as they listened.

Luckily, they didn't understand the words, which were all about sharpened knives, capsizing boats, and bleeding to death!

Through the window I saw Saida cross the yard, almost certainly going for a smoke on the street outside the gate. Mercedes and Gunn I knew were sitting under the parasol over in the far corner, though I couldn't see them from where I was sitting. The water from the sprinkler which the older kids had been playing under earlier on had all but dried up, and the hose had been coiled and put in its place. The toys and bikes had all been taken in.

Fifty minutes before closing.

I turned the music off and found the book we were going to read. The kids gathered around me, they sat close, some almost cuddled up to each other. The little ones didn't distinguish much between their own bodies and others. Was there something animal-like about that? And about them generally, in fact? Their creeping and crawling, their wordless utterings and enigmatic eyes.

'Can you remember what happened when we read yesterday?' I said.

'Mia was having a bath,' said Kevin.

'That's right,' I said. 'And today we're going to read about her going on her summer holiday.'

'We've been on summer holiday,' said Kevin.

'Yes, you have,' I said. 'I have too. Does anyone know what the season after summer is called?'

'I think it's autumn,' said Jo.

'Autumn,' I said. 'That's right. But in the book it's still summer!'

A smell came from one of them. It had to be Liam, he was looking withdrawn all of a sudden, and his face was flushed.

I reckoned it could wait a bit and began to read, turning the book and showing them the pictures every time I turned the page. The older ones grew restless after only a few minutes, fidgeting or looking around the room for something of interest. But the little ones were with me all the way.

At the same moment I finished, the door opened and Saida poked her head round.

'Everything all right in here?' she said.

'Yes, fine. Maybe you could take them outside for a minute, though, so I can change Liam here,' I said, turning towards him. 'All right, Liam?'

He nodded silently and looked at me with his soft brown eyes.

So while the older ones ran about in the yard, I put Liam down on the changing table in the bathroom.

'One, two, three!' I said, and snatched off his socks.

I'd expected him to laugh the way he normally did, but instead he started howling and kicking, and had soon worked himself into a frenzy.

'All right, settle down,' I said, clamping his legs under my arm while I tried to get his shorts off him with my other hand. 'What's put you in such a bad mood all of a sudden? It's a lovely sunny day, and your mummy will be here soon to collect you!'

One of the other kids came in and sat down on the toilet in one of the open cubicles. It was Lillian. She dangled her legs and gave me a cheeky grin while Liam screamed.

'Why is he angry?' she said.

'I don't know,' I said, and took my arm away from his legs. It was impossible to change him anyway for the time being.

Lillian tore off a piece of toilet paper and wiped herself, pulled her knickers up and was just about to go out when I stopped her.

'You've forgotten to wash your hands,' I said.

'Oh, yes,' she said, and went over to the sink where she stood on the little plastic step stool to reach the tap.

Liam was still yelling and kicking. I wondered, as Lillian went out again, whether to change him by force or lift him up and carry him around with me for a bit until he settled down, and then do it.

I looked around for something that might distract him.

My eyes latched on to a cuddly rabbit on the shelf above him. I offered it to him, only he batted it out of my hand.

A proper rage he was in.

'I'm going to have to change you anyway, Liam,' I said. 'We'll be done in no time, you'll see.'

I gripped his ankles in one hand and undid the ties of the nappy with the other. The poo inside was soft and yellow, smeared all over his thighs and buttocks. I lifted his legs and pulled the nappy away, rolled it up and dropped it in the nappy bin. Only then I realised the wet wipes were on the opposite shelf on the other side of the room.

So there I stood, holding on tight to a screaming little boy with his bum all messy with poo.

'Saida?' I called out. 'Can you come and give me a hand?'

But there was no answer.

Either I could let go of him and dart across to get them — it wouldn't take a second, and even if he was on his own on the changing table he wouldn't be able to fall down from there before I was with him again — or else I could lift him up and carry him. But then I'd get poo on me, and poo on the changing table was definitely a better option than poo on my clothes.

'I just need to get the wet wipes, Liam,' I said. 'Just lie still a second, all right?'

By some miracle, he stopped kicking.

With my left hand outstretched and ready to stop him if he fell, I turned round, made a dart to the other side of the room and grabbed the packet off the shelf.

It was empty.

Who the hell left an empty packet there? Quickly, I opened the cup-board where the new ones were kept, snatched a packet and swivelled round just in time to see Liam wriggle over the edge of the changing table. I jumped across, but too late, and he fell to the floor.

He hit his head first.

His eyes were open as I bent over him, but totally vacant.

He's dead, was the first thing I thought.

Oh, no, no.

Then it was as if the part of him that was him came back, and he stared up at me.

He was quite still.

I picked him up and held him tight.

'Are you all right?' I said. 'Did you hurt yourself?'

He wasn't crying, not even a whimper.

It's lino, I told myself. It's soft. And it's a low table.

Everything was all right.

Not a mark on his head, as far as I could tell. Perhaps there'd be a bump after a bit.

I put him down again carefully and began to wash him.

But there was something different about him.

He'll be in shock, I thought, and wiped my T-shirt with a wet wipe before putting a clean nappy on him, then his shorts.

Maybe he'd got a concussion?

That was probably it.

That was why he was different.

I dropped the wet wipes in the bin, picked him up and went outside into the yard where the others were. No one had seen anything, and there was no reason to tell them. Nothing had happened.

I put him down in the sandpit and went over to the others.

Liam sat there staring into the air in front of him.

He must still have been dazed.

'You can go now if you want, Emil,' said Mercedes. 'It's such a gorgeous day!'

'Thanks, that's *really* nice of you,' I said.

'Only because we like you,' she said, and laughed.

A bit further away, Frida's mother came in through the gate, shoved her sunglasses on top of her head and waved at us, and behind her came Jo's mother, pushing a bike.

I told myself I'd better get going before Liam's parents came, and got to my feet. If he was still just as quiet then, they might start asking if something had happened, and I didn't feel like lying to them.

'Hi, Emil,' Frida's mother said. 'Are you going out tonight?'

'I was thinking about it,' I said. 'How about you? Any plans?'

She shrugged and smiled.

'I'm sure we'll think of something,' she said, crouching down as Frida came running up to her.

'See you all, then,' I said, making sure everyone heard, and went out through the gate to where my bike was chained to the fence. I unlocked it, rolled it forward a few steps, got on and started to pedal at the same time as I pulled my phone out of my pocket and pressed Mathilde's number.

'Hi!' she said.

'Are you in?' I said.

'No, I'm at the park. I couldn't stay in on a day like this. Are you off now, or what?'

'Yes.'

'Are you going to come and join us, then?'

'I've got rehearsal,' I said.

'Not until seven, you haven't,' she said. 'Come on, I miss you.'

'OK,' I said, pulling into the side and stopping for a second; the street ahead of me went steeply downhill and was cobbled besides. 'Who are you with?'

'Jorunn and Tuva,' she said.

'OK,' I said again. 'I'll be there in ten or so.'

'Brilliant!' she said.

After I hung up I scrolled through the texts I'd got while I'd been at work. Both Trond and Frode wanted to know if we were going out after rehearsal, Dad was asking us to go out with him in the boat at the weekend, and Fredrik wanted to borrow some cash. He wasn't exactly asking, but I knew it was what he was after.

I called him up.

'When are you going to pay me back, then?' I said.

'What are you on about?' he said.

'You want to borrow some money, don't you?'

'Not any more, I don't,' he said. 'Not if you're going to be so clever about it.'

'You can, though,' I said. 'Only I want it back. How much are we talking about?'

'Five hundred, maybe?'

'OK, no problem. Are you coming up?'

'You're not going down into town, by any chance?' he said.

'I'm down there now.'

'I meant later.'

'Are you in?' I said.

'Yes.'

'Is Mum there?'

'Why would she be? It's only four o'clock.'

'Just wondering. How's she doing?'

'All right, I reckon. You could give her a ring.'

'I will do,' I said. 'Anyway, catch you later.'

'What about the money?'

'Oh, I forgot,' I said. 'I'll be down at Verftet between seven and nine at least.'

'Perfect,' he said. 'See you then!'

I hung up and replied to my texts, put my earphones in and found

Ohia in my music before setting off down the hill. There were people out everywhere, on all the pavements and all the squares, the cafes and restaurants were packed.

Ohia took the top off my high, balancing it out. Ohia's world was dark and depressive, and especially beautiful in the light. Unnervingly beautiful.

Not until I reached the road that ran along the Vågen harbour did the thought of Liam come back into my mind.

A terrible feeling came over me.

He could have injured himself seriously. Maybe he'd started vomiting. They wouldn't understand why.

Or blood might come out of his ears.

Head injuries were dangerous.

I should have told someone. I wouldn't have to say he fell off the changing table, I could have just told them he fell as he was toddling along, fell against something hard, a hard surface. They'd know then, and could take him for a check-up if necessary.

Now it was too late. I couldn't just phone them and say, listen, your son fell down at nursery school today, I forgot to mention it.

It hadn't been my fault.

The fault was not telling someone.

But most probably he was fine. No cause for concern.

I jumped off the bike and pushed it up the hill towards Sydneshaugen, cycled through the park and caught sight of the group on my way down the hill on the other side, they were sitting on the grass below, Mathilde easily picked out in her white bikini.

I pulled up. She wasn't only with Jorunn and Tuva like she'd said, there were three others with them as well. I recognised them, student friends of Tuva's.

Why hadn't she said?

It almost looked a bit lewd, three girls in bikinis, three fully clothed lads lounging in their company.

I felt like turning round and heading home, phoning her to say I'd changed my mind.

But there was every chance I'd already been seen. In which case I was going to look stupid.

I pedalled the last bit and swung in to join them.

'Hello, you!' Mathilde said, looking up at me without taking her sunglasses off.

'So this is where you are, wasting the day away,' I said, and leaned my bike against a tree before bending down to give her a kiss.

'I've got to go to work soon,' she said. 'So you can't be talking about me.'

'How you doing? All right?' said one of the students.

'Yeah, good,' I said.

'You work in a nursery school, don't you?'

'That's right,' I said, and sat down next to Mathilde. She was sitting with her legs tucked underneath her like a mermaid's tail. Sunscreen, her flowery skirt, white top and sandals lay in a little pile behind her.

'Do you want some wine?' one of the others said.

'No, thanks, I'm on my bike,' I said.

I could tell I'd spoiled it for them. They'd have to stop ogling her and chatting her up now.

'I saw the priest again today,' Mathilde said.

'What priest?' I said. 'Oh, that's right, the one who confirmed you.'

Mathilde had been working behind a hotel reception desk for the summer. The previous morning she'd got home and told me the priest from her confirmation had checked into the hotel at half an hour's notice. She hadn't recognised Mathilde, and Mathilde hadn't made herself known to her either, not wanting her to feel like she'd been sussed. Looks like marriage problems, if you ask me, she'd said. Why else would you check into a hotel in your own city? Maybe they're decorating or something, I said, and she'd looked at me like I was thick. At half past twelve at night? I like to think the best of people, I said.

'She came into the chemist's in the shopping centre while I was there,' she said now. 'Have a guess what she bought?'

I shook my head.

'A pregnancy test! So something's going on in her life by the looks of it.'

'Priests can have kids too,' I said.

'It is a bit odd, though, you've got to admit? She goes to a hotel in the middle of the night and then buys a pregnancy test the day after?'

I didn't like gossip, and hadn't thought she did either.

Fuck. Now I was getting negative again.

It was a glorious day, everyone was out in the sun, and I was with Mathilde, who was gorgeous, cool and clever, everything I dreamt about in a girl, and I was even about to go off and rehearse with our band which was really starting to come together.

Only here I was, misery guts, sulking underneath it all.

I lifted my head and looked up at the crown of the tree above us, a torch of green held upright by an ingenious network of roots and branches, and then I looked at her, her pale skin that never tanned and was always cool to the touch, and she smiled at me.

'Are you coming out with us later, Emil?' Jorunn said.

'I don't think so,' I said. 'We're rehearsing tonight and I've got an early start in the morning. But thanks all the same!'

I longed to be on my own with her. We were always so good on our own together, and I never had so much fun as when I was out drinking with just her. But we couldn't spend our lives in a bubble, I realised that.

One thing I'd decided, I'd say yes without a moment's hesitation if she ever started talking about kids. I wouldn't bring it up myself, though. I didn't want to frighten her off, kids were major, and we were so young. Besides, I was scared she wasn't thinking so far ahead with us, that I was just a sort of youthful fling. If I started trying to tie her down, there was every chance she'd dump me.

But we were living together and it hadn't even been something we'd talked about, we just moved in with each other as soon as the chance appeared.

'Anyone fancy a game of pétanque?' one of the students asked. He was tall and lanky with a fringe that hung down over his eyes like a curtain. Every now and then he'd toss his head stupidly to get it out of the way. I seemed to remember his name was Atle.

'Good idea,' his mate Anders said.

'Have we got the energy?' Mathilde said.

'Come on,' said Tuva, and got to her feet, bending down to pick up her skirt and put it on.

I stood up too.

'Think I'll leave you to it,' I said. 'Need to go home and get something to eat.'

Mathilde put her arms around me and looked up at me.

'See you in the morning, bright and early,' she said.

I kissed her. Turning onto the road, I looked back and saw them going over to the sandy pétanque court, all of them together.

An hour and a half later I was sitting at the back of the bus with my guitar beside me, listening to Fela Kuti. As I looked out of the window I tried to push all the houses and buildings into the background, foregrounding the trees and plants to see what the world would look like if *they* were what everything was about instead of us.

It was something I'd started doing while I was still at gymnasium school and got the bus every day. I'd been a deputy in the Nature and Youth organisation and passionate about the environment. I think it came from my art teacher who'd encouraged us when drawing to try and capture the space between the flowers and the leaves in a vase, for instance, or the space between the furniture in a room. Because it was something similar that happened with the trees, they seemed suddenly to step forward and become visible even though they'd been there all the time.

I got off at Klosteret and turned down one of the lanes, then onto the road leading towards Verftet, following the fjord, its blue glaze, the sun glittering on it like little coins of light.

I caught sight of Trond further down the hill, dressed in black as ever, a carrier bag dangling from his wrist, that too a fixture. His drumsticks were in it, I knew that, and gaffer tape and drum keys and gloves, and almost definitely a bottle of Coke as well. I'd bought him a rucksack the Christmas before, but he hadn't taken the hint.

Next Christmas I'd get him some shorts, I said to myself, and shouted his name.

He turned round and waited.

'Hello,' he said.

'Anything new?' I said as we clasped hands.

He shook his head.

His face was broad and freckled, his lips were broad, his nose was broad, his eyes deep and dark, even though they were blue. He was rather short in stature, and stocky too.

We'd been friends since nursery school, so, apart from my brother, Trond was the person I knew best in all the world.

'What's this not coming out with us all about?' he said as we carried on down the road.

'Got to go to work,' I said.

Something dark sprang into my mind.

Liam.

If only he was all right.

'So have I,' he said. 'And I've got to be up at four.'

I shrugged.

'I'm not you. I need more sleep than that.'

'There's not many nights like this in a year,' he said.

'Not here, anyway!' I said. 'Anyway, we'll see. I don't suppose a beer or two's going to make much difference.'

'You're getting less and less rock'n'roll by the month, you do know?' he said. 'Shacking up, nursery school job.'

'Look who's talking! Still living with his mum and dad and working in a bakery.'

'At least I don't go to bed at half past nine.'

'No, you only start yawning your head off at six,' I said. 'Remember when we went to see the Ziggy Stardust film at the film club? Oh, sorry, you wouldn't, would you, you slept all the way through it.'

Further down, the old sardine factory came into view.

'I might have a new song, by the way,' I said.

'Yeah?' said Trond. 'That's good news.'

'Not sure how good it is, though. It's only the lyrics, really. And a rough idea of how it could go.'

'Great,' he said.

'Probably not, actually,' I said. 'Not sure I even want to say what it's called, it's that stupid.'

'What's it called?'

'Shall we go round and see if they're here yet?' I said, indicating with a nod of my head the outdoor cafe area on the other side of the building.

'Don't try and worm your way out,' he said. 'Come on, what's it called?'

I looked at him and grinned without saying anything. He grinned back.

Frode and Kenneth were sitting at one of the tables with a beer each, their guitar cases beside them on the decking. They waved to us and we went over.

'Emil's got a new song,' Trond said. 'Only it's so crap he can't tell us what it's called.'

' "Heartstorm",' I said.

'Mathilde chucked you, has she?' Frode said with a snort.

'What's best, "a storm in *the* heart" or "a storm in *my* heart"?'

'Both sound good to me,' Trond said.

'Neither, they both sound rubbish,' said Frode.

I'd like to see you come up with something better, I thought to myself, but kept my mouth shut. Frode could be a right turd sometimes, but I'd never played with a better guitarist. Never over-embellishing, always getting it right.

'We can always tweak the lyrics,' I said. 'Have you got the key?'

Kenneth, who rarely said anything unless someone spoke to him, nodded.

They drank up and we went inside, into the old factory building to the rehearsal room we used. Just as we'd got set up and tuned, my phone thrummed in my pocket. It was Mathilde.

How come you were so miffed in the park? I LOVE you, you know that, she wrote.

I wasn't miffed! I wrote back. *Just knackered after work. You're everything I want!*

I was about to put it away when she sent another:

Come and see me at work afterwards?

Nothing I'd rather do! I typed back, only then becoming aware of the others standing demonstratively motionless, waiting for me. I slipped the phone back into my pocket.

'Sorry,' I said. 'Shall we run through the set first?'

An hour later, after we'd gone through all the songs, we stopped for a break. Frode and Kenneth went outside for a smoke. Trond and I stayed put.

I read through the lyrics for the new song and felt mostly like keeping them to myself, but messaged them to the others anyway.

A lull at first
then comes the wind
ah, then comes the wind
Then comes the rain
ah, then comes the rain

And the storm is breaking loose
no sign of a truce

A storm in the heart
rain and wind
we were meant to be twinned
A storm in the heart
rain and wind
we were meant to be twinned

The streets of the heart are empty
the words you say torment me
The wind bends the trees of the heart
the rain keeps us ever apart
The heart's heavens are dark
the rain of the heart our mark

A storm in the heart
rain and wind
we were meant to be twinned
A storm in the heart
rain and wind
we were meant to be twinned

A lull at first
then comes the wind,
ah, then comes the wind
Then comes the rain
ah, then comes the rain

Trond's phone pinged behind me.

'Really good, Emil,' he said a minute later.

'Do you think so?' I turned to face him. He was sitting leaning forward with his elbows on his thighs, phone in hand.

'Yeah, really good,' he said.

'Thanks,' I said.

There was a knock on the door, and I went over to let them in.

'The heart is a fart!' said Frode.

'Very funny,' I said.

'You *have* had a bust-up with Mathilde, haven't you?' he said with his biggest grin.

'Can we use it, or can't we?' I said, and went and sat down, picking up my guitar in the process.

'We can,' he said. 'But the heart/apart rhyme might not be the most original.'

'No, you're right,' I said. 'I can mumble it there, though. Michael Stipe style, so no one catches on.'

'Or we can just get rid,' he said. 'It shouldn't make much difference.'

'How about "the trees of the heart fall foul"?' I said. 'And then something that rhymes with "foul"?'

'Growl!' said Frode. '"The bear of the heart says growl."'

Without warning, tears came to my eyes and I turned away. Right, that's bloody it, I said to myself, blinking a few times as I faced the wall, then switched off my amp, unstrapped my guitar and put it away in the case.

'What are you doing?' Frode said. 'It was only a joke! You weren't supposed to take it like that!'

I picked up the case and went towards the door. I knew I shouldn't say anything, just go, and leave them with something to think about.

'I've had it up to here with you,' I said, looking straight at Frode. 'I put my soul into those lyrics, in case you want to know.'

He threw up his arms.

'For Christ's sake, man, it was a joke! How self-important can you get?'

I slammed the door after me and walked slowly through the empty corridor, stopping for a moment outside to give them a chance to catch up with me.

No one came.

They were probably sitting there laughing at me.

But it was my band. They were my songs.

I started off up the hill.

I'd made a fool of myself. Shown them how weak I was.

But I couldn't go back. That would be even weaker.

My phone rang.

It was Frode.

I stood and looked at his name on the display. If I didn't answer, the band would be finished. And it would be my fault.

Was that what I wanted?

I pictured the confusion in Mathilde's eyes when I turned up early, and imagined what my explanation was going to sound like to her: 'Frode was teasing me, so I left.'

It was better to humiliate myself in front of them than in front of her, I reasoned, and took the call.

'Sorry, Emil,' Frode said. 'I didn't mean to hurt your feelings.'

'You didn't,' I said. 'But thanks anyway.'

'Are you coming back, then?'

'Yes,' I said, hung up and turned round.

Far out in the fjord, a ship looked like it was having a piss, a great jet of water arcing out from it into the air. The water glittered in the sunlight. Now and then, the air shimmered like a rainbow. It was like I was dreaming, the humiliation I felt was so enormous it completely took over my whole outlook, as if I had no say in the matter.

I shut out the hum of voices from the cafe and went through the empty corridor to the rehearsal room while trying not to feel anything.

The others pretended nothing had happened, and I was grateful for it. But I couldn't pretend. I'd been too stupid for that.

'I'm sorry I went off like that,' I said. 'I don't know what came over me.'

'Don't think about it,' Frode said. 'Writing's a sensitive business.'

'It's not that,' I said.

'No,' he said. 'I just thought I'd say so to lighten things up a bit.'

'Can we play some bloody music now?' said Trond.

*

After the rehearsal we stayed behind for a few beers, standing at the bar of the crowded cafe outside. We talked about what we always talked about, the band and the songs, and how we could go about recording our material. Fredrik turned up in a pair of marine-blue shorts, white shirt and boat shoes, and hung out with us for a bit for appearances' sake — it was a fair bit of money he wanted to borrow this time — but he couldn't disguise how he didn't belong with us and left again at the first opportunity, when a fat guy with sweat stains under his arms squeezed between us and raised two fingers in the air to indicate his order to the barman. Fredrik, who'd been forced to step aside, caught my attention.

'I reckon I'll be off,' he said. 'See you at the weekend, though.'

'You're coming? Brilliant!' I said.

'It's hard to believe you two are brothers,' said Frode after he'd gone.

'And that he's borrowing from you instead of the other way round,' said Trond.

The guy with the sweaty armpits lifted his two pints high into the air and forged a path through the throng.

'Do you know who that is?' Frode said, lowering his voice and watching him as he went.

I shook my head.

'Lindland. The guy who interviewed Heksa that time.'

'Was that him?'

'Yes. They demoted him to the arts section after that.'

'That would be a promotion in my world,' I said.

'He's a bit of a dick.'

'So's Heksa,' I said.

Frode snorted.

'There's no word for what *he* is.'

'I went to nursery school with him,' said Kenneth.

We all looked at him.

'With *Heksa*?' said Frode.

Kenneth nodded casually and slurped his beer.

'How come you never told us *that* before?'

He shrugged.

'No one ever asked.'

'Of course no one ever asked!' said Frode. 'How the hell were we supposed to know there was anything to ask *about*?'

'What was he like?' I said.

Kenneth shrugged again.

'Just normal. A bit timid, maybe.'

We laughed about it and chinked our glasses together. When I left half an hour or so later, with Trond who had a bus to catch to take him out to Fantoft, I actually had a good feeling in my chest. How idiotic it would have been, to chuck the band in just because a few little feelings had been hurt.

Mathilde looked up from the reception desk when I came in through the door, and the smile she gave me was something no one could have faked.

It made me so happy I leaned across the desk and kissed her, even if she did always keep telling me not to when she was at work.

'You look so incredibly sexy in that uniform,' I said softly, and kissed her on the throat. She shoved me away with a smile, the way you would with a boisterous dog.

'How was the rehearsal?' she said.

'Excellent,' I said.

'Great!' she said.

'What about you?' I said.

Instead of answering me she nodded towards the street outside where two buses pulled up, one after the other.

'It's going to be chaos here any minute,' she said. 'I'm sorry. I didn't know.'

'That's OK,' I said. 'I'm a bit whacked, anyway.'

'Will you phone me before you go to bed?'

'Of course,' I said, and kissed her again.

'I miss you already,' I said as the first of the tourists came in and she directed her smile towards them rather than me.

'Ciao, Emilio,' she said, and flashed her eyes at me.

Outside in the street, where the air, so hot it felt like the Mediterranean, was saturated with darkness, I put my earphones in and browsed the albums on my phone. I hated playlists — apart from the ones I sent

Mathilde, that is. I decided on Bill Callahan's *Apocalypse*. 'He's got a deep voice!' the kids had said when I'd played it to them. And he had, too.

Liam, little Liam, please be all right.

The bus was already waiting behind the shopping centre when I got to the stop. I switched to David Crosby's *If I Could Only Remember My Name* and listened to it all the way up to the hospital. I really liked the warmth of those seventies productions, and the lightness in the playing, all the little licks and riffs they kept tossing in, with no one straining themselves, just dropping by the studio in the afternoon and laying something down before going off to the beach, smoking a bit of grass, having a dip in the sea or whatever they did then, before going back and doing a few more takes. They could *play*. The music was *alive*. The way *people* are alive.

But mostly I liked the warmth of the sound.

At the bus stop outside the hospital I replied to a couple of texts before going into the Narvesen and buying a tube of Pringles, a 7 Up and some sweets. That would get Trond going if he could see me, I thought to myself with a smile. Cola dummies and liquorice caramels instead of heroin.

I took a photo and sent it to him, texting that this was what I wanted on our rider when we got famous.

Better than carrots, any rate, he replied.

And rather a hole in the tooth than a hole in the soul, I typed back.

He replied after I'd paid and gone out.

That's where you're wrong. How many good songs do you know about toothache?

You had to think about that, didn't you? I wrote and started walking up the hill with the phone still in my hand in case he replied. He didn't, and after a bit I slipped it back into my pocket again. The sky above me was blue-black, and the dark fells that loomed on all sides made it seem like I was looking up at the stars from the bottom of a well.

I shifted my guitar case to my other hand and regretted not having waited a bit longer for the other bus that would have taken me all the way, when suddenly the birds began to sing.

I stopped. Above the fells, day was dawning.

It couldn't be!

I swivelled round. On the other side, a light rose into the sky.

It wasn't the sun. It wasn't the moon. It was a kind of star.

But how big it was!

I put my guitar case down, got my phone out and called Mathilde.

The birds were chirping madly all the way up the slope of the fell. A faint, ghostly veil appeared.

'Hi!' she said. 'Off to bed already?'

'No, I'm not even home yet,' I said. 'There's something in the sky. Have you seen it?'

'No?' she said.

'A gigantic star or something. It's really weird. The birds have all started singing. I'm standing on the road just below the house.'

'Oh,' she said.

'You've got to go out and look as soon as you get the chance,' I said. 'It's amazing.'

'I will,' she said.

'OK,' I said. 'I'll call you again in a few minutes.'

I hung up and walked the last bit of the way, turning round all the time to look at the star or whatever it was, which was rising disturbingly quickly now.

We rented the whole of the first floor plus two attic rooms from an old lady who lived on her own, and we paid a pittance in rent. As I opened the gate and went up the path, I saw the flickering light of the TV in her living room. For a brief moment I wondered whether to ring her doorbell and tell her to come outside and see, but it would probably only give her a heart attack, I thought, and instead I just followed the path to our entrance round the back.

As I put the key in the door, there was a heavy rustle from the woods just behind the house.

A deer, I thought.

Something came charging.

I wheeled round and saw a figure come hurtling from the trees. It was a man. He halted abruptly beside the apple tree and bent forward, hands on knees, gasping for breath as he stared back in the direction from which he'd come.

'Hey!' I said. 'What are you doing?'

He looked at me. Even from a distance I could tell he was scared to death. His eyes were wide with fright.

Without a word, he crashed on, through the garden and out into the road.

I stood transfixed until the sound of his running footsteps died away.

Then I let myself in, took the guitar out of its case and put it in its stand in the living room, pulled open the can of 7 Up and phoned Mathilde as I stared at the glowing ball in the sky across the valley.

ISELIN

The old lady came towards me past the confectionery with her shopping bag hanging from her arm. She was wearing a beige overcoat, despite it being more than thirty degrees outside.

'Hello,' I said as she got to the checkout and opened the bag she'd put her items in.

She was small and very thin, and white bristles of hair stuck out from her chin. It was repulsive and I couldn't understand why she didn't get rid of them. Just because you were old didn't mean you had to stop caring about your appearance, surely?

'Hello there,' she said, and began putting her items on the conveyor one by one.

'Very hot today,' I said, looking up at her as I scanned them.

She didn't reply, but took out her purse.

Her eyes were unclear in a way, or watery. The skin of her throat was very wrinkled. That's where you can tell if people have had cosmetic surgery. The throat and the hands. Not that it was relevant in her case!

She wasn't slow, I saw that now. How come I'd always thought she was? Her fingers dipped nimbly into her wallet to pick out her card.

'That'll be 176 kroner, please,' I said.

Without looking at me or saying anything she held her card over the reader.

Although we saw each other maybe three times a week, she didn't know I existed. They say old people disappear and become invisible, that it's a shame for them, but they're not much better themselves. It's so easy to think old people are good and nice, but of course they're just as bad as everyone else, at least the ones who were bad when they were young are.

She put her card back in her purse, put the purse in her bag and went to the end of the little checkout to put her shopping in the bag. When she was finished, she looked up at me.

'Oh, and a packet of mild cigarettes,' she said.

I hadn't seen that coming. Had the old biddy taken up smoking?

'You'll need a slip from the machine over there first,' I said. 'Then come back and pay here, and after that you can pick your cigarettes up from the machine over by the door.'

'What a lot of trouble,' she said. 'Why's that?'

'It's just the way it is, that's all,' I said, and sat back.

I examined my nails while she stood at the machine trying to work out what to do. If she needed help, she could ask. I'd just had my nails done, and the girl who'd done them for me had suggested a pale rose colour that I liked and which now gave me a little tingle of pleasure again. Red, the colour I normally used, made my fingers look small and chubby. They were too, but red drew attention to them. The same with bright red lipstick, it made my mouth look even smaller and my face even bigger and rounder.

'Come and help me out,' the woman said, turning to look at me.

'OK,' I said, and went over. 'What brand do you want?'

'Mild,' she said.

'There's a lot that are mild,' I said. 'Prince. Marlboro. Petterøes. Pall Mall. Camel. Nearly all the brands have a light version as well.'

Three girls came in through the door in a cloud of giggles and perfume.

'Prince,' she said.

I pressed the Prince logo and the selection options came up.

'Just the one packet?'

'Yes.'

When the slip came out I took it over to the till and scanned it. She paid, and I went with her to the cigarette machine, scanned the slip and handed her the packet that dropped into the pickup box at the bottom.

'Thank you,' she said curtly, putting the packet in her shopping bag and going out just as a tall man in his fifties came in and straight away sent me into a panic. I turned round quickly and only just avoided being seen.

Shit.

What was *he* doing here?

In a few minutes he'd be at the checkout putting his items on the conveyor, and there was no one else on except me. Helene was on her break, Dagfinn was in his office, Trude was in and out of the storeroom.

It was Ommundsen, there was no mistaking him, I recognised him straight away even though it had been three years since I left.

It was the last discussion in the world I wanted to have now.

At the checkout in Bunnpris.

Iselin? You're working here?

Me nodding and smiling, shifting uneasily on my chair, looking down at my feet.

Very sensible, earning some money alongside your studies! I imagined him saying. *How's the course going, anyway?*

Oh, fine, I'd have to say.

What was it again? Psychology, wasn't it?

And I would nod.

Lovely seeing you! I've thought about you often since you left. Which doesn't go for all my students, I can tell you.

Maybe he'd even ask me out for a coffee.

The three girls came to the checkout. Three Red Bull and three packets of fags. They couldn't be more than fourteen or fifteen, but I didn't ask for ID, I just wanted them out. They stood there squirming, hardly able to contain their sniggers once they realised I wasn't checking.

Ommundsen was somewhere at the back of the shop now. I got to my feet and walked as quickly as I could down the aisle to the door of the storeroom, there were customers coming in now and the till wasn't supposed to be left unmanned.

He came round the corner and I ducked my head, turning away from him as I went past.

To no avail.

'Iselin?' he said.

I pretended not to hear him, as if I wasn't Iselin at all, but hurried on, went through the storeroom door and out into the yard at the back, where Helene sat leaning against the wall, her eyes closed in the bright sunlight.

'Can you take over at the till for a couple of minutes? I need the loo,' I said.

She opened her eyes and turned her head to look up at me.

'Can't you keep it in for ten bloody minutes? I'm on my break.'

'You can have half mine afterwards. Go on.'

She sighed and got to her feet.

'Two minutes, or else,' she said. The pockmarks on her face were visible close up, and as always when she was on my back it was good to think that she looked so hideous.

I went back through the storeroom into the tiny, stinking toilet, locked the door behind me and sat down on the lid while I started to count to 120 and tried not to breathe through my nose.

My headache came back then. It was like a wire cutting through my brain. During the seconds it lasted, I was unable to think, unable to do anything, searing pain was the only thing there was.

Then, as quickly as it had come, it was gone. I pulled the chain in case anyone was keeping tabs on me outside, washed my hands, pulled some toilet paper off the roll and dabbed my hands with it, dropped it in the bowl, waited for the cistern to fill, and then flushed again.

He had to be gone by now, surely?

But as soon as I came back into the shop I found him standing there waiting for me on the other side of the door.

'Iselin,' he said. 'How nice to see you!'

He was tanned, in an immaculate white shirt, his teeth gleaming.

'Hello,' I said. 'Fancy seeing you here.'

'Yes, in town for the weekend with a colleague. We went to see *Orpheus* yesterday.'

'Sounds nice,' I said.

'How are things with you? You're working here, I see? I thought it was you, and so I asked the girl at the till.'

'Yes,' I said.

He scrutinised me.

'Things are fine,' I said. 'Everything is, really.'

'You'll soon be finished at uni, I suppose?'

'Not quite,' I said. 'Anyway, I've got to get back to the till now.'

'Yes, of course,' he said. 'What time do you get off? Perhaps we could meet up for a drink? If it wouldn't be too odd?'

'No, not at all,' I said.

He looked at me.

'Splendid! How about Café Opera?'

'Fine,' I said, and turned to walk away. 'See you there!'

He came after me with his shopping in a carrier bag.

'You didn't say what time you got off?'

'Eight,' I said.

'Half past eight, then. Would that be all right for you?'

I nodded.

'You mustn't think I go out with all my old students,' he said. 'It would be nice to hear how you're getting on, that's all.'

'Thanks, same here,' I said.

Helene glared at me.

'See you later, then!' I said to Ommundsen, who raised his hand in a wave as he went through the door, while I got back behind the till.

'You just blew your whole break, girl,' Helene said.

'OK.'

I felt like bursting into tears. He was so nice, and he'd really believed in me.

But no way was I going to meet him at Café Opera.

I hadn't eaten anything all day, so as soon as we'd shut I sat down on some pallets in the backyard with a bag of peanuts and a Diet Coke. My skin under my T-shirt was clammy and disgusting. The sun was going down, but the air above the asphalt still shimmered with heat. There was a smell of rotten fruit from the skip a bit further away. I plugged my earphones into my mobile and found my favourite Ariana Grande video, the one she made herself where she lays down a vocal and plays it back while singing the second voice, then plays it back while singing the third, and so on, voice upon voice, harmony upon harmony, until at last she's got a whole choir going there in her bedroom. It's a fantastic video. If anyone's a genius, it's her. People have no idea how difficult that is, what she does there. It should be impossible.

I usually watched it on my break, it was my little reward. That, or anything by Billie Eilish.

I put 'bad guy' on and leaned back against the wall. The music, so incredibly cool, made me want to go out, just fuck everything and go out drinking and dancing.

Helene was standing against the back gate smoking. Seeing me look at her, she opened her mouth and pretended to say something.

Ha ha, I mimed back.

Then she did say something.

I pulled out an earphone and gave her an enquiring look.

'Who was that bloke asking after you?' she said.

'No one in particular,' I said, and put the earphone back in.

She said something else.

'What?' I said.

'Didn't look like it to me,' she said. 'Who was he?'

'An old teacher.'

'Were you shagging him?'

'Oh, for God's sake,' I said, twisting the earphone and turning up the volume before shaking the rest of the peanuts into my hand and chucking them into my mouth.

Couldn't she just get lost? If I was going out, I'd have to put some make-up on, but I wasn't going to do it while she was around. And the toilet was too disgusting.

I turned the music off and pressed Jonas's number, but changed my mind after only one ring, hung up and sent him a text instead.

You got any plans for tonight?

I stood up, went and got my bag, then locked myself in the loo, the only place I could be on my own.

Already out. You? he replied.

If he'd wanted to meet up, he'd have said where he was. So I wrote back and told him I was working late, had been thinking of popping round on my way home, but that I'd see him later in the week.

I put a goldish-looking eyeshadow on that had a bit of glitter in it, darkened my eyelashes and drew a line out from the corner of each eye. It gave me an accentuated look, which I liked, something strong and passionate. Then a paler lipstick than usual, some shading on my cheeks to make them seem that little bit narrower.

I understood him not wanting me hanging around with him and his mates. Even if I wouldn't show him up in any way, having your elder sister in tow was embarrassing enough on its own.

But still it hurt.

I remembered when he was a baby.

Maybe the eyeshadow was plenty, I thought, and took away the black lines. No need to go over the top.

There.

I put away my make-up and changed into a baggy black T-shirt, put my arms through the straps of my backpack and went out.

Helene had gone, thank goodness.

The street outside was crowded with people. One of those giant cruise ships must have come in. Old men in shorts and women in their summer best trying to blend in with the locals who were out on the town. A babble of voices, cries and laughter filled the hot summer air, and Caribbean music came from one of the cafes.

I wiped the sweat from my brow with the back of my hand as I went.

It was boiling hot.

The air was nearly glowing.

I liked it better when it was windy and raining. I could lie in my room then and watch films or read and sleep without feeling guilty about it. The sun was so unsparing. You were meant to be out in it, meant to be out with friends, meant to be having a good time. If I lay in my room then, there'd be something the matter with me, I'd be letting myself down, even though I'd be doing exactly the same thing, and even though my life was my own.

I did what I wanted. So if I didn't want to be out getting drunk, how come I felt guilty?

Fuck it. Fuck all of it.

I stopped and put my earphones in, scrolled until I found *Sheer Heart Attack*, then carried on through the lane leading down to Vågsbunnen, flapping my T-shirt to stop it sticking to my skin.

I was still hungry. There was a Burger King a bit further down. It was cheap, at least. And it was my life, no one decided but me.

All the windows above me were wide open, and the little restaurants with their outdoor tables in the rear courtyards were all full.

But what was that?

An animal scuttled along the foot of one of the buildings. The people in front of me stopped. It was a rat! It crossed the lane, zigzagging through the crowd to disappear under a gate on the other side.

A woman squealed. People looked at each other. There was an alarm of startled voices, and then a few seconds later everything was normal again.

They say that whenever you see a rat there'll always be six others somewhere close by, I remembered, and glanced around me as I walked on. I'd seen rats loads of times in town, especially round the back of the supermarket, but only ever in the evening and at night. Never in the daytime.

I'd never understood why rats were meant to be so disgusting. They weren't exactly cute, like a lynx or an owl, but they weren't exactly horrible either. Their fur was smooth and thick, the tail looked like a little whip, and their front paws resembled little hands with fingers when they held something in them.

Above the islands in the fjord the sun was on its way down, and as I emerged from the lane I had to narrow my eyes in order to see properly. The wharf and the fish market were teeming with people. On this side of the road too, the crowds were huge. I weaved my way among them, grateful for the music in my ears that transported me to another place, making all the faces that surrounded me seem remote and irrelevant.

People were so alike. They squealed when they saw a rat, hit the town in their droves when the sun came out, got married and had kids, forged careers, and then died. And for what? A promotion to departmental manager, partner in a law firm or whatever it was they did. And that was what they worked so hard for?

All just to lie there in the deep soil.

Who cared about their important jobs then?

I crossed over Torgallmenningen into Strandgaten to the Burger King, where thankfully there were hardly any customers and inside was nice and cool.

I couldn't make up my mind between a Bacon King and a Double Steakhouse. I hadn't eaten properly all day, so in the end I went with the Double Steakhouse with extra fries and a Diet Coke.

My mouth was watering as I carried the tray over to one of the tables further inside and sat down.

I opened as wide as I could but still couldn't get the whole burger in for the first bite, the bun crumpled against my top lip as the juicy meat filled my mouth and everything melted together, bacon, beef, bun, onion, tomato, lettuce, ketchup.

I always saved the fries until last, the two things were so different I didn't like to mix them. One juicy and open, the other crispy and dry on the outside, the good, soft part locked inside. The burger I ate quickly, the fries took longer as I dipped them in ketchup and ate them one by one.

And I was still finished all too soon.

I wiped my mouth with the paper napkin and thought about what to do. A man had sat down over by the wall. He was dressed like he worked at the university, in blue jeans, a white shirt, brown blazer, brown shoes. His lips slanted in an appealing kind of way, his face looked like an eighteen-year-old's, whereas the rest of him said he was in his thirties, maybe even forties.

He sat looking thoughtfully out of the window and didn't notice me.

I was full, but wanted some more. The natural thing would have been to get a milkshake for dessert, that was what people did. But there were so many calories in them I could just as well have another burger, maybe the Bacon King with fries I'd been thinking about.

Did I really want more?

Yes.

Why shouldn't I, if it was what I wanted? Who, or what part of me, was it that said no?

Reason. My guilty conscience.

Why not show a bit of willpower, get up and leave?

It was exactly these kinds of situations that were crucial.

I got my phone out and googled 'Orpheus'. A Wiki article came up about a Greek god. Most probably it was the name of a play or an opera too. Knowing him, it'd be an opera.

I typed 'orpheus opera' and searched again.

Gluck's *Orfeo ed Euridice*, that had to be it.

Without thinking about it or looking at how much it cost, I booked

a ticket for Wednesday. Then I took my tray over to the recycling station, emptied out the rest of the Diet Coke, stuffed the cup down the
hole, dropped the rest of the packaging into the bin and went straight
to the counter and ordered a Bacon King and another Diet Coke.

As I put my tray on the table and sat down again, the man looked
at me.

'You eat too much,' he said.

I couldn't believe it.

Did he actually say that?

I looked across at him, my cheeks warm.

He just smiled.

What was I supposed to do then?

I had to say something, I couldn't just sit there.

The shame was burning inside me.

I picked up my burger and lifted it towards my mouth, changed my
mind and put it down again.

'What's it to you?' I said. But my voice was feeble and I hadn't the
courage to look him in the eye.

He smiled.

'I am the Lord,' he said.

Oh, so he's crazy, I thought to myself, and all shame disappeared.

'Leave me alone or I'll call the staff,' I said.

He stood up and came towards me, passed his hand through my hair
and went out.

I sat there with my mouth open and watched him as he vanished
into the crowds outside.

What happened there?

His touch had felt so good.

It had felt so good.

Something soft and warm had spread through my body. It felt like
I'd been filled with warm oil.

I ought to have been angry, I ought to have reported him, he had no
right to touch me.

Christ, what an idiot I was.

No one had touched me for months. Of course it was going to feel
good, another person running their hand through my hair like that.

You eat too much. Yeah, right.

I didn't want any more now, but on the other hand it felt wrong to chuck it all out, so I ate half the burger and a few fries before going over and binning what was left.

Outside in the street, I stood for a moment wondering where to go. I rented an attic room in a house just below the hospital; it had sloping walls and would once have been for the maid. When the sun shone in summer, the way it was shining today, it'd be sweltering in there, it didn't even help to open the windows; by afternoon the place would be boiling, so the thought of going back there now didn't really appeal. But I didn't want to go out either.

I started walking back in the direction of Torgallmenningen. Going about the town on your own was fine, nothing wrong with that, it was actually more unusual for me to be with someone, now I thought about it. It was sitting down somewhere that was the problem, because as soon as I sat down it made me feel like I was so conspicuous. Maybe no one else noticed. But the feeling was so strong it was almost like a light that radiated from me, and everything I did then would have to take place in that light. Whatever it was, reading a book, sipping my beer or wine, or just gazing, I became incredibly aware of it, as if I could see myself from the outside and the inside at the same time. I'm sitting here on my own, she's sitting there on her own. And then in no time at all my thoughts would be churning and dark, I couldn't stand it, and if I was going to stay I'd have to fight it, fight against it the whole time, that light that shone out of me, the extra person inside me who kept such a close eye on everything I did.

Of course, it wasn't like that when I was sitting on my bed in my room. But then it would be other things, like how I should be out instead of staying in, even if it did feel good and relaxing to be drinking tea and eating chocolate while watching some new film on Netflix.

As soon as I stopped walking, it was like a rush of confusion and helplessness went through me. And so I couldn't stop, I couldn't sit down, all I could do was keep walking or else stay at home in my room.

At uni it had made everything impossible. I'd sit there burning in the library, burning in the canteen, burning in lectures.

Thank God for my job, was what I said. At work I could sit there completely exposed without it bothering me. No one cared who I was, as long as I did my job.

The grass surrounding the big pond in the centre of town was crawling with people. Mostly groups of young people sitting drinking by the looks of it. The sky above the fells was a dramatic red as the sun went down into the sea on the other side. The fjord was like a mirror, the air hot and still.

What was it I'd thought in the loo while I'd been doing my make-up?

That I looked exotic with my gold eyeshadow. Arabian nights. Passionate and strong.

On my way out for a date.

Businesswoman.

Lebanon. Beirut. Jordan.

Self-assured. Sexy. Mysterious. A long day, and now a relaxing drink in the hotel lounge.

All these pale Westerners around me with their superficial, commercial lives. The women were like men, and the men were like women.

The man I was meeting was under my spell. He'd drunk from the spring and now would give anything for more.

I could drive them mad, if I wanted.

They forgot about everything but me and what I gave to them.

It was a strange land to which destiny had brought me. Its mountains were so high and so green, its people so cold.

I came past a cafe with outdoor seating. A couple got up and I went over without hurrying, asked them if they were leaving. The man nodded, and I sat down.

The fire in the sky was going out.

I waved the waiter over.

He came.

'Have you got Lebanese wine?' I asked.

'Lebanese, no,' he said. 'We've got Australian, Chilean and Californian. And French and Spanish and Italian, of course. And German white wines. Was it a particular grape you had in mind?'

I made a gesture that was half resigned, half not bothered.

'I'll have a glass of the house red, please,' I said. 'And some olives if you've got any.'

'Will that be all?' he said.

'Yes. Thank you,' I said.

He went away. People strolled along the pond, in no hurry. My eye latched on to three young lads, students probably, one of them pushing a bike, all three with backpacks on. Tanned with summer, lanky, loose-limbed bodies that didn't care about being seen. I saw a mother and father pushing an empty stroller, their little girl toddling along in front, hardly able to walk yet at all.

A flood of longing rose inside me.

If only someone would touch me.

All I had to do was go to a hotel bar later on. There'd always be some-one there who wasn't fussy and would come up and buy you a drink and eventually ask if you fancied going up to his room. Or I could go to Galeien after the clubs had closed, and then just wait. They were younger there, but drunker too, and it'd all feel a bit shabby if I wasn't as out of it as them.

The waiter came with my wine and olives. I took a little sip and tried to go back to where I'd just been in my mind.

Only then the pain came back. The metal wire cutting through my brain like an egg slicer. I closed my eyes, and the darkness was flecked with light.

Aaaargh, I said quietly between my teeth. Aaaargh.

And then it passed.

Nothing in all the world felt better than when the pain passed. Every-thing became good again.

Once, it had lasted nearly an hour. As luck would have it, I'd been at home, because it had made me vomit. But usually it was gone in a mat-ter of seconds.

I sipped my wine. A homeless person came along the street, pushing a shopping trolley full of carrier bags and bundles of rags. Two slender young girls went past him, one in a short white summer dress, the other in a floral-patterned one.

Sensual, strong and mysterious.

Meetings all day, now a well-deserved glass of wine.

If only someone would touch me.

Who had he been, that guy? Why had he done it?

I am the Lord. Yeah, right.

But he hadn't looked crazy.

Who knows what goes on in people's heads?

Not me, anyway.

Take Ommundsen.

For a couple of months or so I'd actually thought he was interested in me. It was embarrassing to think about now. That he could have had feelings for a fat sixteen-year-old. Only he'd often looked at me in class with those warm eyes of his. And he'd helped me with so much.

I could still remember the first time. He came up to my desk after a lesson while I was sitting packing my stuff away.

'Hi, Iselin,' he said.

'Hi,' I said without looking at him.

'Your attendance figures are a bit worrying.'

'I know,' I said. 'I've been under the weather a lot. I'm sorry.'

'I've been wondering if perhaps you might be going through some kind of a difficult time at the moment. Would I be right?'

'No, not at all,' I said. 'Everything's fine.'

He smiled.

'Why do you feel obliged to say that?'

I shrugged.

'Because it's true?' I said, and got to my feet. 'But I'll make an effort with my attendance.'

I left the room without saying goodbye and walked to the bus stop across the road. I was angry and upset. What was it to him?

At the same time, I liked the fact that he was bothered.

No one else was. Mum was away all week in Oslo upgrading her qualifications, Dad had moved out and had a new family of his own now, and Jonas lived with our gran that year.

I was sixteen and old enough to look after myself. It wasn't just something my mum said, I said so too. And it was actually good not having her around all the time.

So the problem wasn't me living on my own during the week. The problem was I hadn't made any friends in my new class. Most of the girls had come from the same school and already knew each other from before. Their cliques weren't open for me, they were already fully formed. Besides, it wasn't cool hanging out with people from your own class. Everyone had their cliques elsewhere.

There were two other girls who were also left out, only they didn't seem to mind. Agnete, who sat by the windows knitting with a wry smile on her face at everything that went on around her, and Sara, who belonged to some kind of Christian sect and always wore a dress and her long hair in a plait. She was really good-looking, but way too weird for anyone to take an interest in her, and she wasn't that interested in other people either. She stuck in at her subjects and got good marks, but she was throwing her life away, it was so obvious. If I'd been as good-looking as her, and as slim, I'd have thrown myself headlong into life without waiting a second.

Mondays were the worst, before the first lesson when everyone was asking everyone else what they'd been up to at the weekend. It was all parties here and parties there, and movie nights with the crew. Occasionally, someone would ask me too, especially Jakob, who always had a thing about including everyone. He was on the student committee, all left-wing politics and wanting to put his idealism to good use wherever he could. A tousle of hair and a face full of pimples, not exactly good-looking, but full of energy, noise and laughter. I had nothing against him, in fact I liked him rather a lot, but not when he wanted to include me in something. He didn't understand it had the opposite effect. That being asked about something by him was like having a mark put on your forehead.

'What did *you* do at the weekend, Iselin?' he said from where he sat in the front row.

I sat at the back, painfully aware that no one could have failed to hear his penetrating voice, shrugged my shoulders and glanced up at him, as if occupied by something else.

'Nothing special,' I said.

But I could only say that a few times before it became conspicuous, so then I started lying, saying I'd been to a party or at Peppe's with my mates, and if he asked about the party, where it had been, for instance, I'd say the name of someone from my old class. No one was going to check anyway.

My dad always said that for any problem there's a solution. If something can't be solved, then it was never a problem.

What was my problem?

That I hadn't made friends at school.

That I didn't get invited to parties.

There was an easy way to solve both problems. I could invite the girls in the class to a party at mine. It wasn't without risk, though, because what if they didn't want to come? It would only make the problem worse.

I wished I could talk to Dad about it, in that half-joking, half-serious way we'd often talk to each other before. He'd said I could come and live with them, but I didn't want to. He'd changed with his new wife and the new baby. He always used to come into my room and talk to me, it was a thing we'd had going for years, but then when he moved in with her he didn't have 'time' any more. He was under her thumb, did exactly what he was told, which meant there was no room for me.

He was just as nice as before, though, and I knew he cared about me, but whenever I was invited to theirs for dinner I could always see straight through him, the way he was scared all the time in case he paid me too much attention compared to her and their kid.

Class parties were something they did in secondary, not at gymnasium school. So I couldn't send invitations out. And I couldn't just ask people if they wanted to come out to mine on Friday, because why would they when we didn't know each other?

But if I was already having a party and then casually mentioned they were welcome to drop by, it wouldn't be that strange. And it wouldn't matter if they didn't come either.

So that's what I did.

To begin with, Mum would leave Oslo on the Friday afternoon and be home by late evening, but after a while she started leaving on the Saturday morning instead, which was good, because then I could have the party on the Friday and have time to clear up before she got home Saturday afternoon.

I came from the kind of village where the boys drive around in cars with their girlfriends in the passenger seat and the girlfriend's mates in the back, and it was such a small place that everyone knew who everyone else was. I said to some of the girls from my old class that I was having a party and they could invite who they wanted as long as it wasn't too many. Then I told the girls in my new class that I was having a party and they could come if they wanted.

The first car came up the drive around six. It was Signe and her boyfriend, and three of his mates. The boyfriend's name was Arild, he was short and had a little moustache and a bunch of keys hanging from his belt. He was full of himself, pretending he knew everyone and everything. But he was eighteen and had his own car, that was why she was going out with him. I didn't know his mates, but I knew they played on the football team.

'*Hi*, Iselin,' said Signe ingratiatingly and gave me a hug.

'So *great* you could *come*!' I said, the same ingratiating tone.

Arild opened the boot and they got two crates of beer out.

I was horrified, but couldn't exactly say anything.

'Where can we put them?' he said.

'In the kitchen?' I said.

Another car came, this time it was Ada and Maja and their boyfriends. They had two bottles of Absolut with them and orange juice to go with it. And then it went on from there. By eight, the area in front of the house was packed with cars, and others were parked up on both sides of the drive all the way down to the road. There were maybe fifty or so. Nobody cared. The stereo in the living room was on full blast, and music was blaring out of some of the cars as well. There were people everywhere, in all the rooms, and still more kept arriving. I didn't know half of them.

At the start, I tried to look after everything, moving stuff from the living room that could get broken, putting things out of the way in cupboards, and there was plenty to keep an eye on, because Mum loved her decorations. I bundled out the two people who were sitting on the floor in Jonas's room smoking pot and locked the door. I decided I needed to hide things from my room that were private, but it was no use, three boys I didn't know were sitting in a row on my bed drinking when I came in, another was rocking on my chair, and someone was sitting on my desk. I gave up then and told myself that whatever happened happened.

It was so awful, and I'd forgotten all about the girls from my new class. Four of them were suddenly standing there staring in the living room. Lea, Hanne, Selma and Astrid.

'You *came!*' I said, and dashed over to them.

'What a lot of friends you've got, Iselin!' Selma said.

The other three sniggered.

They looked like creatures from another world. Everything they were wearing was so neat and finicky and perfect, Astrid in light blue jeans and a blue top with a white floral pattern, a thin white cardigan on top, Lea in a skimpy black Led Zeppelin T-shirt, black skirt and a nice leather jacket.

'Did you come on the bus?' I said.

Lea nodded.

'What are we supposed to do, exactly?' said Selma. 'What do people do at parties out here?'

'Maybe we could just get drunk and then stagger about shouting our heads off?' said Astrid.

They laughed. I did a bit too.

Selma put her hand on my shoulder.

'Lovely to see you, Iselin,' she said.

'Same here,' I said.

'Nice house you've got,' said Lea.

'Thanks,' I said.

'Have you got any wine glasses?' said Astrid.

'Of course,' I said. 'Hang on a minute, I'll go and get some.'

'And a corkscrew, if you've got one,' Selma added as I went.

'If you've got one', what was that supposed to mean? What sort of home wouldn't have a corkscrew? The kitchen was packed with people, the air thick with smoke. A boy I'd never seen before stood unsteadily at the work surface spreading liver paste onto a slice of bread, a cigarette between his lips. Another sat drumming along to the beat of the music with a knife on the edge of the work surface. Not a butter knife, but one of the sharp carving knives. There'd be a mark for every hit. I put my hand cautiously on his upper arm.

'Don't do that, please, you're leaving marks in the wood,' I said.

He stared at me for a moment with listless eyes, without so much as pausing.

Two boys were sitting alongside him, each with a girl in his lap. I'd never seen any of them before either.

'Tarjei, she says you're leaving marks in the wood!' one of them said.

They laughed, but thankfully he got down and walked off, and left the knife on the side. I put it away in the drawer before getting four wine glasses out of the cupboard and going back to the girls. It was as if they were standing in their own little bubble, detached from everyone around them.

'What time's the bus back?' said Astrid.

'You've only just got here,' I said, and straight away wished I hadn't. It sounded like I was begging them to stay.

'I know, I just thought they probably don't run that often,' she said.

Selma twisted the corkscrew into the cork of the bottle she'd brought with her in her little rucksack, and squeaked it out until it released with a pop. The others held out their glasses and she poured.

'Do you want some, Iselin?' said Selma.

'No, thanks,' I said, even though I did.

They stood for a while, sipping their wine without saying anything, huddled together so as not to get jostled all the time. The party was all because of them, but now I wished they hadn't come. They were so uncomfortable, and there was nothing I could do about it. What was I supposed to do, show them my room?

Signe came reeling up.

'Absolutely *brilliant* party!' she shouted.

The fab four exchanged glances and managed to smile.

'Who are this lot, then?' Signe wanted to know, draping her arm over my shoulder.

'They're from my class at gymnasium,' I said.

'Iselin's *so* brainy!' she squawked at them, then laughed theatrically and lurched off.

'She's from my old secondary class,' I said. 'They're all from round here.'

'Thought as much,' said Astrid. 'Is it a yokel theme party?'

I looked around for somewhere for them to sit, but everywhere was taken.

'I like your leather jacket,' I said to Lea. 'It's really nice.'

'Thanks,' she said, and looked down at it.

'Where's it from?' I said.

'I bought it in London.'

'Really?' I said. 'What label is it?'

'APC,' she said. 'It's French.'

'I know *that*,' I said.

'Do you want to try it on?'

'I think probably I'm a bit big,' I said.

Lea went bright red.

'Of course, I wasn't thinking,' she said. 'Sorry.'

There was a lull between us. They looked round restlessly. Guys pissed out of their minds, screaming girls, shouting and laughter. No one dancing, no one just sitting talking.

'The bus goes at ten past until twelve,' I said.

'We can just about make ten past ten, then,' said Astrid. 'We'll have to go now though.'

'It takes nearly an hour into town,' Selma said. 'Which means we'll be back by eleven. I'm really tired, actually.'

'Me too,' said Hanne.

'It was so good to see you,' I said. 'Thanks for coming all this way.'

'Thanks for the invite,' said Selma.

'Yes, thanks,' said Hanne.

'It was nice of you to ask us,' said Astrid.

Selma twisted the cork back in and put the bottle in her rucksack.

'Do you want us to put the glasses in the kitchen?' she said.

'Just leave them on the windowsill,' I said. 'Have a safe journey back!'

'See you on Monday then, Iselin,' said Hanne.

They hugged me one by one and then left. I went to the bathroom for a pee and tried to get myself together. Someone had emptied the drawers and the cupboard under the sink and thrown everything on the floor. Sanitary towels and tampons, old bottles of head lice treatment, Mum's contraceptive pills, packets of paracetamol, disposable razors, deodorants. That was bad enough, but the worst thing was Mum's antidepressants. She didn't take them any more, but the box had been emptied.

I pulled my jeans down and sat on the loo, remaining there a while after I'd finished, my head in my hands.

I'd ruined everything. There was no longer a future for me at school. And Mum was going to be so angry. So incredibly angry.

Someone started hammering and kicking at the door.

'Get a bloody move on in there!'

I wiped myself, pulled my jeans up and flushed the toilet.

'About time!' Arvid said when I came out, his voice a slur. 'I'm fuck-ing *dying* for a piss!'

On the landing, Ada was sitting crying. Maja, who was comforting her, looked up at me and rolled her eyes as I went past. Dad had converted part of the stable into a little flat while he'd still been living with us, with a lounge, bedroom and bathroom, and I decided to go over there and sit on my own for a bit. People had spilled out from the house and were all over the place. One guy was jumping up and down on top of a car, roaring his head off. Another stood pissing up against the outside wall. Some had paired off and were well away, snogging and groping. No one noticed me. I took the key from under the stone and let myself in.

There was no way I could get them to leave, I knew that. The only thing I could do was wait until they left of their own accord.

I locked the door from the inside so no one could come in, and went over to Dad's records, flicking through them until I found something I fancied listening to. Happy Mondays, Black Grape and the Stone Roses had been his favourite bands when he was young, and I picked out *Pills 'n' Thrills and Bellyaches* and put it on.

I imagined I was sitting in my own flat, that the neighbours were having a party and it had woken me up. I was twenty-four and my boy-friend was lying in bed next to me in our bedroom. He slept like a log every night. I drew my legs up underneath me on the sofa and smoothed my hand over the armrest. But nothing could blot out the terrible thing I'd started.

What an idiot I'd been.

Should I text Mum and warn her in advance?

Mum? I threw a home-alone party and I'm afraid it's got a bit out of hand. Please don't be angry!

She'd have a brain haemorrhage.

And I couldn't phone my dad either. He'd have gone to bed ages ago, the baby always woke them up at five.

I changed the record and put some Aretha Franklin on, only to take it off again after a few minutes and go back outside. I crossed towards the house and went into the hall. Someone who looked like Martin was fast asleep on the floor up against the wall. He'd covered himself up with Mum's pale blue coat.

I bent down and shook him.

'You can't sleep here!' I shouted.

He opened his eyes in a daze.

'Get up!' I shouted.

I marched into the kitchen and turned the big light on.

'Everybody out!' I yelled. 'Go on, get out!'

I went into the living room and turned the stereo off.

'Hey, cut it out!' someone protested loudly.

'Everybody out, party's over!' I screamed. 'Out, now! Out! Out! Out!'

I put the big light on in there too.

And then I did the same thing in all the rooms upstairs. Turned the lights on, screamed at them to get the fuck off home.

And it worked. Maybe it was the lights that did it, I thought to myself later, before I fell sleep. The alcohol turned them into nocturnal creatures that shrank back from the light, and all they could do then was leave.

Half an hour after I'd started, the house was empty. Some of the girls from my old class had helped me get rid of the last few boys who'd been reluctant to go.

But Christ, what a mess the place was in. Bottles and glasses everywhere, in Mum's room too, things thrown about, as if a wild animal had been let loose inside, chunks hacked out of the work surface in the kitchen, I knew that of course, but the worst thing was that someone had kicked a *hole* in the bathroom door upstairs, and someone had *pissed* on the sofa. At first, I thought it was beer, but it smelled of piss, so what else would it be? The driveway looked like a bombsite too, bottles strewn all over the place there as well, and parts of the lawn had been churned up by cars.

Even if I spent until Christmas trying to clean it all up, she'd have still noticed.

She was so proud of the place too. She devoted more time to keeping it nice than she did to me.

I couldn't sleep in the mess they'd made of my room, so I cleared up there first and even washed the floor before going to bed. That was all I had to do, one room at a time, I told myself, to get things perfect again, then everything might be all right. The only real worries were the hole in the door, the pissed-on sofa, and the chunks that had been hacked out of the work surface in the kitchen. And the churned-up lawn, of course.

The last thing I thought before I fell asleep was that I could say I'd come home and found the place like this, and that I didn't actually know what had happened. Some sort of break-in, maybe?

I got up early so I could get it all done before Mum showed up. The place looked even worse in daylight, not just because the mess was that much more obvious, but because all connection with the night had been severed. What had been logical then, a load of people coming to my party and doing what they did, now seemed totally mad. Why had the bathroom drawers been emptied onto the floor? Why were there empty bottles in the bath? The fag ends in the plant pots, on the windowsills and floors, the glasses that were everywhere, the mud on the rugs, the used condom in Mum's bed, it was all so over the top. My stomach ached all morning as I cleared up and cleaned. I couldn't even say it had been a success, I'd never be friends with them now. And besides, it had been so obvious what I'd been trying to do. Iselin will do anything to make friends, they'd say. Poor girl.

I went down to the bins at the bottom of the drive with a bulging black bin liner over my shoulder and saw myself and what I'd done as if from the outside, and I burned with shame. Around me already were the colours of autumn, the grass in the meadow was pale yellow and the river brimmed with water that spilled over onto the lower fields. An intense longing for childhood came up inside me. A time when Dad was still living with us and I was just a normal girl who went to ballet classes and liked horses and drawing and painting, and looked forward to school every day.

The bottles in the bin bag made a racket as I slung it into the container. Two more bags were waiting for me at the front door. Once they were out of the way, there was no more I could do.

I sat down at the table in the living room and started some home-work. A presentation in English about the Brontë sisters that I was to give on the Wednesday, and an essay about the Cold War to be handed in on the Friday. From the living room I could keep an eye on the cars that went past on the road below, so that Mum coming back wouldn't catch me by surprise.

She appeared around one o'clock. I gathered my things together as quick as I could and went upstairs to my room, hearing her park the car and then come in through the front door.

'Iselin?' she called out. 'Why is the lawn in such a state?'

Here we go, I said to myself with a sigh.

'Some people came who I hadn't invited,' I called back.

'What do you mean?' she said, looking up at me as I came down the stairs.

'I only invited some friends from school,' I said. 'Then a whole load of people I didn't know turned up in cars.'

She'd had her hair cut in a bob. Her bag was over her shoulder, the car key in her hand, her blue eyes looking straight at me.

'Have you had a *party*?'

I nodded.

'Iselin, how could you be so stupid? I trusted you.'

'I know,' I said. 'I'm really sorry.'

'Is it bad?' she said.

'It *was*,' I said. 'But I've cleaned it all up and put things back the way they were.'

Without putting down her bag or the car key, she started going round the house inspecting, giving the occasional deep sigh and little, despairing groans. 'Oh my God,' I heard her say. 'Oh no . . .'

She was always going to see everything, there was no way I ever could have hidden anything from her. If something had been broken, or if only a mark had been left somewhere, it was the first thing she saw when she came into the room.

She went up the stairs without looking at me.

'Iselin!' she shouted a moment later. 'Come here this minute!'

She'd seen the bathroom door, I realised.

And of course she had.

At first she said nothing, just pointed at the door.

'I don't want to see your face again today,' she said then. 'You can stay in your room.'

'What?' I said.

'You heard me. I don't want to see you, and I won't hear your excuses.'

'Mum, I'm sixteen years old.'

'Then why can't you act like it? Go to your room.'

I hate her, I told myself, closing the door behind me. She was already on the phone to someone about what had happened.

I sat down on my bed.

If that's the way she wants it, I thought after a bit, jumped up and threw some clothes in a bag, packed my school things and went out, down the drive to the road.

She must have heard the front door, because she came out and shouted after me.

'Iselin! Where do you think you're going? Get back here!'

She could have run and caught up with me if she really wanted me back, or she could have come after me in the car.

I phoned Dad from the bus stop.

'Hi, Iselin!' he said. 'What a nice surprise!'

'Can I stay over at yours tonight?' I said.

He was quiet for a second.

'We've talked about this, Iselin,' he said. 'You can come here whenever you want. But you need to give us fair warning. It's not always convenient, you know that. You can't just turn up at such short notice.'

'I'm already on my way,' I said. 'I'm on the bus.'

He sighed.

'I suppose it'll be all right this once. I'll have to clear it with Ulrika, though.'

'If you don't want me to come, I won't,' I said.

'Of course I want you to come!' he said. 'Let me call you back.'

They lived on a new estate on the other side of town, so I had to change buses at the bus station in the city centre. I hadn't had any lunch, so I bought a bag of crisps and a Coke at the Narvesen. I didn't like the idea of eating on the bus where people could see me, they wouldn't know I hadn't had lunch and would think I just stuffed myself with crisps and soft drinks all day. But apart from an old woman and a mum with two kids, the bus was empty, so it wasn't a problem.

Dad didn't ring, but texted me instead.

OK! was all it said.

I took it to mean Ulrika was in a good mood.

They were sitting on the veranda when I got there. Dad got up and leaned over the railing.

'It's open,' he said. 'Just dump your things in your room. Then come up here if you want and say hello to Emil.'

I did as he said, put my bag and my school things down in the spare room that was full of stuff they didn't much use, went up the wide staircase and out onto the veranda through the door at the far end of the living room.

'Hi, Iselin, how lovely to see you!' Ulrika said in her Swedish as she took off her sunglasses. 'How are you?'

'I'm fine, thanks,' I said. 'How are you?'

'Good, as a matter of fact,' she said.

'And here's your little brother,' Dad said, lifting Emil into the air. He kicked his legs a bit and tried to push Dad's arm away.

'Hello, cuddle bunny,' I said.

He looked at me and smiled.

'He likes you!' said Ulrika, now with her sunglasses on again.

'Of course he does, she's his big sister!' Dad said. 'Do you want to hold him?'

I shrugged.

'Can do,' I said.

'You can sit in the chair over there and hold him on your knee,' Ulrika said.

I felt sweaty and horrible and didn't really want to, but Dad handed me the baby and I sat with him on my knee, my arm around him so he wouldn't topple over. He leaned back and looked up at me.

'Ngnnn,' he said, and waved an arm.

'Maybe you could give him a piece of apple?' Dad said, and picked up a plastic box from the table.

'He's just had one,' said Ulrika.

'Not from Iselin, he hasn't,' said Dad, and put the box down again, taking his sunglasses from the table and putting them on.

After a moment he leaned forward and opened the box anyway, and handed me a piece of apple. I held it in front of Emil, who took it and threw it on the floor. Ulrika sighed and picked it up before Dad could reach.

'How's it going at school?' she said, leaning back in her chair again.

'Good,' I said.

Emil wanted to get down.

'Here, I'll take him,' Dad said. 'He's very active. He wants to be doing something all the time.'

Dad looked up at me and smiled.

'Just like you were at that age!'

I smiled back. I was thirsty, but didn't want to ask for something to drink.

'What's your favourite subject? Let me guess. Norwegian?'

'Maybe,' I said. 'I don't know.'

I pulled my hair away from my face and looked across the road at the house opposite. From the corner of my eye I saw Dad and Ulrika exchange glances.

'Is it OK if I have a shower?' I said.

'Of course,' Dad said. 'Clean towels are in the cupboard.'

After I'd showered I made sure to leave everything wiped and clean and hung the towel nicely on the rail before going back to my room and lying down on the bed. I wondered whether to tell them I was going to stay in my room for a bit, because they always wanted to know what I was doing and where I was when I was staying at theirs, maybe because I didn't actually live with them, but I decided I couldn't be bothered. Anyway, there weren't that many other places in the house I could be.

I was lying watching an episode of *Modern Family* on my phone when all of a sudden Dad was standing in the doorway. I pulled my earphones out and sat up.

'What are you watching?' he said.

'Just a series,' I said.

He came in and sat down on the bed.

'Where's Ulrika?' I said.

'Putting Emil to bed,' he said. 'Anyway, how are you? I mean *really*. And you don't have to say "good" now.'

'What are you asking me that for?' I said.

He shrugged. He didn't look like me at all, his face was long and narrow, not round like mine, and his lips were broad and full, not thin like mine.

'You're my daughter,' he said. 'And you don't live here, so it feels like I know less and less about how you're getting on.'

He ruffled my hair.

'I suppose I'm all right,' I said.

'Yes? Have you made new friends at gymnasium?'

I nodded.

'Who?'

'You wouldn't know them, so it doesn't matter,' I said.

'Names, please,' he said, and smiled.

'Astrid, Ada, Selma and Hanne,' I said. 'They're all in my class.'

'What sort of things do they get up to, then?'

'All sorts,' I said. 'Normal things.'

'Were they at the party yesterday?'

He said it in the same casual way he always said things, and wasn't looking at me when he said it.

I felt the blood drain out of my face.

'Yes, they were,' I said, then put my earphones in again and pressed play.

'Can we talk about it?' he said, and I sensed him looking at me even though I was looking down at the screen.

I shook my head.

'There's nothing wrong in having a party,' he said. 'But you must ask first. Do you understand? Especially when you're on your own there during the week.'

'Dad, I'm not completely stupid,' I said.

'I don't think you are, not for a minute,' he said as he got to his feet. 'Dinner in an hour, all right?'

I nodded and he went back upstairs to her.

At school on the Monday, everyone already knew about the party. I got looks when I entered the classroom. I pretended I wasn't bothered. I couldn't change the way they related to me, so I'd just have to change the way I related to them. They meant nothing to me, I decided. And it worked. If I didn't care about them, they couldn't get to me. The same went for school itself. I didn't *have* to get the bus to school every day, I actually could stay in bed and laze every now and then, make myself something nice to eat, sit in my room, do some singing and recording. It was more important to me than maths and geography. Mostly it was hit songs that I sang, but I wrote some of my own too.

No one knew about it.

Sometimes I'd go into town in the lunch break, and sometimes I'd stay there, sitting around at cafes, listening to music or watching videos.

It was after two months of this that Ommundsen had asked if I was going through a difficult time. But I wasn't, I was actually feeling better than I'd done for ages after I stopped caring about what other people thought and believed.

Ommundsen took us for Norwegian, Social Studies and History. I had him too for my elective in music. In one of the music lessons after he'd spoken to me he announced that the school was putting on *Cats*. It was going to be a collaboration between the music and drama classes. He wanted us all to sing for him individually in class to give him an idea about how to cast the various roles, but also so we could start getting used to singing on our own in front of others.

'Iselin?' he said when it was my turn.

'I don't want to,' I said.

'You've a lovely voice, I know you have!' he said from behind the piano, smiling as he looked out at the little group of students.

'I don't want to sing now, and I don't want to be in any musical.'

'But, Iselin,' he said, 'it's only for your classmates!'

'I told you, I don't want to,' I said.

All of a sudden it was too much for me. I sat looking down at the desk with tears in my eyes while everyone stared at me. I jumped up, grabbed my bag and left the room. At first I went to the library, but that was no good either, so I went outside, left the school and went down into town. It was November, cold and cloudy, lines of dirty snow in the streets. I so much regretted having chosen music, because the two things, music and school, weren't supposed to meet, I realised it then. Maybe Ommundsen realised it too. At any rate, he sent me an email in the break, apologising. He suggested I could sing for him on our own. I wrote back from the tea rooms I was in and told him I didn't want that either. He replied straight away and said he respected my choice, but that it was important I came to the next lesson. Which I did, even though I'd made myself an outcast there too after marching off like that.

'Can I have a word, Iselin?' he said after the bell went and we were packing our stuff together.

I nodded.

'I'm sorry I pressurised you,' he said. 'I shouldn't have done.'

'That's OK,' I said without looking at him.

'But I do need to allocate marks, as you know. And singing a solo is part of the curriculum. How about you record something and send it to me? Or we could do it now and be done with it?'

'*Now* now?' I said.

He nodded and smiled.

'OK,' I said.

And so I stood there, with Ommundsen at the piano in the empty music room.

'What would you like to sing?' he said.

'Do you know "Paradise"?' I said.

'Coldplay? I think I can manage that,' he said, and downloaded the chords onto his phone. 'It's a lovely song. Do you like it?'

'Mm,' I said.

'Ready?'

'Mm.'

He played a little introduction and gave me a nod when he wanted me to come in.

When I was finished and the final chord died away, I saw there were tears in his eyes. I turned, went back to my desk and got my bag.

'Iselin,' he said, and stood up.

'Yes?' I said.

'That was absolutely marvellous. You sing so exceptionally well. You've a *fabulous* voice. You *mustn't* hide yourself away!'

Those were his exact words. They made me so happy.

I needed them then. But now, five years on, they meant nothing.

Apart from reminding me how much I'd failed in everything I'd hoped for then. And no way did I want Ommundsen to know that.

I looked up at the fells. The sun had gone and the sky had begun to darken. I took a sip of my wine and checked my phone to see if maybe Jonas had texted without me noticing, but he hadn't. When I looked up again, my eyes met those of a woman at the next table.

What was she looking at me for?

The feeling of being some kind of freak rose inside me.

My body felt like it was starting to burn.

Was anyone else looking at me?

I glanced around, as if looking for someone I knew or something.

Everyone was occupied with their own stuff.

Maybe it was Our Lady who'd been looking at me?

Seeing as how I'd already met Our Lord at the Burger King.

I saw a kind of greyish-yellow mist in my mind's eye, the way I did whenever I thought about God, ever since I was little. It was totally automatic. Only after I became a teenager did it occur to me it was because of the similarity between the two words, gul and Gud — yellow and God. But even though I knew, I still kept seeing that yellow mist.

I never prayed to God in those days, only to Jesus. I couldn't see the point of praying to a mist.

The church attendant at my confirmation had spoken with a lisp, I remembered.

Jethuth Chritht, he'd said.

I'd felt sorry for him. Everyone made fun of him and copied him.

Kids could be so cruel.

I checked my phone again. Nothing.

I didn't have to find Jonas and hang out with him and his friends. I didn't have to sit in a bar and wait to be checked out by some disgusting bloke who wasn't fussy.

I could just as well stay on my own. Walk home through town, have a shower, lie in bed and watch a film, and be good to myself.

Something moved on the ground to my left and I looked to see what it was.

Three rats scurried away hugging the side of the planter boxes, and then three more after them.

Terror ran through my body to my fingertips.

But they weren't dangerous.

It was probably too hot for them. That'd be why they were coming out.

No one else had seen them, so it seemed, at least no one who made a fuss.

I drank up the rest of my wine and put the glass down in front of me.

So that meant there were thirty-six others close by.

Sweat ran from my armpits and I pressed my T-shirt against my skin to absorb it, then lowered my head as casually as I could and sniffed.

The sweat smell had mingled with deodorant and perfume, rank in a scent of petals.

I wanted a man inside me. I wanted to lie on my back and spread my legs and have him up inside me. I wanted him to fuck me the whole night.

I love your cunt, I love your cunt so much, he would say, and would moan, no, cry out, when he came.

And afterwards he'd lie with his head against my chest and his eyes closed while he got his breath back, and he'd kiss me and draw me close, and tell me how lovely I was.

I glanced around sheepishly.

No one was looking.

Only the waiter, who met my gaze.

He came over.

'Another glass?' he said.

I pressed my arms to my sides so he wouldn't be able to smell me, and shook my head.

'No, thanks,' I said. 'Can I have the bill?'

'Certainly,' he said, and went to get it.

No one knew my thoughts.

Maybe some of the other people there were thinking the same.

That little man with the curly hair and moustache, for instance. Perhaps he was fantasising about fucking one of the women at his table at that very moment.

Or me.

Suddenly, there was an almighty sound of breaking glass somewhere above my head. I looked up and saw flames burst out of a window on the top floor, blazing up within seconds. The air crackled and popped.

No one else had noticed.

In no time, the fire took hold of the roof, escalating tongues of flame leaping towards the dark sky, and from inside came the dull thud of something collapsing. Soon the whole roof would be engulfed.

Everyone sat as before.

'Fire!' I shouted.

All heads turned. I jumped to my feet and pointed.

'Up there! Fire!'

They looked up, but remained seated.

What was happening? The building was on fire, couldn't they see?

'Fire!' I shouted again. 'Someone call the fire brigade!'

The waiter came darting towards me.

'All right, settle down,' he said.

'Settle down? What's the matter with you?' I said. 'The place is on fire!'

'There's no fire here,' he said.

'Up there!' I shouted, pointing to the roof.

But there was no fire.

Everything was normal.

The window was intact, the walls likewise.

No fire.

He looked at me.

'But . . . there was a fire,' I said. 'Up there, just now.'

'No, there wasn't,' he said.

'But I saw it!' I said.

He put his hand on my shoulder.

'There was no fire, I promise you. Are you all right? Have you taken something? Do you want me to phone someone?'

Everyone was looking at me.

What had happened?

What had I done?

I pulled a hundred-krone note out of my pocket and put it down on the table, shouldered my rucksack and went out into the street with shame burning in my cheeks.

So incredibly embarrassing.

But I'd seen it!

I stopped at the edge of the pond and wiped my tears away with my index finger. My make-up would have run. But that was the least of my problems.

It was as if they'd been in another world. As if I hadn't been in the same world as them, but a different one.

At the same time as they'd been sitting there looking at me.

I crossed the road in front of the bus station into Lyder Sagens gate. Even there, there were lots of people out.

It had felt like I didn't belong there.

Almost as if I'd been dead and they were living. Or else they'd been dead and it was me who was living.

Oh, the humiliation of it, the humiliation.

I'd stood there shouting and screaming in front of all those people. And there'd been nothing there.

So what was it?

I'd *seen* it. I had.

I turned left and went through Nygårdsgaten the way I always did. The air was so hot it was like mid-afternoon, and my T-shirt felt sticky, decidedly wet under the sleeves. Windows were open everywhere in the low houses that were divided up into bedsits and flats, and here and there music drifted out, occasionally the raucous noise of a party. Darkness rose all around me.

I'd been hallucinating.

But I hadn't taken anything.

And I wasn't mad.

I had to talk to someone about it. If I didn't, I'd *go* mad, that was for sure.

I could call Jonas in the morning.

Maybe go out to his?

He was always good to chill with the day after if we'd been out.

The petrol station was still open, and I went in and bought a hotdog and a Coke, and stood quite openly eating outside the door while wrestling the urge to just run away from it all. A couple my own age went inside holding hands, though only with the tips of their fingers, as if they were only loosely together. Maybe they were, I thought to myself. She had a pair of flowery leggings on, and a white top and sandals, while he had long hair and was wearing army-green shorts and a pair of worn-out Converse that looked like they used to be yellow.

What *was* it that had happened?

I wiped my mouth with the paper napkin, licked the ketchup and mustard off my fingers before wiping them too, then tossed the napkin in the bin by the pumps, took a good swig of my Coke and set off walking again with the bottle in my hand.

But the thought of my boiling-hot little attic room didn't appeal.

Maybe Ommundsen would still be at Café Opera?

It would do me good to talk to him.

Not that I'd pour my heart out, because it was none of his business.

We could talk about *him* for a change.

I could ask *him* questions.

I turned round and started walking back towards the centre. Even if he wasn't there, it was still good to just walk around for a bit.

Soon there were people everywhere again. My thoughts tightened like a web. How could I have forgotten so quickly?

I stank of sweat and was horrible.

But I'd already reached Vaskerelven and to go back now would be stupid.

I put my earphones in even though it was only a few minutes away, and put on 'Blue Lights' by Jorja Smith. It changed the way everything felt around me. Suddenly, everyone was a minor character in *my* life.

A girl stood leaning with her head against a wall in an alley I passed. Three other girls were with her, in high heels and short skirts, though they were looking the other way.

I'd never been to Café Opera before, only walked past. There was no queue, I suppose people didn't want to be inside on a night like this. I paused and removed my earphones, twining the cord around them as I tried to collect myself.

Maybe something was seriously wrong with me. I'd *seen* the fire. I hadn't imagined it, and it wasn't something I'd dreamt either. But what did it mean? What sort of person hallucinated while fully awake, without being high or totally drunk?

I went inside. Ommundsen was nowhere to be seen, so I went upstairs to look for him there.

I spotted him straight away. Sitting on a chair by the window, he was with a woman, they were sitting close and he was holding her hands in his.

It was Emilie, my old English teacher.

But she was married with kids. And he was married with kids.

Were they having an affair?

Ommundsen noticed me and got to his feet.

'Iselin!' he said in a loud voice. 'You came after all. How nice!'

I went over to them, I had no option then.

'And the two of you know each other, of course,' he said.

'Of course,' said Emilie. 'Lovely to see you, Iselin!'

'You too,' I said.

'Can I get you a drink?' said Ommundsen. 'We're not at school any more. And besides, you're past the legal drinking age now!'

'Thanks,' I said.

'What'll it be?'

'Just a Diet Coke, please,' I said.

'Right you are,' he said, and then turned to Emilie. 'How about another bottle?'

'Why not!' she said, and they both laughed.

Ommundsen's face, tanned and clean-shaven, glowed with happiness as he went off to the bar.

Her face glowed too, only a bit milder.

'Martin's been telling me how talented you are,' she said, looking at me with a warm smile.

'I'm not talented at all, I'm afraid,' I said.

'Well, according to what Martin says you are! Do you still sing?'

I shook my head.

'You were his favourite student. Did you know?'

I shook my head again.

She nodded knowingly a few times, as if I'd just said something insightful.

'Are you a couple now, then?' I said.

She smiled again.

'Yes, we are.'

'So you got divorced, and he got divorced?'

'That's right, yes,' she said.

Ommundsen came back and put my glass of Diet Coke and a bottle of white wine down on the table.

'There we are!' he said as he sat down. 'Now, Iselin, how are you?'

'Fine,' I said.

'Enjoying your studies?'

'Yes, definitely.'

'It's psychology you're doing, is that right?' said Emilie.

'Mm,' I said.

Ommundsen put his hand on her thigh, just above the knee, while beaming at me. He looked like he was bursting to say something, only nothing came out but the joyful look in his eyes.

'What are you going to specialise in?' said Emilie.

'I don't know yet,' I said.

'How's the singing coming along?' said Ommundsen. 'I've so often wondered.'

'Fine, I suppose,' I said.

'Do you sing in a band? Or a choir, perhaps?'

I shook my head.

And then I stood up.

'I'm afraid I've got to go,' I said.

'But you've only just got here!' said Ommundsen. 'Stay and talk with us. Or at least drink your Coke!'

'I actually came to thank you,' I said. 'For helping me that time. I never got the chance to say. Only it meant such a lot to me at the time, that you believed in me.'

'No problem,' he said. 'I still do believe in you, in case you want to know!'

I said goodbye, they said goodbye, and I went downstairs and outside into the hot summer night, angry at myself for having been so stupid as to go there in the first place. But at least I'd thanked him, I thought, and put my earphones back in, listening to some more Jorja Smith as I went through the centre of town and carried on walking. I passed the petrol station again, the white building that was the nursing home, the

High Technology Centre, and came out onto the little bridge that ran underneath the big one.

The waters of the fjord were completely still and completely dark, shiny as oil.

Then I saw fire again.

Up on the fell.

I stopped.

No, it wasn't a fire. Something was rising into the sky.

A star.

A megastar.

Was it real? Was it actually there? Or was I imagining this too?

It rose and rose, and its light spread across the sky and glittered on the fjord.

A couple on the other pavement had seen it too, and stood holding on to each other, staring up at it with their mouths open.

Some cars stopped on the bridge above and drivers and passengers got out.

It was the most beautiful thing I'd ever seen.

A megastar.

And it was real.

I carried on up the hill. People at the bus stop outside the old cinema on Danmarksplass stood gaping at the sky. Outside the restaurant a bit further along too, people stopped with their heads tipped back, eyes fixed on the star.

I put *Sheer Heart Attack* on again and followed Ibsens gate. On some of the little boxes that passed for balconies, people stood looking up and talking as I walked by. There was an unusual intensity to their voices. Like fear, almost.

But I certainly wasn't afraid. If Armageddon was coming, it was fine by me.

I stopped and looked up at the star again. It was hard to take your eyes off it. It was so big that it lit up the darkness all the way down to the ground. It shimmered faintly in the crowns of the trees and on the rooftops, on the patches of grass that surrounded me.

It was all over Instagram already. Photos of the star above the Eiffel Tower, the star over Hydra. People had started asking what it was.

There'd probably be a scientific explanation for it in the morning.

I sang along to myself as I went up the road. I'd discovered the album after watching the Queen film. It wasn't really my sort of music, but I loved it all the same. It was like a whole world of its own. And they sang so brilliantly.

I took the shortcut down from the hospital, and as I got to the bottom of the steps and turned into the narrow road where I lived and saw the house, I could see I'd forgotten to switch the landing light off; all three windows shone in the August darkness that was especially dense there, where the ground rose up steeply and a few big deciduous trees grew, thick with leaves.

The couple I rented from had gone to Mozambique three weeks before to work for NORAD, the government development agency. They hadn't bothered renting out the rest of the house, and I'd been tempted a few times into watching TV in their living room and making myself some food in the microwave. But not tonight.

I let myself in and went upstairs to my room on the top floor. It was like a sauna in there. I opened the window as wide as I could, took my clothes off and went into the bathroom across the landing to have a shower. When I was finished I put a clean T-shirt on and a pair of comfy shorts and lay down on the bed with my iPad to watch *Chicago Med*.

It took only a few minutes before my skin was sticky again and the first beads of perspiration began to trickle down my cheek, throat and arms.

I couldn't remember a night that had ever been as hot, not even on holiday.

I fetched a towel to wipe my brow.

The episode I was watching began to blur, looming back at me and blurring again, and soon it dissolved completely.

I was woken suddenly by the sound of someone hammering at the door, and sat bolt upright. The iPad shone in the dark next to me. Let me in! someone was shouting in the street outside. Let me in!

I went to the window and looked down. A man stood thumping his fist against the front door.

Let me in! he shouted again.

Who was it? What did he want?

He was desperate.

I stepped back into the room in case he looked up and saw me.

Mother! he shouted. Mother, let me in!

It was their son.

Should I go down and let him in?

I supposed I had to.

I leaned out of the window.

'Who is it?' I said.

He looked up. His eyes were wide and wild. He was tripping out of his mind.

'Let me in!' he shouted. 'I've got to get in!'

SOLVEIG

'Is that *you*?' the new patient said when I entered the room. He was sitting upright in bed in his blue hospital smock.

I looked at him quizzically.

His face was suntanned and his eyes warm, their gaze bright and alert.

'We were in the same class together at primary school. Don't you remember me?'

I nodded hesitantly.

He smiled.

'You don't remember me,' he said. 'Not that it's any wonder. We moved away halfway through.'

'That rings a bell,' I said. 'A very faint one, though!'

He smelled mildly of aftershave and his cheeks appeared to be quite smooth, so I supposed he must have shaved before I came. For some reason it touched me.

'Well, it's thirty-five years ago,' he said.

'You were rather quiet, would that be right?' I said, a vague recollection having appeared in my mind of a timid little boy with fair hair who might have been him.

'That sounds like me,' he said. 'I sat drawing most of the time. As I remember, anyway.'

'When did you move back?' I said.

'Two years ago.'

'Me too,' I said.

'What was your excuse?' he said, his eyes latching on to me as if it were something he genuinely wanted to know.

'My mother got Parkinson's and was on her own,' I said. 'She deteriorated rather rapidly.'

He nodded.

'I'd been thinking about it for a long time,' he said.

Our eyes met, and I felt myself blush.

I went over to the window and raised the blinds.

The sun was burning high above the town. It gleamed in the body-work of the cars in the car park. A bit further away, the river ran silvery and still towards the fjord.

I turned to him again. He'd folded his hands against his chest.

'The funny thing is I don't feel ill,' he said. 'Not in the slightest. I tried telling them I could walk up here on my own, but were they having it? Not on your life. I had to lie down and be wheeled.'

'Yes, sorry about that,' I said with a smile. 'There are rules they have to follow.'

As soon as I found a minute, I read through his record in more detail. Inge, that was his name. I remembered the moment I saw it. He had a tumour in his brain that hadn't been discovered in time. He'd thought the headaches he'd started getting a few years previously had been migraines, and his GP had thought so too. Not even when he began seeing things that weren't there, or which couldn't possibly happen, did the thought occur to him that something serious might be wrong, and so he never mentioned it to anyone. But then the previous spring he'd had an epileptic fit and a scan had revealed the tumour. It was located in the brain's visual cortex, hence the hallucinations.

I wondered what kind of hallucinations he'd had, what things he had seen.

Perhaps I could ask him about it tomorrow, I thought, glancing up at the board above the door, where a lamp was now flashing. Room number 2, Ramsvik's room. I got up to go and attend to him just as the phone in my pocket began to vibrate. It was Line.

She never called at this time of day, so although I was busy I answered.

'Hi, Line!' I said.

In front of me, Ellen crossed to the coffee dispenser and placed a cup under the spout.

'Hello, Mum,' Line said.

There was a gurgling sound, and only a dribble of coffee. Ellen turned her young, ruddy, rather pudgy face towards me.

'Is everything all right?' I said, pointing at the same time to the coffee maker in the corner.

Ellen gave a little smile and went over to fill the dispenser.

'Yes, of course,' said Line.

'Yes?'

'Yes. But I was thinking I could come out for a few days, if that's OK?'

'Of course it's OK! When do you want to come?'

'Tonight?'

'Tonight? You mean *tonight* tonight?'

'Yes, is that all right?'

'Yes, of course!'

'I'm actually on the bus now. It gets in around sixish.'

'Wonderful! What a lovely surprise,' I said, shaking my head at Ellen who was holding a cup in the air and looking at me enquiringly.

'OK,' said Line. 'I'll let you get on, you're bound to be busy at work. See you later.'

'Yes, see you later. Take care!'

I put the phone back in my pocket.

'Weren't there some biscuits around here somewhere?' said Ellen.

'I think they got eaten,' I said on my way into the corridor.

The sun shone through the window at the far end, giving a sheen to the lino on the floor and making it look almost liquid.

What could have prompted Line to come and stay at such short notice? I wondered. It wasn't like her at all.

And what was I going to make for dinner?

Should I get a bottle of wine?

No, the off-licence would be closed. Anyway, best not to make a fuss. If I went overboard, she'd only realise how much I missed her, I thought to myself, and knocked on Ramsvik's door. Ramsvik, or the Consul as I secretly called him.

He was lying on his back in the bed with his head turned to the side, and was looking straight at me as I came in.

'Hello,' I said. 'How are you feeling?'

He stared at me without moving his head.

'Good . . .' he said hesitantly, elongating the vowel sound. It was as if he knew it wasn't true even as he spoke the word, but was unable to say anything else.

'Are you in pain?'

'Yes,' he said. 'Pain.'

'Where do you feel the pain?' I said. 'Is it in your head?'

'Head,' he said.

'Do you want some more painkillers?'

'Yes. Yes.'

There was something resigned about the look he gave me as he replied.

'Or was that more of a no?' I said.

'Yes,' he said.

Ramsvik was in politics and I'd known who he was when he was admitted. He was often in the local newspapers, occasionally the regional ones too. He was a man of weight and authority, a commanding figure who was used to people doing as he said. He could be blunt, but a gleam was never far from his eye. People liked him. With his beard and his formal style of dress, there'd been something vaguely nineteenth century about him, all he needed was a monocle and he could have been a wholesaler or a consul in a book by Kielland.

Now his imposing demeanour was gone, had seeped away from him like water. All that remained was his body, large still, but weak. He'd suffered a sudden stroke while having breakfast at home. His wife had been alert and made sure he was flown to hospital immediately. The surgery had been successful and the damage rather less extensive than there had been reason to fear. He had been left with a partial paralysis and had difficulty speaking. It was a small price to pay for the life he'd almost lost. But no less traumatic on that account.

I'd seen him with his children when they'd come to visit him, a boy about ten years old and a girl of perhaps twelve. They'd been out of range, he couldn't reach them, couldn't hug them, couldn't talk to them. All communication had been down to them. They'd been frightened, but their fright would diminish and go away. The distance between them, however, was something that had been there to begin with, at least that was the feeling I got. Few things were more devastating to a person than losing the ability to communicate, but occasionally something good would come of it too. And so far he seemed to be dealing with it constructively, without letting himself become angered or frustrated by having to take such small steps at a time, the dependency on other people that had suddenly been forced upon him, but managing instead to turn it into something positive. A new sensibility.

'Live and the children are coming to pick you up tomorrow, is that right?' I said.

'Yes,' he said.

'I spoke to Sunnaas today,' I said. 'Your room's all ready for you there.'

'Thanks,' he said.

'Let me know if there's anything you need,' I said. 'Someone will be with you in a minute to give you those painkillers. And I'll see you before you leave tomorrow, of course.'

As I turned to leave, his gaze slipped away from me and he stared into space.

When I got back from lunch, I was told Inge's wife was sitting on the ward waiting for me, and I went to speak to her.

She got to her feet. Her name was Unni and she was about my age, blonde and slim, her features pretty in a way, if a little indistinct.

'Oh, you're the one who went to school with Inge!' she said when I said my name.

'Yes,' I said. 'Over thirty years ago.'

'How funny,' she said, smiling.

I smiled back.

'Have you had something to eat and drink?' I said.

She shook her head and held her hand up to stop me fetching her anything.

'How long before they're finished?' she said.

'It's impossible to say exactly,' I said. 'But a couple of hours, I should think.'

'And when will I be able to talk to him?'

'The anaesthetist will wake him up more or less immediately after the surgery, and if everything's all right, I imagine you'll be able to see him then. I don't see why not. He will be rather weak though.'

She nodded after everything I said.

'We've got three girls,' she said. 'Will it be all right for them to come and see him after school today?'

'Yes, by all means,' I said. 'Visiting time's until eight.'

I looked at her.

'How old are they?'

'Thirteen, fifteen and seventeen,' she said.

At the same time, Ellen came out of one of the rooms and grabbed my attention, gesturing for me to come. I excused myself and went over to her.

'Can I speak to you a minute?' she said.

'Yes, of course,' I said.

We went into the duty room. It turned out she was concerned about a woman who'd been admitted that morning, or rather it was about her child, an eleven-year-old girl who was at school but would be coming home to an empty house.

'The mother's a bit worse for wear. She says the girl will be fine and is used to looking after herself when she gets home from school, but I'm not so sure.'

'Is there anyone else who can look after her?'

'Her aunt's coming tomorrow, apparently.'

'What do *you* think would be best?' I said.

She hesitated.

'I could get in touch with social services and see if they can help,' she said.

'I think that's a good idea,' I said.

'It's not a bit drastic, you think?'

'No,' I said. 'It's only to make sure she's got the support she needs. Go in and talk to her again, tell her you're going to help out with her daughter. Then you can ring social services and explain the situation to them, and they can take over after that.'

When I came out into the corridor again, Unni was sitting typing on her phone. She knew the operation was likely to go well and that the surgeons would be able to remove nearly the entire tumour. But she had to know too that it would return. In nearly all cases, sooner or later, it would grow back again and would then be fatal.

It could happen in ten months, it could happen in ten years.

Every day would be a gift then, I thought, and looked through the window at the end of the corridor, at the bright houses that seemed almost to have been scattered across both sides of the river, the lush green fellside that rose up steeply behind them, near-black in the shadows at its foot, resplendent in the sunlight that flooded over the ridge at its peak.

Almost three hours passed before Inge's surgery was complete and the orderlies emerged from the lift with his trolley bed. I saw them through the window of the office, got to my feet and went out into the corridor, and followed them into his room.

'There we go,' one of them said, and then they were gone.

Inge's face was drooped and unexpressive due to the anaesthetic. At the same time, the bandage around his head transformed him too, making his face more exposed in a way, more obvious among all the tubes and monitors which surrounded him.

It was my job to help him, help his wife, help their three daughters.

I smoothed my hand cautiously over his cheek before going out again to inform the anaesthetist that he could be woken up and to tell Unni that the operation was over.

The sun burned in the sky all day. There wasn't a cloud in sight, only deep blue space and the fiery ball that slowly passed across it.

And yet I froze. The air conditioning was on full, and in every window on which the sun shone, the blinds were down.

Inge and Unni's three girls come out of the lift, I could tell straight away it was them. They were tall, all three of them, and looked very much like sisters, the same facial contours.

Quiet and sheepish, and staying close together, they came along the corridor until they reached his room.

It felt like I'd intruded on something very intimate that didn't concern me. But I was used to it — in the hospital environment, the boundaries between private and public were in constant flux, it was part of the nature of any hospital and something everyone who worked there had to relate to — and I dismissed the feeling as quickly as it had come.

Before I went off duty for the day, I looked in on him again.

He was sitting up in bed, staring into space with blinking eyes.

'How are you feeling?' I said.

'Bit of a bad head,' he said, and smiled faintly.

'No wonder,' I said, and smiled back. 'I'll give you some more pain relief. Everything all right apart from that?'

'Yes.'

'You're not thirsty?'

'A bit, maybe.'

I filled a glass with water and held it out in front of him. He reached for it slowly, as if it had been a long time since he'd done anything similar and had now almost forgotten what to do, folded his fingers around the glass and lifted it to his lips.

Some of the water ran down his chin.

He made to put the glass down, and I took it for him and put it on the table.

'Thanks,' he said. 'You're an angel.'

He leaned his head back against the pillow, his face pale and expressionless. The edge of his bandage was red with blood.

'What you need now is rest,' I said, and got to my feet. 'I've given you some more morphine now, so the pain should start to go away very soon.'

'Yes, I think I'll have a sleep,' he said.

There were tailbacks at both roundabouts on the way out of town that afternoon, but entering the valley the traffic eased and I could put my foot down. The landscape was glorious, every thinkable shade of green beneath a sea-blue sky. Cattle lay dozing under clusters of trees. Children and teenagers were swimming in the river, bikes glittering between the tree trunks; little piles of clothes lay dumped on the rocks, and here and there, heads, shoulders and arms poked up out of the slowly gliding, gleaming body of water.

I sang.

At the bend that brought the road closer to the fjord, I found myself plunged into the shade of the tall deciduous trees on both sides. I shuddered in what was surely a reflex brought on by the sudden change from strong light to dimness and shadow.

To think that shade existed.

And then I thought about Inge. He'd seemed so unperturbed, cheerful even.

Was he really the same person as that timid little boy I barely remembered?

Had life made him the way he was now?

In that case, his life had been fortunate, I thought to myself.

I picked up my phone and pressed Marianne's number. The ringing tone filled the whole car and I turned the volume down a bit.

'Hi, Solveig!' she said when she answered. 'Can you not make it today?'

'How on earth did you know that?'

'Why else would you be phoning now? Anything else and you'd have told me later on while we were out.'

'Very clever, Sherlock,' I said with a laugh. 'Line's coming tonight, so I thought perhaps we could go out tomorrow instead?'

'Yes, let's do that,' she said. 'How lovely for you!'

'Yes,' I said. 'It'll be nice.'

'I don't think I've seen Line since . . . when would that be? Two years ago? Three?'

'I think she's staying a few days,' I said. 'You'll be able to see her, I'm sure.'

We chatted for a few minutes before hanging up, and then I reached into the glove compartment, took out a CD and put it in the player without looking to see which one it was. I liked leaving things to chance, at least little things like that, it often gave me pleasure.

Oh, I knew this.

What was it now?

I turned up the volume as I reached the end of the valley and the road began its rise over the fell.

Albinoni. Adagio in G minor.

I drove on down the other side, passing along the fjord, the waterfall white amid the green, through the cutting, before another steep, narrow climb.

I felt so uplifted I hardly knew what to do with myself. I could have burst into tears or laughter. I hummed along to the music, which rose and fell like the landscape around me. But music didn't come from the landscape, it came from the sky. Or from within.

Within someone.

Within us all.

Within me.

I drove past a cluster of milking huts and saw some people sitting out, and then the road began to lead down again. At the point where it curved around the big boulder, I slowed down in case I happened to meet a car coming up.

On the other side, a red deer was standing at the edge of the forest.

I'd seen them in the area lots of times, but never as close.

I pulled in to the side, turned the music off and rolled the window down.

It stayed where it was, quite still, its head turned towards me.

So sleek and graceful it was.

It looked at me for a long time, then began to walk away, quite leisurely, before disappearing into the trees.

The distant rush of the waterfall dissolved on the wind that came sweeping through the valley, rustling every tree as it went. I carried on, descending, until at last I could see the blue shimmer of the fjord in the distance, the steep face of the fell that from there resembled a reclining horse.

I put the car key down on the old telephone table in the hall and opened the door into the living room.

Mum was sitting in her chair at the window. Her bony face was in profile, her mouth open, her breathing faint and inaudible.

Behind her, on the other side of the pane, the branches of the tall birch lifted soundlessly in the sea breeze.

Strange how little space she took up when she was asleep, I thought, closing the door quietly and going into the kitchen. The sight of the red deer still resonated in me, a delicate shimmer of joy. I put the shopping down on the work surface, put the items away in the cupboard and fridge, and tucked the folded carrier bag into the bottom drawer.

The rya mat on the floor looked grubby all of a sudden, so I took it into the bathroom and put it in the washing machine, loaded some towels from the laundry bin too, and then started the wash cycle.

When I returned I heard a low hum from the living room. It was her chair, which she could raise with a remote control, making it easier for her to get up.

'Hello, Mum,' I said from the doorway.

Her eyes flashed with anger as she looked at me.

It almost paralysed me, like a hand gripping my heart and tightening around it.

But she couldn't harm me, I told myself. She couldn't harm me.

'Is something the matter?' I said, stepping towards her tentatively. My legs were weak, my body weak.

She tried to say something, but was too enraged, all she could muster was a hiss.

Her anger worked at a different speed from her body, as if it hadn't aged the way the rest of her had.

'Did you want me to come home earlier, is that it?' I said, and took her by the arm, leading her a few steps until she could hold on to her walker and stand on her own. 'Only you know I couldn't get here any sooner,' I said. 'I've a job to look after too, you know that.'

She shuffled forward, her feet barely lifting off the floor, employing all her strength in this single endeavour, to cross the room to the sideboard by the wall.

Was it that watch again?

She tried to pull the drawer open.

I helped her.

'What are you looking for, Mum?' I said. 'What is it you're so concerned about?'

She started rummaging through the drawer.

Then she stopped and whispered something.

I bent towards her.

The brooch. Was that what she said?

'The brooch?' I said.

'Yes,' she whispered.

'Is it not in here?'

I emptied everything out and laid it all on top of the sideboard.

The brooch wasn't there, she was right about that.

It had belonged to her great-grandmother, my great-great-grandmother. Mum had been given it when she got married and had handed it down to me when I got married.

'It must be somewhere,' I said. 'I'm sure we'll find it.'

She looked at me. She knew as well as I did that it hadn't been worn since I moved back home and that the only place it could possibly be was in that drawer in the sideboard.

Someone must have taken it.

It couldn't be Anita, I refused to believe it. But no one else came to the house.

Could she have left it somewhere herself and forgotten about it?

'We'll find it, Mum,' I said. 'I'm sure we will. I'll have a look later on. But first I've got the dinner to make. Line's coming tonight.'

'Line?' she whispered.

'Yes,' I said. 'She phoned earlier on to say she was on her way. I'm picking her up from the bus at Vågen in an hour. Come, let me give you a change.'

I took her arm and walked slowly by her side to the bathroom where I pulled down her underwear, lifted up her dress and helped her onto the toilet.

Her legs, so thin and white, trembled now that the weight of her body no longer pressed them to the floor.

I waited a few minutes before going in again, wiping her, changing her and helping her wash her hands at the sink.

She was calm now and nodded when I asked if she wanted to sit outside for a bit in the sun.

I took a chair out, fetched a rug and placed it over her legs as she sat looking out on the world she'd lived in all her life and loved so much. The pastures, the fjord, the fells.

The sun was high above the mouth of the fjord to the west, and the waters gleamed and scintillated in its light.

*

When the bus pulled in outside the Samvirkelaget co-op, I got out of the car and went over to wait.

Line was the last passenger to emerge. She was wearing a green, army-type jacket with a big yellow rucksack slung over her shoulder.

Perhaps she really was planning on staying a while? A stream of joy ran through me as I lifted my hand and waved to her.

She waved back, looking both ways before crossing the road.

'Hi,' she said.

'Hello, my darling,' I said, hugging her as tight as I could.

'Such a fuss to make,' she said, and dropped her shoulder to remove her rucksack. 'Can you put this in the boot?'

'Of course,' I said. 'Oof, that's heavy! What have you brought with you?'

'Books,' she said, and got in the car.

I closed the boot and got in next to her behind the wheel.

'Anything you want from the Co-op before we go?' I said.

She shook her head.

She wasn't wearing any make-up, and her hair was gathered simply in a ponytail. Together with her oversized jacket, it made me think she was trying to hide, or at least trying not to draw attention to herself.

It wasn't a good thought.

But at least there was some colour in her cheeks, I reasoned, pulling out onto the road as Line took a pair of sunglasses out of her jacket pocket and put them on.

'There's a lasagne in the oven,' I said. 'It should be ready by the time we get home.'

'Sounds good,' she said.

'You're looking so tanned,' I said. 'Have you been out a lot during the summer?'

'I was at a cabin up at the lake last weekend.'

'Who with?'

She glanced at me, then pulled down the visor on her side.

'Some friends,' she said.

The light from the low-hanging sun was refracted by the windscreen in such a way that it was hard to see anything for the glare, and I lowered my speed. There wasn't much traffic once we got away from the town, but the road was narrow and often a tractor would suddenly appear, especially at this time of the year.

'What sort of books have you brought with you, then?' I said.

'Philosophy and theory of science, for the ex.phil. intro course,' she said. 'I was thinking I could do some reading here for a few days where it's quiet.'

'When's the exam again?' I said, and smiled, glad to sense that her grit had returned.

'In three months,' she said.

We crossed the little bridge, passing through the shade of the oak trees that grew there, and I cast a glance towards the trough of the river. There was hardly any water in it, save for the odd pool here and there.

Perhaps not thinking about her appearance like that made her feel she was applying herself more to her studies?

I remembered myself in that same situation. Books and papers everywhere, overfilled ashtrays, unbrushed hair, comfy clothes.

I realised she would barely be able to imagine that I — not that long ago, either — had been a student too, living in a rented room and leading the same sort of life as she was now.

'Gran's so much looking forward to you coming,' I said.

'Mm,' said Line, looking at herself in the vanity mirror, pursing her lips in a way I thought people only ever did when they were on their own.

While Line got herself sorted out in her room, I gave the table in the garden a quick wipe before putting the things out for dinner. It stood among the apple trees, and the dwindling rays of the sun, now low in the west, played in their crowns.

A hawk soared above the pasture below. The way it didn't move its outspread wings, but simply hung suspended in the air, reminded me of a child's kite.

Mum sat watching me as I went back and forth between the kitchen and garden. It was the first time we'd eaten outside all summer, for some reason it seemed such an extravagant thing to do when it was just the two of us.

When everything was ready I gave Line a shout and helped Mum to the table.

She was still well enough to eat on her own as long as I cut her food into bite-sized pieces. It was an exertion for her, and rather pains-taking, but it was important she managed while Line was there. Her helplessness bothered her especially then, I knew. It wasn't the way she wanted her grandchild to remember her.

Line stared blankly at the table as she ate, immersed in her own world, while Mum kept glancing at her, bent over her plate, moving her trembling hand to and from her mouth.

She whispered something and I leaned towards her so I could hear what it was.

Thomas, was that it?

'Thomas,' I repeated. 'Are you asking Line how Thomas is getting on?'

'Yes,' she breathed.

'He's doing fine, Gran,' Line said, remembering to lift her voice. 'He's thinking of going to college.'

'What sort of college?' I said.

'Police college,' she said. 'But he's got to meet the admission criteria first.'

The breeze from the fjord made the branches around us sway and rustle their leaves. Sometimes, when the wind rose, it was as if the trees braced themselves, reaching up onto their toes before releasing again and sinking back.

'Have you told Gran what subject you're going to be doing?' I said.

'No,' said Line. 'I'm sure you have though.'

She looked up at me, as if to gauge my reaction, before looking down at her food again.

I gave Mum some water, holding the glass to her lips. She didn't quite manage to swallow, and some of it ran down her chin. I tore off a piece of kitchen towel and wiped it away hastily, as if by the by.

'Psychology,' Mum whispered.

'Gran says psychology,' I said. 'So yes, we must have talked about it! Are you looking forward to it?'

Line nodded enthusiastically and gave her a smile. I could tell her enthusiasm was affected, but whatever it was that was preying on her mind, it was gratifying at least that she made an effort to please her grandmother.

After dinner, Line went up to her room and I helped Mum into the living room where I put the television on for her before sitting down again outside with a cup of coffee to enjoy the last of the sunshine.

Overhead, some crows came flying up from the fjord. More followed, and soon the sky was teeming with birds. It was like a curtain of living flesh, I thought to myself, beautiful, shimmering patterns of black and darkest blue that a moment later broke up as the crows began to settle in the line of trees leading up to the churchyard a bit further away where they had their nests.

Upstairs, a window opened and I heard the sound of Line's voice, soft and gentle amid the gruff squawking of the crows in the trees.

Who was she talking to?

It wouldn't be Thomas. Although they were involved to a certain extent in each other's lives, they didn't actually have that much in common apart from being brother and sister. I certainly couldn't imagine her phoning him now just for a chat.

A friend, then?

Or perhaps she was going out with someone and hadn't let on?

She was leaning halfway out, her arm resting against the sill, the phone in her other hand. Our eyes met and I smiled. She smiled back before lifting her head and looking out at the landscape.

I hoped she saw the beauty in it. The steep fell, the quiet waters of the fjord, the slowly darkening sky, and, on the other side, the treetops now reddened by the dwindling sun.

In the kitchen, I found the dishwasher had stopped working. It kept stuttering as if it had got stuck, and when I opened it, it was full of water. Presumably, the hose was clogged, perhaps it was calcium build-up. I made a note to phone someone about it in the morning.

I emptied everything out of it and started washing it all up by hand.

The thudding of the dishes against the bottom of the sink, the dull, rounded sound they made, gave me a peaceful feeling. The warmth that enveloped my hands did too, and the networks of tiny bubbles that slid from the surface of the plates as I lifted them up to rinse them in the adjoining sink.

Ever since childhood, I'd connected those grumbling underwater sounds with creatures. Big, stubby grubs, grey and without eyes.

It was one of those things I could never tell anyone, I thought, and smiled to myself.

Oddly, I saw Inge's face as I thought about it.

Had he made such an impression on me?

I was tired, that's all, I thought, and looked up. The sky above the fell on the other side of the fjord was still blue, whereas the details of the sheer fellside, stretching away for several kilometres, were now being erased by the dimming twilight.

I tried to imagine what it must be like to see something that wasn't there. And to believe in it. That the fell didn't actually exist other than in my head. That all of a sudden a man was standing in the kitchen looking at me.

If I turned round now, he would be there.

I smiled again and laid a tea towel on the work surface to put the clean dishes on, instead of the overfilled rack.

The floor upstairs creaked.

What was it that was preying on her mind?

Her footsteps sounded on the staircase and then she was standing in the doorway.

'Going for a walk,' she said.

'Good idea,' I said. 'Where were you thinking of going?'

'Up to the waterfall, maybe.'

A minute later she went past outside the window, putting on her jacket. Everything about her seemed so strangely clear and well-defined against the dusk.

Her high cheekbones and the faintly sweeping line of her eyes made her beautiful.

But she was negative too. A person who demanded and took without giving.

A negative person.

How had she got to be like that?

No, that wasn't how she *was* at all. It was how she was *now*. She was young, still facing off with the world, but a time would come when she would be able to open herself to it and receive what it had to offer, and then she would be able to give.

I heard her voice in my mind. 'Mum, you're so naive,' it said. 'Mum, you don't even believe that yourself, do you?'

I took a clean towel from the cupboard and dried my hands, hung it over the handle of the oven door and went in to see to Mum. She'd dropped off, but wasn't yet quite asleep; as I sat down on the pouffe in front of her, she opened her eyes.

'Do you want me to massage your feet a bit?' I said.

'Yes,' she whispered.

I put her legs up in my lap and began to cautiously bend and stretch them. Her muscles would often stiffen and she would cramp up several times a day, usually very painfully. Massage helped, and walking helped.

I rubbed her calves.

Her arms, stiffly bent at the elbows, trembled as I worked. Her head trembled too, her lower jaw trembled.

It hurt so much to see her that way.

But her eyes were bright.

She whispered something.

'What was that, Mum?' I said, leaning towards her.

'Line,' she whispered.

'How's Line? Is that what you're asking?'

'Yes,' she whispered.

'I don't know,' I said. 'I think something's troubling her. But she hasn't mentioned anything.'

'Ask?' she whispered.

'Yes, I could ask,' I said. 'But I'd rather she came to me of her own accord. I'm thinking it might be why she came. What do you think?'

'Yes.'

I took her feet in my hands and began squeezing and rubbing them.

'Do you remember when I would come home at her age?' I said.

'Yes.'

'I shared everything with you, do you remember?'

'Yes.'

'I don't think you ever told me anything about yourself, though.'

'No.'

Her eyes lit up in a smile.

I turned her foot gently in an arc.

She tried to formulate a sentence.

I heard *you*, I heard *don't*, I heard *self* and I heard *either*.

'You're saying I don't tell Line about myself either?' I said.

She nodded.

'I suppose you're right,' I said. 'But that's because she's not interested.'

I changed feet, slowly describing a circle as I began to repeat the process.

'I don't suppose I was either, come to think of it,' I said. 'Not at that time. I took you for granted, you and Dad.'

Yet those evenings had been so open and full of light, it had been such a good place to come and share my experiences of the world outside.

I put her feet down gently on the floor again.

'Do you want me to help you have a shower?' I said.

She nodded.

'Hair,' she whispered.

I showered her, put a nappy on her for the night, and her nightdress, and had just started to blow-dry her hair when Line came back.

'Mum!' she called out from the hall.

I switched the hairdryer off.

'We're in here,' I called back.

She came in, her face flushed with life after having been out, too excessive in a way for the small rooms of the house.

'Have you seen the baby birds in the gateway?' she said.

I nodded.

'Aren't they sweet?' I said.

'Yes, but why didn't you say anything?'

'There was no occasion,' I said.

'What sort of birds are they? I only saw the babies.'

'There's a pair of wood pigeons that nest there,' I said.

She opened her mouth and was just about to say something when I interrupted her.

'Are you hungry? I could make us a snack before we go to bed?'

She realised I didn't want to talk about the birds, and a look of surprise came over her, but fortunately she didn't pursue the matter, only shook her head slightly instead.

'We'll be finished here in a minute,' I said, and switched the hairdryer on again.

The pigeons came every spring, built their nest in the same place, laid eggs, the eggs hatched and the young grew — but just before they became fledglings ready to leave the nest, often only a few days before, the same goshawk would come and eat them.

It had happened four years in a row and there was nothing to be done about it; I couldn't bring myself to move the nest, so the only thing to do was wait and see and hope for the best.

I hadn't the slightest intention of telling Line. If she found out what the goshawk did — or even worse, if she saw it happen — she'd be devastated. She'd always had such a big heart for animals of any kind — when she was very little she would fill her pockets with worms and spiders, all sorts of creepy-crawlies, and bring them home with her, and even in gymnasium school she was still talking of becoming a vet.

It was one of the reasons she'd liked coming here so much when she'd been growing up. At that time, there'd been animals on the farm — not many, just a couple of cows, often a calf, a horse and some hens, but to her it was an unimaginable wealth.

It had been for me too. I remember thinking that at least she had *that* from her childhood, the summers she spent here, even if everything else should turn out difficult.

I walked Mum into the living room and watched television with her for an hour before putting her to bed in the next room, previously the dining room, now her bedroom.

After closing the sliding door behind me, I went upstairs to Line's room and knocked on the door.

'Yes?' she said from inside.

She was sitting on the windowsill in the dark and looked at me as I came in.

Her rucksack was open on the floor, clothes already strewn about the room, the duvet bunched up.

'Is it not too chilly for you?' I said, sitting down on the edge of the bed.

She shook her head.

'How are things with you?' I said.

'Fine,' she said.

'Are you sure?'

'Yes, I'm sure. Why?'

'You seem a little distant.'

'It's not a crime, is it?'

I sighed.

'We should be able to talk,' I said. 'I mean, properly.'

'What do you want to talk about?'

'You, perhaps?'

'But I don't want to talk about me.'

There was a pause.

'Fine, that's quite all right,' I said after a moment, and got to my feet.

'Good,' she said.

'Anita, the home help, will be coming in the morning,' I said. 'And again at lunchtime. If you'd rather be on your own with Gran and look after her a bit, just let me know and I'll tell Anita she needn't come.'

'I came here to study,' she said. 'Not to look after Gran.'

'OK,' I said. 'As long as I know. Goodnight!'

Instead of going to bed, I put a coat on and went outside. The sky was still light, a thin veil drained of all colour, the way the nights are in the Vestlandet in summer.

Everything was silent. The fjord lay silent in its hollow, the fell rose silently on the other side, and behind me, on the slopes to the north, the trees stood silent too. My feet in the soft grass was nearly the only sound. That, and the occasional, faint murmur of the forest, as if it were slowly exhaling after holding its breath.

I went up to the empty field at the edge of the trees, beyond the pasture, the site of a farm building that had been there once, sat on what remained of the foundation wall and looked back down at the house I'd just left.

I'd always liked to sit there. There could be something liberating about seeing the place from a distance; it made the people inside smaller. It was a thought that had come to me when I'd still been in my teens. Mum and Dad were in there, it was their domain, but only there, for the world outside them was enormous. Who cared what happened in the tiny rooms of that little house?

Now it was me who lived there, but the thought was the same, the only difference being that now it was my own life I could see from afar, my own life that became small. That I wasn't all there was.

In the sky above me, the light of a few stars had almost broken through. It was as if they preferred not to be seen, but knew they had to appear, bashfully pretending not to be there. A bit like Line, I thought with a smile, when she'd been in the school play at the end of term and had looked down at the floor while mumbling her lines so quietly no one could hear.

Then, I became aware of something happening at the edge of my field of vision, and turned my head to see what it was.

A light burst over the treetops on the ridge in the west. It looked like the trees had been set on fire.

For a long time I just sat there and stared.

The light rose in the sky and grew in size, until only a few seconds later it was clear of the ridge. It looked like a star, only its light was so much brighter. It had to be a planet. But what sort of planet would it be, passing by here at this time of the year?

I'd never seen anything like it.

There'd be a perfectly reasonable explanation, I told myself. Anyway, it was such a splendid sight, the glaring light in the pale sky above the dark, tree-covered slopes.

I stood up and followed the low drystone wall along the perimeter of the forest. Soon I could see the village lying as if curled up at the inlet in the fjord, beneath the hills whose presence hid the more distant sea from sight.

The star was higher in the sky now.

So quickly it rose!

I walked on past the pond, its waters black at the forest fringe, and went up to the old mink sheds my grandfather had built and run for a few years and which no one had since been bothered to pull down, situated as they were away from the rest of the farm on rocky ground that was no use for anything else.

Perhaps Inge was the sort who knew the names of the stars and how far away they were?

But why should he be? I thought then, and snorted at such a silly thought. Still, I visualised him standing at the window in the hospital, staring up at the same star as I was looking at now.

It was a silly thought.

I went over towards the barn across the pasture, all the time glancing up at the star.

Could it be a supernova? A star that expanded as it burned out?

There was something quite unreal about it. Or did it make everything else seem unreal?

I stopped at the door of the byre. I remembered so well the warmth and the smell, mellow and yet pungent at the same time, of the cows when I was little, and didn't care to see the cold and glaringly bare stalls now at all, the remnants of dung and hay, now dry and lifeless, the walls that were almost falling down. Nevertheless, I lifted the hook and pushed open the door that had warped and now scraped against the floor. Inside, I threw the light switch, and the next instant the room was flooded with bright electric light.

Something moved in the stall at the far end.

I froze.

An animal came into view, venturing out onto the floor by the manure pit to look at me.

It was a fox.

Its eyes were yellow and it seemed to be weighing me up.

Quite fearless, it stood there. Then, after a moment, it lowered its head, turned and slipped away through the hatch into the barn.

As the bath slowly filled with water, I undressed, folded my clothes and put them on top of the laundry bin. Standing there naked, I considered myself in the mirror. It was seldom I ever did, but now I wanted to see what I might look like to others.

My thighs were white and round, my hips broad. My stomach was soft and crumpled into folds when I bent forward.

I smoothed my hands over my hips. It looked awkward, as if all of a sudden I felt uncomfortable with myself.

I'd spent my twenties and thirties reconciling myself with my body. Now, everything I'd eventually come to accept then had changed, and it seemed like I could start again.

Eww.

It was so much better not to have a man to please. There was no need to think about it then.

I turned the tap off and stepped into the bath. The water was red-hot, but I persisted, lowering myself gently until I was sitting down.

My skin prickled agonisingly for a few seconds, requiring all my resolve to stay where I was. And then it was good.

I leaned back and the hot water assailed my upper body, but again the agony subsided and I closed my eyes.

After the gushing water from the tap, the room was completely still. I heard only the murmur of the television in the living room, the faint rush of the waterfall in the dell.

The dripping tap, droplets gathering and releasing, one after another.

I smoothed a hand over my brow, drew my fingers through my damp hair and was just about to pick up the soap when my mobile started ringing.

It was an infernal invasion. I reached over the edge of the bath, pulled my trousers towards me, extracted the phone from the pocket and saw that it was the hospital calling.

It'll be Inge, I thought. He'll have had a haemorrhage.

But it wasn't Inge, it was Ramsvik, he was on life support and a transplant team was on its way from Oslo.

I dried myself quickly, put the clean clothes on that I'd laid out for tomorrow, and went in to check on Mum.

She opened her eyes when I stopped at her bed.

'Aren't you asleep?' I said. 'Is anything the matter?'

'No,' she whispered.

'Good,' I said. 'I'm afraid I've got to go back to work again. Will you be all right?'

'Yes,' she whispered.

'Do you want me to make you a sandwich?'

'No. Line . . .'

'I'll tell her,' I said. 'She's all right. Don't be afraid to ask her if you need help!'

Everything was quiet as I closed the door behind me and went over to the car. The fjord light and filmy, the fell heavy and silent, the sky clear.

Thank goodness it wasn't Inge!

The thought had been coming back to me all day, that suddenly he would be lying there, his eyes big and black and dead, his brain full of blood.

It happened now and then.

I backed out onto the gravel track, fastened my seat belt, put the car into gear and drove off down the hill, faster than I usually did.

Further down by the gate, an animal was standing in the middle of the track. At first I thought it was a dog, but as I got closer I realised it was a fox. Probably the same one, I supposed. I didn't slow down, presuming it would bolt to one side and run away. Only it didn't.

I braked in front of it.

It looked at me.

I blew the horn, revved the engine, but it didn't budge.

Not until I opened the car door and made to get out did it turn and slink away into the pasture, disappearing a moment later in the tall grass.

Someone must be feeding it, I reasoned, and carried on my way. It was nearly tame. It was a shame, what were people thinking? Wild animals were wild and ought to remain so.

There were hardly any cars out, and I drove as fast as I dared along the narrow roads. On the other side of the fell, where the road into town swung west and the landscape flattened out, I saw the star again, shining low over the peaks. It was almost as if I'd got used to it already, and I savoured the splendour that was all around. The bluish, night-silent landscape, the star shining so brightly and so vividly in an otherwise empty sky.

In Oslo I'd worked as an operating theatre assistant at the Riks-hospitalet. I loved the job, but the intensity it required, the stress that went with it, wouldn't accord with living here, I'd told myself when I decided to make the move back. Sometimes, though, if it was a major operation, they would call on me to assist. I didn't mind, the money was good and occasionally it felt like there was too much administration in my normal work.

Everything was about life and death in the operating theatre. And everyone who'd ever worked there wanted to go back.

Even tonight, I thought as I passed through the stillness of the valley, was about life and death. The patient was dead, but his organs were alive and were to live on inside other patients.

To shield myself from the next thought — that it wasn't just a patient, but Ramsvik — I ejected the CD that was in the player and inserted another.

Eurythmics, 'Here Comes the Rain Again'.

How I'd loved that song.

It occurred to me that I could look in on Inge while I was there. There'd be nothing odd about that, he was a patient on my ward. If I was lucky, he'd be awake too.

Around me the farms segued seamlessly into detached houses, scattered at first, gradually clustering until they at last became a city that lay twinkling below. Passing over the plain after crossing the river, I saw a helicopter coming in low overhead. That would be the team from Oslo, I thought, pulling into the car park in front of the hospital at the same moment the chopper landed on the platform on the other side. The thought of Ramsvik, which had long been a kind of shadow in my mind, now loomed large as I hurried through the car park, entered the building and descended into the basement.

His two children had lost their father tonight.

I breathed deeply a few times. Death belonged to life. Death was natural. It came all the time and took people away. This time it was Ramsvik. It was only natural. Children lost their fathers. That too was only natural.

With these thoughts in mind, which I repeated to myself whenever death came close, I hurried to get changed and then took the lift up to the operating theatre.

Ramsvik lay hooked up to a ventilator in the middle of the glaringly illuminated room, amid tubes and wires, surrounded by monitors.

There were five doctors present. Henriksen, one of our own, stood by
the operating table in conversation with the surgeon I understood to be
leading the transplant team.

Camilla had briefed me on the way in. Ramsvik had suffered a
renewed haemorrhage, so massive there was nothing to be done, the
damage to the brain far too considerable. He'd immediately been put
on life support to keep his organs alive.

It was impossible to comprehend that he was dead. His chest rose
and fell and his heart was beating. He looked like any other patient
under narcosis.

I'd liked him. He'd been an exceptional man.

'Good to see you, Solveig,' Henriksen said. 'Everything all right?'

His eyes smiled above his mask.

'Mm,' I said.

'Let's get ready, then.'

'OK,' I said.

The procedure was for Henriksen to lead the operation until the life
support was switched off and the heart stopped, the Oslo team taking
over from there to remove the heart. Once that was done, Henriksen
would step in and remove the abdominal organs.

Normally, he'd put his music on now. His 1950s playlist — Elvis,
Jerry Lee Lewis, Bo Diddley, but also Frank Sinatra and the other croon-
ers. All a bit silly to my mind, though I'd always liked Elvis. 'Blue
Moon', especially.

Tonight, though, everything was taking place in silence, out of
respect for the deceased.

I stepped up to Ramsvik. His cheeks had more colour now than when
I'd seen him earlier in the day. I began to get things ready, putting out
the hypodermics that would be needed when the chest was opened,
tongs, scalpels, catheters, saw, while Camilla primed the machine that
would keep his blood circulating. The Oslo team stood chatting behind
us with their arms folded.

I checked the monitors. All functions normal. The heart was beating
steadily, comfortably.

Henriksen bent over Ramsvik, glancing up with a nod at Kyvik, who
shut off all infusion. Henriksen then gripped Ramsvik's index finger

and pressed hard against the nail. I looked at Ramsvik's face, which remained motionless. He wasn't anaesthetised, yet the brain registered no pain and was quite without life.

'You can never be too sure!' Henriksen said with a chuckle before straightening up. 'Right! Let's switch him off.'

He did so himself, and I removed the tube from Ramsvik's mouth.

All heads turned to the monitors. Sometimes hours could pass before respiration ceased and the heart stopped pumping. If it took more than ninety minutes, the organs would be useless. But such cases were rare.

It wasn't going to happen now either. The blood pressure dropped as respiration grew fainter, stopping definitively after perhaps a minute.

The curve shown on the monitor levelled off as the heart came to a halt, and after a moment it flatlined completely. An alarm signal sounded.

The ultrasound image showed the heart to be quite motionless.

'Five minutes,' said Henriksen. 'From now.'

He left the room, followed by one of the assistant surgeons.

I stared at the lifeless body that only a few seconds before had been living. For no apparent reason, the gentle guitar chords of 'Blue Moon' came into my head. It was as though the song were actually playing inside me, rather than coming from memory.

I glanced at the others in the room, and a wave of emotion washed through me. I blinked to get rid of the tears, making sure no one saw me, as together with the transplant nurse I began to get things ready for the next and most substantial part of the operation. The body would be opened, the various organs removed, a minutely detailed and time-consuming procedure with no room for mistakes, everything had to take place quickly and precisely.

'Have you done this before?' said one of the transplant assistants, a man who seemed to be in his early thirties. He looked unhealthy, bags under his eyes, but then I supposed we all did in the glaring light.

'I worked at the Rikshospitalet a few years ago,' I said.

'As a theatre nurse?'

'Yes.'

'And you ended up here?'

'It's where I'm from,' I said. 'I wanted to come home.'

'Did you know him?' he said then, with a nod towards Ramsvik.

'He was my patient.'

He shook his head in sympathy. Behind us, Henriksen returned to the room.

'Five minutes gone,' he said. 'Any signs of life?'

'No.'

'Right then,' he said. 'Let's get started.'

I washed the chest, abdomen and groin with disinfecting agent. Kyvik infused the anticoagulant, before Henriksen inserted the tubes of the heart-lung machine into the groin. Into one he fed a balloon that would be inflated just below the brain, ensuring that any remaining blood flow would be blocked. Then, he switched on the machine that would circulate the blood and infuse it with oxygen.

I'd always found this disconcerting, for now the lower body was alive, while the upper body was dead. The head, neck and chest above the heart became cold, gradually turning blue, while the lower body remained living and warm.

There was a flurry of activity around me. I drew the instrument tray with its scalpels, knives and clamps towards me, arranging them one last time before the surgeon began. Ramsvik's corpulent frame lay motionless on the table in front of us; his face was quite white, drained of blood, with a faint tinge of blue.

His whole body, with the exception of the head, chest and abdomen, was covered up. I handed the surgeon a scalpel and he drew a long incision from the throat to the pubis. Fresh, red blood trickled out. When it was done, he returned the instrument to me. I placed it in the holder, then handed him the saw.

I looked up at Ramsvik's face as he began.

His eyes were open.

'The patient's awake!' I shouted.

'Don't be silly,' the transplant surgeon said, immediately switching off the saw. 'He can't be.'

But he too could see that the eyes were open.

'I've not seen *that* before,' he said. 'But I did once have one who shouted after he was dead. Now *that* was scary!'

He started the saw again.

But the eyes that lay open there were not dead. There was life in them, I knew it. It was as if he were looking out at the world from a place far, far away.

Yet the heart was not beating. And the brain had been without blood for some time.

It didn't matter. There was life in those eyes.

'Are we *certain* he's dead?' I said. 'Could there be something wrong with the balloon?'

Both the Oslo surgeon and Henriksen looked at me in annoyance.

'It's just a reflex,' the Oslo surgeon said. 'He *is* brain-dead. The heart has *not* beaten for ages. It's not *possible* for there to be life in him.'

'Look at the X-ray, Solveig,' Henriksen said. 'And at the blood pressure. The balloon is functional.'

'He's as dead as a dead fish,' said the Oslo surgeon. 'Now, let's continue.'

He leaned forward and the saw whined into life as he pressed it to the chestbone. A fine dust filled the air as he cut through the bone, and as the blade slowly made its way downwards, blood trickled forth again, fresh and red.

Ramsvik opened his mouth.

'Stop!' I shouted.

The surgeon stopped the saw again.

'Aaaaaaaaaaaa,' came a voice, barely audible, from the body on the table.

'What the *hell* is happening?' said the surgeon. 'It can't be, it's impossible!'

I looked at the monitor. The heart had started beating again. The curve was low, but it was a curve.

'The heart's beating!' I said.

He was alive.

A kind of panic broke out. The eyes that stared out from above the surgical masks were frightened, darting about as if in search of something concrete to latch on to.

'The definition of death is that it's irreversible,' said Henriksen. 'No one can come back from the dead. Which means that he is not, and was not, dead.'

'Oh, good God,' said the transplant assistant.

'What do we do now?' said the transplant surgeon.

'We sew him together again and then scan the brain,' said Henriksen.

'No organs tonight, in other words,' the transplant surgeon said.

'No,' said Henriksen.

'How can it be *possible*?' the transplant surgeon said, shaking his head. 'There's been no circulation in the brain for *half an hour*. The heart was stopped. And the balloon is functional, yes?'

'Looks like it,' said Henriksen. 'The fact, however, is that he's alive.'

'What will happen to him now?' I said.

'He'll receive no treatment,' said Henriksen. 'No nourishment. So he'll simply expire nice and peacefully. Best for everyone.'

He lifted his voice.

'Not a word outside this room about what's happened here, is that clear? Not a word in Oslo, not a word here.'

I took off my cap, mask and gown, tossed them in the laundry bin and got myself a coffee. Henriksen, scrubbing down, turned his head towards me.

'It can take up to twenty-four hours for the heart to stop after brain death,' he said.

'But his heart stopped after only a few seconds,' I said.

'Yes, yes, yes,' he said. 'It's happened before. There was a time in Sweden, years ago now, when something similar occurred. The patient had been declared brain-dead and they were busy removing his organs when suddenly he opened his eyes.'

'I've heard about that,' I said. 'But they must have been wrong. The patient can't have been brain-dead at all.'

'No,' said Henriksen.

'But *Ramsvik* was dead,' I said. 'We all saw that.'

'Logically, he can't have been,' said Henriksen. 'There must have been something wrong with the balloon. It can't have been working right. That happens too, of course. Nothing's infallible.'

He smiled.

'Anyway, it's still early. We're off for a drink. Fancy joining us?'

He winked at me.

'No, thanks,' I said.

'OK,' he said. 'Some other time, then.'

He produced a little spray bottle, sprayed three times into his mouth, wiped his lips and dropped the bottle back in his pocket.

'Nicotine,' he said. 'See you later, Solveig!'

I waited a few minutes before taking the lift down to the ward. Jorunn appeared from the duty room as I stepped out. She must have heard it stop.

'Hi, Jorunn,' I said. 'Everything all right? Just come to get something.'

'Have you been assisting with the transplant?' she said.

'Yes,' I said.

'Poor man,' she said.

'I'll say,' I said, and went into my office, put an unused ring binder into a plastic bag and went out again, to Inge's room.

I knocked cautiously and opened the door.

He was sitting up in bed supported by pillows and turned his head towards me as I came in. His face was pale, there were dark rings around his eyes and a shadow of stubble on his cheeks and chin. His eyes glowed.

'Are you *still* on the job?' he said. His voice was faint, but not weak.

I nodded.

'I had to assist in theatre. I'm on my way home now, though.'

'All right for some,' he said.

'How are you feeling?' I said.

'I'm alive,' he said. 'That's the important thing. It is to me, anyway!'

'So your head's still hurting, is it?'

He nodded, albeit reluctantly.

'Not that it's any wonder,' he said. 'They were rummaging around in there for hours.'

I smiled.

He smiled too.

'Just ring for help if you're in too much pain,' I said.

'I will,' he said.

There was a pause.

Then we both started to say something at the same time.

'Do you think you can −' he said.

'Have you seen —' I said.

We smiled again.

'What were you going to say?' I said.

'You first,' he said.

'No, you,' I said.

'It was nothing earth-shattering,' he said. 'I was just wondering if you could do me a favour and pull the blinds up? I can't sleep, and it's nice to lie here and look out.'

'Of course,' I said, and went over to the window.

The new star shone down from high above the town.

'What do you think it is?' I said.

'The new star?' he said.

'Yes,' I said, looking up at it.

'It's a new star,' he said.

'The new star's a new star?' I said.

'It has to happen,' he said. 'New stars forming in the universe.'

'Yes,' I said.

'What were you going to say?' he said.

'It was nothing,' I said. 'You must try and get some sleep, or at least rest. I won't disturb you any more now. I just wanted to see how you were getting on.'

'I'm fine,' he said. 'Will you be here tomorrow?'

I showered hastily in the changing rooms in the basement, dressing alone before going out into the warm night air. It was sticky and I wondered if there was going to be a thunderstorm.

I was happy and unsettled at the same time. The music came on when I turned the ignition, it was loud and belonged to another frame of mind, so I switched it off, rolled the window down, pulled out onto the road and crossed the river. The traffic lights at the junction were red and I looked down at the barrack-like club venue they called Riverside on the bank below. Perhaps twenty youngsters were hanging around in the car park outside, some leaning against the cars, most with a bottle or a glass in hand. As so often when something intense had happened at work, it struck me how different the world outside was. None of the young people down there had a thought for what went on inside the hospital day and night. Of course not, why should they? Death was always somewhere else. Right until it came close to them, as it would, and for a while encroached upon the life they led and pushed it into the background.

The lights changed to green and I turned onto the empty main road that led out of town and into the valley, the new star at my rear. A large herd of cattle, a strain that had been imported into the area a few years before with a view to enhancing meat production, lay in the field and resembled boulders in the grey nocturnal light of the late summer. They stayed out all year round, and I saw them every day. One winter morning, I'd seen one of them lying dead on the ground; by the time I drove back the other way in the afternoon it had been removed. And that spring I'd seen a newborn calf get to its feet for the very first time, its legs trembling, its mother lowering her head towards its little frame and licking it clean.

They were such beautiful creatures and seemed to live such a harmonious life, even when they stood bracing against the wind and snow in winter.

The image of Ramsvik flashed into my mind as he'd lain there on the operating table with his eyes open. The faint, tormented sound that had come from him.

I was only glad it wasn't me who had to fill in the operation report.

What could it say?

The heart had stopped when he'd been taken off the life support. The blood circulation in the brain had ceased. So he must have been dead. The heart not beating for a short while didn't have to be decisive, many patients had regained consciousness after relatively long periods with no cardiac activity. Brain activity was the decisive factor.

What was it Henriksen had said? Death is irreversible. No one can come back from the dead. Ramsvik having done so meant only that he hadn't been dead.

The white farmhouses that lay scattered about the landscape around me gleamed dully yet intensely in the greyish light. Most of the windows were dark. I looked at the clock on the dashboard: almost two.

*

The downstairs lights were all on when I got home. I sighed to myself. Line never gave a thought to others, never assumed responsibility for anything.

Still, it was too late to educate her now.

I was exhausted, but made myself a cup of tea and buttered myself a slice of bread which I ate while standing at the window, before looking in on Mum to see if she was all right.

She was fast asleep and I switched off all the lights, put some more milk in my tea so that I could drink up in one gulp, went upstairs to my bedroom, undressed, folded my clothes, pulled the duvet aside and got into bed, making myself comfortable on my side, hands folded under my cheek, the way I'd done ever since childhood.

I lay awake for some time, too tense to sleep.

My bedroom was directly above Mum's, and when she'd moved downstairs I'd thought it would be an advantage, allowing me to hear if anything was wrong, but in practice it was a source of unease, for there was never a sound from down there and often I would imagine her no longer breathing, but lying dead in her bed.

It was the same unease I'd felt after Line was born.

As if breathing were something that occurred in defiance and the natural condition, for infant and elderly alike, was not to be breathing, the breathless state being an equilibrium to which they were naturally drawn.

It had happened once to one of the other women in the mothers' group I'd attended, she'd been in a lift, the baby had been lying in its pram and had stopped breathing. Fortunately, she'd noticed something was wrong, and without thinking, she recalled, she'd lifted the child into the air by its feet and shaken it.

The child began to breathe again.

We'd laughed when she told us, finding her description comical, but we'd all recognised the fear.

How long ago it was.

Twenty-one years.

And the last thing I was afraid of when it came to Line now was that she would stop breathing. She was in the midst of breath's very realm.

Mum, on the other hand, was at its perimeter.

I lifted my head, pulled the curtain aside and looked down towards the neighbouring farm, where the lights in the attic shone yellow above the veranda. My eye followed the road to the forest where it disappeared from view, consumed by motionless spruce towering dark in the night. I could hear the rush of the waterfall, lay down again and closed my eyes. The last thing I remember was an owl hooting three times in the distance. But it could have been a dream.

KATHRINE

Perhaps it was the twin brother of the man I'd met at the airport, I thought as I left the church and crossed over to my office again. Perhaps he'd come to Bergen for the funeral. It was hardly likely, but certainly possible.

He had looked exactly the same.

But how well did I actually remember that face?

It could have been someone who just looked like him, nothing more than that.

That would be it.

I smiled at Karin and closed the door behind me, sat down at the desk and began attending to the pile of emails that always accumulated so quickly. But I found I couldn't concentrate, so I went out and got myself a glass of water and an apple from the fruit bowl in the conference room, sat down again in my office and looked out of the window as I munched. The lawn outside was scorched yellow, white almost where it met the gravel of the car park. Behind the wall of the churchyard beyond, I saw water showering into the air and picked out the rhythmic tick-tick-tick of the sprinkler, though so faintly I could easily have been imagining it.

I looked at the photo of Gaute and the children; it was from the summer before, they were sitting on the smooth rocks at the shore and looking at the camera, Marie on Gaute's knee, Peter leaning close to him.

My people.

I wondered if I should get Peter a mobile phone. We'd be able to text each other during the day. It would give him an extra sense of security.

He was special, Peter, not like other boys, and the other children in his class had begun to reject him. He didn't understand why, and tried to impose himself in the ways that were available to him. He thought it would help if he knew better than them. That they would want to be friends with him if only they understood how clever he was, and how good at things.

His teacher had rung me up one day in the spring. There had been an incident involving Peter and a boy with a stutter. Peter had mimicked the boy in front of the others and tried to make him say difficult words. I did not take the matter up with him when I got home, hoping instead that he might tell me about it himself. When he didn't, I went into his room before he went to sleep. Lying with his cheek against the pillow, he looked at me quizzically. He'd just had a bath and was clean and delicate. The look he gave me was innocent, but immediately became tinged with fear: he knew.

I sat down on the edge of his bed.

'Your teacher phoned me today,' I said.

He said nothing, but stared vacantly into the air in front of him, abruptly depleted.

'He told me you'd been teasing a boy who stutters. Is that right?'

'I didn't mean it,' he said quietly.

'What did you do, exactly?' I said.

He didn't answer.

'Peter, what did you do?'

'It wasn't just me,' he said. 'The others were doing it as well.'

'That's no excuse,' I said. 'You were bullying him. Have you thought about how he feels? Have you?'

His eyes filled with tears.

'I didn't know it was wrong,' he whispered.

'Of course you knew it was wrong,' I said.

'No!' he almost shouted, and started to cry.

It was as if something took possession of him. His body squirmed under the duvet, he sobbed loudly, his tears now running down his cheeks.

'Peter,' I said.

'I — didn't — know!' he sobbed.

'You must make amends,' I said. 'You must apologise to him. And never do it again.'

'I — didn't — know!' he sobbed again, writhing, his eyes wild with despair.

'Peter, settle down,' I said, and smoothed his hair with my hand.

Howling sounds began to issue from him. His body thrashed.

He was hysterical.

'Peter!' I said, and tried to pin him down. 'That's enough!'

'Aaaaaaaahh,' he howled. 'Aaaaaaaahh, aaaaahhhh.'

'That's enough, Peter,' I said again, and got to my feet. 'You'll apologise to him at school in the morning, and let that be the end of it.'

I put my hand on his shoulder and bent over him.

'Goodnight,' I said.

He looked up at me.

I switched the light off, closed the door behind me and went downstairs into the living room where the TV was on, a frozen image on the screen of a man getting out of a car in what appeared to be an English village.

'Gaute?' I said.

'In here,' he said from the kitchen.

He was sitting on one of the bar stools at the kitchen island, eating leftovers from dinner with his phone lit up in front of him. He was almost in darkness, only the light above the cooker was on.

'How did it go?' he said.

'Fine,' I said, and took a glass from the cupboard, filled it with water and drank as I leaned against the work surface, supporting myself with my other hand.

'I heard him crying.'

'Yes, he was full of remorse.'

'How do you think he's feeling now?'

'He's still crying, I imagine.'

'And you just left him?'

He looked at me.

'He must learn to manage his emotions,' I said. 'And he must learn on his own.'

Gaute's eyes met mine for a second, before looking away.

It meant he didn't like what I had said.

It meant disagreement.

'Don't go up to him, OK?' I said.

'He'll go to sleep soon enough, I suppose,' he said, and glanced at me quickly before lowering his gaze again.

The slices of lamb on his plate, which only a few hours earlier had been soft and succulent, were now stiff and white with coagulated fat. He was eating them with his fingers.

'What are you watching in there?' I said, putting the glass in the dishwasher next to him.

'*Inspector Morse*,' he said. 'Or maybe it's *Lewis* now, after his assistant took over?'

'Yes,' I said. '*Inspector Lewis*, is that it?'

I turned and looked out of the window. The lights in the houses along the gentle slope of the road were soft, at least compared to the starkly illuminated industrial buildings that lay dotted along the road too. There were some new rows of housing, and then the fell began, rising dark and tree-clad against the grey-black sky.

'Shall we watch the rest of the episode together?' I said.

'Yes, we could do,' he said. 'I'm halfway through, though.'

'I don't care much for detectives, anyway,' I said.

He smiled and opened the fridge door, scraping the uneaten pieces of lamb from his plate into the plastic container with the rest of the leftovers.

'Are we really going to eat that?' I said. 'I keep throwing leftovers out from there.'

'We can do a spaghetti bolognese with lamb instead of mince,' he said. 'It's rather good, actually.'

'OK,' I said, and went into the living room. Pausing in front of the sofa, I stood and listened. It was all quiet up there. Water ran from the tap in the kitchen, Gaute washing his hands.

I sat down, picked up my phone and checked the local paper, skimming the headlines there. He would go up and look in on him, I knew it.

'Start, if you want,' he said behind me. 'Just need to go to the loo.'

'It's all right, I'll wait.'

He would go into Peter's room first, I guessed, hearing him go up the stairs. He would sit down on the edge of the bed and comfort him for a minute before going into the bathroom and flushing the toilet in the belief that I would hear it and assume he'd been in there all the time and was now finished.

In so doing, he would undermine what I had said. It wouldn't be the end of the world, but the worst thing was his secrecy. He didn't have the guts for even a minor confrontation with me. The few minutes he stole to be with Peter up there weren't about Peter, regardless of what he thought. They were about him. He didn't know what to do with his emotions. He never did.

Suddenly, it struck me that my increasing irritation, which had been coming to the fore more and more frequently, and which I could not always keep to myself, to the extent that it would occasionally turn into anger, could be a form of self-justification.

That something inside me was blaming him so that something else inside me could be denied.

He'd done nothing wrong. And he hadn't changed either.

The water ran through the pipes from upstairs.

I breathed in deeply.

My need to be alone was so great it almost caused me to panic.

But I controlled it, switched the television on with the remote and turned my face towards him with a smile as he came down the stairs.

'You started it, then,' he said.

'Five seconds ago,' I said.

He sat down beside me.

'Do you want anything?' he said. 'Coffee? Tea?'

'It's a bit late,' I said.

'Drink, then?' he said.

'No, thanks,' I said.

He put his feet up on the coffee table, resting his arm on the back of the sofa behind me.

'You can have one, if you want,' I said.

'I'm fine,' he said.

We watched the episode in silence. When it was finished, I switched off, went into the kitchen and began emptying the dishwasher. He came in after me.

'Is something the matter?' he said.

I shook my head, putting the glasses and the cups in the cupboard two by two.

'All right,' he said. 'I'll go to bed, then. Are you coming up?'

'In a bit,' I said, and smiled. 'Just need to have a look at something first.'

'OK,' he said.

I went into the study and started on some work. Upstairs, I heard him turn on the shower and sighed: Gaute only ever showered before bed when he wanted sex.

It was hardly surprising that he thought I was being unfaithful, I told myself as I sat absently looking out of the window with the apple core in my hand. Although we clicked reasonably well once we did go to bed together, my aversion towards sex was growing. It was as if there were a distance I needed to traverse, and that distance kept increasing. Once it was behind me, something else would take its place and the resistance and doubt I'd felt would sometimes go away completely then, so it wasn't that. It was something else that was in the way.

It didn't matter much to me, it was more that I felt guilty towards him. But I could hardly have sex with him just because I felt guilty, it would be a form of prostitution.

He wondered, of course, and realised there was something wrong. And then when I hadn't come home the night before, he'd put two and two together.

I understood the logic.

But I didn't understand how he could think so badly of me.

Did he really know me no better than that?

I stood up and dropped the apple core in the waste bin. The funeral was in fifteen minutes. I went to the toilet and had a wee, and when I returned to the office I sat down and closed my eyes and ran through the entire liturgy in my mind in order to focus on what was about to happen and to bring with me as little as possible from my own life.

A few minutes later I crossed over the open space to the church. The sun was so strong it felt almost as if it were scorching my face. The temperature outside had to be at least thirty degrees. And not a breath of air. The leaves on the trees above me hung quite still.

But within the ancient thick stone walls of the church, the air was cool.

I put on my vestments in the sacristy as the bells began to ring, and returned to the church interior. The organist, Erik, struck up the prelude. The two undertakers sat next to each other on the first row of benches, their heads bowed. The coffin was black, which was rather uncommon nowadays, and I wondered why it had been chosen when there had been no specific request for it.

I began to sing. The two undertakers lifted their heads and accompanied me in seasoned voices, without embarrassment.

It felt strange to sing only with them, as if it merely drew out the feeling that we were performing a theatre piece, with no attachment to the situation and the deceased, yet it felt right and dignified too, as if the hymn took on particular importance by virtue of none of us present having known him as a person to whom we could say goodbye.

'Grace to you and peace from God our Father and the Lord Jesus Christ,' I enunciated to the empty rows of benches. 'We are gathered here today to say a last farewell to Kristian Hadeland. Together, we will surrender him into God's hands and follow him to his final resting place. For God so loved the world that He gave His one and only Son, that whoever believes in him shall not perish but have eternal life.'

I looked down at the coffin. A wreath with the words *Rest in Peace* had been placed on top of it — from 'Friends', as custom dictated in those circumstances.

The thought passed through my mind that it couldn't possibly have been the deceased's twin brother I'd seen. If it had, he would have been present. The idea that the deceased could have a twin brother not in attendance at his funeral was strange in itself, but even stranger was the notion that he would have contacted me at the airport, the priest who was to lay his brother to rest.

Such coincidences did not occur.

But who was he then, if not his twin brother?

Could I have been mistaken?

I raised my arms slightly, palms turned upwards.

'Jesus says: Come to me, all you who are weary and burdened, and I will give you rest.'

The two men were looking straight ahead. Their faces revealed no emotion; they were at work.

'Let us pray,' I said.

I folded my hands together and bowed my head.

'Lord, you have been our dwelling place throughout all generations. Before the mountains were born or you brought forth the whole world, from everlasting to everlasting you are God. You turn people back to dust, saying, "Return to dust, you mortals." A thousand years in your sight are like a day that has just gone by, or like a watch in the night. Teach us to number our days, that we may gain a heart of wisdom.'

I looked up again. The bright light outside made the colours of the stained-glass windows gleam red and green and blue, the otherwise dull walls of the church interior shimmering faintly. Everything accentuated the emptiness of the space. As I stepped towards the pulpit, I visualised his round face. His eyes, at first merely friendly, albeit perhaps rather imposingly so, had later seemed almost to be inciting. As if he had known something about me, I thought. As if he had known who I was.

If it *was* him, it would be ironic, given that I was now laying him to rest knowing nothing about him.

But it *couldn't* be him.

I had to stop thinking it.

I glanced at Erik. He smiled at me and gave me a thumbs up, the idiot. Dignity was everything in that space, no matter how many times you were there in the course of a day.

I breathed in.

'Kristian Hadeland was born on the sixth of June 1956 at Haukeland Hospital in the city in which we stand,' I said. 'And he died here, in this same city, on the twenty-third of August, sixty-seven years old. We are gathered here today to say farewell to Kristian, and to remember him. In normal circumstances, the next of kin would have spoken to me about the life of the deceased, their time in education, their work and family, the events of a life, great and small, and either they or I would have shared those recollections with the bereaved in a memorial tribute. Today, at the coffin of Kristian Hadeland, circumstances are sadly different. None of those present are able to remember him. All we know about you, Kristian, is that you lived here on this earth for sixty-seven years. You were an infant, innocent and doted upon, and then you were a child, growing into the world. You saw the sun and the moon, you saw the trees and the flowers, you saw houses and cars, you saw the sea and the sky. You were an adolescent, filled with the emotions of life, and then you grew into adulthood and became a man, following the path of your life, whether you felt it to be of your own choosing or to have been chosen for you. Now all that is behind you. Now your days on earth have been numbered. Now you are in God's hands. You were a human being, for better or worse, and we remember you as such here today. Life is hallowed, and it is death that makes it so, and the meaning of life is God.'

The younger of the two undertakers, who until then had let the liturgy wash over him without resistance, as if it were a kind of wind, suddenly looked up at me in what seemed to be puzzlement. But when I nodded to Erik and he struck up the first chords of 'Deilig er jorden', they both sang with gusto.

Fair is creation
marvellous God's heaven,
blest the souls in their pilgrim throng.
Through realms of earthly
loveliness onward
we go to paradise with song!

Ages lie waiting,
ages quick in passing,
generations that form a throng.
Music from heaven
never falls silent
in this the soul's glad pilgrim song.

Angels first sang it
to the wond'ring shepherds,
sweet was from soul to soul its sound:
Peace and rejoicing
be to all people,
for us a saviour now is found!

The music faded. I didn't even know if he had been Christian. Whether he had believed in God. Probably not, hardly anyone did any more.

Did I?

But I would never entertain such a thought. And certainly never in church.

'Let us hear what the Word of God says about life and death, the final judgement, and our hope in Jesus Christ,' I went on.

I opened the Bible in front of me and began to read.

' "And I saw a new heaven and a new earth: for the first heaven and the first earth were passed away; and there was no more sea. And I saw the holy city, New Jerusalem, coming down from God out of heaven, prepared as a bride adorned for her husband. And I heard a great voice out of heaven saying, Behold, the tabernacle of God is with men, and he will dwell with them, and they shall be his people, and God himself shall be with them, and be their God. And God shall wipe away all tears from their eyes; and there shall be no more death, neither sorrow, nor crying, neither shall there be any more pain: for the former things are passed away. And he that sat upon the throne said, Behold, I make all things new." '

'This is the word of the Lord.'

I closed the book.

'The scripture I have just read, from the Revelation of St John the Divine, is one of the most widely used of all in funeral services,' I said. 'This is so because it gives hope, and concerns hope, a release from all that is painful in life, but especially that which is painful to us when someone close to us dies. There shall no longer be sorrow, nor crying, nor pain, and neither shall there be death — "for the former things are passed away". It is easy to dismiss such words as the wishful thinking of a tormented individual, the wish for a new world in which all that is wrong with the present one will no longer exist. But if we think of what John's revelation describes to us as being the kingdom of God, and if we think then of what God is, the words make sense. God is not sorrow and pain, God is joy. God is not death, God is life. And, not least: God is eternal. And all of this is present now, in the place in which we stand today. Joy and life and eternity are with us. We share in the joy, as we share in life and share in eternity. But we *are* not joy, we *are* not life, we *are* not eternity. God is those things. We share, in a way, in God, as the minute

perhaps shares in eternity, even though it is finite, and we do so even
when we are crushed by sorrow, absence or pain. We are always a part
of God. And what Jesus showed us is that God is a part of us. "Behold,
the tabernacle of God is with men," the scripture says. It means that we
are never alone. The fact that we sometimes feel ourselves to be alone is
another matter. When we do, it is perhaps because we have shut God
out, and shut ourselves in, with our sorrow and pain. Indeed, we can
imagine such a life, locked in darkness while the light shines outside.
What is the truth of that life? That it is dark in itself? Or that it has
turned away from the light? If we open ourselves to God, through Jesus
Christ, who is the light, we open ourselves to joy, life and eternity. All of
which are present even in darkness, even in loneliness, even in pain.

'We are never alone.

'No, we are never alone.'

I stepped forward to the coffin, bowed my head, and folded my hands.

'Let us pray.

'Eternal God, Heavenly Father, you have in your son, Jesus Christ,
given us victory over death. We ask that you lead us by your Holy Spirit,
so that we never lose hope in you, but live our lives by faith in your
Son, and one day come into eternal life in your kingdom, through Jesus
Christ our Lord.

'Into your hands, O God, I commend my spirit.

'You redeem me, O Lord, O faithful God.

'Into your hands, O God, I surrender my spirit.

'Glory be to the Father and to the Son and to the Holy Spirit.

'Into your hands, O God, I surrender my spirit.'

I nodded to Erik, who began the postlude as the two undertakers
rose, gripped the catafalque and rolled it up the aisle towards the doors.
I walked behind the coffin as I had done so many times before. But this
time I was close to tears. It very seldom happened. Perhaps because
normally my attention would be directed towards the bereaved and
their grief, which always seemed to fill the church so much more than
the presence of the deceased, which in this case was all there was. Everything was so empty around him and the power of the liturgy seemed
to come to the fore in such circumstances, where no sorrowful faces
were congregated to absorb it. For it concerned not only them, as was

so easy to think when they broke down sobbing all around; it concerned every one of us.

I narrowed my eyes as we emerged into the sunlight. How unbelievably hot it was.

And how still.

How could they bear their dark suits in such heat?

Not that my cassock was much better.

They rolled the coffin along the gravel paths, following the yellow-white perimeter of scorched grass that became greener further inside the churchyard beneath the tall, shady deciduous trees, passing among the scattered gravestones.

The new grave was over by the wall in the far corner. The brown sides, the brown earth, made it look like a wound in all the green. And the planks that were laid across it, the little crane that stood there waiting, brought to mind a building site. I'd never cared for this makeshift aspect, the act of committal became so prosaic and mechanical. At the same time, it was how the world was, unfinished and in constant change. It would have been quite as wrong to close one's eyes to it.

The two undertakers transferred the coffin onto the cradle that was attached to the crane. It was heavy, and they shoved more than lifted, labouring to bring it into position with a brief thud.

'And now let us sing hymn number 570,' I said.

Deep and glorious, word victorious,
Word divine that ever lives!
Call thou sinners to be winners
Of the life that Jesus gives;
Tell abroad what God hath given;
Jesus is our way to heaven.

Saviour tender, thanks we render
For the grace Thou dost afford;
Time is flying, time is dying,
Yet eternal stands Thy word;
With Thy word Thy grace endureth,

And a refuge us secureth.

By Thy spirit, through Thy merit,
Draw all weary souls to Thee!
End their sighing, end their dying,
Let them Thy salvation see!
Lead us in life's pathway tending,
To the life and bliss unending!

As we stood there singing I saw us as if from afar. Three people standing among grass and trees, singing in front of an open grave in the corner of a churchyard, while cars drove by on the road outside and aeroplanes passed across the blue sky. Our voices, rising into the air and dissolving, so brittle and weak. And the coffin with the lifeless body inside it above the grave, the sunlight that made its black varnish gleam.

I opened the Bible at the passage from which I was going to read. The white page was a glare.

I was pregnant.

That was why I'd felt sick.

I was going to have a baby.

Oh no.

But that was why.

I couldn't have it.

Not with Gaute.

I lifted my gaze and looked at the two undertakers standing at the graveside waiting, their hands behind their backs.

"'Jesus says, Fear not; I am the first and the last: I am he that liveth, and was dead; and, behold, I am alive for evermore, Amen; and have the keys of hell and of death."

'Let us pray.

'Lord Jesus Christ, let Kristian Hadeland rest in peace under the sign of the cross until the resurrection day. Help us to put our faith in you, both in life as well as death.'

The younger of the undertakers started the motor while the other stood next to him with his head bowed and his hands at his back.

Slowly the coffin was lowered into the grave, whose soil was dry at the top where the sun had shone, but moist, glistening and dark at the bottom.

I bent forward and picked up the shovel that had been placed ready for me.

'In the name of the Father, the Son, and the Holy Spirit,' I said, putting the shovel into the small mound at my feet and casting earth into the grave.

There was a short and rather harsh sifting noise as the earth struck the wood of the coffin.

'From earth you have come,' I said.

And a second time.

'To earth you will return.'

A third time.

'From earth you will be resurrected.'

I bent forward, put down the shovel, and straightened up again.

'Our Lord Jesus Christ says: "I am the resurrection and the life. The one who believes in me will live, even though they die; and whoever lives by believing in me will never die.'

I turned to the two undertakers.

'Receive the blessing,' I said. 'The Lord bless you and keep you. The Lord make his face shine upon you and be gracious to you. The Lord lift up his countenance upon you and give you peace.'

I stepped over and shook them by the hand, as if they were indeed the bereaved. With that, the formalities were concluded, and as we walked back through the churchyard this was made plain by their body language; suddenly their movements were different, looser and more relaxed, the younger even humming softly to himself, a song I recognised after a few seconds as 'Wonderwall'. The other man took off his jacket as we went and slung it over his shoulder, his index finger hooked through the little loop in the collar.

'Do you mind if I smoke?' the younger of them said.

'No, not at all,' I said. He took a packet of Marlboro from his inside pocket, lighting the cigarette he put between his lips with a lighter he retrieved from his trouser pocket.

'That was a nice sermon,' he said. 'Very good indeed.'

'Thank you,' I said.

'But what you said about death making life hallowed, where did that come from? It's not in the scriptures, is it?'

'Funny you should mention it,' I said. 'Because I'm not really sure. It was just something I said. Something that came to me without my having thought about it.'

'A bit fortunate no one else was there, then?' he said.

'What do you mean?' I said.

'It probably goes against everything the liturgy's about, wouldn't you say? Death is there to be conquered, isn't it, not to make life hallowed? You're right in what you say, absolutely as far as I'm concerned, but not theologically or liturgically. In fact, what you said probably verges on heresy, don't you think?'

I looked at him as we came to a halt by the hearse. He smiled and gave a shrug.

'Have you studied theology?' I said.

'Not theology, no,' he said. 'Philosophy. Years ago now, though.'

'So in other words you don't know what you're talking about,' I said, realising that I had raised my voice.

He smiled again, hesitantly this time.

'And yet you accuse me of heresy. I am a priest in the Church of Norway. I have just buried another human being. Do you think you're being appropriate? And by what right do you criticise me?'

'Steady on,' he muttered. 'I didn't mean it like that.'

'I know exactly how it was meant,' I said, turned and went back inside the church.

Shortly afterwards, I heard the hearse drive away.

He had overstepped a boundary, I told myself, still seething as I began to get changed in the sacristy.

I hung my white vestments in the cupboard, put on my skirt, put my arms into the sleeves of my blouse and buttoned it, sat down on the chair and fastened the straps of my sandals.

I felt completely empty.

But then I always did after a funeral, there was nothing unusual about that.

What was more, I had a right to be angry. His criticism had been inappropriate and stupid. Not to mention insensitive. Did he think priests were completely unmoved by what they were involved in?

I stood up and brushed my hair in front of the mirror, tied it in a bun and put on some lipstick.

The shadows under my eyes, always there, were now even darker.

The white blouse didn't exactly help.

What did I have in the cupboard in the office? I wondered. Winter things, mostly.

It had been rather a long time since I'd bought myself something new. Perhaps I could do so today.

It would be nice, I thought, putting the lipstick back in the little make-up bag I kept in the sacristy and taking a last look at myself in the mirror.

I put my hands to my abdomen.

Could I really be pregnant?

JOSTEIN

Outside the windows where I sat working, the sun was shining and the sky was empty and blue. I sensed the bars and restaurants were starting to fill up, so I submitted the piece I'd been working on just before three, even if it could probably have been better. No one cared anyway, least of all me. It was an interview with a female artist who was opening her first solo exhibition that same evening, out at Abildsø Galleri. She'd given me the tour there that morning. Pale and dark-haired, in an oversized sweater and roomy trousers, the sort builders wear, with pockets all over the place, she was waiting for me outside when I got there with the photographer. It was saddening to see how much she was looking forward to seeing herself in the paper. I wanted it all done as quickly as possible and suggested straight away that we go inside and look at her paintings together. They were all of clouds, white on a blue background. Why clouds? I asked. I don't know, she answered. She went around with her hands in her pockets, shoulders hunched, staring at the floor in front of her a lot, hardly looking at me at all. Perhaps because clouds are constantly changing in their form, at the same time as they're always the same, she said. That presents a challenge to any artist. Why's that? I said. What happens when something that's in constant flux becomes . . . well, fixed in its form? she said. I looked at her without saying anything. OK, so what happens, then? I said eventually. She had no answer to that for a while, and we walked slowly past a few more pictures with neither of us saying anything. But then she thought of something. It had to do with time. Time, she said, stops in the painting. But it doesn't stop outside the painting. No, I said, you're right about that. But what's it got to do with clouds? Everything, she said. It's got everything to do with clouds. OK, I said, and altered tack. Would you say your paintings present a new take on clouds? She laughed and said she hoped not. But maybe, if it wasn't too ambitious, she said, she hoped they might give someone a new take on painting. What kind of take would that be? I said. How do you mean? she said. Well, you said you hoped your pictures would give people a new take on painting. What sort of take do you mean? That bit was a joke, she said. OK, I said. What does this exhibition in Bergen mean to you as an artist?

I've got nothing against artists as such, it's the ones who think they're artists I don't like, the endlessly self-obsessed, pretentious little people who think they know something the rest of us don't, think they see something the rest of us don't, and feel they have to lecture us about it. The truth is they know less and see less, and that it ought to be us giving them a bloody lecture. But I had a job to do, and the questions I asked her were respectful enough. Nonetheless, it must have been clear what I thought about her and her art while we'd been talking, because her gallerist rang a few hours later and complained to Ellingsen, the arts editor. He came over to my desk and told me what the guy had said. I said he could read the piece himself and tell me if he saw anything disrespectful or condescending in it. He didn't, so that was the end of it. I knew he wanted to tell me to watch myself, but I knew too that he hadn't got the guts.

Idiot.

Before knocking off, I checked my emails and noticed that Erlend, the photographer, had sent his photos. I wrote back and told him they were good, put my jacket on and left the hideous open-plan office behind me, not for good, unfortunately, but at least for today. No one looked up as I walked out, they were all sat bent over their keyboards, staring at their screens. Those who weren't writing were most likely checking how many hits their pieces had got. It was the dearest thing to their hearts.

I needed a piss, but getting out of the building took priority. I didn't like pissing alongside the new colleagues. Could always take a cubicle of course, but then people would think I was embarrassed about pissing in company. They can say what they like about me, but neurotic's not a label I'd care for.

On the pavement outside I paused and lit a fag. The sun glittered in the glass facade behind me. The air was hot and the street was full of traffic and people, it was like being abroad. But the city was mine, no doubt about that: on Sydneshaugen, the Johanneskirken towered above me, below lay Torgallmenningen, beyond it the Fløyen fell, and behind that, obscured from sight, if not from mind, the Ulriken.

Where should I go?

Verftet was good for sitting out when the sun was going down, but it was such a bloody trek. Wesselstuen would do for a Monday night.

On my way there I phoned Turid.

'Yes?' she said.

'What happened to hi?' I said.

'Hi,' she said. 'What do you want?'

'Nothing,' I said. 'Are you at home?'

'Yes.'

'I'm done for today. Going for a beer at Wessel's. Should be home around sevenish.'

'OK,' she said.

'Are you tired?' I said.

'No, not especially. Why?'

'You sound tired, that's all. What time's your shift start?'

'Eight.'

'We'll have an hour together, then. Have you made any dinner?'

'It's in the oven.'

'Is Ole in?'

'What a lot of questions all of a sudden!'

'It's the journalist in me,' I said.

She laughed.

'He's in his room,' she said.

'Is he off out tonight?'

'I don't know. I shouldn't think so. Phone him and ask.'

'He doesn't speak to me.'

'You shouldn't give up.'

'Anyway, I'm there now. See you later.'

I hung up and turned the corner, then carried on down the hill in the direction of the Hotell Norge. A swarthy little type from Eastern

Europe was sitting on his haunches on the pavement with a cap in his hand. It couldn't have been much of an earner for him sitting there, I thought, people only passed by. If you really had to beg, you needed to do it somewhere where it was natural for people to stop, or somewhere where they spent money and felt guilty about it. Outside the super-markets was best, where people came trundling out all the time with their trolleys overflowing with food; they could hardly do anything else then but give a few bob to some poor sod who they thought was starving.

He peered up at me as I went past. I couldn't see his eyes, only two narrow, wrinkled flaps of skin.

The way they bowed their bloody heads.

We'd not had their kind in town the last hundred years, I was sure of it.

It put me in a bad mood and I looked the other way.

Why did they have to humiliate themselves once they got here?

I was no adherent of communism, but the two-bloc set-up, one good, one bad, one where capitalism was king and one where the state was everything, and then clusters of poor countries on the fringes where the actual conflict was played out, had been nothing if not stable.

I remembered the demos back in the day, the marches entering Tor-gallmenningen, flags and banners waving. Down with the USA, down with the war in Vietnam, down with NATO, down with nuclear weap-ons. They were demonstrating against themselves, I understood that even then, even if I was only in my early teens.

But no one demonstrated at all these days, I thought, surveying the square that was teeming with people. A group of youths were sitting on the Blue Stone, more still on the step below, and everywhere people were crossing the open space on their way to one place or another.

Or no, that wasn't entirely right, they demonstrated for the climate and against the apocalypse. But that was like being in favour of life and against death.

Tearfulmenningen, I'd called it in an article I did once.

Lot of positive feedback for that one.

I carried on the last bit to the cafe and scanned the outside tables with all their gleaming pints to see if there was anyone I knew. There wasn't.

I could sit on my own, only it didn't look like there was a single table free.

This bloody heat!

Fortunately, I'd got my jacket on. The sweat stains under my arms made me look unhealthy. And I couldn't exactly tell people I was actually in good shape.

Maybe I could go on to Ole Bull?

I glanced towards the place. It looked like it wasn't as busy, so maybe I would.

But just then a group of four got up from where they were sitting. I didn't think twice. Two girls who'd been standing at the bar were already on their way over, so I threaded my way through and quickly put a hand on the back of a chair, enquiring if the seat was vacant only seconds before the two lasses got there.

'Sure,' said one of the group who were now on their way. 'Go ahead.'

'Cheers,' I said, and gave the two girls an apologetic shrug before sitting down.

'We could share the table, maybe?' one of them said.

I shook my head.

'Some others coming in a minute,' I said. 'Sorry.'

They turned round and went back to the bar. I took them to be students. Humanities, I reckoned, going by the clothes.

Slender and gorgeous, both of them.

Should have taken them up on it, I reflected, and lit a fag while looking across at them; they'd gone back to where they were standing before, each with a glass of white in one hand and their other elbow on the counter, jangly earrings, eyes on the lookout.

They'd likely have been interested if I'd told them I was an arts journo, they'd have wanted to talk then.

But for a start I'd only have to go through a load of bollocks to keep them interested, and even then they were still only in their early twenties, meaning I'd have to surpass myself if I was going to make enough of an impression to shag one of them.

No sense kidding myself.

I lifted an arm and wiped the sweat from my forehead with my jacket sleeve. Then, as I put another cigarette between my lips, I noticed a woman looking in my direction. She nodded and smiled half-heartedly, and raised a hand in a tentative wave. She had dark curly hair and was in her fifties, a bag strapped across her chest even though she was sitting down. I'd seen her before, but couldn't remember who she was. I gave her a little nod in return, and then remembered, she was one of Turid's former colleagues.

In fact, the whole table were, I realised then.

It'd be a bit odd if I didn't go over.

Only then I'd have to take my jacket off to keep my seat.

Just then, a waiter appeared at my table. He was dressed like a proper waiter, white shirt and black trousers, but his face lacked the dignity. A teenager with an empty look and big lips he obviously couldn't shut.

'Lager,' I said.

'Draught Hansa? A pint?' he said.

'Of course,' I said. 'What do you take me for?'

He smiled. I didn't smile back.

While I waited for him to return, I got my mobile out and checked what they were doing on the paper. The top story was an explosives accident in Arna, one dead, one injured. It was barely worth the mention, but it had only just happened, so of course it had to go top. Next was local councillor Rafaelsen's admission that he'd been fiddling his travel expenses.

Who hadn't?

Only then had they got the disappearance, third from the top. SEARCH INTENSIFIES FOR FOUR YOUNG MEN, was the headline. In other words, nothing new.

It was a case that had me itching, I had to admit. The missing kids weren't just four *young men*, but four members of a death metal band. They posed with swastikas, claiming it was just an ancient Indian symbol. They used pig's blood at their concerts, and worshipped the Devil, but were so dense they worshipped Odin at the same time, and everything Norse.

The fact of the matter was they were just a group of gangly, spotty-faced lads full of social anxiety and scared stiff of women, but the satanist black-magic drivel they dabbled in, the death symbols and the allusions to violence, worked, and people thought they were mean and evil.

They'd been missing four days now. My guess was they'd collectively topped themselves and were lying dead in the forest somewhere. The paper had interviewed some of the parents, completely normal middle-class folk from out in Åsane, they were out of their minds with worry, of course, but I had to laugh when I saw it, because if those four lads were alive, their parents had destroyed everything they'd been trying to build up, just by that one story. Come home, Helge!

My pint was put on the table in front of me, golden and mouth-watering.

'Would you like to pay now?' the kid said, the empty tray clutched under his arm at his side, his mouth still open.

'I'll likely be having a few more,' I said, dropping the phone back into my pocket. 'But listen, can I ask you something?'

'Yes?' he said.

'You're from round here, right?'

'Yes, from Loddefjord.'

'Do you know the lads out of Kvitekrist?'

'The ones who've gone missing?'

'That's them, yes.'

He shook his head.

'I know who they are. But I don't know them myself.'

'Do you know anyone who does?'

'Why do you ask?'

'I'm a journalist,' I said.

'Oh,' he said. 'I know someone who knows the brother of one of them.'

'Which one?'

'Jesper. The drummer.'

'Can you get hold of his number?'

He shook his head and glanced around a bit uncomfortably.

'I don't think so,' he said.

'You don't think you can get hold of it, or you won't because you don't trust me?'

'I've got nothing to do with it,' he said. 'I don't know why you're asking me.'

He turned and went back to the bar. I swallowed a mouthful of beer, wiped the froth from my lips and lit a fag.

Was beer good, or was it good?

I got the feeling it was going to be a decent night. There was so much expectation in the air, laughter and high spirits at the tables around me, so many people in the streets. It was like the whole town was out.

And the sun was still high in the sky.

Someone behind me put their hand on my shoulder. I turned my head and looked straight up into the smiling face of Geir Jacobsen.

'So this is where you've been hiding,' he said, sliding onto the seat next to me.

'Long time no see,' I said. 'Been a while. Where have you been?'

'Same place as always,' he said. 'I should be asking you. Arts and culture now, isn't it, from what I've heard?'

'Afraid so,' I said, stubbing out my fag before taking a slurp. 'Fancy a pint? I'm just about to order another.'

'No, thanks all the same,' he said. 'I'm on my way to work. Saw you from the street and thought I'd come over and say hello.'

He got to his feet.

'Still got the same number?'

'Yes,' I said.

'I'll give you a buzz. We'll have a pint then.'

'OK,' I said. 'Good to see you.'

'Speak to you soon,' he said, and picked his way back between the tables and out onto the street.

I looked over at a waitress and when I managed to catch her eye I held a finger in the air. She nodded and came over shortly after with a fresh pint. I emptied the first one and handed her the glass.

Meeting Geir like that had given me an appetite for company, so I phoned John to hear if there was anyone still at work who might be up for it. He wasn't sure, he said. He was on his way home himself, but he thought there might be a crowd meeting up later on, though he wasn't sure where.

'Do you want me to ask for you?' he said.

'No, no need for that,' I said. 'Just wondered, that's all.'

I hung up.

Should never have rung in the first place.

Do you want me to ask for you?

What was he using for brains? Did he think I was fifteen years old?

I looked over at the bar. The two girls weren't there any more. I looked around to see if they'd managed to get a table.

They must have gone.

So tomorrow I'd have a piece about a woman who painted clouds.

What would a man like Geir make of that? If he even read the arts section, that is.

Not that he was thick or anything, unlike many of his colleagues. He'd just have a chuckle about how daft it was, at the same time as acknowledging the spot I was in.

I'd have to have that piss now. Couldn't sit there with my legs crossed like a kid.

I stood up and draped my jacket over the back of the chair. The stains under my arms were as big as bathing rings, it was hard not to think about it as I passed between the tables on my way to the bogs, the urge to piss becoming greater the closer I got, I'd be bursting in a minute. Once I was through the door I sensed relief, only to discover there were three people queued up in front of me at the urinals, and some others waiting for a cubicle.

I felt a dribble, not much though, nothing the old undies wouldn't absorb. I could live with that. Only next time it wouldn't be a dribble but a splash.

I shifted my weight onto my other foot.

Two ahead of me now.

I wasn't going to make it.

As soon as one of the men already at the urinals gave his tackle a shake, zipped up and turned round to go, I barged in front of the guy whose turn it was and stepped up to the white bowl.

'Hey, what do you think you're doing?' he said. 'There's a queue here!'

It was so good to let go I felt like breaking into song.

I turned my head to look at him as my piss sprayed hard against the porcelain. He had a scraggly beard and glasses, and looked like he fixed the computers in a small business.

'Thanks for letting me in,' I said.

'I didn't, you barged in front of me!'

'Yeah, all right,' I said, turning round again and finishing off. 'There you go! Your turn.'

He shook his head to tell me what an idiot I was, but it was only in resignation, nothing to pull him up about.

On my way back, I stopped at the table where Turid's old workmates were sat. It'd be odd not to talk to them, and Turid definitely wouldn't be pleased if she got word I hadn't.

'You all right there?' I said.

The boozy faces that turned towards me beamed gormlessly.

'Hello,' said the one with the curly hair, whose name I suddenly remembered was Jorunn. 'Out on the town, are we?'

'No, just a beer after work,' I said. 'You lot look like you're in for the long haul, though!'

'We miss Turid,' she said.

'I'm sure she misses you, too,' I said.

'Sit yourself down and have a beer with us,' said a bloke whose name was Frank, a small, stocky fellow with a moustache who I'd never been able to stand. 'Seeing as you're on your own over there!'

'Thanks, just the same,' I said. 'I'm waiting for the rest of my crowd. Where are you all off to?'

'Zachen, maybe,' said Jorunn. 'We'll see.'

'All right,' I said. 'Nice to see you!'

'Say hello to Turid!'

'Will do,' I said.

Left a little trap for myself there, I thought as I sat down again at my own table. If they didn't leave soon, they'd see that nobody else came and think 'the rest of my crowd' was something I'd made up. And why would I do that? Because, they'd think, he didn't want to be seen as someone who drank on his own. And why would that be? Could it be that Turid's husband is lonely?

I knew everyone in this fucking town. High and low, from King Solomon to Harry the Hatter.

I was having a couple of beers after work, that was all. I didn't give a toss what they thought.

Still, might be an idea to move on somewhere else, new pastures and that. Maybe Verftet after all? They did a nice sunset out there. Always a good feeling, tanking up as the sun goes down.

Sounded like a poetry collection.

Tanking Up. Poems, Jostein Lindland.

Not as good as the old favourite, though.

Setting Sun-days. Poems, Jostein Lindland.

Or did it need the hyphen?

Setting Sundays.

That was cleaner. Better.

Hemingway always had good titles. *The Sun Also Rises*. *For Whom the Bell Tolls*. *The Old Man and the Sea*.

I took a good slurp and lit a fag. There wasn't a woman under forty in the place now. They looked like hens the way they sat clucking with their croaky voices. And the men were like cockerels, sticking their chests out and trying to impress.

Like that little squirt at Turid's work. He'd been lifting so many weights his arms pointed out from his sides when he walked, as if they were branches rather than arms. But who would fancy a dwarf with bulging biceps and a barrel chest?

No, time to move on.

I got my phone out and held it to my ear.

'Yes?' I said, and paused. 'I'll be right there.'

I put the phone back in my inside pocket, picked up my ciggies and got to my feet, lifted my hand in a wave and smiled in the direction of Turid's colleagues, before going to the bar and paying the bill.

The trees threw long shadows across the square. The windows of the apartments on the other side twinkled in the sunlight. If I hadn't known better, I could have been in Paris, I thought to myself. Wide boulevards, rows of leafy trees, pavement cafes, people everywhere. And if the Mariakirken wasn't exactly Notre-Dame, it was at least from the same period. Or was it?

I'd have to check that someday, I thought as I passed the music shop on the corner and crossed over to the theatre side.

Two homeless people were lying in sleeping bags up against the wall. One had a shopping trolley next to him full of stuff, the other a bike laden with all sorts of bags. One of the two faces was partially visible, brown as a nut, leathery as an old wallet.

The summer must have been good for them too.

Maybe it wouldn't be all that bad? Let go of everything, no

responsibilities, totally free. A bit of begging, a bit of thieving if needs be. If you'd already given in, it'd hardly make much odds. Drink yourself senseless whenever you liked, or all the time for that matter.

Cold in winter, true.

Not much fun sleeping out, true.

But some of the sleeping bags these days would keep out minus twenty, at least. Nick one of them. Thermal undies and a good thick coat, some decent footwear for the winter.

It was the drugs that destroyed them, nothing else.

At the bottom of the gentle hill that leads down towards Nøstet, my eye passed over the old swimming baths. I'd always liked walking by there because of the smell of chlorine that streamed out of the ventilation system. Not any more, though, not since the place had been turned into an arts venue. Close on a billion kroner it had set them back. And for whose benefit?

Experimental theatre groups.

Christ on a bike.

Once, a few years back, I'd been stupid enough to buy tickets for one of their theatre festivals. A French theatre group was putting on *Faust* in the old tram sheds at Møhlenpris. I'd never seen such rubbish. And I'd seen rubbish in my time. Four or five performers in black coats and long beaks instead of noses, warbling about the stage and mumbling for four hours straight. That was it. All the way from France to Bergen for *that*.

Freezing cold too, it'd been.

But the worst thing was no one called them out. It was all smiles and nods afterwards, everyone agreeing how 'powerful' it had been, how 'intense' or 'existentially disturbing' — and those were just a couple of the comments I overheard. They didn't mean a word of what they were saying. But somehow people have got it into their heads that they *have* to like what they don't like, that it's *actually* good, thereby legitimising the shite so you can be sure there'll be more shite to come, instead of putting a plug in it once and for all.

A billion kroner! For a bunch of layabouts screeching and carrying on and pretending they're giving us something of value, whereas what they're actually doing is taking. Taking our money, taking our time, and taking our self-respect too, because that's what we lose if we keep saying something's good when it isn't.

The only thing they give us is shite.

Those clouds were a fulfilment by comparison, pure Michelangelo.

Faust, my arse.

All right.

The smell of exhaust fumes and seawater that filled the air down by the harbour wasn't bad either.

I stopped and lit a fag before carrying on up Murallmenningen into Skottegaten. Unbelievably, it was no more than five o'clock.

Should I phone Turid and tell her I'd be late?

Because I would be. No point in conning myself.

She'd be off to work at quarter to eight, besides spending at least a quarter of an hour getting ready. So there was no sense hurrying home for that half-hour.

I could text her just before seven and tell her I was running late. How late would be up to me, she wouldn't be there then.

And Ole wouldn't care.

Or would he?

I wondered what he thought about me.

Better give him a ring now, in case I was too pissed later on.

I dropped my fag end onto the pavement and stepped on it as I took my phone out of my pocket.

In the building on the corner, up the stairs on the first floor, was where the first girlfriend I'd been with had lived. Agnes, her name was. She'd shared the place with a mate of hers. What was her name again? Mari? No. Marit? No. Margit, that was it.

Agnes and Margit from Sandnes.

I scrolled down until I found his number and then tapped it.

While it was ringing I looked up at the windows and tried to remember what it had looked like in there, what kind of furnishings there'd been.

A light grey wall-to-wall carpet, as I recalled.

Pinewood coffee table?

A red armchair.

Oh, I'd shagged her in that chair once. She'd sat there in the nude with her legs apart and her fanny all wet, and I'd leaned over her and dipped my cock inside her.

The phone rang four times and then went dead. Ole had declined the call. Maybe just as well, for the thought of Agnes in that chair had given me a hard-on.

I stuck my hands in my pockets and carried on, stroking my knob with the fingers of one hand as I went. Giving it a little squeeze now and then. Oh yes. Now I'd have to nip out to the bogs when I got there, get the job done properly. I just had to keep it going until then.

She might not have been the best looker in the world, Agnes, but what a body she had. Big, firm tits. Nothing I'd liked better than standing behind her and cupping them in my hands. Supple and pliant, she was too.

It was beyond me now, how I could have got sick of it and chucked her.

What I'd give to be able to ring that doorbell again.

I looked down the hill at the blue water of the fjord that was visible above the rooftops while I imagined her figure coming down the stairs, how I'd follow her up, into her room, into her bed . . .

By the time the old sardine factory came into view I'd gone limp again, and no amount of stroking and squeezing was getting me hard as I turned round the side of the building onto the decking where the outdoor serving area was.

A bit of effort in the bogs and it'd be no problem, I thought to myself, but getting it back up from a standing start, was it really worth the effort? It wasn't, I decided, so I passed among the tables and sat down at one that was free at the far end.

The hills out on Askøy were a lush green across the fjord, which was still and shining, only a slightly darker shade than the sky. For some reason, there was a mist further out, a foggy kind of light that blurred the colours there.

In the middle of the fjord was what looked like a salvage vessel, a huge jet of water arcing into the air from it and plunging back into the sea. Another vessel appeared from behind the first one, so there was plenty of activity out there.

I bought two pints, it'd save me the bother of going twice.

Ole.

Did I have to think about him now?

I took a slurp, lit a fag, leaned back in the chair while fidgeting with the beer mat on the table in front of me and looked out over the water.

There was nothing to think about, because there was nothing I could do.

Turid had suggested not long ago that I take him on a trip somewhere, just the two of us, a father and son thing. Most likely she'd got the idea from a film she'd seen.

'And where were you thinking we should go?' I said.

She'd shrugged then and turned her palms upwards, the way she always did when leaving something to me.

'Anywhere you like.'

'Are we talking Scandinavia or Europe now? Or another continent? Should I take him to Africa, do you think?'

'No need to be sarcastic,' she said. 'What about Copenhagen? Stockholm?'

'I'm not going to bloody Stockholm with him, that's for sure,' I said.

'Copenhagen, then.'

'And what are we supposed to do there?'

She shrugged again.

'Have a nice time together?'

'The only thing he's interested in is his gaming. I know exactly what it'd be like. We'd sit there at one restaurant after another without saying a word to each other. Do you realise how unbearable it'd be?'

'It wouldn't have to be like that. Maybe the two of you being together there instead of at home would make things different,' she said.

I hadn't a clue how she'd got it into her head that things could be different. Perhaps it was a mother's love for her son. That kind of love could make you blind too. Not that I was going to present the truth to her, I kept that to myself. But the truth was that our son was a loser.

That made me a loser too.

A year ago we'd driven across the fells to Oslo, he was starting uni there, on the Blindern campus. Biology, he reckoned he'd choose after the foundation year. He'd hardly been in a forest in his life. I glanced at him in the rear-view every now and then as he sat in the back staring out the window. Silent and withdrawn, not a smile in sight.

'Cheer up, back there!' I said. 'You're free at last!'

He just gawped at me in the mirror.

He'd got a room in halls up in Sognsvann. We carried the few things he had with him inside, and then Turid and I went off to a hotel while he spent his first night in his own place. The next day I took him out to IKEA. Turid went to see her sister and her sister's family out in Nittedal, and even if a trip to IKEA with Ole wasn't exactly a dream scenario, I was glad to avoid seeing them.

'You'll need a frying pan. Will this one do you?'

'I don't know.'

'We'll take it, then.'

'OK.'

And that's how it went on, the trolley filling up with glasses and plates, kitchen utensils, rugs and plants. I was determined it wouldn't get me down and tried my best to keep a conversation going in the cafeteria afterwards. He sat there poking at his food, muttering a yes or a no every now and again.

He'd got into the habit of cutting his own hair with the clippers. It was like a centimetre-thick mat on his head. He never looked anyone in the eye, so it was impossible to engage with him, all you got was evasion and avoidance.

But avoidance of what?

I didn't like talking about him with Turid, and I didn't like the psychologising people came up with as soon as things weren't going like clockwork in a life — what does it help to put a name to something? — but on our way back over the fells that Sunday a year ago I made an exception.

'Do you think the lad's depressed?' I said. I stared at the road ahead that ran straight as a die across the moors and between the rocky outcrops, but I could see out of the corner of my eye that Turid was looking at me.

There was a silence for a moment.

'Why are you asking that?' she said.

'He never smiles. He never talks. He hardly eats. There's no energy in him. No strength.'

I glanced at her as I changed gear and overtook the motor home that had just turned out of a lay-by onto the road in front of us.

'He's always been quiet,' she said.

'True,' I said, noting in the mirror that the motor home was already a good way behind us.

She fell silent again.

But there was more to come, if only I waited.

'He's never had much of an appetite either,' she said after a bit.

'No, he hasn't,' I said.

'What makes you think he's depressed?' she said.

'I'm not saying he is,' I said. 'It was a question, that's all.'

We drove on for a while with neither of us speaking. A tarn appeared and was gone, its surface roughened by the strong wind, and we passed two cyclists who from a distance had looked like red balloons, the wind filling their jackets.

I reached out and switched the radio on.

'Do you think he'll manage on his own?' Turid said.

'He'll have to,' I said.

But of course he couldn't. He said he was fine, said he was attending lectures, said he'd made friends, but none of it was true. Turid had a feeling something was wrong and turned up to see him unannounced. I told her not to, that it was the stupidest thing by far that we could do, but she brought him back home with her anyway.

And he was still there.

I was angry just thinking about it.

So I paid it as little attention as I could. And there was definitely no point now, I thought, sitting at my table on the decking at Verftet that last day of summer, gazing across the water to Askøy, savouring not only the warmth of the sun that had begun to sink in the sky to the west, but also the buzz that was kicking in from the two pints I'd already drunk.

The tables around me were nearly all full now. People were in high spirits, the voices loud and animated, the laughter buoyant and loose.

Students, people from the arts and culture sectors, university lecturers, journalists, the occasional actor. The care workers and lorry drivers were certainly few and far between.

I got to my feet to go for a dump and draped my jacket over my chair, the whole issue of sweat stains now somehow seeming utterly pointless.

As I passed through the cafe interior, I noticed a crowd from the paper go past outside the window. Lucky I hadn't still been sitting there, I thought. They'd have seen me drinking on my own then, it would have put them in a dilemma: join me or ignore me. Either way, it would have been uncomfortable. Now I'd be able to go over to their table, as if from nowhere, strike up some conversation, pull up a chair, and that'd be me sorted for the duration.

The Man from Nowhere. A novel, Jostein Lindland.

Sitting down on the bog, I first checked my email, then texted Turid.

Dragging out a bit, sitting with a bunch from work, I typed.

OK, she replied a second later, as if she'd been ready waiting.

Then came another.

Just remember you've got to get up tomorrow as well.

Yes, boss, I wrote back, squeezing out a hard little lump that turned out to be as black as coal when I stood up to wipe myself and peered into the bowl.

The phone lit up next to the sink. I dropped the paper, pressed to flush and watched it all whirl away into the underworld before checking what she'd written.

When did the two of us last go out?

Christ, was I supposed to feel guilty now?

You work nights, I typed back.

Not every night.

Dinner at Klosteret Saturday then? I wrote.

:) she replied.

It wasn't exactly what I needed, but at least I'd have some peace for a bit.

I slipped the phone into my pocket and went back outside. The crowd from the paper were sat around two tables nearest the water. They'd already got them in, there were pints everywhere.

'Lindland,' said Gunnar as I came up after retrieving my jacket.

'Here he is,' said Erlend.

'Room for one more?' I said.

'If you can find a chair,' said Gunnar.

'I'll need a pint or two first,' I said, and went and joined the queue at the bar. I lit a fag while I waited, got my phone out, checked my email. Nothing. Opened the one from Erlend so I could say something about his photos if needs be.

The artist was standing in the middle of the concrete gallery space, her pictures a blur in the background, all you could see was some white and some blue. Her hands were in her pockets and she was staring at the camera with her head lowered slightly so it looked like she was gazing into her innermost being.

They knew how to pose, many of our so-called artists and writers.

I zoomed in on her face.

She didn't look half bad, now that I didn't have to listen to her.

Nice eyes.

Lips a bit narrow, maybe.

But a nice shape to her face.

Her eyes were so blue it almost looked unnatural. As if they were made of glass with the colour painted on.

I hadn't noticed when I'd been interviewing her, but then she'd been looking at the floor most of the time.

I pinched apart again to look at her chest.

Her sweater was too big to be able to see what was underneath.

Maybe she wasn't as skinny as I'd thought. Maybe she was soft and gorgeous under all those baggy clothes.

I took a drag of my cigarette and flicked away the ash, caught the bartender's eye and held two fingers in the air. He nodded and started to pull the pints.

Returning to the table, I put them down, picked up a chair from the adjoining table and sat down between Gunnar and Sverre. There wasn't quite enough room, so I had to sit slightly drawn back. It didn't feel right, I was by far the most experienced among them, a nestor of investigative crime reporting I'd once been called, but there was nothing to be done about it, and it was only because I'd come last anyway.

'Anything new?' I said, leaning back and crossing my legs so as not to sit demurely like a woman with my knees together, the way a couple of them were.

'Like what?' said Olav.

'No idea,' I said. 'But those lads are going to be found sooner or later, I hope. Should make a good story.'

'They've probably just gone off on a cabin trip,' said Sverre. 'Either that or they've gone to Oslo to stab someone to death.'

He looked at me and smiled. The others laughed.

'If you ask me, they're lying dead in the forest somewhere,' I said, regardless. 'Suicide pact. They're just the sort who would.'

My phone rang. Stupidly, I'd forgotten to mute it.

It was Ole.

I declined the call and turned the sound off. Couldn't talk to him there. Didn't want to get up either and thread my way between the tables with the phone pressed to my ear, it signalled something intimate that I didn't want to display to them.

When I slipped it back into my inside pocket, the conversation had moved on from the missing kids to some removal men Sverre had hired at some point during the summer; they'd been sober when they turned up at the old house in the morning, he said, only their behaviour had become more and more erratic as the day wore on, until eventually he'd realised they were drinking, and by the time evening came round they were pissed out of their minds.

'Unpacking the boxes the next day, I couldn't find the cognac. They must have drunk it.'

'What did you do about it?' said Olav.

'What could I do? I couldn't prove anything.'

'I had some builders in once who kept leaving the bathroom in a hell of a mess,' said Gunnar. 'There was shit all over the toilet, up the sides of the bowl and on the rim. And this was happening every day. Couldn't do a thing about it though.'

'Where were they from?' I said.

'What does it matter?' Gunnar said.

I shrugged and gave him a smile.

'Poland?' I said.

'It's not relevant,' said Gunnar. 'The point was I couldn't do anything about it, not where they came from.'

'So they were from Poland,' I said.

He didn't reply, and I had to laugh before taking a slurp of my pint and lighting another fag.

There was something miserable about Gunnar, I'd always thought so. It wasn't that he never said anything, because he did, or because he didn't smile or laugh, because he did that as well. But with him it was forced, his natural state was misery. In misery he went through the corridors, in misery he sat at his desk in front of his computer.

He was from Kinsarvik, though no one would ever have guessed, he looked like a Spaniard, his cheeks and throat a shadow of stubble before he got to lunchtime.

He worked in the opinions and editorial section and his own editorials were always the ones that got read the most, so he was incisive enough.

I couldn't stand them though. They were like a barometer of all the right opinions.

He was the type who put his finger in the air to see which way the wind was blowing before he went to work.

'It's all going to pot in Poland now,' said Olav. 'It's as bad there as it is in Hungary in many ways. It's the strangest thing. After the Nazis were there, and the Communists were there, they choose of all things to go in for nationalism.'

'Hardly surprising, though, is it?' I said. 'They've always been squeezed between the superpowers, so when the chance finally comes around it's no wonder they want what's theirs. Which is Poland. The Polish nation state.'

'They've passed a law making it a punishable offence to mention Poland in connection with the Nazi extermination camps,' said Sverre.

'Controlling history's part and parcel of building any nation,' I said. 'And the camps were actually German, weren't they? Even if they were in Poland.'

'Are you defending it?'

'Not at all,' I said. 'I'm just explaining it, that's all.'

Everyone went quiet for a few seconds, looking at the floor or looking away, absorbed in the greying fjord all of a sudden. I drained the rest of my pint, put the empty glass down on the table, picked up the other one and took a slurp.

'I was in Warsaw last winter,' said Sverre. Some would say he was the diplomatic type, others that he shied away from conflict, but whatever he was he knew everyone and was liked by the majority. 'I was in the Old Town, it was just before Christmas, so there was a Yuletide market with lots of little stalls. It looked like you would have imagined it in the Middle Ages. But there was something not quite right about it, there was no atmosphere. I looked it up when I got back to the hotel and realised that the old part of town had been totally destroyed during the war and then rebuilt exactly as before. I hadn't known, but I'd sensed it.'

'Same as Dresden,' said Gunnar. 'Have you been there?'

Sverre shook his head.

What a bunch of halfwits, I thought to myself, and gazed across the water to Askøy, where the sun had now almost disappeared behind the hills.

Darkness rose imperceptibly, filling the space between the fells on both sides of the fjord.

And I was bladdered. No doubt about it.

I looked at Erlend.

'Nice photos you took today, Erlend,' I said when his eyes caught mine.

'Thanks,' he said. 'Nice piece, too.'

'Is it up yet?'

'Yes,' he said. *'Does Bergen really need more clouds?'*

He laughed.

I wanted to look it up and see for myself, but couldn't bring myself to do it in their company.

'Did you like the pictures?' he said.

'The paintings?'

'Yes.'

I grinned and leaned back in my chair.

'Understood,' he said.

At the same moment, I noticed one of the city's writers coming along with a trail of youngsters after him. Students from the writing academy, no doubt.

As they passed our table, he lifted an index finger to his forehead in a kind of salute.

'Lindland,' he said.

He managed to make my name sound almost like an insult, and I straight-faced him.

They sat down at some tables a bit further away.

'Anyway,' said Sverre, drinking up and getting to his feet. 'Tomorrow looms.'

All of a sudden they all got to their feet.

A sense of terror gripped me.

What was I supposed to do now?

'Just need to pop to the loo first,' said Gunnar. 'Anyone fancy waiting so we can share a taxi?'

'I need to join you,' said Olav. 'But you'll be going to Fyllingsdalen, won't you?'

'That's right, sorry,' said Gunnar.

'Sorry because you live there, or because I can't share your taxi?'

'Both,' said Gunnar.

Olav looked at me.

'You live out in Åsane, don't you?'

'Breistein, yes,' I said. 'Only I'm not going home yet. Meeting someone at Bull's Eye later on.'

Olav winked at me.

'I'll have to get the bus, then,' he said, and began squeezing his way between the tables with Gunnar and Sverre following on behind.

'What's your plan?' I said to Erlend, who'd stayed put.

'I'm just going to finish this and then get off home,' he said. 'I only live round the corner.'

'Where's that?' I said.

'Below Dragefjellet.'

'Nøstet?'

'Kind of. Heggesmauet.'

'Never heard of it,' I said, and picked up the pint Olav hadn't finished, downed what was left, then looked out across the water, where the sun had gone down and darkness poured out over the hills.

'What's that?' said Erlend.

'What's what?' I said.

He pointed in the direction of Laksevåg. A light shone from the top of the ridges, pale and shimmering as if from a full moon.

But the moon hung dull in the sky further to the east.

Bloody hell.

The light intensified, growing and growing in strength until moments later an enormous star burst into the sky above the trees.

'What the hell's that?' Erlend said.

'I don't know,' I said.

Everything had gone quiet around us. Everyone was staring up at the light. Some had got to their feet. Then, as if they'd been waiting for the signal, their voices returned again. A babble of theories and conjecture, trepidation and excitement broke out around us.

'It's only Armageddon,' I said with a laugh. 'It had to come sooner or later.'

'No, seriously,' said Erlend. 'That's the strangest bloody thing I've ever seen. It's got to be a comet of some sort. Don't you think?'

His face was completely unmoving as he looked at me. But his eyes were scared.

'Maybe. Whatever it is, there'll be a perfectly natural explanation.'

'It's right overhead, for Christ's sake!' said Erlend.

I felt sorry for him.

'It just looks like it is, that's all,' I said. 'Enjoy it while it's there.'

It wasn't often the word beautiful came into my mind, but now it did. Beautiful and unsettling.

Why was it unsettling?

Because it was completely silent. It just hung there, completely silent in the sky.

But then so did the sun and the moon, for fuck's sake.

'Shall we get going?' Erlend suggested, all casual.

I smiled.

'Afraid to go on your own?'

'Ha ha,' he said.

'How old are you again?' I said.

'I thought it might be pleasant,' he said. 'Forget it.'

I laughed.

'Going to have a mope now too, are we? Come on, only kidding. Let's go.'

All around us people sat gazing up at the star, but no one was standing any more. Erlend slung his bag over his shoulder and I lit a fag, reminding myself to buy a new packet at the 7-Eleven before following him away from the serving area and onto the road outside the sardine factory.

'They used to hang people up there in the old days,' I said, pointing to the left.

'I imagine that's why it's called Galgebakken, don't you?' he said.

He walked quickly and I was soon short of breath, but I could hardly ask him to slow down.

He kept glancing up at the star that was now high in the sky, owning the heavens. I could tell it bothered him; at one point he shook his head.

The column of light that had first come into view over Puddefjorden had now disappeared. Instead, a faint, ghostly illumination reflected in its waters.

If he didn't want to talk, then fine by me. But did he have to walk so bloody fast? Maybe he thought his flat would protect him from Armageddon?

We parted company when we got to Nøstegaten and I carried on towards the centre of town on my own. Of course, I could have gone home, that would have been the smartest thing. The day after would have been easier then, less resentment in the air.

But Bull's Eye would give me some alone time for a bit of serious drinking before they closed. After that I could just glide home nice and pissed through the empty streets in a taxi — few feelings were better.

Taxi Home. Poems, Jostein Lindland.

But that could be in the daytime too. Whereas the whole experience lay in driving through darkness.

Taxi Home at Night. Poems, Jostein Lindland.

Nah, too fussy.

How about *Taxi Nights*?

Not bad.

Taxi Nights. Poems, Jostein Lindland.

Wait a minute.

The New Star. Poems, Jostein Lindland.

Bloody brilliant.

I went past the National Theatre, along Markveien to Torgallmenningen, where I remembered to buy cigarettes, and then on to the Hotell Norge. There were people everywhere, a lot of them looking up at the sky every now and again, I noticed, as if to make sure the enormous star was actually there and not just something they'd imagined.

I paused and lit a fag, looking up myself.

Weird stuff.

At the same time, my phone vibrated against my chest.

It was Turid.

'What's up?' I said.

'Where are you?' she said.

'Why do you want to know?' I said.

'Ole's not answering his phone.'

I sighed.

'I tried earlier on,' I said. 'He didn't answer, of course. He just doesn't want to talk to us.'

'So you're not at home.'

'On my way to the bus now, as it happens. Have you seen the new star?'

'What do you mean?'

'A great big new star, just appeared in the sky.'

'No, I've not seen it.'

'Well, you should.'

'Give me a ring when you get in,' she said. 'I'm a bit worried.'

'Don't be, there's nothing to be worried about. He's either gaming or gone to sleep.'

'I hope you're right. Bye.'

So that was her in a sulk, I thought to myself as I dropped my phone back into my pocket. It'd be worse yet, though!

There was hardly anyone in the pub when I got there. The weather was too good, I suppose. But it suited me fine. I got a vodka and Red Bull in, and a pint and a Jägermeister, sat down in one of the booths and knocked back the hard stuff before settling in with the pint.

The room was dark, all nooks and crannies, the way it had to be with so many ugly buggers sat there drinking. The dim light erased their features and made them seem, if not pleasant-looking, then at least ordinary. After a few more drinks they'd be checking each other out like they were models.

The darkness was good for business, pure and simple.

Not that the punters gave it a thought, but it was surely there in the subconscious, drawing them to the place without them knowing why exactly.

It couldn't be the price of the beer that brought them out.

The New Star.

How would the first poem begin?

An August day?

An August day by the fjord?

The fjord, August?

Nah.

An evening in August, that was more like it.

It was good.

An evening in August
as the sun sank
and spirits rose
I beheld the new star

Bang on! First go!

I wrote it down in a text to myself before going up and getting another round in. Vodka and Red Bull, two Jägermeisters and a pint. Again, I knocked the hard stuff back first, one after the other, then went outside for a smoke.

As I crossed the floor, everything went black for a second or two.

I couldn't see anything all of a sudden.

Christ, am I going blind now? I thought, and stopped, standing still there for a minute with my heart thumping like mad in my chest.

Then it passed. Five seconds, maybe ten, it lasted.

Blood pressure, I reckoned. Low blood pressure.

And the alcohol.

I carried on towards the door, glancing around discreetly to see if anyone was staring at me.

Jesus, that was unpleasant, I thought as I lit a fag and gazed in the direction of the pond, Lille Lungegårdsvannet.

But I felt fine again now.

People who drank meths went blind.

Surely they weren't putting meths in the vodka?

Not at the Hotell Norge.

The star wasn't visible from where I was standing, but the faint gleam in the water of the pond told me it was still there.

My mother used to faint now and again, and that had been low blood pressure. She'd get up and fall down. It could happen if she had to stand up for a long time as well.

The old bat.

Low blood pressure, that'd be it.

And alcohol.

When I stood up.

Only now it was all right again. No reason to panic.

I stubbed out my fag in the ashtray stand outside the door and went back inside. Took a couple of slurps of beer and got my phone out to see what they were doing up there.

The weather, of course.

Full-on summer! the halfwits had come up with.

The next story was about a policeman who'd been sending a young girl so-called 'sex messages'.

He shouldn't have, of course.

I wondered who it might be.

And what he'd written.

I'd have to remember to ask Geir next time I ran into him.

I scrolled down to the bottom.

My piece wasn't up yet.

But hadn't Erlend said it was?

They must have put it straight into arts and culture. No link on the main page.

Couldn't blame them. She wasn't exactly a name.

On the other hand, the name on the byline was mine.

Didn't that count for those arse-lickers any more?

I'd lost interest in reading it and went back to zooming in on her photo to make sure I hadn't been seeing things before.

Nope.

Definitely all right.

And she was still in town.

What time was it, anyway?

I swiped the news page away. Just gone nine.

Could that be right?

Nine, was that all?

In which case the opening would still be on!

OK, I could go over there. I'd covered the exhibition, it wasn't like I was going to get stopped at the door.

A couple more shots, and then: bang! Lindland's on his way. It'd be like Gulliver in Lilliput.

Ignore the arty-farty stuff, grin and bear all that, then get her into bed.

Fuck the art out of her.

I stood up, a bit gingerly this time so as not to go blind again, got three more Jägermeisters in, and a pint to go with them, and drank them with a feeling of excitement. There was a lot to be positive about all of a sudden. The title, the first poem, nailed, and then the thought of what she was hiding underneath that big sweater of hers. It warmed me inside. I felt my throat tighten.

Twenty minutes later I was on my way to Engen again. I hadn't felt so good in ages. It was like everything I saw just glanced off me and was gone.

Supreme, that was what I was.

The gallery was on a pier, brick-built, big and grey. Outside, torches were burning and two or three little clusters of arts people stood smoking with wine glasses in their hands, all dressed the same way.

Inside, the place was heaving. No one was looking at the paintings any more, this was a party. Or rather, it was a reception, everyone on their best behaviour. Polite chatter and laughter everywhere.

Where was the artist?

I looked around.

There she was.

In one of those trouser suits, or whatever they were called, that looked like a dress but were actually a pair of trousers, that women seemed to like so much.

I went over to an unmanned counter in the corner that was decked out with wine by the glass and took a glass of white, not drinking it, but holding it sophisticatedly by the stem, and began to walk, slow as you like, from picture to picture while pretending to be giving them my most careful consideration.

I didn't look at her, of course. Not so much as a glance in her direction.

As I got to the final wall she came over.

'What are you doing here?' she said.

It wasn't exactly pleasant surprise, more like disgust. But she'd come over, that was the main thing.

'I thought I'd have a closer look at your paintings,' I said. 'There was so little time earlier on.'

'Don't tell me you're interested in art,' she said. 'That interview is the worst I've ever done. Which is saying quite a lot.'

I didn't respond, just carried on looking at the paintings on the wall in front of us.

'You know what they call you here?'

'No,' I said. 'What do they call me here?'

'The idiot from the local rag. When I said you were going to be interviewing me, that's what they said. What, that idiot from the local rag is going to interview you?'

'I've been called a lot worse than that,' I said. 'I suppose you know that *idiot* is from the Greek and means "ordinary citizen"? I'm quite happy with that.'

She looked at me for a few seconds, then turned and went away.

I finished studying the paintings, drank what was in my glass, went and got another and then went outside for a smoke.

The idiot thing was something I remembered from school. The history teacher had been a dithering old fellow who used to give us that same lecture every time he heard the word. Which wasn't seldom, because of course that was what we called him, Idiot.

Among those smoking outside I recognised a radio guy from NRK, the national broadcasting network. I kept bumping into him, we saw each other at all the same press conferences, but I'd never exchanged more than a couple of words with him.

Normally, I'd stay well away, but it wouldn't be a bad thing if she saw me with people she respected, and I assumed he'd interviewed her too earlier in the day, in that smarmy arts journo way of his, so I went over to him.

'What do you reckon, then?' I said.

'About what?' he said. He had a beard and glasses, and the brown corduroy jacket he was wearing made him look like he was stuck in the seventies, athough he could hardly have been born then.

'The paintings,' I said.

'Exquisite,' he said, then looked up at the bright star high above the city. 'Even if they do pale a little compared to this. My God.'

'True,' I said. 'But then everything does compared to the stars.'

'It's different tonight though, isn't it?' he said. 'I mean, this is absolutely bloody astounding.'

'It is, yes,' I said, holding out my packet of cigarettes and offering him one. He shook his head.

'What's your verdict, anyway?' he said after a pause.

'The paintings?'

'Yes.'

'I like them,' I said.

There was another pause. He looked around. I thought I might as well get in a bit of practice, and went on before he could say he had to go.

'I like the way they consider time. I mean, clouds share the concept of time with us, don't they? Constantly changing, in flux above our heads. Rather as if they were measuring the moment for us. Then, when they're painted, time stops, do you understand me? Bang, stop. But the pictures are in there,' I said, indicating the door behind us. 'Sharing time with us, though no longer changing. So if she's lucky, the artist who painted them, they'll still be here when we're dead and gone. The time they inhabit is therefore conceptually different altogether. If you understand what I'm saying?'

'Of course,' he said. 'But listen, I'm dying for a piss.'

He went away, and I looked at the others who were standing around. A politician with a professional interest in the arts and culture, in a red dress and a black jacket. What was her name again? Jensen. Same as the speed skater. Eva Jensen.

Was it gold or bronze she won at Lake Placid?

Bronze, wasn't it?

Bjørg Eva Jensen, that was her.

But this one was plain Eva Jensen.

Her laughter was excruciating, both the laugh that came out when she wasn't actually laughing, which was a kind of gurgling, and what came out when she found something funny, long, birdlike noises that began way up the scale before gradually descending.

I reckoned it had to be hell being a politician. Never being able to get pissed, at least not in public, and always having to mind what they said and think about how they came across.

How did she get to where she was?

Was it because she understood more than others? Was she more capable than others?

Of course not.

She knew people, that was what it was about. Workers' Youth League to begin with, courses and training, camps, loads of contacts. Then straight onto the city council while still in her early twenties.

You saw her all over, at every event going.

I'd have no problem drinking and being a politician at the same time. No one could ever tell how drunk I actually was.

It had to be one of my most useful talents.

I followed her with my eyes as she walked past me towards the entrance. She stopped in the doorway to allow someone out.

Who else but the artist herself?

She was with two others, a man in a suit and a woman in a suit. They went round the corner and sat down on the edge of the pier.

So, she was a smoker. Good. That meant we had something in common.

No sense in being coy, I reasoned, and went over to them.

She looked up at me with annoyance.

'What do you want?' she said.

'I just wanted to say that I think your pictures are really good,' I said.

'Who cares what you think?' she said.

'I know that interview was a bit rough,' I said. 'My background's in news. I've probably carried a bit too much of that over with me. But what does it matter, for God's sake, we're consenting adults. And your pictures have been growing on me. I wanted to tell you that.'

I turned round and walked off.

There was no point in hanging around, not with the animosity and bitterness she obviously felt towards me, but then there was no point in letting all that free wine go to waste either, so I went back inside, took a glass and drank it while standing back against the wall, and then another one after that.

That would have to be it now.

Tomorrow looms.

I put the glass down on the counter and was heading for the door when everything blacked out. It was like a wave of darkness came crashing down into my brain, and the last thing I sensed was my legs suddenly being too soft to keep me upright.

The next thing I knew, I was in a darkness beyond the world. Desperately, I tried to remember who I was and what I was doing there.

Then, in that darkness, I saw a room. I wasn't in the room, I was outside it, and yet I could see it from underneath.

Faces were staring at me, mouths opened and spoke.

Who was I?

Where was I?

Who were all these people?

When were they from?

It was as if all time and all space were wide open.

And yet it was to that same place that I returned.

'He's coming round,' someone said.

I was Jostein.

I was lying on a floor.

I tried to get up, but fell back.

The opening.

The artist.

Was that her bending over me? On her knees?

'Here,' she said. 'Drink this.'

A glass was put to my lips. I drank.

'What's happening?' I said.

'Are you all right?'

'Yes, I am now,' I said. 'I went blind. I can see now.'

'You passed out. You've had too much to drink.'

I sat up. Someone came and gripped my arm, helped me to my feet.

'Are you OK?' the guy said.

'Fine,' I said.

'You've had rather too much to drink,' he said. 'Time you went home.'

'I'll call a taxi,' the artist said.

'There's one at the door,' the guy said. 'He can have that one, can't he?'

'Yes,' I said. 'I'm OK. Nothing to be concerned about. I can walk on my own.'

And I could.

Christ, what a scene. People were staring at me as I went through the room and out the door.

I got into the taxi.

'Have you booked?' the driver said without turning round.

'Someone has,' I said.

'Going to Sandviken?'

'No, Breistein,' I said.

'This one's for Sandviken,' he said.

'Oh, to hell with it, then,' I said, and opened the door to get out.

The guy who'd booked the cab must have come just after me, because he was standing outside already reaching forward as I opened the door.

'It was me who ordered a taxi to Sandviken,' he said. 'Only there's been a change of plan.'

'OK,' said the driver, and I closed the door again and leaned back in the seat. 'Breistein it is, then.'

The clock on the dashboard said ten thirty.

It couldn't be right.

It felt like I'd been out for years.

Half ten?

The buses were still running. I wouldn't even have to wait for the night bus.

'I've changed my mind,' I said. 'You can put me down at Torgall-menningen.'

'Seriously?' said the driver.

'Yes,' I said.

He can be pissed off all he wants, I told myself after we pulled into a bus stop and he handed me the card reader. But no way was he getting a tip for such a short ride.

What actually happened back there?

I ought to sit down somewhere and get myself together, I thought. Not Bull's Eye, though, I was well past that stage.

It was strange, but my head was clear and I felt fine, as if the darkness had cleansed me.

The darkness.

It hadn't been a normal case of passing out.

Even if I'd never passed out before, I knew it couldn't have been.

I stopped between the Narvesen and Dickens.

Café Opera?

Henrik?

No, the place would be jumping. I wasn't in the mood for people now.

Maybe the bar at the Norge?

A man could sit in peace there.

No sooner said than done. After a brief visit to the bogs, where I splashed my face with cold water and dried myself with some paper towels, I ordered a beer at the bar and sat down at one of the low tables beside the wall. The place was half full, but quiet nonetheless; a lot of people were sitting on their own, a few with laptops in front of them.

The beer tasted sensational.

Just what I needed.

What had happened wasn't good. Too many people there who knew me. *Lindland passed out drunk, have you heard?* But it hadn't been the drink. It was in the family. My mother used to pass out.

She never talked about what it was. Maybe there wasn't much to talk about.

Still, I was pretty sure she never woke up beyond the world in darkness, the way I'd done, peering into that bright room of faces and voices in some other place.

What had happened?

It had all been in my mind.

It just didn't feel like it had.

I drank the pint and got another. As I put it down on the table and was about to sit down again, I noticed a familiar figure come into reception. The artist herself.

Was she staying *here*?

It looked like it.

But how could she afford it?

Blagging funds out of the arts foundation, I shouldn't wonder, though most of them got a pittance, I knew that much.

She said something to the receptionist, who nodded and typed something into her computer.

Then she turned round and came towards the bar.

What was I supposed to do then?

She was too full of animosity and bitterness for me to give it another go.

But I wasn't going to hide from her either.

When she saw me, she nearly stopped dead, but composed herself at the last minute and carried on as if nothing had happened. She ordered a drink at the bar without turning round, then took the drink, a gin and tonic by the looks of it, with her to one of the tables across the room where she sat down with her back to me.

As if I was going to be bothered.

Cold and scrawny, she was, and pretentious as they come.

I got my phone out and googled *clouds in paintings*.

Forty-two million hits. So we weren't talking about originality here.

I opened a couple of pages. John Constable seemed to be an important name.

An hour, that's what it took him to paint a picture of some clouds.

A damn sight better than hers.

There was life in them. It was like seeing clouds in the sky. Grey and dirty.

In the corner of my eye, I saw her get to her feet. I looked up as I slipped the phone back into my inside pocket. She came towards me, stopping three paces from where I sat.

'I just want to say that I think you should go home now,' she said. 'Everyone who saw what happened was concerned for you. Strictly speaking, you should go to A&E.'

I smiled my widest, most supreme smile.

I still couldn't make out her boobs, the outfit she had on was too loose for that.

Or maybe she hadn't got any?

'Thanks for the thought,' I said. 'But you're not my mother. You're not my wife either. So what you think basically doesn't count.'

'And thank goodness for that,' she said. 'Anyway, I've said it now.'

She went back to where she was sitting.

Decent enough arse, though. Nice and full under the soft black fabric. Gave me a stiffy.

I crossed my legs, leaned back and slurped my pint.

What was she doing drinking on her own, anyway?

Was she an alcoholic?

Didn't look the type.

Still, you never could tell.

I thought about going to the bogs for a wank.

Or maybe give it one last go?

It wouldn't do any harm.

I went to the bar and ordered two gin and tonics. Drank one while standing there, then took the other one over to the table where she was sitting.

She looked up at me without speaking. The look she gave me was more exasperation than annoyance.

'I'd like to apologise for what I said just then. And to thank you for your help earlier on. I'm actually not proud of myself for what happened, so it was easier to be dismissive, I suppose.'

'All right,' she said. 'Apology accepted.'

She turned away from me and stared straight ahead, as if I'd already gone.

'One more thing,' I said. 'Your pictures really did move me. It's important to me that you understand that, after the interview.'

She glanced up at me again.

'Why didn't you say so in the article, then?'

'I didn't really see the pictures properly until this evening,' I said. 'I was more interested in you while we were doing the interview.'

'Interested in criticising me, you mean.'

'It's my job to be critical,' I said. 'It's not normally the way in arts journalism, most reporters there are servile, but I believe that's a mistake. There's no reason to be soft on artists or writers.'

'I don't like you,' she said.

'So I gathered,' I said. 'Which is fair enough. But why is it so important to tell me?'

'Because you keep turning up. And because it's intriguing to me that my pictures should move you. What could an idiot like you possibly see in them?'

'I might not have words for that sort of thing,' I said. 'Idiots often don't.'

'Are you hurt now?' she said with a laugh. 'Don't tell me you're hurt!'

'But I can try,' I said, and sat down on the chair next to hers.

'What are you doing?' she said.

'I just want to tell you what I saw in your pictures,' I said. 'Then I'll leave you alone. It's time I was getting off home, anyway.'

She said nothing, but turned the glass in her hand.

'You probably won't agree, but the way I saw them they were empty.'

'I see,' she said.

'If you look at John Constable's clouds, they're full of life, aren't they? Do you know what I mean? His clouds are often dirty. But your clouds are pristine and empty. And that emptiness is *existential*.'

'What do you mean exactly?' she said, looking at me.

'Nothingness,' I said.

'You mean the nothingness of existence?' she said.

'Yes,' I said.

'And why would that move you?'

'Because I'm going to die.'

'What are you saying?'

'No, no, not like that,' I said. 'But one day I'm going to die. And you are too. I wonder if that's why you painted them.'

She nodded a few times without speaking.

I drained my glass and stood up.

'Have a nice journey home, then,' she said.

'I thought I'd have a smoke first,' I said.

She said nothing, and made no move to follow me either, withdrawing into her own thoughts again, so I went out on my own, stood in front of the big window and lit up.

When I came back in, she looked up at me.

'Weren't you on your way?' she said.

'Yes, I am,' I said. 'Just need to pay the bill first.'

At the bar, I turned and looked at her again. She was sitting with her back towards me. I went over.

'Do you fancy another?' I said. 'Before I close the bill?'

'Are you making a play for me now?' she said.

'What if I was?' I said.

'Then you could go to hell.'

'In that case, I'm not. I'm buying you a platonic drink. OK?'

She nodded.

What was it with her? I wondered as I went up to the bar and ordered. What happened to the introverted artist staring at the floor and not knowing what to say?

'You're on the G&Ts, right?' I said, putting the glass down in front of her.

'That's right, yes,' she said. 'Thanks.'

She took a big slurp.

'I was wrong about you,' she said. 'You're not an idiot at all. You're just an unlikeable man.'

She laughed, as if to herself.

Could she be mentally unstable?

Of course she was. She was an artist.

'I realise you only want to fuck me,' she said. 'We needn't pretend.'

I said nothing.

'Only you're a bit too fat for my liking.'

'OK,' I said.

She laughed.

'You should see your face now,' she said. 'No, I think you're all right. Shall we go?'

'Go where?' I said, and instantly felt my throat tighten.

She lifted an eyebrow ironically and stood up.

I stood up too.

I didn't like this. She was way too unstable.

I went with her to the open lift. The door closed and she pressed the button for the second floor.

'I've got a rule,' she said on our way up. 'No kissing on the mouth.'

'That's what whores say,' I said.

'Exactly,' she said, and laughed.

I stepped up close to her and put my hand between her legs. She shoved me away.

'What would your wife say?' she said.

'She wouldn't know,' I said, pressing against her again.

'Patience,' she said.

The lift came to a halt, the door opened and she stepped out. I followed her along the corridor.

No, I didn't like it one bit.

Only she'd given me such a hard-on.

She stopped outside the room, found her key card, tapped it against the reader, opened the door and went in. Before I could do anything, the door slammed shut in my face.

Fucking whore.

She'd been having me on.

Or was it a game she was playing?

I knocked as hard as I could.

No answer.

She'd been out to humiliate me all along.

But I wasn't having it.

Fucking prick-tease.

She was nothing, a zero of an artist.

I knocked again.

No answer.

Right, then.

If that was the way she wanted it, then fine by me.

I turned and began walking away along the corridor, only then something happened. Suddenly, I felt the blood streaming through my body, a light pressure in every vein, and my head seemed to tingle from these new sensations. Then all at once the wave of darkness from before returned, rising quickly inside me, flooding my consciousness.

I've no idea how long I was gone, but when I came to I was adrift in darkness. Beneath me, the corridor area shone brightly, no bigger than a postcard. The body I thought I could discern on the floor seemed unconnected to me, though I knew I belonged to it. I couldn't get my thoughts together, they were all over the place. Nothing I could see made any sense.

And then, without warning, I was back inside that shining space, the corridor stretching away with all its doors.

Again, the artist woman was crouching beside me.

I was on my stomach, my cheek against the wall-to-wall carpet.

'Can you hear me?' she said.

'Get away from me,' I said, slowly pulling myself into a sitting position.

'You need the hospital,' she said. 'I'll go with you.'

'I'm fine. Leave me alone.'

I got to my feet and started walking down the corridor.

I sensed her come after me.

Like the last time, my brain felt cleansed. I saw everything around me more clearly, more distinctly. But my legs were still wobbly and shaking increasingly with every step. Halfway to the lift it felt like they were about to give way, and I stopped and held on to the wall for support.

'Do you need help?' she said, standing a couple of paces behind me.

'No, I fucking don't,' I said.

'But you are going to the hospital?'

'No.'

'But you must. It's serious. You may have had a stroke.'

'You mean a mini stroke.'

'Yes,' she said.

'Listen,' I said, and started walking again. 'I passed out, that's all. It runs in the family. And now I'm going home to get some sleep. And you can stay out of my way.'

She said nothing.

I made it to the lift and pressed the down button. When I turned round, she was standing in the middle of the corridor with her arms by her sides.

'Seriously, I'm concerned about you,' she said. 'You can't go off on your own in that condition.'

I stared at the metal door and heard the whirr of machinery in the shaft. I was so tired I didn't know what to do.

What was I using for brains?

I had to exploit the situation.

'OK,' I said.

The lift door slid open. An elderly man was standing inside. His face was singularly soft and round, like someone much younger, at the same time wrinkled and furrowed like a seventy-year-old's.

He smiled politely and was about to step out, when suddenly he paused.

'This isn't reception, is it?' he said.

'No,' I said.

'Are you going down?' he said.

'No, changed my mind,' I said.

The door closed. The artist woman looked at me and burst out laughing.

There really was something way too bloody unstable about this.

'Sorry,' she said. 'I only wanted to get my own back.'

She laughed again.

'There was no *only* about it,' I said.

'No,' she said, and walked slowly beside me as we went back down the corridor.

Why were my legs so weak?

Maybe it *was* a mini stroke?

I sensed the smell of her perfume and got a stiffy again.

She unlocked the door while I stood and waited. My hand was in my pocket, discreetly stroking. She smiled and looked down at the floor.

So, demure again now, was it?

'This time you can come in,' she said.

'Because I passed out?' I said.

'Yes,' she said. 'What other reason would there be?'

'None,' I said, and stepped inside. 'It's the only one I can think of.'

'There could be plenty of reasons,' she said. 'Do you think I'd have let you get this far, if I didn't want you to fuck me?'

What?

I looked at her. She turned and went into what I supposed was the bathroom.

To get herself ready.

If she wasn't having me on again.

The room was only small, an armchair, a tiny desk, a wardrobe and a minibar.

Her suitcase lay open on the floor, her clothes seemingly tossed about the room in anger, they were everywhere.

But it was a big bed.

I didn't care for women calling it fucking. They ought to say making love, or at a push screwing.

Maybe I should just go?

She was trouble.

But I couldn't do a runner from this. A willing woman in a hotel room? What would that make me?

It wasn't like she was dangerous or anything.

I opened the minibar and took out a whisky and a vodka. How small are those bottles? It was ridiculous.

'Do you want a drink?' I called out as I sat in the chair.

'In a minute!' she called back.

I downed the whisky in one.

Pictured the fabric of her outfit gliding down over her gorgeous arse. Her bending over. Me kneeling behind her, licking her arsehole.

The door opened and she stepped out. Still with her clothes on.

What had she been doing in there?

'You've passed out twice tonight,' she said. 'That can't be good for you.'

'Feels all right to me,' I said. 'What are you having?'

'Is there still some red wine?' she said, sitting down on the bed. Now she was all quiet and timid again.

Was she putting it on?

I couldn't get my head round her, but made like I wasn't fazed by the situation, twisted round and grabbed the bottle of red that was on the shelf behind the chair, and tossed it onto the bed beside her.

She picked it up and unscrewed the top while looking around at nothing in particular.

I took one of the glasses that had been next to the bottle and tossed it to her as I'd done with the bottle.

'Thanks,' she said, and smiled.

I watched her pour the wine into the glass.

She sat with her back half towards me and sipped. Neither of us spoke for a while.

'What do we do now?' I said eventually.

She turned her head and looked at me over her shoulder.

'Perhaps we should just go to sleep,' she said.

'Is that all?'

'Or do you want me to be your whore?'

'I wasn't thinking of paying for it,' I said.

She laughed.

I stood up.

She looked at me, and then she stood up too.

I stepped up close to her, pressed my body against hers and grabbed her bum cheeks with both hands.

'Well, there's a thing,' she said. 'Have you been sitting there thinking about me?'

'Yes,' I said.

I tried to kiss her, only she turned away.

I unzipped the back of her outfit and pulled it down over her shoulders, down over her body, while she unbelted my trousers.

Lying back on the bed in her panties and bra, she looked up at me as I stood in the middle of the room and got my trousers off in a hurry.

I was too heavy to get on top of her. Instead, I lay down beside her and tried to get her panties down.

'Take your shirt off,' she said.

'No need for that,' I said, using force to get them down over her knees, which for some reason she was pressing together. 'I'm fine as I am.'

'I want to see you,' she said.

'No need for that,' I grunted, pressing against her.

'Relax. I've got nothing against fat men,' she said.

Couldn't we just do it? Couldn't I just get my cock inside her?

'OK,' I said, undid the shirt and pulled it off.

She smoothed a hand over my belly, gripping my cock with the other.

'How do you want me?' she said.

What a fantastic question.

'On all fours,' I said.

'OK,' she said, turning round. As I got into position behind her, I saw us reflected in the mirror on the wall above the bed. Christ, is that me? I thought for a second, wriggling forward on my knees a bit so I could get close enough to stick the steel inside her. I tried not to look in the mirror, only my eyes kept going back to it as I pumped. I looked like some kind of animal with my big belly and flabby cheeks, and she looked like an animal too, getting fucked on all fours with her head lowered and her hair hanging down, but at the same time it felt so good, oh, it felt so good inside, that the man and the woman in the mirror could have been another couple entirely.

'You're so gorgeous,' I groaned. 'You're so good.'

Any second now and bang.

'You're so gorgeous,' I said again. 'You're so lovely.'

Aaaahhh.

I squirted for what felt like an age inside her before flopping down on my side.

She flipped onto her back with her cheek on the pillow and her eyes closed.

'Was it good?' she said. 'Was I good?'

'It was brilliant,' I said.

There was a silence.

'I didn't seen this coming,' she said after a bit. 'You won't tell anyone?'

'What?' I said.

'You won't tell anyone, will you?'

'What do you take me for?' I said. 'Who would I tell?'

She sat up, took a towel off the chair and wrapped it around her.

'Your friends?' she said on her way to the bathroom. I heard her turn the shower on. I got my underpants on and was buttoning my shirt when she poked her head round the door.

'You're not leaving, are you? You can't!'

'It's not even one o'clock yet,' I said. 'I can still get home before it gets too late.'

'I can't be on my own now,' she said. 'You can't do this to me.'

Oh Christ, now for the complications.

On the other hand, if I stayed, I could fuck her in the morning again before going to work. I couldn't do that if I went home.

'I wasn't sure you wanted me to,' I said. 'Of course I can stay.'

'Thanks,' she said.

Once she'd closed the door I sat down in the chair and checked my phone. No texts, no emails. The top story on all the news sites was the new star or whatever it was.

I'd forgotten all about it, with one thing and another.

I opened the text I'd sent to myself.

The New Star

An evening in August
as the sun sank
and spirits rose
I beheld the new star

It still worked.

It was good.

You can never be sure. Sometimes you get a moment's inspiration and it turns out rubbish.

I put the phone down on the low shelf above the bed, peeled my shirt off and got under the duvet. Should really have had a shower, I thought, stinking of cunt most likely, only it felt so good to be lying there, all my fatigue came creeping back, like a mudslide, increasing in velocity, until after only a few moments it swept me away into its obscurity.

When I woke up, the room was pitch-dark. On the shelf above my head, my phone was vibrating. I groped for it.

'What's that?' the artist woman said. She must have got back into bed without waking me up.

'Phone's ringing,' I said, and answered it.

It was Geir.

At half past three in the morning?

'Hello?' I said.

'I've got something for you,' he said. 'Come out to Svartediket now, right away.'

'What? What is it?'

'We've found the lads from the band.'

'Straight up?'

'Or rather, we've found three of them.'

'Are they dead?'

'I'll say. Murdered. Horrific, never seen anything like it. It looks like some kind of ritual. They've been butchered.'

'How do you mean, ritual?' I said, feeling around with my other hand until finding my shirt on the floor.

'They've been skinned.'

'So we've got a serial killer in Bergen?'

'Yes. Get here as soon as you can.'

'I haven't got the car.'

'Then get a taxi. You can't drive all the way out here anyway. Get him to drop you off at the waterworks, then follow the reservoir for a bit on the right. You'll find us easy enough. OK?'

'Why are you doing this for me?'

'Let's just say I feel sorry for you. Now, get a move on.'

He hung up. I got out of bed and put my shirt and trousers on in a hurry while the artist woman peered at me.

'What is it?' she said. 'Where are you going?'

'It's work. Emergency.'

'I thought you were arts and culture?'

'Not any more,' I said. I bent down to put my shoes on, grabbed my jacket and was out the door.

TURID

J ostein of course hadn't come back by quarter past seven and I had to get off to work. That was his problem, not mine, I thought, but still I waited as long as possible before switching the oven off, going into the bedroom and getting ready. It was boiling hot in there even with the window wide open. Outside, in the garden, everything was still. I stood looking at it for a minute. The grass on the slope of the lawn was parched and yellow, although I'd been watering it as much as I could all summer. It still pained my heart to see the stump by the fence where the chestnut had stood. How lovely it used to be in spring with its white flowers and thick foliage. But that was life. Even trees got sick and died. There was so much else that was good, I told myself, leaning forward to see the climbing roses that had come into bloom a few weeks before, their clusters of white flowers.

I wondered whether to close the window as I was leaving the house, but Ole would be here, and Jostein would be home as well before too long, and wouldn't like it if it was too hot in there.

The sound of my breathing filled the room, then my feet as they slid through the legs of my jeans. And from Ole's room next door came the incessant tapping of his fingers at the keyboard. I changed into a white bra and put on a white T-shirt. Stood in front of the wardrobe for a moment wondering if I should wear a thin jacket on top, the night would be cooler, but dismissed the idea. I'd be indoors, so it wouldn't matter.

I checked my phone to see if he'd sent another one of his excuses. He hadn't, and so I put it away in my bag along with my sunglasses and my inhaler. Then I knocked on Ole's door.

He was sitting with his back to the door in that big ergonomic office chair of his, in the same grey shorts and black T-shirt he'd had on all week.

'Everything all right, love?' I said.

He swivelled halfway round in the chair and looked up at me.

He was different, I could tell straight away. It was written all over him.

'Yes,' he said, and smiled. 'Now it is.'

Had something happened? What had happened?

'That's good,' I said. I didn't know what else to say. Normally he'd have given a sigh and said, 'Yes, Mum.' Or else he'd be more riled and ask why I wanted to know, not even bothering to turn round then, sick of me asking.

'Yes,' he said. 'Everything's fine.'

Could he have met someone?

But how could he when he never went out?

And what girl would be interested in someone who always had the same shorts on? And with such greasy hair?

'All right, then, Ole,' I said. 'I'm off to work now. Your dad'll be home soon.'

'OK,' he said. 'Have a nice time.'

'Thanks,' I said. 'Give me a ring if you need to.'

'OK.'

At the bottom of the stairs I had to stop to get my breath back. It was getting bad now; it used to be only when I went *up* the stairs that my windpipe would tighten like that.

It was like having to breathe through a straw.

And it affected my head as well, the only thing I could think about was everything I couldn't do. It was like all my power had run through my fingers.

Not that I had any power. But all the things I was used to doing.

The air shimmered above the tarmac as I stepped outside. Two sparrows sat pecking at an apple each in the apple tree, completely unperturbed by the shiny strips I'd hung up in the branches to keep them away and which glittered in the sunlight. I waved my arms at them and they fluttered off. I knew it was no use, they'd only come back again the minute I was gone, but it gave me a little feeling of satisfaction nonetheless.

I went to the car and dipped a hand into my bag for the key.

But where was it?

I rummaged through the contents with both hands. Glasses cases, glasses, scarves, house keys, paracetamol, chewing gum, inhaler refills, inhaler, all sorts, only no car key.

Where had I put it?

I went up to the house again, a bit too quickly, and had to pause for breath on the top step. I went inside and looked on the table in the living room, the table in the kitchen, the bedside table in the bedroom. But no key anywhere.

It was already half past seven. I'd still be on time if only I could leave in the next couple of minutes.

'Ole?' I called out.

'What?' he called back from his room.

'Come here a minute.'

I heard him open his door.

'Where are you?' he said.

'In here,' I said. 'I need your help. I can't find the car key.'

He appeared in the doorway. I sat down on the chair.

'Mum's a bit short of breath,' I said.

'And Mum can't find the car key?' he said. 'Is Mum helpless?'

'That'll do,' I said. 'I don't know where that came from.'

'Where what came from?'

'Saying "Mum" like that.'

'No, it was a bit weird,' he said. 'But I'll find the key. You have a sit-down.'

He searched where I'd already been, but I didn't say so. I could have missed it, and besides it was good to sit down.

'Nope,' he said.

Why was he in such a good mood all of a sudden?

'Has something happened?' I said.

He stopped and looked at me.

'No,' he said. 'What would that be?'

'I don't know,' I said. 'You seem different, that's all.'

'Happier?'

'Yes.'

He stared out at the garden.

'Does it worry you, me being a bit happier?' he said.

'Don't be so silly. Of course not.'

It was odd how unlike his father he was. So sensitive, and so delicate.

His features were different too, and his whole physique.

Jostein had been a handsome man. I could still see it in his face, his bright blue eyes. The powerful, compact body he used to have had gone fat, but there was still nothing slack about him, not like Ole with his rounded shoulders and soft, formless features.

As a baby he'd been irresistible.

As a child shy and physically awkward.

He would lose the puppy fat if only he'd start getting out a bit, get some sun on him, find himself some friends who could spur him on, encourage him to pull himself together, start training perhaps, and start dressing properly . . .

A good attitude was half the battle.

'Found it!' he called out from the bathroom.

I got to my feet.

'Oh, good,' I said. 'Thank you, love. Do I get a cuddle before I go?'

'Does Mum want a cuddle?' he said as he came up to me.

I smiled.

'I told you I didn't know why I said that. It was how we talked when you were little, that's all.'

He handed me the key.

'Thanks,' I said.

Without a word he put his arms around me. I put my cheek to his chest.

'OK, Mum,' he said, and stepped away. 'You'd best be off.'

'Text me when you go to bed,' I said. 'So I can say goodnight.'

'Will do,' he said, and went back to his room, while I went outside to the car I'd sensibly left in the shade under the cherry tree when I'd come back from the shop that afternoon, so the temperature inside wouldn't be quite as unbearable.

There was a waft of barbecue and I glanced over the hedge into next door, where Jensen was standing on the patio with his back to me, trying to make himself useful, his hands in a pair of barbecue gloves. He was on his own there and my eye ran through the garden until I saw his wife crouched in a pair of red shorts in front of one of their many flower beds, brandishing a pair of pruning shears.

How idyllic.

I got in the car, started the engine and turned out onto the road, pulling away past our row of houses and gardens, then out onto the main road. It was twenty to now, so I'd be two minutes late. Nothing anyone could pull me up for.

Apart from Berit.

She'd pull me up for it. She collected other people's errors. And she was always on my back.

Criticising a person was the same as putting yourself above them, telling them you're better than they are. There was no other way of looking at it.

Being in charge of the unit meant she was within her rights. But it wasn't exactly beneficial to the working atmosphere. And going on years of service I was her senior by far.

Anyway, you didn't have to be a brain surgeon to work with the intellectually disabled.

I sighed without realising until I heard the sound it made, which bordered on a groan.

When I was at home I managed to shut out all thought of work, if not a hundred per cent, then at least eighty. But as soon as I was in the car on my way there it all came pouring in.

Every day, I dreaded it. It hadn't always been like that, but now it was.

And then there was Ole.

It seemed like it was never going to stop with Ole.

What had that look been in his eyes?

What had I seen there?

Perhaps he'd decided something and everything appeared brighter to him now? I'd told him so many times that going to university in Oslo wasn't everything. That it might make better sense to start at the university here. He could even live at home then, if that was what he wanted.

But that was just the problem. He had no life of his own. Having to stand on our own two feet sharpens us. It hones us. It gives us an outside, instead of just an inside.

I visualised his face. His kind eyes.

There was nothing wrong with him. He was good all the way through.

Why wasn't that enough?

The Shell station appeared ahead of me. I glanced automatically at the petrol gauge. Three-quarters full.

And then I thought about cigarettes.

What a treat it would be to sit on the veranda and have a smoke tonight.

Just the one.

But that would be it then. I knew it would. One cigarette would be enough to get me started all over again.

Anyway, the petrol station was behind me now and I turned onto the old main road where unbelievably there were still a couple of small farms with sheep and cows before the new housing developments began, the new church without a steeple, which everyone hated apart from the people who'd commissioned it, who thought it was fantastic, so very modern.

It looked about as inviting as a deep freeze, if you asked me.

Anyway, God wasn't modern.

It was those lunatic devil worshippers who'd burned the old church down. Everyone knew about it as soon as it happened. The news spread like ripples in a pond. The church is on fire, the church is on fire. It had never occurred to me until then that people actually cared about the church. Or that I did. It wasn't just a building, as everyone had thought.

Jostein had managed to get an interview with one of the ones who was behind it, a young man they called Heksa. The police went and picked him up straight away and he ended up inside. Jostein had always held that he'd never had anything to do with it. But there were rumours, and not long after they moved him over to arts and culture. Restructuring, was the reason they'd given.

People could say what they liked about Jostein, but he was a very good crime reporter, one of the best even. They took that away from him.

And now he was clinging to what he had.

I'd have thought he had more pride, to be honest.

Now he went looking for excitement elsewhere.

He was like a kid, wanting adventure.

Only not with me.

I came round the bend where the landscape suddenly dropped away towards the fjord, and saw the rooftops of the tall, rectangular buildings at the perimeter of the grounds standing out red in all the green.

My chest tightened.

I breathed in slowly and imagined a gentle breeze passing over a wide meadow. Air streaming freely through my throat, streaming freely into my lungs.

Streaming freely.

And out again, streaming freely.

After the bus stop I turned onto the narrow drive that wound its way through the trees of the hospital grounds. Two carers I didn't know came pushing a couple of residents in wheelchairs. Behind them came another two residents. They stopped when they saw the car, as they'd learned when they were children; it was etched into them.

I lifted my hand in a wave and they stared with open mouths.

The woods behind the buildings were bathed in light. The sun twinkled in the rows of windows as I passed. There were only four units left now, so a number of the buildings stood empty.

The clock above the entrance of the administration building said eight o'clock exactly.

Parking outside A2 and turning off the engine, I heard distant cries from inside, like the bellowing of a bull. I picked up my bag and opened the car door. At that moment, my phone pinged. I sat in the seat with my feet resting on the ground outside while I found it. It was Jostein.

Dragging out a bit, sitting with a bunch from work.

'You don't say,' I said out loud to myself. 'What a surprise.'

OK, I texted back.

He was probably well oiled already, and it was only eight o'clock.

Just remember you've got to get up tomorrow as well, I typed.

I regretted it straight away. I wasn't his mother.

Sure enough.

Yes, boss, he wrote back.

I looked up at the windows on the first floor. All were wide open. The veranda door of the duty room was too. It must have been sweltering in there all day.

No faces to be seen.

I felt like talking to him. He'd been in a good mood earlier in the day, and I wanted to tell him about Ole. But those two minutes would soon be ten. And if he was with people from work he wouldn't want to talk anyway, especially not if he was getting drunk. He wouldn't be serious then. Or else he would opine, rather than talk.

When I had him to myself, he was different.

Occasionally, at least.

When did the two of us last go out? I texted.

You work nights, came his prompt reply.

Not every night, I typed.

Dinner at Klosteret Saturday then? he wrote then.

I sent him a smiley in reply, put the phone back in my bag and made my way slowly to the entrance. But still there was a tightness in my chest. It was like there was a barrier in the way, blocking the passage of air. And if the heart started pumping hard then, the body would cry out for oxygen and everything tightened. But I couldn't breathe deeply enough to let the air come streaming into my lungs and give them what they craved. I was forced to take short, quick breaths that didn't help, and my whole body would hurt and cry out until my pulse's violent and unreasonable demands for more air died away.

So I had to walk slowly, take things easy.

I took my sunglasses off and stood without moving for a moment before keying in my code and pushing the buzzing door open.

The corridor was empty and still. They must have gone out somewhere, I said to myself as I reached the duty room. The door was locked, and I unlocked it. Two flies rose up from the sofa as I put my bag down. They buzzed about in the air. I poured a coffee from the big dispenser. I could see it wasn't steaming and taking a sip discovered it was tepid and bitter. It would have to do. I sat down on the sofa, my eyes following the flies for a moment as they flew this way and that, then I looked out through the open door at the building across the sports field, the woods behind it.

Footsteps sounded in the corridor.

Berit came in without noticing me, went over to the desk in the corner and picked up the green report book.

'Hi,' I said.

'Oh, hi,' she said. 'Are *you* here now?'

She went out again.

The cow.

The absolute cow.

I swallowed a mouthful of coffee and put the cup down. Got to my feet, only to think better of it. I didn't have to prove anything to her, so I sat down again.

If she could look straight through me, I could look straight through her.

She was only in her thirties. But she was more like an old woman. Small and grey and bony, with pointy little teeth that made her look like a mouse.

Gnawing away at everyone and everything.

So efficient. And so officious.

But she worked here. Meaning she couldn't be that brilliant. No one who had a choice would work here.

One of the flies landed on my knee. I sat quite still and watched it crawl about for a bit. When it paused and raised its forelegs to its head, a bit like a cat washing itself, I lifted a hand cautiously towards it. My dad had taught me the method when I was little. If the movement was slow enough, the fly wouldn't see it. Once my hand was just above it, I held still for a few seconds and then struck as hard as I could.

The fly was squashed and some yellow matter came out. I picked it up by one of its thin legs and dropped it in the bin.

Dad used to say too that flies were the dead. That was why there were so many of them, and why they stayed close to us in our homes. They were dead souls. I'd never known whether he meant it or not. But ever since the first time he said so I hadn't been able to look at a fly without thinking about it.

No.

Best get started.

I went out onto the ward. The corridors and rooms were completely quiet. Behind the glass wall of her office, Berit stood dishing out their medication into their dispensers.

Thank goodness she'd soon be going home.

As long as she didn't lock the door after her.

But why would she do that? I asked myself as I went into the kitchen. She'd never done so before.

There were some flies buzzing about the kitchen too. I counted at least five, likely there were more. They had a habit of settling on dark surfaces where they couldn't be seen as easily.

It was because the building was so close to the woods that there were so many of them.

I turned round. Berit was looking at me from her office across the dining area.

Not wanting to give the bitch a chance to criticise me, I bent down and began to unload the dishwasher that was full after their hot meal.

'Perhaps you could give the residents your attention first, before the dishes?' Berit said behind me. She'd left her office and stood staring at me from the dining area.

I sighed and closed the door of the machine.

'The dinner things are meant to be put away before the night shift turns in,' I said.

'There's no rule,' she said, and went back to her office again.

I was going to say I thought they were all out, only I remembered the cries I'd heard before. Georg was here, of course.

I knocked on his door and went in.

He was lying in bed, staring up at the ceiling while making little noises. Spit dribbled from the corner of his mouth. He turned his head to look at me and smiled.

There was a dreadful smell. Man-muck, as they called it up north, in a room hot with sun.

'Gaaaaa!' he said.

'Hi, Georg,' I said, stepping towards him and ruffling his hair. 'Shall we give you a change?'

'Gaaa, gaaa, gaaa.'

I opened the window first. The air outside was just as hot. I took a nappy and a packet of wet wipes from the cupboard, and then a towel.

Leaving him alone in his room on a day like this, what were they thinking? He was only parked with us for a few weeks until his local authority had a flat ready for him, but still. Surely they could have found a place for him where there were others like him, so he wouldn't have to be left behind just because the bouncers, as we called them, couldn't be bothered taking him out with them.

I pulled the cover aside and tried not to breathe through my nose. He was wearing a pair of green shorts and a white singlet. His legs were round and soft, and almost as white as the sheet. They were completely dead, they just lay there as I pulled his shorts off him, heavy as logs.

There was a big scar down one of his thighs. Someone had once left him too near a wood burner, so I'd heard. Left him there to get burned. And he hadn't moved, or even made a sound.

I undid the sticky fasteners of his nappy and opened it. His mushy excrement was smeared over his hairy buttocks. I swallowed and began to wipe. His scrotum was covered in it too, and the inside of his thighs.

I dropped the wet wipes one by one into the soiled nappy as I used them up.

'You should really have a shower,' I said. 'But it'll have to wait until the morning. Is that all right?'

I put my lower arm under his thighs and lifted them up slightly in order to put the clean nappy on him.

His penis lay like a small dead animal between his legs.

'Nice and clean now, Georg,' I said. 'How's that for you?'

He'd just lain there during the whole process, staring at the ceiling.

I pulled his shorts up again, folded the soiled nappy and took it with me to the toilet where I put it in the bin before washing my hands thoroughly.

As I stood there, a white minibus came up the drive. It swung round the corner and stopped. I heard shouts and excited voices, the short swish of the sliding door in its rail, the thud as it slammed shut again.

All was quiet for a moment, and then came the bedlam as they spilled into the ward.

I closed the gate into the kitchen area before getting on with my work. The residents were seen to their rooms and the noise died down.

I stood with a spiky handful of cutlery, putting it away piece by piece in the drawer where it belonged, when I heard Torgeir dragging himself along the corridor. His legs were useless, thin and withered below the knees, and his feet pointed the wrong way, so when he was indoors he moved about by swinging himself along on his arms.

Whish, whish, whish.

He stopped outside the gate and looked up at me.

'Hi, Torgeir,' I said.

His face could have belonged to almost any male in his forties. His forehead and nose were red from the sun, and a shadow of stubble had already darkened his cheeks even though he'd been shaved that morning.

But appearances deceived. He couldn't talk, and his mind was stalled.

I disliked him intensely.

He didn't like me either.

'Have you had a nice day?' I said.

He hissed as he breathed, and glared at me.

Perhaps because he sensed that my interest wasn't heartfelt.

Did he hate me?

It certainly seemed like it.

His eyes were fixed on me.

'Do you want some coffee?' I said.

His breathing stopped.

I took a mug from the cupboard and filled it halfway with coffee from the pot I'd just made.

He began to breathe again.

Then I got a carton of milk out and poured until the mug was full.

'There we go,' I said as I handed it to him over the gate. He reached up and gripped it. His eyes closed blissfully.

He never seemed to have more than a single thought at any one time.

If he even had thoughts, and not just urges.

He gulped the coffee down in one.

Beggingly, he held the mug out towards me.

On the other side of the corridor, Berit stood up and locked the medicine cabinet.

I took the mug from his hand and only then said no, so that he couldn't hurl it against the wall.

'You can't have any more,' I said. 'You know that. You won't be able to sleep.'

Berit closed the office door behind her. I looked up at the clock on the wall. Another half-hour and she'd be on her way home.

Torgeir didn't move, but watched me as I put away the last of the things from the dishwasher. A fly settled on his head. It wandered about a bit without bothering him. Down his temple and onto his cheek, underneath his eye it crawled. Then someone turned the TV on in the TV room and Torgeir spun round and headed towards it.

I poured myself a coffee. I liked being in the kitchen best, behind the gate, at least when they were awake. So I always took my time there.

I got the big serving tray out and the sandwich things. The cheese I'd already sliced, saveloy, liver paste, salami, cheese spread with bacon. I always sliced some cucumber and tomato as well, to make it a bit nicer for them, but they never touched either. On Saturday nights they had pizza, and on Sunday mornings I boiled them some eggs.

Three of them couldn't butter their bread themselves, so I did it for them. They were Torgeir, Olav and Kenneth. All three could be violent.

Olav had bitten me one of the first days I'd been on the ward. I was shaving him as he sat in the bath, and there was something I didn't do right, which made him howl. He gripped my arm and sank his teeth in until he drew blood. One of the male carers had come running and dealt with him.

They weren't really carers at all, but worked on the ward because they were big and strong and could handle violent behaviour. Most of them were bouncers on the side.

I'd had to have a tetanus injection. After that, I asked to go on nights. I didn't tell them I was afraid, but I think they understood.

The bouncers weren't afraid. They messed about and played games with them, gave them big hugs, were severe when necessary, but laughed a lot. The residents liked them, they felt secure when they were around, and taken care of.

Even Kenneth. His head was empty. He wandered about the ward eating whatever he came across. Even the fluff on the floor he'd put in his mouth, and when he'd still had hair he would pull out great tufts and eat them. Now his scalp was kept shaven. I'd seen him eat an onion raw, as if it were an apple, I'd forgotten to close the gate and there he was at the fridge, munching away as the tears ran down his cheeks. He was slim and athletic, and looked like a sportsman. Once, he'd been left behind at a petrol station and had been found several kilometres away, wading across a field in deep snow, heading towards the forest. They told me when I started in the job that he would walk until he dropped. Not because he wanted to get away, but because once he got going he couldn't stop.

When he was sad, he banged his head against the wall. One time, he managed to crack his head open before they got to him. And if he worked himself into a rage, it took three grown men to deal with him.

The strangest part was he was so handsome.

He wasn't bothered about me, but I was afraid of him anyway.

But it was Olav I was most scared of. He weighed people up. Sometimes when he saw me he'd bare his teeth.

The nights were no problem, they were medicated then and wouldn't wake until morning when the day shift came in. So in that way the job was all right.

I put the kettle on before carrying the plates, mugs and cutlery over to the dining table. They were all made of plastic and had been in use for so long their colours were dulled, their surfaces rough.

As I opened the fridge for the milk and juice, Karl Frode appeared from his room. He looked bedraggled, his curly hair was in disarray, there were stains on his sweater and the socks on his feet were coming off.

'Good evening, Turid,' he said mechanically, as if repeating a formula he'd learned. He never looked at anyone he spoke to, including me.

'Good evening, Karl Frode,' I said. 'Are you hungry?'

'Yes, I'm hungry,' he said, pulling out his chair and sitting down at the table.

I put the cartons out in the middle.

'Have you had fun today?' I said.

'Yes,' he said.

'What have you been up to?' I said, going back into the kitchen area to get the tray with the sandwich things.

'Don't pester me,' he said.

'I won't,' I said, bringing the tray to the table. 'I promise not to pester.'

'Nice weather today,' he said.

'Yes,' I said, 'it's been lovely. Have you been outside?'

He slammed his hand down hard on the table.

'You weren't to pester!' he said, his voice rising several octaves.

'I won't pester,' I said. 'Do you want us to be quiet?'

'Yes,' he said.

'All right,' I said, unlocking the drawer where the sharp knives were kept, before cutting the bread and arranging the slices in the big bread basket.

'Butter,' he said when I put the basket on the table.

'You're right, I forgot the butter,' I said. 'Thank you, Karl Frode.'

He smiled and stared at the table.

'Butter!' he said. 'Butter! Butter!'

'Butter coming up,' I said.

Karl Frode could be dangerous too. If he flew into a rage, he could throw the furniture about and smash up everything in his path. But he did so only rarely, and it hadn't happened at all while I'd been there. The fact that he could talk made him seem less threatening too, in a way.

A student who'd worked with us a few weeks earlier that summer had said that Karl Frode looked like a philosopher. Vidgenstein, I think his name was. Something like that. He'd shown me a photo on his phone, and he really was the spitting image. The same curly hair, the same round, staring eyes, the same long face and downturned mouth. Karl Frode was slightly fuller in the cheek, but apart from that they were as alike as twins.

He'd lived at the hospital nearly all his life. After the days when they used to strap them down at night, he'd developed a habit of wearing his trouser belt as tight as possible. Another twisted thing was his masturbation. He could only do it standing in the bushes outside the building while staring up at the windows. And what he saw in the windows could only be the reflections of clouds. They'd take him out at various times when there wasn't much risk of him causing offence and would wait round the corner, smoking with their backs turned while he stood with his trousers down having a wank. It was harmless, but still, no one ever mentioned it.

I put the margarine down in front of him.

'Ha ha. Ha ha,' he said.

'What is it, Karl Frode?'

'That's not butter, it's margarine,' he said.

'Yes, you're right,' I said. 'But we still call it butter, don't we?'

He sat without moving, staring at the table. A fly settled on the edge of the margarine. Another was crawling on the cheese, conspicuous against its yellow colour.

I waved them away. Karl Frode didn't seem to even register the movement, but kept staring. When he was in a good mood, he would lean back and cross his feet, prattling away and laughing, occasionally getting so excited he would lose control of himself and start to stutter, spit spraying from his mouth.

I went into the TV room and told them their tea was ready. Kenneth was sitting on the lap of one of the carers, rubbing his head against his chest like a baby. Olav was almost lying down in his chair, his hands dangling over the armrests. The other carer, Gunnar, sat in a chair next to him looking at his phone.

They got to their feet and I carried on to the duty room. Torgeir was sitting in the corridor outside the open door, staring into the room like a dog waiting for a treat.

'Tea's ready,' I said to Berit, who was sitting on the sofa writing in the report book on her knee.

'I've noted down that you were fifteen minutes late again today,' she said, and looked up at me.

'I see,' I said.

Wild horses wouldn't make me apologise.

She stood up.

'Everyone was out anyway,' I said.

'But you couldn't have known that,' she said, stepping past me.

Then Gunnar appeared.

'Give me a hand with Georg, will you?' he said.

I helped get him into his wheelchair, which Gunnar then wheeled in and positioned at the end of the table. I tied a bib under Georg's chin and he grinned. He was in a good mood.

Fortunately, Berit never had tea with us when she had the afternoon shift. After dispensing their medication, she went and got her bag from the office, said goodbye to the residents and carers at the table, and went off busily down the corridor. Not long after, I heard her start her car outside, and shortly after that the sound of its engine was gone.

The residents tucked into their sandwiches and gulped down their juice and milk. I fed Georg, while Gunnar and Hans watched the others with apathy.

They took me for granted. I might just as well have been a chair or a curtain.

'Where did you go this afternoon, anyway?' I said.

'Hellevangen,' said Hans. 'They had hot dogs and ice cream. It was like Christmas, wasn't it, Kenneth?'

He put his strong arm around Kenneth and gave him a shake. Kenneth reached out for some more bread and shoved half a slice into his mouth. It was as if he was in a different room from us.

'Sounds like a nice time,' I said.

'Tea,' said Karl Frode.

'Oh, yes,' I said. 'I forgot the tea.'

I went into the kitchen and switched the kettle on again.

Outside, the sun was going down. The trees on top of the hill were a reddish glow. A single pine, on its own on a small outcrop, looked like it was on fire. The sky was still blue, but lower down, above the grass and between the trees, the colours were dwindling.

The air from the open window was warm and full of dry smells.

As I turned round, Karl Frode was staring at me.

'The Deevel's out there,' he said.

Gunnar and Hans laughed.

'You and that Deevel,' said Gunnar.

He didn't look at them. He was looking at me.

'The Deevel's out there now,' he said, and pointed at the window.

I took four plastic mugs from the cupboard and put a tea bag in each. As I began to pour the boiling water, he got to his feet.

'Shut the window!' he shouted. 'Shut the window!'

'All right, Karl Frode, settle down,' said Gunnar.

'Shut the window, woman!' he almost screamed, his arm outstretched as he came towards me.

My heart pounded in my chest.

All of a sudden, I couldn't breathe.

Gunnar got to his feet.

'Stop, Karl Frode,' he said.

But Karl Frode didn't stop, and Gunnar darted after him, threw his arms around him and held him tight.

'All right, Karl Frode,' he said. 'Relax now. Settle down.'

But Karl Frode was having none of it, shouting and writhing in Gunnar's arms.

'The Deevel's coming!'

I gripped the edge of the work surface with both hands as I heaved for air.

Behind us, Torgeir dashed his plate to the floor, followed by his mug. Hans got to his feet. Torgeir launched himself from his chair, overturning it in the process and hurtling off down the corridor at top speed in the direction of the TV room. Hans ran after him. Kenneth began to howl. Olav glared at me and bared his teeth.

'The Deevel's there!' Karl Frode shouted again, spitting and spluttering, twisting to escape from Gunnar's grip.

'If you could just close that window,' Gunnar said to me firmly. 'Just close it.'

I turned round. The window seemed so very far away. Everything was a mist.

'Do it now!' Gunnar said.

I staggered a few steps towards it, reached out too early and almost lost my balance, but somehow managed to close it. And then, the deepest of breaths: there was nothing there, no barrier in the way, no cord tightening around my lungs.

'There, you see, Karl Frode,' said Gunnar. 'The window's closed. The Deevel can't get in now.'

Karl Frode settled immediately.

Gunnar looked at Olav and Kenneth.

'You guys sit there nice and quietly, OK?'

And he took Karl Frode by the hand and led him to his room.

Olav was still glaring at me. I went over and closed the gate. In the TV room, Hans raised his voice.

How terrible a place it was.

I looked at the clock. Hans and Gunnar were due off in forty minutes, the same time as my night-shift colleague arrived. But they were so unsettled that night. If it carried on, we wouldn't be able to cope on our own.

Should I ask one of them to stay until they went to sleep?

Or call in an extra hand?

Kenneth howled, a low monotone, the way he did when he was dissatisfied with something.

Thankfully, Gunnar came back.

'Maybe they could have that tea now?'

I took the tea bags out and dropped them in the bin, added milk almost to the brim of each of their mugs and carried two of them over to the table. Then I sat down and went back to feeding Georg, who seemed quite unperturbed by all the commotion.

I was more relaxed now that my breathing had settled. Only my legs were still a bit wobbly.

'What do you say, Olav, a nice cup of tea?' said Gunnar. 'Calm the nerves?'

Olav downed the lukewarm tea in one. Kenneth stared at his own mug, then tipped it over, spilling the contents all over the table.

'All right, Kenneth, that'll do,' said Gunnar. 'There's no need to touch it, if you don't want it.'

I fetched some kitchen roll and soaked up the mess while Gunnar took Olav and Kenneth into the TV room and Hans wheeled Georg back to his room. I began to clear the table, putting the food back in the fridge and the mugs and plates in the dishwasher. When I went to the laundry room after that, I saw Gunnar take Kenneth to his room.

Apparently, everyone was settled.

So the coast was clear.

I went back through the corridor. Pausing outside Berit's office, I made sure no one saw me before opening the door and going inside. The medicine cabinet was locked. She kept the key in the top drawer of the desk, and the key to that drawer on the top shelf next to her ring binders.

I took it and unlocked the drawer.

But the key wasn't there.

What?

So where *was* it?

Carefully, so as not to leave a sign, I lifted everything inside the drawer in case the key had somehow slid underneath.

But no.

Shit, shit, shit.

I checked the other drawers as swiftly as I could.

Nothing.

I could feel my pulse throbbing in my neck, like someone jabbing an index finger.

I couldn't spend much more time in there.

I locked the drawer and put the key back on the shelf, slipping out into the corridor just as Gunnar emerged from Kenneth's room.

'Have you seen the report book?' I said in case he wondered what I'd been doing.

But I didn't seem to have awakened any suspicion.

'Could be in the duty room,' he said.

'I hope so,' I said, stepping past him.

'It might be an idea to close all the other windows too,' he said as I walked away. 'Before our friend notices.'

Why can't you do it? I thought to myself, but said nothing.

I went into the laundry room again, unloaded the tumble dryer and dumped the dry clothes in a basket, took the wet ones out of the washing machine and put them in the dryer, then switched it on before loading the washing machine with more dirty laundry, putting a squishy pod of detergent in and starting the cycle.

I looked out of the narrow window. The sky above the hill was flaming red and yellow. The trees were dark.

Someone must have frightened him with stories about the Devil when he was little.

Or the Deevel, as he called it.

Where could she have put that key?

Surely she hadn't cottoned on? Had she found out and taken it home with her?

No, she would have reported it, and I'd have been summoned.

I went into the duty room and sat down on the sofa, then got my phone out of my bag. Nothing from Ole. Or Jostein.

I texted Ole.

Hello, love! I typed. *Hope all's well at home. Text me or phone before you go to bed. Thinking about you. Mum.*

Now that it looked like I wasn't going to get hold of any pills, the unrest I'd started to feel got worse. It was all I could think about as I sat there.

The door at the end of the corridor opened. That would be Sølve.

I looked at the time.

Ten minutes early, as always.

Maybe she hadn't locked the cabinet!

I hadn't checked.

Please let it be true! I said to myself as Sølve came in.

'Hi,' he said, bending his head slightly to take off the messenger bag he was wearing across his chest.

'Hi,' I said.

He put the bag down on the sofa, removed the bike clips from his trouser legs, opened the bag and put them inside as he let out a deep sigh.

'Anything new?' he said, looking at me for the first time since he came in.

'They were a bit unruly at tea.'

'Oh?'

'Karl Frode thought the Devil was in the woods.'

'The Deevel, you mean. Nothing new there. Are they settled now?'

'I think so,' I said.

Sølve was in his early thirties. Dark hair and brown eyes, a narrow face with a scraggle of beard. He could have been attractive if he wasn't so intense and always feeling sorry for himself. The first time we worked a shift together he told me all sorts of private things about himself and his wife, things I didn't want to know. Things about people he'd worked with too. Everyone was against Sølve, so it seemed.

I imagined he confided in me thinking I didn't pose a threat to him. I hated it, hated his incessant moaning, it made me physically sick. While he, no doubt, thought his confidences were a gift he was giving me.

'I'll make a quick round, then,' I said, and got to my feet.

'You do that,' he said. 'Have the bodybuilders gone yet?'

I already had my back to him and pretended not to have heard.

The chances of her having forgotten to lock the cabinet were minimal, but as long as it was a possibility I couldn't leave it untried.

I felt a warmth in my chest just thinking about it.

Both carers were out of sight as I opened the door of the office and went inside.

It was locked. Of course it was.

She'd probably just put it down somewhere without thinking.

I paused in the middle of the room and looked around me.

Nothing.

Perhaps it had been on top of an envelope or something else she'd thrown out, I thought, and rummaged quickly through the waste-paper basket.

But no.

The bitch had taken the key home with her.

On the other side of the window, Sølve came into view. He went into the kitchen without seeing me. I stepped out of the office and closed the door behind me, as if there was nothing untoward about it.

'There's fresh coffee in the Thermos,' I said.

'Oh, thanks,' he said.

In the duty room, Gunnar sat hunched over the report book making an entry, while Hans was standing outside on the veranda gazing out. The white bark of the birch trees in the woods shimmered faintly in the fading light of the dusk.

'Right,' said Gunnar, and stood up. 'Have a good shift, then.'

'Thanks,' I said.

He put his leather jacket on and picked up his helmet from the table in the corner.

'Any sign of the Deevel out there?' he said.

Hans turned round.

'No,' he said with a laugh. 'He must be there somewhere, though, if Karl Frode says so!'

They left together. Shortly afterwards I heard Gunnar start up his motorbike. The evening was so still that the noise it made didn't die away until he was somewhere up on the main road.

I checked my mobile. Not a word from Ole.

I phoned him.

Why wasn't he answering?

Maybe he'd already gone to bed, I thought. Or maybe he'd run out of battery.

I put the phone back in my bag and went out onto the ward. All the residents were now in their rooms. If I looked in on them to see if they were asleep, I ran the risk of waking them up, so normally I left them in peace.

Sølve was sitting in the TV room watching TV, his mug balanced on the armrest.

My throat was dry. I went to the kitchen and drank a glass of water.

The skin of my upper arms stuck to the skin beneath my armpits and I lifted my elbows for ventilation.

My brow was sticky too.

Outside, the sun had gone down. The pine that shortly before had looked almost like it was ablaze on its rocky outcrop had receded into darkness.

I cupped my hand under the tap and splashed my forehead and cheeks, then dabbed myself dry with a paper towel.

An owl hooted.

Where could she have put that bloody key?

A single Sobril was all I asked for.

I went into the office again. There was still a tiny chance the medicine cabinet wasn't locked at all and was only jammed, so I stuck my fingernail in the crack of the cabinet door and tried to work it open.

When I couldn't, I started looking for the key in places less logical than before. Inside ring binders, underneath piles of papers.

I felt like crying.

It was such a small thing to ask. Such a very small thing to ask.

On my way back to the duty room it struck me there was another medicine cabinet downstairs on the ground floor. What routines might they have there? I wondered. For all I knew, it could have been left unlocked. Or the key could be lying in a drawer for anyone to take.

I had to think of a pretext.

It didn't have to be much. Soap powder for the washing machine, milk, coffee.

Suddenly, everything looked brighter.

Sølve was still in his chair with his mug on the armrest.

Had he fallen asleep?

If he had, I wasn't going to wake him.

I switched the light off in the duty room and went out onto the veranda, where I sat down on one of the two chairs there.

A thick darkness had descended among the trees in the woods. But above their crowns, a faint ray of light stretched away across the sky.

The moon must have risen on the other side.

It was so completely still out there.

If I asked the downstairs night shift for soap powder, they'd only go and get me some. So I'd have to go in without making myself known, and hope I wasn't seen. If they saw me, I'd have to say what I was doing there. It would be a bit odd just walking in without a word, but it wouldn't be suspicious, surely?

I breathed deeply, slowly.

A movement against the sky made me turn my head.

An enormous bird came gliding towards the woods. It was barely visible in the darkness.

What could it be?

A heron or something?

And then it was gone, vanished into the dark just above the trees.

Another came sailing by, closer this time. It flapped its wings, a leathery, creaking sound. As it passed through the faint light from the building, it turned its head.

A stab of terror went through me.

It was a small human.

The face of a child looked at me.

Then, as it dissolved into the darkness to disappear like the first, I realised I'd been fooled, that of course it was just a trick of light and shade.

But how dreadful it had been!

The head had indeed seemed human, but there had been wings and feathers, and long, thin legs.

How big could a heron be, anyway? Or a stork?

They were big birds.

I stared up at the sky, but there were no more to be seen.

If only I had a cigarette.

And then I thought about Ole.

Maybe he'd answered by now.

I went and got my phone.

Nothing.

I pressed his number as I sat down again.

Come on, love, answer.

I let it ring until the voicemail kicked in. I rang again, and again after that.

And then I sat for a moment, staring into the darkness.

Something was wrong. I knew it. I was his mother.

He never ran out of battery. Not when he was at home, anyway.

And he wouldn't have switched it off, surely?

Or would he?

But why?

I called Jostein.

'What's up?' he said.

He was drunk.

'Where are you?' I said.

'Why do you want to know?' he said.

I hesitated a few seconds, knowing he was going to make light of it.

'Ole's not answering his phone,' I said.

He sighed.

'I tried earlier on,' he said. 'He didn't answer, of course. He just doesn't want to talk to us.'

'So you're not at home,' I said.

'On my way to the bus now, as it happens. Have you seen the new star?'

'What do you mean?'

'A great big new star, just appeared in the sky.'

'No, I've not seen it.'

'Well, you should.'

'Give me a ring when you get in,' I said. 'I'm a bit worried.'

'Don't be, there's nothing to be worried about. He's either gaming or gone to sleep.'

'I hope you're right,' I said. 'Bye.'

I got up, put the phone in my pocket and went inside to the ward. I needed that medication, now.

But first I really did have to make sure they were asleep.

Cautiously, I opened the door of Olav's room. He was lying on his back in bed, fast asleep with his mouth open, almost like any other middle-aged man. On the wall was a photograph of him as a child together with his parents. I knew he hadn't seen them in twenty years.

Kenneth was asleep with his back to the door, his cheek resting on his arm, the scars on his scalp quite visible against the white linen.

Karl Frode was sound asleep too, snoring peacefully on his back, his cheeks saggy in repose.

As I closed his door again, Sølve came out from the TV room.

'Everything all right?' he said.

I nodded.

'Just checking,' I said.

'I'll start on the cleaning in a minute,' he said. 'Need some more coffee first, though. You having any?'

'No, thanks,' I said, sidestepping him on my way to the room at the end of the corridor, which was Torgeir's. He had nothing in there, no furniture, no pictures, no decoration of any kind, just a blue mattress on the floor. He didn't even have any proper bedding, but slept in his clothes with a blanket over him.

He tore everything to pieces.

There was no door to his room either, he wouldn't have been able to open it, so instead they'd built a partition to provide him with some form of privacy.

I heard the heaving sound of him breathing inside. He often hyperventilated, but never when he was asleep.

When I went in, he was crouched in a corner, masturbating. He was naked. His penis was very big and pointed up diagonally from between his legs, his hand moving up and down.

He looked at me with wide, hateful eyes, and his breathing became a hiss.

I turned away quickly.

'Time for sleep now, Torgeir,' I said on my way out.

Sølve looked at me from the doorway of the duty room.

'Is he not asleep?' he said.

I shook my head.

'He was busy,' I said.

'Aha,' Sølve said, and smiled.

I didn't smile back, but got my phone out of my pocket, pressed Ole's number and put the phone to my ear as I went towards the laundry room.

No answer.

He was probably just asleep.

Ole didn't sleep like other people, but would grab a couple of hours here and there.

That would be it. He'd just forgotten his promise to text me, that was all.

The sight of Torgeir had unsettled me, and as I emptied the remaining soap capsules for the washing machine into a bag, tied a knot in it and dropped it into the bin, I kept seeing him in my mind, even though I didn't want to. His feet pointing the wrong way, his big erection poking up between his withered legs, his powerful upper body. The grin on his face.

What did he fantasise about?

Oh, for goodness' sake.

I took the dry clothes out of the tumble dryer, put the wet washing in and loaded the machine again, only I left it open this time. I carried the clean clothes into the TV room, folded them and sorted them into piles on the table there.

That done, I went into the duty room where Sølve was sitting on the sofa doing nothing.

'Better get started, I suppose,' he said.

'We've run out of soap for the washing machine,' I said. 'I'm going to pop down to B and borrow some.'

'I can do that,' he said, getting up. 'I've not done much yet tonight.'

'No, you stay where you are,' I said. 'I know who's on duty down there, it'll give me a chance to say hello to her.'

'OK,' he said.

A long-drawn-out screech came from the woods. It sounded like a cross between a bird and something more reptilian.

A shudder went down my spine.

Sølve turned his head and peered into the darkness through the open door.

'I wonder what that was,' he said. 'Did you hear it?'

'No idea,' I said. 'Could it have been a heron?'

'A heron, yes, that'd be it,' he said. 'Have you heard herons before?'

I nodded.

'They sound quite prehistoric,' he said.

He got up and went out onto the veranda. I checked my phone again. Nothing. And yet what felt like a thrill ran through me. It took me a few seconds to realise why. The medicine cabinet downstairs.

The blood began to throb in my temples as I went down the corridor. If I was found out, I'd lose my job. No question about it.

But I wouldn't be found out.

It was a crap job anyway.

I opened the door at the far end and went down the stairs into the dark hallway. The exertion made me short of breath and I stopped at the bottom to steady my pulse and allow my eyes to adjust to the dark.

If I went in like it was the most natural thing in the world, no one would suspect a thing.

A sound from upstairs made me look up.

But it was only the door shutting.

The outside door had to be unlocked too, and I pulled out my keys as I stepped slowly across the floor, found the right one, the only one with a rubber key cover, and after fumbling for a moment managed to insert it and open the door.

The air outside was as hot as a holiday abroad.

In the darkness behind me someone suddenly came running. I turned, only to be shoved aside as a figure hurtled past me.

In the light from the parking area, I saw that it was Kenneth.

He turned the corner and was gone.

He was stark naked.

Oh Christ.

I'd really dropped myself in it now.

I hurried after him as fast as I could round to the other side of the building.

He wasn't there.

He'd run into the woods.

My chest ached and I leaned back against the wall as I tried to catch my breath.

What was I going to do?

I had to sound the alarm. A resident absconding was a serious matter. And this one was naked and had disappeared into the woods. The police would be brought in. With helicopters, I shouldn't wonder.

And all because of me.

Oh no.

I imagined how Berit was going to react.

She'd give me the sack.

There was no doubt about it.

But no one knew *when* he'd escaped.

What if I tried to find him myself? Maybe he was sitting on a stump just inside the trees.

And if I didn't find him, I could claim he'd only just gone missing.

If I could just find him myself! Who was to say I couldn't have a bit of luck now and again like everybody else?

I was about to call his name when I remembered that the door onto the veranda above me was open. Sølve was probably still sitting there.

Without a sound, I crossed the narrow strip of lawn between the building and the woods, and stepped among the trees. The pale light from the windows dissolved after only a few metres, and darkness closed around me.

ARNE

I woke up in such acute pain that for a few seconds I didn't know where I was or what had happened. All that existed was the searing sensation in my face, my pounding head.

I put my hand to my nose. My fingertips were at once wet with blood and a sharp pain stabbed at my skull.

I'd crashed the car.

The headlights were still on, pointing at the trunks of some trees.

I passed my tongue over my upper lip, sensing blood. The salty, metallic taste almost made me heave.

I opened the door and climbed out.

The car had come to a halt against a tree a few metres from the road. The right side had taken the impact. The headlight casing was smashed, the wing crumpled.

Everything was still. Not even a murmur from the sea.

And no traffic, thank Christ. No one to call the police.

No houses nearby.

I couldn't remember a thing about whatever had happened. But I couldn't have been going very fast.

I'd been driving while drunk.

How stupid was that?

I touched my nose again, as if somehow I needed the dull pain to detonate, no matter how much it hurt.

Ow, bloody hell! Ow, ow, ow!

After a moment it subsided and only a constant, throbbing ache remained.

I was still a bit drunk, I realised, losing my balance and gripping a tree for support as I staggered back to the road to get my bearings. It was like there was some kind of membrane in between me and what I could see.

I stopped in the middle of the road. The air felt hot, like at the height of afternoon, and completely dry, a faint scorching sensation against the skin.

So strange.

Through the trees on the other side I could see the moon reflecting on the surface of the sea below, and more distantly, to the right, a cluster of small lights that could only come from the houses out on Vågsøya.

I was at least twelve kilometres from home.

How was I going to get out of this?

I could switch the engine off for a start. No sense in lighting up the whole scene.

I got in and turned the key.

Maybe I could remove the number plates and just leave the car here? Walk home.

But then the police would be involved.

Tove?

She was too far gone to be of any help.

Wait a minute, didn't I have a packet of fags somewhere?

I leaned across the passenger seat and immediately a shot of pain went through my head again with the sudden build-up of pressure.

But there they were, on the floor. A shiny, red-and-white packet of Marlboro cigarettes. And, next to them, my mobile.

I lit one straight away.

A trickle of blood ran down my lip. I licked it away, and this time there was no sudden urge to vomit.

I opened the glove compartment and found a packet of tissues, tore it open and pressed the soft paper gently to my face.

Then I phoned Egil.

He answered immediately.

'Arne?' he said.

'Hi, Egil,' I said. 'How's it going?'

'Fine,' he said. 'You? It's not like you to be calling. Not this late, anyway.'

'That's the thing,' I said. 'I'm in a spot of bother.'

'Oh?'

'Yes. I've crashed the car into a tree.'

'OK.'

'Do you think you could get out here? I'm a bit drunk, you see.'

'Understood,' he said. 'Where are you?'

'At the side of the road just before you get to Vågsøya. Keep going after the shop and you'll see me after four kilometres or so.'

'What state's the car in? Can it be driven?'

'I don't know. I reckon so.'

'OK.'

'Are you coming, then?'

'Yes. I'll come in the boat, then I can drive you and the car home.'

'Brilliant.'

'Mind what you say. You might have to do something for me one day.'

'Of course, no problem,' I said.

'Maybe something you don't want to,' he said. 'See you in a bit.'

He hung up.

I tossed the glowing end of my cigarette into the road and lit another. The bottle was still intact, I noticed then, firmly in place in the holder in front of me.

It wouldn't look good if someone came and saw me drinking in the car, so I took it with me and went back over the road into the trees on the other side.

And then I remembered the strange star. The crabs on the road.

So it wasn't moonlight, I realised, looking up into the sky behind me.

There it was, shining brightly.

Smaller now, further away.

Or maybe it had only looked bigger and closer before because I was drunk.

Was that where the heat was coming from?

Oh, don't be so stupid.

The stars were out there, beyond an endless expanse of icy darkness. This one was no exception, no matter how close it seemed.

The forest floor was bare and dry, carpeted with yellow needles. Above, the trees stood straight and tall, spreading their branches from a height of some five metres or so, but as I went on they became lower and more twisted in shape where the wind blew in from the sea, and I found myself having to forge a more convoluted path until at last I emerged onto the pebbled shore.

A heavy log had washed up a few metres below the last line of trees. It looked like it had been in the sea for a long time. I passed my hand over its surface, it was completely smooth, and had not yet begun to rot. I sat down on it, lit a cigarette and stared out at the sea. It was calm, and my gaze was drawn to the point where it dissolved into the thick, velvety darkness that rose up above the world like a belljar. A darkness in which light shone through the tiniest holes. At least, that was how the madman Strindberg had construed it, I thought to myself, and gulped a swig from the whisky bottle.

I hadn't checked the message I'd got yet. I supposed it was from Ingvild. But I couldn't help her sitting here, whatever the matter was, and I reckoned she could cope perfectly well on her own anyway. She was dependable. So exceptionally unlike her mother.

What a bloody mess.

Mother manic. Father pissed. Car wrecked.

How did it get to this?

And how could I dump so much responsibility on Ingvild?

She was only fifteen.

I took another swig.

Ahh.

The strong alcohol not only burned in the back of my throat, shifting my mind from the throbbing pain I felt in my face, it cleared my head too. I could almost follow it in my thoughts, the path of the alcohol as it spread with the blood through the brain, removing all detritus. Yes, the function room was being cleared now after the party, dirty plates and glasses taken away, new tablecloths laid on all the tables, the floor washed, the run-down candles making way for new ones. Soon it would be pristine again, gleaming and ready.

And then I could dance.

I took another swig.

The dark sea lay motionless in front of me. Apart from a gentle, rhythmic, almost inaudible clacking of pebbles where the water lapped at the shore, everything was silent.

What a night.

I felt an urge to go down and dip my hands in the water. In this heat it was surely well above twenty degrees by now.

The thought of crouching down and splashing my face filled me with such sudden desire. How good it would be!

I stood up and realised I still had the phone in my hand. I slipped it back into my front pocket, where it rested against my thigh.

It wouldn't do me any good knowing what the situation was at home. I couldn't do anything about it anyway until I got back.

The round stones I stepped on occasionally knocked together, a sound that was at once hollow and sharp. It felt like it could be heard several hundred metres away.

I stopped and listened into the darkness. He'd be here soon.

Nothing.

I went towards the three big rocks I could see a bit further away, which I recalled so well from when I was a kid. I used to climb on them whenever we came here with Mum and Dad. One of them looked like a priest with a bulging belly in his black cassock, perhaps mostly because of the grey-white band that resembled a cleric's collar where the rock narrowed towards the top.

I ought at least to *read* her message. Maybe she'd only texted to say everything was all right?

I put both my hands against the big rock. It was warm, almost warmer than my hands in fact.

But it couldn't be.

I bent down and touched one of the stones at my feet.

It was just as warm.

Could it be some kind of volcanic activity under the ground? That had warmed up the rock?

No, not here. In Iceland, maybe, but that was a couple of thousand kilometres away.

OK. I decided to rinse my face first, then go back to the log, sit down, have a fag and then read her text.

It was a good plan.

Dark objects didn't just absorb heat, they stored it too, so obviously the rock temperature was going to rise.

Relieved to have come up with an explanation, I went down to the water's edge, sat on my haunches, cupped my hands and filled them with water at the same time as leaning my face forward.

The water was warm and soothing; I dashed my face with it several times before the salt, which I hadn't thought about until then, began to sting in my wounds.

But that too felt good, etching into my flesh.

I looked across the sea.

At the same moment I heard the distant hum of an outboard. It was like an auditive zip opening up the stillness.

I went back to where I'd been sitting before, drank what was left of the whisky and lit a smoke. He was still some way off, so I had plenty of time to check that text, as I'd told myself I would.

But as long as I was here it didn't make much difference what I knew or didn't know.

They were probably all asleep anyway.

A whitish churn became visible on the surface to the north-west, the sound of the outboard growing in intensity.

I got my phone out, opened it and tapped on the text from Ingvild.

Dad I'm scared when are you back

Oh no.

What could it be?

I stood up.

Maybe it was the new star that had scared her. The fact that there were no adults around.

But Tove was there.

Should I phone her?

No, it would be meaningless, given the state she was in at the moment.

I went down to the water's edge again. The body of the boat was visible now, cutting a wide arc as it came towards land.

It occurred to me he didn't know where I was.

The outboard slowed abruptly.

A few seconds later, my phone rang.

'Where are you?' he said.

'I can see you,' I said. 'I'm standing on the beach.'

'OK,' he said. 'I'll moor in the inlet here. Where are you standing exactly?'

'About halfway along. You know the rock that looks like a priest?'

'Yes.'

'I'll meet you there.'

'OK,' he said, and we hung up.

I lit a fag.

If I phoned Ingvild, I might wake her up, and not being there meant I'd only make things worse.

Should I text her?

If something serious had happened, she'd have phoned.

Wouldn't she?

The boat slid into the inlet and disappeared from view behind the trees.

I tapped on her number and put the phone to my ear as I looked up at the stars in the darkness above my head.

Please, God. Don't let anything bad have happened. Let everything be all right.

'Dad, where are you?' Ingvild's voice said.

'I'm with Egil,' I said. 'I'm on my way home now. Has something happened?'

'It's Mum,' she said. 'She keeps going in and out of the house and wandering around the garden all the time. I can't get through to her. It doesn't matter what I say, all she says is "Are you sure?" or "Sorry" or "I don't know". The twins were frightened.'

'Are they asleep now?'

'Yes. I've been sitting with them, they've only just dropped off. But there's someone downstairs.'

'What?'

'There are noises coming from downstairs. I'm too scared to go down. You've got to come. Please, Dad.'

'I'm on my way,' I said. 'No need to worry about Mum, she just needs to shut everything out at the moment, that's all. A bit of rest and she'll be fine again, you'll see.'

'A bit of rest in the hospital, you mean?' said Ingvild.

'Yes,' I said. 'She'll be able to rest there.'

'It's so awful,' said Ingvild. 'It's like she doesn't see us! She looks right at me and still can't see me! And she keeps walking all the time. Heming wanted to know why you couldn't come home and hold her.'

'I'm on my way, Ingvild. Where's Mum now?'

'I don't know. Out somewhere.'

'OK. It's nothing to be worried about,' I said. 'All right?'

'But what about the noises? I'm so scared. It sounds like someone's down there.'

To my left, a figure emerged out of the woods onto the shore.

'I'm sure it's nothing. Probably just the cat.'

'It's not the cat, Dad. There's someone down there.'

'I'm sure there isn't, sweetheart. Don't be scared. We're on our way now. Home in fifteen minutes, maybe. Half an hour at the most. OK?'

'OK. But hurry.'

'You're such a good girl, Ingvild. You've been so strong and brave tonight.'

She sighed and hung up.

Heavy with despair, I turned towards the figure further along the shore and lifted my hand in a wave. But he was on his way towards the three rocks and didn't see me.

'Egil!' I shouted. 'Over here!'

Everything was all so hopeless.

He looked around in bewilderment for a few seconds before he saw me.

'Thought you said the priest!' he shouted back.

I lit another cigarette as I watched him traverse the stony shore.

He stopped in front of me, out of breath.

'The state of you,' he said.

I put my hand towards my nose, a reflex, halting the movement at the last second.

'Your nose looks broken,' he said. 'Is it?'

'I don't know,' I said. 'It hurts, though.'

'I should think it does,' he said. 'Where's the car?'

I nodded in the general direction.

'We need to get going,' I said. 'Tove's not well and the kids are on their own with her.'

'While you're out drink-driving and smashing the car up?'

'No need to rub it in,' I said, and started to walk. 'It's serious by the sounds of it. I think she's getting psychotic.'

'She definitely didn't seem good today,' he said.

'No, maybe she didn't,' I said. 'It's just always so hard to tell where it's going.'

'That's what you always say,' he said.

He made his way up the slope beside me, his chest wheezing. Tall and upright, with his little paunch, his unruly hair.

'So what are you going to do?' he said.

I ducked beneath the low branch of a pine tree, the pain immediately throbbing in my nose. I straightened up, but too soon, the branch whipping back into my neck.

'Christ,' I said. 'I hate these bloody woods.'

Egil opted for a longer way round, vanishing for a moment behind a curtain of foliage.

'What are you going to do, then?' he said when our paths converged again.

'I don't know,' I said. 'About Tove, you mean?'

'Yes.'

'I need to know what sort of a state she's in first,' I said.

'Psychotic, you just said.'

'Perhaps. I don't know. If she is, I'll have to take her to the hospital.'

Egil looked up at the new star as we crossed the road, but said nothing.

'This is where I'm parked,' I said.

'Doesn't look too bad,' he said. 'Give me the key and I'll see if I can back her out.'

'It's in the ignition,' I said.

He opened the door and got in. A moment later, the engine started and the left headlight came on. He revved a couple of times like a bloody racing driver before putting it into gear and reversing steadily and slowly through the heather and scrub.

Once it was back on the road I got in the passenger side.

'So far so good,' he said.

'Thanks, Egil,' I said.

'No problem,' he said, reversing across the tarmac, twisting the wheel and then arcing forward again to bring us onto the right side of the road.

'How are the kids taking it?' he said.

'Ingvild's scared,' I said. 'The twins are asleep.'

'OK,' he said.

There was a silence.

'I'm not exactly good with kids,' he said. 'But if you drive her to the hospital, I can stay with them, at least.'

He looked at me.

And then he laughed.

'No, you can't take her to hospital looking like that,' he said. 'They'll have you in too!'

'Didn't you hear me? Ingvild's scared. A psychosis is no laughing matter.'

'A person who's been as stupid as you've been tonight ought to be able to take a joke,' he said. 'I'll take her in, you can stay home and take care of your kids.'

I didn't answer him.

Why did he have to moralise now?

And who did he think he *was*, anyway? Living on his own in a summer house, fifty years old and without a job. Not much of a life to boast about.

We came out of the woods onto the high flatland where the crabs had been crossing the road. They were all gone now, apart from the odd shell that lay crushed here and there.

I glanced at Egil.

He was staring straight ahead and changed gear as we got to the bend on the other side.

I couldn't be bothered telling him about the crabs.

I leaned my head back and closed my eyes instead.

'Thanks for coming out,' I said.

'No problem,' he said.

'Did I wake you when I rang?'

He didn't answer, but I sensed him shake his head.

'I was reading,' he said.

'What are you reading?' I said.

'A book about the Lion-man.'

Something about his tone of voice told me he was now expecting a question about who the Lion-man was. He wouldn't get it from me, that was for sure.

'Oh, right,' I said, and opened my eyes. We passed the road leading down to the marina. What I'd told Ingvild was true, there was no need to worry about Tove. But it was unsettling, nevertheless. To see a person vanish into their own world and become unapproachable was unsettling in itself. And this was their mother.

As the road swung north, the star was above us in the sky.

It was beautiful.

As beautiful as death was beautiful.

'We haven't talked about the new star,' I said. 'It's a bit weird.'

'Maybe,' he said. 'But you've got other things to think about.'

'Yes,' I said.

There was a silence. We turned onto the gravel track that was our road, and Egil took his foot off the accelerator, the car almost sailing like a boat between the empty houses.

'What do you think it is, then?' I said. 'A comet? A supernova? Or a new star?'

He shrugged.

'I don't know. Probably a new star. It's happened before in history.'

'Has it?'

'Yes, lots of times.'

He looked at me.

'Have you heard of the *Augsburg Book of Miracles*?'

'No,' I said.

'It's an illustrated manuscript from sixteenth-century Germany. It wasn't found until quite recently. Anyway, here we are,' he said, pulling up in the driveway next to the house. 'We can talk about it later.'

'Yes,' I said.

He switched the engine off and engaged the handbrake.

'Do you want me to wait here while you check on the kids?'

I unclicked my seat belt.

'If you would,' I said. 'You can still drive her to the hospital?'

'Of course.'

'OK. Wait here a bit, then.'

I opened the door and got out. All the outside lights were on, every lamp and light in Tove's studio likewise, the garden an illuminated island in the dark.

The rooms appeared empty as I went up the paved path along the front of the house. There was no one in the garden either.

The door was wide open.

And then I focused on what Ingvild had said about the noises from downstairs, that someone was there.

I hesitated in the doorway and peered inside.

Everything seemed normal.

I went in and opened the kitchen door.

Everything normal there too.

'Dad, is that you?' came Ingvild's voice from the landing.

'Yes,' I said, and went up the stairs.

She was standing at the top, leaning forward with a hand on the banister. Her mouth opened as our eyes met.

'What's happened? What have you done? You're injured!'

I didn't know what she was talking about at first. Then it came back to me.

'It's nothing,' I said. 'Bashed my nose a bit, that's all. It doesn't hurt. Don't worry about it. How are things here? Are you all right?'

I came to a halt and put my arms out towards her.

She did the opposite, folded her arms across her body and looked down.

'You've been drinking,' she said.

'It's all right,' I said. 'Let's concentrate on what's been going on here. Give me a hug?'

She nodded, but remained standing as before, as if curled up inside herself. I put my arms around her.

'My grown-up girl,' I said. 'Everything's going to be fine, you'll see. It'll all work out in the end.'

'Dad, you've been *driving*,' she said, and pulled away.

She looked me in the eye.

'Are you still drunk?'

'Let's just sit down nice and quietly, and then you can tell me what's been going on,' I said. 'We'll sort things out. Are the twins still asleep?'

She nodded.

I stepped past her and went into their room. They were lying on their sides, cheek to arm. Everything about them was closed, not just their mouths and eyes, but their bodies too in a way, and the thought flashed in my mind that life is something that takes place inside us.

I turned towards Ingvild who was standing looking at me.

'You need to sleep too,' I said. 'Come on, let's go into your room.'

'Can't you find Mum and take care of her first? Now?'

'Taking care of you is more important.'

'What do you mean?' she said, and looked at me with what seemed like suspicion.

'Mum won't remember any of this,' I said. 'It's like she's dreaming. But you'll remember. That's why you're more important. And Asle and Heming too.'

'Go and find her now,' she said.

She had the moral high ground with me being drunk and not having been there for them. But I couldn't let her boss me about either.

There was a noise from downstairs, a heavy thud, and then something breaking.

Ingvild jumped.

'Did you hear it?' she said. 'There *is* someone down there.'

'It sounds like the cat to me, Ingvild,' I said. 'Nothing to worry about. I'll go down and let her out.'

She stayed where she was, her eyes following me as I went down the stairs.

What could it be?

It wasn't the sort of noise a cat would make.

I paused at the front door and glanced out to see if Tove was there, but the garden was as empty as before. Then, cautiously, I opened the dining-room door and peered inside.

Nothing.

I tiptoed through the room to its other door. Put my ear against it.

Someone or something was rummaging around in there.

Could it be a dog?

I felt like walking away from it. The door was closed, so whatever was in there wouldn't be able to get out.

Unless it was a someone, rather than a something.

It didn't sound like it, though.

Full of trepidation, I pressed the handle down and opened the door.

It was completely dark inside. And the noises stopped.

I felt for the switch on the wall, and when instantly the light came on, a badger was standing in the middle of the room looking at me.

It growled.

I closed the door again in a hurry.

'What is it, Dad?' Ingvild said from the hall. 'Dad? What is it?'

'There's a bloody badger in there!' I said.

'What?'

She came into the room.

'How can it have got in?'

'No idea,' I said. 'Let's just leave it for now. I'll go and look for Mum first, then we can deal with the badger after that.'

'You're going to leave it in there? Aren't badgers dangerous?'

'No, they're not dangerous,' I said. 'Anyway, it can't get out on its own, can it?'

I smoothed my hand over her head.

'You go to bed, sweetheart, get some sleep.'

Quietly, she began to cry.

I put my arms around her.

'Are you going to take her to the hospital?' she said after a bit.

'Yes.'

'And leave us on our own here? I don't want to be on my own.'

'Egil can drive Mum, I'll stay here with you. OK?'

She nodded.

'You get some sleep,' I said.

She nodded again.

I got the key from the drawer in the kitchen and locked the badger in, then went outside to Egil who was sitting quite still in the car with the door open.

'The kids are fine,' I said. 'Tove's not in the house, so I'm going to go and look for her now.'

'Do you want me to help?'

'I wouldn't mind,' I said. 'By the way, there's a badger in the living room. Behind a locked door now.'

'Really?' he said. 'I didn't know there were badgers around here.'

'Apparently, there are,' I said. 'Are you coming?'

He got out.

'She likes a walk along the shore,' I said. 'I reckon we'll find her there. Unless she's just gone off down the road, of course.'

'Have you looked in the studio?' he said.

'Just from outside. Looks empty to me.'

'Maybe we should check first, before going off somewhere else,' he said.

'You're right,' I said. 'You wait here, then.'

I went to the door and opened it.

Tove was asleep on the sofa below the window. Her mouth was open and she was snoring. She was lying on her back with one hand on her chest, her feet flat on the sofa, knees in the air, legs splayed.

It was over, I thought to myself. At least for now.

I picked up the blanket that was draped over the armrest and was about to cover her up when I noticed her other hand was covered in blood. Thick and red, as if she'd dipped her hand in a bucket of blood.

What the hell?

I lifted her arm tentatively and examined her hand. There appeared to be no wound of any kind.

I stood still for a moment and looked around.

Where could it have come from?

I went into her work area in the other room. And there, on the desk, lay the head of the cat. It had been torn from the body, sinews and threads of flesh protruded from the blood-soaked neck.

The eyes were wide open, bright yellow against the dark fur. They looked so alive.

Some sketches of the detached head lay in a small pile next to it.

Oh Christ.

What's happening to you, Tove?

I switched the light off, went over to the sofa to make sure she was still asleep, switched the light off there too and then went back outside to Egil who was standing with his hands in his pockets looking in the direction of the winking mast.

'She was inside,' I said.

'I thought she might be,' he said. 'Was she asleep?'

'Yes.'

'What are you going to do now?'

'I'm not going to wake her, that's for sure. She hasn't slept for days. Maybe she'll be all right once she wakes up. Anyway, all we can do now is wait and see.'

'So you won't be needing me any more tonight?'

'No,' I said. 'Or wait a minute. If it's not too much to ask? Only there's that badger?'

He nodded.

'It's in the living room,' I said, going into the house with Egil behind me. I paused at the door and turned the key.

'How are we going to tackle this?' I said.

'Maybe just open the door and then move away?' he said. 'It'll find its own way out, I reckon.'

'What if it goes upstairs? The twins are up there.'

He laughed.

'A badger taking the stairs? You think so?'

'What do I know?' I said. 'I'll just pop up and make sure their door's closed anyway. Won't be a sec.'

Ingvild's door was closed, I could see as I glanced down the corridor. And the boys' was too, upstairs.

'OK,' I said to Egil. 'Shall we let it out?'

The badger must have known we were there, for it was standing motionless, looking up at us as I opened the door.

It growled and bared its teeth.

'Oh, yes,' said Egil. 'It seems to be in a bad mood. Let's leave it alone and see what it does.'

We went back out into the hall.

'I'll stay here until it's gone,' said Egil. 'How about a beer while we're waiting? We can sit in the garden and keep an eye on it from there.'

'Good idea,' I said, and got two bottles from the fridge, taking them with me to the table outside where we positioned the chairs so we could see the door.

Had she killed the cat? And torn off its head?

I could hardly believe it.

But the head was there on the desk.

'Cheers, then,' Egil said, lifting his bottle to mine.

'Cheers,' I said. 'And thanks for your help.'

We sat quietly for a bit. Beyond the pools of artificial light, the darkness of the August night lay thick over the land and everything around us was still.

The bridge of my nose throbbed with pain and it occurred to me that it must have been hurting the whole time, though I hadn't sensed it until I sat down.

High above us shone the new star.

I sat looking at it for a while as Egil hummed softly to himself and examined his fingernails, as was his habit.

'Nice beer,' he said eventually. 'What is it?'

'It's from Nøgne-Ø,' I said. 'Good brew, but bloody expensive.'

He nodded.

At the bottom of my field of vision I registered a movement and saw the badger poke its snout through the doorway.

'There he is,' said Egil.

'Shh,' I said.

It looked right and then left, then right again, as if it were a schoolkid about to cross a road. Then it emerged and shuffled off, hugging the outer wall only a few metres in front of us. Its low centre of gravity made it look like a kind of trolley trundling along the path.

'It's a splendid animal,' said Egil.

'Yes,' I said. 'Strange that they exist here.'

'How do you mean?'

'They look like something out of a fairy tale. Or something exotic from a faraway land. It seems hard to grasp that they belong here.'

'What animals do you think belong here?'

'Dogs and cats. Cows and sheep.'

He looked at me with a grin on his face. As so often before, it felt like he knew something about me to which I myself was oblivious.

I gulped the rest of my beer and put the empty bottle down on the table.

'Fancy another?' I said.

'It won't do any harm, I suppose,' he said.

'Actually, I might be promising more than I can deliver,' I said. 'I'm not that sure I've got any more, come to think of it.'

I got to my feet and went inside, first to Ingvild's room thinking I'd look in on her, only to change my mind when I realised that if she was still awake she'd only berate me for drinking again. The fact that it was only beer wouldn't mean a thing to her. Instead, I went to the bathroom for a piss.

Christ.

The bloody state of me.

My nose was swollen and bent, and crusted with blood. My eyes were red, and my hair was all over the place.

I took a cloth and wrung it out in some hot water, then dabbed gently at the congealed blood.

My piss, once I'd cleaned myself up, was dark yellow, brown almost. Probably the hot weather, I told myself. All my fluids had come out in sweat.

There was only one bottle left in the fridge, but there, at the back, behind two cartons of juice, was a can of Hansa.

'Cheers,' said Egil when I handed him the bottle.

'All quiet?' I said as I sat down.

He nodded.

'I'll be making tracks after this. It's been a long day. When are you off back anyway?'

'Day after tomorrow was the plan. It depends on how things stand with Tove now, though.'

'When does school start?'

'Wednesday.'

He nodded again, as if my kids' school was something he cared about.

Could a psychosis make her do something like that?

I'd have to remember to get rid of the head before the kids woke up.

We sat for a bit without speaking. His face glistened slightly with perspiration in the dim light from the outdoor lamps. My skin too felt clammy, my thin shirt stuck to my chest and upper arms. I picked at the fabric and it barely lifted away.

'What was that book you mentioned? The Duisburg something-or-other?'

'Augsburg. *Das Wunderzeichenbuch. The Book of Miracles.*'

'Oh yes?'

'It's a sort of illustrated catalogue of all the miraculous signs and portents that have appeared in the world from the days of the Old Testament until the book was produced in 1552.'

'And you've got it?'

He laughed.

'I'm not that well off, I'm afraid. There's only one copy. Fortunately, Taschen published a facsimile edition a couple of years ago.'

'And what about it?'

'In 1103, on the first Friday of Lent, a new star appeared in the sky, it says. It was visible for twenty-five days, always during the same interval. And in 1173 a new star was again recorded. That was during a solar eclipse, so it may not have been visible until then. On the other hand, it was much bigger than the other stars. And in December 1545 two new stars appeared in the sky. They too much bigger than all the other stars.'

'You've got a good memory for detail, I'll give you that much,' I said.

'Not at all,' he said. 'But I can remember the details because they're so interesting. There are lots of other signs in the book too, of course. Blood rain, comets, birds falling out of the sky, earthquakes, solar eclipses, celestial swordsmen, you name it. A fish with a human face, a chicken with four legs.'

'Aha,' I said. 'For a moment, I thought we were talking about some kind of scientific record of celestial phenomena. But it's all just nonsense and superstition?'

'Is that star up there nonsense?'

'No,' I said. 'But it's not a sign from God either.'

He smiled.

'Since when were you an authority on God?'

'Come on,' I said. 'You believe in miracles now too?'

'I don't need to believe,' he said, and lifted his gaze towards the star. 'It's enough just to look.'

'So it's a sign, is it?'

'Everything's a sign. That tree over there. The leaves. Signs, everything.'

'Of what?'

'I don't know.'

'All right, then. Signs *from* what? Who's contacting us?'

'The world is contacting us. The signs are from the world. From that which is.'

'You're going to get my back up in a minute,' I said, patting my pockets in search of my cigarettes.

'On the table,' he said.

I picked up the packet, tapped one out and lit up.

'Let's just move on, shall we?' I said.

'Fine by me,' he said. 'It's time I got going, anyway.'

'How long will it take you to walk home?'

He got to his feet and finished off what was left of his beer.

'Half an hour, maybe,' he said as he put the bottle down on the table.

At the same moment, a long-drawn-out squeal came from somewhere close by.

'What was that?' I said, glancing around.

There it was again.

'Sounded like it came from over there,' Egil said, nodding towards the shrubbery by the wall of the house, the foliage green and luminous in the light of the outdoor lamp above.

I got up and followed him over.

He drew the bush aside with his hand.

'Blimey,' he said.

'What is it?'

'A dead cat. And that kitten you were looking for.'

He reached into the shrubbery, turned and straightened up with the kitten in his hands. It squeaked and squealed.

I bent forward and saw the cat lying there smeared with blood, its head missing.

'Must be the badger,' he said.

'Do you think so?' I said, drawing myself upright again. 'Would a badger take a cat like that?'

'They can do, yes. Here, you'd better look after this poor thing.'

He handed me the squirming kitten.

It was warm and soft and terrified.

I held it to my chest in both hands as it struggled to get free.

'All right, then,' said Egil. 'Catch you later.'

'Yeah, see you,' I said. 'And thanks again.'

I stood for a minute as he went towards the drive.

He stopped and turned.

'What about tomorrow by the way?' he said. 'Who's going to look after the kids if you've got to take Tove to the hospital?'

'I'll give my mother a ring,' I said. 'You've been more than enough help for now!'

He lifted his hand by way of goodbye and a moment later was round the corner and gone.

'Poor thing,' I said, stroking my hand along the animal's thin spine. My first thought was to take it into Ingvild's room, she loved cats, but then I realised the explanation would have to involve some facts she probably wouldn't appreciate being woken up for. And anyway, she'd had enough drama for one day.

'So you'll have to stay with me,' I said as I went back into the house, stepped out of my shoes and went upstairs to the bedroom as quietly as I could, clutching the kitten to my chest.

I closed the door behind me and put the kitten down on the floor so I could get undressed. Immediately, it scurried away and hid under the bed.

In just my underpants I knelt down and tried to retrieve it, but it cowered out of reach and all I could do then was get into bed and go to sleep. I'd thought it could lie under the cover beside me where perhaps it would feel safe. Now it would have to lie on its own there on the floor, with its pounding heart and gleaming eyes, I thought to myself, or pictured in my mind — for thoughts come as both pictures and words, a bit like light, which comes as both particles and waves, one could imagine, as indeed I had, many times.

KATHRINE

The air shimmered above the pavement; the whole street seemed like it was swaying in the heat, the shadow sides of the buildings having taken on a dreamlike, stooping appearance against the sky that was so blue, the rays of sun that made everything they touched glitter and glow. The lawns surrounding Lille Lungegårdsvannet were packed with people. But inside the shopping centre, so delightfully cool, there was hardly a soul. I went slowly down the rows of shelves in the pharmacy, taking various items I needed, toothpaste and new toothbrushes with pirate designs for Peter and Marie, two kinds of sugar-free chewing gum they liked, cotton buds and cotton wool balls, a deodorant and a packet of paracetamol, things I imagined would make the pregnancy test I'd come to buy less conspicuous. Still, I couldn't help but glance around me when I took it from the shelf, as I did again when placing my items on the counter in front of the assistant.

She looked up at me before scanning them one by one.

Was it an enquiring look she gave me?

Did she know who I was?

Or was it simply because she thought me too old to get pregnant?

As I opened my bag to get my money out I noticed my phone light up, still muted after the seminar. I took it out and saw that it was Gaute. I hesitated a moment before declining the call and dropping the phone back into my bag.

I needed to get myself together first.

'Would you like a bag?' the assistant asked.

I shook my head.

'That'll be 420, then, please,' she said without looking at me.

She was small and round, with fair hair and glasses that had thick black frames, and she wore the quasi-medical uniform in which all the pharmacy staff were clad, her large breasts making hers seem rather tight across the chest. She looked like the child-bearing type, someone who could give birth with ease. But that was just prejudice, I told myself as I held my card to the reader, for surely it wasn't true that curvy women were more fertile than those of more slender form?

I put my items away in my bag and went back out onto the main concourse, taking the escalator up to the cafe on the top floor, which was quite deserted apart from an old man sitting at the window eating a piece of chocolate cake with trembling hands, shreds of coconut stuck to his lips, a pair of crutches leaned against the chair beside him.

I went to the ladies' room and into the cubicle, texting Gaute first to say I'd call him back shortly, then I opened the test kit, hitched up my skirt and pulled down my pants, and sat down on the toilet.

How silly I felt, hysterical almost. What had got into me? I was forty-two years old and on the pill. How could I be pregnant? The nausea I'd been feeling could have any number of explanations. Was it some kind of unconscious autosuggestion?

But why would my subconscious want me to be pregnant?

The door opened and someone came in.

They rattled the handle of the cubicle. Couldn't they see it was occupied?

I stood up and rearranged my clothing, put the test back in the packet unused, flushed the toilet and went out. A girl in her early twenties stood waiting, staring at the floor. There was something familiar about her face, but I was unable to place it. She did not acknowledge me in any way, but went straight into the cubicle, so clearly I was imagining things, I told myself as I washed my hands.

In the cafe, I bought a Diet Coke and sat down over by the window, at the table furthest away from the old man, almost drinking the whole glass in a single gulp, so much more thirsty than I'd realised. I then sat for a short while, looking out on the square below where people milled about and birds fluttered.

Was it perhaps a sign that I should stay? My subconscious telling me it understood my life with Gaute and the children to be good, doing what it had to in order to prevent me from removing myself from that life?

Anchoring me with another child.

I'd have been happy too. Another child would have been such a joy. Only not with Gaute.

Could I turn things around?

A step sideways, and everything would be good.

Dear God, please let me take that step. Let life with Gaute fill me with happiness again.

The shadows outside were growing long. The cries of the gulls, so melancholy as they issued into emptiness, were faintly audible through the windows.

How strange the episode had been with the bird of prey the day before. I'd never heard of anything like it.

Why was the thought of it so unsettling?

It wasn't the way things were supposed to be. It was a change in what was supposed to be unchanging.

The door of the ladies' room opened and the girl came out. She glanced at me before descending the escalator. Now I remembered her. It was the girl from the reception desk at the hotel.

So I hadn't gone completely senile.

I got my phone out and called Gaute.

'Hi,' I said. 'You rang just before. I was in a meeting.'

'Yes,' he said. 'I wanted to apologise, that's all.'

'For what?'

'For my accusations yesterday. I don't know what came over me. I'm very sorry about it.'

'I understand,' I said.

'What, that I'm sorry?'

'No, that you suspected me. I haven't been quite myself for a while. It's better now though.'

'Is it?'

'Yes.'

'What was the problem?'

'I'd rather not talk about it over the phone. Tonight, perhaps? I could buy some wine and something nice to eat?'

'How about a barbecue?' he said. 'The weather's glorious.'

'Good idea,' I said. 'Perhaps we could have some people round too?'

'I thought the two of us were going to talk?'

'We can talk afterwards. Shall I ask Sigrid and Martin?'

After we'd spoken, I sent Sigrid a text asking if they'd like to come over for dinner. I'd known her since school and we'd always kept in touch even when we'd been living in different places, though not always that frequently. When she moved back to town a few years earlier, we began seeing each other again. She was the idealistic type, her first job had typically enough been with the *Klassekampen* newspaper, and since then she'd worked for an aid organisation in Mozambique for five years and for a charitable foundation in London after that, before they had children, Helene and Theo, and she decided to come back home and began writing for the regional newspaper. She was cynical too, and I liked that combination, the idea of her working with illusions without illusion. Sometimes, I could see myself doing the same thing, but *that* was definitely an illusion, my own job being concerned with emotions and relations, and about being near to something none of us really knew anything about, though all, or at least many of us, perceived. Theology was not the study of God but of how we could talk about God, to open ourselves to the Divine, so the Divine might flow. Sigrid understood this, her cynicism was aimed at the ways in which God was talked about, by the clergy especially, whom she called small-minded. 'It's all the wrong people talking about God,' she said once. 'So it's hardly surprising no one believes any more. There's something wrong from the outset with a man who wants to be a priest, and it is still mainly men.' 'Who else should talk about God?' I asked. 'The best minds, I suppose,' she said. 'The exceptional talents of any generation.' And then she laughed and looked at me, and said that her criticism didn't count in my case.

I liked Martin, her husband, too, even if I wasn't always sure how good he was for her. They'd got together when they were students, and Martin was still a student. He'd done a PhD in philosophy, then changed direction, becoming a radiologist and working at the hospital for a time before going back to uni and doing some kind of computer course, only then to start another PhD, this time in biology, which was where he was at now. We'd stopped joking about it; it was as if an eccentricity had now become more of a fate.

Sigrid answered immediately, they'd love to come, and I drank up the last of my Coke and took the escalator down again. It was too hot to eat meat, I thought as I emerged onto the street and was struck by the heat. Prawns, and perhaps some crab if they had any, that would be better. A chilled white wine to go with it.

I walked down to the fish market and stood in line among the crowds. The light under the awning had a reddish tinge, like when you look at the sun with your eyes closed, at the same time as it appeared to scintillate from every surface. I stared for a while at one of the tanks in which some rather large fish were swimming. The cool green hue of its water was soothing on the eye. And the movements of the fish, their appearance, seemed so alien there on land, among shorts-clad tourists, buildings and cars.

'Can you give me three and a half kilos?' I said when it was my turn, indicating the prawns with a nod of my head.

The man serving me, a big fellow with a heavy, bald head and a white apron on over his red T-shirt, began scooping the prawns into a bag.

'Perhaps you could give me a discount if they're not fresh?' I said.

It was obvious from the antennae, many of which were broken, that they'd been frozen. I could tell because a girl I knew used to work there when we were still teenagers, she told me they often ran over to the supermarket and bought frozen prawns when they started running out.

'These are fresh,' he said without looking at me as he put what had now come to two bags on the scales. 'So that'll be six hundred kroner exactly.'

'If you say so,' I said. 'I don't suppose there's much of a difference anyway.'

He threw me a glance as he dropped the paper bags into a plastic carrier and tied the grips together. Some beads of sweat ran down the skin of his throat.

'I need some crab as well,' I said. 'Four, I think.'

He nodded and leaned forward, gathering up four of the crabs that lay on their bed of crushed ice.

'Are they Norwegian?' I said.

'The prawns are fresh and the crabs are Norwegian,' he said. 'That'll be nine hundred altogether.'

I took out my card and he handed me the reader. Just then, my phone rang. I hurried to key in my PIN, my other hand dipping into my bag to find the phone.

It was Mum.

'Hi, Kathrine,' she said. 'How are you?'

'I'm fine,' I said, clamping the phone between cheek and shoulder as I retrieved my card with one hand and picked up the carrier bag with the prawns and crabs in it with the other. 'Talking to you yesterday helped.'

She laughed drily.

'I'm sure it didn't. But you sound like you're feeling better. Have you spoken to Gaute?'

I put the card back in my wallet, my wallet in my bag, and began walking.

'Not yet,' I said. 'But I'm not going to say anything.'

'Why not?'

'There's nothing to say.'

'Well, it's the right thing,' she said. 'Every relationship has its ups and downs. One must learn to let things ride in the down periods.'

'And grit one's teeth?'

'No. It's not torture we're talking about. But patience.'

There was a pause. She was in the habit of ending our conversations rather abruptly, but not this time.

'How are things with you, anyway?' I said. 'Are you at work?'

'Yes. But I'm going out to the summer house as soon as I get off.'

'That sounds nice,' I said.

'It's not because I want to,' she said. 'Only I can't get hold of Mikael. He's not answering his phone. Which means I have to drive out there and make sure he hasn't had a heart attack in the heat.'

'Are you worried, seriously?' I said. 'Does he always answer when you phone him?'

'Mikael? No. He's notorious. Can't be trusted when it comes to keep-ing in touch. I can't help wondering if something might have happened to him though.'

'I'm sure nothing has,' I said, coming to a halt at the crossing, where the light was on red.

'No, likely not,' she said. 'He's probably just lost his phone while out fishing. It'll be ringing somewhere at the bottom of the sea.'

'What a fine image,' I said.

'Of what?' she said.

'Oh, I don't know,' I said. 'Anyway, I must go. Give me a buzz when you get there, will you?'

'Will do,' she said. 'Bye for now.'

A small, dirty, somewhat dented car was blocking the entrance to the supermarket car park. An elderly woman with thin white hair was sit-ting inside, and she glanced nervously at me several times as a man the same age approached the vehicle on foot from the other side. They weren't just old, I thought, they were also rather shabby, the way alco-holics or drug addicts become shabby. I could have reversed and driven around them, but I was in no hurry and imagined they'd soon pull out of the way. However, I couldn't help feeling it was what I should have done, for the woman quickly appeared to be so consumed with guilt, she gestured aggressively to the man to make him hurry, before her frightened eyes darted back to me.

She leaned across and opened the door for him. He was tall, with a narrow, stubby head and a mane of grey-white hair that was pressed flat on one side, his skin brown and rough-looking and etched with fur-rows. He put something inside the car before trying to get in himself. But he was too stiff, and could hardly squeeze himself into the confined space and onto the seat; it looked almost like he was stuck and unable to move at all. The woman shouted at him, or so it appeared from the way her mouth was moving.

She glanced at me again, then grabbed him by the T-shirt and pulled. The car behind me beeped its horn as she leaned across the now seated man and yanked the door shut.

Strange that she could be so sensitive to the needs of others and yet live the kind of life she apparently had, I thought to myself as they pulled away, leaving me to find a space in the row closest to the supermarket entrance.

I didn't need to buy much. Some wine, a few bottles of beer, lemons, mayonnaise, some good bread, soft drinks for the children. And ice cream, of course.

And butter. I mustn't forget butter.

I picked up a red basket from the stack inside the entrance and crossed through the cool, gleaming food hall that didn't look the slightest bit like a hall, the shelves drawing one's gaze down towards them. All the different colours, all the different logos, the sheer variation in all the packaging, a storm of signs all meaning different things, everything compellingly commanding attention.

I never thought about it apart from at times like these, coming directly from a funeral.

The great beyond.

I'd talked about it in some of my sermons, about lifting one's gaze, about seeing the bigger picture, though talking about it wasn't enough, it had to be perceived. It had to come from inside.

But at the graveside everyone saw the great beyond, I thought, pausing in the fruit section, my eyes passing over the shiny apple varieties, oranges, mandarins, bananas, searching for the lemons, finding them at the end of the row, bright yellow against the green felt.

I tore off a bag and put six of them inside, then moved on to the bakery where I took two white loaves and two baguettes.

Did anyone still call it French bread?

There weren't many customers. It was probably still too early for the influx of people on their way home from work. And of course there was the fine weather. The very last days of summer, before rain and wind and darkness.

I stood for a moment in front of the shelves of beer, at first to decide what kind, then how many we would actually need. Three each? That made twelve. But three wasn't many if they stayed late, especially not in this weather. Four made sixteen. In which case I could just as well get a crate. We'd have some in hand then.

It wouldn't look good, though, the priest lugging a crate of beer through the supermarket.

Or the priestess, as Mum sometimes called me.

Still, would anyone be bothered?

I put the basket down on top of a crate, bent forward, picked up the crate and carried it to the checkout.

After I'd paid and stood bagging my items, I somehow got the feeling of being watched. I turned round and looked straight at the man from the airport. He was standing over by the kiosk, staring at me.

Without thinking, I started to go towards him.

He turned on his heels and hurried for the exit.

'Hey, you!' I shouted. 'I need to talk to you.'

He darted through the door. I left my shopping and ran after him.

By the time I emerged into the car park he was perhaps twenty metres away. The bashed-up car from before pulled up alongside him. He turned to face me and lifted his hand in a wave. It looked like he was smiling. Then he opened the car door, got inside, and the vehicle, accelerating with a jolt, pulled out onto the road and was gone.

Half an hour later, I parked on the gravel outside the house, opened the boot and took out the bags of shopping. I left the crate of beer where it was, thinking Gaute could bring it in.

The kitchen windows were open and music was coming from inside. Even in the shade of the tall birch tree the air was sweltering hot.

Gaute opened the door before I'd come up the outside stairs.

'Hi!' he said, and put his arms around me. 'Glad you're home!'

He kissed me on the mouth; it felt almost like an assault as I stood there with a carrier bag in each hand.

'I'm glad, too,' I said, stepping into the kitchen with the shopping. 'Did you have a good day at work?'

The music was coming from the radio, a pop station for a younger audience. At least it would have been in 1995, I corrected myself, recognising The Wonder Stuff from my student days.

'Same as usual,' he said. 'Apart from the kids being a bit manic. It's the weather that does it.'

'Yes,' I said as I put the crabs and prawns in the fridge. 'People die more too when the hot weather comes. And after that the cold.'

I took a bowl out of the cupboard and put the lemons in it. Gaute came up and embraced me from behind. I straightened up and turned my head towards him. He kissed me on the cheek.

'I'm sorry,' he said softly.

I could feel that he was hard.

'You've nothing to be sorry about,' I said, pulling away to take the bread from the bag and put it out on the side. 'I thought we'd have prawns instead. I didn't really fancy a barbecue in this heat.'

'Is something the matter?' he said, his arms at his sides now as he stood looking at me.

The fine networks of lines that radiated from the corners of his eyes were clearly visible in the bright light of the kitchen, and suddenly I saw what he looked like, now. The corners of his mouth had begun to droop and the deep cleft in his brow had become permanent. His curly, faintly red hair had always been so thick and made him look younger, and his natural vigour and enthusiasm had given him such a lively face. But not any more.

My poor husband, I thought, and smiled at him.

'No, nothing,' I said. 'Just a hard day at work, that's all. I held a funeral for a man in an empty church. It got to me. I don't know why.'

'Of course it got to you,' he said. 'It's hard to understand how you cope with so much grief every day.'

'It's not my grief,' I said.

'No, but you see it. You talk to those who grieve.'

'Listen,' I said, 'there's a crate of beer in the boot, would you bring it in?'

'Well, I say,' he said. 'You bought a whole crate?'

'I thought it'd be good to have some in the house,' I said. 'Especially in this heat.'

'Sounds good to me,' he said, and went outside to fetch it.

I turned the radio off and went into the living room, opened the window at the far end and sat down in the chair next to it, only to get up again a moment later, to lean my elbows on the sill and look out. I was still unsettled by what had happened at the supermarket.

Obviously, it couldn't have been Kristian Hadeland I'd seen there, even if for a few minutes I'd thought so. He was dead and buried. But all the same, the experience was unpleasant, for why had that man appeared in my vicinity again? And what did he have to do with that shabby old couple?

She'd looked so frightened the way she stared at me.

The reason wasn't necessarily that she'd been uncomfortable blocking my way, as I'd thought. It could quite easily have been something else, something to do with the man from the airport.

She'd stared at me with a frightened look in her eyes, and not long after that he'd stared at me too, and then he'd taken off with them. Almost as if he'd been making a getaway.

Why did he run when he realised he'd been seen?

Gaute came in and I turned round.

'The basement's the best place for that, don't you think?' I said as he stood there with the crate in both hands.

'Yes,' he said. 'We'll want some in the fridge first though.'

'What time will Peter and Marie be back?' I said.

He paused in the middle of the room.

'Sevenish. I was thinking maybe they could stay the night there. Have Martin and Sigrid round without the kids to worry about.'

'But they'll be bringing their own,' I said.

'OK,' he said, and went into the kitchen.

It had all been a series of coincidences, I told myself. Nothing on which to expend time and energy. I'd run into a man who happened to look like someone I'd since buried, and then I'd run into him again shortly afterwards, quite by chance. There was nothing more to it than that.

At seven thirty on the dot, Sigrid and Martin's red Passat pulled up in the drive. She was wearing a short white blouse that was knotted at the waist and a long, splashy cotton skirt, her hair in a ponytail, and she had sunglasses on. I noticed too how tanned she was, her confident, self-assured bearing as she got out of the car.

She'd always looked good that girl.

'Hello there,' I said as she looked up.

'Hi!' she said. 'Lovely to see you!'

Martin opened the back door so the children could get out. He had on a pair of olive-green shorts and a black T-shirt that was rather too tight, revealing a slight paunch on his otherwise slender frame. His skin was as white as chalk, and along with his dark hair and somewhat awkward demeanour it made him seem like his partner's direct opposite.

'Do we go round the back or should we come up first?' Sigrid said, the car key still in her hand.

'Just go round the back,' I said. 'Gaute and the children are there already.'

The sun was low in the west and the horizon was edged by a ribbon of orange-red light. Through the open window came the sound of voices from next door's front patio, jaunty and expectant, I thought, as if they were awaiting some major event.

I put my head out slightly and saw four or five people standing with wine glasses in their hands while Vroldsen, the head teacher at Gaute's school, emptied a bag of charcoal into the barbecue. Faintly, I heard voices from our garden too, the children laughing and shouting.

I took two large dishes from the cupboard and the paper bags containing the prawns and the crabs from the fridge. The prawns spilled out, scraping against each other in their hues of reddish-pink as I upended the bags into the china.

I placed one dish on top of the other and carried them outside into the garden, where the grown-ups were sitting at the table on the patio, the children playing in the little playhouse Gaute's father had made for them.

'What a good idea to have prawns,' Sigrid said, immediately getting to her feet. 'Our first time all summer, in fact.'

She gave me a hug. Martin got up too and waited his turn behind her.

'Hi,' he said, putting his cheek towards mine and placing a hand in the small of my back, though without our cheeks actually touching to complete the manoeuvre.

He avoided looking at me too.

Sometimes I got the feeling he was attracted to me and that the reason he so conspicuously kept his distance was that he didn't want anyone to suspect.

'Hi, Martin, how are you?' I said.

'Fine,' he said, and sat down again, glancing at Sigrid as he did so. 'I'm fine, aren't I?'

'Yes, you're fine,' said Sigrid.

'Anything new?' said Gaute, leaning back and crossing his hairless legs, tilting his head somewhat arrogantly, I thought.

'New isn't something I connect with Martin,' said Sigrid with a laugh.

Had they been arguing before they came out? I got the feeling they had.

'Wine or beer, Kathrine?' said Gaute.

'Perhaps a beer,' I said, sitting down.

The table looked so nice with the prawns and lemons, the bread and the butter, the blue glass plates, and a tall, slender green wine bottle, all set off against the white tablecloth.

'Come and get something to eat, you kids!' said Gaute.

The children came crawling out of the playhouse, sat themselves down at the little table next to our big one and began helping themselves to sausages and bread that they turned into hot dogs.

'Do you know what I saw today?' Sigrid said to them.

They shook their heads and stared at her.

Did *they* think she was beautiful?

No, that sort of thing didn't start until later.

Perhaps Peter did?

'I was sitting in the garden when I heard a noise behind the fence. Then all of a sudden a fox jumped up onto it.'

'A fox?' said Marie.

'Yes!' said Sigrid. 'It just sat there and looked at me. For a long time. And then it jumped down and ran off into the woods again.'

'Are foxes dangerous?' said Marie.

'No, of course they're not,' said Peter.

'How strange,' said Gaute.

Martin said nothing, although he almost certainly had an opinion about it. He extracted some meat from one of the crab shells and spread it onto a slice of bread, hunched over his plate, eyes fixed on what he was doing.

'What have you been up to since we last saw you, then?' said Sigrid.

'Kathrine was away at a seminar last weekend and I was here with the kids,' said Gaute. 'We went swimming out at Nordnes, it was lovely.'

'In the sea?'

'No, no, in the pool there. Apart from that, just working all week. No great shakes. How about you?'

'Work's been quiet,' said Sigrid. 'The world hasn't really got going again yet after the holidays.'

'There must be something happening somewhere, surely?' said Gaute. 'Those four lads who've gone missing, for instance?'

'That's not really my department,' said Sigrid. 'Martin's just made an interesting decision about *his* work, though. Haven't you, Martin?'

Martin looked at her, and something resembling anger flashed in his eyes.

'Maybe,' he said. 'I'm sure we've got better things to talk about than that, though.'

'No, go on,' said Gaute. 'What sort of a decision?'

'He's giving up his PhD project and wants to start another one instead,' said Sigrid.

'I thought you were nearly finished?' said Gaute.

'Not exactly,' said Martin. 'It'll need another six months or so yet.'

'So why are you giving it up?' I said.

He gave a shrug.

'He wants to write about how trees think,' said Sigrid, and laughed.

Don't laugh at him, I thought.

He looked at her. Then he put his napkin down on the table, and for a moment I thought he was going to get up and leave.

'That sounds really interesting!' I said.

'No, it doesn't,' said Sigrid. 'It sounds *totally* brainless, if you ask me.'

'Let's hear it from the man himself,' said Gaute. 'What's the thrust of it?'

Martin sighed.

'I haven't actually decided I'm going to yet,' he said.

'Yes, you have,' said Sigrid.

If they hadn't been arguing before they came, they certainly would be once they left, I thought to myself.

'*Can* trees think?' said Gaute.

Something sank inside me as soon as he said it. Sometimes he could be so . . . well, *stupid*.

At the same time, it got the situation on an even keel again, Martin taking his cue.

'No, not *as such*,' he said. 'But if I do have to explain it, that's not the right place to start. Everyone knows what thoughts are. But we don't know what they *actually* are.'

'Chemical and electrical impulses in the brain, aren't they?' said Gaute.

'Yes, but to get from the biological processes to actually *thinking* something is rather a leap. What's a thought?'

'Wouldn't you like to know!' said Sigrid, and laughed.

Fortunately, Martin smiled.

'Human consciousness is the biggest mystery that exists. No one knows what it is. Or even why it's there. Nietzsche believed we could all do very well without it.'

'Eternal return,' said Gaute. Martin glanced up at him before going on.

'The mind is a kind of place where we become visible to ourselves. But why? What's it good for? When we see ourselves, we see ourselves from without — the way others see us, in other words. That was what Nietzsche understood, that the mind exists for the good of the community. It's there for what goes on between people. And that's where some scholars believe there to be other kinds of consciousness too. Other forms of intelligence. The forest, for instance. The point being that those kinds of consciousness — intelligence, if you will — are so alien to us that it's hard for us to see that they even exist.'

'That's very interesting,' I said.

'But in six months he'd have been finished and could have got himself a job,' said Sigrid.

'So a tree can't think,' Martin went on. 'But the trees can. The ecosystem as an entity can. The fact that such an idea is being talked about now is probably down to people trying to construct forms of AI. We don't know what that's going to look like either.'

'What what's going to look like?' said Gaute.

'Artificial intelligence,' I said. 'But these thoughts aren't new, Martin.'

'How do you mean?'

'People believed long ago that everything was living, that the forest was populated by spirits, even that the forest was a being itself.'

'That was superstition,' said Martin. 'This is science.'

Martin's little talk was followed by a brief lull before everything picked up again and we sat eating, drinking and chatting about a variety of other things. The sun set behind the trees, the blue sky dimmed and dissolved into darkness. The strange thing was that the air did not cool as the sun went down, but remained hot, burning hot almost.

After a while, Gaute and Martin took the children inside to put them to bed. Sigrid lit a cigarette as soon as they were out of sight and leaned back in her chair.

I fetched the paraffin lamp from the shed, put it on the table and lit the wick.

'Do you want some more wine?' I said.

'Yes, please,' said Sigrid.

I poured some into her glass first, then my own.

'Cheers,' I said.

'Cheers,' she said. 'Here's to thinking trees!'

'I wouldn't worry too much, if I were you,' I said. 'As long as it doesn't affect you financially, I mean.'

'It's not that,' she said. 'It's just that I get so bloody down about it. He can never see anything through, you know? Nothing ever comes of it. There's never any result, never anything palpable to show for it all, not even a completed dissertation. All he does is plod about. I mean, he's supposed to be a role model for the kids. They're supposed to learn what a man is by looking at him. And now he comes up with this!'

'It *is* actually quite interesting,' I said.

She made a face like an idiot and looked at me, then took a drag on her cigarette and gulped a mouthful of wine.

Behind the fell on the other side of the valley the sky started to brighten. It could only be the moon, I reasoned, turning round to look up at the children's room, the two windows where the light was on.

'But you're a priest,' said Sigrid. 'So you're disqualified when it comes to fantastic theories about invisible powers.'

'There's a lot we don't know,' I said.

'Not true. It's the other way round. There's a lot we know.'

What on earth was that?

'Look!' I said.

Sigrid turned.

'Jesus Christ,' she said.

An enormous star rose up above the fell.

'Hey!' Gaute shouted down from the veranda. 'Have you seen that?'

It seemed almost to wipe everything else out.

'It's hard not to,' Sigrid shouted back.

It's as if it's watching us, I thought.

Gaute and Martin came back across the lawn, Gaute's movements were hectic.

'What do you think it is?' he said, stopping to look up at the sky. 'A UFO? Ha ha ha!'

'It's a supernova,' said Martin. 'A star flaring up somewhere in the galaxy before burning out.'

'But it's so close,' said Sigrid.

'It only looks close,' said Martin. 'The reality is it's very distant. What we're seeing now is actually something that happened hundreds of years ago.'

'What do you think, Kathrine?' said Gaute.

'I don't know,' I said. 'But what you say sounds convincing, Martin.'

For a while, we all looked up at it. The sight filled me with a terror I tried to counter with rational thought, telling myself it was a natural phenomenon, not a sign, and that a star couldn't see us, couldn't think about us, couldn't judge us.

Then, after a few minutes, it was as if we could look at it no longer, as if we'd seen all there was to see. Gaute poured some more wine into our glasses and sat down again, Sigrid lit another cigarette, I began to wonder whether to bring some dessert out or just coffee. But the star did not vanish from our minds, for we kept squinting up at the sky, I too, and even when I wasn't looking at it, I was thinking about its presence.

Were the others scared?

They didn't seem to be.

'Are they asleep up there?' said Sigrid.

'Far from it,' said Gaute. 'At least they don't have to get up for school tomorrow. They're having a whale of a time.'

'They've always got on so well together,' said Sigrid. 'Peter is Theo's hero.'

'Still?' said Gaute.

'Yes, he mentions him all the time.'

'What are they up to, if they're not asleep?' I said.

'They're devising a play,' said Martin. 'Peter and Helene are writing and directing and playing the main parts, Theo and Marie are extras.'

'I'm amazed they're not on their iPads,' I said, and got to my feet. 'Who's for coffee?'

As I went in, I remembered that Mum was going to give me a ring when she got to the summer house. I put the plates down on the work-top and checked my phone. Nothing. Martin and Gaute came in with the rest of the things from the table. She must have forgotten, I thought. It was unlike her, though.

'Where should I put these?' said Martin.

'Just on the side there,' I said. 'Thanks.'

I emptied the shells into a bag and tied a knot in the top before pressing it into the bin under the sink. When Gaute started loading the plates and glasses into the dishwasher I went to my study, closed the door and called Mum's number as I looked up at the star. It was higher in the sky now and no longer as unsettling.

She didn't answer.

I called again. Behind me the door opened. I turned round. It was Gaute. As soon as he realised I was on the phone, he closed the door again.

Either something was wrong or she'd forgotten to charge her phone.

Everything all right? I texted, and went back into the kitchen. Gaute had put the coffee on, put the berries out in a dish and taken the cups and glasses from the cupboard.

'Do you need a hand?' I said.

'You could go and look after our guests, now that you've finished on the phone,' he said without looking at me.

'I'm sure they can look after themselves for a few minutes without my help,' I said. 'Is something the matter?'

'No, not at all,' he said, opening the fridge door and pulling the drawer out from the freezer compartment.

'OK,' I said. 'I'll take as much of this as I can manage.'

I stepped past him as he straightened up with a tub of ice cream in his hand, took out the big serving tray that was wedged between the wall and the microwave and began putting cups, bowls and glasses on it.

'Who were you talking to?' said Gaute.

'My mother,' I said.

'At this hour?'

'Yes, she said she was going to call when she got to the summer house, only she hasn't, so I just wanted to check on her.'

'I see,' he said, still without looking at me.

Upstairs there was an eruption of children's voices and laughter, coming closer as they emerged from their room onto the landing.

'Can we put on our play for you?' said Peter when the little troupe spilled down into the kitchen a moment later. 'Please?'

'Aren't you asleep yet?' I said. 'It's way past bedtime!'

'Of course you can,' said Gaute. 'We're dying to see what you've come up with!'

Ten minutes later we sat and watched our children's premiere. Peter was a snowman, he'd wrapped a white sheet around himself and borrowed my white knitted cap to wear.

'I'm wandering in a strange land,' he said, pacing up and down on the lawn in front of us. 'It's so hot here! Oh no, I'm melting! I'm dying!'

He sank to his knees.

Enter Helene with Marie's tiara on, and wings on her back, a magic wand in her hand. After her came Theo and Marie, each with a pillow tied around their waists with belts, and knitted caps on their heads, though it wasn't entirely clear who they were supposed to be.

'I'm wandering in a strange land,' said Helene, pacing up and down with the two smaller children trailing in her wake. Suddenly, she saw the snowman.

'Who are you, and what are you doing here?' she said.

'I'm Sam, a snowman,' said Peter. 'Help me, help me, I'm melting!'

'But I can't help, I can't command the weather and wind. But I know someone who can,' said Helene. 'Wait here!'

'Hurry, hurry!' said Peter, sinking even further as the three others began pacing up and down again. Then Peter got up, took off his sheet and cap and stood staring dourly into the sky.

'Wizard, Wizard,' said Helene as she approached him. 'Can you command the weather and wind?'

'I can,' said Peter. 'Do you want it hotter or colder?'

'Colder, please. There's a snowman in the desert and he's melting.'

'Oooh, wind of the North! Oooh, snow and frost!' said Peter, reaching his arms in the air. 'Come and make the weather colder!'

'Thank you, dear Wizard,' said Helene, stepping aside then with the two little ones while Peter put on his sheet and cap again. This time he lay down.

'I'm dying,' he said. 'But wait! It's getting colder. A miracle has happened!'

Slowly he got to his feet. The other three came up to him.

'Thank you, Good Fairy, for saving me!' he said. 'Will you marry me?'

'Yes, I will,' said Helene, and took his hand.

We clapped our hands. Gaute shouted 'Bravo!' Peter looked embarrassed.

'Very well played, everyone!' I said. 'But now it's time for bed.'

I stood up and took them inside. Peter clung to me.

'Did you think it was good, Mummy?' he said.

'Yes, of course I did,' I said, and ruffled his hair.

'I was thinking about the climate,' he said.

'I realised that,' I said. 'But next time perhaps you could let the others play more of a part?'

He looked at me.

'But I was the one who thought it up,' he said. 'The others didn't have any ideas.'

'That's all the more reason for you to include them, isn't it?' I said. 'Come on, let's get you off to bed.'

He dashed off, up the stairs and into their room. When I went in he was lying in bed with his face to the wall. The others bedded down on their mattresses.

I sat down on the edge of his bed.

'What's the matter, Peter?' I said, and stroked his hair.

He didn't reply, but lay there stiff and unmoving.

'You were very good,' I said. 'It was a very fine play.'

He didn't reply.

I stood up.

'Sleep well,' I said. 'Your mummy and daddy will come and take you two home soon,' I said to Helene and Theo.

'Goodnight, Mummy,' said Marie.

I switched the light off and went out.

On the veranda I stood for a moment and looked up at the star. It was as if it had redefined the sky completely. Now it was the only thing that seemed important.

Something terrible was going to happen.

That was what it said.

Something terrible was going to happen.

It was well past midnight when Sigrid and Martin carried their sleeping children to the car. After they'd said their thanks and pulled away down the road, Gaute and I went back up into the kitchen and began to clear away and wash up the rest of the dishes. We always did so after having people round; no matter how tempting it was to go straight to bed, it was nothing compared to the feeling of waking up to a clean and tidy kitchen after a late night. Usually, we talked about the people we'd been with and the things we'd discussed, but on this particular occasion we didn't exchange a word. Silent and sullen, Gaute rinsed the bowls and glasses, while I emptied the dishwasher, and when I began to load it again he disappeared without saying a word, presumably to fetch whatever was still left on the table.

I was tired and a bit worried — Mum still hadn't been in touch — and couldn't be bothered with making an effort to lighten the mood. Besides, it would only give him an opportunity to start an argument.

I dropped a pod of detergent in the little compartment in the

dishwasher, closed it and switched it on. Without waiting for Gaute, I
went upstairs, removed my make-up, washed my face, brushed my
teeth and undressed. I was about to get into bed when I saw the pregnancy test packet on my bedside table.

Had I put it *there*?

I couldn't remember.

But I must have done, I told myself.

I picked it up and tucked it between the bed leg and the wall before
pulling the duvet aside and getting into bed. It was far too hot to lie
under a duvet, but I couldn't manage without, there was something
unnatural to me about going to sleep without a cover. A sheet was no
good, and whenever we were on holiday in the sun I'd always have to
rummage in the cupboards for a proper duvet. It was the weight and
the sense of security it gave, but it was also habit.

The solution was to lie on my side with one leg underneath it and
the other on top.

What a strange day it had been.

And how sensitive Peter was.

It made him quite dysfunctional at times. He needed to toughen
himself up, be more resilient.

Why hadn't Mum phoned?

Should I try again?

I half sat up, then lay down again.

I couldn't be bothered.

Fortunately, the nausea had gone.

Not that it meant anything. It was the mornings that were telling.

Of course I wasn't pregnant.

Where did all these fantasies come from?

The doppelgänger. The pregnancy.

I hoped that was it: a fantasy.

I was too old. The risk of chromosomal defects increased with every year.

Would I not receive it?

A gift from God?

A child?

I'd have to.

Did God know all my thoughts?

Don't be silly. God is omniscient, God is omnipotent, but He is not personal.

So I'm quite safe.

But what a dreadful idea it was, that someone could know everything a person ever thought. And then, when life was over, confront them with it.

So many stupid thoughts. And so many awful and malicious ones too. Not to mention those whose only purpose was to justify something.

What was wrong with Gaute?

I hated it when he was like that. It filled all the rooms, and was impossible to escape.

I ought to just laugh it off.

He couldn't contend against laughter.

But I was unable.

What a dreadful idea that was, of eternal return.

But someone knowing your each and every thought was even worse.

Why was that?

Because it *was* dreadful, wasn't it?

The idea of eternal return meant that we had to do as much good as possible. Because everything we did we would have to do again into infinity. But if someone knew our every thought, then we had to *think* as much good as possible. And that was untenable.

Oh, this heat.

I turned onto my other side, the duvet cool for a brief moment then against my skin.

Gaute came up the stairs, his footsteps heavy.

I opened my eyes and saw him standing in the doorway.

'So who got you pregnant?' he said.

I sat up.

'What are you talking about?'

'I've a right to know, I think.'

'Goodness me, Gaute,' I said. 'Is that what you think?'

'What else would a pregnancy test be doing in your bag? And why have you hidden it now?'

'You mean you've been rummaging in my *bag*?'

'That's beside the point. Answer the question.'

'I've been feeling sick, and the idea came to me that I might be pregnant.'

'By whom?'

'By no one. I'm not pregnant. But if I was, it would only be you, of course.'

'We don't have sex any more,' he said.

'It's not that long ago,' I said. 'Anyway, this is absurd. I can't talk to you if you're presuming things like that.'

'Who were you phoning earlier on, when you slipped away to your room?'

'Oh, stop it,' I said. 'I told you, I was phoning my mother.'

'Let me see your phone, then.'

'I certainly will not. You've gone too far now, Gaute. I won't have you not trusting me. Do you seriously believe I'm lying to you?'

'Yes.'

He turned and went down the stairs again.

I flopped back and stared up at the ceiling. I felt like I was suffocating.

It couldn't go on like this.

I couldn't stand it.

I turned onto my side, laid my head on my arm and closed my eyes.

My blood pumped heavily in my veins.

What an awful day.

How little he was.

A little man, that was what he was.

I opened my eyes again. A faint wash of light shimmered above the floor. I hadn't noticed until then. At first I thought it was the moon. But it was the new star.

Music drifted up from downstairs.

It sounded like one of Dylan's albums from the seventies.

I got up and went to the open window, and looked up at the star that shone from on high. There it was, in the cold, dark sky.

Why couldn't it be a sign of something good?

Of new creation, new life?

On the bedside table behind me, my phone lit up.

It could only be Mum.

I opened her text.

Hi, Katie, sorry not to have called before. At the hospital with Mikael, he's had a minor stroke. Fully conscious though, and every chance of complete recovery. On the ward with him now, so can't talk. Will call you tomorrow. Hugs, Mum.

ISELIN

He was still pounding on the door as I went down the stairs, and shouting too. I was scared, he sounded completely out of it, but he'd seen me, and in a way it was his house, so I forced myself to go all the way down to the front door.

It shuddered every time he hit it.

'Let me in, for Christ's sake!' he shouted.

I held the latch between my fingers. But I couldn't get myself to open the door. Instead, I turned round and started back up the stairs, as quietly as I could. If he hadn't got a key, it wasn't my place to let him in.

I was only the lodger. And he was out of his head on drugs.

He could be dangerous.

I stopped.

What did it matter?

Something was happening. Something out of control and unpredictable.

I went down again, only this time I wasn't bothered if he could hear me.

I paused in front of the door. He was still hammering on it.

I unlocked it.

But he didn't realise, he just kept on battering with his fist, so I opened it cautiously.

As soon as he saw it open, he came barging in, shoving me back against the wall as he went.

'Lock the door! Lock the door!' he shouted, and ran up the stairs.

The door of one of the rooms up there slammed shut after him.

I locked the front door and went up to my room on the top floor, locked my own door and got into bed again. I switched off the iPad, wiped my face and throat with a towel, closed my eyes.

From the floor below me came a loud, piercing scream.

'AAAAARRRGH!' he screamed. 'AAAAARRRGH!'

I sat up in fright.

I'd never heard anyone scream like that.

'AAAAARRGH!' he screamed again. 'AAAAAAARRRGH!'

He must have taken something really powerful. Ketamine. That made you hallucinate. Or LSD.

The poor sod.

I had to help him. Or did I?

He could be dangerous. He might think I was after him and kill me. All it took was a knife in his hand and it'd be no more me.

But he could hurt himself, too.

He was completely out of it.

I got up and stood there without knowing what to do. Then he screamed again and I made a decision. I got a knife out of the drawer just in case and went slowly down the stairs. The door into their part of the house was open.

'NO, NO, NO,' he shouted from inside.

I stepped into the hall, not knowing where he was, waiting for him to scream again. Only now it was all quiet.

For some reason I knew right away he was behind the door furthest away. His old room.

I opened it carefully.

He was on his knees in the middle of the room with his hands folded. There was no light on, but I could see that his eyes were closed.

'Hi,' I said softly.

Abruptly, his eyes opened and he got halfway to his feet, almost throwing himself back against the wall at the same time.

'NO!' he shouted. 'NO! NO!'

He pressed himself against the wall, staring at me with terrified eyes.

What was he seeing?

'It's only me,' I said, gripping the knife tighter behind my back. 'The lodger. There's nothing to be scared of. Everything's all right.'

He was hyperventilating. Pressing back against the wall like a trapped animal. I didn't move, and after a bit it looked like he was starting to calm down.

'What's that behind your back?' he said.

'Nothing,' I said. 'There's nothing behind my back.'

'Show me your hands,' he said.

I tried to smile, as friendly as I could.

'There's nothing there,' I said.

'SHOW ME YOUR HANDS!' he shouted, and came suddenly towards me. I jumped back, turned and ran out of the room and up the stairs. I looked over my shoulder as I got to the top. He hadn't come after me. I locked my door and lay down on the bed, my heart thumping in my chest as I tried to catch my breath.

Bloody hell.

He was out of his mind, and inside the house.

What was I going to do?

I held my breath for a few seconds and listened.

It was all quiet down there.

I got my phone out and scrolled through my contacts.

As soon as I started breathing properly again, I phoned the owners. I had both their numbers, but chose hers. Her name was Anne.

She answered straight away.

'Iselin,' she said. 'Is something the matter?'

'Hi,' I said. 'Someone was at the door. I think it's your son.'

'Jesper? Is he *there*?'

'Yes. But he's out of control. Screaming and shouting. I tried to talk to him, but he chased me upstairs. I think he must be on something. It's like he's hallucinating. I don't know what to do. I know you can't really do anything from where you are. But I thought you might know someone I could call.'

'Jesper's been reported missing,' she said. 'We're in Amsterdam at the moment, on our way home to find him. But he's there, you say? Are you sure it's him?'

'I think so. He was shouting for his mother at the door. What do you think I should do? I'm a bit scared.'

'What's he doing?'

'He keeps screaming. It's like he's possessed or something. There's no talking to him.'

'This is awful,' she said. 'We won't be home until late in the morning. Listen, I'll call you back in a few minutes, OK?'

'OK,' I said.

With the phone still in my hand, I stood up and went to the window. I leaned out. The heat out there was massive.

Downstairs, he screamed again. It cut right through me.

It had been almost as if he'd seen something else when he looked at me. It was like he was in a different world altogether, where everything meant something different.

The phone rang.

'Iselin?' she said. 'Are you still there?'

'Yes,' I said.

'We've called the police. They should be there very soon. What's going on at the moment?'

'I'm not sure. I'm up in my room. He just screamed.'

'I'm so sorry about this, Iselin,' she said. 'Thanks for bearing up. It'll soon be over, I'm sure.'

When I hung up the place was quiet. I lay down on my bed again. Sweat ran from my armpits and down the insides of my arms. I scratched myself and wiped my face with a towel.

Now it was the silence that scared me.

Had he killed himself?

I wouldn't have put it past him.

But he'd probably just fallen asleep.

I got up and went over to the window again. The street was a dead end, so the police could only come from the one direction.

Nothing yet.

I knew I should wait until they got there, let them in and leave it to them. Only the thought of him lying dead or injured wouldn't leave me alone.

I turned the little key and unlocked my door, then crept down the staircase, stopping to listen on the landing.

Not a sound.

A car came up the road outside and I turned to look out of the window. It was the police. The blue light was flashing, but there was no siren. Two men and a woman got out. They stood talking for a second as they looked up at the house.

It was still completely quiet in there.

Then there was a knock on the front door, and it was like an actor in a movie you were watching suddenly appearing in your room.

I went as quietly as I could down the last flight of stairs and opened the door.

'Hi,' the policewoman said. 'Are you Iselin?'

I nodded.

'Is he upstairs?'

'Yes. But it's all gone quiet. He might be asleep. He was completely out of it just now, though.'

'Has he harmed you in any way?'

I shook my head.

'He's just been screaming like mad. And then he came at me, but I got away and he didn't come after me.'

'You rent a room in the attic, is that right?'

'Yes.'

'Do you mind showing us what part of the house he's in? You can go back to your room. We'll take care of things.'

They followed me up the stairs.

'He's in there,' I said, and they stepped up to the door and knocked while I carried on up to my room. I left my door open and stood still for some time so I could hear what was happening down there.

But there was nothing.

If they'd already taken him away, they'd certainly been quiet about it.

No screams, no scuffles, no violence.

After a while, someone came up the stairs. I pushed the door to without closing it and sat down on the bed.

There was a knock.

It was the policewoman.

'We can't find him,' she said. 'He doesn't seem to be here at all.'

'What?' I said. 'But he must be. I can hear everything in this house. If he'd gone out, I'd have heard him.'

'Could he have got into the rooms on the ground floor? The door's locked down there. You wouldn't have a key, would you?'

I shook my head.

'OK,' she said. 'In that case, there's not much more we can do. Call this number if he comes back. I'll get in touch with his mother now.'

She handed me a card and I put it down on the table.

'Thanks for your help,' she said, and then went down the stairs again. After a few minutes, they started their car and pulled slowly away down the road, without the blue light this time.

I closed the door, got into bed and shut my eyes. I was sure he was in the house somewhere. I'd have heard him go out if he wasn't.

Unless it had all been in my head?

I sat up.

Like the fire?

It wasn't possible. It couldn't be.

Everything had been so real. He'd been hammering on the door, shouting his head off. I'd gone down and let him in, and he'd shoved me out of the way and run up the stairs. I'd gone into his room. He'd thrown himself back against the wall and had been scared to death of me.

My brain couldn't possibly have made it all up.

So where was he now?

I went to the window, put my hands down flat on the sill and leaned out. The sky above the fells had grown lighter, the stars had paled and were now barely visible at all. Only not the new one. The new one shone, bright and clear.

JOSTEIN

I might not have been the happiest man in the world as I closed the door behind me and hurried along the corridor to the lift, but it wasn't far off. A triple murder wasn't exactly an everyday occurrence. And if Geir was saying it was the most horrific thing he'd seen, it had to be bad. A serial killer on the loose in the city, it didn't get much better than that. What's more, it gave me an alibi in case Turid happened to ask. How was she to know what time I'd been called out? And for all I knew, that little artist piece in the room back there might even be sticking around another day yet. I could pop back and check once I'd got the article done.

Coming down into reception, I was somehow expecting it to be winter, snow piled up in drifts against the buildings, a black sky full of whirling snowflakes. Only it wasn't. It was summer and hot as hell. The air outside was like walking into a wall, anyone would have thought it was the middle of the day.

The taxi rank was deserted, not a cab in sight. I lit a fag and typed the address into the app. For destination I put Svartediket, but deleted it again thinking no one in their right mind was going to take me up there at this time of night. Instead, I looked the place up on Google Maps to see what roads led up there. The junction of Svartediksveien and Stemmeveien looked all right.

Six minutes away, it said.

I stood and watched as the little black car icon turned round on the map and headed towards the centre of town.

Torgallmenningen lay empty and desolate in front of me. From one of the top-floor apartments, some music blared all of a sudden. I looked up and saw three people step out onto a balcony, each with a bottle in their hand.

Butchered, he'd said.

And killed with what? A slaughter knife? Or maybe a good old-fashioned axe?

Skinned, too.

That was extreme.

Why had he done it?

Or why had they? There'd been four lads in that band. That meant there could be more than one killer. But didn't he say only three had been killed? So where was the fourth?

The fourth one had killed the others. And they hadn't got him, he was still out there. Maybe down here in town now, with me standing about.

The taxi was on its way through the tunnel. I flicked my fag end onto the pavement and went towards the road where he'd soon come into view.

The birds had already started twittering in the trees above me. Cheep-cheep, you fat creep. Cheep-cheep, and no sleep. Wasn't that what they were saying?

I didn't notice him until then, but there was a man standing back against the wall on the other side of the road, staring at me. Or staring at something. He was probably just a drunk stood gawping while he tried to find the strength to walk the last bit of the way home.

I looked up the road in the direction I was expecting the taxi to come from. There wasn't a car in sight, so I opened the map to check. It told me he'd pulled up outside the Hotell Norge.

I looked around.

Those maps weren't always that exact.

No taxi anywhere.

You could phone them directly now, couldn't you?

There was a phone icon, anyway. I tapped it and put the mobile to my ear, pacing back and forth impatiently now. They were up there with their bodies gathering their crime-scene evidence, and it wouldn't be long before other reporters got wind either.

The phone kept ringing.

Eventually, I gave up and went back into the hotel. There was no one on reception. I hit the bell hard with the flat of my hand.

A lanky beanstalk of a bloke in a black suit that was too big for him came out from the back and looked at me all superior, though he was the one with the horsey teeth and pockmarks in his cheeks.

'How can I help you, sir?' he said.

'Can you get me a taxi?' I said. 'I've tried, but no luck.'

'Are you a guest of the hotel, sir?'

Just order the cab, you bloody tool.

I shook my head.

'I'm a guest of someone who is,' I said.

Been upstairs for a shag, he most likely thought. But what did I care? He nodded and pressed the button, then handed me a chitty with an order number on it.

I went back outside.

If only it would get a move on. It was eating me up, hanging around knowing what was going on out there.

I lit another fag.

No one could deny me anything if I was first on the case.

Three bodies in the woods, butchered and skinned, and one journalist. Come on!

'You must be impatient,' a voice said behind me.

What?

I spun round. It was the guy who'd been staring at me. I'd thought he was somewhere in his twenties, only now I could see he was forty at least, if not fifty.

'Are you talking to me?' I said.

All he did was smile. He didn't look drunk at all. So what did he want? Was he a homo, or what?

'Yes,' he said. 'There's no one else here.'

'You could be a lunatic talking to yourself,' I said. 'You look a bit like one too, frankly.'

He put his hand on my shoulder.

'What the hell do you think you're doing?' I said, and twisted away. Just then, the taxi pulled up and I stepped resolutely towards it, opened the door and got in the back, shaking my head in disbelief at the guy.

'Did you order?' the driver said without turning round.

'Yes,' I said, and waved the note at him.

'Svartediksveien?'

'That's right. And bloody sharpish too. If you get a move on, I'll make it worth your while.'

The homo was still standing there smiling at me. As the driver swung the car round and pulled away again, he lifted his hand in a wave, as if we were friends now.

Bloody idiot.

I was going to give him the finger, only then I thought maybe it meant something completely different in the homo world, so I looked away instead.

'Live out there, do you?' said the driver, and glanced at me in the rear-view. He had a high voice, a bit throaty, that didn't match the age of his face. His brow was lined with wrinkles, sad eyes behind his glasses.

'What if I did?' I said as dismissively as I could, looking out at the buildings and trees as they flashed by the rear window.

He'd probably seen that guy touch me and got all sorts of ideas.

An odd sense of calm washed through me, slowly, it was like I was floating. I was angry, so it wasn't what I wanted, only I couldn't do a thing about it.

If it carried on, I'd start crying. That was what it felt like.

'Big emergency response out there tonight,' the driver said.

'Oh yeah?' I said. 'Fire, was it?'

'No, a police matter, I think. You don't live there, though?'

I didn't answer him.

He was probably on his own a lot, smoking and drinking, I thought, as we turned into Kong Oscars gate. Not a soul about. It was seldom I saw the city at this time of night. Either I'd be too pissed to notice or asleep.

When was the last time I cried?

Must have been a kid.

I took my pocket knife out and unfolded one of the blades, put the point to the tip of my finger and pressed down, harder still, until the blood began to appear and the pain, thin as a needle, was all that existed for a few seconds.

'But you're from here, I can tell from the way you talk,' the driver said.

'Didn't you get the message?' I said, licking the trickle of blood from my finger. 'Keep your nose out and get a move on. There's not another car in sight.'

'Right you are,' he said.

We went through Kalfaret at speed. Svartediket was only a few minutes from the centre of town, though it was hard to believe seeing how deserted it was out there. Good place for devil worshippers, though. They could carry on as they pleased with no one to bother them.

How had he pulled it off, three killings? Had they been asleep, maybe? But why?

Most likely off his head on some shit or other.

Or else the devil worship had got to him. Made him think what they were doing was for real and not just for show.

All that obsession with evil, it was so half baked. Like worshipping the sun. The sun rose every day, no need to worship it to make that happen. Same thing with evil. Evil was already there, and getting along quite nicely on its own.

My phone vibrated in my inside pocket.

It was Turid.

She'd be at work, so she was probably just making sure I wasn't still out.

I declined the call and switched the phone off completely.

The driver turned off Kalfarveien onto a narrower road leading left. A few moments later, he pulled into the side after a junction.

'Here we are,' he said.

I got my card out and stuck it in the reader he held out to me, then keyed in my PIN. He'd been too nosy to get a tip.

He was so pissed off about it he didn't say a word when I got out.

As if tips were a right they had.

I stuck my wallet in my back pocket and started walking, past the silent houses, towards the big, grey dam.

I looked at the time and hoped the fun wasn't going to be over before I got there. But it was still only less than half an hour since Geir's phone call.

They couldn't have got much done in that time.

He'd said right at the waterworks, hadn't he?

Yes, he had.

I turned down a narrow road that led in front of the dam, passing first a small five-a-side pitch, then a basketball court, the sound of rushing water rising as I went.

I stopped. About seven police vehicles were parked up by the woods on the other side of the channel. Three uniformed, all young, all armed, were hanging about chatting, one of them leaning against the bodywork of a patrol car.

They didn't look like they'd noticed me and I stepped back a bit behind the waterworks building where they couldn't see me.

What was I going to do?

I lit a fag and looked up at the wall of the dam. I could just go up to them, of course, explain things the way they were, that I was a reporter and had received a tip to go to the scene. They weren't going to shoot me, but they'd have a good laugh, that was for sure. There was no way they were going to let a journo in there now.

But it was a free country, as we said when we were kids.

And this was a residential area, they could hardly stop me crossing the bridge and going along the road on the other side. From there I could go up the side of the fell and then get round them through the woods.

A bit of a nuisance, maybe, but worth it.

I tossed my cigarette away and started walking down. All three police officers clocked me as I went over the little bridge, and I glanced back at them inquisitively, the way I reckoned anyone else would do who just happened to be passing by.

I could feel their eyes following me and tried to concentrate on just walking normally, but as soon as I'd got round the corner and was out of sight I relaxed again and started looking for a suitable place to scramble up the slope.

There were houses all along the road, so I'd just have to go through one of the gardens. Likely no one was up at this time anyway, I thought, and opened the nearest gate, walking up the steps into the garden that rose steeply towards a red-painted house. The windows were dark, everything was quiet, and I went as quickly as I could, out of breath before

I'd even got past the house, up through the back garden into the trees, where I paused, bent double with my hands on my knees to get my breath back.

It was still dark, the terrain was pathless and the wood was dense, so this was definitely not going to be fun. But if I was lucky, the bodies would be relatively close by. They were a feeble lot, that satanist crowd, they probably wouldn't have been arsed to go very far.

I started walking. Below, I could see lights from some of the houses through the trees, and after a bit from the waterworks too. The best thing was probably to keep some height, the police were most likely going back and forth between the vehicles and the scene. I kept having to duck under branches, climbing higher when I couldn't get through, dropping lower where the ground got too steep. The bushes tore at my legs, here and there was a drystone boundary I had to clamber over, and at one point, as I squeezed through a thicket of spruce instead of going round, I scraped the skin off one cheek.

I hated forests.

Why couldn't they have killed each other in a flat?

After ten minutes, I stopped again. The strength was gone from my legs and I was too out of breath to push on. Sweat ran down my brow and stung my eyes with salt.

At least I'd got as far as the reservoir. I could see the dark water below me through the trees.

Somewhere in the distance came the thwapping noise of a helicopter.

Chances were it was on its way to the hospital, hardly more than a kilometre from the waterworks.

I wiped the sweat from my face with a sleeve, rubbed my eyes with the other and forged on.

Perhaps sticking to the water wouldn't be such a bad idea, I thought. For all I knew, I could have already gone past the crime scene.

I started down the slope. My legs were as soft as flower stalks, it felt like they'd give way any minute.

The chopper came closer. It wasn't going to the hospital, that much was obvious. It could only be the police.

It came in over the fellside and I stopped and looked up. A moment later it went past, dark and hard against the grey-black sky.

I carried on down. The vegetation was barely penetrable, the ground so steep in places that the bare rock showed through.

I heard the chopper turn at the bottom of the valley and come back. It flew in low along the fell.

What were they doing?

I held on to a branch with one hand and peered up at it.

It was going slower now.

No sooner had it passed above me than it turned round again and came back. This time it hovered directly above.

Surely they couldn't have seen me?

I crouched down under a spruce just in case.

I could no longer see it, but the rotor blades kept thwapping for maybe half a minute before abruptly the sound of them changed and it flew off at something like top speed.

Emerging from my hiding place, I carried on making my way diagonally down the slope. Only then did it occur to me that the killer might still be around. That he could be lying low in the woods, waiting for things to settle.

No, he couldn't be, they'd have the dogs out searching, hunting him down. He'd be well away by now, back in town. He could even be on the other side of the country. If he had a driving licence, that is. Could satanists drive? He couldn't be stupid enough to have flown or taken a train, surely?

I found myself on some flatter ground and realised I wasn't that far from the water now. The sky was still dark, I still couldn't see the hues of the vegetation that surrounded me, but at least I could see where I was putting my feet.

'POLICE! LIE FLAT OR WE'LL SHOOT! NOW!'

I dropped to my knees as quick as I could and held my hands over my head.

'JOURNALIST!' I shouted back. 'DON'T SHOOT!'

'LIE FLAT! ON YOUR STOMACH! NOW!'

I threw myself down, pressing my face into the ground. A second later, some figures came crashing out of the undergrowth from all sides.

'I'M A JOURNALIST!' I shouted, my voice muffled by my prone position. But the idiots didn't care. They descended on me. A knee thrust into the small of my back and a hand pressed my head down as my arms were pulled back behind my shoulders.

'Ow, for Christ's sake!' I said. 'You're hurting me! I'm a journalist, I told you!'

A pair of handcuffs snapped around my wrists and I was hauled to my feet.

That was when I got my first look at them. Three kids from the special operations unit in full commando gear.

'What are you doing up here?' one of them said, doing his best to stare me down. He had a scraggy beard, most likely to make him look older.

'I've told you three times. I'm a journalist. I'm covering a case for my paper. Now, do you mind being a good boy and taking these cuffs off me? This is bloody ridiculous.'

'Name?'

'Jostein Lindland. Google me if you want.'

He kept staring at me. I wasn't going to play his game, so I looked up at the fellside instead.

After a second, he gestured, a nod of his head and a raised eyebrow, and the two other lads grabbed me by the arms and started leading me down.

They'd obviously decided that was how they were going to do it, so I said nothing.

As we approached the water, a path appeared and we followed it. After a bit, it opened out into a clearing below a cleft in the fellside, and when we emerged I finally saw where the killings had taken place. A little patch of grass, no bigger than ten by ten metres, flooded with light from powerful spots, teeming with police. I saw Geir at once, standing outside a white tent that was open at one end, talking to a small guy I took to be Gjertsen. Both looked up, and Geir immediately came towards us.

There was a faint smell of something burnt. Like the site of a house fire a week after the event. There was another strange smell too. Oh, what was it? It wouldn't come to me . . .

'Lindland,' said Geir, coming to a halt in front of us. 'What are you doing here?'

'My job,' I said. 'Only I got attacked in the woods.'

He smiled.

'Their job,' he said.

He looked at the guy with the scraggy beard.

'You can take those off him now.'

The guy nodded and released the cuffs.

I rubbed my wrists, absorbing everything I saw around me while try-ing not to look too inquisitive.

Was it gunpowder I could smell? Old-fashioned gunpowder?

Gjertsen, who until then had been typing something on his phone, looked up at us again, put the phone back in his pocket and came over.

'Thought you were arts and culture these days,' he said.

'I am,' I said, brushing some pine needles and bits from my trouser legs. 'I'm doing a piece on a band. Kvitekrist. I heard they might be here.'

Both Geir and Gjertsen grinned.

'Who told you that?' Gjertsen said.

'I've got my sources,' I said.

'How much do you know?'

I shrugged.

A forensics officer in a white bunny suit came out of the tent. Two others, side by side, were inching along the fringe of the woods, heads down, eyes fixed on the ground at their feet. A bit further away were the remains of a bonfire. The logs were charred, but not completely consumed. Around the bonfire, stones had been laid out in what seemed to be a pattern. It was hard to tell, but it looked like it could be a pentagram.

'Well, we can't have you hanging about here,' said Gjertsen. 'I'll get someone to take you back.'

He went towards the forensics officer outside the tent.

I looked at Geir.

'Are they still here?' I said.

'Who?'

'The bodies.'

'Mm,' he said.

'Can I see them?'

'You must be out of your mind. Of course you can't. It's bad enough you just being here.'

'Photos, then?'

'You know enough to write your piece,' he said.

I desperately wanted to see them: devil worshippers, ritual triple killing, he'd never seen anything like it, he'd said.

Over by the trees, one of the forensics guys bent down and picked up an object. It looked like a book, black or else burnt.

The other one held out a transparent evidence bag and he dropped whatever it was into it.

'Is it the drummer who's not here?' I said.

Geir glanced at me before he managed to hide his surprise.

'No comment,' he said.

'Thanks,' I said.

'I never said anything.'

'OK. But if it is him, I know someone who knows him quite well. I spoke to him only yesterday, as a matter of fact. Before this, of course.'

'You're not the only one who knows people, Lindland,' he said.

'Who's to say you know who I know? And the person I'm talking about knows a great deal. I doubt he's going to talk to you after today, though.'

'How would you know?' Geir said.

'I'll find him before you lot, just watch!' I said, and laughed.

Geir took a black vape out of his pocket and stuck it in his mouth. A mist rose up and clouded his face.

He put it back in his pocket.

'You're just going to see them, OK?' he said. 'And you're not going to write a word about what you see. Because if you do, you'll never get anything out of me ever again.'

'Understood,' I said, and felt an immediate stab of pleasure in my chest.

I followed him over to the tent, where we stopped in front of Gjertsen.

'Lindland's coming in,' Geir said.

'Come off it,' said Gjertsen. 'You know he can't. They'll crucify you.'

'He may be able to help us with something. And he won't be reporting what he sees.'

'Can we trust you?' said Gjertsen, looking straight at me.

'I can give you my word,' I said.

'Is that worth anything?'

What was this?

The little twerp.

I got the urge to tell him something about men with tiny dicks, but I was there at their mercy, so I kept it to myself and offered him my best smile instead.

'I've never broken a promise to you lot,' I said. 'And you did get your hands on Heksa thanks to me. It cost me my job, in case you've forgotten? Of course you can trust me.'

'All right,' said Gjertsen. 'But he's your responsibility, Geir.'

As if to underline the fact, he walked away from us.

'Steel yourself when you go in,' said Geir. 'It's a bloody gruesome sight, I can tell you. So don't puke or anything. OK?'

'Yeah, fine,' I said.

'And not a word about what you see, in the paper or anywhere else.'

'So you keep saying,' I said. 'Can we go in now?'

He drew the tent opening aside and I stepped in behind him. The light in there was glaring, almost white, it made the grass look oddly artificial. In the middle were what I supposed were the bodies, covered by a tarp, likewise white. A forensics officer was combing the ground; he was on his knees and didn't look up when we came in. Another person, who I took to be the pathologist, was sitting on a folding stool typing on his phone, surrounded by boxes and cases of various kinds.

'Are you ready for this?' said Geir, crouching down at the tarp and looking up at me.

I nodded.

He pulled the tarp away and drew himself upright.

Oh, Christ.

Oh, bloody hell.

The three lads were lying on their stomachs, their heads wrenched back, facing the wrong way, it was like they were looking down their noses at their arses. All the skin on their bodies had been stripped off, leaving a bloody mess of flesh and tendons, with veins and arteries exposed here and there. But from the neck up, the skin had been left. It was as if they were wearing masks. Where their throats were supposed to be there were just gaping holes. The fingernails were still attached to their fibrous-looking digits. And the tops of their heads had been taken off.

They didn't look like humans.

They looked like someone had tried to construct humans but hadn't quite managed it.

'Seen enough?' said Geir.

I nodded and he covered them up again.

'Do you understand now?' he said as we stepped outside.

'Who could have done a thing like that?' I said. 'I mean, how did he manage? It must have taken days! And he must have been strong too.'

Geir got his vape out again.

'I don't get how you can be so calm,' I said. 'You've got a triple murder and a deranged killer on the loose. *Here*, in this town.'

'Deranged is about the right word,' he said.

'Best of luck, is all I can say,' I said. 'And thanks for the gander.'

'What d'you reckon?' said Geir.

I shrugged.

'Not my job, fortunately,' I said. 'But whoever it was must have been completely out of it on something. Something that gave them super-human powers to boot.'

'The way the heads have been yanked back, you mean?'

'That's right.'

'Two could do that,' he said. 'But as far as we can make out, there was only one other person here.'

'Maybe you should poke about in cowboy and Indian circles,' I said. 'What with them being scalped like that!'

'Try putting that in your write-up,' he said.

The three young police officers who'd been posted at the waterworks must have been told I was coming, since all they did when I came back from the woods was nod.

I stopped behind the big administration building, lit a fag and switched my mobile on to call a taxi.

Turid had phoned forty-seven times.

Forty-seven!

Something must have happened.

Maybe she'd forgotten her key and couldn't get in because Ole was asleep?

Whatever it was, I couldn't help her, not now, I had to get down to the paper and get the piece written, double bloody quick.

I couldn't be bothered faffing about with the app, but called the taxi company the old-fashioned way before switching my phone off again.

Fifteen minutes later I was sitting in the back of a cab watching the houses sail past outside, many with lights on in the windows now, the day beginning to start. There were people in the streets too, not on their way home, but on their way to work, cyclists with their helmets on, their lights flashing hysterically, buses with their cargoes of labour. The sky was dark blue and completely clear, the sun on its way up above the Fanafjell, and on the other side, above Askøy, the new star was still there.

It had all gone better than I could have hoped.

What a story I'd got my hands on.

A satanist death metal band, or at least most of one, massacred in the most gruesome manner. A killer on the loose.

And no one knew about it yet!

I wouldn't have minded knocking on the door of her hotel room for a quickie, only time was too short, I couldn't afford to lose it.

When the taxi pulled up outside the newspaper building, I gave the driver a small tip. He'd kept his mouth shut all the way, and this, this was my day.

At last it had come.

TURID

In the darkness among the trees I saw nothing at first. I stood still for a minute to allow my eyes to adjust, and to listen out for Kenneth.

There wasn't a sound.

He must have been way ahead of me.

How could he run here?

I'd have given anything to be able to run after him, hurtle through the undergrowth flat out, catch up with him and take him back with me.

But all I could do was plod. And even then my chest tightened.

Gently does it, Turid, you old slowcoach.

Gently does it.

Take your time.

Nothing's happened yet.

He's not going to die, you'll find him, he's going to be all right.

Breathe easy.

Think easy.

The forest floor was so dry it crackled underfoot. I could hardly see the outlines of the tree trunks, but went slowly among them with my hand out in front of me so as not to walk into the branches that kept suddenly appearing from the murk.

After twenty metres or so the ground got steeper and I halted.

This was hopeless. He'd be long gone by now. And I'd no way of knowing what direction he'd taken either.

But I couldn't lose a patient.

There'd be a gigantic search. And all because of me being so stupid.

What was Berit going to say?

He *could* have stopped and sat down somewhere.

It was as if the ears had to get used to the quiet the same way the eyes had to get used to the dark, I thought, because now suddenly I could hear all sorts of little rustling noises all around me.

'Kenneth!' I said out loud into the darkness, then held my breath for a second.

Nothing.

I decided to keep going for a bit. At least then I'd have done what I could.

'KENNETH!' I called out.

Nothing.

But he never listened to anyone, he was too stupid for that, more stupid than a dog he was, so why should he answer me now?

Slightly further on I came to a path leading off up the slope to the left, doubling back to the right, then continuing left again. The moon paled the ground, the trees not nearly as dense now, and the going became easier, even if thick tree roots here and there meant I had to watch out. They looked like serpents in the moonlight.

I paused every twenty metres or so, my hand on a tree trunk for support as I listened. Little rustling noises in the undergrowth, the murmur of night in the depths of the woods, but no footsteps, no hurtling madman, no demented howling.

Eventually I emerged onto a small, treeless plateau where I turned round and looked back at the illuminated buildings below, the little roads that ran between them. The woods stretched darkly towards the prison, which was perhaps a kilometre away, an island of light in the darkness.

I could pack the job in, it occurred to me. I dreaded coming in every day, so there was no sense in clinging to it. Especially not after tonight.

When I turned back round, I saw that it wasn't the moon that was shining above the trees, it was a planet.

As a child, I'd thought it was the Star of Bethlehem. We all did.

Oh God, if only I could go back. To Mum and Dad and little Tore.

The baby on the rug in the living room, his smile as I bent down to pick him up and then pulled a face at him.

Those cheeky little eyes of his.

The softness of his skin!

The reminiscence felt so real as I forged ahead, and for a few moments the new baby was so very near to me and filled me with a sense of infinite goodness that streamed through my being.

Jostein once said that was what heroin did. It gave you the same feeling of being protected and cared for that you had when you were little.

Mum and Dad. The duvet snug around my body, a grown-up getting to their feet, smiling and saying goodnight before turning out the light. Good and warm and safe.

I looked up at the Star of Bethlehem again and stopped.

'Dear God in Heaven,' I said. 'Please let this end well. Let me find Kenneth. Let Ole be all right.'

Five more minutes, I told myself. Then I'll go back and raise the alarm.

Sølve would be wondering where I'd got to soon.

If he wasn't asleep.

'KENNETH! KENNETH! COME BACK!' I called out, pressing on.

I suppose mostly it was for my own sake. So I could say I'd done all I could.

On the other side of the plateau the trees rose up like a wall, but beyond them the ground sloped away again, the trees were further apart, and the ground was carpeted with heather. There was no path any more, but the walking was easier.

And then I saw a light. Between the trees, maybe a hundred metres further on.

It looked like it came from a fire.

Kenneth would be drawn to it. If he saw it, he'd go there.

But who would have lit a fire in the woods?

Kids drinking in secret, perhaps.

They wouldn't care that open fires were prohibited.

I went diagonally down the shallow slope, my feet swishing through the heather. At the bottom, two enormous trees lay toppled on the ground, while behind them the woods grew dense again.

The fire seemed just as far away as before. Maybe it was because I was no longer seeing it from above. And then, as I zigzagged my way between the tall, dark spruce, the opposite seemed to be true and it appeared to be a lot closer than I'd thought.

There, in a small boggy-looking clearing among the trees.

All I could see was its glow. Not a sound came from anywhere.

Surely no one would leave a fire burning in the woods?

Maybe they were asleep.

Yes, that'd be it.

And Kenneth, of course, wasn't there. Why would he have been?

It was as if during the last few minutes I'd forgotten what I was actually doing. How desperate a situation I was in.

And how far I'd walked!

I looked at the time.

I hadn't been away more than twenty minutes.

Could just as well go over and have a look.

I walked forward following a narrow stream that had almost dried up to a trickle, in places quite hidden beneath the branches of the spruce that grew on both sides.

Somewhere close by, there was a sound. I froze, and abruptly it stopped.

It had sounded like someone coming through the undergrowth.

'Hello?' I said, the feeblest croak. 'Is anyone there?'

And then, an eerie clicking noise sounded out harshly through the trees.

There was a reply, the same sound from a different place.

I was so terrified I couldn't move.

Then, above my head, as loud as a human cry, came a birdlike squawk.

KRUUAAA!

My heart thumped in my chest, for as I tipped my head back and looked up, a great shadow came gliding from out of the tree where I stood, sailing through the air above the dell, dissolving into the darkness on the other side of the stream.

The clicking sounded again, only now it was so very close by.

I wanted to scream.

But if I did, they'd come for me.

Petrified, my whole body trembling, I stood and peered into the darkness from where the sound had come.

That bird, that great bird, had been covered in scales.

I couldn't see anything.

Nothing in the clearing in front of me.

And everything was quiet again.

Not a sound, not a movement.

It was as if an enormous wave had come crashing down on me, only then to retreat again as quickly as it had come.

I had to get away.

But I was too frightened to move.

Cautiously, I started towards the little clearing again.

The fire dwindled. The flames subsided, the light they gave diminished.

Out of the trees on the other side came Kenneth.

He walked slowly, as if in sleep.

In front of him, the fire died out.

The clicking started again, from several directions at the same time, though softer now than before.

kalikalikalikalik

He stopped, his naked body shimmering faintly in the light from the firmament.

And then he knelt.

kalikalikalikalik

There was a rustling in the undergrowth close to me. A shadow flitted away. A few seconds later it emerged into the clearing. It was a man. He moved quickly, fitfully almost, his motions fluid and yet at the same time oddly stiff. His head was large and heavy, like that of an ox. Three plaits of hair hung down his naked back. The fingers of his enormous hand splayed out into the air. His other hand held a vessel.

kalikalikalikalik

He halted in front of Kenneth.

Kenneth lifted his head and looked up into the sky.

Leaning forward, the man dipped his hand into the vessel and placed it on Kenneth's brow. A shudder went through Kenneth's body and he fell backwards onto the ground.

The man turned and looked at me.

His eyes were yellow, only it wasn't a man. It wasn't a man.

SECOND DAY

SECOND DAY

EGIL

The morning did not begin well. I hadn't gone to bed until nearly four and having forgotten to draw the blind I woke up as soon as the first sunlight flooded the room somewhere around half six. There was no way I could fall asleep again, I knew that, but I tried nonetheless, for few things are worse than those pointless hours in the morning when you haven't had enough sleep to be able to concentrate — and can no longer, as I could no longer, have a drink or two to help get you going.

Or rather, I *could*, I thought to myself, tossing and turning under the cover in the first warmth of day. The restriction was self-imposed, which meant I could lift it myself at any time.

Why were there two of me? One who said no, and one who egged me on. One who wanted to, and one who did not. How much easier human life would be if inner agreement had been our default setting.

And then everything that had happened the evening and night before came crashing down on me.

The new star.

Was it still there?

I got up and went out onto the veranda.

The star was still shining in the north. Even then, in the morning, with the sun in the sky.

Clearly, it was strong. Or close.

A morning star.

I am the bright Morning Star, Jesus said.

But in Isaiah the Morning Star was the Devil.

Wasn't that right?

I'd have to check.

I stood with my hands on the rail, angled forward as I looked out over the sea. It was dark blue and so still that its surface didn't appear to be fluid at all, but comprised of something firm. A kind of blue glass in which the sun glittered and gleamed.

Some gulls soared in the air above me. They seemed almost to be enjoying the warmth and stillness.

A stillness so seldom here.

I ran a hand through my hair and realised how greasy it was.

It was too hot for a shower, but maybe a swim instead?

I went inside and took a towel from the cupboard in the bedroom, put a pair of trunks on and a shirt, slipped my feet into my sandals and went back out again, pausing at the desk in the living room where the typewriter was, pulling out the sheet of paper I'd been typing on when Arne rang, putting it on top of the pile next to the typewriter without reading what I'd written.

The star was obviously a sign.

But of what?

It would become apparent soon enough.

But where, and to whom?

I followed the path below the house to the smooth, flat rock at the shore. I'd swum from the same place ever since I was a child, dark, gently sloping rock sheltered by a sheer outcrop with a deep pool at its foot. It felt like the spot belonged to the property, and it always annoyed me if other people used it, though of course I never said anything, we didn't own the rocks.

But I was alone.

The water looked inviting with its unruffled, deep blue surface, but I wasn't twelve years old any more, I knew that the first seconds of immersion would be an icy shock regardless of how warm the water actually was, so I took off my shirt and sandals and sat down first to gather courage and soak up some sun.

There had been something rather nightmarish about the evening before, I thought, as I stared at the hazy horizon. Arne's bloodied face on the beach, the car crashed among the trees, the enormous star in the sky. The heat in the dark of night, the badger inside the house, the cat with its head torn off. And Tove, her manic demeanour.

It all seemed such a far cry from the peacefulness that surrounded me as I sat there on the rock.

It was all their own doing, and yet they acted like it was something that just happened to them, like it was the same for everyone.

I wondered for a second whether I should look in on them later, but dismissed the idea almost immediately. I liked talking to Arne, so it wasn't that, it just seemed to come with a price I wasn't ready to pay for the moment. It was impossible to be in that house without it leaving a mark in some way, as if when I left bits of their chaos would be stuck to me and I always had to struggle to get rid of them again. They were a family in need, only they didn't realise it.

How stupid to accept those beers.

I needed to stay *well* away.

Even if it had only been a couple of beers and I'd been nowhere near drunk, it was the contact with it that mattered. It being so near to me the whole time.

Why was it so bloody hard to stick to a decision?

I got to my feet and clambered up the rock, stood on the edge, raised my arms above my head and dived in. Cold, briny water engulfed my warm skin. I opened my eyes to a swirling effervescence of tiny bubbles, the bottom shimmering green a couple of metres beneath me. I took a few short strokes, pulling myself downwards before turning, launching myself upwards and breaking the surface with a splutter.

It was good.

I climbed up onto the low rock, rubbed myself dry with the towel, put on my shirt without buttoning it, slipped my feet into my sandals and went back up to the house again.

The summer house is all I want, nothing else, I'd told my father when the issue of inheritance had been raised. If I can't have it, then so be it, but I won't have *anything* else.

And so he gave it me. As well as a generous sum of money transferred to my account every month. I hadn't asked for that, but I hadn't turned it down either.

It wasn't good, taking the money. I assumed he despised me for my lack of pride, the way one hand refused to take what he was offering, while the other accepted it. But he'd never said so, not with a single word.

And I needed the money.

I walked round the side of the house to the end that faced west, to see if the spider had caught anything in its web. I referred to it as the King, an enormous beast of a thing that seemed to have been around for several years. It moved about a bit, spun its webs, hid itself away, first in one place, then another, according to its own unfathomable logic. It had been settled at this side of the house for a couple of months now.

A bumblebee hung suspended in the web. It looked like it was dead, but it was hard to tell. I leaned forward and peered up under the beam, where the King at present resided.

There he was, yes.

Quite unmoving, his legs tucked into his body in the darkness, the intricate structure he'd woven stretched out beneath him.

No way could evolution be blind. No way could something so sophisticated and yet so simple have arisen by chance, no matter how many millions of years chance had at its disposal.

I prodded the bumblebee cautiously with the tip of my finger and watched it sway a couple of times back and forth.

How on earth could a spider manage to eat such a thing?

I went back up onto the veranda, slid the big glass door open, fetched a can of Pepsi Max from the fridge, picked up the novel I was reading, my cigarettes and an ashtray, and sat down in my chair outside.

There still wasn't a cloud in the sky, and if it hadn't been for the rocks at the shore and the islets that seemed almost radiantly white in the sunshine, the world would have been completely blue from where I was sitting.

I opened the can and took a slurp, lit a cigarette and tried to read for a bit. I was halfway through Hemingway's *Islands in the Stream*, but the Caribbean world in which it was set was impossible to conjure up in the sun-drenched Nordic coastal landscape that surrounded me. I saw pine forest, Scandinavian summer homes and pebbled beaches, not palm trees and colonial mansions. Besides, I was rather too tired to concentrate properly. And the heat was already exasperating, to put it mildly.

A *smeigedag*, I thought, putting the book down on the table next to me. Wasn't that what they were called, days like this? Or maybe that wasn't quite right. The word was unconditionally positive in its associations, used to refer to those long and lazy summer days that miraculously opened up to us after the interminable winter season, but this heat had something sick about it that could only be endured, not enjoyed.

And yet, going by the number of plastic tubs, with and without sails, that had now begun ploughing the waters out there (I refused to call such vessels boats), people were somehow doing just that.

The phone rang in the bedroom. I stubbed out my smoke and went inside, bending down to try and see the number on the little display in the bright sunlight that fell into the room.

It was Camilla.

What did she want now?

I waited until it stopped ringing, muted it and dropped it into my shirt pocket, put on a pair of shorts, a straw hat and sunglasses, went out the other side, got on my bike and pedalled off down the narrow gravel track, past the pontoons in the bay and onto the road, which although paved was barely wider than the track.

The hot air rose up in columns between the trees, and the smell of the woods, of bare, dry leaves and sun-baked soil, wafted towards me as I cycled.

Willowherb in the roadside ditches, on the sloping ground that swept towards the water, raspberry bushes clinging to the crash barriers.

She'd called the evening before. I'd answered then. Fool that I was. She told me she was going to Rome and that I'd have to look after Viktor for a week. She was leaving today!

I'd told her I couldn't, that it was impossible at such short notice.

I'd kept a civil tongue and been quite rational. She was angry. Furious, more accurately.

But it was unreasonable, to say the least.

Why couldn't you have told me before? I said. It wouldn't have been a problem then.

But I only got to know today, that's what I'm saying! she shouted. You never spend time with him. And this is a big chance for me, I can't possibly say no!

No need to shout, I told her. What about your parents?

My parents are in fucking Thailand!

Your brother, then?

But you're his *dad*. For fuck's sake, Egil!

Can't you take him with you? I suggested.

But then she hung up.

I missed the boy, of course I did, so it wasn't that. But he couldn't just come at the drop of a hat. I had to prepare, get in the right frame of mind. Because when he was here, he took up my whole time. Took up all my space.

I'd reached the foot of the hill leading up towards the woods, and stood up on the pedals.

Bilberry, heather, liverworts and mosses carpeted the ground between the trees. White shimmering trunks of birch could be glimpsed further within, where the bogland began.

Why wasn't this good enough? Why wasn't it sufficient in itself?

Passing through the woods, the air was if anything even hotter, and I felt the sweat trickle down my neck and the length of my spine as I sat down again and pedalled on.

I am here, at this moment in time.

It's enough.

No smartphone, just a small Nokia, no GPS, no engine, only pedals, wheels, the hot air against my body, the woods.

The last few kilometres were easy, the road either flat or sloping gently away, and after fifteen minutes or so I was at the place where Arne had crashed his car the night before. I wheeled the bike down the path towards the stony beach, lugged it over the rocks and through the trees in the direction of the inlet where I'd moored the boat. It was hard going, boggy areas of blackthorn and thorny rose hip over which the bike had to be lifted before I could carry on were a hindrance, and the low, wind-pressed pines that were more like bushes would have been difficult to negotiate even without a bike. And all because of that idiot Arne, I thought, leaning on the handlebars as I paused for a moment.

In some strange way he seemed to bask in Tove's madness. It made him important, or so he seemed to believe.

But anxiety is hell. Depression is hell. Psychosis is hell.

The path on which I now stood was dry earth, carpeted with twigs and yellow pine needles, edged with rocks and scrubby vegetation. The sun beat down on it, its golden light shimmering in every detail, as if everything had been accorded its own little halo. I lit a cigarette, noticing a large anthill a bit further on, in a small glade between low, crooked pines.

I pulled the branches aside and went up to it, crouching down with my cigarette in my hand. The mound was crawling with ants, its whole surface seemed to be in motion, as if it were alive, a creature in its own right. A moment later, the first ant crawled onto my foot. Brown and black in colour, its tiny body perfectly articulated, it proceeded fearlessly across the strap of my sandal. More followed, and I wondered what they would do. Bite me to chase me away? Or did they think I was a kind of tree they should climb?

I brushed them away carefully, straightened up and turned to go back.

But there was something strange, glistening in the sunlight by one of the tree trunks beside me. At first I thought it was a coat, half rotted and shapeless, but when I stepped towards it and bent forward to investigate I saw that it was a skin of some kind that had been sloughed off. Dry and translucent, like the snakeskins you could sometimes find in the woods in spring, only this wasn't from a snake, it was far too big.

I gripped it tentatively between my thumb and index finger and pulled it towards me.

Christ almighty.

It was as long as a child was tall.

What kind of animal could it have belonged to?

Thin, dry and scaly.

I drew myself upright and looked around me.

Everything was still, not even the sea made a sound.

And then: the drone of an outboard at the top of its register, passing towards the mouth of the sea in the west.

A smartphone would have been handy, I thought as I went back to the bike. I could have taken a photo of the skin, if that's what it was, and maybe googled it too. The same thing with the Morning Star, that strange double reference in the Bible to the Devil and Jesus. I'd have to sit and pore through books now.

Not that it was any particular sacrifice. In fact, it was better that way.

It meant there was a time lapse between question and answer, a space that opened up: a span that had to be bridged, an effort to be made.

The knowledge gained would be the same, but the effort increased its value.

Wasn't that right?

Or was it just harking back to the eighties? A time when friction was a marker of quality? Noise in music, unreadability in literature?

I picked up the bike, rested the frame on my shoulder and walked the last bit of the way through the wood and down to the boat, which was still there, the outboard and everything else exactly as I'd left it. I untied the mooring and drew the boat in, hauling it up slightly onto the narrow shore, put the bike down in the bottom, pushed out while wading alongside, then climbed in, took up the small anchor, started the engine and drew slowly away.

The weather was as boiling hot as before, but the heat wasn't nearly as oppressive on the water.

I turned round and saw the waves spread in my wake, the landscape that seemed almost to come down to greet the sea, sloping towards its surface, its vegetation thinning and diminishing, until at last it faded into it and was gone.

I got my phone out to see if Camilla had sent me an abusive text, as I was expecting. The light was so strong I had to hunch up and shield the display with my hand so as to create enough shadow to be able to see.

Yes, there was a message from her.

I opened it.

Viktor's on the bus on his way to you. Collect him at the bus station 11.40. Camilla

What the hell?

Had she gone mad?

She couldn't do this to me.

There was no agreement!

What if I was ill?

I'd told her I couldn't!

I couldn't!

And who was supposed to look after him then?

Didn't she think of what might be best for *him*?

I felt like hurling the phone into the sea, but then thought better of it, put it down next to me on the thwart and opened the throttle until I regained some equilibrium.

Bloody bitch.

11.40?

It was nearly that now!

I picked up the phone again and texted her while glancing up now and again to make sure there were no other boats coming towards me.

I can't collect him. So he'll be on his own at the bus station. Egil

She wasn't the only one who could play games, I told myself, the phone in my hand so that I could see as soon as she replied.

I was clear of Vågsøya and described now a wide arc as I turned towards the east. With the speed I was doing, I'd be back in a matter of minutes.

By the time I eased off the throttle again and the bow sank back, the boat slowly gliding in towards the jetty, she still hadn't answered. I moored, lifted the bike ashore, took the fuel can with me and went up to the house.

It was gone ten o'clock.

I'd have to go and collect him, there were no two ways about it. And then I'd put him on the next bus back the other way.

I put the fuel can in the shed, lit a cigarette and got myself a beer from the fridge, put the parasol up on the decking and sat down with my feet up on the rail.

I took a long slurp. And then phoned her.

No answer.

She had to have some kind of contingency plan in case I didn't turn up, surely? It would be totally unlike her to run such a risk.

But I couldn't be sure.

What would happen if no one picked him up?

It'd be a case for the authorities then. The child protection system.

Which would hurt her more than me, seeing as she had custody.

But what if they took it away from her? Would it then be passed on to me?

I *couldn't* have him full-time. It wasn't even an option.

Did she have a contingency plan?

I phoned again.

No answer.

I finished my beer, went into the kitchen and put the empty bottle in the crate next to the fridge, then stood there for a moment staring into the room without really seeing anything.

My phone vibrated as a text came in.

Not answering your calls. So now you know how it feels. Boarding flight now. Enjoy yourself with Viktor!

Her triumphant tone filled me with loathing. I saw the look on her face, the smirk she put on when she knew she was right. Her eyes, at once goading and as cold as ice.

At least we weren't together any more, that was one good thing.

Can't collect him, I'm afraid, I typed. *Hope for your sake someone does. You're the one with custody.*

That would give her something to think about.

I fetched the fuel can from the shed again and went down to the boat.

She knew I'd cave in eventually, knew how weak I was. She'd seen me with tears in my eyes when we'd argued. But also when something unexpectedly good happened, she'd seen me cry then too.

It was beyond her comprehension. That a modicum of goodness all of a sudden could bring me to tears.

I couldn't have stayed with her.

With the fuel can beside me on the jetty, bright red in all the blue, I drew the boat in, stepped on board, untied the moorings and connected the fuel line to the outboard, backed out carefully in a tight crescent and threw the motor into forward gear before setting off.

If I ever wrote a love poem, I'd dedicate it to the skerries here. To the maritime life, where the water is the way and boats the mode of transport. I'd never been able to express to anyone what it meant to me, what lifted inside me when I saw the jetties in town where people moored up, the ferries that plied between the islands, the water lapping towards the bank building, the hotel, the warehouses that lined the road, the fish processing plant where the mackerel lay on their beds of ice in polystyrene crates, the flags that flapped in the sea breeze, flaglines snapping against their poles. The cormorants out on the islands, the grassy hollows of the islets, the lighthouse at the mouth of the sea, the fish in the depths, the crabs on the barnacles at night. I'd tried many times over the years, to explain to friends and girlfriends I'd had, and to a point they'd understood, nodding and agreeing how pleasant it all was. But that wasn't it at all! Whenever I looked around, at the waterways and the boats, the houses that were turned towards the sea, the sea buffeting the land, be it the islets and islands, inlets or towns, whenever I saw all that, what struck me with such force was that it was so alien, so *other*, as if it were the inception of a different world altogether, a world of water. And when I crossed the square with my carrier bags of groceries and went down the steps to the boat that lay moored there in the middle of town, and sailed slowly out through the channel towards the open sea, it was as if I inhabited Italo Calvino's novel *Invisible Cities*.

It was a feeling that never ran down. On the contrary, it became more entrenched with every year I lived here.

It was by no means unthinkable that Viktor in time would relate to the place in the same way, though it was hardly likely, I thought to myself as I entered the narrow strait between the two main islands, where the houses stood huddled together on both sides, red or white, an occasional yellow ochre, windows glittering in the sunshine. He was a city boy and preferred the indoors.

But maybe we could enjoy a few nice days here together anyway.

A bit of fishing, a bit of swimming. A trip into town now and then for an ice cream.

What more could a ten-year-old want?

But a whole week was a long time. I already longed to sit down and read, go for a walk afterwards, read again as darkness fell, and perhaps do some more writing too.

I sailed at the sedatest of paces among all the boats in the strait. People didn't care once they were out here, but lay sunbathing on their decks, filling themselves with food and beer, music blaring as if they were at home, not a thought for being in a public space.

I wished they weren't here. That the strait was devoid of boats, the islands devoid of people. So it all could emerge in its true form and come into its own. Or perhaps that wasn't the way to put it. I just wanted the sense of being *here*, here in this particular place, a place on earth. I wanted the place to inhabit me, and I it.

That's how it was in autumn, throughout the winter and early spring. So I couldn't complain.

And other people had just as much right to be here as me.

But they were encapsulated in something else when they were here. They turned up their music, listened to their radios, exchanged chat and banter, immersed themselves in their phones. They brought their own worlds with them and barely absorbed this one.

I entered the more open part of the strait and picked up speed. It was quarter past eleven already, but I still had plenty of time.

Between the green trees growing on the two islands, houses and out-crops of rock projected in explosive displays of colour and detail. At the end of the strait lay the town, as if vibrating beneath the blue sky, white-painted houses clinging to its steep streets, the old radio mast rising up from the top of the hill.

Jesus had been a loner, he had all the features. He rejected his mother and brother, didn't want to know about them. The disciples he attracted were no substitute family — the relationship was one way only: Jesus spoke, the disciples listened; Jesus dictated, the disciples obeyed. Weeks in the wilderness. A clear longing for death.

What had he done in the thirty years before stepping out as the Saviour?

Had he reimagined himself? Was that why he suddenly emerged into the open and became visible?

Emerged from what? From what existence, from what life?

One of the things I'd been thinking about most that summer was whether religion — specifically Christianity — was mainly a social phe-nomenon or whether conversely it was turned away from the social domain. The teachings of Christ were of course highly social in nature, to the extent that they were all about turning the other cheek and look-ing after the weak and infirm. That all men were equal was easy enough to proclaim, and indeed many did, but the full implications of such a standpoint were in fact almost inhuman. In an essay he once wrote about Rembrandt, Jean Genet goes off track and describes a situation in a train carriage in which a hideous and loathsome-looking man is

seated opposite him, and Genet is struck by sudden, terrifying insight
as he asks himself whether such a man could be his equal. Are *you*
equal to *me*?

Idiots, liars, murderers, wife-beaters, paedophiles. Equal to *me*?

Yes, and yes again.

It was the social aspect of Christianity that Nietzsche railed against
and so brutally exposed. In Christianity, the weak discovered they could
browbeat the strong. So weak became strong, bad became good, sick-
ness became health. Morality constrains, oppresses, hinders. No true
development, no true freedom, no true greatness is possible under the
tyranny of the weak. But Nietzsche was impossible to read without consideration of the fact that he himself was a loser, weak and alone, and
that everything he wrote about will, about power and about the strong,
was to compensate for his own inadequacy. His thoughts were by no
means poorer on that account, for there is no doubt that Nietzsche was
one of the greatest thinkers since the classical era, the freedom in his
thoughts, their sheer power, was unrivalled — but they remained just
that, thoughts. The thoughts of Christ changed the world. Nietzsche's
thoughts changed merely thoughts. And Jesus was not weak, his
unprecedented power shines throughout the Gospels, though they
were written so long after his death.

But it wasn't the message of love for one's fellow men that turned
me towards Christianity. On the contrary, in fact. The great problem of
our time was that everything was about human beings and nothing
existed any longer outside the sphere of the human. No matter which
way you turned, you encountered human eyes, or something human
eyes had seen. In a way, I was as far removed from faith as could be.
From the moment I opted out of the Church of Norway at the age of
sixteen, I'd felt nothing but contempt for Christianity — and all other
religions too, for that matter — but I was still interested in faith as a
phenomenon, what it meant, basically, to believe. Faith was something
that gave meaning to life, I assumed, and meaning interested me. But
to believe seemed to me to pander to a system, a package as it were of
conceptions and values, something ready-made and compiled by others, and the price to be paid for being rewarded with that meaning was
constraints on one's freedom. Faith was for the feeble of mind, those

lacking independence, the submissive, who gladly allowed themselves to be led. I read Kierkegaard's *Fear and Trembling* and realised there was another way of believing, and a Christianity other than the one Nietzsche had attacked — issuing from the idea of the social realm. Kierkegaard's book contains a number of strange vignettes concerning the weaning of a child from the mother's breast, that first relationship in a child's life, the symbiosis, warmth and security it was suddenly denied, and one could almost see the desire for what no longer was there, and the turning outwards towards everything else, which to the child as yet barely existed. Other people, the social world, society. Faith was thus a turning away from the realm of the social, again towards something that as yet barely existed. This was where Abraham went when he climbed the mount to sacrifice his son to God. He was filled with a father's love, and his faith directed him towards an abyss. Perhaps what awaited him there was simply emptiness, the terrible void. His faith surmounted his fear, which made faith inhuman, for what person can kill his son with intent and leave the human realm to face the unknown that perhaps indeed was the terrible void? I found the thought compelling, but it meant nothing to me, it was without consequence, there was no way I could absorb it into my own life.

But something must have happened, unbeknown to my conscious self I must have been working away at it, because during the winter I had become converted. In an indescribable moment of joy, everything slotted into place. The insight, for that's what it was, had since faded somewhat, and I strove continually to approach it once more. And although the days were dark, its light was somewhere always shining, whether in my soul I was in the forest or on the sea, all I had to do was go towards it.

I had basically vegetated all that winter, sleeping long into the mornings, my phone muted, not bothering to wash or change my clothes, still trying to get out for a walk during the daytime, but mostly lazing around on the sofa. I had started drinking as soon as the light began to fade. In previous years, I'd often thought about how fantastic it would be to live on my own in the summer house, and then, after Camilla, I'd actually moved out here. It wasn't that fantastic any more. Of course, I realised it wasn't the house, or the landscape, or the hermit-like existence that was the problem, it was me. I didn't care for my own company. This was ironic. For all the years I'd been in various relationships I'd always yearned to be alone, and when eventually I took the consequences of that yearning, it merely led me to yearn even more. But to where? For what? I'd been running away all my life, a person didn't have to be a psychoanalyst to see that. I'd thought I was running away from the others — my father and brothers, Torill and the whole shebang, my home town, and home country, the conformity of education, Therese and Helene and Hanne, and all the women I'd had in between, when I was king of the castle — but it was so clearly myself I'd been running from.

It was an embarrassing insight, all the more so for it being so obvious. Those around me had surely recognised it for what it was all along.

Was everything a person did down to the disposition of their soul?

I had refused to accept it, and yet, lying there on the sofa that winter, with that key in my hand, all doors were indeed opened.

I was cowardly, shied away from conflicts, from work, from people. I avoided every demand, sought the path of least resistance, drank too much, thought only of myself.

It had led me here.

The first days of the new year had brought snow, thick and still. The temperature had been around zero, a fog had settled heavily on the sea and woods. When I went for my daily walks, usually in the afternoon just before dusk, always the same route, following the smooth, rounded rock of the shore, along the pebbled beach and back again through the woods, the stillness was so apparent as to seem ominous. Fog deadens all sound, packing the landscape in its dampness, and no one else was out here at that time of year, the nearest road with any traffic to speak of was several kilometres away.

All I could hear on my walks were my own footsteps, my own thoughts.

The air grew colder, a thin layer of ice covering the rocks, the fog retreating, but not the clouds, which hung like a dark curtain over the horizon. A wind picked up as the snow fell once more, the air a flurry of tiny shards tossed this way and that. Even the few steps to the shed to fetch wood became an expedition requiring scarf, woolly hat and gloves. Returning inside, I placed three logs from the pile I held in my arms in the stove, dumping the rest in the box next to it, then I removed my outer garments and lay down on the sofa. It was only just gone eleven o'clock, but it was so dark outside that the fire already reflected faintly in the windowpane. The sea roared.

Then: church bells.

Or rather: at first I couldn't place the sound that was only just audible against the storm, dissolving almost completely into the rushing of trees, the battering wind that raced up from the shore, the low, thunderous rumble of the sea.

Ding, ding, ding, they said, so faint and so apart from the other sounds out there that it was as if they came from a land beyond.

I hadn't even known it was Sunday.

I'm going, I said to myself, and got to my feet. It would do me good to listen to something other than just my own thoughts. And if I couldn't stand what I heard, at least there'd be something to look at in there.

I had put a thick sweater on, anorak, hat and gloves, wound a scarf around my lower face and gone out. It had stopped snowing, though no one would have believed it, for the air was still whirling with snowflakes whipped up by the wind, thrown about at its will.

The church stood on top of a ridge above the sea and was visible from afar to anyone approaching the land by boat, yet almost completely hidden if you came from the road on the other side, as of course most people did nowadays. An outer wall of stone and brick dated back to the twelfth century when the first church had been situated there, whereas the rest of the structure was eighteenth century and made of timber.

I'd been up to the church several times before on my walks, it was only some twenty minutes away and I liked to emerge from the woods to see it there on top of the ridge: there was something fascinatingly archaic in our modern age about a house of God in the midst of nature. But I'd still never been inside.

When I opened the door on that particular morning, the service was already under way and the few people who were seated inside — hardly more than six or seven, eight at most, and all elderly — turned as I entered. I pulled off my hat and gloves and nodded tentatively, then

tucked myself into one of the rows of benches at the back, unwinding
my scarf and unzipping my anorak. My face felt warm on the inside
after my bracing walk, cold on the outside because of the biting wind.
I rubbed my cheeks a couple of times as I looked straight ahead at the
priest. He was elderly too, with a saggy face and glasses whose lenses
were so thick, their frames so obtrusive, that they wholly dominated
his appearance. His white collar was barely noticeable in comparison.

They had come to the confession. The priest looked down at the floor
as he led the congregation:

Holy God, our Creator,
look upon us in mercy.
We have sinned against you
and broken your commandments.
For the sake of Jesus Christ, forgive us.
Set us free that we may serve you, preserve the Creation
and love our neighbours as ourselves.

Had I possessed faith, I thought to myself, I'd probably have found
comfort in the words. But since I did not, the words had no force, were
connected to nothing. There was no one to look upon us in mercy, no
one to forgive us, no one to set us free.

I looked up at the ceiling. It was green with white clouds painted on it.
The green colour was beautiful, but unexpected: why not sky blue? The
hue reminded me of the sea over a deep sandbank on a summer's day.
The clouds were crude representations and quite identical. Suspended
from the sky hung a large model of a sailing ship. What kind of Christianity was this? Rococo clouds under an eighteenth-century maritime sky?

The rows of benches terminated in a kind of portal with a large, styl-
ised lion on each side. Here and there were paintings showing biblical
motifs, which must have been even more unfamiliar then, before the
advent of photographs and film, in an age when none of the people
who came to sit in the church would have been able to travel to Israel
to behold with their own eyes the Sea of Galilee, Jerusalem, Bethlehem
or Nazareth.

It must have been like a fairy tale.

As the maritime eighteenth century with its forests of masts in the harbour was now like a fairy tale to us.

It felt strange to be present in a space that was so dense with meaning, in the woodland at the edge of the sea, but even stranger, I thought to myself, that none of that meaning remained valid. The insights that were immersed in those symbols, their deposits of meaning, were no longer relevant to us.

Only a few dithering old folk cared enough to come here now. To them, the church was a kind of spiritual walking aid. Their voices as the priest led them in the hymns were crackled and dry. A single woman, however, sang brightly and with gusto, and perhaps then she heard again her twenty-year-old self, though her song projected now backwards rather than forwards in life.

Towards the end of the service, the priest said the creed and I pricked up my ears:

I believe in God, the Father almighty,
creator of heaven and earth.
I believe in Jesus Christ, his only Son, our Lord,
who was conceived by the Holy Spirit,
born of the Virgin Mary,
suffered under Pontius Pilate,
was crucified, died, and was buried;
he descended to the dead.
On the third day he rose again;
he ascended into heaven,
he is seated at the right hand of the Father,
and he will come to judge the living and the dead.

I believe in the Holy Spirit,
the holy catholic Church,
the communion of saints,
the forgiveness of sins,
the resurrection of the body,
and the life everlasting.
Amen.

This too was like a fairy tale. Born of a virgin, yet son of a king. And 'the third day', why not the second or fourth?

Then followed the intercessions, the repeated confession and prayers that concluded the service, and the attendant, a squinting man in his sixties with wiry white hair who licked his lips incessantly, passed among the congregation for the collection. I found a couple of crumpled 500-krone notes in my trouser pocket, which I gave him, mostly because I felt sorry for him, only a small handful of coins lying at the bottom of the small woven basket he held out towards me.

Outside: the wind, the mighty sea, the darkened sky.

Cars, turning one by one in the car park, pulling away onto the road in the flurrying snow.

I followed the old cart road through the woods, where the wind squeezed its way past the trunks of the trees, dumping its snow against their bark, and emerged after a while into the wide-open space that a few decades earlier had been used as a shooting range and before that, during the war, had served as a landing strip for German aircraft. Now its only purpose was as a place for people to leave their cars when they came to swim and laze on the beach in summer. The concrete ruins of abandoned German fortifications faced the sea, from where the wind now came whipping. It was conceivable, I thought to myself as I crossed that empty space, my head bent against the elements, that it was merely their way of worship that was archaic, belonging to a bygone age, whereas what they believed in was immutable, had always been there and always would be there, and that faith would be able to find — as perhaps it always had found — new pathways to deliverance, from the different places that were the cultures of our different ages?

The problem in that was Jesus. There was absolutely nothing timeless about him, and nothing immutable. He'd lived in a particular place, in a particular age, at the same time as others known to us from history. Augustus, Herod, Pontius Pilate. And what happened to him happened only once and was never repeated, as is the case for all of us, in all our lives, in the natural circumstances of time under which we live.

The worship of Jesus Christ amounted to a hallowing of ourselves, did it not? Making God one of us?

Was this perhaps the germ of the total humanisation of existence in which we now lived?

I reached the end of the clearing and followed the path on into the woods. Everything around me seemed to be in a state of turmoil. The wind rushed in the trees, whose branches creaked and groaned; the waves roared and crashed; the air was a howl. I felt invigorated, though more by the church interior than by the ritual that had taken place there; the sense of being in a space so filled with meaning had been good, even if that meaning was less than relevant to me.

What did they believe, those who believed?

I'd never quite understood it.

Below me, great waves rose up like sea monsters hurling themselves at the shore. The sea crested white as far as I could see; above, the sky was grey-black and low. Where the path veered to the north, the sea disappeared from view, but its noise remained, lingering among the trees as if disconnected from its origin.

I wanted meaning in my life. But I couldn't believe in something I didn't believe in. I couldn't just plunge in and hope something out there would gather me up, quite simply because I didn't believe there *was* anything out there.

I paused and stared ahead. Tall, straight spruce swayed like ships' masts in the wind. Further in was a thick belt of pine, their branches waving, flailing, though the trees themselves stood almost unmoving. There was a different weight about them, a different darkness.

'God, give me a sign!' I said into the air.

Did I really say that? I asked myself in the very next instant.

Was I, a grown man, really standing there in the woods asking God for a sign?

Embarrassed and ashamed, I forged on, burying my lower face in my thick, wide scarf, my woolly hat pulled down to my eyes. Suddenly all I wanted was the sofa, bed, sleep, darkness.

Something moved above me and I looked up.

A large, black bird came flying out of the storm. It flapped about, for a moment hanging suspended on a gust, though its wings were beating still. Then it settled on a branch just above me.

It was a raven, and it looked straight down at me.

I didn't know what to make of it.

It opened its beak, tipped its head back and squawked three times.

Krroaa! Krroaa! Krroaa!

With that, it flapped its wings, flew up above the treetops and vanished from sight.

Bewildered, I began to walk again. I had asked for a sign, and a bird had come. It was a coincidence, it had to be! If there was a God, an almighty, He surely wouldn't care what I did or said!

And yet: a bird had come. It had looked straight at me. And it had cried three times. Not two, not four.

After I'd been pondering the fairy-tale aspect of Jesus spending three days in the kingdom of the dead.

The path skirted a small rise in the landscape before leading down towards the sea again. An old sand quarry lay gaping. Not a soul to be seen. Nor any beast or bird.

When I'd moved to Norway at sixteen to start gymnasium school, I'd spent some time during that first autumn term discussing religion with one of the girls in my class, Kathrine her name was, she was a Christian and defended her faith fiercely. My opinions then hadn't been that important to me, and the things I said were intended to goad her more than anything else, and to make me interesting to her. In fact, for a few months I hardly thought about anything else but her. One day, she brought a picture with her to school that she wanted to show me. It was a column of light breaking through dense cloud. You say God doesn't exist, she said, that He's just an invention. But this is no invention, she said, holding the picture up in front of me. But that's just the sun, I said. You worship the sun? I was genuinely surprised at her naivety. It hurt her, of course. And now all of a sudden I was the one seeing signs of God's presence, not in the sun, but in a bird, and not as a credulous sixteen-year-old, but as a grown man at the midpoint of life.

By the time I got back to the house and let myself in, I'd distanced myself sufficiently from the occurrence to be able to smile at my folly. I stamped the snow from my boots against the door sill, took off my outer layers and hung them on two chairs I pulled up in front of the wood burner, placed three logs on top of the embers, knelt down and blew until the flames began to wrap around them. Then I went into the bedroom, switched the light on and stood in front of the bookshelf. Reading *Fear and Trembling*, I'd become so enthused by Kierkegaard's thinking and the style of his writing that I'd immediately ordered his collected works from the Danish publishers. They amounted to more than fifty volumes and to my shame I'd yet to open a single one, since my fervour over the knight of faith and the sphere of infinite resignation, and all the other things Kierkegaard wrote about, had evaporated during the time it took for the box of books to arrive.

Now my eyes passed along their blue spines. One title contained the word 'bird' and I pulled it out. *The Lily of the Field and the Bird of the Air*. Flicking through the pages, I realised it was a sermon. An interpretation of a passage in the New Testament. I took it with me to the desk in the living room, sat down and began to read.

When I'd finished, it was dark outside and the wind had subsided.

I was filled with an emotion so immense I hardly knew what to do with it. Thoughts were suddenly nothing, nada, nichts.

I closed the book and crouched down in front of the wood burner again, crumpled some newspaper, placed some bits of bark, twigs and other dry sweepings on top, leaned three logs up against each other as if to form a tepee, struck a match and watched as the fire flamed yellow and a circle of black spread across the newspaper, which at the same time curled in on itself and was consumed.

God's kingdom was here.

I turned round and felt the clothes that were hung from the backs of the two chairs. They were quite dry now. I put them on, sat down on the stool by the door and put my boots on. The snow from earlier had melted into little pools that still lay on the floor, slight, lustrous distensions on the varnished floorboards. The flames leapt in the wood burner. Apart from the hiss and crackle of the fire, the room was quite still.

God's kingdom was here.

I got to my feet, opened the door and went out. The snow-covered ground leading down to the sea in front of me was without movement. Stars shimmered in the clear, dark sky. The temperature had dropped dramatically; it felt like minus five, perhaps even minus ten. A snowdrift was blocking the door of the shed. I decided I might as well shift it, went round the side of the house to the little extension where my father used to keep the car, fetched the spade, went back and began to dig.

I suppose all of us have yearned for freedom at some stage in life. That yearning is like a spring, pressed tighter and tighter together, packed ever harder, until it reaches the point where its compacted force can be compacted no more, and the spring releases. Often, this happens first at the age of seventeen or eighteen, when the young adult leaves the home of the parents, and again in one's forties, when our new family is torn asunder by it. But it's not only our need for freedom that changes as we proceed through life, our understanding of it does too. I like to think of society in such a way that a key concept like freedom is construed differently by different groups, and it's the force that arises in their interactions in the friction of dissimilarity, that drives society forward — or back, if that's where the momentum is directed, or round in circles. The yearning for freedom, if acted upon, leads to departure and thereby to something new. We break up, and break away. That the new is so often the same as the old, precipitates counter-insights, which too are prevalent, living their lives alongside our yearnings for freedom, our urges to break away, our beliefs as to the future, they too graduated, from mild to bottomless resignation, from the considerate desire to preserve, to the brutal compulsion to stagnate.

Hans Jonas, the Jewish philosopher who penned the standard work on Gnosticism, a pupil of Heidegger who, like other prominent pupils of Heidegger, distanced himself from his philosophy, not primarily by condemning it — though he did that too — but by expanding it, outlined towards the end of his life a proposal for a philosophy of biology in the framework of which he traced back such an ethically charged concept as freedom to a time long before man emerged; right back, in fact, to the very first origins of life. Reality, in this conception: matter in the thrall of material forces, without will, constrained by mechanical patterns of action. Streaming lava cooling into mountains, oceans evaporated by sun to become clouds, plummeting atmospheric pressure becoming winds, winds that cause the seas to storm, water eroding the rock, sand carried on the wind. Electrical charges dissecting the sky, bolts of lightning striving towards the ground. Indeed, the burning sun, the twinkling stars, the moon that orbits the earth that orbits the sun, in a disc-shaped galaxy that sails through the universe. Life, even its very first, unimaginably primitive forms, frees itself from this matter and the mechanics of this matter. Life is itself matter, and this is the miracle, that matter frees itself from matter and can do as it will, more or less independently of any system. That for those first hundreds of millions of years such will is so constrained, its room for manoeuvre so immeasurably small, is of no consequence in relation to the gigantic and unfathomable leap from matter that life entails. But the freedom that so occurs is not unconditional, for what happens when matter is set free is that at once a dependency arises, it too new and unprecedented. Life demands ever-constant supplies of nourishment, whether from the sun, water, soil or other life forms, and if such supplies are curtailed the living matter will revert to dead matter and freedom will come to an end. The dynamic between freedom and dependency is in other words fundamentally the same for monocellular life and bacteria as it is for us.

When I was sixteen, I saw only the one side of freedom. I held it above everything else and called myself an anarchist. What I had in mind then was a kind of absolute freedom: *no one* should have the right to decide over me, I should be able to do *only* as I pleased, and the same should apply to *everyone*. There should be no authorities, no societal superstructure, no boundaries between countries. In discussions I entered into at that time, my opinions naturally met with fierce opposition and much shaking of heads. Society would collapse without some form of hierarchy, and crime would flourish. 'What if you got the urge to kill someone, would that be OK, if no one was allowed to decide over another person's actions and there was nothing to stop you?' 'Of course,' I'd tell them, 'if you want to kill someone, go ahead, feel free. But you *wouldn't* kill another person, would you, even if you could? There's something stopping you? Those are your morals. It's *your* morals that set the limits, no one else's. People kill each other as it is, don't they? Even though we've got laws against it, and prisons and police, and even though it's the biggest taboo that exists. People are always going to kill other people, an anarchist society is no exception. But I think there'd be fewer cases. Because it's not just down to laws and rules of conduct imposed on people, there's also a huge pressure on people to live up to society's demands on them to fit in, earn money, obtain goods and status symbols, and those who fall by the wayside find freedom in criminality. Do you understand what I'm saying? In a society where that kind of pressure doesn't exist, where there's freedom for everybody, crime, at least to a very large degree, will cease.' 'Oh, you're so naive,' they'd naturally reply. 'No, you're the ones who are naive,' I'd come back at them, quite as naturally. 'Man is fundamentally good, it's society that turns him bad. Have you ever known a bad baby?'

It wasn't difficult to see where these opinions had come from. My father had taken over the family shipping business from his father, and as the eldest son it was expected that I should do likewise. He never said so in as many words, and when I began moving in a different direction, one that quite clearly was incompatible with a career in business, he expressed no disappointment. I understood that he'd already given up on me a long time before. But *I* felt the pressure, *I* felt that I'd disappointed him.

Dad was always working while I was growing up. Usually, he wouldn't be home until after I'd gone to bed, and although he never laid a hand on me and barely ever raised his voice against me, there was something about him, no matter how mild-mannered and restrained he came across, that told me he didn't like me. I was overweight as a child, which I'm sure displeased him, and I was so shy that I couldn't look any visitor in the eye or utter anything sensible, much less comprehensible. He put up with it when we were on our own as a family, but when visitors came I saw that it vexed him, even though he made light of it. Most of all, I liked to play on my own; even when I was twelve years old, my room was filled with action figures and I wasn't afraid to play with dolls either. My brothers were quite different, Harald especially, who was only a year younger and exploited my weaknesses the best he could when we were children. Powerful is he to whom we give power, as Nietzsche said, but of course I was oblivious to it then and would put up with being treated like a dog if it meant I could be left in peace. If I cried on account of a conflict with Harald, it wouldn't be Harald who got told off, but me, because I was the eldest and ought properly to be chastising my brother instead of the other way round.

Later, in adulthood, we got on fine together, and there was nothing wrong with my upbringing for that matter either, not really; we simply belonged to different worlds. Dad stepped down when he reached sixty, and Harald, who had attended the London School of Economics and gone on to enjoy a very successful spell working for Goldman Sachs in the City, stepped up to head the company in his place. Gunnar, three years younger than me, took a similar path and was now CEO of a medical company he'd got involved in while it was still little more than a start-up and which now, having developed a new antidepressant, basically a hallucinogen, was in explosive growth. All three continued to be based in London. Dad had sold the house in Hampstead and taken up residence at a central hotel. He was doing fine, as far as I knew, cultivating his hobby as a collector of art, visiting the exhibitions, private views and dinner parties that were important to him in that respect. His particular interest was for constructivism. There was much that I hadn't the heart to say to him as far as his art interest was concerned. In his business life, he'd been the fulcrum, in control of everything and generally savvier than most about the way things worked. He appeared to think this carried over to the art world, not least because he found himself so welcome wherever he went. But what made him welcome was his money, and if artists, gallerists and curators listened patiently to him as he held forth about his beloved Russian constructivists or American pop artists, whose work he also purchased in quantity, it was not because they found what he had to say interesting, but because they were being indulgent towards him, the truth being that he most likely bored them. My father was rather small in stature, self-confident without being self-obsessed, dapper and well dressed with his white shirts, blue suits, brown shoes, ties and cufflinks, but his eyes, although kind, could turn cold whenever his cynicism, which I took to be more practised than hereditary, kicked in. He could assess a man rather well, but a lot of things went over his head, there being very little depth in him.

He had met Torill in the Norwegian expat community when she was working as an au pair in London, a Scandinavian beauty whose life when the two of them got together took a turn she almost certainly could never have envisaged. Something of a neurotic, she loved me more than any other. Torill had depth, but was also unreflecting, her

emotions totally unsorted, everything was intense for her. She took me
with her to the cinema even when I was a small boy, and before I was
thirteen or fourteen I'd become quite the film buff. Films were her
emotional release, allowing her to let go instead of keeping everything
in, which must have felt like a blessing.

They divorced during the summer of my sixteenth birthday, and we
brothers moved back to Norway with her. Torill was a master in making me feel guilty, forever spinning her little webs in which I would
become trapped. She was only forty years old then, and still very good-
looking, but something had unravelled inside her, perhaps because
she'd never built anything of her own, and in that respect it was no
help at all that her family lived in the same town; in fact, if anything,
it probably only infantilised her somewhat.

Physically, my development had really taken off the year before we
moved, and by the time I started gymnasium school I was no longer
overweight. I looked all right, though without it having any noticeable
effect, and the same was true of me coming from London, something
I'd thought would automatically make me popular. The other kids
found me a bit odd, presumably because I was introverted and never
instigated anything on my own, preferring instead to keep well out of
things, but also I think because I took such an interest in many of our
lessons. Torill would occasionally ask me about girls at school, and I
answered her as truthfully as I could, but I never mentioned Kathrine,
although by remaining silent about her it felt like I was betraying her.
There was nothing between us, but she was sacrosanct to me, a place in
my heart that I would guard as I lay on my bed reading, dreaming
about getting up, leaving the room and never coming back.

I discovered Bjørneboe's books and identified strongly with him, he
too the anarchist son of a shipping magnate. I read Kaj Skagen's *Bazarov's
Children* and Erling Gjelsvik's *Dead Heat*, which led me to Hemingway,
from where it was a short step to Turgenev, and from there an even
shorter one to Dostoevsky.

I fantasised about killing someone, not Torill, although it would
have turned my life into something fantastical, but someone random.
The chances of being caught in such a case, where there was no connection between the murderer and his victim, were, I knew, immeasurably

small. But in view of my propensity to feel guilt — I couldn't actually kill a fly without feeling torment — I realised that I would surely give myself away. I couldn't leave Torill either. And contradict my father? Not without tears welling in my eyes.

I put it all behind me the summer I finished gymnasium, and standing on the deck of the ferry on my way to Denmark, watching Norway disappear from view, I was consumed by a feeling of happiness. I was planning on being away for a year, travelling around the continent, taking odd jobs here and there to earn some money; in my rucksack was a book called *Vagabonding in Europe* which listed different jobs that were easy to get, picking oranges in Spain, for instance, or labouring on French docks. But I still wasn't completely free, Torill having insisted that I was to phone her every day, something I'd been unable to refuse. To start with, heading towards Munich, from where I was going on to the Alps, I ventured not to call her a couple of times, only she'd felt such despair, had been so worried about me, that I hadn't the heart to do it again.

I zigzagged through Italy, and from Brindisi caught the ferry to Athens, from there sailing out to some of the islands before plotting a course north again, arriving in Zurich in late September. There I succumbed to a kind of collapse, gripped one evening by a sudden fear, frightened for my life, frightened about everything that could happen, and when morning came I found myself unable to get out of bed. I lay there the whole day, trying to sleep to get away from it, but little helped, and when darkness fell I descended into such panic that my whole body trembled. I was hungry, had nothing to eat and was quite unable to go out and get something. And the fear I felt doubled, for being scared only scared me that much more, and being alone in a foreign city made it even worse. I couldn't phone Torill, I realised that even in the fragile state I was in. And I certainly couldn't phone my father, which would have been too great a failure. But eventually I did so, and sat trembling on the floor with the phone in my hand, dialling his number at the tone.

'Stray speaking,' he said at the other end.

'It's Egil,' I breathed.

'Sorry?' he said. 'Who did you say it was?'

'Egil,' I said.

'Egil!' he said. 'Where in the world are you?'

I started to cry.

'Is something wrong?' he said. 'What's the matter? Has something happened?'

I couldn't speak, all I could do was weep, and then I hung up. I hadn't the strength to go to bed and could only lie down on the floor. After a couple of minutes, the phone rang. I picked up the receiver and held it to my ear.

'Egil?' said Dad. 'I've found out where you're staying. If you can't answer me now, so that I can hear you, I'll send a trusted friend to help.'

'Yes,' I breathed.

'I don't know what's happened,' he said. 'But we'll sort it out. It's no problem.'

I started crying again, disintegrating into sobs, not wanting him to hear me, and again I hung up.

An hour later there was a knock on the door. I was lying in bed and couldn't get up to answer. A besuited man in his forties came in. He was wearing glasses, rectangular lenses in a very thin frame, his features rather nondescript, in fact he would have been quite anonymous had it not been for the fullness of his lips and a somewhat oblique smile.

'Hello there, young man,' he said in German. 'Not doing too well, I hear?'

All I could do was stare at him while I shook inside.

'My name is Dieter. I'm a friend of your father's. I'm here to help you.'

He smiled. His hair was thin and sandy-coloured. His eyes were blue.

'First we must get you out of here,' he said. 'Are you able to get dressed?'

I said nothing.

'All right,' he said. 'I'll help you.'

He opened my rucksack and took out some clothes, holding my blue-green paisley shirt up in front of me.

'Will this do?'

I didn't answer him, couldn't answer him, and he smiled again, picked out a pair of trousers and then sat down on the edge of the bed, drew the cover aside and began to dress me. Once I'd got the trousers on, he slid his hand under my back and raised me into a sitting position, helping me on with the shirt as if he had all the time in the world, doing up the buttons, then proceeding to the shoes, a jacket.

He packed my bag, slung it over his shoulder, took me by the hand and pulled me upright. His arm around me, we left the room. He'd already paid the hotel, he said. Now we were going back to his house, where I would spend the night, and in the morning I was booked onto a flight to London, where my father would come and pick me up.

'How does that sound? A good plan?'

I burst into tears.

He had two kids of his own, he told me as we drove out of the city. Six and eight years old and a right handful, but I wouldn't have to worry about them.

'Are you hungry?'

I nodded.

He parked outside a rather swish residence, got out of the car and came round to open the door on my side, where I sat without moving. His wife, whose face was gentle with a smattering of freckles running across the bridge of her nose and dispersing over her cheeks, her eyes rather narrow and creased at the corners, was in the kitchen rinsing vegetables in the sink when we came in.

'This is Egil,' said Dieter. 'Egil, this is my wife, Annika. Egil isn't feeling that good, so we're putting him up for the night. Is there something for him to eat?'

'Yes, of course,' said Annika.

How I got through the evening and night I can't remember. I assume I slept. The next morning, a nurse came to the house, she was to accompany me all the way to London. Dieter drove us to the airport, where he bid me a hearty farewell, embracing me as if we were old friends. My father was waiting for me at Heathrow, welcoming, if rather measured. There was no one to help me where he was living, he said, so he'd put me into a small private clinic close by where I could rest until I was well again.

He was no doubt thinking a week, perhaps two. I stayed there for six months. I remember hardly anything from that time, it seems such a blur. I know that I was unable to read, unable to listen to the radio or even to music. It wasn't that I couldn't concentrate, though I couldn't do that either, it was more like there was no room in me for anything that came from outside, everything from outside hurt. It even hurt to look at a vase of flowers or a curtain. It was terrible. The most terrible thing was perhaps that as such there was no way out. All I could do was exist in the same darkness, the same hurt the whole time. I spoke to no one, and for six months opened my mouth only to take in nourishment.

It was spring by the time they let me out. I remember *that*. Dad came and picked me up sometime in the morning. I'd packed and got myself ready. Torill was going to come too, only I'd told her not to. She was staying at a hotel, waiting to meet me. But that's not the reason I remember that day so well, at least not the only one. Because when I followed my father out of the door and walked to the car beneath a mild, white spring sky, it was with the very strong feeling that the world did not wish me well. That nothing good would come of my life.

It was all so very ironic. I'd had a kind of vision on one of the Greek islands, not Patmos, of which I knew nothing at the time, and not Hydra either, but a totally unknown and unimportant little island where I'd been staying for a week or so. It was no major vision, certainly nothing that was worth telling anyone about, yet it was significant enough to me. In the mornings I would wade out to a small islet some way off the beach, taking with me some food, a towel, a change of T-shirt and a couple of books in a bag I carried above my head, and I would spend the day out there on my own, reading and swimming and taking in the sun, while back on the island in the evenings I would eat at one of the restaurants, have a few beers and pass my time people-watching. I felt restless during my stay there, anxious even, it was as if I didn't really want to be there, as if there was something I was longing for without really knowing what it was. It wasn't people, because in the little village in the evenings there were people all around me, which made me want to go somewhere else — especially if someone tried to strike up a conversation — though again it wasn't something that exerted any

great pull on me. One evening, I decided to go for a walk. I walked up
through the narrow streets to where the village came to an end and the
mountain began, and carried on upwards, determining all of a sudden
to reach the top. There was a tall radio mast there, blinking red in the
darkness. I sat down and lit a cigarette, and looked out at the sea that
was quite black with little dots of light from the ships out there, and at
the sky, it too black, though more velvety than I was used to from the
night sky at home. Occasionally, lights blinked there as well, from
planes on their way to or from the airport in Athens.

Could a person live without a name? I wondered at once.

Without identity?

Could a person exist without being connected to anything?

Unbound to any past or history, family or society?

Could a person simply be *a human being on earth*, who could go wherever they wished without interpreting what they saw in terms of any
kind of system, but thinking quite freely? In other words: seeing what
they saw as if for the very first time, in every instance? Could a human
being simply *exist*? Without ambition, without plan, without theory?
Could I live, not as Egil Stray, but simply as someone, anyone, no one?
A human being through which the world streamed without attaching
itself, and who for his part likewise streamed through the world, without attaching himself?

Or, to put it differently: could a person be *completely* free?

That was the vision I had. To be a person without a name, without a
history. *To be nothing more than a human being.*

It was, on the surface of it, so threadbare an idea that it couldn't
have made sense to anyone but me. Certainly, those with whom I subsequently shared it did not understand it the way I did. It was so simple
a thought that it could barely be called a thought at all. 'Yes, of course.
To not have a name, yes. And no identity. Interesting. A bit like an animal, yes? Is that what you mean?'

Yet to me, the thought was flesh and blood and quivering nerves. I
knew it could not be brought to fruition, but I considered that it could
be something to strive for, an ideal for life, as it were.

But how could a person disconnect?

I could, for instance, have bought myself a boat and set off around the world, on my own, sailing wherever I wanted, going ashore wherever I wanted; my father would more than likely have given me the money if only I'd asked him, and even if he would have disapproved, he'd seen the direction I was heading and had probably already written me off. But even then, I think, I'd begun to realise that the ties that bind are inside a person, and that disconnecting from the external world was unlikely to make a difference.

Nevertheless, the idea became precious to me in the weeks that followed and, so I thought, would remain so for the rest of my life. But then when I had my breakdown, everything changed, my whole life turned around at once, because after that everything was about making sure I would never end up there again, in that terrible place inside me. The doctors talked about keeping firm structures, firm contexts, maintaining an overview, developing routines. Which of course was the very antithesis of simply existing as a human being.

All this, indeed everything in my entire life, became catalysed that winter day in the summer house, suddenly and unexpectedly slotting into place in my conversion.

How can I explain it?

I can't.

When later I read *The Lily of the Field and the Bird of the Air* again, it was hard to understand exactly what had made such an impression on me the first time round. I couldn't trace back the grand emotions I had felt to any single sentence or paragraph, though many had been underlined in what seemed to be a state of inner fervour. But this is a mistake we make time and again, we think thoughts are isolated units, apart not only from our emotions, but also from the surroundings in which they are conceived. Which is probably why philosophers have always been so concerned with building systems, for in the system a thought is given its own designated place, independently of whatever happens outside of it; thoughts are thus protected from the world and may appear as entities in their own right, so pure and impersonal that they may be thought by anyone, over and over again, wherever and whenever. But the fact of the matter is that thoughts cannot get by on their own. When Nietzsche conceived the notion of eternal return, the apex of his thinking, it was as if he became so gripped by emotion that he was barely able to contain himself, the letters he wrote about the great discovery he'd made were manic in their enthusiasm, at the same time as he was unable to reveal in a single word what *exactly* it was he had thought that was going to change everything. This would be his labour, trying to put the thought and its implications into words, for the thought in itself, naked and bereft of emotion, was indeed anything but grand and fabulous, and actually, when at last it could be considered, manifested as black ink on a white page, rather banal. Its grandness lay in the storm it had precipitated inside him, and it was the storm he wanted to convey, not the thought on its own. The thought had to be supported from below, underpinned and lifted by the thoughts that surrounded it, in order that it might produce the gasp of awe that he considered it to be worth.

As different as they were, Kierkegaard had in common with Nietzsche that his writing was so personal that it was nigh on impossible to take his thoughts and make them one's own, at least not without mutilating them. When he wrote

> Would that in the silence you might forget yourself, forget what you yourself are called, your own name, the famous name, the lowly name, the insignificant name, in order in silence to pray to God, 'Hallowed be *your* name!' Would that in silence you might forget yourself, your plans, the great, all-encompassing plans, or the limited plans concerning your life and its future, in order in silence to pray to God, 'Your kingdom come!' Would that you might in silence forget your will, your wilfulness, in order in silence to pray to God, 'Your will be done!'

these were not unfamiliar thoughts to me, apart from the fact that I would never have put God into that equation. Abandoning oneself to the Divine, giving up the self, was of course a well-known component of any religion, which had given rise to systems of prayer and worship and meditation, something that had never interested me, seeming to me to be a simple matter of suggestion, a mere trick of the Low Church. But Kierkegaard's abandonment was different. The silence in which one might forget oneself was like the silence of the lily and the bird, they were our teachers, but also like the silence of the forest and the silence of the sea. Even when the sea rages loudly, he wrote, it is nonetheless silent, and these words I read as the sea raged loudly outside the house in which I sat. The forest keeps silent, even when it whispers, he wrote, and I listened to the forest as it whispered, and to the silence in its whispering, and I knew that silence, for the clamour of my own inner life resounded so clearly against it. When I was with others, I never heard it, the clamour then being everywhere, generated by our every will, our every plan, our every ambition, our every quest for pleasure, but when I was out walking here, in the silence that is here, I heard it.

In a strange way, what I read coincided with what I was. I read about the raging sea as the sea raged, I read about the whispering forest as the forest whispered, and when I read that to pray was not to speak, but to become silent, that only in silence could God's kingdom be sought, God's kingdom came.

God's kingdom was the moment.

The trees, the forest, the sea, the lily, the bird, all existed in the moment. To them, there was no such thing as future or past. Nor any fear or terror.

That was the first turning point. The second came when I read what followed: *What happens to the bird does not concern it.*

It was the most radical thought I had ever known. It would free me from all pain, all suffering. *What happens to me does not concern me.*

This required absolute faith and absolute abandonment to God, as the lily of the field and the bird of the sky exemplified. Even in deepest sorrow, with so frightful a tomorrow, the bird was unconditionally joyful. Sorrow and tomorrow did not concern it, but were given over to God.

To be obedient as the grass when bent by the wind, I thought, and looked up: outside, the storm had abated, all was dark and still; the faint light of the moon, reflected by the snow, made the smooth rock of the shore seem as though it were levitating.

God's kingdom was here.

And I existed for God.

*

In the half-year that had passed since that night, those thoughts had been like a place to which I could return. It was as if the insights I'd gained there continually needed renewing in order to be maintained; I fell so easily back into old ways. I read extensively in the Gospels and saw everything as if in a new light. The light of freedom and the unbidden, and the light of God's kingdom. When Jesus said, 'If any man come to me, and hate not his father and mother, and wife, and children, and brethren, and sisters, yea, and his own life also, he cannot be my disciple,' I understood what he meant, he was preaching the message of total freedom, disconnection from every relationship. And when he said, 'Foxes have holes, and birds of the air have nests, but the Son of man hath not where to lay his head,' what he was talking about was disconnection from every place. Jesus lived in the open, or aspired to live in the open. The idea of cutting all ties to other people, to one's own past and to all places, may sound self-centred and egoistic, but is in fact the opposite, for only thereby, only as *but-a-human*, do all humans become equal, only then may all be seen for what they are: *but-a-human-humans*. And the following brief passage in Luke, 'And he said unto another, Follow me. But he said, Lord, suffer me first to go and bury my father. Jesus said unto him, Let the dead bury their dead: but go thou and preach the kingdom of God. And another also said, Lord I will follow thee; but let me first go bid them farewell, which are at home at my house. And Jesus said unto him, No man, having put his hand to the plough, and looking back, is fit for the kingdom of God,' underlined the radicality of the message of Jesus and reinforced the importance of freedom for the coming of the kingdom of God. No past, no future, only a vast now, and in its light God assumed form.

That was the light I saw that night in the summer house.

Not the work of creation itself, not the crooked pines with their tassels of needles, not the clear, burning fire and the crackling logs as they gradually turned into ash and cinders. Not the stars that shimmered in the dark and unendingly still night sky, not the ice-mantled rock of the shore. Not the foxes that lived in the forest, with their thick coats and wily-looking faces, not the big gulls that screeched and soared over land and sea, in their white-and-grey plumage, with their yellow beaks and black, beady eyes. Not the cod that lay motionless above the shallow banks off the islets, yellowy-brown and white, and utterly silent. Not the kelp that grew beneath the water, nor the clusters of blue-black mussels that clacked against the rocks in the pull of the waves. Nothing of what existed, but its *consequence*: in this, God emerged into being.

I had thought about this all through the summer, and read accordingly, though of course without ambition of coming to any conclusion, for God was not something firm that allowed itself to be easily grasped. But, I thought as I stood steering the boat through the strait, the town looming up ahead, at least I knew what to look for, and in which direction to look. In the social realm, only the social was visible, the human sphere was everything there, even animals and trees vanished from view, and that was why true religion turned away from the social. People are created not *in*, but *for* the image of God, as Hans Jonas wrote. And only he who hates his father and mother, his wife and children and brethren and sisters, and his own life too, will be able to see it.

Even in the wind of motion, the air in the strait felt like an oven, so it was no wonder the water close to shore was teeming with people, their pale little heads bobbing like seals, thin white bodies wading out or clambering back.

The colourful array of towels spread out on the beach.

Ahead, the details of the town began gradually to emerge. I saw people in the streets and seated at the pavement cafes, carrier bags gleaming in the sunshine, even the tiny white dots of the ice creams some of them held in their hands.

Ten minutes until the bus arrived. I'd be just in time, I thought, slowing down as the little ferry came chugging from the jetty, on its way to one of the outlying islands. I opened up the throttle again after it had gone, slowing once more a couple of minutes later as I entered the wide channel leading into the harbour itself.

I found a space, moored and went into town.

Maybe I could have a beer when he got his ice cream?

One beer never hurt anyone.

There was a church bazaar on across the road and I looked up at the church building itself with its red-brick walls, its green copper roof and copper spire, and it struck me that I'd always overlooked it, taken it for granted. I'd certainly never been inside.

But it would have to wait. It was hardly the kind of thing a young boy would be looking forward to.

The clock on the tower told me I still had a couple of minutes. I crossed the road and hurried the last bit of the way to the bus station. A big, sleek coach, white with red and blue writing on the sides, came gliding in just as I got there. That would be it.

It pulled into the bay, the doors opened and people began to file out, most gathering at the side to wait for their luggage, others walking directly away into the town, free men and women.

I couldn't see Viktor anywhere.

I went over to the huddle of passengers where the driver had now opened the luggage compartment and begun to unload the bags.

'Excuse me,' I said. 'Is this the bus from Oslo?'

He didn't reply, his upper body momentarily consumed inside the cavernous compartment as he tried to extricate a pushchair. His white shirt was soaked through with sweat all the way up his back.

'It's from Oslo, yes,' a young man said.

'Thanks,' I said, and went to the door, up the steps and into the bus to see if he was there. Coming from the bright light outside, I could barely see a thing at first. A funny taste filled my mouth, it reminded me of a particular apple variety, only then it was gone, my eyes adjusted to the half-light and I went up the aisle.

Viktor was sitting at the back, his knees wedged against the seat in front. He didn't look at me as I came towards him, but stared harshly out of the window.

'Hi, Viktor! Good to see you!' I said.

He ignored me.

'Have you had a good trip?'

No answer.

A slight curl of his mouth told me he wasn't completely indifferent.

'Come on,' I said. 'Let's go, shall we?'

I touched his shoulder.

'Have you brought any luggage? If you have, we'll need to get it.

We're going by boat to the summer house. It'll be fun. I was thinking we could get an ice cream first.'

'I don't want an ice cream,' he said, flashing me a glance.

'Suit yourself,' I said. 'But we need to get off the bus now, come on.'

'I'm not coming,' he said. 'I want to go home.'

'It's only for a few days,' I said. 'You'll be home again before you know it.'

'I want to go home now.'

'Well, I'm afraid you can't, mate.'

'I'm not your mate.'

'All right,' I said. 'But you can't sit here. Everyone else has gone now.'

'I don't give a shit,' he said.

'That's enough, Viktor,' I said. 'I won't have you swearing. It's not nice.'

'I don't give a fuck,' he said. 'And you're a dick.'

'Don't call me that,' I said. 'I'm your dad.'

'Fuckwit,' he said.

'Viktor,' I said, 'don't call me that.'

'Fuckwit,' he said. 'Fucking dick.'

'That's enough now,' I said.

His eyes stared straight ahead. Then, a smile passed fleetingly over his face before his hardened expression returned.

I couldn't believe it.

Was he really that *wicked*?

I'd thought he was upset and angry at his mother having left him. But then he wouldn't have smiled, surely?

'Come on,' I said.

'No,' he said.

Outside, the driver drew himself upright. There were only a couple of suitcases and bags in front of him now.

'Viktor, we've got to *go* now,' I said. 'You know full well we do. You can't stay here.'

He said nothing, but sat without moving, staring out of the window.

I took his arm gently and tugged.

'Come on, Viktor,' I said.

He looked down at my hands.

'Cunt,' he said.

A sudden rage welled inside me.

'That's ENOUGH!' I said. 'You're coming with me, NOW!'

I dragged him to his feet. He gripped the seat in front and clung to it.

'HELP!' he shouted. 'HELP!'

Just then, the driver came up the steps at the front of the bus. I let go of Viktor.

'What's going on here?' the driver said, coming towards us.

'It's all right,' I said. 'My son here refuses to come with me, but we'll sort it out.'

'Viktor, wasn't it?' he said. 'You know I promised your mother I'd look after you? You'd better do as your dad says.'

'He's not my dad,' Viktor said.

'You heard me,' said the driver. 'I promised your mum. So you go with your dad now and pick up your luggage out there before someone runs off with it.'

'OK,' said Viktor after a moment's hesitation, and stood up without looking at me.

I followed him out and we went to where the luggage had been left. A small carry-on suitcase and a little rucksack.

'If you take the rucksack, I'll take the suitcase. OK?' I said.

'You can take them both,' he said.

'All right, no problem,' I said, as I swung the rucksack over my shoulder and picked up the suitcase.

How come he did what the driver said, when he wouldn't listen to me? I wondered as we started to walk, Viktor keeping a couple of paces in front of me. Being his father presumably meant I was someone he felt safe with, thereby allowing him to feel he could take things out on me, whereas the driver was a stranger. Moreover, the man's black trousers and white shirt looked a bit like a uniform, which automatically instilled a form of respect.

I ought to have taken him by the hand and led the way. After all, he was only ten. But I held back in case he rejected me again.

'How about an ice cream?' I said. 'It's so hot!'

'I said I didn't want one,' he said. 'Are you deaf?'

'Right, we'll go straight to the boat, then,' I said.

He was wearing a pair of green shorts of a kind that looked more usual for an adult, and a yellow T-shirt with a surfing print across the chest. His skin was as white as chalk and only highlighted by his mother's choice of colours for him, I thought. His arms and legs were thin, his head rather small, eyes narrow, his lips, too, narrow and tight. He never looked anyone in the eye, and when his mother and I had still been together I'd suggested we should perhaps take him to a specialist and have him examined, it being a sign of autism.

She hit the roof, so we never did.

But there was definitely some issue there.

He stared at the ground as we walked, his hands in his pockets. When we got to the crossing, he glanced up at me and I was relieved to see a trace of uncertainty in him, regardless of everything else.

'Cross over here,' I said.

I stayed a couple of paces behind him. Then, so that he wouldn't have to reveal his uncertainty to me again, I said:

'Turn left down to the jetty a bit further on. Can you see where I mean?'

Outside the old post office, I recognised a face coming towards me. It was Tore. He lifted his hand in a wave as he saw me. Despite the heat, he was sporting a pair of long black trousers and a black T-shirt, his eyes hidden behind big, black sunglasses. A bag hung from his shoulder.

'There's a turn-up,' he said.

'Long time no see,' I said. 'How's things?'

I saw my own reflection in his sunglasses and wished he would take them off.

'Oh, you know,' he said. 'You?'

'Good,' I said.

Viktor had come to a halt and was standing a bit further away pretending not to know me.

'Still out in the summer house?' Tore said.

'That's right,' I said. 'Just came in to pick up my son.'

'I didn't know you had one,' he said. There was surprise in his voice, but as long as I couldn't see his eyes it was hard to tell if he was having me on or not.

'Didn't you?' I said. 'He's ten years old now.'

'Just goes to show,' he said. 'You never said.'

'Didn't I?' I said. 'He lives with his mother most of the time, so he's not here that often.'

I looked at Viktor.

'Hey, Viktor, come and say hello to a friend of mine!'

He stayed where he was, as if he hadn't heard me.

'He's a bit shy,' I said. 'Anyway, what about you? Been up to much?'

'Not really. Still slogging away at the opera.'

'Oh, I'd forgotten about that!' I said. 'It'll be nearly finished now, surely?'

He nodded.

'And there's a decent chance of it running at the arts centre in the spring.'

'Wow!' I said. 'I'll look forward to that. Listen, I've got to get going. But look after yourself, and see you again soon, I hope!'

'Yes, likewise,' he said, walking away as I turned towards Viktor again.

'Who was that?' he said.

'His name's Tore,' I said, and smiled at him, glad that he'd said something without being asked. 'An old friend of mine.'

'Why didn't you tell him about me?' he said.

He looked up at me.

A chill went through me.

'Of course I told him,' I said, starting to walk. 'He was only joking. He's never seen you before, that's all.'

'It didn't sound like he was joking,' said Viktor.

'Well, he was,' I said. 'Come on, the boat's just over there.'

Wasn't there something I could distract him with?

He didn't want an ice cream.

A Coke or a lemonade?

But that would mean sitting down somewhere, which would give him time to reflect and perhaps ask more questions.

No, the boat would be best.

In my mind's eye, I suddenly saw myself walking along the jetty with a carrier bag in each hand, bending forward to put them down in the boat.

I'd forgotten to do the shopping. There was no food for him out there.

'It's just the way he and I talk to each other,' I said. 'We pretend to be stupider than we are. It's a bit hard to explain. It's called irony.'

He didn't even turn round.

There was no reason for him not to believe me. It was true as well, in a way; Tore could have forgotten I'd told him, or he could have been joking. It would be like him.

We went down the steps onto the jetty. Viktor came to a halt by the boat without looking back at me.

'I'm impressed,' I said. 'I wouldn't have thought you'd recognise it.'

It struck me immediately that what I'd said undermined our relationship. Of course he recognised it.

'There are so many boats here,' I said. 'And so many that look the same.'

I put the luggage down on the ground, drew the boat in and stepped aboard.

'Will you hand me the suitcase?' I said.

He picked it up and handed it to me.

'And the rucksack?'

He handed that to me too, then got into the boat himself. His face was serious, determined almost. But at least he was no longer refusing to go with me. That was always something, I thought, loosening the mooring.

'I want a life jacket,' he said.

'I haven't got one,' I said. 'Sorry about that. But I promise to take care. You'll be fine. You can swim, can't you?'

'It's against the law not to have a life jacket,' he said.

'Not exactly,' I said. 'It's not the smartest thing to do, but if we go easy, it'll be all right, you'll see. Then we can buy you a life jacket tomorrow. OK?'

He said nothing and I started the motor and backed out a bit before turning and heading off. The sun was high in the sky, beating down without a cloud in sight. Its rays glittered and twinkled from windows and cars, bikes, outboards, railings, benches and tables, the water in the harbour a scintillating display of tiny, trembling flecks, while further out, towards the horizon, they seemed to pool in great, sweeping rivers of light.

Viktor sat with his back to the prow, staring at the gradually diminishing town as we picked up speed and the boat planed.

He could manage a smile, surely?

The salty wind that ruffled his hair, the warm air and the blue, blue world that surrounded us.

My own childhood hadn't been that easy either. Fat and repugnant as I was then. But I couldn't recall being aggressive. I liked being on my own, and I'd been shy too. Definitely. But not angry. Not impudent like that. And I couldn't have hurt anyone if I'd tried.

I had to treat him kindly and be patient with him.

He was only ten.

I looked up at the new star. It seemed more distant now, in the great glare of day, but it still shone brightly.

I pointed to it.

'Have you seen the new star?' I shouted.

He stared up at it. But his face revealed no interest, and again he turned his attention to the landscape we left behind.

Twenty minutes later, we drew into the marina.

'Are you coming into the shop with me?' I said.

He shook his head.

'Are you going to be all right sitting here on your own, do you think?'

'Yes,' he said.

'OK. There's not much can happen to you here, I suppose,' I said, and stepped ashore, mooring the boat before going inside the freezing cold supermarket where there wasn't another customer in sight. I tried to make do with buying as little as possible, basically potatoes and vegetables to go with the fish I caught, and then some crispbread and cheese, and I'd need cigarettes, of course. But what was I meant to get for him?

I wondered what he might like.

Leaving my basket in the shop, I went back outside to ask him. He was sitting with his arm on the gunwale, his cheek resting on top. Seeing me come towards him, he straightened up.

'Is there anything in particular you'd like me to buy?' I said.

'No,' he said.

'What do you like?'

'I don't know.'

'Crisps? Chocolate? Pizza? You can have what you want, it's up to you.'

'I don't know,' he said.

'Anything at all?'

'I don't care.'

'All right,' I said. 'I'll see if I can find something nice.'

Back in the supermarket, I tried to remember what sort of things I'd liked when I was his age. I put a bag of paprika-flavoured crisps in the basket, then another kind, salt and vinegar, some salted peanuts and popcorn. A couple of bottles of fizzy drink for him, a few beers for me. A steak for each of us. Bearnaise sauce. Chocolate bars. Chocolate pudding, raspberry jam, vanilla sauce. And half a dozen raisin buns.

After I went to the checkout and started putting my items onto the conveyor, it occurred to me I should get a couple of pizzas in as well. I put the basket down, went back and got four different ones from the frozen counter.

'Any cigarettes today?' the assistant at the checkout said, a young guy of about eighteen with pale skin and dark hair, a red spot on his cheek, bursting with yellow pus. I seemed to remember his name was Simon.

'Oh yes,' I said. 'Thanks for reminding me.'

'No need to thank me,' he said, and smiled hesitantly, the way he often did. 'Every cigarette you smoke takes two minutes off your life, isn't that what they say?'

'I believe so,' I said, bagging my items as they came down the line. 'They never say which two minutes, though, do they? It could be the ones we could do without.'

He smiled again, and turned to open the cigarette display behind him.

'How many? Three as usual?'

'That'll be fine, yes,' I said. 'Thanks.'

Behind me, the door opened and a slight woman of about sixty came in, removing her sunglasses and putting them away in the bag that hung from her arm.

'Hello, kiddo,' she said. 'How's it going here?'

Her voice was throaty, her skin rather blotched. It was clear that she smoked a lot.

Simon, if that was his name, pushed the card reader towards me.

'Fine,' he said. 'Not exactly busy, though.'

'No one can be bothered in this weather,' she said.

'Not in the middle of the day, they can't,' he said.

I inserted my card and keyed in my PIN. I was surprised by the familiarity of the tone between them, and reasoned that she was his mother, in which case I might have expected him to be more reserved there in public, only he wasn't.

'Thank you,' he said when the transaction was approved, and I picked up the two carrier bags.

'Thanks a lot,' I said. 'See you again.'

The heat outside was a shock even if I did know it was coming. The air shimmered here and there over the empty car park. The woods, extending all the way down to its far end, were green and dry. But the air smelled of salt, not of the woods, and it wafted towards me as I turned the corner, the jetty stretching out into the still and blinking water.

Viktor had sat down at the edge and was tossing small stones into the water. When he saw me coming, he got up without a word and climbed into the boat again. I stepped past him, a bag in each hand, and when the boat rolled more than I'd anticipated under my additional weight, I crouched and put them down. The bottles chinked, and Viktor looked first at the bags, then at me, with narrow, peering eyes.

'How many beers did you buy?' he said.

'Just a couple,' I said. 'To go with the dinner. And some pop for you.'

'Mum says you're a sad alky,' he said.

Another chill ran through me.

I tried to contain myself, mustering all my willpower as I stowed the bags away, one on each side, making sure they weren't going to tip over, before sitting down on the thwart in the stern.

Viktor stared at me.

'Is that what she says to *you*?' I said.

He shook his head.

'She said so to Milo. She didn't know I was listening.'

'Who's Milo?' I said.

'Her boyfriend, I suppose,' he said.

'She's got a *boyfriend*?' I said.

'Yes,' he said. 'Milo.'

'And she told him I was an alcoholic?'

'No. She told him you were a sad alky.'

'Well, I'm not, Viktor. It's very important that you understand that. It's not true.'

He said nothing, but leaned over the side and dipped his hand in the water.

'I may have a beer with my meal now and then,' I said. 'But that doesn't make me an alcoholic.'

Nothing suggested that he was listening. I started the outboard and backed out. The boat came to an abrupt halt.

I'd forgotten the mooring line.

I put the motor into neutral and stepped forward into the bow, knelt down next to Viktor and drew us in, undid the knot, shoved off, went back and sat down on the thwart again, then shifted into forward gear and opened the throttle. I didn't care what the speed limit was inside the harbour, all I wanted was to get back home as fast as possible.

Not long after, we were there. If Jesus had not where to lay his head, as it said in the Gospel, because he wanted to be completely free and be just a human being, unconnected to anything or anyone, something I totally understood, *I* could not let go of *this*. I loved the sight of the storehouse at the jetty, in its coat of thick red paint, nestled in the little inlet, the smell inside it, of tar and salt, as I loved my house itself, yellow ochre in colour, long and low on the crest of the rise, and of course the woods, the smooth, bare rock of the shore, the jetty. The decked veranda, the living room with its wood burner, the little kitchen.

Without that anchor, I'd be lost. I wasn't strong enough to drift about, even if it really was what I wanted. But the world had opened itself up to me anyway, and it was here that it had opened.

With a carrier bag in each hand, I followed Viktor's delicate frame up the path to the house. He wasn't exactly agile; the rough terrain seemed to be difficult for him to manage, there was something awkward and uncoordinated about his whole body, he was rather knock-kneed, and his arms never quite seemed to be under control.

It broke my heart to see it.

After I'd put the groceries away in the kitchen, I went back down to the boat and got his case and rucksack, while Viktor stood on the veranda and pretended I didn't exist.

'Don't you want to sit down?' I said as I came back towards him and saw him still standing in the corner.

He shook his head.

He'll come round after a bit, I reasoned, and left him in peace, putting his things on the floor in the little bedroom, where I paused and lifted the duvet to my nose. It was clean, but it had been ages, perhaps six months, since I'd changed the bed clothes, so it didn't exactly smell fresh.

But kids didn't care about stuff like that, the important thing was that it was clean. If he complained, there were several sleeping bags in the loft in the garage.

I pulled the curtain aside and looked out at the woods. Shafts of sunlight slanted down from bough to bough, the way water might run from rock to rock as it made its way down a fellside, though only the fewest beams penetrated into their deepest depths, the light therefore seeming that much brighter there, in the darkness and gloom of the woodland floor.

They could say what they wanted about me, but I wasn't an alcoholic.

Why had she said that?

To come across as a victim in the eyes of her new boyfriend?

Milo. It sounded like a detergent.

I straightened up. It didn't concern me. It didn't concern me in the slightest.

I was the person I was.

Let it go. It makes no odds. Don't rise to it.

I went out onto the veranda and lit a cigarette. Viktor had gone down to the shore and was sitting on the rock prodding a stick at something by his feet.

In the blue sky high above him, three gulls soared. They were sent, to that place, to that time.

Yet they brought no message but their presence.

Which was mysterious enough in itself.

I turned round and looked up at the star.

What message did it bring?

The Morning Star was important in the Bible. But in conflicting ways.

Now it was important in our world.

I needed to check what the Bible said about it once Viktor was asleep.

I went into the kitchen and got him a bread roll, thinking it would be good to offer him something when I went down to see what he was doing. Maybe a soft drink as well?

No, that would be overdoing it. He'd think I was pandering to him.

A roll was fine.

He looked up at me as I came back out onto the decking. Then, as I went down towards him, he looked away again.

'Hi, Viktor!' I said, crouching down beside him. 'I brought you a bread roll, in case you fancied something.'

'I'm not hungry,' he said.

'Come on,' I said. 'You've got to eat. And you might as well enjoy yourself now you're here. Sulking's not much fun. It's a dead end.'

I put the roll down next to him and stood up.

'I reckon this must be the finest day of the year so far,' I said. 'Do you fancy a swim? Or maybe we could fish for some crabs? Or we could go out somewhere in the boat, if you want. To one of the islands. The lighthouse!'

'I want to go home,' he said.

'This *is* home,' I said. 'But if you'd rather sit and sulk, that's fine by me.'

He looked up at me with that narrow-eyed smile.

Was that what he wanted, for me to get angry? Was he goading me on purpose?

If he was, he was in for a disappointment. I wasn't going to lose my temper with him, it didn't matter what happened.

I went back up to the house, and as I reached the veranda again I had an idea. Arne's twins were about the same age as Viktor. We could go over there. They could play together. Maybe he could even stay the night there. Arne owed me more than one favour.

I pressed his number, leaned my elbows on the rail and looked out at the sea.

'Hello, Egil,' he said. 'I'm in the car and you're on speakerphone. Tove's with me.'

'OK,' I said. 'How is everything?'

'We're on our way to the hospital.'

'OK. When are you going to be back, do you think?'

'No idea. Why?'

'Viktor's here,' I said. 'Surprise visit.'

'Viktor? Is that your son?'

'That's it. I was thinking maybe he and the twins could hook up?'

'Yes, of course,' said Arne. 'They're at home, as far as I know. My mother's there to keep an eye on them.'

'Oh, right,' I said. 'In that case, perhaps tomorrow would be better?'

'Up to you,' he said. 'I'm sure she'd be happy to see someone.'

'I'll have a think about it,' I said. 'But thanks, anyway. Speak to you soon.'

For a few seconds, I thought about mixing myself a drink, an ice-cold gin and tonic would have done rather nicely, but I went and got myself a Pepsi Max instead, pressed some ice cubes out into a glass, cut a slice of lemon and put that in too, before pouring the drink and taking it out with me onto the veranda.

'Viktor!' I shouted. 'Come and get something to drink!'

I hadn't expected him to react, but he did, getting to his feet and trudging back up towards the house.

'What would you like?' I said as he stepped onto the decking. 'There's Villa Farris, Solo and Pepsi Max.'

'Solo,' he said.

'Bottle or glass?'

'Bottle,' he said.

I opened a bottle for him in the kitchen. He gulped a mouthful before going back down to the shore with the bottle in his hand.

Was he going to stay there all week?

I sat down in the chair outside with the Bible in my lap and began skimming through Isaiah until I found the quote I was looking for.

The volume had belonged to my paternal grandfather, it was as heavy as a small child and wonderfully elaborate, but now it was mine and bestrewn with my underlinings and comments.

It turned out I'd already underlined the passage about the Morning Star.

How art thou fallen from heaven, O Lucifer, son of the morning! How art thou cut down to the ground which didst weaken the nations!

For thou hast said in thine heart, I will ascend into heaven, I will exalt my throne above the stars of God: I will sit also upon the mount of the congregation, in the sides of the north:

I will ascend above the heights of the clouds; I will be like the most High.

Yet thou shalt be brought down to hell, to the sides of the pit.

The Morning Star was called Lucifer in Latin, which meant 'bearer of light'. Here in Isaiah, Lucifer was the son of the morning, and the son of the morning could normally hardly be anything else but God, the creator of all things. Lucifer was thus aspiring to become His equal, but was banished from heaven into the kingdom of the dead, over which traditionally he was then considered to rule.

On the face of it, the passage would have us believe that Lucifer was the son of God. But in the oldest parts of the Bible, the relationships between the different characters are often unclear, the nature of the angels being particularly inscrutable; in one place we are told that the angels mingled with the daughters of men, who begat them children who for a time wandered the earth as giants, while elsewhere the distinction between God and the angels is often fluid and uncertain. Moreover, the word 'son' could of course be construed in a looser sense meaning 'created by'. But it was striking nonetheless that in other passages Jesus, who *was* the son of God, was likewise referred to as the Morning Star, which is to say Lucifer.

The angel Lucifer, the Morning Star, had been banished from heaven to earth. Now the Morning Star shone once more from the sky. So what did that mean?

Not that I believed the star to *be* Lucifer or Christ. The star was a star. But I had no doubt that it was a *sign* of something.

I swallowed a mouthful of Pepsi. It was diluted now, the ice cubes already melted.

You only had to look at it, I thought, and tipped my head back to gaze at it. The star was filled with meaning. It affected everyone who saw it. Something silent and intense streamed from it. It was almost as if it possessed a will, something indomitable that the soul could contain, but not change or influence.

The feeling that someone was looking at us.

I snapped back at a sudden noise from the shore. Viktor was standing up, focused on something on the ground in front of him. I realised he'd smashed the bottle against the rocks. I put the Bible down, stubbing out my cigarette as I got to my feet, and dashed down to where he was standing.

'Did you *smash* that bottle?' I said.

He nodded and smiled.

'But, Viktor, you know you can't do that! There's broken glass everywhere now, people can injure themselves. Animals too, for that matter. That's not what you want, is it?'

'It's so boring here,' he said.

'You might think so,' I said. 'But there's lots of things to do, if you bother to think about it. Come on, how about a swim? It's like the Mediterranean out there.'

'I don't want to,' he said.

'OK,' I said. 'How about something to eat, then? You must be starving by now. I bought pizzas.'

He said nothing.

'Are you hungry?'

He nodded.

'Good!' I said. 'But first we've got to pick up all this broken glass. Come on!'

'You can do it,' he said.

For a moment, I wasn't sure what to do. I knew I ought to insist, maybe even force him, because disrespecting nature was one of the worst things I knew, and that was something he had to learn. On the other hand, I had the distinct feeling he was only going to be obstructive and that I'd end up doing it myself anyway. If I forced him, the rest of the day and the evening too would be ruined.

I crouched down beside him.

'Listen, Viktor,' I said. 'Somebody might injure themselves on that broken glass. An innocent animal could cut itself and perhaps be prevented from finding food because of it. And we don't want an innocent animal to die because of something you did, do we?'

'Who cares?' he said. 'It's only some glass. You can pick it up yourself, if it's so important to you.'

'OK,' I said. 'But if you do it again, I'm going to be angry with you.'

I went up to the house and came back again with a plastic bag to put the shards in. They were spread over a fairly large area, and although I probably didn't retrieve them all, I was reasonably sure I found the biggest bits, at least.

Now and then, I looked up at Viktor as he sat by himself on the rock, small and hostile. It was hard to believe that he belonged to me.

I dropped the plastic bag into the recycling bin at the front of the house, and then had a look in the garage to see if there was anything there that he could play with, finding an old dartboard and a set of darts that I took out onto the veranda and put in the corner for later on, before going inside to make us something to eat.

I never fussed about setting the table properly when I was on my own, naturally, but now I took out two of the best plates, which according to my father were from the mid-nineteenth century, and two wine glasses, even if we were only having pizza and soft drinks.

Viktor came as soon as I called for him, grabbed a piece of pizza and stuffed it in his mouth even before he'd sat down. I hadn't eaten frozen pizza since the time I'd been living with Torill and she'd had one of those days where she just lay in her bedroom.

It tasted like cardboard then, and it tasted like cardboard now.

'Have we got any ketchup?' Viktor said, without looking at me.

The joy of him saying 'we' was immediately offset by the realisation that I could only disappoint him.

'Sorry,' I said. 'I forgot to buy some.'

He grabbed another slice, his fingers digging into the topping, and devoured it.

'Are you sure you don't want to go for a swim?' I said. 'It's just the weather for it.'

He shook his head.

'Don't you like swimming?' I said. 'The water's not cold in this heat.'

He stood up and went behind his chair, and before I'd managed to react or even knew what was happening, he'd lifted it above his head and brought it crashing down onto the table with all his might, smashing the plates and glasses in the process.

He let go of it, turned and walked out.

My heart was thumping in my chest.

I remained seated for a minute to collect myself, noticing that he'd gone and sat down at the same place on the shore.

There was something seriously wrong with the boy.

I went into the kitchen and got a bin liner and a dustpan and brush, and started to clear the table, then I dumped everything, the pizza, the shards of china and glass, into the bin outside. Once I'd got things reasonably straightened up inside, I went out onto the veranda and lit a cigarette. I was still trembling all over.

He'd done it for the sake of attention. Or to make me punish him.

I wasn't going to punish him. And I wasn't going to give him any attention for such a wanton act of destruction.

The best thing I could do was ignore him.

It would give him something to think about.

Again, I felt the strong urge to mix myself a gin and tonic. It was something to do with the taste of it in the heat, the cold glass in the palm of my hand. The liquid's gentle rotation as the hand drew its little circles. The chinking together of the ice cubes, small and slick. The green slice of lime in the gleaming, transparent refrain of it all.

Why was he so angry?

It couldn't be that bad out here, not even for a ten-year-old.

He was more than angry. It was as if a rage were set inside him, deep in the marrow of his bones.

What was he thinking now?

Was he pleased at what he'd done?

Was he even thinking about it?

I couldn't remember what I thought about when I was his age. I hadn't the faintest idea.

It was too hot for coffee.

Or maybe an espresso? Three little mouthfuls.

A slight wind came in from the sea. I could see it ripple the surface at the shore. The pennant at the side of the house lifted on its breath, like an animal after a long sleep.

I'd always disliked these sea breezes intensely, even when I was little. It was something to do with the world, hitherto so polished and still, becoming unsettled. The surface of the sea became unsettled, the flowers and bushes became unsettled, the trees became unsettled, and then the flaglines would begin to rattle against their poles, the worst sound in all of my childhood.

Why did the world become unsettled? What tormented it? What was on its mind?

I went into the kitchen, put some water in the bottom of the espresso pot, poured some coffee into the little metal cylinder, screwed the top on and put the pot on the ring of the cooker, where it soon sizzled and spat.

How strange that I'd tasted apple when I stepped inside the bus, I thought, at the same time picturing myself sitting down next to Viktor out there on the shore, putting my arm around him and hugging him tight.

He would only twist away, perhaps get to his feet and stomp off.

But perhaps it was what he wanted?

All children, surely, wanted to be hugged?

I decided to do so, as soon as I'd drunk my coffee. He'd just have to run off, if that was how he wanted it.

The coffee pot hissed.

That taste of apple had been so distinct, there was a recollection attached to it, but I couldn't work out what it was, it was like a dream you try to pin down, only for it to keep dissolving.

I went into the living room and looked out.

Viktor wasn't there any more.

I heard footsteps and rummaging from the veranda outside.

When I went out, he was trying to lean the dartboard up against the window, but seemed to have realised it wasn't such a good idea and stepped back to stand there holding it in his hands.

I wasn't angry with him, I sensed as I saw him there, his slight frame awkwardly askew, as if bent oblique by the wind, his face as ever resembling a grin, with its narrow eyes and prominent cheekbones. But I didn't feel any affection for him either.

'We can nail it up somewhere, if you like,' I said.

He nodded.

'To a tree, maybe?' he said.

'No, trees are living. We shouldn't put nails in them. How about round the front? On the side of the garage, perhaps?'

He nodded again.

'I just need to see to something in the kitchen first,' I said. 'Are you going to wait here? Or do you want to go round on your own?'

He shrugged.

I wondered if I'd been too appeasing as I went inside again. The coffee pot was hissing louder now, but the water had yet to come to the boil.

Should I wait for it, or turn it off and go back out?

If I made him wait, the initiative he'd taken could disintegrate.

But it would only take a few moments for the coffee to be ready. Wouldn't it be ruined if I turned the cooker off now?

I pressed the pot down hard against the ring, and the hissing got louder. I took a cup from the shelf above the cooker and put it out on the counter, then fished my mobile out of my shirt pocket to see if anyone had phoned.

Johan. Three times.

Unlike him, I thought to myself, and as I heard the coffee start to bubble up to the upper chamber of the pot I decided to call him back later on. I took the pot off the ring, turned the cooker off and glanced out of the window while I waited for the coffee to settle.

A sailing boat was putting in next to the boathouse. It was using its outboard. A woman stood at the rudder, while a man stood aft with his arm outstretched, a gaff in his hand. Two kids sat in the bow, looking down, their heads lowered, no doubt immersed in their mobile phones.

This was my property.

I'd never put a sign up, not believing in private property rights in that sense, and it was OK by me if it was only for a couple of hours, but something told me they were planning on anchoring up for the night.

I poured the coffee into the cup and went round to the front of the house with it. Viktor stood throwing darts at the garage wall, trying to make them stick.

'This is a good place,' I said. 'Hang on a minute, I'll get the hammer and some nails.'

I drank the coffee in one go, put the cup down on the ground next to my bike and went into the garage, to the corner where my dad's toolbox was kept. There were plenty of loose nails in the bottom of it, and I found a small hammer too.

'How about here?' I said, holding the dartboard against the wall about a metre and a half off the ground.

Viktor nodded, and I drove the nail into the wood.

'There we are,' I said. 'You're all set now.'

I picked up my cup and was about to go back inside, already looking forward to sitting down, the light streaming in, the Bible in my lap, pausing now and then to ponder the sea, but then it struck me that here was a chance to get close to him, and I put the cup down again.

'I thought you were going in,' he said as he took aim, moving his arm backwards and forwards from the elbow a couple of times, before launching the dart.

It fell flat against the board and dropped to the ground.

'Bad luck,' I said.

A swarm of midges hung in the air by the wall, each tiny insect whirring this way and that, though without the shape of the swarm altering in any way.

The apple tree in the woods. That was where the taste had come from. The wild apples I'd eaten as a child. There was something fairy tale about a tree no one owned, blossoming alone in spring, quite apart from the trees that surrounded it, to bear such copious fruit in late summer.

'You try, then, if you think it's so easy,' said Viktor, handing me a dart.

I threw without thinking, and a wave of regret washed through me as the dart buried itself in the board only a hair's breadth from the bull's eye.

'Beginner's luck,' I said. 'Your turn.'

He aimed again, making the same movement of his arm before throwing his dart. The arc it described was far too short, and it struck the wall side-on below the board and dropped to the ground again.

'OK,' I said. This time I was more aware of the situation as he handed me the dart, and my throw pierced the wall above the board where it remained.

'You see,' I said.

'See what?' he said.

'That my first throw was just lucky.'

The sunlight poured down from above and seemed to refract from even the smallest surface, radiant in every tree of the sloping woods, particularly the birch that were almost shimmering as they trembled in the breeze.

The soil that bordered the track looked like dust that would whirl up at a glance.

Viktor concentrated again.

Perhaps we could go into the woods and see if there were apples on the tree?

He lifted a foot from the ground and lunged forward as he threw. This time, the dart struck the board properly, but lacked the thrust to penetrate.

He spun round and walked away.

'Hey, where are you going?' I said.

'It's boring,' he said.

'I can show you how to do it,' I said.

'You're no good at it either,' he said, and disappeared round the side of the house.

I picked up the darts, then threw them quickly in succession. They ringed the bull's eye like a bunch of flowers. I felt deceitful, and turned round to make sure Viktor hadn't come back unexpectedly and seen me throw. He hadn't, and I removed them from the board, putting them down on the ground and leaving them there. Going back inside, I got my phone out and pressed Johan's number.

'Well, if it isn't my old pal!' he said in his Swedish, as if I were calling out of the blue.

'Johan,' I said. 'How's things?'

'Excellent, I must say. How about you? Still in that *hut* of yours? Ha ha ha!'

'I'm doing fine,' I said, leaning forward with my hand on the windowsill as I looked down towards the inlet. 'I can see you phoned earlier on?'

'I did, yes. Have you seen the news today?'

'Not yet, no.'

They'd put a tent up down there. Only now they were nowhere to be seen. Maybe they were on the boat, below deck.

'So you've not heard about Kvitekrist?'

'Them going missing, you mean? My guess is they've gone into hiding.'

'Well, you're wrong there, I'm afraid. They've been done in, the lot of them, and rather brutally, so it seems, too. It's even made the news here in Sweden today. They're saying it looks like a ritual killing. The whole of Bergen's buzzing about it.'

'Seriously?' I said. 'All of them?'

'Well, three of them, anyway. All suspicion's on number four, the drummer.'

'Jesper? Never, I don't believe it. But . . . where did this happen? And when?'

'Up at Svartediket. You know the place, you've been there yourself.'

I sat down on the floor and leaned back against the wall. I felt sick.

'What are you going to do with all the footage you've got? Every TV station in the world's going to be after it now. CNN, Fox, you name it. And please don't say you're going to keep it to yourself!'

'Why not?' I said. 'Why would I want to sell?'

He sighed at the other end.

'Then finish the film, at least! I can put everything else on hold if you want.'

'I'll have to think,' I said. 'When did you say it happened?'

'They were found yesterday.'

'And they were definitely murdered?'

'Three of them, yes. Murdered and mutilated.'

'Christ,' I said. 'They were just kids.'

'Not any more,' he said. 'Anyway, call me if you decide to go ahead. You know where to get hold of me. And listen, you need to finish that film! Please?'

After the call, I lit a cigarette and went back out onto the veranda. Seeing Viktor sitting there, I stubbed it out again and went over to him.

'We must find something to do, Viktor,' I said. 'I agree darts is a bit boring. But we can't just sit and do *nothing*.'

He didn't answer.

'Do you want to phone your mum?'

He shook his head.

'Maybe we can go to the garage and see if we can find something? There's all sorts of stuff in there. There's bikes, too. We could go out somewhere on them, if you want? Or go off in the boat? I'll let you steer?'

'Haven't you got an iPad?' he said.

'No. I've got no internet here. Not even on my phone. But hey, I know this apple tree in the woods. Do you want to come with me and see if there's any apples on it yet?'

'Who are they?' he said, pointing at the boat in the inlet, the four figures who were walking back along the shore towards it.

'No idea,' I said, and got to my feet. 'Tourists, that's all.'

'What are you going to do?' he said.

'Nothing in particular,' I said. 'Read a bit, perhaps. I quite fancy a swim now, too. There aren't many things better than a swim in the sea on an evening like this. Have you tried it?'

'I can't swim,' he said quietly.

'You can't *swim*?' I said, realising immediately it was a stupid thing to say. 'Well, you can learn in no time here,' I said, quickly making amends. 'I can teach you.'

The sea had darkened in the last hour. It lay there in front of us, deep blue and still. The smooth rock was aglow in the light of the descending sun. The wind had died down completely.

I could hardly believe they were dead. All three?

What could have happened?

Jesper was alive. I had to call him. But he'd be in custody if they thought it was him?

Was he crying?

'Hey, Viktor, what's the matter?' I said, and sat down next to him.

'I don't like it here,' he said. 'And I hate you.'

'OK,' I said. 'Hate's a very strong word. What have I done to make you hate me?

He got up and walked away.

I let him go, not even looking to see where he went.

What had she done to the boy? Calling me an alcoholic and turning him against me. He'd be grown up before he understood who I really was. Telling him was no use. Don't believe what your mother says. I'm not an alcoholic. I'm actually quite a decent person.

But there was more wrong with him than Camilla could be blamed for.

The family had continued their walk, passing along the shore below me now, no more than twenty metres away. It felt like an intrusion, they were well inside my personal space, and I got to my feet and went back inside. Viktor was lying on the sofa. I tipped a bag of crisps into a bowl, opened another bottle of soft drink, and put both things on a tray along with a dessert bowl and a spoon, a carton of chocolate pudding and another of vanilla sauce, and carried the whole lot into the living room.

'I'll put this here on the table for you, in case you feel like it,' I said, then went outside again, lit up a smoke and sat down in the chair with my feet up on the rail. I called Jesper's number from my contacts, only to get through to a generic voicemail saying the person at that number couldn't be reached at the moment.

What could have happened?

It couldn't have been coincidence. They were too preoccupied with violence for it to be that, filling their lives with all its symbols.

Could it have been one of the other bands?

I typed him a text.

I'm hearing all hell's broken loose and you're in trouble. Call me if you need help or want to talk with someone unconnected / Skallgrim

I sat and looked at it for a moment, deleted *Skallgrim* and put *Egil* instead, then sent it. Skallgrim was their name for me — because of

Egill Skallagrimsson, of course, from the Viking sagas — but using it myself made it look like I identified with them, which I certainly didn't. I'd found them interesting, yes. Had even been rather fascinated by them, for a while. But my interest and fascination was precisely down to my *not* being able to identify with them. I couldn't understand them, and it was impossible for me to see how I could ever have become like them if I'd run into their kind when I'd been twenty. They were naive, their symbols and posturing nothing but an act, all about bigging themselves up — but still it had led them, consciously or not, into something else more dangerous, and infinitely more radical. The devil the satanist scene worshipped stood for the transgression of every law and rule, every notion of human kindness and solidarity; it was an egotism so great it could easily have driven them to kill another person and remain unmoved by it. As one adherent had said: a person dies every second, so why make a fuss about a single murder? He was in prison now for killing a random man in a park, a crime he probably would have got away with if he hadn't boasted about it.

After spending a few weeks with them, I'd understood with dismay that in their eyes what they were doing was all about freedom. And that to them freedom and violence belonged together. Death was something they asserted and cultivated, believing, so I realised, that a person could only be free when death, whether one's own or someone else's, was no longer something to be feared and avoided. At that point, compassion for others came to an end, and such ruthlessness was of course freedom's fundamental condition.

Nietzsche and Bataille were the philosophers of freedom, and ruthlessness was alien to neither, but their thoughts were only thoughts, their words only words. Bataille, and other members of the secret society that went by the name of Acéphale, had toyed with the idea of human sacrifice by decapitation, even going so far as to select a victim, though falling short of actually carrying it out. Kvitekrist, however, and the circles in which they moved, translated such ideas into action and made them real, presumably with little knowledge of either Nietzsche or Bataille, though the most charismatic scene members, Skjalg, or Heksa, had read Zarathustra, or at least claimed to have done. That was what made me get in touch with them.

Two of those I'd interviewed, and whose lives I had followed to a certain extent, committed suicide, one during my months of filming them, the other a year later. The whole thing was so toxic that eventually I pulled out, archiving the footage and dropping the project, whose working title had been *The Devil in the Valley*, for good.

I decided that as soon as Viktor had gone to bed, I was going to dig out the material and see what I'd got. I'd no idea how many hours of footage there was, but nothing had been edited. Some of it I'd never even seen.

Or maybe it wasn't such a good idea, I thought a second later, reaching for my cigarettes. Maybe I'd just leave it alone. Three were dead now. And there was nothing anyone could do about it.

Far away in the east, it looked like the sky was darkening, more black than blue, rising up like a wall above the sea. It was hardly surprising with the temperatures we'd been having, I thought, and lifted the Bible onto my lap, proceeding to flick through the Gospels to see if I could find the passage where it said Jesus was the Morning Star, but it was hopeless as long as I didn't have the slightest idea where to look, and so I put it down again, took a deep drag on my cigarette and gazed towards the sea.

The tourist family had appropriated my space, the grown-ups sitting on the rocky outcrop, the two kids swimming silently in the pool below. A gull cried piercingly, its horrid noise emitting into the open and immediately dissolving. I sensed the stillness that remained, the stillness of evening, leaned back in my chair and closed my eyes.

I awoke in the twilight.

A strange noise came from the woods behind the house. A throaty, clicking kind of noise.

kalikalikalikalik

Immediately, there was a response from further away.

kalikalikalikalik

What could it be?

An animal of some sort, but what? I thought, getting to my feet. Only then did I see the campfire that was burning down at the shore, its flames bright and distinct in the gloaming.

A bird?

Herons made a prehistoric sound. But this wasn't a heron.

I went inside. Viktor was asleep on the sofa, lying on his back with his mouth open, his eyes partially so, enough for me to see the whites.

Bless him.

I lifted him up and carried him into his room. His head lolled back, and he opened his eyes. They looked completely vacant, as if his soul had left him.

'Just putting you to bed,' I said.

'Mmm,' he said. 'Mmmm.'

Once under the covers, he curled up in the foetal position. I couldn't tell if he was asleep or not.

'Goodnight, little man,' I said, stepping back out and leaving the door open in case he woke up and panicked when he didn't know where he was.

I opened a bottle of Delamain and poured myself a glass, drinking it standing on the veranda. I knew nothing better. A couple of drops on the tongue were enough for the magnificent taste to well in the mouth, and yet it was such a thin liquid. I ordered six bottles at a time from the state off-licence twice a year, ever since tasting it with my father some years previously.

The air was still warm, though moister now, almost steaming in the dusk.

Whatever kind of animal it was, it was quiet now.

My body was stiff after having slept for so long in the chair. I felt a bit of a chill, too, despite the warmth.

I went into the bedroom and took off my shirt, wiped the sweat away with a towel, put on a clean shirt, lightweight cotton, and a pair of white socks, then sat down on the stool in front of the sliding door while I tied the laces of my running shoes. After that, I looked in on Viktor to see if he was asleep. He was, well away by the looks of it.

I went outside, down onto the rock, though staying above the path for a while so as to avoid the tourist family from the boat.

A band of rose-coloured light edged the horizon behind me, enough to still bring out the colours of the landscape, albeit only just: the dianthus were more grey than pink, the grass that grew in all the little hollows more ashen than yellow, but the rock itself was a tawny hue, and the sea below still blue.

It felt good to walk. And it was good to see the light slowly being absorbed from the ground by the hazy veil of darkness that so quickly grew dense in these last days of August.

If I was quick about it, I'd be able to find the tree while there was still enough light. I went up the stony beach towards the woods behind, where there was a small clearing perhaps a hundred metres in. Wasn't there a little stream there too?

Yes, there was.

Lightning flashed in the black sky above the horizon. The thunder that followed sounded distant and faint. How strange that the sky in the west could be so bright and clear, while in the east it was thick with thunder clouds.

It would be an hour, at least, before the rain came.

I hurried over the stones, cutting towards the woods along a path that ran between bushes of sloe and rose hip whose tops were like barbed-wire fences, entering then among the trees, which at first were no taller than me, though as I walked on they began to strive towards the sky, until the tallest rose up, ten and twenty metres, like watchtowers in every quarter.

The first part of the woods extended some two hundred metres before being traversed by the road; beyond the road were some open fields, and then the trees stretched away once more. There was a big pond in there, where as a boy I'd swum, but its water was so thick with algae now one could almost walk on it.

I followed a gravel track that ran through the fields, then a path that went up the hill into the woods on the other side. The darkness was falling faster than I'd anticipated, and I began to regret having come so far. But I liked there being a point to my walks. The clearing I was aiming for wouldn't take more than a few minutes to reach, and Viktor had been so fast asleep he wasn't likely to wake until morning.

Something rustled in the undergrowth close by.

For some obscure reason, the thought came into my head that it was a dead person unable to find rest.

But the dead were hardly likely to make a sound, I told myself, and smiled at the thought.

I'd only just written about a dead person I'd seen, so it wasn't so strange that the thought had occurred to me like that. It had been lingering in my subconscious. But it was something I'd seen only once, and I wasn't sure if what I'd seen had been real or not, whether it had been something inside me or something external. What's more, I'd never know, I told myself, and just then I saw something move across the path in front of me.

I halted, standing quite still for a moment as I stared, but whatever it was had disappeared into the undergrowth.

A snake, most likely, I thought, and stamped my feet down hard as I went on, making sure it would know I was there. It had been moving away from me, but it was when they were surprised that they attacked. If it was an adder, of course. But it could have been a grass snake.

I hadn't seen a snake since the spring, when I'd come across a number of them coiled up in the sun on the warm stones at the beach, as yet cold and sluggish from the winter.

Again, something moved in front of me. This time I saw it quite clearly as it slithered across the path into the bushes, its flat head slightly raised.

It was an adder.

But two in the same spot at this time of year? Or maybe there were even more?

My fingertips and toes tingled. Rationally, I wasn't afraid of them; they weren't dangerous, at least not if you were careful, but there was something about them as creatures that filled me with terror. It was a terror that had existed on earth as long as the snake itself.

Wasn't it around here somewhere?

Yes, through that little dell there.

I walked on a bit, following the low outcrop of bare rock. After some fifty metres, the woods opened out into a clearing.

Sure enough, a stream ran beyond it on the other side.

And the apple tree was there ahead of me, set apart from the other trees.

I went up to it. Its branches were heavy with fruit. The summer had been good to it, I thought to myself, reaching out and gripping one of its apples, twisting it free and sinking my teeth into it.

Mmmm.

The taste, at once sweet and tart, was exactly as I remembered. A faint suggestion of bitterness that wasn't there in any shop-bought apple, something unusual, unique.

The old world.

It was my uncle who'd brought me here first. My dad's younger brother Håkon.

Distant in manner, gruff and stern.

But always good to me. He told me things about my dad that I'd never have known otherwise. It must have amused him, I thought, picking some more apples so that Viktor could taste them too, filling my pockets. And then, as I was about to go back, something moved again in the grass next to me.

Another adder.

It stopped and raised its head, its tongue flicking the air.

It seemed to be looking straight at me. But snakes could barely see a thing.

I stamped my foot hard on the ground, and then again.

It thrust its head forward, the movement transmitting through its body as it wound away towards the trees.

I looked around to see if there were any more. To see so many in such a short space of time was unusual. Were they gathered here to mate? Or perhaps their food was particularly plentiful here?

All was peaceful and still. The grass was grey in the dusk, darker among the trees, the tallest of which stood black against the sky.

I went over to the rock, whose slope was gentle enough for me to scramble up without using my hands.

From behind me came the sound I'd heard earlier.

kalikalikalikalik

I turned and surveyed the clearing. It had come from close by, perhaps from the trees across the grass.

If it was a bird, it was of considerable size.

There were no birds like that in this landscape, not as far as I was aware.

I climbed the hill and was making my way back down the other side when I saw what could only be a fire among the trees, not far from the pond.

There was a band of more open terrain there, sheltered by rock, slanting away towards the pond. I'd been there many times as a child. One summer, I'd found a dead cow there, lying in the stream. I remembered I'd poked a hole in its belly with a stick. The stench had been indescribable.

Unable to imagine anyone camping there any more, I decided to go over and have a look.

The pond was tranquil, edged with reeds. The banks, which I remembered to be claylike and slippery, were now dry and cracked apart. And yet the memories returned; I recalled features and details of the place moments before my eyes picked them out, much as when I returned to a book I hadn't read in years and thought I'd forgotten.

I stopped at the foot of the narrow, open incline. The fire was burning above it, at the fringe of the wood.

I couldn't see anyone there.

But they had to be close by. Who would leave a fire in the woods in a dry period like this?

I went slowly towards it.

There was no one to be seen.

I came to a halt at the fire, which burned gleefully in the dim late-summer night.

'Hello?' I called out. 'Is anyone there?'

Not a sound.

I looked around, peering into the darkness among the trees.

What the hell was that?

Further in, between the wood and the rock, was a kind of mast.

I'd never seen it before.

'Hello!' I called out again.

Strange.

It stood some fifteen metres tall, sheltered by the steep rock face. At its foot, two wooden ramps had been constructed, the mast itself rising up between them, thin and delicate, made of what looked to be wire mesh.

It wasn't a radio or telephone mast, but seemed to be completely home-made.

A student project of some kind?

Whoever made it had probably lit the fire.

They could have gone back to their car to fetch something. It wasn't far to the road.

In fact, I could go back that way, I thought. It would be quicker.

I followed the path into the trees. There was no one else around, and the car park was empty too when I came to the road. Whoever lit the fire must have gone for a walk, somewhere close to the pond, and felt sure the fire wouldn't get out of hand.

It had been a well-constructed fire.

I went along the road until coming to the fields and the gravel track that led back towards the beach, from where I soon saw the light from the house in the distance, as if suspended in the air.

Reaching the smooth ribbon of rock that rose out of the water along the shore, I went up the slope to the right and followed the fringe of the woods for a bit before heading down again where the terrain flattened out.

The tourist family's campfire had gone out.

Lights twinkled from a few boats further away, but apart from that the night was dark and black.

August night.

I paused and lit myself a smoke, sitting down on the still-warm rock. The cover of cloud was so dense now that not even the new star was visible.

Thunder rolled in the distance.

Unrest in the land beyond, I said to myself, and got my phone out to see if Jesper had replied. He hadn't. But there was a text from Camilla.

You two getting on all right? C

Fine, I replied. *You?*

Fantastic, she wrote back promptly.

That good? I replied.

She sent a smiley back. From some Roman restaurant, I imagined, out with that Milo bloke.

Who cared?

Lightning lit up the sky out there.

Ten seconds later and there was a peal of thunder.

It was louder now.

I stood up and went the last bit of the way towards the house. I stopped above the inlet and looked down at the sailing boat as it lay white and motionless in the darkness. No sign of the tourists. No doubt they were tucked up down below. Strange to think of people sleeping there, afloat inside that thin shell. Helpless, to all intents and purposes. Anyone could go on board.

Another lightning flash illuminated the sky. I counted the seconds. Seven before the thunder came.

Suddenly there was a scream.

I wheeled round.

It was from the house. It was from Viktor.

I started running.

Another scream, more protracted, more sustained.

I got to the veranda, pulled the sliding door open and dashed into the living room.

Viktor was standing back against the wall staring at me. His face was distorted in terror.

'Viktor, what is it?' I said. 'Is someone here? What's happened?'

He pointed to the bedroom door. It was closed.

I jumped forward and opened it. The room was empty.

I spun back to Viktor.

'There's no one there,' I said, and stepped towards him.

He was crying, and I put my arms around him.

'What is it? What's the matter?' I said.

'A man,' he sobbed.

'Was there a man here?' I said, thinking immediately of the man from the sailing boat.

Viktor nodded.

'At . . . at . . . at . . .' he sobbed. 'At the wi . . . window.'

'A man at the window? Outside?'

'Y . . . y . . . yes,' he said.

I didn't like what he was saying, but I couldn't let him know.

I crouched down.

'There's nothing to be afraid of, I promise. It was probably just someone going past who thought they'd look in.'

'No, no, no,' said Viktor.

I ruffled his hair.

'I'm sure it was,' I said. 'You woke up and saw someone at the window, and you thought you were all on your own here. No wonder you were frightened! But there's nothing to be afraid of, I promise.'

'But there is,' he said, and clung to me.

'We're safe here in our little house. And nobody's been in. It was just someone out for a walk, that's all, who was curious to see what was inside. They shouldn't have looked in, but some people are a bit like that. It's happened to me too, twice at least.'

'But . . . he . . . he . . . didn't look . . . like . . .'

'Like what?'

'A . . . hu . . . hu . . . human,' he sobbed.

Not like a human, is that what he was saying?

Like what, then? Like a dead person?

Had the gates of hell opened?

'You stay right here, Viktor, and I'll go out and have a look.'

'No!' he cried.

Oh, the poor kid.

'Of course it was a human,' I said. 'It's dark outside, that's all. Things often look strange and different in the dark. Even quite normal things.'

'No, Daddy,' he said. 'It . . . wasn't . . . a human . . .'

'Could it have been an animal, then, do you think?'

He shook his head as the tears ran down his cheeks.

'All right,' I said. 'I'll go into your room and open the window and look out. There's nothing there, but I want you to be quite sure, OK?'

'OK,' he said.

I went into the room, turning round to give him the thumbs up before opening the window. The trees in the darkness swayed in the wind that had gathered over the sea and now rushed about the land. Everything was sighing and creaking out there.

'Is anyone there?' I called out.

No reply, obviously. I felt stupid. But I'd done it for Viktor's sake, not mine.

I closed the window and returned to him.

'You see, there's no one there,' I said. 'Perhaps you just imagined there was?'

He shook his head firmly.

'Then I'm sure it was only an inquisitive walker,' I said. 'Listen, shall we do something cosy?'

He looked at me without speaking.

What would he find cosy?

'How about some chocolate pudding?'

He shook his head.

'We could light a candle and sit for a bit? How does that sound?'

He shook his head again.

He was scared out of his wits. It was more than just waking up on his own and feeling frightened. He must have seen something.

I felt there was some kind of underlying angst in him, too.

I put my arms around him. He was as stiff as a board.

'Everything's all right, Viktor,' I said. 'There's nothing to be afraid of. Come on, let's sit outside for a bit.'

I led him tentatively towards the door. He allowed me to guide him, and a moment later we were sitting in our chairs on the veranda. The sky above the sea split with lightning every now and then. He looked out, expressionless.

I was concerned. Something clearly wasn't right.

The new star. The great skin I'd found shed in the woods. The crabs on the road.

The dead girl.

And now Viktor seeing something that wasn't human.

But then again, I had no idea what films he watched, what games he played.

'I got a text from your mum just before,' I said. 'She's having a nice time in Rome.'

'Mhm,' he said.

'Are you and Mum getting on all right?'

He turned his head and looked at me for a second, then looked back at the sea.

It was impossible to tell what he was thinking.

'Do you fancy some crisps?' I said after a moment.

'OK,' he said.

I got up and fetched the tray I'd left for him in the living room, a candleholder and four candles.

He leaned forward and took a handful of crisps as I lit the candles.

'Are you still frightened?' I said, sitting down again.

'A bit,' he said.

'But you know there's nothing to be afraid of now, don't you?'

He shrugged.

I poured some soft drink into his glass. He drank it in one go.

'It's like being at the cinema, this!' I said.

It really was magnificent, watching the lightning in the dark sky in front of us.

Viktor took another handful of crisps, and stuffed them into his mouth, flakes and crumbs dropping onto his chest.

He hadn't been taught any manners, that much was obvious.

But he did seem calmer now.

I reached out and picked up my cigarettes, tapping one out against my palm and then lighting up.

There was that sound again, from behind the house.

kalikalikalikalik

What *was* it?

I stood up.

'I'm just going to get something from the garage,' I said. 'Won't be a minute.'

'Don't go!' said Viktor.

I couldn't take him with me, and I couldn't leave him on his own.

I sat down again. From the sea came a faint, thrumming sound. It was the rain beginning to fall. And then, moments later, the first drops struck the rock in front of us, spattering everywhere within seconds, and all of a sudden we were as if in a dome, sheltered on the veranda from the elements that raged around us.

We sat for a while without speaking.

'Is there something else you're afraid of?' I said after a bit. 'I understand you being scared seeing someone at the window like that. Especially if you thought you were on your own. But is there anything apart from that?'

'No,' he said.

He picked up his bottle of pop and drank from it.

'That's all right, then,' I said. 'Because there *is* nothing to be afraid of. You know that, don't you?'

'I know,' he said.

'But listen,' I said, 'it's late. I think you should go to bed now, don't you?'

He shook his head.

'Are you frightened of being on your own in your room?'

'No.'

'You can sleep in my bed, if you want.'

'What about you?'

'I can sleep on a mattress on the floor.'

'OK,' he said.

I followed him into the bedroom. He took his shorts and T-shirt off and his pale, skinny body crept under the duvet.

I sat down on the edge of the bed, but when I made to run my hand through his hair he turned away.

I got up.

'Where are you going?' he said.

'Just onto the veranda,' I said. 'It's a bit early for me to go to bed yet.'

He sat up immediately, picked his shorts up off the floor and put them on.

'Viktor, it's bedtime now,' I said. 'Do you want me to sit here with you?'

As soon as I said it, he pulled off his shorts again and got back into bed.

'You mustn't go when I'm asleep,' he said.

'I won't,' I said.

'Promise?'

'I promise.'

He closed his eyes, and I sat down on the floor with my back against the wall. His breathing was calm and steady, and I sat for several minutes without moving, sensing that he wasn't quite asleep.

'Daddy?' he said abruptly.

'I'm here.'

'I *am* afraid of something.'

'What are you afraid of?' I said.

For a long moment, he didn't speak.

I turned my head and looked at him. He was lying quite still, staring at the ceiling.

'I'm afraid of death,' he said quietly.

I didn't know what to say. But he was waiting for an answer.

Perhaps he'd never told anyone before.

If there was one thing I wasn't afraid of myself, it was death. It could come only as a relief, a liberation from life's torment, its badness and petty malice; from those who constantly craved, who took and never gave.

'Everyone is from time to time,' I said after a pause. 'Even grown-ups.'

He said nothing. It was almost as if I could *hear* him think.

'But you've a long life to look forward to,' I said. 'There's nothing to be afraid of. OK?'

He didn't answer.

Twenty minutes later, he was fast asleep.

I crept out and sat down outside. The darkness was alive with pouring, dripping rain. I wondered if the rain was warm, and whether to go and see what was making that noise. But I dismissed the idea, put my feet up on the rail and lit a cigarette.

kalikalikalikalik, came the noise from the woods behind the house.

kalikalikalikalik, came the reply.

SOLVEIG

W hen I went out into the garden the next morning, it was to bird-song everywhere. Strings of chirping undulated through the air, a swinging network of sounds, some wistful, others full of joy, underpinned here and there by the throaty, angular coo of a wood pigeon, and all set against the cawing of hundreds of crows now start-ing their day in the trees a bit further away.

I put down my bowl of yogurt and my mug of coffee on the little table that stood up against the house wall, sitting down in the chair beside it with my face lifted towards the sun that had just risen above the spruce on top of the ridge to the east.

My body ached with fatigue. But with only a little breakfast and some coffee it would recover. It always did. Fatigue didn't matter, all one had to do was stick it out. It had its various phases, too, and often concealed itself to the extent that one hardly noticed it.

I wiped my mouth with the back of my hand as I swallowed, and reached for my coffee. My whole mouth tingled with the yogurt's acidity.

One of the pigeons came flying towards the house from over by the woods. Turning my head to watch it, I saw that the star was still shin-ing, high in the sky.

I took out my phone to see what the papers were saying about it. Above, a window opened. I tipped my head back and looked up, but saw no one. She must have gone straight back into bed.

The experts were having a field day. Most, it seemed, considered it to be a supernova. A rare phenomenon, though by no means unprecedented. What puzzled them was that they were quite unable to identify it.

Inge's theory, that it was a new star, seemed not to figure at all in their considerations.

454 KARL OVE KNAUSGAARD

I smiled and put the phone down on the table. As I finished my yogurt, a calf came into view by the fence that marked the boundary with the next-door farm. It shook its head from side to side a couple of times, no doubt bothered by flies, horseflies perhaps, before beginning to graze. Behind the hillock, two cows appeared, wandering sedately in the same direction as the calf, before they too began to graze.

Surely it wasn't unthinkable that something new could occur? Something that had never occurred before?

I scratched an itch on my lower leg and closed my eyes to the sun. When I opened them again, I saw a little sparrow come flitting from the tall birch onto one of the branches of the apple tree. It performed a little twirl in the air before settling, as if in glee.

I would have liked to have sat there a while longer, but Mum may have been awake and I didn't want her to have to lie helpless in bed, so I swallowed the last mouthful of coffee, got to my feet and went back inside to the kitchen, rinsed the bowl and mug and left them in the sink before opening the door of her room.

She was asleep, in exactly the same position as when I'd last looked in on her.

I put a hand on her shoulder.

'Mum,' I said. 'You've got to wake up now. I'll be off to work soon.'

She opened her eyes and looked at me.

Her gaze was clear and bright the very instant she awoke, revealing no doubt at all as to where she was, or who I was.

It was a comfort to see.

'Anita will be here any minute,' I said. 'Do you want me to sit you up, or do you want to lie for a bit?'

Her lips shaped the word *up*, and I took the remote control from underneath her pillow and pressed the button for the upper part of the bed to lift slowly into the air with a hum.

'I'll go and get myself ready,' I said. 'Is there anything you need while I'm still here? A glass of water, perhaps?'

She shook her head.

'The radio?'

She opened her mouth to whisper a barely audible *no*.

I opened the curtains, smiled at her and went out into the passage, where I got some clothes out and took them with me into the bathroom. I showered quickly, dried my hair with the hairdryer, put some make-up on and got dressed just in time to hear what could only be Anita's car come up the track.

It stopped outside, the door opened and shut, footsteps crunched the gravel, and then from the passage came a bright and cheerful: 'Good morning!'

When I came back in, she was standing beside Mum, who was sitting with her feet on the floor, slowly moving her trembling hands to the walker that had been placed in front of her.

'Hello, Anita,' I said.

'Hello,' she said. 'She's had a good night, I understand?'

'Yes. I think so,' I said.

I liked Anita, whose breezy nature could only be a boon to my mother. My only reservation about her was that she often talked to me over Mum's head, as if she wasn't there.

Mum turned slowly towards me, her eyes seeking mine. She opened her mouth to say something.

I stepped closer and lowered my head, placing my hand on hers, which was warm.

Line, it sounded like she was saying.

'Line's still in bed,' I said. 'She probably won't be up until much later. But she's going to be here all day.'

She whispered something else.

'What was that?' I said.

She whispered again.

Realising that I still hadn't understood, she became frustrated, her arms trembling violently. Her eyes filled with rage.

I smoothed my hand over her upper arm.

'What's on your mind, Mum?' I said, putting my ear to her lips.

But her breath was the only thing left now, not a word could she utter.

I had no idea what was troubling her, it could have been anything. Perhaps she wanted us to have something for dinner that Line liked, or perhaps she wanted me to tell Line that her grandmother was fine on her own, that she didn't have to worry about her, but could do as she pleased?

Her whole body shook now.

'Are you thinking about what Line's doing today?'

He eyes were veiled with protest as she looked at me. So it wasn't that.

'What is it, then?' I said.

Again, she whispered something, but I still couldn't work out what it was.

It was exasperating, for I was already running late.

'Let me help you up,' I said, taking her by the arm and lifting her upright with Anita's help.

'I've put some clean clothes out for you in the bathroom,' I said. 'I've got to go now. See you this afternoon. We can talk then. Have a nice day with Line!'

She stood with her mouth gaping, her arms still trembling, following me with her eyes as I went out and closed the door.

I was worried as I went towards the car, as if something serious had happened. It didn't help telling myself it was nothing more than Mum having a little problem with making herself understood.

She became so small in those situations, with the importance she attached to even the most unimportant of matters. I was well aware, of course, that in all likelihood her mental and emotional faculties were undepleted, it was just that she could express so little, and anything of even the slightest complexity was impossible for her to convey.

What had she been trying to say about Line?

I stopped in the gateway and looked up at the nest that was partially hidden there among the climbing plants. Only when I took a step to the side did I see the chicks, huddled together, their small, orange-yellow beaks reaching up towards the sky.

As I stood there, one of the parent birds came sailing over the roof of the house again. Unfazed by my presence, it settled on the edge of the nest, leaned forward and began feeding its young. Its movements were quick, abrupt almost, as if it kept changing its mind.

I continued round the side of the house and got into the car, which for some reason I'd forgotten to lock when I'd come home the evening before. Perhaps it was with Line being home, I thought as I dumped my bag on the back seat, started the ignition and turned my head to reverse out onto the track. The unusual overriding the usual.

And then there was Ramsvik.

An unpleasant feeling came over me.

He'd been dead. The body lying there on the table had been a corpse, only then it had opened its eyes and emitted a low scream. As the surgeon was cutting open its chest.

I drove down the shallow slope of the gravel track and turned out onto the road that ran along the fjord. The sky in the west was still a haze, the fell above the fjord veiled.

There was a natural explanation for everything, including this, I told myself. He hadn't been dead, that was all there was to it. The monitors had been wrong.

I came past the Co-op. There wasn't a soul to be seen so early in the morning, apart from a man sitting on a bench outside. He was always there, there was something the matter with him. Not much, but enough to compel him to spend his days there, on the bench, watching people come and go, occasionally engaging in chat.

The boats in the inlet lay motionless on the fjord; they looked almost as if they were floating in mid-air.

Then the road led into the valley, leaving behind it the yellow pastures, white houses and shimmering red barns. Trees rose up densely on both sides. Flecks of light played among their green shadows. A small stream glittered here and there between the trunks, emerging elsewhere into the open, as if borne by its light, sandy bed.

I found myself singing 'Would I Lie to You?' Where did that come from? I wondered, as the waterfall appeared a bit further ahead, the road bending before rising to ascend the fell.

Eurythmics, in the car last night.

That was it.

I'd played that album all summer when it came out, couldn't get it out of my head.

Be Yourself Tonight.

How ironic that was!

Sverre giving me the eye as I came walking from the jetty on my way up to the community hall with Therese and Marit and Anna. A bit tipsy already, my hair rather wet, showing off my white dress in the summer rain, my raincoat still tucked under my arm, a bottle of Liebfraumilch in my other hand.

Be Yourself Tonight. It was to Sverre I had lost myself, and for so many years.

'Would I Lie to You?' One of the first things he said after we became intimate and started talking seriously was that he'd had cancer and had almost died.

There was no reason for me not to believe him. Who would lie about such a thing?

I'd walked with eyes open straight into disaster.

But it was over now! I was free. And moreover I was home, I thought to myself as my eyes saw the bogland, yellow and dry after the long summer, the low-slung hills strewn with bilberry shrubs, the fjord then re-emerging to reflect the green fellsides.

Half an hour later, as I crossed the car park outside the hospital, a helicopter came in from the fells, tiny, at first, as a dragonfly.

Strange how the noise of that small machine could so dominate the sky, I thought. And how ominous it always sounded.

I went down to the changing rooms and put my uniform on, and as the helicopter came in resonantly and landed outside I got myself a coffee from the machine and took the lift up to the ward, just in time for morning conference.

On my round afterwards, I went first into Ramsvik's room. His condition was unchanged, Renate had said. His heart was functioning unaided, and the CT scan had revealed brain activity, so he was definitely alive. Though not sufficiently to allow any dignified life: the doctors had decided against IV therapy, which meant that his days were numbered. How long it took would depend on how strong and wilful he was. His wife had been informed of the decision and expressed her agreement. She was with him, I knew, as I knocked on the door. And I knew too that his children would be coming in the afternoon to say their goodbyes.

She was sitting in a chair next to the bed, holding his hand, and looked up at me with a smile.

She was rather small, with round cheeks and a look of mildness, the corners of her eyes and mouth finely creased.

'Hello,' I said, closing the door gently behind me.

'Hello,' she said.

'I'm so sorry about this,' I said.

She lifted her eyebrows and pressed her lips together in an expression of hopelessness. We can do nothing about it, her face seemed to say.

'It happened quickly and without pain,' I said. 'If that's any comfort.'

'He's not dead yet,' she said.

'No,' I said.

'Won't he be in pain when he's not receiving any nourishment? He'll starve to death, won't he?'

'He's not conscious of anything,' I said. 'I don't think he'll be aware of any pain.'

It looked like he was asleep as he lay there with his eyes closed. His face seemed naked without his glasses. His beard was still neatly trimmed. I knew that underneath his pyjama jacket his chest was heavily bandaged, but I wasn't sure if she realised.

'What exactly happened last night?' she said.

'He suffered two massive strokes,' I said.

'I know that,' she said. 'They rang and told me, and said I needed to come in. They said he was brain-dead. That his organs were being donated. He'd registered, apparently. But then they phoned again and I was told he wasn't brain-dead after all.'

She gestured towards him, a slight movement of her hand.

'And his organs hadn't been donated. What's going on? Do you know? What happened last night? Now the doctors are saying there's brain activity, but that he's not going to wake up again.'

'They did a CT scan, and that scan revealed no brain activity. That must have been when they called you in. Apparently it was wrong. I don't know how that could happen, I'm afraid. But when they did another in the early hours this morning, some brain activity was detected. That's all I know.'

She turned and looked at him, still holding his hand, stroking it gently.

'If there's anything you need, don't hesitate to ask. Or if you've any more questions. The best thing is for you to have a word with the consultant, Dr Henriksen. I'll ask him to look in on you.'

'Thanks,' she said, and smiled.

I smiled back and went towards the door.

'Is there no chance he'll wake up again? Not even the smallest chance?'

'I'm afraid not,' I said. 'It was a massive haemorrhage.'

'I know, of course,' she said. 'It's just that he looks so alive.'

She smoothed her hand over his cheek and I closed the door behind me and went out into the corridor.

I understood all too well what she meant. He looked as if he could wake up at any moment. That his brain was lifeless seemed therefore more like a hypothesis, a theory put forward by the doctors.

She must have had her children rather late, I thought. She looked to be at least fifty. They'd have an old mother and no father. But she seemed to be the type who could cope with most things.

Ellen came towards me.

'How did it work out with that little girl?' I said. 'Is someone taking care of her? Is she all right?'

'We sorted it out,' said Ellen. 'She stayed the night at a friend's from school. Her aunt's coming today to look after her.'

'Well done, Ellen!' I said. 'And the mother?'

'Not so good. Withdrawal symptoms. They're letting her go home tomorrow, though.'

'We can't do anything about that,' I said. 'But at least now the children's social care team are aware of the situation. Let's hope they can make a difference.'

'They take kids away from their parents,' she said.

'Not always. And sometimes it's the best option,' I said.

'Not in this case,' she said.

'You'll just have to let it go and hope for the best, I'm afraid,' I said, and went into my office, where I skimmed through the records of a new patient who'd been admitted the evening before. His name was Mikael Larsen, he was seventy years old and had suffered a mild stroke, had been found by his wife after a few hours, was unable to speak and displayed paralysis on his left side. He was due in surgery at some point during the day, to drain a clot from between the cerebral membrane and the skull.

He was in the same room as Inge, who'd been moved that morning.

I closed the document and massaged my forehead with the palm of my hand while staring at a photo of Line and Thomas; they were three and two years old and were standing holding hands in the road as they looked at the camera, Line with a wide smile, Thomas looking serious. Two toddlers, little mini-people I could lift into the air, carry and hold.

So much love they gave without knowing. And how delightful it had been when they used to lay their heads against my chest, their little faces all chubby cheeks and wide eyes.

The grief of that time being gone fluttered inside me for a moment, a shadow of loss. But a shadow nonetheless, I thought, made by the light. They weren't dead!

I got up, went out to the staff toilet and splashed some cold water on my face at the sink, carefully dabbing myself dry before going to see the new patient.

Inge's bed was hidden behind a curtain. I could hear he was listening to the radio, the volume turned down low, as I went to the other bed. The patient was awake and looked at me. A woman in her sixties, who'd been sitting in a chair reading when I'd come in, put her book down and stood up.

'I'm Hanne,' she said, putting her hand out. 'And this is Mikael.'

'I'm Solveig,' I said. 'I'm in charge of the ward here. Please, have a seat!'

She remained standing. Her face was meagre and pale, her features sharp. Red hair, green eyes.

'How are you feeling?' I said, turning to Mikael, who seemed younger than his seventy years. His hair, rather long and dark, was swept back, a few locks spilling forward into his eyes. He looked like a fading film star from the fifties.

His mouth drooped at one side.

'O . . . kay,' he said.

'He's having difficulty finding his words,' his wife said. 'He knows what he wants to say, but not how to say it. Is that right, Mikael?'

'Yes,' he said.

'Have you spoken to Dr Mattson?'

'Oh yes,' she said.

'Good. So you're aware there'll be some surgery this afternoon.'

'That's what we've been told, yes,' she said.

'There's a cafeteria where you'll be able to wait, if you like.'

She nodded dismissively.

She looked down on me, I could tell. I was only a nurse in her eyes, so she was probably someone high and mighty. If she wasn't trying to make up for her fear and uncertainty, that is.

I touched her arm.

'Don't hesitate to buzz,' I said. 'If there's anything you're not sure about, or anything you need.'

'Thank you,' she said, and sat down again. 'We've got everything we need for the time being. Haven't we, Mikael?'

She looked at her husband.

'Yes,' he said.

'Good,' I said, moving then to Inge's side of the room. For want of a door, I tapped the knuckle of my index finger against the frame that held the curtain.

'Come *in*,' he said playfully.

I drew the curtain partially aside and stepped forward.

He was sitting up in bed with his bandaged head, in his blue hospital smock, smiling.

'I thought that was you on your round,' he said.

'How are you feeling?' I said.

'Fine, thanks,' he said. 'A bit of a bad head, but I suppose it's part of the package. They were rummaging about in there quite a while. And of course they had to saw the lid off first. No one's done that to me before.'

'I should hope not,' I said. 'Nothing unusual apart from that?'

'No,' he said. 'No seizures, no hallucinations. The drudgery of hospital life, that's about it.'

'Excellent,' I said with a smile I was unable to hold back.

'Yes,' he said. 'As long as it lasts.'

There was a silence.

'What did you see exactly?' I said after a moment.

'The hallucinations, you mean?'

'Yes.'

'One time it was two trees floating by the side of the road. I was on my way to work, so it was early morning, the sun was up, and there above the fields were these two trees, roots and everything hanging down. The funny thing was,' he said, 'it didn't occur to me that it was an hallucination. To me it was real! I saw it with my own eyes!'

He shook his head.

'Another time, I saw a car in flames. The sun was out then as well, and there was snow on the ground. The car was in the middle of the road, engulfed. I slammed on the brakes and jumped out, only then there was nothing there. I thought I'd gone mad. But I'd seen it with my own eyes! It wasn't something I'd imagined, it had been right there in front of me. Eventually, I didn't know what to believe and what not.'

'That must have been terrible,' I said.

'Yes, it was,' he said.

There was another silence.

'They're discharging you tomorrow,' I said. 'Are you ready for that?'

'Just about,' he said. 'It'll be good to get home.'

Beside the radio on the little bedside table was a framed photograph. Not of his wife or children, but of an owl with outstretched wings, taken a moment before landing. Because the wings were curbing rather than propelling its flight, it looked like the bird was unnaturally suspended in mid-air.

It was a powerful image.

'Do you like it?' he said.

I nodded.

'Did you take it?'

'I wish I had! No, it was a proper photographer. He knocked a pillar into a field, and another one next to it with a camera and a self-timer on it. He wanted to pull the birds out of the sky, he said. And that's what he did. That one's an owl. Amazing, isn't it?'

'It is,' I said.

I wondered if he knew that people in the old days associated owls with death. If you heard an owl screech close to your house, it meant someone was going to die. Owls were thought to inhabit the borderland between night and day, life and death.

If he didn't know, I didn't want to be the one to tell him.

When I entered the duty room, Renate, Ellen and Mia were standing laughing at something one of them had said. Renate was dishing out medication, Ellen was seated at the computer, while Mia stood with a cup of coffee in one hand, her other fidgeting with a cigarette.

'It's quiet today,' I said, pouring myself a coffee.

'The lull before the storm,' said Renate.

'I just looked in on Mikael Larsen,' I said. 'His wife's a bit prickly. Does anyone know what she does?'

'No idea,' said Renate. 'They don't live here, anyway. They've got a summer house out at Hellevika, on one of the islands in the fjord. I think maybe they own it. The island, that is. So they must have some money.'

'That would explain it,' I said, and sipped my coffee, glancing at the screen above the door, where a lamp had started flashing. Room 2. Ramsvik's room.

I put my cup down and went out. Behind me in the corridor, someone came running. I turned. It was Henriksen.

'Solveig,' he said. 'Major traffic accident coming in. A car and a bus. No word as yet as to how many injured or dead, but it looks like we're going to be busy. I need your help. A helicopter's on its way in now. And there'll be ambulances too. Can you get someone to take over here?'

'Yes, of course,' I said. 'Give me two minutes.'

I went back in and explained the situation to Renate. She was to call in some extra help and cancel surgery. I took the stairs up to theatre, rather than the lift, giving me a chance to call Line and tell her I was going to be late. She didn't answer, so I texted her instead before switching off my phone and hurrying up the final flights.

There was a bustle of activity all around me as I changed and got ready. Everyone still remembered the bus crash a few years earlier involving forty schoolchildren, seventeen of whom had lost their lives. I hadn't been there then, but several of my colleagues had, and I knew it was still traumatic for them. The images in the mind from that day would never quite go away.

The trolley carrying the first of the patients emerged from the lifts a few minutes later. A child passenger from the car, a girl about five or six years old. Major, life-threatening injuries to her head and chest. Her face was hidden behind the ventilator, but her hair was matted with blood and it looked as if half her skull was open. They'd put her on a morphine drip in the helicopter, so she was breathing, her heart was functioning and her blood loss was under control, but Henriksen shook his head as he bent over her and I cut away her clothing.

Behind us another patient came in, and then another.

'She's practically dead,' Henriksen said from behind his mask. 'How her heart can still be beating I don't know.'

'But it is,' I said. 'She's battling.'

'Haemorrhaging in the brain and chest, probable pneumothorax. No doubt internal haemorrhaging elsewhere too.'

She was wearing a little necklace, it looked like she'd made it herself, plastic beads in all sorts of colours, with little boxy letters in the middle spelling the name ALICE.

Henriksen took her hand in his and pressed his thumb hard against one of her fingernails. Her eyes remained closed. He squeezed her shoulder blade between his thumb and index finger. She drew her arm away at the same time as she opened her mouth. The sound that came out was low and protracted and didn't seem to belong to her at all.

They wheeled her in for a CT scan and Henriksen leaned over her sister, who was around ten years old, she too seriously injured and comatose.

'Oh God, what a mess,' he said. 'She's nothing but blood and bone.'

He picked some shards of bone from her skull with his fingers.

It was evening by the time I left theatre. The family from the car were all still alive. One of the two girls had suffered life-changing injury to her brain, assuming she would get through the days that followed. The same applied to the father. The mother and the two eldest, while having escaped without head injury, were nonetheless critical.

No one could ever expect to survive the injuries they had all sustained. And yet they had. At least so far.

I lingered under the shower, strangely unable to acknowledge my surroundings; I felt as if I was still in the operating room, and the shower cubicle with its white floor tiling was something I was dreaming.

They'd been on their way home from holiday. A lapse in concentration from the bus driver as he rounded a bend and they'd lost everything.

All the little moments they'd taken for granted, perhaps barely even noticed, would never return. Breakfast before going to school, the youngest dangling her legs on her chair as she ate her cornflakes, the two older ones arguing about clothes upstairs while the coffee maker gurgled and morning radio filled the room.

How innocent our lives were.

I turned the water off and took the towel from the hook, pressing it to my face and holding it there. Fatigue came over me again, and at once I felt drained.

I draped the towel over my shoulders like a cape, stepped out into the changing room and sat down on a bench.

Even the thought of getting dressed seemed insurmountable.

I needed to sit for a bit.

But then I'd have to get a move on. Mum and Line would be needing me at home.

I could barely stand up, and got dressed still seated.

I couldn't even be bothered to switch on my phone.

But I had to, I told myself.

It helped slightly to get outside, where the world opened up around me. The weather had changed, the sky was overcast now and the air was dense with rain. Not even the new star could be seen.

A white broadcasting vehicle was taking up space in the car park. I glanced towards the main entrance, where a dozen or so people, some with TV cameras, stood in a huddle.

It struck me how absurd it was that everyone had to know when an accident had happened, even people far away in other parts of the country.

I dipped into my bag for the key, pressed it and saw the lights of the car flash, the wing mirrors slowly open out like the ears of an animal that had suddenly become aware of something.

I got in, put my bag down on the passenger seat and switched my phone back on.

Four texts from Line.

Is it the accident on the news?

Making waffles for Gran!

Where's the waffle iron?

Found it!

An intense feeling of gladness unfurled inside me as I typed a reply.

Lovely! On my way home now. See you soon!

I put the phone back in my bag, turned the ignition, put the car into gear and pulled away.

That was the last thing I'd expected.

It meant she felt at home, even if she hadn't grown up there. And despite me not having been there with her today.

It was the house itself that was looking after her.

And the fact that Mum was there too.

I opened the window a bit to get some air in so I wouldn't fall asleep at the wheel. There was hardly any traffic on the roads, and very little in the way of distractions that might keep me awake once I'd got out of town onto the main road, which I could have negotiated with my eyes closed.

Once, I'd driven Thomas and three of his teammates to a football match after work and had been so tired that I'd dropped off, only for a few seconds, but long enough for the car to veer towards the rock face at the side of the road. One of the boys had suddenly shouted, 'Watch out!' and I'd woken just in time to avert an accident.

Fortunately, I don't think any of them ever realised how close it had been. But what a shock it gave me. I was responsible for three boys and my own son, and had nearly got us all killed.

A few heavy raindrops dashed against the windscreen. I closed the window and switched the radio on, only to switch it off again almost immediately. There was no space left inside me to take in talk.

The river ran dark among the trees. Not a soul to be seen.

How good it would be to climb into bed and sleep.

I could make us a light supper. Fried egg and cutlets, perhaps. Give Mum a massage and a shower, and then to bed.

The big oak trees rose up like dark citadels in the flat valley. The cattle had gathered underneath them to shelter from the weather. Not the smartest place to stand if it began to thunder.

Why hadn't they died? I wondered, putting the wipers on full speed as the rain battered down. Something was keeping them here. It was almost as if their hearts had been working on their own, beating of their own free will, beyond the control of the brain.

That poor girl.

Alice.

Several passengers on the bus had been seriously injured too. But none had died, at least not yet. It was hard to believe.

The miracle in the Sædalen.

That should be the headline.

Without taking my eyes off the road, I opened the glove compartment, took out an old CD and slipped it into the player.

It was Beethoven's Symphony No. 7. I skipped straight to the final movement and turned up the volume.

'Bam baa ba, baam ba ba!' I sang, the rain drumming on the body of the car, the dark sky hanging low over the changing landscape.

I wondered what sort of music Inge listened to.

I barely knew anything about him. But I felt sure he'd like Beethoven.

The thought of sitting in a car with him while listening to music made my pulse race.

How silly I was.

Tomorrow he was being discharged and would disappear out of my life for good.

Out of my heart.

Stop it, I told myself.

I didn't even know him. Had hardly even spoken to him.

And I wasn't sixteen any more.

On the other side of the fell, the fog lay like a lid over the valley. Descending through it, I could hardly see a thing and was forced to slow to a crawl. Below the big boulder where I'd seen the red deer the day before, I followed an impulse and pulled into the side. A few minutes wouldn't matter, I thought, turning off the engine and opening the window.

The rush of the falls resounded from the fellside. There was more water in the river than there'd been before, I noticed; it covered more than half the stony bed now. The headlights shone through the fog and made it glisten.

I'd almost been expecting the deer to be there again. It wasn't, of course, but it was nice to sit there for a moment anyway. It was a good spot, with the waterfall, the pool below, the narrow river that on sunny days appeared golden because of the sandy bottom and its yellow-white stones. The enormous boulder that according to legend had been hurled across the fell by a giant and split down the middle when it landed. And all because the church bells down at the fjord had annoyed him so dreadfully.

I looked across at the trees that grew on the other side of the river. The road made it seem almost like the forest started here. Which of course it didn't. In fact, I was almost in the middle of it now.

Was that the deer?

It *was*!

There between the trees, it stood looking at me.

The car must have made it curious. Perhaps the beam of the head-lights? It probably couldn't see me at all.

It lifted its head and seemed to sniff the air for a long moment. Then it walked forward. Its coat was dark in the dim light, apart from the legs, the backs of which were white.

Out into the river it went.

To drink?

No, it came straight across.

It paused again, only a few paces from the car now.

There was no longer any doubt. It was looking at me.

Its great, dark eyes.

I leaned forward tentatively.

'Hello, beautiful creature,' I whispered. 'What do you want?'

It stepped closer and then stopped, its head only an arm's length away.

As cautiously as I could, I reached my hand out. It lowered its muzzle and sniffed me, its hot breath against my palm.

'Hello there,' I whispered again.

It looked at me. It gaze was warm and open, but quizzical too.

In the seconds that passed before it lifted its head once more and wandered off, it struck me that it had looked at me in the same way as I had looked at it.

After it had gone, I sat for a moment to collect myself before driving on. After the serenity of my encounter with the deer, the car engine sounded like an inferno. There was no traffic on the road, and only a few minutes later I pulled up outside the house.

A new wave of fatigue assailed me. I could barely open the car door and get out. Certainly, I couldn't remember ever having felt so exhausted. I was often tired, of course, but this was different. It was as if it took all my strength just to walk from the car to the house. But I'd feel better in the morning, I told myself as I stepped into the passage and put my bag down on the chair. A good night's sleep was all I needed.

Mum was no doubt asleep already, and Line would likely be upstairs in her room, for the house was completely still.

Yet the lights were on in all the rooms.

When would she learn?

I opened Mum's door and looked in.

The bed was empty. The chair as well.

'Mum?' I said.

No answer.

Where could she be?

I went into the kitchen. No one there either. But the waffle iron had been left out on the counter, along with an empty bowl of batter and two plates.

'Line?' I called out.

Not a sound.

I went up the stairs and opened the door of her room.

It was empty.

Could they have gone outside?

But Mum was far too unsteady on her feet. Unless Line had thought of the wheelchair.

No, they wouldn't be out at this time, in this weather. She wasn't that silly.

I went slowly down the stairs again. If something had happened to Mum and the ambulance had been here, Line would have phoned.

I stopped in the passage and listened.

There was no one in the house.

'Mum?' I called out again, louder now.

I went and got my phone out of my bag and called Line's number.

She'd switched it off.

Could they have gone to the hospital?

There was no other explanation.

And how badly I needed to sleep. But I couldn't now. I couldn't do anything but wait.

I put the kettle on. Normally, the fell across the fjord would be visible all night in summer, a dark, impenetrable wall against the slate-grey sky, but now it was completely obliterated by the fog. It was as if the world ended at the rowan trees on the other side of the fence, I thought to myself, taking a mug from the cupboard and a tea bag from the box in the pantry, the milk from the fridge, then looking around for the sweetener, which I found by the porridge oats Line had left out on the side.

As I waited for the water to boil, I went down into the cellar to see if the wheelchair was still there. It was, tucked away between the wall and the freezer, ugly and covered in dust.

I emerged into the kitchen again just as the kettle switched itself off and the faint, pale blue light at its base went out. I filled the mug with boiling water and left the tea bag to steep for a minute, added some milk, clicked in a couple of sweetener tablets and sat down in a chair with the mug in my hand.

I ought to ring the hospital.

But first I needed to go to the loo.

Even that seemed like an effort.

I took a sip of the tea and put the mug down on the table, got to my feet and went to the bathroom.

Mum's walker was blocking the doorway.

Oh, goodness.

There she was, lying on the floor. She wasn't moving. Her arm stuck out at a terrible angle.

I moved the walker out of the way, crouched down and felt for her pulse.

But her eyes were open, and she looked at me.

'Mum, what's happened?' I said.

She tried to say something, but couldn't.

'You've broken your arm,' I said. 'I'll call the ambulance. Everything's going to be all right.'

I dashed back to the kitchen, grabbed my phone and called the emergency number, darting into the living room to get a blanket as I spoke.

'It's Solveig Kvamme here,' I said. 'My mother's fallen in the bathroom and broken her arm. Can you send an ambulance right away? She's elderly, she suffers from Parkinson's and is rather frail. It's an emergency, in other words.'

I gave them the address and took the blanket with me into the bathroom. Carefully, I adjusted her position so that she was lying more comfortably, put the blanket around her, fetched a glass of water from the kitchen and put it to her lips, encouraging her to drink, talking to her the whole time.

She closed her eyes and drifted into sleep, or perhaps passed out. She must have struggled to stay awake while waiting for me to come, I thought to myself, feeling despair pumping around my body with every heartbeat. She must have heard me come in, must have heard me call out for her.

I sat down beside her on the floor and tried to call Line again. At the same moment, the front door opened.

I went into the passage. Line was hanging up her raincoat on the peg and looked at me as I appeared.

'You're home!' she said. 'Well, I knew you were. I saw the car.'

'Gran's had a fall and broken her arm,' I said. 'I'm waiting for the ambulance to come.'

'What?' she said. 'How? She was asleep! That's why I went out. She was asleep!'

'It's not your fault, love,' I said. 'She must have got up herself to go to the loo and just fallen, that's all.'

'Oh, poor Gran!' she said. 'Is it serious?'

'She's rather frail as it is, so it's not good,' I said. 'Hopefully, she'll mend all right. She's a tough old bird.'

'Is there anything I can do? I mean, anything at all?'

I shook my head and passed my hand over her cheek.

'Thanks, Line. I'm just going to sit with her until the ambulance comes.'

'OK,' she said.

I turned to go back to the bathroom.

'Are you going to the hospital with her?' she said.

I turned round.

'Yes, that's what I'm thinking,' I said.

'Do you have to?' she said. 'The doctors and nurses there will take care of her, won't they?'

'It can be a rather daunting experience, even so,' I said. 'Being taken away in an ambulance to a big hospital like that.'

'OK,' she said again, and stepped past me, her eyes downcast, before going upstairs to her room.

Mum's eyes were still closed when I returned to her. I put my hand cautiously to her brow. It was cold and clammy. This wasn't good, I thought, and sat down on the floor with my back against the wall. It wasn't good at all. Her breathing was so faint I had to stare at her chest for a long time to detect any movement.

It was as if she needed less of everything now, even air.

I hoped she wouldn't die.

Her mouth was open and drawn, and her cheekbones were again as pronounced as when she was a young woman.

Of course I had to go with her in the ambulance, it didn't matter how exhausted I was. I could sleep there and go straight on duty in the morning, it wasn't a problem.

But Line wouldn't want to be on her own in the house all night. She'd always been afraid of the dark, ever since she was little.

She was just too proud to admit it now.

And Mum wasn't conscious. Perhaps I could go in early in the morning and see to her then?

I'd be needing strength for the two of us.

I heard the sound of a vehicle coming up the track from the road. I went and opened the door, and watched as the ambulance crew got out, took a stretcher from the back and came towards me, the reflective bands on their uniforms faintly luminous in the light from the windows.

VIBEKE

Åse woke up at the crack of dawn, standing cheerfully in her cot at first, hands gripping the bars, but since I took my time, having already been up at four o'clock to feed her, after which I'd lain awake hoping she would quickly go back to sleep again, she soon began to scream, and then to wail.

Helge stirred beside me.

'What time is it?' he mumbled at first. And then: 'For goodness' sake, can't you see to her?'

I put my hand on his chest, pressed my cheek to his, which was rough with stubble, and kissed his throat.

'Happy birthday, old man,' I whispered.

He opened his eyes and turned his face sleepily towards me.

'Oh, I'd forgotten,' he said, reaching out his hand and ruffling my hair. 'Thanks. What time did you say it was?'

'I didn't. But it's half past five.'

'Oh God,' he said.

'You go back to sleep. I'll see to her. It's your day today.'

He turned over and pressed his head into the pillow, bending his neck back as far as he could, and in a matter of seconds his breathing settled and his mouth fell open.

I got up, taking my nightgown and putting it on as I went over to Åse's cot in the corner.

She reached her arms up towards me, her teddy in one hand.

'You certainly woke me up early today,' I said, lifting her up to sit on my hip. She put her head to my shoulder and dug her little hand into my back.

'You're such a good little girl, Åse,' I said, and kissed her on the forehead. 'Do you want to go downstairs?'

'Nn,' she said, meaning yes. *Nn* could also mean no, but the intonation then was different, rising instead of falling.

My phone. I'd need my phone.

I went over to the side of the bed and picked it up off the nightstand.

His sleeping position looked so uncomfortable, but it was the only way he *could* sleep, I'd learned. With his head tipped back as far as it would go.

Perhaps it was to give easier passage to sleep's dark cloud, for he always fell asleep so abruptly. And slept so soundly that I doubted he'd ever actually seen *me* sleep.

'Daddy's asleep,' I said softly to Åse, who stared at him as she sucked on her dummy.

'Nn,' she said, squirming then in my grasp, wanting to move on.

I took her with me into the bathroom and put her down on the floor while I sat and had a wee. She toddled over to the bath, peered over the side, then squatted down to pick up the toys that had been left on the floor, before throwing them one by one into the tub.

'Bang!' I said.

She looked at me and smiled. It warmed my heart.

Downstairs, I opened the door onto the terrace so that she could go in and out as she pleased, then got some coffee on the go and turned the radio on. The sun hadn't come up yet, but the sky was bright and the air outside unbelievably warm.

With a cup of coffee in my hand, I stood looking out over the rooftops towards the fjord below, the fells beyond. Åse trundled her big ladybird trolley back and forth over the slate flooring. Her nappy hung heavily between her little legs and I went and got a clean one from the bathroom, picked a light blue cotton dress out of the tumble dryer so as not to disturb Helge upstairs, laid Åse down on the sofa and changed her.

On the radio they were talking about the new celestial phenomenon that had appeared out of nowhere the evening before. An expert from the university was explaining about supernovas. His voice was eager and proud; he knew what he was talking about, and at last his moment had arrived.

'Here we are, my little lovely,' I said as I carried her over to the high chair, took a yogurt from the fridge and began to feed her. At first she sat quietly, opening her mouth when the spoon arrived, swallowing and then opening again while looking into my eyes the whole time. There was such an unfathomable warmth and trust in her eyes, I thought, and such openness. Not a shadow, not a cloud.

'Hello there,' I said. 'What are you thinking now, I wonder?'

Suddenly she shouted and waved her arm in the air. Her attention had shifted to something behind me.

I turned round to see what it was.

'Aha!' I said. 'You want your own spoon, is that it?'

'Nn,' she said.

I got one out of the drawer and handed it to her. She clutched it tight and proceeded to make some unsuccessful prods into the yogurt pot, before losing patience and grizzling loudly in frustration. I held her wrist to guide her hand, but she was having none of it.

'Rrraaaaa!' she wailed.

Let go, Mummy, it meant.

When finally she managed to get the spoon in the pot, she could only flip a big dollop of yogurt onto my chest. And before I could stop her, she picked up the whole pot in her hand and threw it to the floor.

She looked at me, her eyes enquiring and goading at the same time.

'Do you want some bilberries?' I said.

'DAAA!' she shouted.

I tipped some into a bowl and put it down in front of her. She picked them up one after another between her index finger and thumb, putting them into her mouth with the utmost concentration and without a sound.

'They're good, aren't they?' I said, licking the finger I'd used to remove the yogurt from my nightgown, before fetching the cloth and wiping the floor by her chair, rinsing the plastic pot and dropping it in the bin for recycling. I poured myself some more coffee and drank it standing in the light from the modular skylighting as I checked my schedule on my phone. I was supposed to be working from home today, but that was only a ruse, the real plan being to get things ready for Helge's birthday. He'd said he wanted no fuss, no guests, no party — we'd booked a trip to Rome at the weekend to celebrate quietly on our own — but this was his sixtieth, and this time there'd be no wangling his way out.

I'd joined forces with Tore, his brother, and we'd invited fourteen people round for this evening. Drinks on the terrace, osso buco, his favourite, for dinner — one of the chefs from Sjølyst, his restaurant of choice, was coming in the afternoon to get started — and then to round everything off a specially made cake, not of the spectacular kind, but a regular soft sponge cake his mother always used to serve on his birthdays when he was growing up, and which I was going to make as soon as he got off to work.

Most things were already prepared. But I still had to buy flowers, wine, spirits, fruit and mineral water, pick up his present from the picture framer, iron the tablecloth and the napkins, set and decorate the table, and drive Åse up to my mum's — all the myriad little things that always had to be done before any party, and for most of the day I'd have Åse with me, as well as having to remember to reply to some important emails and make a couple of phone calls.

I ought to give a speech, too.

I'd have to think about what I was going to say as the day went on.

All these things gave me such pleasure, and had done so for some time already. I obviously enjoyed conspiring and keeping secrets. Perhaps because it was so far removed from my nature?

I could hardly wait to see his face when he came home and realised he was being celebrated, and in style.

Åse was scrutinising me and so I put my phone away, lifted her out of her chair and sat her down on the floor, took her bowl and put it in the dishwasher, picked up my coffee and, seeing her toddle onto the terrace, followed her outside.

The ridges of the fells to the east were an orange glow. Not long after, the first rays came spearing over.

At Joar's fortieth, his wife had given a speech in which for some reason she'd decided to say how things were between them. None of the guests had known quite how to react; discomfort spread, people looked at the floor, exchanged glances, and afterwards the meal had continued in silence, broken only by the clinking of cutlery on plates. Forty was when you met yourself in the doorway and could take stock one last time, before it was too late to change direction. It was an age of truth, no matter how unpleasant. But a celebration wasn't the place! A celebration was about the good things, the broad, sweeping lines in life that were so dominant as to exclude anything bad. For the bad things were always so petty.

Not that I had anything bad to say about Helge.

He was obsessed with his work, yes, and indifferent about things that didn't interest him, which was to say everyday life, yet always well meaning. Self-absorbed. Energetic. Stubborn in certain areas, weak in others. Flush with an unacknowledged fear of ageing.

But none of this said anything about who he *was*.

He was the kind of person you didn't want to see leave a room, no matter how many other people were there. A person who said things you'd never thought of before. Someone you wanted to be near.

I looked at Åse. She was sitting quite still, staring at something in front of her. Prodding it, whatever it was, with her finger.

I got up.

'What have you got there?' I said, bending over her.

Five ladybirds were crawling around on the slate flooring.

'Oh, how lovely!' I said. 'Ladybirds!'

'Nn,' she said.

'*Ladybird, ladybird, fly away home*, we used to sing when I was little,' I said, nudging one onto my finger and letting it crawl there for a moment before standing up and flicking it over the railing. Immediately, it opened its little wings and drifted away on the air.

'There, she flew away,' I said.

Only then did I see that there were lots of them. Twenty, thirty, at least. Some of them were settled on the railing, others on the tiles, while others simply flew about.

How strange.

'Look, Åse,' I said, and lifted her up.

Now that I'd become aware of them, I saw still more. All the dots that were filling the air would be ladybirds too. There was a whole swarm on its way.

At the same moment, they began to settle all around us.

'Daa!' said Åse, flapping her hands in glee.

The tiles were alive with them all of a sudden. A few landed on Åse too, crawling on her dress and in her hair, and instantly three appeared on my nightgown. I brushed them away as I endeavoured to take Åse back inside without stepping on them, but it was impossible, there were so many now that they crunched under my bare feet as I retreated towards the open door.

I slid it shut behind me and put Åse down carefully, picking the ladybirds out of her hair, brushing them from her dress onto the floor, where they began to crawl about with the others that had managed to get in.

Outside, the terrace floor was now covered with them. The glass door and the big windows were almost alive.

I felt sick.

'What a lot of nice ladybirds,' I said, Åse sitting on her haunches to stare at them as they crawled around on the parquet. 'But let's go and put the television on, shall we? Then Mummy can do some tidying here.'

I found the remote on the sofa and switched the TV on, lifted Åse up and scrolled to the kids' programmes, selecting an episode of *Teletubbies*, which she loved, and as soon as the sun with the baby's face rose up on the big screen on the wall and she was fully immersed, I hurried back into the kitchen and got out the dustpan and brush.

It felt so unpleasant to be sweeping up living creatures as if they were crumbs, but it was even worse to have them crawling about the living-room floor. Strangely, they offered no resistance, attempting not to fly or even get out of the way, but lying still on the dustpan as I carried them through the room to the kitchen window, which I opened with my free hand before scattering them into the air outside.

Behind me, Helge came down the stairs.

'No need to do the cleaning on my account!' he said.

He hadn't put his glasses on and his face looked oddly exposed, his eyes innocent, as if somehow they weren't yet used to the world.

'Happy birthday,' I said, going towards him.

He kissed me lightly on the mouth.

'Do you have to keep reminding me?' he said. 'It's a dreadful day!'

'You're a man in the prime of life,' I said. 'What could be better than that?'

He laughed.

'That's the worst euphemism I've ever heard.'

'Have you looked outside?' I said. 'On the terrace? There are thousands of ladybirds out there.'

He turned and walked towards the door at the other end of the room.

'Good Lord,' he said. 'That's amazing!'

'I get an end-of-the-world sort of feeling,' I said.

'Nonsense,' he said. 'They're just swarming, that's all.'

'Why would they do that?'

'They're looking for food or somewhere to see out the winter, I imagine.'

'How come I've never seen it before, then?' I said.

He shrugged.

'Have you?' I said.

'Seen it before?' he said.

I nodded.

He shook his head.

'So how do you know it's natural, then?'

'Insects swarm. The ladybird is an insect.'

He turned to where Åse was sitting motionless, staring at the television as she sucked unremittingly on her dummy, then went over to her and lifted her up.

'Hello, my lovely one!' he said, and tossed her into the air.

She started crying.

A shadow passed over his face.

'Nothing can drag her away from *Teletubbies* once she's settled down with it,' I said quickly. 'She won't have it if I try to move her.'

'It's all right,' he said.

He put her down again, and at once she was quiet.

'Have you had breakfast yet?' he said, looking at me as he absently ruffled her hair.

'I was waiting for you,' I said.

'Do you mind if I go for a little run first?'

'On your sixtieth birthday?'

'*Especially* on my sixtieth birthday.'

'It's your day,' I said with a smile. 'Anyway, it suits me fine. I can make some breakfast while you're gone. What would you like? Eggs? Omelette?'

'Porridge,' he said. 'But you should make something nice for yourself.'

I first met Helge at a taxi rank. I'd been to London and come back on an evening flight. Normally, I'd have taken the shuttle service into town, but work was paying, so I'd thought I might as well take a taxi with it being so late.

It was raining, there were no taxis, and the only other person waiting was a tall, slim man with an umbrella in one hand and a briefcase in the other.

I'd recognised him straight away. It was Helge Bråthen, the architect. He was often on TV and in the newspapers, and there'd even been a documentary made about him which I'd seen.

A lone taxi pulled into the rank. He folded his umbrella and gave it a shake, and when the taxi stopped in front of him, he opened the door and got in. Only then did he appear to notice me.

'Where are you going?' he said.

'Into town,' I said.

'We can share, if you like? Save you standing here waiting.'

'Thanks, that's very kind of you,' I said, and went round and got in the other side.

He sat looking at his mobile, and I checked mine for any messages. At exactly the same moment, we each put them away and looked out of our respective windows.

He didn't seem to notice the synchronicity.

The windscreen wipers moved rhythmically, soporifically from side to side. The wet surfaces gleamed in the headlights and street lighting. Where the light petered out, the darkness was completely impenetrable.

'You're interested in art, then?' he said.

I looked at him in surprise.

Then I realised. The tote bag in my lap, from the Tate.

'You could say,' I said, and smiled. 'How about you?'

I saw no reason to appeal to his ego, which I assumed was big enough to begin with, and made no suggestion that I knew who he was.

'Oh, you know,' he said, looking at me through his round, black-framed glasses. 'You could say. I ask because I saw you at the Blake exhibition in

London yesterday,' he went on. 'It was you, wasn't it? Unless I'm much mistaken?'

I nodded.

'Did you enjoy it?' he said.

'Yes,' I said. 'I'm fond of Blake. The exhibition on the whole was a bit overwhelming, though, I thought. Too much, in a way. Not enough space around the pictures. So they died a bit for me.'

'I agree,' he said. 'The manuscripts were wonderful, though, don't you think?'

'Yes,' I said.

We fell silent again. I was glad of the lull, not feeling particularly inclined to chat, especially with someone I didn't know. I must have signalled it, because he didn't speak again until we approached the centre of town and he asked me where I wanted to be dropped off.

Apart from mentioning it at work the next day, that I'd shared a taxi with Helge Bråthen, I gave no further thought to the encounter. I certainly wasn't looking for a new relationship. Marcus and I had only split up a few months before, and although that had mostly been my own initiative I was still feeling low about it, because I still cared for him a lot. And then there was my exhibition. Properly speaking, I was far too young and inexperienced to be in charge of such an ambitious undertaking, the museum's most far-reaching exhibition in many years, but the concept had been mine and I'd done much of the groundwork myself, the thought being precisely that it would be harder then for them to task anyone else with the curation — if they even ended up liking the idea.

They had, and for the next eighteen months I'd worked exclusively on the project.

At the opening, to which were invited all and sundry in the way of artists, politicians, sponsors and local celebrities, Helge Bråthen came towards me pointing his finger at me.

'The Blake exhibition in London!' he said. 'Am I right?'

I nodded.

'So you're not just interested in art, it's your job too? What else would you be doing here, I ask myself.'

'You could say,' I said. 'How about you?'

'No, I'm only an architect,' he said. 'What do you think of the exhibition, then? You were rather critical of Blake, I remember.'

How could he remember that? He surely met all sorts of new people every day?

I smiled.

'I like it rather a lot,' I said. 'How about you? What do you make of it?'

'Some of it I like,' he said. 'And some of it not so much.'

'What parts of it don't you like?'

He looked at me as he ran his hand over the stubble on his scalp.

'The lighting in room 2 is awful,' he said. 'Far too dark. It gives the wrong atmosphere. Atmosphere must come from the pictures, not from the bloody lighting. The colours on the walls are awful too. Same reason.'

'But what about overall? The art itself? It works pretty well, wouldn't you say?'

Now it was the stubble on his chin that he rubbed.

'To an extent,' he said. 'It's just so very difficult to mix up different ages like that, even if there is a thematic link. It makes things so obvious. Do you follow me? What you want is for the pictures to work together, as it were, to play off each other. Rather than just representing the age to which they belong.'

I nodded.

'But the crows, now that's *very* good. And Vanessa Baird's pictures. I love Vanessa Baird.'

'Me too,' I said.

He looked at me as if confused for a second, as if he'd forgotten who he was talking to, before nodding and smiling at me. Then he glanced around, presumably in search of a waiter with some wine.

I nodded and went off to mingle.

The next day he phoned me.

'Helge Bråthen speaking. Blake in London, if you remember?'

'Oh, hello,' I said.

'You pulled one over on me yesterday! Pretty emphatically, too. I would never have said what I really thought about the exhibition if I'd known *you* were the curator!'

I laughed.

'It was interesting to hear your opinion,' I said. 'And the lighting's been sorted now. Thanks for bringing it to my attention! You were right, of course.'

'No, not at all,' he said. 'Let me make it up to you. Can I take you out to dinner?'

'Yes, I'd like that,' I said.

'Tonight?'

'I can't tonight,' I said, and sensed myself smiling. 'It's our public opening.'

'It can't go on all night, surely?'

'Until ten.'

'Meet you after that, then?'

'There won't be any kitchen open then, will there?'

'Not a problem. They'll stay open for us. Shall we say ten thirty? Restaurant Sjølyst?'

We said ten thirty, and not many months after that I moved into his apartment. I saw that he was happy then, but I saw too that he was concerned.

'What do you actually want with me?' he said the first evening after I moved in. 'I'm not far off sixty. You're thirty-three.'

'I want to have a baby with you,' I said.

He stared at me in disbelief.

'You are joking, aren't you?'

'No.'

'What on earth do you want *that* for?'

'Because I love you.'

'You do?'

'Mm.'

'As much as that?'

'Mm. And besides, you've got good genes.'

I put the porridge on while he went and showered. Then I heated some rolls in the oven, made more coffee, fried an omelette and pressed three glasses of orange juice, all of it ready when he came down the stairs.

'Well, I must say,' he said, rubbing his hands together as he sat down.

'Don't just make do with the porridge,' I said, lifting Åse into her chair and then holding a glass of juice to her lips. Her face twisted into a grimace at the first sip, but then she wanted more.

'Why not?' he said.

'It's what solicitors and businessmen eat when they're going in for the Birkebeiner race. I can't think of anything worse, to be honest.'

'Yes, you can,' he said, dropping a dollop of butter into the middle of his porridge and sprinkling cinnamon on top. 'Industrial livestock farming, the oil industry, the extinction of the species. Just to name a couple of examples. All worse than porridge.'

'You forgot whaling,' I said.

'That goes under extinction of the species,' he said.

He began to eat, and looked up at me.

'Can't you sit down?'

'I'm just about to,' I said, and nodded towards the brown Gudbrands-dalen cheese. 'Perhaps you can cut her a piece?'

I sat down and he placed a piece in front of her, which she took and put in her mouth, as quiet and as concentrated as when she'd eaten her bilberries.

'Isn't she lovely?' I said.

'That's an understatement,' he said. 'She's fantastic.'

'Which of us do you think she looks like today?'

He looked at me, then at her.

'Your eyes, thank goodness. My nose. Your mother's facial shape. Your sister's hues. But everything taken into account, she's very much her own person. With her own soul.'

She watched him attentively as he spoke. Sometimes I felt they admired each other from a distance. They hadn't entirely got the hang of each other yet, but they would.

We had talked no more about it that first evening, and neither of us mentioned it in the days that followed. But then in the car one day, on our way to the supermarket after work, he put his hand on my knee.

'It's fine by me,' he said. 'Let's have a baby. But looking after it will have to be your job. I'm too old to go to work *and* be a modern dad. And you've got to be completely sure. It has to be something you really want. Bear in mind that I'll be seventy by the time the child's ten.'

'I'm competely sure,' I said, and squeezed his hand.

Now he pushed his empty plate aside, cut a roll in two halves and placed a slice of cheese on each.

'You must have some omelette too,' I said. 'It's very good, even if I do say so myself.'

'Mm,' he said, and took a bite of his bread, leaning forward over his plate so the crumbs from the crispy crust didn't end up in his lap.

'What have they got in store for you at the office today, do you know?' I said.

He shook his head and swallowed, then took a slurp of his orange juice.

'A cake in the shape of the new post office or some such nonsense, I shouldn't wonder,' he said. 'I've told them I want no fuss this time. No doubt they think I was only joking.'

'Weren't you?'

He snorted.

'Fifty was all right. I hadn't yet grasped the gravity of the situation. Sixty's another matter altogether.'

We were quiet for a few minutes, all three of us. The radio kept repeating the interview I'd heard earlier in the morning, the eager astronomist over and over again.

'Listen to that idiot,' Helge said, leaning back in his chair. 'The way these people drone on about how everything that happens must have happened before and will happen again in exactly the same way. Science is built on the notion. Everything following certain laws which are unchangeable. I've always thought it can't possibly be true. Well, not always, but at least since my twenties. It's no more than three hundred thousand years since man emerged. And that was something completely new, something that hadn't been there before.'

This was Helge's guiding idea. That the world wasn't governed by laws, but by habits. He'd taken it from Peirce, whom he'd read with some friends in their student days. He'd even called his thesis 'Architecture and Habit'. I'd visited the university library and borrowed it the day after our first night out, and I'd been impressed. Subsequently, he'd left theory behind and had never pursued the ideas that nevertheless were still so important to the way he understood the world.

'But that's biology, evolution. Surely there's no contradiction between that and the laws of nature?'

'But our whole experience is about change!' he said. 'It's not that long ago since they split the atom, for instance. And only a few generations back there were no such things as cars or sewing machines or planes or computers or space rockets or what have you.'

'That's just man exploiting the laws of nature to his advantage,' I said. 'That doesn't exactly nullify them, does it?'

'But try and imagine a world without natural laws. No eternally recursive patterns, no boundaries for what can occur and what can't. But where everything nonetheless evolves and *everything* has a history.'

'So gravity, for instance, just evolved?' I said to provoke him, though he clearly didn't grasp the intention.

'Exactly! It was never a given! Matter simply began to behave in that way. It became a habit, and after billions of years it's become a habit so difficult to turn around again that we think it to be an eternal law. To begin with, though, it was merely a case of improvisation. Everything in nature is improvisation. Some solutions just turn out to be better than others, and so they become entrenched.'

'But how does matter know how to behave? Habit presupposes some kind of conscious mind, doesn't it?'

I looked at him with a smile.

'You don't believe matter can think, do you?'

'Let's say the idea sounded right, the utterance less so,' he said, and smiled back. 'Still, let's entertain the idea for a moment that matter can think. Or perhaps not think as such, but that it possesses some form of consciousness. Consider atoms, the way they slot into patterns that work. And that everything new that happens strives to do likewise, to slot into patterns that work.'

'I'm not sure I understand the difference,' I said. 'The end result's the same, gravity exists no matter what.'

'But there's a huge difference!' he said. 'If evolution applies to everything, then something completely new can occur at any time. Take that supernova up there, for example,' he said, poking a finger upwards. 'What if that's something completely new? Science won't be able to embrace it, because they've already decided that nothing new can happen. They won't be able to see it.'

'What do you think, Åse,' I said, running my hand through her hair. She'd been sitting quietly, watching Helge gesticulate as one by one she placed the dry cornflakes I'd given her in a line on the table in front of her.

'You realise, of course, that it was probably the first metaphysical thought in the world?' I said.

'What was?'

'That everything is alive, even matter.'

'There's no reason to believe their thoughts were any poorer than our own,' he said, getting to his feet. 'What are your plans today, anyway?'

'I was thinking I'd try and get a bit of work done, if Åse will let me. I might take her into town with me later, too.'

'That sounds nice,' he said, and downed the rest of his coffee, wiping his mouth with the back of his hand. 'I seem to be running a bit late now. See you this afternoon.'

As soon as he left the house, I put Åse back to bed, and once she fell asleep I started on the cake. The ladybirds were all gone from the terrace, and while the sponges were in the oven I sat down and dealt with some emails.

The temperature outside had already risen to thirty degrees, and it would almost certainly get even hotter later in the day.

I texted Atle, Helge's eldest son, who'd promised to help me carry things.

Are you still up for it? I wrote.

Of course, he wrote back. *What time?*

Ten. See you then. And thanks!

I went back into the kitchen and looked at the sponges through the oven glass. They were still rather pale-looking, so I went upstairs, had a quick shower and got changed, Åse still sleeping, her arms and legs outstretched like a little starfish, before going back down, taking the sponges out of the oven, savouring their delicious smell and golden hue, and leaving them to cool on a rack. One had sunk a little in the middle, but not enough for it to matter.

I cleared the breakfast things from the table and had just started the dishwasher when Åse began to cry.

'I'm here, Åse,' I called out as I went up the stairs, finding her standing up in her cot, warm and sweaty, her face creased and tearful.

'What a long sleep you've had,' I said, lifting her up. 'Let's change your nappy, shall we? Then we can go into town. That'll be fun!'

She grizzled a bit, and I handed her the hairbrush to play with as I put her down.

I packed her bag with some nappies and wet wipes, some fruit purée and a couple of small cartons of milk, pressed an empty feeding bottle into one side pocket and a bottle of water into the other, made sure I'd got my money, the car keys and my sunglasses, then carried her out into the hallway with the backpack on and my own bag on my arm, and took the lift down into the basement.

I hardly ever drove anywhere, preferring to cycle or walk, but now we were going to the big shopping centre on the outskirts of town, so there was no other way.

Helge had taken the Mini as usual, so it was the Audi I backed slowly out of the space in the cramped residents' garage, before emerging into the bright sunlight with Åse safely belted into the child seat behind me.

Once we were on the main road, I phoned my mum.

'Hi,' I said. 'Is it all right if you pick her up at ours instead? It looks like I'm going to be too busy to come and drop her off.'

'That's fine,' she said. 'When do you want me to come? The same time?'

'Yes. Or any time before five,' I said.

'The sooner the better?' she said.

I laughed.

'Yes,' I said.

'In that case, I'll be there around three.'

'Brilliant,' I said. 'See you then!'

Mum was almost the same age as Helge, there was only a year between them, and I knew she found it a bit hard to relate to, though she'd never let on.

It was one thing that they could conceivably have been a couple themselves, but it was quite another that he, a man her age, was sleeping with her little girl — for that's who I still was in her eyes — which no doubt to her mind, though again she'd never say so in as many words, was tantamount to paedophilia. Or if not that exactly, then at least something against the order of nature, the way things were supposed to be.

What was such an old man doing with such a young girl? And not just any young girl, but her own daughter?

We'd never talked about it. She wanted to let me live my life, which I was grateful for. But it was *inconceivable* for her not to despise him, a man her age running around after girls only half his own.

I ought to bring it up with her sometime.

But she would never admit it, not even to herself.

And what would I say? All I could think of were clichés.

Age is just a number.

But it was true!

The person Helge was, that which was *him*, had no age. It was swathed in sixty years of lived life, and for many people this was something that made the path to the core so long and convoluted that the person inside remained unto themselves, a tone that was theirs and theirs alone, amid all their thoughts and feelings, which no one else had access to any longer. But in Helge's case, the path to the core was short. As when he bubbled with enthusiasm about a matter, or when he was feeling down about something, or found something else so indescribably hilarious that he completely lost himself in laughter.

It made him vulnerable, and his vulnerability was something I loved.

'I'm thinking about your daddy!' I said, reaching my hand behind the seat and finding hers.

She pushed it away.

'Do you want an ice lolly afterwards?' I said, immediately wishing I hadn't. *Afterwards* wasn't a concept she understood.

'Nn!' she said.

And then, when no ice lolly transpired:

'UAA! UAA! UAAAARGH!'

'You'll have to wait a bit, Åse,' I said. 'We'll soon be there, and then I'll buy you an ice lolly.'

But it was too late, she was already screaming.

A petrol station appeared just ahead. Without hesitating, I flicked the indicator and turned in.

'Come on, we'll get you an ice lolly,' I said, releasing the safety belt from her seat and lifting her out.

The heat dithered above the asphalt. Traffic rushed by, a merciless racket. The air was thick with exhaust and petrol fumes. Åse hadn't yet understood why we'd stopped, she wailed and kicked her legs and was almost impossible to carry.

But when I slid back the lid of the freezer display and took out an ice lolly, she went quiet immediately. I opened it for her, she put the lolly in her mouth and I handed the wrapper to the man at the till, who scanned it. I paid and we returned to the car, and a few minutes later turned back onto the road towards town.

I parked on the shopping-centre roof. We were early, and Åse was still hypnotised by her ice lolly, so I switched on the radio and sat waiting for her to finish.

I thought about what Helge had said, about everything in the world being the result of improvisation and that the laws of nature were basically just habit.

Ideas didn't have to be true to enthuse him, nor even probably true. It was enough for them to be new.

But what if ideas behaved in the same way?

An idea was conceived, and when first it was conceived it would occur again, over and over, spreading throughout society, until after a few generations our ideas were so entrenched and habitual that what they conveyed became construed as laws of nature.

Mum had told me that towards the end of his life my grandfather, on seeing the politician Jo Benkow on the news, had suddenly said, 'What's that damned Jew doing on my television?' She'd been appalled, her father had never before expressed anti-Semitism, nor any other form of racism. Had he held such views all along, but kept them to himself, knowing them to be stigmatising, only for them to escape him after he had become old and begun to lose his bearings?

Was it the case that such ideas, with all the prejudice they contained, had been held for so long as to become a part of our fabric, even though we had not conceived them ourselves? Was that why they were so difficult to break down, why new ideas were so infrequent and met with such resistance? But when first conceived, they would occur again, over and over, until they too became galvanised by habit, if not to become laws, then at least possible truths.

There was hope in that, wasn't there?

For the impossibility of changing the course of the world, as like a moth we steered directly into the flame, was only seeming. I thought about saving the rainforests. I thought about banning fossil fuels. I thought about how terribly we treated animals. And if I thought about those things, others would too, and a pattern would form, more and more people would share those same ideas, until eventually they became a truth with which our actions could only accord.

And precisely because of the nature of ideas, their gathering together in clusters could only make them increasingly inescapable.

Or was that just idealistic nonsense?

My mobile pinged. It was Atle.

Here now, he wrote. *Are you on your way?*

With you in five! I typed back, then got out of the car, opened the boot and took the stroller out, unfolded it and put Åse in it.

'Look at the state of you!' I said.

Her face was covered in ice lolly, her dress soaked with it all down her chest.

I took a handful of wet wipes and washed her face, then lifted her up and sat down on the back seat, planted my feet on the ground and Åse in my lap, pulled the dress over her head, found a clean one among the things I'd packed and put it on her before putting her back in the stroller.

'There we are!' I said, threading my arms through the straps of the backpack, tucking my own bag onto the storage rack under the stroller and heading for the lift.

I could get most of what I needed in the shopping centre. The only other thing I had to do was to pick up Helge's present from the picture framer's. I could do that while Åse was with my mum, I thought, turning the stroller so that Åse could see herself in the mirror.

I pressed the button for the ground floor and crouched down beside her as the doors slid shut.

'Look,' I said, pointing at our reflection. 'It's us! Åse and Mummy. Can you wave?'

She curled the fingers of one hand together and then opened them again in that incredibly cute way that small children do.

I chuckled and gave her a kiss on the cheek before getting to my feet again, pushing the stroller out into the ground-floor shopping area and going over to the off-licence where Atle stood waiting.

He was wearing a pair of khaki-coloured shorts, white shoes and a blue shirt. His sunglasses hung from his breast pocket. His hair was slicked back, his beard trimmed short.

How Helge had produced a son as vain as Atle was beyond me.

'Hi, Vibeke,' he said, checking me out with a fast look he presumably didn't think I'd notice, a once-over, lingering for a fraction of a second on my breasts, before stepping towards us and giving me a hug. 'Great idea, throwing a party for him!'

'Yes, isn't it?' I said.

Åse stared up at him.

'Hello, gorgeous,' he said, and smiled at her.

Inside the off-licence he took a shopping trolley while I pushed Åse round in the stroller.

'The chef's instructed us to buy either Barolo or Barbaresco,' I said. 'So what if we get seven of each? Will that be enough, do you think?'

'How many people are coming?' he said.

'Fourteen in all.'

'I should think that'll do, then,' he said. 'Which of the Barolos do you want?'

'This one, perhaps?' I said, pointing.

'The most expensive?' he said with a grin. 'Why not the best?'

'I like it,' I said.

'All right,' he said, and took seven bottles from the shelf.

Why had I asked him of all people to help? I wondered, already dreading the next choice I had to make.

Maybe it was best just to let him get on with it.

'I didn't grow up with wine, so I'm a bit unsure,' I said. 'But you realised that, didn't you?'

'At least you didn't take the second most expensive,' he said. 'That's what people do when they've got the money, but don't know what they're doing. They think going with the most expensive wine is too vulgar. The second most expensive will still be a good wine and nearly as posh, so they reckon.'

'You can choose, if you want,' I said.

'I'm no expert,' he said. 'But I can do, of course.'

'We need some dessert wine too,' I said. 'And spirits. Gin and vodka and whisky. I think that should cover it.'

'Cognac, maybe? He likes his cognac.'

'Yes.'

Atle put the bottles up on the conveyor while I got my card out of my bag.

'He'll realise what you're up to, won't he? If he checks the account?' he said.

Was he putting me down? Or was that seriously what he thought?

I put the card in the reader and keyed in my PIN.

'It's not the sixties,' I said. 'I've got my own job. And my own bank account.'

I put the card back in my wallet and began bagging the bottles.

'And even if I *had* used your dad's account, I very much doubt he'd be checking. It's not exactly his style, is it?'

'No, I suppose not,' he said. 'He's not got much control over his finances.'

Åse threw her teddy to the floor, followed a second later by her dummy.

'Are you bored?' I said, picking them up again. She shook her head briskly and I put them away under the stroller.

'We're going in a minute,' I said.

'I'm ready,' said Atle, now with several carrier bags divided between both hands.

"Perhaps we should put all this in the car before we go on,' I said. 'Those must be terribly heavy.'

'I can do it, save you the hassle with the buggy and everything. Where are you parked?'

'In the car park on the roof,' I said, and handed him the key. 'Right next to the lift.'

It struck me that anyone who saw us would think we were out shopping with our little daughter.

'I'll go to the florist's while you're at it,' I said. 'I'll meet you there!'

Once he was out of sight, I phoned Helge.

'How are my two favourite girls?' he said.

'We're fine,' I said. 'We're at the shopping centre getting a few things in.'

'Like what?' he said.

'Like some flowers, for instance. It is your birthday, after all. And Åse's had an ice lolly, which she liked very much, and now we might just go to a cafe or somewhere. What are you up to?'

'Nothing much,' he said. 'It's too hot to work, so I'm just hanging around really.'

'Haven't you got air conditioning?' I said, pausing outside the florist's.

'Yes, yes. It's the general mood more than anything. Too much summer, it makes a person restless. Anyway, where are you exactly? I could come and meet you. Have you had lunch?'

'Who has lunch at ten o'clock?'

He laughed.

'All right, how about in an hour, then? Can you endure the inferno until then?'

'Well, I can. Not sure about Åse, though.'

'We needn't have lunch just to see each other,' he said. 'Where are you? I'll come right away. I could do with some new shirts. A pair of shorts too, in fact.'

'Listen,' I said, 'it's not that convenient just at the moment.'

He went quiet.

'OK,' I said. 'I might as well come clean. I'm busy with something secret.'

'Ah, I'm with you,' he said.

He'd be able to guess now, I thought to myself as Atle came out of the lift some distance away.

'It's just a little thing,' I said. 'But I can reveal that it's something special that I think you'll like. That's what I'm hoping, anyway.'

'As long as it's not a cake in the shape of some church in Malmö,' he said.

'Was that their surprise?'

'Yep.'

I laughed as Atle came up.

'Did it taste nice?' I said, putting my index finger to my lips.

'Yes, as a matter of fact, it did.'

'They obviously love you,' I said. 'I do too!'

Everything felt better going into the florist's. The shop was bursting with gladioli and I bought a big bunch, all white, another that ran through the spectrum of pale pink to deep red, and another that took in yellow and orange, pink and red. And then, for good measure, two bunches of anemones, red, white, purple and blue.

'You're certainly going for it,' said Atle, his arms full of flowers as he waited for me to pay.

'Sunflowers are your dad's favourites,' I said. 'We ought to buy some of those too, even if they don't really go with these.'

'What about you?' he said.

'What about me?'

'Your favourite flowers.'

'Have a guess,' I said. 'Gladioli, obviously.'

The assistant wrapped some sunflowers for me too, and after I'd paid for them we went into the supermarket and bought fruit and mineral water. Åse was starting to get unsettled, twisting in her stroller, grizzling increasingly, but she liked going in the car and once I'd got her securely fastened in the child seat she was uttering only happy little gurgling sounds and was quite serene.

'I think I can manage on my own from here,' I said to Atle after he'd put the flowers on the back seat.

'No, it's no trouble,' he said, getting in. 'You've already got your hands full with Åse.'

'A bit, yes,' I said with a smile. 'Thanks a lot!'

He put his sunglasses on and looked out of the side window without speaking as we drove off between the big, box-shaped retail outlets.

I knew rather a lot about him, but everything I knew came from Helge. I had no idea what the world looked like from his own perspective.

When we got onto the motorway he took his phone out.

'Looks like we've got a serial killer on the loose,' he said.

'What?'

'They've found the lads out of that band who disappeared. Three of them killed. The fourth one's still missing.'

'Oh my God,' I said, checking my wing mirror before changing lanes.

'They were playing with fire,' he said.

'Literally,' I said. 'Weren't they the ones setting churches ablaze?'

'Not them exactly. But they belonged to the same circles.'

He rolled the window down on his side and rested his elbow on the frame.

'How about some music?' he said.

'What do you want to hear?'

'Something from your playlist. Anything.'

'OK,' I said, and put the album on that I'd been playing last.

His hand patted the beat.

'Beach House,' he said.

'Do you like them?'

'I do, yes.'

We entered the tunnel, and he closed the window.

'How are you doing back there?' I said, reaching my hand out for hers. There she was.

'I liked your exhibition, by the way. Very much, in fact.'

'*The Soul and the Forest*?'

'Have you done any others?'

I laughed.

'Not on my own, no.'

'Anyway, it was really clever. I was impressed. And I didn't even know you then.'

'Thank you, Atle,' I said.

A lull ensued. I left the motorway, slowing down as we went up the exit ramp, pulling out into the city streets that were teeming with people, though fortunately not with traffic. Turning into the street where we lived, I felt under the handbrake for the remote to open the garage door when unexpectedly his hand touched mine. It was as if an electric shock went through me.

'Here it is,' he said, handing me the remote.

I took it, casting a glance at him at the same time. He was looking straight ahead as if nothing had happened.

It must have been unintentional.

'Thanks,' I said, pressing the button and seeing the door twenty metres ahead of us begin to retract.

'What's it like, anyway, being married to my dad?' he said.

I looked at him before slowing almost to a stop and changing down to first to come safely through the narrow entrance into the confined parking area.

What was he trying to do? Establish some kind of intimacy between us?

'That would strictly speaking concern only your dad and me,' I said, turning my head to back into our space. Åse looked at me.

'Mummy!' she said.

'What was that? Did you say *mummy*? Did you?'

'Mummy!' she said again, triumphantly this time.

'I was just wondering,' he said. 'Always interesting to get different perspectives on a person. Especially when he's my dad.'

'You're right, I'm sure,' I said. 'Excuse me a second, I just need to send a text.'

Åse said mummy! I typed, and sent it to Helge.

Fantastic! he wrote back. *That's your girl!*

I put the phone back in my bag, undid my seat belt and got out, unfastened Åse and gave her a big hug, while Atle opened the boot and unloaded all the shopping bags.

'I'll come back for the flowers,' he said.

'Great,' I said.

Upstairs in the apartment I changed Åse, while Atle put the wine and other drinks out on the worktop before going back down again. I just wanted him to leave, but felt out of politeness that I should at least offer him a coffee or something. After all, he'd given up his morning to help me.

'Where do you want them?' he said, appearing in the doorway with the flowers.

'Just put them down next to the drinks,' I said.

'Do you want me to put them in water?'

'I'll do that myself in a minute,' I said. 'You've already been very helpful.'

'It's no trouble,' he said. 'No trouble at all.'

'There's no need, really,' I said. 'Would you like a coffee before you go? Or something cold, perhaps. Diet Coke? Beer?'

'I wouldn't say no,' he said. 'To a beer, that is.'

Åse sat with her music box, opening and closing the drawers one after another. She looked around for things to put in them, picking up a plastic horse that was too big to fit, looking up at me quizzically.

I wound the key on the back, making the ballet dancer turn to the music that came out. She shut the lid, and the music stopped.

Atle studied the pictures on the wall.

'That wasn't what you wanted, was it?' I said. 'You wanted things to put in the drawers!'

I picked up some small toy animals, some other figures and a few Lego bricks, and put them down beside her.

'I grew up with these pictures,' Atle said. 'But I've never really looked at them until now.'

'Nn,' said Åse, pulling open a drawer.

I went into the kitchen.

'Do you like them, then?' I said, stepping past him on my way.

'Yes,' he said. 'The Gustav Aase especially.'

'The one with the bird?'

'Yes, it's amazing, really. I was afraid of that bird when I was little.'

'I can well imagine,' I said, taking a can of Carlsberg from the fridge.

The painting showed a great, black bird reaching its head to the sky, its beak wide open, towering high above the people, who were tiny.

'Here you are,' I said, handing him the beer.

He took it with one hand. His other touched my upper arm.

'Thanks,' he said, looking me straight in the eye.

I stepped back, glancing towards Åse, who was sitting on her knees watching us.

He smiled, took a sip, and turned his attention back to the picture.

I couldn't say anything. He hadn't done anything. If I said something, he'd say I was hysterical. He was only being friendly.

'I think I'll put Åse to bed for her nap,' I said. 'She's tired out.'

'Yes, of course,' he said. 'I'll sit outside for a bit.'

I picked her up and she rested her head heavily on my shoulder.

'You can have a nice sleep now,' I said as I carried her towards the stairs. Softly, so that Atle wouldn't hear me, I said:

'Can you say *mummy*?'

'Mu-mmy!' she said.

'Oh, you little star!' I said, and hugged her tight.

She was really tired and didn't protest at all when I tucked her in. I turned the air conditioning on, drew the blinds, then went to the bathroom and splashed my face with cold water.

Atle was sitting smoking on the terrace, the green can in his hand.

'Is she asleep?' he said.

'She's well on her way,' I said, and sat down in the chair across from him, on the other side of the terrace door.

'Aren't you having one?' he said.

I shook my head.

'There'll be plenty to drink tonight, I shouldn't wonder.'

'And he still doesn't know?'

'No. I don't think he's cottoned on yet.'

There was a silence.

I was dying for something to drink, but if I went and got myself a Coke, it would only prolong the situation.

He put the can down on the floor. I could hear it was empty.

I stood up.

'I've got lots to do,' I said.

'I'll give you a hand,' he said.

'That's kind of you,' I said. 'But I need time to myself before everything kicks off.'

'I can take a hint,' he said with a smile. He stubbed out his cigarette and got up.

I followed him out into the hallway.

'Thanks for your help, Atle,' I said.

He stepped forward and gave me a hug.

His hand moved down my back.

He drew me close.

'Atle,' I said, and tried to extricate myself.

'Yes,' he said, and kissed me on the mouth.

'What are you *doing*?' I said, immediately pulling away. 'Have you gone mad? You fucking idiot!'

'I thought you liked me,' he said. 'It seems I was wrong.'

'I'm your stepmother!' I said.

'Technically, yes,' he said. 'Although I am older than you.'

'You're leaving, now,' I said.

'Yes,' he said, and he turned, opened the door and went out into the corridor before stopping.

'Don't say anything to Dad,' he said. 'I'm asking you.'

I closed the door without replying and locked it behind me.

I didn't want to cry, but I did.

Cried as I went back through the apartment and up the stairs to take a shower. To wash it all away.

What had I done to make him think he could have me?

I closed the door of the bedroom where Åse was asleep, undressed, turned the shower on and let the water jet out over my body.

Why had he done it?

What was it about me that had put such a thought in his head?

I couldn't tell Helge. He'd be devastated.

I soaped my entire body, washed my hair, rinsed out the shampoo, dried myself, hung the towel on the rail and went cautiously into the bedroom.

She was fast asleep, her little chest rising and falling like a bellows.

He was her brother.

Damn him.

I picked out a white cotton dress.

But it was too short and too low-cut; suddenly I didn't feel like putting it on, and I took out a pair of shorts and a shirt instead.

Downstairs I started cutting the flowers, thinning the foliage and putting them into vases.

They were lovely, at least.

As I was about to fetch the tablecloth and iron it, I remembered the cake. The longer it stood with its pastry cream and filling, the more delicious it would be, his mother had said.

I moved the bottles of wine and drink we'd bought back against the wall, got out the biggest chopping board we had and put it on the counter, carefully sliced the sponges into three, and placed the layers next to each other in the right order so I knew how they were to be put back together.

Then I mixed the pastry cream, stopping the mixer every now and then to listen out for Åse.

When the cream was done, I realised I needed to go down into the basement and get the jam and berries from our storage room down there.

It should have been the first thing I did. Åse was more likely to wake up now.

It would only take a few minutes though. Five at the most.

I stood without moving and listened.

She was all quiet up there.

OK.

I picked the keys out of the bowl on the bench by the door, then stood and waited a few seconds for the lift to arrive while looking out of the window. The lawn that sloped down to the courtyard was empty and bathed in light. I pressed the button for the basement. There was no need for concern, even if she did wake up. A few minutes on her own wouldn't harm her.

Down in the basement, where the various apartments had their storage rooms, the lights went on automatically as I stepped out of the lift.

But what was that?

The door of our room was open.

Had there been a break-in?

I craned and peered in.

A figure was lying on the floor.

A homeless person or a drug addict.

I only hoped he wasn't dead.

I switched the ceiling light on inside and stepped cautiously towards him.

It was a young man.

I crouched down beside him.

He was breathing.

Most likely sleeping it off.

But he couldn't lie there.

I stood up.

What was I supposed to do?

My phone was upstairs. I couldn't leave Åse on her own much longer either.

Close the door on him and call the police?

He looked to be about twenty. Seemingly not a drug addict.

Probably a student who'd had too much to drink the night before.

I leaned forward again, put my hand on his shoulder and shook him gently.

He opened his eyes. As soon as he saw me he recoiled against the wall, scrambling back like an animal.

'You can't sleep here,' I said.

'Help me,' he whispered. 'You've got to help me.'

ARNE

I woke up in the middle of the night, needing a piss. For a while, I resisted and tried to go back to sleep, but the pressure on my bladder merely increased and eventually I got up and went downstairs. Instead of using the bathroom, I went out into the garden and pissed in the rose bed in the middle of the lawn. I did so now and again, when everyone else was asleep, it gave me a sense of freedom, or maybe it was ownership: I owned the house, I owned the garden, I could do as I liked there.

It was so warm there was no difference between outside and in. My skin was moist even though I was only in my underpants. The new star shone from the dark night sky, so much brighter than the others, and its light made the vegetation shimmer faintly.

I'd have to pull myself together from now on, I thought, my piss splashing against the flowers in front of me until I started spreading it from side to side so the sound was less conspicuous.

I wasn't drunk any more, but my head was thumping and it hurt every time I moved.

When I was finished, I opened the door of her studio to see if she was still asleep.

She was lying in exactly the same position as before. Her mouth hung open and she was snoring slightly. Thank goodness for that. Sleep drew her back down to earth again, and I needed her here now. We were going home the day after tomorrow. The kids were going back to school, and my own term was starting then too.

I was desperate to get back to work. My plan had been to press on with my novel during the summer, only it hadn't turned out that way.

It never did.

It wasn't for lack of ability. It was the will that was missing, that last bit of will.

But I could lecture. And writing *about* literature came easily to me. I could do both with my eyes shut.

I crept into the adjoining room.

The torn-off head of the cat was still there on the desk.

Christ, it was so macabre.

The vacant eyes, the grinning mouth, the blood.

She'd never done anything like it before.

Probably best to get rid of it now, before the kids woke up and found it.

I went and got a bin liner, a pair of yellow rubber gloves, a spray bottle of detergent and a cloth from the kitchen, filled a bucket with hot water and went back. She was fast asleep, lost to the world, but still I shut the door behind me before putting the gloves on and gingerly picking up the head with both hands while trying to push every thought from my mind. Yet even the gentle pressure I exerted flattened the fur to the skull in such a way that I couldn't help but think how much smaller it looked as I dropped it into the bin liner. The dead yellow eyes, the vicious wound that had matted the black fur with blood, the little thud as the head hit the floor.

I washed the blood away as quickly as I could, emptying the bucket onto the lawn before fetching the spade and going over to the redcurrant bushes with the bin liner, the house still quiet.

I put the bin liner down and thrust the spade into the ground where I'd buried the kitten. They were mother and baby, so I thought they could share the same grave. It was a stupid, sentimental thought, but there was no reason not to pursue it.

I was the only person there.

And yet, in the same instant, it felt like I wasn't alone.

The feeling was compelling, and I straightened up.

It wasn't like someone was standing watching me in the darkness. It was more like someone was inside me.

That I was being watched from within.

'Have *you* lost your mind now?' I said softly to myself, stamping the spade through the layer of bark chips, deeper into the firmer soil, which

I dumped in a pile at the side. After a few minutes, the hole was per-haps half a metre deep.

The kitten wasn't there. I must have been in the wrong place, the grave from earlier had to be further along. I picked up the bin liner and was about to tip the head out into the hole when something stopped me and I took it out carefully with my hands instead. No reason not to be dignified about it.

Or maybe the kitten had been alive after all and somehow managed to escape?

But even if it hadn't been dead, it surely couldn't have scrabbled its way out? I put the head in the hole, then went back and got the rest of the body from the bushes next to the house, placing it in as natural a position as possible, before filling the hole and patting down the soil.

After cleaning up, I washed my hands thoroughly in the bathroom sink. I went into the kitchen and took some slices of salami from the fridge, rolled them together and put them in my mouth.

The feeling that someone was watching everything I did, knowing my every thought, was still there.

If it was all an exam, I'd have failed, I thought with a smile.

Had we got any chocolate or something?

I opened the cupboard next to me. The kids still had some sweets left in a bowl at the back, which I'd put away behind a bag of flour where they wouldn't be able to find them, and there was half a packet of Krokanrull milk chocolates there too, which I devoured on my way back to bed.

And then I remembered the other kitten.

Luckily, I'd closed the door, so it was still there.

I got down on my knees and looked under the bed. There it was, curled up in the corner, though not asleep, two shiny little eyes peering back at me from a furry ball.

'Pss, pss, pss,' I said.

It didn't move.

'We'll have to give you a name,' I said. 'You're the oldest cat here now. How does that feel?'

I stood up again and got into bed, folding my hands on top of my chest.

'Are you wondering what you're called down there?' I said. 'Mephisto, was that it? Black as you are?'

I closed my eyes and must have fallen asleep immediately, because the next thing I knew the room was filled with light and loud voices were coming from the living room downstairs.

The twins were arguing.

I got up and pulled the curtains aside. The sun shone from a completely blue sky, and not a breath of wind disturbed the leaves on the trees.

I got a pair of shorts and a short-sleeved shirt out of the wardrobe, dressed and went downstairs.

Heming was sitting in the wicker chair in a sulk, while Asle was on the sofa gaming with the iPad on his lap.

'How are we, people?' I said.

'Good!' said Asle, looking up to send Heming a glare.

'What about you, Heming?' I said, ruffling his hair.

'Asle took the charger, but I was using it!' he said.

'How much battery have you got left?' I said.

'Three per cent.'

'And how much have you got, Asle?'

He shrugged.

'I don't know.'

'Well, have a look,' I said.

'Fourteen,' he said.

'OK, then let Heming have the charger. When he's got fourteen per cent, he can give it back to you.'

'But, Dad, it's *my* charger,' he said. '*His* charger doesn't work. Why should I have to suffer?'

'You're not exactly suffering,' I said. 'Anyway, I'm the one who decides here, so you'll do as you're told. All right?'

'All right, then!' he said, and yanked the cord so hard that the charger shot out of the wall.

'Hey, what do you think you're doing?' I said. 'Treat things properly!'

He jumped to his feet demonstratively and stormed out of the room with the iPad in his hands, leaving the charger behind on the floor.

'Have you had any breakfast?' I said to Heming, who had already taken his brother's place on the sofa.

He shook his head.

'What about Asle?'

'No,' he said.

'I'll make some now, then,' I said.

'OK,' he said, without moving his eyes from the screen.

Someone came walking along the road, and I bent forward to see who it was.

Kristen, who else? In the blue overalls he always wore. A regular pair in summer, thermal in winter. He had a full carrier bag in each hand. Amazing how sprightly he still was, I thought. He'd be eighty by now?

I turned towards Heming again.

'Heming?' I said.

'Mhm?' he said.

'How were things here yesterday when I was out?'

'Not very nice,' he said as a volley of beeping battle sounds came from his iPad.

'How do you mean, not very nice?' I said.

'You know,' he said.

'No, I don't,' I said. 'I wasn't here, remember?'

'Mum was acting strange,' he said. 'She kept saying the same things all the time.'

'Mum's not very well at the moment,' I said. 'She gets like that when she can't sleep. In fact, it's a bit like she's sleepwalking, don't you think?'

'Yes,' he said.

'It's nothing to be frightened about,' I said.

'I know,' he said.

'And Ingvild was here,' I said. 'That helped, didn't it?'

'A bit,' he said.

'OK,' I said. 'Breakfast in fifteen minutes!'

I should have gone upstairs and spoken to Asle about his behaviour, but it would have to wait. It was more important to find out how Tove was doing.

I drank a glass of water in the kitchen, opened the two windows wide to let the summer in, and went over to the annexe, only to find it empty.

She must have gone for a walk, I thought, sitting down at the table in the garden. I wanted the summer to fill me too. So fresh air could banish all that had happened the night before.

If we were going home in the morning, I'd have to start packing soon, and then there was the tidying up and cleaning to be done on top of that.

I gazed at the summer houses across the bay, where a car came gleaming along the road towards the blue, glittering sea beyond.

Damn it, the kitten!

I'd forgotten all about it.

I only hoped the door up there was closed.

How was I going to tell the kids that not only was one of the kittens dead, the mother, Sophi, was too?

The badger story was perhaps too brutal for them. Especially if it was supposed to have happened so close to the house.

I didn't want to lie to them any more.

Tove came walking along the shore. In the five minutes it took before she came into the garden, a whole range of different feelings for her passed through me.

She went by the table where I was sitting without acknowledging me, as if she couldn't see me at all, and disappeared into her studio. She had on a white shirt, beige-coloured shorts and a pair of clogs. I got to my feet and went after her. She was wandering about in there, in a world of her own. Her clogs clacked against the floor.

'Tove,' I said. 'We need to talk.'

Fleetingly, she looked at me.

'Are you sure?' she said, and went outside again.

I went after her, catching up with her on the lawn.

'We're going home tomorrow,' I said.

'Are you sure?' she said.

'Yes, I'm sure,' I said.

She went down the drive onto the road.

'Sorry,' she said.

'You've nothing to be sorry about,' I said.

'Are you sure?' she said.

'Tove,' I said. 'Won't you come inside with me?'

'I don't know,' she said.

'I think it's best we go to the hospital.'

'Are you sure?'

I put my hand on her shoulder to stop her. She carried on.

'Where are you going?' I said.

'I don't know,' she said.

I stopped. I wasn't going to use force, at least not while the kids were there.

She was already striding away.

'Tove,' I said, raising my voice slightly. 'Come with me now!'

'Are you sure?' I heard her say again.

I wasn't comfortable about letting her go; she didn't care about anything, she just kept walking all the time. But there was nothing else I could do.

I ought to take her to the hospital straight away.

The question was, was she poorly enough? What was I going to say? That she kept walking round the garden? That I couldn't get through to her?

She wasn't a *danger* to anyone.

But what about the cats?

I went back inside and got my mobile from the bedroom, then stood in the garden and phoned my mother.

'Hello, how are you?' I said when she answered.

'Hello, Arne,' she said. 'I'm fine. Ingvild and I had such a nice time together. What a good-looking girl she's become.'

'Yes, she has,' I said.

'How are things with you, anyway? That's far more interesting than how I am!'

'That's partly why I'm calling,' I said. 'Tove's having a down period, quite a bad one. I'm going to have to take her to the hospital, I think. I'm a bit hesitant, though. It's rather a drastic step. And of course she might be better once she's got some sleep.'

'How's she behaving?'

'I can't get through to her. She just keeps wandering about on her own.'

'And the children are there with you?'

'Yes, of course.'

'Arne, you must get her away from there. For her own sake, but for the children's too.'

'Yes, you're probably right,' I said. 'I can't leave them on their own again, though. Do you think you could come over and look after them?'

'Of course. I'll come right away. Is there anything I should bring?'

'No, I don't think so. Perhaps some plums for the kids?'

'All right, will do. See you soon, then.'

I hung up and looked up at the house. The two open windows in the kitchen looked like wings, I thought. As if the house had just landed and would soon take off and fly away again.

Ingvild.

I went inside and knocked on the door of her room.

'Come in,' she said.

She was lying on her stomach on the floor, legs bent at the knee, feet in the air, putting some make-up on with the mirror in front of her.

'Hi,' I said.

'Hi,' she said.

'Mum's not too good,' I said. 'I'm going to have to take her to the hospital.'

'I thought so,' she said, and I watched in the mirror how she blushed her cheeks with the brush while shaping her mouth into a little O.

'Gran's coming over to look after the twins.'

'Good,' she said.

'You're not still angry with me, are you?' I said, smiling as our eyes met in the mirror.

'Angry will do for the moment,' she said, peering into her make-up kit.

'I see,' I said.

'Only it's Mum we've got to think about now, isn't it?' she said.

'Yes, you're right about that,' I said. 'I just thought I'd apologise for last night. For leaving you on your own.'

She didn't answer, but shaped her mouth into a slightly larger circle to put on her lipstick.

'I'll be back as soon as I can,' I said.

'Are we still going home tomorrow if Mum's in the hospital here?'

'I haven't thought about that yet,' I said. 'We'll have to go home at some point, though.'

She raised herself onto her knees, retracted the lipstick and dropped it back in the box, got to her feet and went over to the bed.

'Is everything else all right?' I said.

'Yes, fine,' she said. 'Why wouldn't it be?'

She gave me a faux smile, picked up a book from the windowsill and began to read.

I looked at her for a few seconds, but when she gave no sign that she intended to do anything else but carry on with her reading, I stepped out and closed the door behind me.

I stood motionless for a moment in the corridor, not knowing what to do.

I could go after Tove and bring her home. But she'd only go off again, and I couldn't exactly lock her in.

I needed to talk to the kids too, about the cats. We were meant to have taken the mother and kittens back home with us in the car, so I'd have to make sure they knew in good time before we left.

But the last thing we needed now was more emotion.

Maybe the best thing would be to start packing until Mum arrived. After that I could go and find Tove and take her to the hospital, then do the rest of the packing when I got back.

I didn't like Ingvild being angry with me, but it was no use talking to her, words were no help now. I'd have to give it time, and then it would pass on its own. I understood her reaction, what I'd done wasn't good, but she could only see it from the outside and had no idea what it looked like from the inside, the reasons I'd had, how much of it had been bad luck, pure and simple, and bad timing.

I went into the kitchen, tipped some Nescafé into a mug, filled it with hot water from the tap and took it with me into the garden, to the table that was now shaded by the willow.

Had it been an ordinary day, I'd have taken them for a swim somewhere. Spent the whole day at the beach.

It was such a waste, sitting inside on a day like this. The temperature was at least thirty degrees.

Maybe I could put the badminton net up? They liked badminton, once they got started. And there wasn't a breath of wind. I'd be able to pack while they were playing.

Tove appeared between the house and the annexe. Without looking at me or paying any attention to anything in her surroundings she went straight into the house. A moment later, she came back out, went past the annexe and out through the gate on the other side.

What could be going on inside her?

I looked at the time. Mum would be here in forty minutes, if she'd done as she said and left right away.

A scratching noise made me turn my head. It was the squirrel again, darting across the wall, this time followed by another. Over the fascia board they went and along the roof, their bushy tails waving in the wake of their supple little bodies.

Suddenly, I remembered something I'd dreamt that night. How vivid it was now: I'd been lying in bed and heard a voice singing downstairs; I went down, opened the door into the kitchen, and there, in the middle of the floor, sat the cat, singing.

Watch the sunrise, it sang.

I smiled and got to my feet. Not only had it been singing in English, its head had been on too and it had seemed so very satisfied, happy even.

I opened the shed door and stood for a moment while my eyes adjusted to the dark, then took the badminton net with its thin poles from the shelf. It was rolled up tight, almost like a fishing net, and I took it outside onto the lawn and began to untangle it. Planting one pole solidly in the grass, I unfurled the net and pulled it taut before thrusting the other pole likewise into the turf and going back for the rackets and shuttlecocks.

'Asle and Heming!' I called into the house.

'Yes?' said Asle from upstairs. 'What?' said Heming from the living room.

'That's enough sitting inside!' I called out. 'Come and play some badminton!'

I could almost hear them sigh as they put their devices down. But I knew it would only take a few minutes for them to become completely immersed and forget about everything else.

'Gran's coming soon,' I said as they emerged into the passage. 'But you've got a good half-hour until then, at least.'

'Why is Gran coming?' said Asle.

'Why didn't you tell us?' said Heming.

'She's coming to look after you,' I said. 'While I take Mum to the hospital. She needs to rest and get well again.'

'Can't she sleep here?' said Asle, sitting down on the step to put his trainers on.

'No,' I said. 'But she'll be able to sleep at the hospital. It's nothing serious.'

'Is there anything fizzy to drink?' said Heming, who never undid his laces, but simply crammed his feet into his shoes and wriggled them into place. I kept telling him not to, it made him look lazy, and for a short time he'd listened and done as I said, but now he'd fallen back into the habit again.

He cast a glance at me to check my reaction, so it wasn't as if he'd forgotten.

'*Is* there anything fizzy to drink, Dad?' said Asle, getting to his feet. 'It's so hot!'

'You can have some when Gran gets here,' I said.

'OK,' he said, and went out onto the lawn, closely followed by Heming.

Once they'd begun playing, I went upstairs to start packing. For the third time, I remembered the kitten as soon as I saw the closed door of the bedroom. How on earth could I keep forgetting? It would be starving by now. I fetched some water and some liver paste from the kitchen, opened the door carefully, crouched down and pushed the two bowls as far under the bed as I could. The kitten had moved a bit and lay with its head to the floor, its paws stretched out in front of it as the bowls came sliding towards it.

'Here you are, Mephisto,' I said softly. 'Some food for you. I'm going to start the packing now, but there's nothing to be afraid of.'

I dropped the piles of clothes from the shelves into the two big suitcases, cramming them full before taking them out into the passage, then filling the big sports holdall with the twins' clothes and dumping it next to them. There wouldn't be time for a proper clean before we went, but I could get a cleaning company in to do it for us and leave the key with Egil so he could let them in and lock up afterwards.

Through the open door, I heard one of the boys shout:

'Hi, Mum!'

I went outside. She was crossing the lawn, most likely heading for the path to the shore. The boys had stopped their game and stood watching her.

'Where have you been?' said Asle.

'I don't know,' she said.

'Where are you going?' said Heming.

'I don't know,' she said, turning and coming towards the house.

I reached my arm out to her as she passed me, and touched her shoulder. She carried on, through the passage into the living room, then out again, following the line of the house in the direction of the road.

The boys didn't know quite how to react, standing with their rackets in their hands, their bodies signalling aversion.

I went towards them.

'What's wrong with Mummy?' said Asle.

'She's not very well,' I said. 'It's nothing to worry about. She'll soon be all right again.'

'But she keeps walking all the time,' said Asle. 'Can't you stop her?'

'I'm afraid I can't,' I said.

'Can't you hold her tight?' said Heming. 'Maybe she'll stop then?'

'I'm taking her to the hospital in a short while,' I said. 'When Gran gets here. You carry on with your game. Who's winning?'

'No one. We're not playing for points,' said Asle.

'I hope they keep her in the hospital for a long time,' said Heming. 'So that she's completely well when she comes home again.'

I nodded.

'She will be, I'm sure,' I said. 'When she comes home, she'll be well.'

She came back towards us, passing between the house and the annexe.

The boys stared at her.

She turned left and was gone again.

'Do you want that fizzy drink now?' I said. 'You look like you're thirsty, the way you're sweating.'

They did, and drank at the table in the shade. I left them to it. There was less than half an hour until Mum was due, and I'd plenty to do in the meantime.

As I unloaded the dishwasher, it occurred to me that Ingvild might tell my mother about what had happened. That I'd been drink-driving and had crashed the car. Even if it hadn't actually happened like that, it quite conceivably looked that way from her point of view.

I filled the dishwasher again, switched it on and went and knocked on her door.

She was sitting in her chair, scrolling on her phone.

'What are you up to?' I said.

'Looking at my phone?' she said.

'I can see that,' I said. 'What are you looking at?'

'Insta.'

'Mind if I have a look?'

She looked up at me and snorted, turning the display face down against her thigh as I stepped towards her.

'You don't keep secrets from me, do you?' I said.

'Ha ha,' she said.

'Gran's on her way over,' I said. 'I was thinking about what happened last night. It's probably not a good idea for her to know everything. She worries, you know. She's starting to get on.'

Ingvild looked at me.

'You're so unreal,' she said, and jumped to her feet, barging past me through the door.

'What?' I said. 'What's the matter?'

The bathroom door slammed shut behind her.

The look she'd given me, her voice, had been full of disdain.

She was always so idealistic. Everything had to be so correct. But life wasn't like that. She would understand soon enough.

Yet something had sunk inside me. She was my daughter, and she despised me. Or at least despised what I'd done.

As if I didn't have enough to be getting on with.

I went to the kitchen and cleared the things away, giving the surfaces a quick wipe with a cloth, continuing with the living room and dining room.

On the other hand, I thought, she was a teenager, and what were teenagers known for if it wasn't hating their parents?

I'd been the same. Not hated them exactly, but disliking them intensely for a while, and feeling ashamed of them.

She came into the kitchen as I put down the glasses and bowls I'd found left about the house.

'Isn't it about time you took care of Mum now?' she said. 'She needs help. She's completely out of it. You can see that, surely?'

'Of course I can,' I said, opening the dishwasher. Steam billowed out, the water still sloshing and dripping inside. 'I'm taking her to the hospital as soon as your gran gets here.'

'Can't you just go now? I can look after the twins.'

I put the glasses and bowls inside and closed the door again.

'I'm doing the best I can, Ingvild,' I said. 'We're going home in the morning, so I've got to start packing and tidying up before we can go to the hospital. Besides, there's nothing I can do for her when she's like this.'

'But what about her?' she said.

'What do you mean?'

'Are we going home without her?'

'It looks like we'll have to,' I said. 'School's starting, and I've got to go back and plan for the new term.'

'We can't put her in hospital *here*,' she said. 'How are we supposed to come and visit her?'

I sighed.

'No, it's not ideal,' I said. 'But there's not much else we can do. Maybe she can be transferred to a hospital back home. I'll have to ask them about it.'

'You're just glad to get rid of her, aren't you?' she said, wheeling round and marching off to her room again.

I was angry now, but resisted the urge to go after her, closing the windows instead, the ceiling and work surface already crawling with flies. I took the fly swatter from the bottom drawer. My first swipe took three out at once, one splatting against the beam, the other two dropping motionless to the floor. I picked them up by the wings and flicked them into the sink. My next foray resulted in another two, but then they started getting cautious, either taking to the wing and buzzing about in the air, where they seemed to know I couldn't harm them, or else settling on the dark surfaces where they were hard to see, or in places other than where they normally could be found and where consequently I didn't look.

There was an intelligence there that had now kicked in, that much was obvious. But it only made it all the more satisfying when my swipes occasionally hit home and in a split second delivered one of them from life.

Not all died, however. Some were merely stunned, unmoving for a few seconds before finding their legs and attempting to stagger off. These ones too I picked up by the wings and dropped into the sink, and when eventually they'd accumulated into a little pile, I turned the tap on and swilled them away down the drain.

I looked out at the boys in the garden. They'd become good at badminton during the summer, arcing the shuttlecock high into the air, backwards and forwards between them.

I'd forgotten the breakfast.

Christ.

At the same moment, a car came up the road, and as it passed by the window I saw it was Mum's blue Fiat.

She could make them some brunch instead, I thought, and went out to meet her. She reversed slowly into the drive and parked next to my car. I watched her as she took off her sunglasses and put them in her bag on the passenger seat, then opened the door and got out. Behind me, Heming and Asle came running.

She looked rather stooping, her movements slower than I seemed to remember.

'Well, if it isn't Asle and Heming!' she said, receiving them each with a hug. They squirmed a bit, but they liked it too, I could tell.

'Have you got anything for us?' said Heming.

'Let me see, I think I might just have something, yes,' she said, glancing up at me with a nod.

'Hi,' I said.

'Have you been in an accident?' she said.

'Nothing serious,' I said.

She turned and looked at the car.

'When did that happen?'

'Yesterday. But I think the boys are more interested in what you've got for them.'

'Oh, it's nothing to get excited about,' she said. 'Just some sweets.'

She opened her bag and took out a bag of Twist.

I saw their hearts sink in their chests.

'You'll have to share,' she said. 'You can manage that, though, I'm sure!'

'Thanks, Gran,' said Heming.

'Thanks,' said Asle.

'You can sit down at the table over there and eat a few now, if you want,' I said. 'I need to talk to Gran.'

They did as I suggested.

'I'm sorry to have to call on you like this,' I said. 'Bit of a crisis on, as I said. It looks to me as if she might be psychotic. It's impossible to get through to her.'

'Where is she now?' Mum said, putting her sunglasses on again in the glaring light.

'Walking around somewhere. I don't know exactly. I'll soon find her, though. Do you think I could borrow your car? Not sure I want to risk it with mine.'

'Of course,' she said. 'Is Ingvild here?'

I nodded.

'I'm afraid they haven't had any breakfast yet. Do you think you can fix them something? I'll be back as soon as I can. It'll take about an hour to get there, but then I've no idea how long it'll take after that. Hopefully no more than an hour or so. That should mean you'll be able to get back tonight, if you want. But I'd better get going now. Have you got the car key?'

She handed it to me.

'I'll see you later, then!'

'Aren't you taking anything with you?' she said.

'Like what?'

'A bag with some things she's going to need. Clothes, for instance.'

'Good idea. I hadn't thought of that,' I said, and went inside, opened the biggest of the suitcases and rummaged through the piles. Underwear, a pair of sweatpants, some T-shirts, a pair of jeans, a sweater, some socks. I emptied a bag I'd filled with bathing costumes and swimming trunks, and crammed it all inside, fetched a deodorant from the bathroom and told myself that should do it, not really knowing what else she might need.

Some ID would probably be a good thing.

I opened her bag that was hanging from the peg in the passage. It was full of medication, pills in their hundreds. Why had she left them there? I wondered, unzipping the front pocket where her driving licence and credit cards were.

I didn't like nosing into her things at all, but I had no choice with her being as ill as she was, so I tucked her driving licence away quickly in my own wallet and went back into the garden, where Mum had sat down with the boys.

'Right,' I said. 'I'll get going, then.'

She looked tired and pasty. But her eyes were bright and keen, and as wilful as ever.

She smiled. At the same time, Tove appeared over by the gate.

It was the last thing I needed. If she wouldn't come with me of her own accord, I'd have to force her, something I didn't want to do with the boys watching.

I went towards her.

'Tove,' I said, 'I think it's best we go to the hospital now.'

'Are you sure?' she said.

'Yes,' I said.

'I don't know,' she said.

Tentatively, I took her hand. She let me do so, and went with me as I started to walk towards the car.

'Can you say goodbye to the boys?' I said under my breath.

'Are you sure?' she said.

I put my hand in the air and waved to them, as if from us both.

'We'll be off, then,' I said, lifting my voice again. 'Have a nice time with Gran!'

'Bye,' they said.

We stopped at the car. I opened the door without letting go of her hand. She was about to get in when suddenly she stiffened.

'It's all right, you can get in,' I said. 'We're going to the hospital now.'

She looked at me.

'Are you sure?' she said.

Her voice was calm, but her eyes were filled with terror.

'Get in, Tove,' I said. 'There's nothing to worry about.'

Sensing she was about to walk off again, I put my hands on her shoulders, pressed her gently down into the seat, lifted her feet inside and closed the door. As casually as I could, I then walked round to the driver's side, opened the door and got in without so much as glancing up.

I leaned over and pulled her seat belt out, fastened it, started the car, fastened my own seat belt and reversed out, waving to them, only to notice they were no longer looking in our direction.

She said nothing on the way into town, but simply stared straight ahead. I still wasn't sure if we were doing the right thing. They could refuse to take her on the grounds that she wasn't ill enough. After all, she was basically only wandering about and giving the same answers whenever she was asked a question.

I don't know. Are you sure? Sorry.

That was what she said in the car too, if I asked her something.

It was like a tool she'd discovered, something she could keep at hand in the knowledge that no matter what she was asked she would always have an answer at the ready.

But she'd decapitated the cat.

The sun shone from the middle of the sky, dousing the landscape with cascading light. The blue sea glittered, the green hills were radiant, even the tarmac sparkled.

I pulled up at the traffic lights at the top end of the town, by the lake, the park teeming with sunbathers, accelerating away when red changed to green, preparing to join the motorway on the other side. Tove gripped the door with one hand, the other reaching towards the glove compartment, bracing as if we were going to crash.

I put my foot down as we went down the slip road, flicking the indicator for us to merge.

'Stop!' she shouted. 'I want to get out! We're going to crash!'

'Are you sure?' I said, casting a quick glance at her. If she got the irony, it would all have been a charade.

'Stop!' she shouted again, her hand now groping for the door handle.

'It's all right, Tove,' I said. 'We're not going to crash. We're on the motorway now, that's why we're going fast. That's what it's there for.'

She fell back in her seat.

'Sorry,' she said.

'It's all right,' I said, and picked up my phone, checking to make sure Bluetooth was activated before connecting to the radio and tapping the last album I'd been playing.

Bowie, *Blackstar*.

'No, no,' said Tove as the music started.

'But you like Bowie,' I said.

'It's evil,' she said.

I looked at her.

'What do you mean?' I said.

'Death,' she said.

'Yes,' I said. 'But it's a fantastic album.'

'TURN IT OFF!' she yelled.

'OK, OK,' I said, picking up the phone again and scrolling down as I tried to keep my eye on the road in front of us, which fortunately was deserted.

I put *Lodger* on instead.

'I'd just dropped the boys off at school when I found out Bowie had died,' I said. 'For some reason, it was *Lodger* I played that day. Of all his albums. I didn't think I liked it that much.'

She said nothing, just kept staring straight ahead.

'Tove?' I said.

'Are you sure?' she said.

OK, I thought, indicating and pulling into the outside lane to overtake a lorry. It was laden with timber, and as we passed it I noticed she gripped the door again.

She'd never been scared of driving before.

I indicated again and pulled back into the slow lane. The forest was thick on both sides, rising up here and there with the hills, sinking occasionally and opening itself towards the sea.

If she wasn't ill enough to be admitted, they'd think I was trying to offload her. The thought had occurred to me every other time too, that

I'd be looked on with suspicion, as someone trying to do her harm by having her put away in the madhouse.

But Mum had been in no doubt.

The music receded abruptly and a ringtone took its place.

I could see it was Egil, and tapped the screen to answer.

'Hello, Egil,' I said. 'I'm in the car and you're on speakerphone. Tove's with me.'

'OK,' he said. 'How is everything?'

I looked at Tove. She was sitting the same as before and didn't seem to react to his voice at all.

'We're on our way to the hospital,' I said.

A sign said thirty-two kilometres. If I drove at ninety, that meant it'd take a third of an hour. But how much was that?

'OK,' said Egil. 'When are you going to be back, do you think?'

'No idea,' I said. 'Why?'

'Viktor's here,' he said. 'Surprise visit.'

Viktor?

I didn't know who he was talking about to begin with.

Then I remembered. Viktor was the son he never saw. Wasn't that what he was called?

'Viktor? Is that your son?' I said.

'That's it. I was thinking maybe he and the twins could hook up?'

'Yes, of course,' I said. 'They're at home, as far as I know. My mother's there to keep an eye on them.'

'Oh, right,' he said. 'In that case, perhaps tomorrow would be better?'

'Up to you,' I said. 'I'm sure she'd be happy to see someone.'

'I'll have a think about it,' he said. 'But thanks, anyway. Speak to you soon.'

Twenty minutes, I made it.

'Did you know Egil had a son?' I said.

She didn't answer. I hadn't thought she would either.

Ingvild was right. I was glad to get rid of her. I had to be honest with myself. But it wasn't for the reason she probably thought. It was just that everything became so difficult, chaos grew up around her, and the thought of her not being there was a relief. *Everything* would be easier then. Breakfast, no problem. School in the morning, no problem. Work, no problem. Dinner, no problem. Homework and TV in the evenings, no problem.

That was why I felt guilty and felt like I was having her put away, because things were so good when she wasn't there, which wasn't the way it was supposed to be at all.

The empty forest through which we'd been driving for some time gradually thinned out into industrial estates, shopping centres, car show-rooms. A few trees were all that remained, scattered here and there like ruins in a now disrupted topography.

Strange, Egil having a son. I couldn't imagine him as a father. Oblig-ing and submissive as he was, a breath of wind and he'd blow away. How would that work in a family?

I want to fuck Egil.

What had he got that I hadn't?

He could barely look after himself. I looked after everyone. He had no job, lived on his father's handouts. I was a university professor, with a responsibility towards hundreds of students.

Did she think there was some kind of depth to him that wasn't there in me?

If she did, she was wrong.

I could see how it might look that way. He was shy and unassuming, and held himself back, which made it easy to think there was a lot more to him than met the eye. She'd once said he had an artist's nature, and being an artist herself that meant she felt some kind of affinity between them.

But what had he ever done?

Nothing of artistic merit as far as I knew. His films were documen-tarism. Journalism.

Whereas I'd written just over 150 pages of a novel.

Perhaps I should let her read it.

Yes, I would. As soon as she got better and they let her out again. She wouldn't underestimate me any more then. At least not in the same way.

It was a good thought, and I turned to her and smiled.

She was staring into space, as if hardly even aware that I was there.

I picked up my phone and scrolled down through Bowie's music, selecting *Hunky Dory*, my favourite album of his.

Up ahead, the bridge arced over the strait. After that, we'd be at the hospital in minutes.

It wasn't Egil's fault though, I thought, skipping 'Changes', which I'd listened to so many times, and going straight to 'Oh! You Pretty Things'. She was the one who'd written that she wanted to fuck him, he'd had nothing to do with it. Anyway, I liked him.

'Do you remember when I first played you this?' I said. 'And you hadn't even heard the album?'

I wasn't anticipating any answer, but I had no way of knowing how much she took in.

'You were so out of my league. You knew that was how I felt, didn't you? A student of the National Academy of the Arts on her way to becoming an artist, and beautiful as a dream. And yet you thought Bowie started with "Let's Dance". You'd never heard of Nick Cave, and you thought "Love Will Tear Us Apart" was by Paul Young!'

I laughed to myself.

She was as mute and as withdrawn as before.

'That was the first time I got the feeling I might just be all right. That there was a chance. It sounds daft, doesn't it? Just because you hadn't a clue when it came to music. But that's how it was.'

We'd entered the outskirts of the town now. Housing blocks strewn over the flatland through which we passed, schools and the odd super-market. The first signs appeared for the hospital. On the other side of the river, after coming through the tunnel, I turned off to the right and car-ried on a few hundred metres until it was there in front of us, a large, recently built complex comprising an array of different buildings.

I found a parking space and looked at her.

'Are you ready?' I said.

'I don't know,' she said.

I went round to the passenger side and opened the door for her. She let me take her hand, her eyes quite vacant, and I led her over towards what I took to be the main building, where there was an infographic showing where the various departments were located.

The psychiatric department was round the other side. We walked between two buildings that were joined by a corridor that hung like a bridge above us. Tove walked slowly, still wearing her clogs. But something about her had changed, for when I looked at her, a wry smile appeared on her face.

The door at the rear of the building was locked. I rang the bell. Tove stood looking at the river, quite uninterested in what I was doing. The lock buzzed and I pushed the door open, holding it for her, but having first to put my hand on her shoulder and guide her cautiously forward before she stepped inside.

There was a small waiting room, a few chairs and tables, a reception office behind a glass partition. A young, dark-haired man with a beard sat talking to himself, next to him another man, likewise bearded, though a little older, family of some sort. I went over to the reception, where a woman sat looking at the computer screen in front of her. Tove remained in the middle of the room, standing behind me.

'Hello,' I said, bending towards the little hatch.

The woman, in her late fifties, with glasses, her hair tied up in a bun, narrow-lipped and with tired eyes, looked up at me without reply.

'I'm here with my wife,' I said. 'She's been manic for some days now and I can't get through to her any more. She can't look after herself.'

I spoke in a low voice, not wanting Tove to hear me talking about her in such a way.

'I think she might be a bit psychotic. I'm wondering if someone might have a look at her.'

'Have you phoned?' the woman said.

'No,' I said. 'We came straight here.'

'You should have phoned first,' she said.

'Yes, sorry about that,' I said, turning back to Tove. She was standing motionless with her head bowed, staring at the floor with a little smile on her lips. It was a smile that had nothing to do with what was being said, but seemed rather to stem from somewhere deep inside her.

The woman made a few clicks of the mouse.

'Name?' she said.

'Mine or hers?'

She sighed.

'Hers,' she said. 'Your wife's. What's her name?'

'Tove Hovin Larsen,' I said.

'Has she got any ID with her?'

'Of course.'

Where was the bag?

I looked around. It wasn't there.

I couldn't remember bringing it in with us.

It had to be still in the car.

Damn it.

'She's got her driving licence, only we've left it in the car,' I said. 'Do you want me to go and get it now?'

'We'll do it later,' she said. 'Date of birth?'

Once I'd given her all the particulars, she told us to sit down and wait. I looked at Tove and she looked back at me with a little smile, giggling almost. I wondered what was going through her mind. The way she was smiling made it look like we were up to something. Something that to her mind was exciting and good, whose effects would be far-reaching.

The young man with the beard was speaking English to himself, I heard now. His brother, if that's who he was, ignored him.

Outside, someone shouted. The door opened and an elderly woman came in, flanked by two men. She was around seventy years old and giving them hell, writhing and squirming, flailing her arms as she kept shouting: 'He's lying, I'm not Anne! He's lying, I'm not Anne!' They led her across the room and through a door on the other side.

Tove sat unperturbed in her own world.

'Do you want some coffee?' I said. 'There's a machine over there.'

'Are you sure?' she said.

I went over and dropped some coins in the slot. The machine began to whirr, a white cup was ejected and filled. The plastic was so thin it became darkened by its contents, and so hot that in order to carry it I was forced to hold it gingerly by the rim, which wasn't that much better since the steam then rose against my palm. I put it on the table and was just about to sit down again when a male nurse came in. It wasn't us he'd come to collect but the two brothers, who duly followed him through the door, the younger still muttering to himself while making angry little tosses of his head.

'The kids are back at school the day after tomorrow,' I said, sitting down. 'So we're going to have to drive home in the morning.'

'Are you sure about that?' she said.

'With a bit of luck we might be able to get you transferred. I can't promise anything though.'

'Sorry,' she said.

'It's not your fault,' I said.

My phone pinged a message, and I took it out to see who it was from. It was Ingvild.

How's it going with Mum?

Everything's fine, I typed back. *We're waiting at the hospital now. How's everything at your end?*

Fine.

Has Gran baked you some buns?

Apple crumble.

Lovely! See you soon.

Hug Mum from me and tell her I love her.

I sent her a heart and put the phone back in my pocket. In the office behind the glass partition, another woman had come in and the two colleagues sat chatting, the new one gesticulating all of a sudden, which made the first one laugh. I was annoyed by it, and was about to go over and ask how much longer we'd have to wait, when the door opened again and another nurse entered the waiting room. She was young, in her late twenties, pale-skinned and freckled, her mouth bearing the slight irregularity that suggested she'd been born with a cleft lip.

She was very attractive, and I had to make an effort to look at Tove and not at her when she stopped in front of us.

'Hello,' she said. 'My name's Benedicte. You must be Tove?'

'Are you sure?' said Tove.

'If you'd just like to come with me?' she said.

We followed her down a corridor, at the end of which was another waiting area.

'If you'd just like to take a seat for a second, the doctor will see you in a minute,' she said.

'Thank you very much,' I said.

A loud, heart-rending scream came from somewhere close by. It was desperation, I thought, rather than pain.

Tove stared at the door.

'Ingvild just texted and I'm to say how much she cares for you,' I said.

'Are you sure?' she said.

And then the door opened, and another nurse came out to collect us. She was in her fifties and spoke with an accent I took to be Eastern European. She led us into a room without windows, where Tove and I sat down on separate chairs. The nurse herself sat behind the desk with some papers on it.

'Hi, Tove,' she said.

Tove didn't answer, but stared at the opposite wall.

'Can you tell me your full name, Tove?'

'I don't know.'

'Tove Hovin Larsen, it says here. Is that right?'

'Are you sure about that?' said Tove.

'Your date of birth?'

'I don't know.'

'Can you tell me the reason why you're here today?' the nurse said.

'I don't know,' said Tove, and brushed something invisible from her thigh.

'What else are you called besides Tove?'

'I don't know.'

'Do you know what day it is today?'

For a brief moment she appeared to be trying to work it out, but then she let it go and looked down at her hand on the desktop.

'I don't know,' she said.

'How are you feeling?'

'I don't know.'

'Have you seen anything unusual today? Or heard anything unusual?'

'I don't know.'

The nurse looked at me.

'Perhaps you can help me out? Can you tell me what made you come in today?'

'Tove's been manic for some days now,' I said. 'Yesterday it became impossible to get through to her. And today she's just been walking non-stop around the garden. We've got three children and it's rather frightening for them, so I thought it best to bring her in and maybe have her admitted for a few days.'

'Is that right?' the nurse said, looking across at Tove.

Tove nodded.

'OK,' the nurse said. 'If you'd just wait here a minute, the doctor will be along soon to have a word with you.'

She went away and we were left on our own in the little room. It reminded me of the times we'd been expecting a baby, and would go for various check-ups and have to sit and wait in similar rooms, the two of us on our own. But we'd been full of expectation then about all that was going to happen, and at least we'd been together in that.

Now I no longer knew if we were together at all.

We had the children, of course. They would always be ours. But did we have anything besides them?

The door opened again and a man in his fifties came in. He introduced himself as Nygård, and his face, small eyes above baggy cheeks, inspired little immediate confidence. But no doubt he was competent enough, I told myself as he looked at Tove through the rectangular glasses on his nose, pen at the ready. Six years of training and more than twenty years of experience, I reckoned.

He asked much the same questions as the nurse had done, an exception being whether Tove had any children.

'I don't know,' said Tove.

'Who's this?' the doctor then said, nodding at me.

Tove looked at me.

'I don't know,' she said.

He put down his pen and leaned forward slightly, his elbows resting on the desk.

'I think it'd be best for you to stay here until you get better, Tove.'

'Are you sure about that?' said Tove.

An hour later, I was finally able to leave the hospital. I paused outside and lit a cigarette, crossed the car park with it smoking in my hand, stopped beside the car and took a last couple of drags before getting in. It was swelteringly hot inside and I opened all four windows as I pulled away towards the exit.

After the doctor had gone, we'd been taken into another empty room, this time on the closed ward, with windows facing the corridor through which patients and nurses kept passing, the former often shouting or screaming, though their behaviour didn't seem in any way to affect Tove, who sat quietly next to me as if unaware even of my own presence.

Once the paperwork was completed, the red-haired nurse took us out into the corridor, where someone else came and showed Tove to the room that was to be hers. White plasterboard walls, a grey linoleum floor, a bed, a chair, a bedside table.

'Have you eaten anything today?' the nurse asked.

Tove shook her head.

'I'll fetch you something. Have you brought any things with you?'

'I don't know,' said Tove.

'She's got a bag in the car,' I said. 'I'll go and get it.'

When I got back, Tove was sitting on the bed with her hands between her knees. There was a plate on the bedside table, with two slices of bread on it, an apple and a glass of juice.

'I'll be making tracks, then,' I said. 'It'll be good for you here, I think. I'll phone you every day.'

'Are you sure about that?' she said, getting to her feet and putting out her hand.

She wanted to give me her hand in farewell, as if I were a stranger. I took it, and it struck me that we'd never shaken hands before.

'Everyone's dead,' she said, and looked at me earnestly.

'What?' I said. 'What did you say?'

'We're all dead.'

I sighed.

'We're alive and well,' I said. 'All of us. I'll phone you tonight. OK?'

'Sorry,' she said.

Even before I'd left the room, she'd sat down again to carry on staring at the floor.

Now, in the car as I left the hospital area, I thought to myself how significant everything was. Her saying that she didn't know me was significant. Her shaking my hand instead of hugging me was significant. Regardless of whether she was psychotic or not.

And what she'd said about us being dead: it meant we were dead to each other.

Psychoses were like dreams, I knew that. They made you think in symbols and images, seeing meaning everywhere where there was none.

But it was true. We were dead to each other.

I stopped at the junction and checked my mirror to make sure there was no one behind me, took out my phone and was about to text my mother to say I was on my way home, when it occurred to me that she didn't know how long things had taken, and that I now had the chance of an hour on my own somewhere.

I slid the phone into the hollow underneath the handbrake, put the car into gear and pulled out, passing first through a residential area before joining the main road. Soon I was speeding back over the bridge, the sea gleaming and open, the sun lower in the sky now, and in the east, occasionally visible from the road that cut its way through the forest, a curtain of dark cloud.

The star. I'd forgotten all about it.

It was almost a shock to see it shining so brightly in the oceanic blue sky up there.

The crabs, the crash.

I'd forgotten it all.

And all those bloody fish in the cellar!

They'd be reeking to high heaven by now. I *had* to do something about them before we left.

I picked up my phone again, my eyes glancing through the albums that were stored on it as I drove. Not Bowie, because that would just remind me of her and taking her in to the hospital. Maybe Peter Gabriel? His first solo album, the one with 'Here Comes the Flood'? I'd played it regularly ever since the first time I'd heard it at the age of twelve, though not at all this past year.

It was a relief to be on my own.

All of a sudden, there were no problems any more. At least none that were insurmountable.

The music came on and I turned it up.

When I was a boy, the road followed the coastline, passing through the little towns that lay there, winding through the inlets, past the small farms. Now they'd straightened it out so that it ran a few kilometres inland. It was quicker, but I was in no hurry, so I turned off at the next junction and drove towards the sea, finding the old road soon enough and following it instead. It must have been there ready in my brain, for I knew what was round every corner. Memory and reality merged, past and present collaborated. In one way it felt like I was driving the car in my mind, in another like it was my mind doing the real-time driving.

A small river cascaded down a weir, whose steps gleamed darkly in the shade of great oaks. A wrought-iron gate glittering in the sun separated from the road what had once been a large manor farm; a red barn, red outbuildings, the main house painted white, a pennant flag in the Norwegian colours drooping motionless from a flagpole.

Suddenly I remembered the hotel in the little bay with the sandy beach. One Sunday in every month, Mum and Dad used to take us there for dinner, the Sunday after payday. Surely it would still be open? I could sit and have a beer in the shade before carrying on home. Perhaps I'd even have something to eat. The kids would be all right with my mum, and it occurred to me that I hadn't eaten a thing all day.

As I approached the place, 'Here Comes the Flood' came on, and I sang along. I'd never thought about what the lyrics meant, even if I did know them by heart. They'd always just been words. It was the same with anything I listened to. Johannes from my department, a huge Dylan fan who'd written a book about his lyrics, mocked me for it. Who plays Dylan without listening to the words? he'd say. The words are the whole point!

But now I listened: strange signs, omens, early warnings.

Egil believed in signs. But what did that mean? Signs from what, from whom, from where? What if the crabs did invade the land, and a new star did appear in the sky? It didn't mean there was some omniscient being behind it all, using those occurrences to 'speak' to us.

I couldn't understand how he could believe such a thing.

Of course, those signs didn't have to be random and meaningless on that account, either. When the animals started behaving differently, or were suddenly dying in strange circumstances, it was a sign that the balance of nature had shifted, that the ecosystem itself was breaking down. And the heat we were experiencing was a sign that the climate protecting us was likewise breaking down.

These were rational signs from a system of which we were ourselves a part. There was nothing mystical about it, nothing supernatural, no God 'speaking' to us.

And the star was a supernova. Another natural phenomenon.

Ahead of me now, nestled among trees, lay the hotel. I turned in and slowed down. The car park was full. Clearly, I wasn't the only one to have had such a bright idea, but I managed to squeeze into the far corner, in the shade to boot.

On the terrace, too, I was fortunate and found a table, a couple with a child rising to leave just as I appeared.

My lucky day, I thought, and turned round on my chair to catch the attention of a waitress.

How could I think such a thing when I'd just put Tove in the hospital?

But it didn't weigh heavily on me. I felt unburdened.

And happy?

Yes, to be honest.

The waitress saw me and came over. She was about my age, stockily built, with dark hair that looked to be dyed.

'What can I get you? A drink?' she said in English.

'No need for the English,' I said in Norwegian. 'It's still a Norwegian restaurant!'

'I'm sorry, I don't speak Norwegian very well,' she said.

'Oh, I see,' I said. 'Where are you from? And please don't say Sweden!'

'No, I'm not from Sweden,' she said, without grasping the joke. 'I'm from Lithuania.'

'Good for you,' I said, and ordered a pint of lager and a chateaubriand.

No, I ought to be feeling down, I thought, my eyes following her as she went through the dark double doors into the restaurant itself. The fact that I wasn't told me I was lacking in empathy, something that occasionally concerned me, because empathy was something you were supposed to have. The propensity to care about other people. Mum and Dad both had it in abundance. So it wasn't down to upbringing. Presumably it was some genetic throwback.

I did care about her, it wasn't that. Just not all the time, that's all.

She was in a room on her own in a madhouse and didn't even know who I was.

It was terrible. But then so was her behaviour. She left the kids to fend for themselves, couldn't care less about them. Only an hour ago she'd refused to acknowledge she even had any.

She was psychotic, but even so. It was still revealing of the person she was inside.

At least I cared about the kids.

I'd looked after them all summer.

But I had to remind myself that she was their mother, if only to remain aware of how difficult it was for them. It was no good.

It was no good at all.

The waitress came out again with some drinks on a tray. I picked up the cold beer she placed on my table and downed a large mouthful as I looked out across the glittering surface of the sea.

The Flood *would* come. The Flood was the rising sea, the sin it was to purge was our galloping consumption.

I texted Mum to say I was on my way.

Which I was, technically.

Jolly good! she wrote back. *All well here. How's Tove?*

Tove's been admitted to the closed ward, I typed. *Not sure for how long, but probably a few weeks.*

The poor girl, she replied.

I didn't know what to say to that, so I put the phone down and took another slurp of my beer. She probably thought I was driving, I told myself, so it wouldn't be strange if I didn't add anything.

I picked up the phone again and called Lothar.

He answered straight away.

'Hello, Lothar, how's it going?' I said.

'Arne,' he said. 'I'm all right, how about you?'

'Not too bad,' I said. 'What are you up to?'

'Now, you mean?'

'For example, yes.'

'Lubricating a bicycle chain while the kids are in the paddling pool. You?'

'Sitting outside at a restaurant, looking at the sea.'

'Sounds nice.'

'Could be worse,' I said. 'Anyway, we're heading home tomorrow. That'll give me a couple of days to prepare. You'll have been working all summer though, knowing you?'

'Not at all, nothing but holiday here. OK, so a small amount of work, maybe.'

'Have you written anything?'

'A bit, yes.'

'Like what?'

'A piece on Heidegger's black notebooks. Have you read them?'

'Sort of,' I said. 'Skimmed them a bit. At yours actually, now I come to think about it, back in May or whenever it was. What have you got to say about them?'

'Nothing interesting,' he said. 'I'm just trying to explore the Nazism and anti-Semitism, how it comes through in the notebooks and how it relates to his more regular philosophy from the same period.'

'That sounds *very* interesting,' I said.

'No, not at all,' he said. 'Everyone's doing it now. But I'm doing it mainly for my own sake. I've always been fond of Heidegger.'

'You want to rescue him?'

'No! That's the last thing I want! I'm just trying to look at it with an open mind.'

'Peering into the abyss?'

'Looking the Devil in the eye.'

'I'm with you,' I said. 'I've been peering into an abyss of my own today, as it happens. Tove's had to go into hospital with a psychosis. I'm on my way back from there now.'

'Oh dear,' he said. 'That's bad news. Poor Tove. And poor you and the kids. How are they coping?'

'They're doing fine,' I said. 'I'm trying to shield them as best I can. It's not the first time she's been ill, though.'

'So she's going to be staying in the hospital down there?'

'I think so, yes,' I said. 'Hopefully, she'll be well enough to come home soon. A psychosis like that often clears up rather quickly, apparently.'

'I'm really sorry to hear about this, Arne,' he said. 'Let me know if you need any help with anything when you get back.'

'Thanks,' I said. 'It'll be fine, though. Anyway, good to speak to you.'

'Same here. Have a safe journey home!'

I hung up and put my phone in my pocket. I always thought it was poor manners to leave it on the table while eating, even if you were on your own, and I could see the food was arriving now.

The steak wasn't completely tender, but more than satisfactory. There were chips to go with it, in a kind of a basket thing. They were crisp and delicious.

The table behind me was occupied by Germans, the one on my right by some Brits, while everyone else within earshot was from Eastern Europe. The beach was teeming with people, the sounds they made came like arrows through the air, laughter, conversation, shrieks and cries.

I should have brought the kids. Now we'd have to wait until next year.

I drank the rest of my beer and patted the pockets of my shorts in search of my cigarettes, realising immediately that I'd left them in the car.

'Here Comes the Flood' came to me again, and I sang silently to myself.

For some reason, I couldn't quite believe in the climate crisis, not really, not in the way it was going to play out in my lifetime. I knew it was happening, so rationally I did believe in it, but not emotionally. I wasn't frightened by it, basically because it didn't feel like it was anything to be frightened of.

Could people be varyingly empathetic towards nature too?

Get a grip, man. Anguish won't get you anywhere.

Besides, even if my powers of empathy were poorly developed, who was to know? I wasn't exactly going around showing it off to people.

I turned towards the waitress again. She was on her toes, even if she couldn't speak the language, and came over immediately.

'Could I have the bill, please?' I said in Norwegian.

She understood, and nodded.

Lothar had run bang into a midlife crisis, turning up one morning in the department in full lycra, mud splattered up his back, helmet in one hand, backpack with his books and papers in the other. He even asked if I wanted to see his bike in the lunch break, and when I googled it afterwards I could see he'd lashed out thirty grand on it.

Thirty thousand kroner!

For a bike!

I smiled and got my card out of my back pocket, putting it down on the little plate with the bill she'd left on the table.

When I first got to know him, he was all beard and hair, his body little more than an appendix to his mind. Now he'd had a haircut and tidied himself up, was slim and tanned, and looked more like a financial analyst than a professor.

Why couldn't they bring the card reader out with the bill? The way they did it was such a bind, first they brought the bill and then they went off somewhere so you had to wait for them to come back before you could give them your card and pay.

What was the idea? Was it to allow the customer time to study the bill first? But surely the customer could do that while they waited with the card reader?

No, Heidegger wasn't my man. I'd tried reading his analyses of Hölderlin and couldn't help thinking he was committing the beginner's error of inserting his own agenda into the poem, instead of drawing elements out of the poem and then cautiously blowing on them until they started to flame. The poem had to be read in its own light, it was the only sure method. What he wrote was no doubt good enough on its own terms, but it had little to do with Hölderlin.

At last, the waitress returned to my table with the card reader in her hand. I added ten per cent, for the service had been good and the food not bad at all.

Five minutes later I was on my way towards the motorway again. No reason not to get a move on now, I thought. Besides, something inside me longed for speed.

Mum's car was barely more than a sewing machine, but I got it up to 130 before it started to rattle and shake.

I listened to the War on Drugs for the rest of the way. The melancholy was a perfect match for the mood I was in, and for the landscape through which I drove, the dark wall of weather slowly approaching through the bright sunshine.

White boats in the strait, the supermarket car park filled with cars, two cyclists wobbling their way up the approach to the bridge, bikes heavy with luggage, laden like mules.

What if she was right? I thought all of a sudden. What if we *were* dead, and this was the land of the dead?

I smiled and pushed the lever to squirt some washer fluid onto the windscreen, whose true, filthy state was revealed in its encounter with the sunlight.

The notion that the division between the realms of the dead and the living was not as sharply drawn up in the classical age as it was now was a subject I was going to talk about next week. But that this world could be the realm of the dead was not something I'd considered before. Maybe it would be a good place to start? Or would that be confusing things too much? They'd probably have no idea what I was talking about. Their brains were so unbelievably conformist, I could hardly depart an inch from the world they knew without them bombarding me with criticism and scepticism.

Perhaps I could invite a priest to give a guest lecture. Or was that a bad idea?

The Church of Norway's line on life after death?

No, it would be interesting, of course it would. There were so many mutterings going on there now, so much sidestepping that it was impossible to know what they actually believed. Everything dissolved in a fog of good intent.

I crossed the bridge and followed the sweep of the road to the left, past the bay with its pontoons and into the woods, the occasional clearing opening out into meadow, then turned left at the crossroads, carrying on a few kilometres before the gravel track appeared on the right and the white-painted house and annexe at last came into view, at right angles to each other, the grass in between.

Mum was reading at the table outside, I noticed as I pulled up. Next to her, Ingvild lay on a bath towel, soaking up the sun.

'Hi,' I said as I went towards them. 'Everything all right here?'

'Everything's fine,' Mum said, taking off her sunglasses.

Ingvild sat up.

'How long's Mum going to be in the hospital?' she said.

'They're not sure,' I said. 'Hopefully not too long.'

'Is she going to be transferred to the hospital at home?'

'Not just yet, I don't think. Perhaps in a few days, once she starts feeling a bit better.'

'Did you ask them?'

'There was so much else to think about,' I said. 'But I'll be in touch with them every day. I'll ask when it's appropriate.'

She said nothing, but snatched up her towel and went inside.

'What are the twins doing?' I said.

'They went in,' Mum said. 'Complaining about the heat.'

'They've got a point,' I said, and sat down.

There was a jug of water on the table, beside it three drinking glasses in a little stack. I took one and filled it up.

'It may be none of my business,' she said, looking at me. 'But there's beer on your breath.'

I stared at her.

'Yes, you're right,' I said. 'It's none of your business.'

'All right,' she said, picking up her book again and starting to read.

'I stopped off at the hotel where we used to have Sunday dinner,' I said. 'I had something to eat and a beer to go with it. I'm forty-three years old, you know, and in charge of my own life. I hadn't had a thing to eat all day. And I'd just put my wife in the psychiatric ward.'

She looked up at me and nodded.

'So that's why you can smell beer on my breath,' I said.

She put the book down.

'Ingvild and I had a talk,' she said.

'Oh yes?' I said calmly, though bracing for the worst.

'She told me what happened here yesterday.'

'And what did she say?'

'She said you got drunk and crashed the car while they were on their own with Tove. Tove, who's going through a psychosis.'

'Firstly,' I said, 'I wasn't drunk. I'd had two beers, that was all. Secondly, I only popped out to get some cigarettes. Yes, I know it's stupid, but I've started smoking again. Thirdly, Tove was asleep at the time.

And fourthly, the reason I crashed was because the road was crawling with crabs all of a sudden, which I swerved to avoid.'

Mum stared into space for a moment, as if she needed time to process what I'd said.

'The point is that you weren't here for them when they needed you,' she said in a measured voice. 'Ingvild was very afraid. She still is afraid. They need stability, especially with Tove being as unstable as she is. And the only person who can give it to them is you.'

'I know,' I said. 'It was a combination of unfortunate circumstances, that's all.'

I stood up.

'I'll go and see what the twins are up to,' I said. 'When were you thinking of going back?'

'That depends on how long you need me here,' she said.

'Well, I need to get things ready for driving home tomorrow,' I said. 'I'm sure it would be good for the kids if you stayed until then. Until we get going, I mean.'

'Then I will,' she said.

The rain came stealing in as I packed and tidied up, an inky curtain of cloud that darkened further as twilight descended, gradually blocking out the world. By the time the first drops fell, it was as if only the house and the garden existed. Beyond them, everything was black.

The last thing I did was carry the suitcases and bags to the car and put them in the back. The advantage of the car was that you didn't have to think too much about what to take, the way you did if you were flying somewhere, so I filled every space that was left with carrier bags full of stuff, and various items that either wouldn't fit in the suitcases or I'd forgotten to pack and discovered only when going through the rooms to check that we'd got everything.

It wasn't the best way of doing things, but if I could get hold of a cleaning firm to come during the week, the house would be spick and span for when we came back next summer.

I hadn't asked Egil yet if he'd be able to come and let them in, or to check on the house now and then, and put some heating on once autumn came round, but that was just a formality. He hadn't got much else to do out here in the winter season, and he was helpful by nature.

I closed the boot and went and inspected the damage again. One headlight wasn't working, the indicator on the same side likewise, but I'd just have to chance it. If we were unlucky enough to get stopped, the worst that could happen would be that they removed the number plates, which would be bad enough, but most likely I'd only be handed a small fine.

And in all the years I'd been driving, I'd never been stopped once.

A raindrop splashed against my forehead, another on the back of my hand, and as I looked up into the darkness, the rain began to drum against the bodywork, a slow patter at first, then faster and faster.

I went into the kitchen and phoned Egil as I looked out at the garden, strips of which were illuminated by the light from inside.

He didn't answer, and I hung up.

Mum was sitting in the living room, watching a film with the twins. Ingvild was in her room. We'd had dinner, so there was nothing more to do for the evening.

I had to tell them about the cat. I didn't think it could wait until we left and they realised she wasn't with us.

Should I tell them she'd probably been run over?

But *probably* would only give them hope, so that was no good.

And if I said she *had* been run over, they'd want to know the details, how I knew, and where I'd buried her.

I phoned Egil again, turning back to face the kitchen, looking at the empty work surface and my own blurred reflection in the window above it. Three flies scuttled across its surface in different directions. What does a fly think when it sees another fly? I wondered. Do they know they are many?

He still wasn't answering. It wasn't unusual for him. Often, he left his phone behind when he went out in the boat. Or anywhere else, for that matter.

I could pop over.

A smoke and a drink on the veranda would be all right.

Providing it cleared up, of course. It wouldn't be much fun in this weather.

I looked in on the boys, who were sitting on either side of their grandmother, immersed in the film. She was knitting and made do with glancing at it now and again.

'Is that *Howl's Moving Castle* you're watching?' I said.

They nodded.

'It's really good,' I said. 'I think it's my favourite of those Japanese films.'

'Mm,' said Asle.

'Can we have some sweets?' said Heming.

'Of course you can,' I said. 'We're leaving in the morning. So you can have what you want.'

'An ice cream?'

'You'll have to see if there's any left in the freezer,' I said.

Asle pressed pause, and they both shot off into the kitchen.

Mum carried on knitting.

A flash of lightning lit up the darkness faintly for a second. I counted without thinking, making it seven seconds before the thunder came.

'Perhaps you could visit Tove in the hospital, if they're going to keep her for a while?' I said. 'I'll see if I can get her transferred, but it might take time.'

'I will,' she said. 'Though I'm not sure it'll suit her.'

'Of course it will,' I said.

'There's no of course about it.'

I sighed and turned towards the door as the boys came back in.

'Can you two come with me a second?' I said.

'Where to?'

'Upstairs. There's something I want to show you.'

Stepping into the bedroom, I closed the door behind us and crouched down.

'The kitten's under the bed,' I said. 'We'll take him with us in the morning.'

They knelt and bent forward to see, their ice creams still in their hands.

'He's got a name now,' I said. 'Mephisto.'

'Is he scared?' said Asle.

'Where's Sophi?' said Heming. 'Isn't she meant to look after him?'

'Yes,' I said. 'But I'm afraid something not very nice has happened. Sophi's dead. She was killed by a badger. Luckily, we've still got Mephisto, though. He'll be our cat now.'

'A badger?' said Asle.

'Is Sophi dead?' said Heming.

I stood up and tousled their hair in turn.

'Yes,' I said. 'These things happen in the animal world. But she had a good life with us. And Mephisto's her baby. So we'll take good care of him, won't we?'

'But . . .' said Heming. 'Where . . . ?'

'In the woods,' I said.

'Did you find her?'

'Yes.'

'When did you find her?'

'Last night, while you were asleep,' I said. 'And I buried her in the garden and gave her a fine funeral.'

Some tears trickled down Asle's cheek.

'No need to cry,' I said. 'She had a good life.'

'I didn't say goodbye to her,' he said.

'You were always very good to her, both of you,' I said. 'Anyway, come on. Tomorrow you can help me get Mephisto in the travel box. Perhaps we can give him something extra nice to eat. He'll probably cry a bit, but only because he won't understand what's happening. He's never been in a car before.'

They followed me downstairs and sat on the sofa again.

Relieved that they'd taken it so well, I went over to Tove's studio for a smoke. I didn't know what things of hers to take. Clothes weren't a problem, but what about her work? I had no idea what she'd be needing once she was home, and just left everything as it was.

With a cigarette smouldering in my hand, I looked through the canvases that were leaned up against the wall facing inwards, the way she always stored them.

For some time, I stood gazing at a flat landscape she'd painted with some girls in it, their small figures among some pine trees, out of place in a way, in their jeans and T-shirts as they bent forward to pick berries, half hidden by the stems. She'd used oil paints, the colours were bright and vivid, the feeling of forest quite overwhelming. There was something vaguely unsettling about it too.

Behind it was one that was even more unsettling. It showed a naked man, he too in the forest, but here against a background of dense spruce in the half-light of dusk. He was walking away, his head bowed, holding something spherical in one hand.

I turned the desk lamp towards it for a better look, the drooping ash of my cigarette dropping to the floor before I could do anything about it, and I took another deep drag, feeling the filter become hot against my lips.

It wasn't a man, I saw then, but a humanoid being of some sort. The body was that of a human, though exceptionally strong-looking, the head bald apart from a pigtail of hair that ran down between the shoulders from the rear of the scalp, while the face . . . The face was crude, like a Neanderthal's. The ears looked like animal ears, and the eyes . . .

But the strangest thing was that a star was shining brightly above the forest.

I touched a corner of the canvas and examined my finger. It was dry. She must have painted it before the new star appeared.

Unless she'd added it to something she'd already done?

Tentatively, I put my finger to the star.

It was just as dry.

When had she painted it? I definitely hadn't seen her working on it.

And the star!

It had to be a coincidence, but strange all the same, I thought, and I put it back among the others, switched off the light and went outside into the rain as I pressed Egil's number again.

Still no answer.

He must have run his battery down, I thought, stepping into the living room.

'I'm just going to pop over to Egil's,' I said to Mum. 'He's not answering his phone and I need to sort some things with him about the house. Will you be OK? You can read to the twins when they go to bed, if you want. Or they can manage themselves. Can't you, boys?'

They both nodded.

'Don't be too long,' Mum said.

'I won't,' I said. 'I'll stop for a coffee on his veranda, that's all.'

She followed me out into the passage.

'Is this absolutely necessary?' she said. 'In this weather?'

'It won't take long,' I said, and put my rain jacket on.

'There's something restless about the house tonight,' she said. 'Can't you feel it?'

'No,' I said. 'Just the opposite, in fact. The restlessness is all gone now Tove isn't here. You're just being a bit sensitive, that's all. It'll be the weather.'

'Perhaps,' she said. 'Are you going in my car?'

'Yes,' I said, opening the door to the noise of the pouring rain and wind. 'If that's OK?'

She nodded.

'Drive carefully,' she said, and went back into the living room.

I turned the wipers on full and backed out onto the track. Great puddles had already collected in the potholes, picked out by the beam of the headlights. I felt a childish glee at the forces that were loose, the rain, the lightning, the thunder, and there wasn't another car out, so as soon as I got onto the road I could put my foot down, speeding through the weather and darkness, the trees on either side of me, like the walls of a tunnel.

She must have painted the star later, I reasoned. She probably saw all sorts of things in her mind's eye when she was psychotic, but I doubted that she had psychic abilities too.

I only hope the children haven't inherited whatever it is she's got, I thought to myself, slowing down the last bit of the way, where the road narrowed and ran along the curve of the inlet, offering poor visibility to anything coming the other way. The whole bay was in uproar, waves crashing against the shore, boats tossing and heaving at their moorings.

His car was there, I noticed, as my headlights flooded his garage further up the slope. His bike too. But of course he wouldn't be mad enough to cycle anywhere in weather like this. Certainly not with his son.

I pulled up, turned the engine off and got out. The rain battered against the roof and rushed in the woods, and from the shore came the thunderous clamour of the waves as they pounded the land.

I knocked on the door.

Stood there and waited a while before pressing the handle. It was locked, so I went round the back to the veranda. Perhaps he'd be sitting in the living room with a book in his lap, under the light of the single lamp where he usually read.

A bolt of lightning ripped the sky.

Bloody hell, that was close!

The crash that followed only seconds later sounded like an explosion.

I crossed over the rock and stepped up onto the veranda.

The door was open. I assumed it meant they were home, only it was dark inside, so maybe they'd gone to bed.

Should I wake him?

I'd come all this way, I reasoned, and knocked on the glass.

'Hello?' I called out. 'Egil?'

The place was quiet.

Entering the house while they were asleep wasn't really on. But then again, I could say I was worried about them, the door being open in the storm and all.

I stepped inside, pausing in the middle of the room.

'Egil?' I said. 'Are you here?'

The only sounds to be heard were the sounds of the storm.

I went into his bedroom. It was empty. The bed was unmade, as if someone had been lying in it and had then got up again. But it was no use thinking of normal behaviour when it came to Egil, I thought with a smile. I couldn't really imagine him making his bed.

It struck me they might be sleeping in the other bedroom.

But it too was empty.

They weren't here.

I switched the ceiling light on and looked around me.

An enormous Bible had been abandoned on the floor. It was the only unusual thing I could see. That, and the food that had been left out in the kitchen.

I went over to the typewriter on the table and cautiously turned the pile of papers next to it to look at the title page.

On Death and the Dead
An essay by Egil Stray

Was that what he'd been writing about?

I looked around, expecting to hear his voice all of a sudden: *What are you doing here?* But there was no one there, and instead I began to leaf through the pages, reading now and again at random.

'*As we know, death is not necessary*. Thus Georges Bataille in 1949, and ever since I read that sentence for the first time, it has lived inside me,' it said at one point.

'What is occurring with death is that it is becoming smaller and smaller, and so compelling as this development has been, it is no longer inconceivable that death at some point will reach its nadir and vanish,' I read elsewhere.

It was a relief to see how pretentious it was. Here sat the rich man's son, alone in his summer house, thinking himself a philosopher!

I flipped the pile and left it exactly as I'd found it, turning round again to make sure he wasn't standing in the corner watching me.

'Egil?' I called out.

Wasn't there a sleeping space in the garage too? They could be spending the night there, a bit of adventure for the boy.

I swiped down on my phone and tapped the torch function as I went round the side of the house again, into the garage where the old Saab was, and shone the beam on the platform below the roof.

'Egil?' I said, knowing that there was no one there, the way a person knows such things.

I closed the door behind me.

Where could they be?

I decided to check the boat for good measure, tied the hood of my jacket tight and went out into the storm that roared and surged around me, lashing from the sea as I lit a path down to the boathouse.

His boat was inside, tossing up and down.

It was only what I'd expected.

Unless they'd gone out before it began and been taken by surprise? Maybe they were stranded on some islet out there?

But then his boat was hardly likely to be here, I realised, and laughed at how stupid I was.

The vessel tore at its moorings like an animal trying to writhe its way free.

The foaming waves hurled themselves at the flat rock of the shore, now and then bearing down from a great height.

I returned to the house, switched the light off, pulled the sliding veranda door shut and went back to the car. With his car, boat and bike all still here, the only explanation could be that they'd gone for a walk to enjoy the thrill of the storm.

In which case, they would soon be back. But I couldn't be bothered to sit and wait, we had an early start in the morning, so instead I turned the ignition, put the car into gear, backed out towards the woods and set off down the hill, the beam of the headlights forming an illuminated tunnel in the darkness, lacerated by rain.

TURID

I was so scared I closed my eyes to escape it all. But the terror remained, he could come for me without me sensing it, and so I opened them again.

He was standing with his body angled away from me.

He tipped his head back and stared up at the sky, baring his teeth. Then he walked towards the trees and slipped away between them.

Everything was suddenly quiet. Not a sound from the woods.

I stood motionless for some time, my eyes glancing this way and that. Nothing moved. Kenneth too was still.

Everything inside me trembled. My legs were so weak and soft that I had to hold on to a tree so as not to fall.

Was he really gone?

I stood there for perhaps ten minutes before slowly walking forward into the clearing. I stopped, looked around me, continued a few paces, stopped.

Everything was quiet.

There was no one there.

It was over, I told myself. The creature was gone.

I bent down beside Kenneth. He was lying on his back with his arms at his sides as if he'd been shot.

I felt for a pulse, and found it, beating between my thumb and index finger.

I hardly dared say his name out loud, afraid that my voice would call them back.

I smoothed my hand over his cheek.

'Kenneth,' I whispered. 'Kenneth.'

He opened his eyes.

At first, he looked vacantly into the sky above us.

'We're in the woods,' I whispered. 'We've got to go home now.'

He scrutinised me as he sat up.

His gaze frightened me. There was something different about it. Something that hadn't been there before.

The way he looked at me.

'Come on,' I said softly. 'We're going home now.'

He got to his feet.

I looked around, but saw no movement, heard no sound.

I took his hand, and he let me. When I started to walk, he walked too. Away, along the stream, between the two fallen trees, slowly up the bank, through the heather.

Kenneth didn't seem to know he was naked, or else attached no significance to it, for he seemed quite unperturbed.

It would be someone from the prison, it occurred to me. An escaped prisoner. Some of them looked terrifying. Pumped up on steroids. Big as oxen. Raw, brutal faces.

That would be it.

He'd escaped from the prison and was lying low here until they stopped looking for him.

The great birds were just birds.

The darkness, and my anxiety, had made everything so harrowing.

And Kenneth's gaze was unchanged, I told myself, glancing at him discreetly. His eyes were fixed straight ahead, showing no emotion. It was the way Kenneth had always been, a single face was all he had, and his staring eyes. Not vacant entirely, but expressionless. As if nothing was ever of any concern.

My breathing became laboured about halfway up the slope, and I stopped. I couldn't get enough air. It felt like every capillary tightened, to twist and writhe inside my body. My heart pounded and I bent double, my body crumpling, though I knew I had to stand straight and open my lungs.

It felt like the only air was coming in through a tiny straw, yet my lungs were so big, how could they ever be filled?

hhhhii hhhhaa, hhhhii hhhhaa

I sensed Kenneth staring at me.

hhhhii hhhhaa, hhhhii hhhhaa

And then the blockage seemed to release. Air streamed abruptly into my lungs, into my blood, and the pain ceased.

I drew myself upright and realised we'd been holding hands the whole time.

'We can carry on now, Kenneth,' I said. 'We'll soon be home.'

I looked down from the top of the ridge at the institution's cluster of buildings. They seemed almost to be asleep beside each other in the flat terrain. The prison looked different, a harshly illuminated rectangle in the dark forest, wide awake and angry.

But the vessel and the blood, what was that about?

He must have killed an animal and butchered it. Probably out of his head on something, and then Kenneth had appeared.

We followed the path cautiously through the last bit of the woods.

Now I had to get him back inside unnoticed.

I crossed my fingers for Sølve to be asleep. If he was, it'd be as if nothing had happened.

The light from the buildings fell faintly over the ground in front of us. After a few moments I saw the windows and the lamps from which it shone, and then we were crossing the lawn.

There was no one on the veranda, at least. And no one to be seen about the buildings either. If they'd found out we were gone, there'd have been some sort of activity.

But there wasn't a soul.

I unlocked the door while Kenneth stood passively waiting.

In the corridor, I opened the door to the toilets, moistened a paper towel and wiped away the red mark on his forehead. It was sticky and could only be blood.

Now that we were back inside, it was the only sign that something had happened. As for him being naked, all I needed to say was that he'd tried to get away, only I'd managed to stop him. He couldn't talk, and there was no way he could communicate anything else. I certainly wasn't going to tell anyone, not even Jostein.

Not that he'd believe me.

I went up the stairs, leading Kenneth by the hand, his face expressionless as always, his movements stiff and mechanical.

The corridor was empty. Tentatively, I went towards the duty room and looked in. Sølve was sitting on the sofa. His head was tipped back and his mouth was open.

Thank God for that.

'Come on, Kenneth, we'll get you to bed,' I said, and opened the door for him. I stood for a moment in the doorway and watched him as he pulled the duvet aside and climbed into bed.

'Sleep well,' I said.

He turned his head and stared at me, then opened his mouth as if about to speak.

His eyes blinked several times in succession.

'Ah ah ah,' he said.

'What's that? Is there something you want?' I said.

He coughed.

'Yuh . . .' he said.

'Do you want some water, is that it?'

He was still staring at me.

'Yuh . . . a . . . ahh . . .' he said.

His voice was a faint rattle from somewhere deep inside him.

You are?

Was he speaking?

No, of course he wasn't. He was making sounds, that's all.

'Goodnight, then,' I said.

'You . . . ahh . . .' he said again.

Was he speaking? Were the sounds words?

He put his hand in the air.

'You . . . are . . . doomed . . .'

And then he lay down, closed his eyes and turned his back to me.

'What was that? Did you say something? Kenneth, did you say something? What did you say? Kenneth?'

I stepped forward and touched his shoulder, trying to make contact with him.

He was lying heavy and still, breathing with the regularity of sleep.

I went back out into the corridor. He can't talk, he can't talk, I told myself. It was sounds, that's all. Turid, it was only sounds.

Could I be suffering from withdrawal, was that it?

Seeing and hearing things that weren't there?

If I couldn't get my hands on some Sobril tonight, at least I could have a smoke, I thought, and went into the duty room, opened Sølve's bag, not caring if he woke up or not, found a packet of Prince Mild and a lighter in the side pocket, and went out onto the veranda, where I sat down in the chair and lit up.

'I must have fallen asleep,' said Sølve's voice from the doorway. 'Did I miss anything?'

'No,' I said. 'What would you do if I reported you?'

'You wouldn't, surely?' he said.

'Maybe,' I said, drawing the smoke into my lungs with a splutter.

'I didn't know you smoked,' he said.

I didn't answer him, but coughed and gasped for breath in succession. I couldn't smoke with my bloody chest. I knew that, it stood to reason.

Such a bloody bind.

I bent forward and stubbed it out on the concrete.

'I don't suppose you've got a Sobril on you?' I said.

'Sobril? No. I've got a Xanor, though. Do you want one?'

'You haven't? Seriously?'

'Yes, I have. Relax. But if I give you one, it means you're not going to report me, right?'

He laughed.

'Have you got two?' I said.

A moment later he handed me two pills and a glass of water.

'Good old Turid,' he said.

I sighed and swallowed.

I'd be paying a high price for the favour. We were partners in crime now.

He sat down in the other chair.

'Can you leave me on my own for a bit?' I said.

'What?' he said. 'I just helped you out!'

'Please? Just for a bit. There's something I need to think through.'

He got up without speaking, and went in. I leaned my head back and looked up at the sky. The pills wouldn't kick in for another half-hour, I knew that, but it felt like they were already helping.

Yuh ahh duu md

It was sounds, that was all.

Yuh ahh duu md

After what had happened in the woods, anyone's imagination would run riot. It had been running riot then too, for that matter.

Birds with scales on them, and primitive monsters.

I'd been hysterical.

Kenneth running off naked into the woods was mad enough on its own, and me having to run after him.

That was a story I could tell one day.

Not that Ole was likely to give me a grandchild.

Poor little love.

I went in and got my phone to call him. Sølve had started washing the floor in the corridor by the sound of it. The deal between us was he did the kitchen and the toilets, and I did the floors. But now he was miffed and was trying to make me feel guilty by doing my work too.

No answer.

This time I wasn't worried. Either his battery had run down, or else he'd gone to sleep with his phone muted.

It was no use calling Jostein. He'd be well away, if he'd been out on the booze.

A whispery sensation from the pills spiralled gently through my body, drawing a veil through the passages of my brain, settling softly on my nerves, calming and soothing. I felt so peaceful that even my most angry thoughts dissolved.

What was it I'd thought to myself up there on the hill?

A thought that had shone so brightly.

Now I remembered.

That I could pack the job in altogether.

That was it.

I was getting on, but I wasn't exactly old. I'd got experience, I was bound to be able to get another job.

Maybe even something completely different?

Something with flowers, perhaps. A nursery again? Or even better, a florist's. Tying bouquets, arranging sprays.

Colours and shapes, life and joy.

If I could live my life again, that would be what I'd do. Become a florist, with my own shop.

I'd have chosen art at gymnasium school, and kept it up, painting and drawing.

And not gone to work that spring day in 1986.

But then I wouldn't have had Ole.

Forget that.

Marrying Jostein needn't have stopped me having a florist's shop.

And he hadn't exactly pulled the wool over my eyes that day he appeared at the nursery. He was the same then as he'd been since. So what I'd got was what I'd wanted.

The sky was blue that day, and the sun was shining, but there was a cold wind too, and planting bulbs that afternoon meant my fingers were numb and red with cold.

I'd never have remembered if it hadn't been the first time I saw him.

A car had come up the track, whirling up the dust, and through the grubby panes of the greenhouse I'd watched as it pulled in and a young man got out with a camera in his hand. He stood talking to Erlend in the office at first, but then came back out to take some pictures and exchange a few words.

He wasn't that tall, but well built, and his clothes were all on the small side. His trousers were slightly too tight around the thighs, his suit jacket a tad too short. His mouth was wide and his chin rather angular, and his hair was blond. But what I noticed about him, what everyone noticed about him, were his eyes. They had this bright blue colour I'd never seen in anyone else.

He worked for the local paper and was doing a series about different careers for the weekend supplement, he said. He got us to show him around and asked a lot of questions as we went. He laughed a lot, in a very confident way, as if he didn't care what anyone in the world thought of him.

We talked about him when he got back in the car and drove off, but I didn't think of him again after that.

Then, the week the article appeared — Erlend posted a copy of it on the office wall and another on the noticeboard in the greenhouse — Anne came to get me, there was someone on the phone for me. And it was him, Jostein Lindland. He'd been thinking about me, he said, and was wondering if I'd care to have dinner with him.

'I don't know about that,' I said. 'I don't know you.'

He laughed.

'That's the whole point!' he said. 'So we can get to know each other!'

'It can't do any harm, I suppose,' I said eventually, and he'd been reminding me about it ever since. If ever we were doing something special, he'd say, 'It can't do any harm, I suppose!'

You couldn't keep him down in those days, always laughing at the slightest opportunity. That was all gone now.

I didn't bring him any joy any more, and he kept Ole at arm's length.

Such a little family, and I hadn't even managed to keep it together.

I took another of Sølve's cigarettes. Surely I could have a smoke without coughing my lungs up, as long as I inhaled gently?

Of course I could.

I heard him come into the duty room and sit himself down with a sigh.

'I'm just having a little rest,' I said. 'I'll do the rounds in a minute. And my share of the cleaning.'

'I've done it,' he said. 'Thought I might as well, you wanting to be on your own and everything.'

How could he still be miffed? I wondered, stubbing the cigarette out in the ashtray as good as unsmoked.

'Thanks,' I said. 'You didn't need to, though. Everything quiet in there?'

'Quiet as the grave,' he said.

He sat checking his phone and didn't look up as I went past him into the corridor. Parts of the floor were still glistening wet, others were already dry. There was a smell of detergent, but not enough to mask the pungent smell from the toilets, which always seemed to be so latent, though I suppose it was no wonder after fifty years.

I opened the door of Kenneth's room and looked in. He lay snoring on his back. That only an hour or so earlier he'd been lying in the forest as if he'd been dead hardly seemed believable.

With that giant tramping around him.

What had *happened*, actually?

I closed the door again and looked in on the others in turn. All were fast asleep.

As light slowly returned to the sky and the first cheeping birds made themselves heard on the other side of the windowpanes, I got the breakfast ready for the morning shift. Boiled the eggs, hard and soft, toasted some rounds of bread, put cheese and ham and salami out on a dish, got the jams and spreads out, and set the table.

The last thing I did before they came in was fold the clean and dry clothes and get another wash on the go.

Sølve was still sulking and left without saying goodbye, and when I opened the report book to see what he'd written, I saw that he hadn't bothered.

I sat down with the book on my lap and scribbled a few lines about Kenneth and Torgeir having been a bit unsettled before bed, though the night had been uneventful.

If I'd put down what had actually happened, Kenneth on the loose, running about starkers in the woods, no one would have believed me. Certainly not if I'd reported everything I'd experienced out there.

But that was all down to anxiety and imagination, nothing else.

Not until Berit came into the corridor did I realise I'd forgotten to make the coffee. It was a major sin, about being considerate towards your colleagues. It wasn't unusual for things to overlap a few minutes, but to be on my own with her now was the last thing I needed.

'Have a good shift,' I said, going out just as she entered.

I half expected her to call me back, but she didn't. Most likely she was as glad to avoid me as I was to avoid her.

On my way downstairs I ran into Unni, all in white in a cloud of perfume.

'Quiet night?' she asked without stopping.

'Oh, you know,' I said. 'Same as ever.'

'Sleep well, then,' she said, going in through the door, while I carried on down into the entrance and out into the car park. The sun was still low, but the air was warm and still. It always felt strange to emerge into the morning from a night shift, especially on such a fine day in summer, when the sun had been up for a few hours and the day had long since begun. I never quite managed to make it join up, because in my head I was already facing the night.

I rolled the window down and drove slowly through the hospital grounds, which at this early hour were still all but deserted. Reaching the main road, I picked up speed and had to roll the window up a bit as the air inside the car became increasingly agitated.

Ole hadn't phoned me back, he must have gone to bed early. Which was good, because maybe then we could have breakfast together. Jostein had probably gone off to work already. He was always an early starter, it didn't matter how much he'd had the night before.

Breakfast with all three of us was seldom good anyway.

Maybe I could set the table in the garden?

I coughed a few times. I mustn't smoke any more, I told myself. In any case, it was never as good as I thought it was going to be. I'd have to remind myself.

I turned down the road that led through the estate where we lived. The lawns lay yellow and parched between green hedges and trees. A front door opened and a man came out. A car reversed out of a drive-way. Apart from that, everything was quiet.

The trees stood motionless, as if asleep.

Mornings such as these seemed to contain an invisible darkness *behind* the bright sunlight. I saw it, of course, because day was my night, but it was no less real on that account.

I pulled up on the gravel outside, engaged the handbrake, picked up my bag and got out.

It must have been about twenty-five degrees already.

Wasn't it watering day today?

Yes, I was sure of it. I hadn't watered yesterday, so it had to be.

I went round the back of the house and uncoiled the hosepipe that hung from the wall, clicked the sprinkler onto the nozzle and placed it on the slope of the lawn before turning on the tap.

A watery hand rose up and unfolded into the air, showering the dry grass as if with a sigh.

I stood and watched it for a minute. It felt so good. There was some-thing life-giving about the wet water falling on the dry ground.

Inside, I put my bag down on the table in the passage and went upstairs to the kitchen. Everything was still as I'd left it. Neither Ole nor Jostein seemed to have eaten anything.

The lasagne was untouched in the oven.

I wasn't hungry, but I hadn't eaten since the evening before on the ward, so I opened the fridge and looked inside to see if there was anything I fancied.

Not really.

There were some eggs and milk, though. I could make him some pancakes, like when he was little? How he used to love them!

Nowadays he could just as easily come in and say he didn't want any. In which case it wasn't worth the effort. A boiled egg, then. He never said no to a boiled egg. And that was simple enough.

I took three eggs out and a packet of sliced ham. Pierced a little hole in the dumpy end of each egg, filled the kettle with water and switched it on, sliced a tomato and arranged it on a plate, and some cucumber too, then got the bread out of the bread bin and the knife from the drawer.

The trees threw long shadows outside. The sky was so blue and clear.

I stood at the window in the living room to watch the sprinkler. The water glittered in the air, falling soundlessly to the ground.

I'd have to ask Ole to move it while I slept. Three times it needed, at least.

I went into the kitchen again, poured the boiling water into a saucepan, put the eggs in, cut some bread and put it in the toaster, then set the table for two. Got the juice out of the fridge, and the liver paste in case he wanted any. If he did, he'd be wanting some pickled cucumber on it, so I got that out too.

When the eggs had boiled for exactly four and a half minutes, I took the saucepan off the hob, drained the water off, put it down in the sink and filled it up with cold water from the tap before taking the eggs and putting two on his plate, one on mine.

Then I went and knocked on his door.

'Ole?' I said. 'Are you awake?'

When he didn't reply, I opened the door.

His bed was empty.

He wasn't at his computer either.

'Ole?' I said, stepping inside. Sometimes he'd be sitting on the floor up against the wall with his mobile. Only he wasn't.

The room was empty.

Fear struck me like a blow.

'OLE!' I shouted, going back out onto the landing. 'OLE! OLE!'

Maybe, just maybe, he'd gone out and met up with a friend. Stayed the night at his.

I hurried downstairs again, got my mobile out of my bag and called his number.

Faintly, I heard his phone ring somewhere in the house.

He'd never have gone out without his phone.

I called Jostein. He didn't answer. I called him again, pressing his number over and over as I went through the rooms, shouting Ole's name. My heart thudded harder and harder, my throat tightened, I couldn't breathe, I had to bend forward and support myself against the wall. There was no air coming in, my chest felt like it was going to explode, everything went dark, and then a tiny passage opened, a tiny stream of air whistled into my great big lungs, the passage expanded, and at last I could gulp in oxygen, deeply, several times in quick succession.

He'd killed himself.

I knew it.

I screamed.

The scream filled my entire being, and when it stopped it was as if I'd been abandoned by it.

It wasn't certain, I told myself frantically in this new silence. It wasn't certain, it could be something else, he could have been awake all night and have gone for a walk.

Why shouldn't he have gone for a walk?

Ole had gone for a walk. His bed was made, because he hadn't slept in it.

I called Jostein again.

Ole had gone for a walk, I told myself, and put my phone back in my pocket. All I had to do was wait and then he'd be home.

But I couldn't wait.

He'd killed himself.

He'd gone for a walk.

He'd shot himself with Jostein's shotgun.

I crept down the stairs and stopped in the passage.

If the shotgun was in the storage room, he hadn't killed himself.

I looked at the door.

All I had to do was go in and look.

But I couldn't. As long as I didn't know if the shotgun was there, he was still alive.

He'd gone for a walk. Up to the woods, to the foot of the steep rock face where he'd built a den when he was little. It was his place. That would be where he was.

I put my sandals on and went out to find him.

My little love.

My baby Ollie.

You haven't done anything stupid, have you?

I went through the garden, over the fence and up the path, where humming insects dithered in the air. Past the overgrown football pitch, up the slope behind it, to where the rock face rose.

'OLE!' I shouted.

His place was a little patch of grass in front of the rock, tucked away behind some oak trees. One of them he called the Giant Tree.

His jacket was there.

So he'd been here.

It was a good sign, surely?

Unless he'd been saying goodbye to the place.

I called Jostein again. Only he could help me now.

I called and called his number all the way home.

Ole wasn't in the house. He wasn't in his place.

He'd gone for a walk without his phone.

But why had he seemed so happy and untroubled all of a sudden the night before?

He'd found a way out.

'NO!' I cried, halting at the fence. 'NO! NO!'

I buried my face in my hands.

All strength, every emotion drained away from me. Only a canvas of fear remained, white and cold. I crossed the lawn slowly, continuing round the house to the garage. I opened the door and went inside. It was dark and cool in there. I switched the light on. Ole was slumped against the wall in a pool of blood. The shotgun lay across his legs. He'd shot himself in the chest. His head drooped against his shoulder. His eyes were open. They were empty and lifeless.

I reached forward and felt for a pulse. His heart wasn't beating.

I was standing in his blood.

I crouched down, put my cheek to his and held him.

'So cold you are, my dear little boy,' I whispered. 'I'll get you a blanket.'

I pulled the phone out of my pocket and called the emergency services while going in to get the blanket, the phone to my ear. There was blood on it, on my hand, my chest, my cheek.

'My son is dead,' I said. 'He's shot himself in the garage at home. The address is Rogneveien 11. My name is Turid Lindland.'

I tucked the blanket around him snugly and sat at his side, stroking his hair, until the ambulance arrived. I got to my feet and went towards it as it pulled up behind my car. Two men jumped out.

'He's in here,' I said.

They followed me inside. One of them crouched down to check his pulse.

He looked up at us.

'His heart's beating,' he said. 'It's faint, but it's beating.'

I gasped. The two men darted out. I fell back against the wall.

They came running with a stretcher and two big cases. I couldn't watch as they attended to him, but went outside instead, calling Jostein's number repeatedly.

A few minutes later they came out with Ole on the stretcher, an oxygen mask over his face, a catheter in his arm, and slid him into the ambulance. One of them got in the back with him, the other turned to me.

'You can sit in the front,' he said.

JOSTEIN

I didn't tell anyone either from the desk or the editors' office what case I was on. I just sat down on my chair and started writing, not even bothering to take my jacket off, even if it was covered in crap, and of course it soon got noticed that I was sitting there stinking of drink and how's your father, typing away like mad, because not many minutes passed from Ellingsen clocking in to him standing in front of my desk.

I didn't look up.

'What are you writing?' he said.

'A piece of major importance,' I said.

'About what?'

'Wait and see,' I said.

'I don't recall you mentioning anything at the editorial meeting? Or to me?'

'I didn't,' I said. 'Listen, do you mind going away now? I've got to get this done. It's urgent.'

'I don't care for your attitude,' he said, trying to big himself up by sitting down on the edge of my desk with his arms across his chest. 'Have you come straight from a party?'

I shook my head. I'd got a royal flush, and they could go to hell.

'This won't do,' he said, standing up again. 'It's not the eighties or nineties now, you know. We need to talk. The two of us together. Shall we say one o'clock in my office?'

'You can say what you like,' I said, and looked up at him with the widest smile I could muster.

By one o'clock, I'd be an arts journalist no more, that much was certain.

Half an hour later I was done and went to find the news editor. He
was sitting in one of the conference rooms, or glass cages as I called
them — everything had to be so open and transparent now — and I
knocked so hard on the pane it made him jump.

'Not now, Lindland,' he said. 'Can't you see I'm busy?'

He was only just in his early thirties, so his patronising tone got my
back up. But I kept my cool.

'Got a piece for you,' I said. 'You should read it, *now.*'

He sighed.

'Iver's your chief, give it to him.'

'It's a news story,' I said. 'And you should read it now. If you don't,
you'll regret it.'

He glared at me.

'Have you gone mad? You stand here, reeking of alcohol and looking
like I don't know what, and dare to *threaten* me?'

'For fuck's sake, man,' I said. 'What's happened to this newspaper?
I've got a massive scoop here, and you're sticking to formalities and
don't want to know?'

'All right, I'll read it,' he said. 'On past merit.'

Past merit? Who did he think he was? To him, the past barely went
back to last week. He had *no idea* who he was talking to.

'But right now I'm in a meeting. Send it to me and I'll get back to you
this afternoon.'

I shook my head.

'You read it *now*. Is that too hard to understand? When *I say* it's a
scoop, it's a fucking *scoop*, all right?'

He glared at me again.

'I don't care for your attitude, Lindland,' he said.

Un-bloody-believable.

I spun round in anger and left him without a word. Went straight to
the editor-in-chief and knocked on her door. She was about sixteen and
I had zero faith in her, but the final word in the place was hers.

She looked up at me from behind her enormous desk.

'I've got something,' I said before she had time to speak. 'The police
have found those lads out of Kvitekrist. Three of them have been murdered. You can't imagine the carnage. The bodies are up at Svartediket.

I was there last night. Talked to the police. No one else knows. Kavli wouldn't read my piece because I'm arts and culture.'

She hadn't said anything yet, but sat looking at me.

'Send it to me,' she said.

'OK,' I said, closed the door after me, went back to my desk and sent it.

Five minutes later, she comes over with Kavli in tow.

'We're running it,' she said. 'But it's got to be checked first. Karsten and Hans are doing that now.'

'Good,' I said. 'But it's my case. And I follow it up.'

'We'll have to see,' she said.

I shook my head.

'No, we won't,' I said. 'I've got the contacts, I know the satanist scene, and I was first to it. I'm not having some wet-behind-the-ears little squirt taking this on. It's mine.'

I saw the way they exchanged glances. I saw too that Kavli was saying no.

Fucking idiot. Prestige, prestige, prestige.

'All right,' she said. 'But you cooperate with Hans and Karsten and Kavli. And it's this case only.'

'Fine by me,' I said, and got to my feet. 'I'll get off home and grab some kip.'

Outside in the street, the city flooded in sunlight, I lit a smoke and decided to go back to the little artist piece at the hotel. Technically, I was at work, and Turid would be asleep after her night shift, so she wouldn't miss me or suspect anything. I could have a shower and we could have a nice little quickie before going home.

I didn't want to drag reception into anything, so I took the lift straight up and knocked on her door.

There was no one in. Either that or she didn't want to see anyone.

She was unstable, I had to remember that.

I went out again, lighting another smoke while checking the news on my phone. Nothing yet. Maybe they couldn't get hold of Geir or anyone else who could confirm it.

Fifty-three notifications from Turid now. But the last one was over an hour ago.

The best thing to say was that I'd run out of battery and had no idea she'd been trying to get in touch.

I turned and went up the hill towards the theatre, then got into a taxi there.

'Can you stop for a minute at the Shell station?' I said as we headed towards Sandviken.

'Right you are,' said the driver, who was so fat he could hardly fit in the seat; his two little eyes peered at me in the rear-view from out of his blubbery face.

What a day.

The fjord was blue and still as a millpond. The islands were lush green and dashed with orange or red where the houses were. One of the catamarans was on its way north. A thin wisp of white water trailed like a tail in its wake.

The driver pulled in behind the pumps at the Shell station and I went in to buy a packet of chewing gum in case I happened to meet Turid before I got a chance to brush my teeth, and some more cigarettes, but as I stood at the till and was about to pay, I suddenly felt hungry, it was like a cavern opened up inside me, and I bought three hot dogs and a Coke to go with them. The driver eyed the food as I got in, maybe it even made him feel underfed. It was something of a meal, I'd give him that.

I'd just got it down me as we approached the houses where we lived. I licked the dressing and ketchup off my fingers, wiped my hands on my trousers and got my card out.

'You can stop here on the corner,' I said. I didn't want her to see me coming home in a taxi, it'd only set off a chain of questions.

Still, it felt a bit odd ambling up the road at this time of the morning when it wasn't the weekend. Not a soul to be seen, of course.

I opened the door quietly and went into the passage, stopped and listened. All was quiet, she was sleeping like the little baby she was. I went into the flatlet we'd once rented out to a loony and which afterwards I'd nabbed for my own — I had my desk there, a sofa and a TV, a bathroom and a little cubbyhole I'd used as a darkroom aeons ago — and got undressed, dumping my suit jacket, which reeked to high heaven now, at the bottom of the cupboard and making a mental note

I'd have to get it dry-cleaned at some point, got in the shower, turned it on and stood under the hot water while I sighed with delight.

I had a shave and brushed my teeth, and put a clean pair of undies on, then wondered for a minute if I should sleep there or upstairs in the bedroom. There was the most practical, seeing as how I was only going to grab a couple of hours before getting back to work, but it could raise questions, so I rolled some deodorant under my arms and went up to the first floor.

Turid wasn't in bed, and she hadn't slept in it either, it was still made.

Maybe she'd left me?

Was that why she'd rung me all those times?

Had someone seen me? One of her workmates? And tipped her off?

For crying out loud.

I pulled the duvet aside and crumpled the sheet so it looked like someone had slept there, in case she was just running late for some reason, then put on a pair of shorts and a shirt and went to the kitchen to make myself a coffee. If we were going to have a serious talk, I'd need coffee and cigarettes.

Maybe her mother had died?

It was possible.

She'd have gone straight there in that case, and tried to get hold of me a million times.

I couldn't have been seen. It had all gone on in a hotel room!

Maybe I didn't need any sleep? Now I'd had a shower and got my summer togs on, I felt rather fresh, on top of things even.

I took the steaming mug with me into the garden and sat down at the table in the shade of the veranda. Stared for a bit at the water from the sprinkler as it sparkled in the sun. There was a hissing sound from somewhere along the hose, it probably meant there was a hole there, but not a big one, because the water pressure looked fine.

Might as well grab the bull by the horns, I thought, switched my phone on and called her number.

'Jostein,' she said.

'I can explain everything,' I said. 'I got this fantastic tip-off while I was out with that lot from work. It's the story of the century. And it's mine. I was out all night working on it, then went straight back to the office and wrote it up. It's big. It's going to be on CNN, Fox News, BBC, you name it. I've just popped home for a shower and a change of clothes and now I'm on my way out again. Looks like I'm going to get my old job back now too. So everything's good.'

I took a sip of my coffee and reached for my cigarettes.

'Jostein,' she said again.

I sensed the worst. There was something about her tone of voice.

'What is it?' I said.

'Ole's touch and go.'

'Ole? What are you saying? What's happened?'

'Oh, Jostein. He's shot himself.'

'Ole? You mean he's tried to kill himelf?'

'Yes. Yes. Yes.'

'Oh Christ. The *bloody* idiot,' I said.

'Jostein,' she said. 'You've got to come, now.'

'Christ,' I said again. 'But he didn't succeed, is that what you're telling me? He's still alive?'

'I think so. I don't know. They've got him in surgery now.'

'Shit,' I said. 'What made him do it, do you think?'

She started crying.

'Come now. We need you.'

'I'm on my way,' I said, nearly adding that I just needed to finish my coffee first, but fortunately I didn't. She wouldn't have understood.

I needed time to take this in.

The bloody idiot. How could he do such a thing to his own mother?

We didn't kill ourselves in our family.

We just didn't.

We put our troubles aside. And he was his mother's only joy.

Hadn't he thought about that?

Could he only think of himself and his petty little problems?

Killing yourself because you've got no mates.

How sad was that?

And how wrong!

Why couldn't he give life a go?

Sitting at home feeling sorry for himself.

No wonder.

I stood up and paced the patio while I smoked.

Christ.

The bloody idiot.

It was so stupid it could make you cry.

Ahhhh!

I threw my cigarette to the ground, trod on it and went back inside. I'd have to take her car, but where she'd put the key was anyone's guess.

Luckily it was on the table in the passage.

Did I need to take anything with me?

Credit cards and driving licence in my back pocket.

That was it.

I locked the door behind me, went to the car and got in. It was boiling inside. The seat was burning hot against my thighs and I twisted round to see if there was a blanket in the back that I could sit on. And then I was blacking out. The darkness came washing over me, like a premonition at first, as if I knew what was going to happen before it happened. In that split second, I felt fear, the realisation that the wave from before was coming back to consume me, but for some idiotic reason I put the key in the ignition and started the engine, as if somehow I could drive away from it.

The darkness rose in me like water in a bottle being filled from a tap, and then everything became black.

No, everything became nothing.

How long it lasted, I don't know. Time didn't exist.

But suddenly I was in a place.

I recognised it.

The darkness was all around. But far down in the depths before me was a shimmer of light. And there I was, in that light, in the car with the engine running.

Only this time I wasn't coming back. I didn't want to come back.

I looked around.

A black abyss behind me.

Could I get there?

I was there already, I fell, and everything was darkness again.

*

It didn't feel like I fell *through* the darkness, it felt like I became *as one* with it. That I *was* the darkness. But without knowing until afterwards, when I'd left it and opened my eyes, at first not knowing who I was, or where I was, only *that* I was.

I was lying on the ground. The sky above me was grey, the air raw and cold. I could hear running water somewhere close by, but apart from that everything was completely still.

I half expected someone to be there, trying to revive me. But I was all on my own.

It was because I'd gone the other way, I thought, and sat up.

I found myself by a rock face in a forest. The trees surrounding me were without leaves, the trunks glistening with moisture. The soft, damp cushion on which I sat was moss.

For some reason, I was as thirsty as hell.

I got to my feet, clutching the nearest tree trunk for support, and looked up at the dark branches that latticed against the grey sky.

Was it something I was imagining? Was I actually still in the car, with everything I was seeing simply going on in my head?

The tree was an oak, so tall and thick it could easily have been a thousand years old. The bark was at once rough and smooth, robust and disintegrating.

No, there was no doubt I was actually here, by this tree, in this forest.

I looked to where the sound of the water was coming from. Some slender tree trunks radiated white among the green and grey. Birch often grew by water or in wetlands. I remembered from when I'd been in the scouts.

So there was probably a stream.

But where was I, exactly?

And what was I doing there?

Christ.

Could I be dead?

Had I had a heart attack in the car?

It would make sense, in a way. That it was my soul that had been out there in the darkness and gone another way to end up here.

I looked down at my body.

What was it doing here then?

Belly and all.

So many bloody questions all at once.

I needed something to drink first. Then I could think.

I set out over the soft floor of the forest, leaving the great oaks and entering a thicket of much younger trees whose trunks were no fatter than my arms; densely they stood, their thin, smooth branches yielding to the pressure of my body, whipping back into place, the crowns swaying above me as I forged my path.

I hated forests.

Wet and cold and thirsty as hell, I came to the copse of birches. The sound of rushing water was loud and seemed to be so close by, but there was no river in sight, not even a stream.

And yet the water rushed.

I closed my eyes. It sounded like it was coming from below. A subterranean river?

I opened my eyes again, lay down and pressed my ear to the ground.

The sound was hollower now, as if the water were running through some great system of caves beneath me.

I followed it, wondering if it might run out into a lake nearby, or well up into a pool somewhere, or a spring.

I was cold. I tried to work some warmth into my body by going faster.

Everything was still, no animals to be seen or heard, and no birds either. Only tree upon tree, bush upon bush, thicket upon thicket, bog upon bog, motionless in the mist that occasionally passed unhurriedly through the air, as if it were blind and were feeling its way forward.

There were no signs of human activity anywhere, not a bottle top or a soggy orange peel, nor even the slightest imprint of a heel in the soil or moss.

I was no pathfinder, my time in the scouts had extended only to a few weeks one autumn, until I'd had enough of their holier-than-thou ethos and packed it in, so there could quite easily have been tracks all around me, I just couldn't see them.

That said, I thought, rubbing my hands up and down my arms a few times, because I was getting seriously cold in my shorts and summer shirt, surely a person could sense if a place was deserted or not?

I bent down and pulled up a handful of moss, pressed it to my mouth and tried to suck some water out of it without getting a mouthful of soil and plant matter at the same time. Enough seeped in to moisten the inside of my mouth, though not without a taste of earth and bits of moss stuck to my tongue.

I spat and carried on.

In front of me stood a large oak.

The same bloody one.

I'd been going in a circle.

I stopped and put my hand against its enormous trunk as I looked about.

I'd gone *that* way. So maybe I should go *this* way now?

As I started walking again, it occurred to me there was something familiar about the place. The rock face and the big oak. I'd seen it before.

But where?

I turned round.

It was like a dream. The harder I thought about it, the further away it drifted.

I carried on down a bank, emerging a few minutes later into a small clearing. From there I could see the ridge of a hill, and I recognised it.

I saw it every day from my kitchen window.

I looked around me, and every feature of the landscape suddenly fell into place.

Our house was there. The neighbours' there. The road ran there.

But there was just forest everywhere, nothing but trees.

Where were the houses?

Had I come to another time? Before it was all built?

Don't be stupid.

But what could it be?

I was standing pretty much exactly where the car had been. There was no doubt about it.

Or was there?

My throat was parched like I'd never known before. The need for something to drink tore at me and I hurried on through the housing estate that wasn't a housing estate but a forest. I was freezing now. A night outdoors in this temperature, in these clothes, wasn't a prospect, that was for sure. There had to be people here *somewhere*. And where there were people, there was warmth. I could break into a cabin if I could find one, or knock on the door of a remote farmhouse, or just keep walking until I came to some village or town.

The sound of running water came back. Here and there just a babble, elsewhere a deeper, thundering roar, where I imagined it crashing through great subterranean channels.

I looked up at the grey-white sky. It was the same sky I'd always seen. The light suggested it was the middle of the day, and probably late autumn, considering how cold it was.

What kind of shit *was* this?

If only the darkness would come back. So I could wake up away from it all, return to my senses in the car.

All I could do was go on and hope it was going to happen.

The forest grew thicker again. It seemed older here, many of the trunks and lower boughs mouldy-looking and covered in moss. Next to them grew straight and slender young trees that reached perhaps twenty metres into the air, and then pine, so close together their branches intertwined, giving the impression there was only one, a great bloody giant of a thing.

I paused by a birch, stuck my neck out and licked the smooth bark. It only gave me a taste for more. My throat was like sandpaper, but that wasn't the worst thing, the worst thing was the sucking sensation inside me, as if my whole body was contracting around this fierce craving for something I was unable to give it.

But it wasn't a desert I was wandering in, under a scorching sun. That was the irony, because there was moisture all around me, in the air, in the trees, in the twigs and leaves at my feet.

I went in a wide arc around the pine, no longer hearing the river underground. But on the other side of that dense cluster, the forest opened itself around a treeless furrow, and there, brown and still, ran a stream.

It was perhaps a metre in depth, the sandy bed shimmering faintly through the cloudy water. I knelt at its bank, my knees sinking into the soil, but what did I care when, from my cupped hands a moment later, cold water ran down the funnel of my throat?

I lapped and slurped like a hound.

Afterwards, I sat on the ground and leaned back against a solitary birch growing up at the very edge of the stream. The lower trunk was quite black, the bark only transitioning into white some five metres above.

The water had been so cold. Its coldness seemed to spread not only from my throat and into my thorax, but also from the cavity of my mouth and into my head. But it was a different coldness than was in the air. This one was pleasant, as if smoothing and enfolding. And what was inside me became clearer to me, too. My heart beating with such simple beauty. The blood streaming to every part of my body. Yes, the blood streaming, the heart beating, and the emotions too, likewise of such simple beauty, diffusing in a different way from the blood, moving more like shadows on the ground when the sun passed behind a cloud, suddenly to re-emerge, flooding everything, first in one way, which was joy, then in another, which was sadness. And all as the heart beat and beat. And the trees grew, the water ran, the moon shone, the sun burned. The heart and the blood. Joy and sadness. Trees and water. Simple and beautiful. Beautiful and simple.

'So well you beat,' I said.

The sound of my own voice there in the stillness of the forest surprised me, and I got to my feet.

Where on earth was I?

My knees were wet, and soil stuck to them.

And in the mud on the bank were prints. Footprints at first, then the indentations made by a pair of knees.

Were they mine?

They had to be. There was no one else here.

Did I live here?

In the forest?

Or was I just out?

Who was I, anyway?

Didn't I know?

'Hello, my name's . . .' I said in the hope a name would come. But it didn't.

Was I anyone at all, if I didn't *know* who I was?

A nobody? A somebody?

All I needed was just that little fragment of something familiar, I sensed, then everything would fall into place.

I started walking again, in search of whatever it might be that could unravel the mystery for me. Past a thick array of pine, into an older wood of fallen trees, mouldy and rotten, bracken brushing my legs.

From somewhere came the sound of a river once more. Not gentle as the stream I'd just left, but fierce and roaring. It was on the other side of the ridge, surely?

But when I climbed up and stood on the top, there was no river to be seen.

The sound of it was all there was.

Could it be some kind of ghost river?

What a load of bilge, I told myself, and descended to where it *ought* to have been, pressing my ear again to the ground, and discovering the sound became louder, and I realised then that it *was* subterranean.

I pictured some kind of cave system down there, with walls that were faintly phosphorescent. Fish with eyes that had grown over, blind toads, stoats that could see in the dark and had found a way in to gorge themselves.

So I knew what fish were, and toads and stoats.

What more did I know?

I knew what cold was, and what rain was. I knew trees and moss, hills and sky.

But nothing beyond all this?

There was something there, but it felt like somehow it was concealed behind a smooth-faced wall. I knew it was there, but I couldn't scale the wall to get to it.

A vault of precious thoughts.

So I knew what a vault was, and thoughts.

Something told me I should go on, and so I continued through the forest as it sloped gently upwards. The trees here were so tall they took all the light, the forest floor was bare beneath them. I looked up at the grey-white sky between the crowns as I went. Like milk in the dusk, I thought for some reason, and pictured a glass of milk on a kitchen table, the only light falling in from outside. It was a laminated table, Respatex, with a marbled pattern and metal legs, four stools tucked up to it, with light blue upholstery, they too with metal legs. On the table, besides the milk, were two brown plates, empty apart from the crumbs that remained of two sandwiches, and another glass too, empty, though its rim was edged with milk.

This was a fragment of something, but it fell short of what I needed, stopping there.

Who had drunk the milk and eaten from the plates?

When?

And where?

Strange how still it was here, I thought. No birdsong, not even the throaty caw of a crow. And no wind.

A short distance in front of me, in between the trees, a rock face rose up, glistening faintly in the mist.

Someone was sitting there!

Back against the rock, hands at their sides.

'Hey, there!' I called out, and went towards him as fast as I could.

For a he it was. A young man, I saw as I came closer.

I'd seen him before.

He was connected to me in some way.

Hair cut short above a round, as yet immature face, skin pale. Strikingly bright eyes.

He looked up at me as I came towards him and halted.

'Dad? What are you doing here?' he said.

He was my son.

I had a son.

'I don't know,' I said.

'Are you dead?' he said.

'Dead?' I said. 'Of course not. I just . . .'

He looked down at the ground as if abruptly he'd lost interest in me.

'I just can't remember anything,' I said. 'Nothing. Can you help me?'

He was holding something in his hand, I noticed now. It looked like a cuddly rabbit.

It *was* a cuddly rabbit.

He clutched it to his chest and looked up at me again. His features were indistinct in a way. No, inconstant. His features kept changing in front of my eyes. But it was him all the time.

'No,' he said. 'I can't help you.'

'Can *I* help *you*?' I said.

He shook his head.

'Not any more,' he said, then got to his feet and began to walk away.

'Where are you going?' I said.

'Don't follow me,' he said.

He moved unsettlingly quickly through the trees, seeming almost to glide over the ground.

'Wait!' I called out, and hurried after him. But although I ran, the distance between us increased, and soon he was out of sight. I carried on in the same direction without knowing if he had actually gone that way, but it was all I had to cling to.

The terrain became easier and easier to negotiate, the trees more scattered, and after a while I found myself emerging from the forest to stand before a wide heathland that was clad in heather, purple tinged with tawny yellow. It seemed to stretch out for some kilometres. The lighter areas looked like bogland. Here and there were patches of shrubs and bushes.

I could see a figure in the distance. It had to be him. I set after him at a run.

Beyond the Heath, fells rose up, dark and grey beneath the sky that was now growing dark.

Was that where he was going?

He stopped and turned, and saw me coming, and for a moment it looked as if he might wait for me.

'Son!' I called out. 'Wait!'

But he went on, at a wander.

Then stopped again.

In front of me, a patch of thorny vegetation. I halted, though against my will.

I couldn't spill blood here.

I knew this, while at the same time I knew that I had to reach him.

My son.

I had a son.

I remembered a kitchen.

I was here.

That was all.

I didn't even know his name.

But he looked at me.

'Come!' I shouted.

Reluctantly, he began to move towards me.

His eyes shone like two lights.

'I can't remember anything,' I said, as he came to a halt no more than a few paces away, the thorny bushes between us. 'I can't even remember your name!'

His face was older now than when I'd seen him before. But as I stared, it altered imperceptibly, and he came to resemble a sixteen-year-old, though the features remained distinctly his own.

I was filled with the warmest feelings for him and wanted only to reach out my hand and smooth his cheek, embrace him, feel his body against mine.

'I just want to help you,' I said.

'I don't need help,' he said.

'But then I need to know what we're doing here,' I said. 'And who I am. Do you know? Or have you forgotten too?'

'I don't know what you're doing here,' he said. 'But I've got to go on.'

'I think I'm here to bring you back,' I said.

'Maybe you are,' he said. 'But I don't want to go back.'

He turned and began to walk away again.

'Then I'm coming with you,' I shouted after him.

He didn't reply, and his figure grew smaller and smaller. Soon he was gone completely.

What was I to do now?

Where was I to go?

There was something familiar about the fells he'd gone towards. The shape of them.

Maybe I lived here and saw them every day.

Did I live with Son?

And his mother, perhaps? Did I have a wife?

I closed my eyes and tried to think of Wife. No face appeared, not even when I tried to picture Son, to conjure up an image of Wife.

I was exhausted to the core of my soul. Cold and hungry too.

Darkness came swiftly, more swiftly than I was used to. I needed to find shelter for the night. The only place I could think of was the place where I'd found him. Maybe he'd go back there. It was certainly more likely than me finding him somewhere by chance, I reckoned, and I began to head back.

In the shelter of Son's rock face was a rather deep cleft, sloping steeply downwards to rise up again on the other side, and across the cleft someone had laid logs to form a roof covered with branches of spruce. Just outside this refuge was a campfire, a circle of stones in whose middle lay the charred remains of firewood in ash. On closer inspection, I discovered a number of small bones, as from chicken or rabbit, white and smooth, quite without flesh or sinew. Against the rock wall, small logs were stacked for burning, and dry twigs had been collected for tinder. Someone was clearly using this place on a regular basis.

I sat down with my back against the rock.

Something told me it wasn't Son, but someone else.

I took three of the logs and stood them up against each other, broke some bark from one of them, snapped the twigs into smaller lengths and laid it all out around the base. Intuitively, I patted the six pockets of my shorts, and then my breast pocket, where I found my lighter and cigarettes.

So I smoked.

Prince Mild.

I saw a dry field on which the sun was shining, and I saw myself lower my head and shield the lighter's flame with my cupped hand, for it was windy, and then I saw two girls standing beside each other, in wellington boots and overalls, thick sweaters underneath, one with her hair gathered in two pigtails, hands covered in soil.

That was all.

Again, it was a thread I couldn't unravel.

It stopped there.

But the girl with soil on her hands, could she be Wife?

I lit the bark and twigs and immediately they caught. Only when the fire began to grow, devouring the darkness around it, did it occur to me that being seen might be dangerous.

There were others here. Someone had made the shelter and arranged the stones around a fire site.

But I needed warmth.

I could go without food until morning, but not warmth.

Tomorrow I had to find Son. He was in need, I knew that, and I was meant to help him, I knew that too. I didn't know what I was meant to help him with, or how. But I felt certain that he did. Besides, he knew who I was.

I was here because of Son.

I reasoned it was all I needed to know, and stared into the fire, the flames rising and falling, the play of colour, shifting from orange to yellow tinged with blue, ghostly, yet unchanging in its core.

The wood crackled and popped, occasionally surprising with a louder, more explosive report.

I began to drop off. Perhaps more pictures would come back to me then, I managed to think in the moments before sleep. Didn't they usually?

But somewhere close by something rustled. My eyes snapped open. Probably just an animal on its way through the undergrowth, I told myself, and reached for a new log, placing it carefully on the fire.

I got the feeling I was being watched.

Maybe it was because I was so visible in the light of the flames and could see nothing myself in the surrounding darkness.

I tried to dismiss it.

A few minutes later, my eyes gazing absently into the fire, I'd already forgotten about it, when a voice suddenly spoke.

'Who are you?'

I jumped to my feet and peered out.

'It's all right,' the voice said, with a chuckle. 'I can't harm you!'

It was a woman. She must have been studying me for some time.

'Who are *you*?' I said. 'Come here so I can see you.'

Soundlessly, she emerged into the light. She was rather small and looked to be in her seventies, slightly stooping, her face lined and leathery, the way elderly women often looked in old photographs. She smiled, but only with her mouth, her eyes impassive, bright blue and cold.

'I've not seen you here before,' she said. 'When did you come?'

'I don't know,' I said.

'Who are you, then?'

I shook my head and held my hands up in a shrug.

'Have you drunk of Lethe?' she said.

'What's Lethe?' I said.

'A river,' she said.

'I drank from a stream earlier today,' I said, and sat down. 'But I don't know its name.'

'That was Lethe,' she said. 'It's why you can't remember.'

'Who are you, anyway?' I said.

'Why do you want to know?' she said, sweeping her hair to one side, a gesture that looked like it went back to when she was young.

'Or maybe you don't know yourself?' I said.

She snorted and sat down where the rock was flat.

'I do,' she said. 'But it's not relevant here.'

'And yet you asked me?'

'I've not seen you before, that's why.'

'I've not seen you before either,' I said.

'True enough,' she said, and smiled. 'But it wasn't so much your name I was wondering about as what you're doing here. And why you lit a fire.'

'I was cold, obviously,' I said.

'The cold will not harm you,' she said. 'You must remember that you are dead. No one dies twice.'

I looked at her. Her face was solemn. No trace of irony.

'What do you mean?' I said.

'Are you a Denier?' she said.

'What are you talking about?'

'Are you denying that you're dead?'

'This is absurd,' I said. 'I'm freezing, I'm hungry, I'm tired. I have a body, and what's more I've got a packet of cigarettes on me. Not many dead people would be able to say that, I don't think.'

'It's all the same to me,' she said. 'No one has ever had a reasonable conversation with a Denier. It can't be done.'

She stood up to go.

'OK,' I said. 'Let's say I'm dead. Doesn't that make you dead, too?'

'Indeed,' she said, and melted away into the darkness.

'Wait!' I called out.

No reply.

I jumped up and went after her. The darkness was so thick I could hardly see a hand in front of me.

'Wait!' I called again, pausing a moment to listen for her footsteps.

But there wasn't a sound.

If I couldn't see anything, then neither presumably could she. Which meant she had to be lingering somewhere very close. Still, I reckoned I'd be better off looking for her when the light returned, so I went back to the fire.

Was I dead?

It didn't make sense.

But if I was alive, where was I? And how did I get here?

Could I have been in some sort of accident and lost my memory? Wandered away into the woods?

Had Son been in the same accident?

I'd have to find the old woman again in the morning, I told myself, and lay down on my side, as near to the fire as I dared, before closing my eyes.

I woke at dawn. It was raining, and while the roof I was sheltered under appeared to be watertight, I was freezing cold and trembling. I sat up, rubbed my arms briskly, and looked out at the miserable wet and misty forest as I tried to hang on to the dream I'd been having. I'd been out on my bike with a friend, he was about twelve, like me. Ahead of us, in the sunlight that came down through the trees, a huge ship appeared. It was an oil tanker, and it was moored up. Two men were playing tennis on the deck, apart from that it was deserted. The ropes that were keeping the ship moored were almost as thick as our bodies.

That was it. But it gave me hope, because now there were three sequences I remembered — the kitchen scene, the girls by the field, the bike ride with my friend — and if they kept coming to me like that, in a few days I'd be able to piece together some kind of a past and perhaps find out who I was.

Also, Son was here. And I recognised the fells on the other side of the plain.

But Son was the key.

I needed to find him and help him.

I started off towards the fringe of the forest. The plan was to follow it all the way along the Heath and hope that from where it ended the way forward would be obvious. It wasn't inconceivable either that things would come back to me as I walked, then maybe I'd have more of an idea as to which way to go.

The rain poured and dripped everywhere. The mist lay so low and was so dense that in some places I couldn't see the tops of the trees.

At the foot of the shallow slope I followed, maybe thirty metres below me, there was a channel I hadn't noticed the day before. Along its bank stood ample spruce trees with grey trunks and a tangle of bare, wispy branches at the bottom, heavier green boughs further up.

I stopped in my tracks.

Was that someone sitting there, in the undergrowth?

I was sure of it.

My eyes glimpsed a pale, flat face, the dark outline of a body.

My heart quickened, and without being aware of what I was doing I realised I'd got my cigarettes out and had lit up a smoke.

The figure wasn't moving.

Maybe they were dead?

The smoke I blew lingered a moment in the air in front of me before dispersing.

I took a drag, so forcefully it made the filter hot.

No one dead ever smoked.

The old woman had been having me on.

I dropped the fag end on the ground and trod on it, then made towards the spruce, slowly and tentatively so as not to frighten whoever was there. But not even when I stopped in front of them, and saw the face as plain as day, did the figure move.

Its eyes were open though, and there was life in them, they shone strangely, as Son's had shone. As if a little flame were burning inside them.

'Hello?' I said softly, and crouched down.

The figure turned its head towards me. It looked at me like it was blind. The mouth hung open. Its gaze seemed not to fix on me. Sparse tufts of hair hung from its scalp, as if someone had pulled its hair out. It was a man, or what was left of a man.

'Hello,' he said, his voice cracked with age.

An icy chill ran through me, and I stood up abruptly and stepped back, glancing around, but there was no one else.

'Who are you?' I said.

'I . . . don't . . . know . . .' he said, reaching his hand out slowly towards me, as if he wanted to touch me, not knowing I was out of arm's reach.

'What is this place?' I said.

He withdrew his hand just as slowly as he'd extended it, and turned his head away from me. I couldn't get a hold on what he actually looked like, his facial features were nigh on impossible to pin down. Only his eyes were clear, shining brightly in their blindness, in the dim light beneath the tree.

'I . . . don't . . . know . . .' he said again.

'Talking to the Undead?' a voice called behind me. 'Then you're stupider than you look.'

It was the old woman, bustling down the slope.

My heart sank at the sight of her.

So I didn't care for her, I reasoned.

I should have gone straight down to the Heath, not stopped here.

She halted a short distance from me.

'They remember nothing. They know nothing. All they do is go about here.'

'I can't remember anything either,' I said.

'But you think. You're a Denier, not an Undead.'

'Didn't you say I was dead yesterday?'

'Indeed, and dead you are. But not an Undead. What did you say to him?'

'I asked him who he was. And what place this is.'

The Undead had turned his face towards us, or to where he heard our voices were coming from. With his mouth hanging open, he looked like he was listening.

'He can hear us, can't he?' I said.

'Indeed. But he understands little, the poor creature.'

She stepped forward, reached into the undergrowth to grip a tuft of his hair, and then pulled.

'Up we get,' she said. 'Come on, up we get!'

The Undead twisted in her grasp, yet rose slowly to his feet. Once he was standing, she shoved him on his way. He stumbled forward before finding his balance and walking away from us into the trees, where he vanished from sight.

She smiled.

'They're harmless,' she said.

'Who are they? Who was he?' I said.

'No idea,' she said, sweeping her hair to one side in the same coquettish manner as before.

At that moment, as she lowered her head and appeared to me in profile, I recognised her.

I'd seen her before. Many times.

But who was she?

Behind her, at the top of the slope, three men came into view. They weren't Undead, but like her. They came to a halt and looked down on us.

She became aware that I was staring at something, and turned.

They came towards us.

I understood from her reaction that they weren't dangerous, but started nevertheless in the direction of the Heath.

'Where are you going?' she said.

'To find Son,' I said.

'Have you a son here?' she said.

I didn't answer. She came up alongside me.

'How can you remember?' she said.

'I saw him yesterday,' I said. 'And now I'm going to find him again. Goodbye.'

She stayed put. I carried on. Not until I came out into the open a few minutes later did I look back.

No one had come after me.

I followed the line of the forest, watching the whole time for any sign of movement out on the Heath that stretched away, vast and empty, into the distance. Only the odd bird could be seen above it, small and dark, soaring high in the grey sky.

It was a relief to be on my own, and a relief to be on my way. I was still cold, and hunger gnawed at my stomach, but something must have happened, because in a strange way it didn't bother me. It didn't seem to have weakened me either, I felt a strength in me as I strode on.

After a while, I stopped and looked back every so often, as if something was forcing me, something I couldn't control. I was catching myself doing it with increasing frequency. I kept telling myself I had to press on, but the next minute I was turning my head again and looking back.

The feeling that something was wrong grew in me, almost with every step. It was like I wasn't supposed to leave the place, it was where I was meant to be, and the certainty of this tore at me. At the same time, the certainty that Son had gone this same way and the urge to find him were quite as strong.

It felt as if two magnets were pulling on me from different directions. Or no, it was as if one magnet was pulling me back, while I myself tried to strive ahead. If that's how it was, I thought, then things could only get easier, because the pull would get weaker and weaker the further from Home I got, until eventually it would release completely.

After a while, the Heath transformed, no longer heather and thorny bushes, but boggy and yellow, and here and there were glinting pools and ponds. When small knolls and more sweeping ridges began to appear, and the ground became grassy, I left the forest fringe and set out across the plain itself. Before long, what seemed to be a cluster of towers appeared in the distance. There were three, and I made for them.

As I came closer, I saw the air was ribboned with smoke, a belt extending from one end of the Heath to the other. It unsettled me, and the urge to return to Home grew so strong it forced me to stop.

In front of me, in the knee-high grass, lay something red.

I went towards it. It was a small pile of clothing, a red shirt on top. T-shirts, underwear, jumpers and trousers. Next to it, almost hidden, lay several pairs of shoes and sandals.

I crouched down and saw a brown leather wallet lying open and face down on the ground. Turning it over to examine it, I found it contained a strip of photo-booth images showing two girls, perhaps fourteen or fifteen years old, and tucked behind it a single snapshot of a boy the same age, seemingly cut from a larger photograph. There were two fifty-krone notes too, some coins and a bus pass.

I stood up again and surveyed the landscape ahead.

The rest of the way to the Towers appeared to be strewn with items of clothing left in the grass, increasingly so the closer I came, along with shoes and glasses, wallets, bags.

It wasn't smoke, I realised, but steam. And it looked to be coming from a river that seemed to dissect the plain.

Approaching the embankment, I realised that the Towers were on the other side of the river. Perhaps thirty metres apart, they formed a triangle. At the foot of each, two broad ramps led up, apparently constructed from timber, and from these ramps the towers themselves reached maybe twenty metres into the air, slender and delicate-looking, made, as far as I could see, out of some kind of wire meshing.

The grass surrounding them had been trampled down over a large area some hundred metres in length and breadth. Heaps of clothing, as tall as a man, lay everywhere.

What place was this?

It seemed to be some kind of assembly point, perhaps for thousands of people.

The towers — could they be churches of some kind? Did they symbolise something?

I lifted my gaze. The sun was visible as a paler, faintly yellow area of light in the grey.

Far above, a great bird circled slowly on a current of air.

I didn't like it, there was something ominous about it, and I felt exposed, the only figure visible as far as the eye could see.

I went up the embankment and down the other side to the river, bent down and cautiously dipped my hand in the water. It was red-hot.

No one could get over here without being scalded.

I looked towards the towers.

Who could have built them?

And what were they for?

My eyes searched the sky for the bird. But the sky was white and empty.

A new image dislodged from the vault of my memory: I was climbing a mast, it was grey and made of metal, the air was cold, the sky was blue, the sun was shining. Patches of snow lay beneath me. I was thirteen, it was spring and I was thirteen. Easter! Long, lazy days. Below stood Gaute with the curly hair and impish smile.

It must have been a radio mast, I thought, looking up towards the top of the tower, which culminated in a long metal pole.

I hadn't recovered that much information in one go since I'd lost my memory.

A sorrow went through me when I thought about it.

He didn't want to know me.

Had I done something to him?

What could it be?

He was Son.

He'd said he had to go back.

Back where?

It could be anywhere.

I returned to Home in the afternoon. It felt good, though I was missing Son. I sat with my back against the rock, looking out into the forest without really seeing anything, and that too felt good. When darkness came, I lit a fire.

It was as if my body absorbed its hunger, like the planks of a wooden boat will swell with moisture to seal their joins.

I dozed by the fire as I had done the previous evening, and again there was a rustle close by.

'Is it you, old woman?' I said.

Without a word, she emerged into the glow from the flames and sat down.

I paid her no attention, only reached backwards and picked up a new log which I placed on the fire.

'Did you find your son?' she said.

I shook my head.

'How far did you go?'

'To the river on the Heath,' I said.

'Did you cross it?'

'No, I didn't.'

'There's a cable ferry there — didn't you see it?'

'No.'

'Not on the Heath, but in the forest.'

I sensed her looking at me.

'What's on the other side?' I said, without returning her gaze.

'The same as here,' she said. 'Forest and water.'

'So why would he want to go there?'

'There's a bridge there.'

'And?'

'He wants to cross the bridge to the other side. It's the only thing he wants.'

'What place is it?' I said.

'The land of the dead.'

'I thought this was the land of the dead?'

She shook her head.

'This is the land of those who are not.'

And then we were silent.

Presently, as if from nowhere, a deep and resonant hum rose above the forest. It passed through the sky like thunder, though it was not thunder, but a persistent tone that reverberated in the landscape around us.

I got to my feet to go down to the Heath, for this was its command, but Old Woman gripped my arm and held me back.

'Don't listen to it,' she said urgently. 'Stay here.'

I pulled free and went out into the darkness. It was as if the hum overrode all else. Inside me there was room for it alone. It was so beautiful, all I wanted was for it to go on. And I wanted to obey it. To become a part of it.

And that was why I went to the Heath, for the hum told me to.

Yet when I came to the stream, the hum stopped.

Its absence brought pain to my chest.

I halted.

All around me I heard a rustling, and whispered voices.

It was the Undead. But not just one or two, they were everywhere, passing among the trees, like people in a dream. Their clothing was dark, their faces and hands white and shimmering in the darkness. And their eyes, their eyes shone.

One of them went past me. It whispered something, though not to me, for it seemed not to notice me at all. It was whispering to itself.

The great hum rose and sounded again.

It filled me up.

Oh, how beautiful it was.

I carried on.

If only I could be like it, or become a part of it, I would never ask for anything ever again.

'Jostein!' a voice called out behind me.

Jostein?

That was me.

I was Jostein.

I spun round.

Old Woman was coming down the slope after me.

'Don't go there, Jostein!' she shouted. 'Come back!'

She stopped in front of me and took my arm.

'Come. We're going back.'

'But it's so beautiful,' I said. 'Can't you hear it?'

She shook her head.

'How do you know my name?' I said. 'I know you, don't I?'

I was Jostein.

It was as if the name opposed the hum, coming between me and it, and it no longer filled me as before.

She tugged on my arm, and I followed her back to Home.

For a long time, the hum filled the landscape around us with its great, plaintive tone. I did not speak, for I was still immersed in it, even though it no longer held me in its thrall. She too remained silent.

Then, as abruptly as it had arisen, the hum ceased.

'I'm your father's mother,' she said.

I looked at her. She stared at the ground, prodding the earth absently with a stick.

'Farmor?' I said, and tears welled in my eyes.

'Do you remember me?'

I shook my head.

'Your father died when you were fifteen. I couldn't bear the grief and succumbed. You were sixteen then. Do you remember now?'

'No,' I said. 'But I recognised you.'

We fell silent.

'Where is Father now?' I said. 'And is Mother alive?'

'Harald is in the land of the dead. Ellen in the land of the living.'

She looked at me.

'Do you know enough now?'

I wept. I remembered nothing.

She passed her bony hand over my cheek.

'What about Son?' I said.

'I don't know,' she said. 'No one gets over the bridge any more, they say. I imagine he's there waiting.'

As soon as day broke, I set out for the bridge. For some hours I followed the line of the forest until I came to the steaming river. I followed it into the forest. It was raining, and the rain was cold, but I froze no longer. She'd said that Son was not reconciled and was therefore confused. He was filled with longing, but knew not for what. Does the hum reconcile? I'd asked her then. Yes, she'd replied. But had you given in to it, you would no longer have been able to help your son.

In front of me, on a sandbank at a bend in the river, was a raft. Above it, two cables were stretched between the banks. I shoved the raft into the water and stepped onto it with caution, gripped one cable and pulled myself slowly to the other side.

Would there be anyone here?

I'd seen no one all day. The landscape had been quite empty.

But there were people here, I knew it.

I looked around.

Nothing but trees and bushes, water and steam, sand and stones.

I stood motionless for a while to see if I might catch any movement in my vicinity.

But no.

I walked as quickly as I could along the river and emerged onto the Heath again. It felt safer there, for I could see so much further.

The towers on the Heath were barely visible in the mist. If I hadn't known they were there, I might not have seen them at all, I thought, and continued towards them, glancing back over my shoulder the whole time into the forest. The thought of turning back and returning to Home occurred now with diminishing frequency, and by the time the Heath petered out, funnelling into a trough-like dale, it had vanished completely. Now I felt the urge only to push on, towards the bridge and Son.

A road of sorts, more of a track than a road, led into the dale. In the softer, muddier parts, I saw hoofprints and human footprints, and also narrow wheel tracks which looked like those that might be left by old-fashioned carts or wagons.

But not a soul did I see.

Why was there no one here?

It struck me that the road might be perilous, that a person would stand out and be visible, and that this might be the reason it was deserted.

But Son had followed it. And Son needed me, even though he didn't know it himself.

I carried on through the dale. After a while the road forked, and I went right. But the path I'd chosen led only to a sheer face of the fell, forcing me to double back and try to find a navigable way over the ridge. It was hard going, but I managed to scramble to the top.

The sea.

It was perhaps a hundred metres beneath me. Extending grey and heavy towards the horizon, dotted with a myriad islands, most covered by forest, shrouded in mist.

And there in the distance was the bridge, its shallow slope rising away from the land, dissolving from sight in the vaporous air.

A shiver ran down my spine.

Not just because I was now close to Son. But also because I knew this place like the back of my hand.

It was where I was from.

I lived here.

The names of the fells were on the tip of my tongue.

But no names were forthcoming.

In all its familiarity, everything remained alien. For it was only the contours I knew.

The place I came from didn't look like *that*, did it?

But then what *did* it look like?

I sat down on a rock and got my cigarettes out. I only had eight left, and there wasn't much chance I'd be able to lay my hands on any more round here. Still, there was no point in saving them, I thought, and lit up.

I closed my eyes and tried to think of what the place had looked like before.

Nothing came to me.

When I opened them again, a boat came gliding round the point below, hugging the coastline. It was big, I counted twelve pairs of oars, all working as one. There was a mast too, but the sail was down.

Two great birds soared above it. They seemed clearly to belong to the boat in some way, accompanying the vessel like an escort towards the cove in between the fells.

On my way down into the dale I caught sight of a figure on the other side, or what I took to be a figure, a glimpse of blue was all I saw. Above, the sky had darkened, and for a moment I thought I might have imagined it. But when I got to the bottom and set out along the track that led in the direction of the cove, I saw several figures, of these there was no doubt, for some appeared only a few metres from where I walked.

None of them looked at me, and none looked at each other.

And then they were everywhere, in the forest and on the fellsides.

But one, an old man with sunken cheeks, a big, fleshy nose, large ears and watery eyes, looked at me as I passed him, and when in the same instant I realised this and turned towards him, he raised his hand and pointed at me. His mouth opened, but not a sound came over his lips. Shortly afterwards, my eyes met the gaze of a woman, she too decrepit with age, her head shaking slightly, but her eyes, her eyes were open wide.

There seemed to be nothing frightening about them. They moved slowly and rather heavily, as if the force of gravity were too great.

Nevertheless, I walked on as quickly as I could, and sought to avoid further contact.

Presently, the dale opened out in front of me, and there, at the end, the bridge rose, almost invisible now in the dusk.

A short distance away, bonfires were burning.

There were people everywhere, on the area below the abutment. Most stood without moving, as if they were waiting for something. Yet their faces revealed no expectation, their eyes and bodies signalled only apathy. The few who were moving around were met with irritation by those who were not. I gave them as wide a berth as possible, not wishing to draw any attention to myself, but the very fact that I was walking, rather than simply standing or shuffling about in little circles, made me conspicuous. Moreover, I was forced to scrutinise them in my search for Son, and they did not care for my attentions at all. In some cases, hatred flared in their eyes, while others showed merely puzzlement. The darkness grew closer and soon they would become but shadows among shadows, I told myself, as I too would become but a shadow to them.

'Son!' I called out softly.

Sighs and groans went up at once.

'Son!' I shouted.

'Shut up!' a voice growled back.

It was hopeless. I was never going to find him like that, certainly not in the dark.

He might even have crossed the bridge already.

Farmor had said it was closed, yet nothing I could see as I approached suggested this was true. There were no barriers, the structure just projected away from the land before rising to melt into the darkness. As far as I could see, though, there wasn't anyone on it, either standing or walking.

Maybe it was closed off further along? Or on the other side?

Around me, people stood so close together that I could no longer pass through them without resorting to force.

'Son!' I shouted again.

'AAAHH!' someone cried.

Many lifted their hands slowly to their heads and pressed them to their ears.

My need to find Son was so compelling now that I didn't care what happened around me. I forged my way forward, forcing a path through the bodies, causing sighs and groans and little cries in my wake, while hands sought helplessly to cling to me as I passed.

And then I was away from the throng and standing before the bridge.

Had he crossed over?

I went towards it. If he hadn't crossed over, he would at least be able to see me clearly up there.

No! I thought, halting in my tracks.

What was I doing?

I couldn't go up there.

I had to stay here.

Sensing relief, I turned and went the short way back. Not into the crowd, but skirting its edge, as if I were an officer inspecting his troops.

'Son!' I called out as I went, studying every face.

Again and again I called.

But from Son came no reply.

When the crowd thinned, I stopped.

What was I supposed to do now?

I looked around. It was then I noticed the boat now moored at the other side of the cove, perhaps a hundred metres away.

Something was happening there.

Three bonfires were burning on the shore, and a number of figures seemed to be wandering back and forth in the flickering light.

Was Son there?

I circumvented the crowd and approached. There were people gathered there too, though none appeared to be interested in what was going on.

The figures moving on the shore were different, their faces of crude and brutal appearance, their heads shaved, as big as the heads of oxen, though with long pigtails dangling down between their shoulder blades from the rear of their scalps. Their movements were singular and lurching, slack and stiff at the same time. Some held in their hands a trough-like wooden vessel from which they occasionally drank. To the left of this scene, in the half-light, stood a number of tents where people went in and out.

It was as if they were all waiting for something.

I ventured closer. At one point, I accidentally bumped into someone, a woman whose eyes flashed with anger and whose mouth opened as if to speak. But not a sound did she emit, and a second later her alarm subsided and she became impassive once more.

To the rear of the bonfires, barely visible behind the flames, a kind of scaffolding had been erected. With a litter of some sort, supported by four long poles. On it, a figure lay.

After a short time, two of the Ox-heads emerged from one of the tents, carrying a human between them. It was a woman. Her arms were stretched above her head and bound together at the wrists, as her legs were bound at the ankles. She was naked. From another tent, a second woman was borne, likewise bound. Not a sound did they make, yet they were alive, I saw their mouths open and close.

They were laid out on a bench.

From between the tents, two horses were led to the open area in front of the boat.

The Ox-head who led them placed his hands on their necks and whispered in their ears as if to calm them.

Yet they were unsettled, snorting and stamping.

Two more Ox-heads stepped forward, each with an axe.

The others gathered around them.

They raised their axes and at once brought them down on the necks of the horses. The beasts fell to their knees, their legs scrambling as if to find foothold, one letting out a cry, only for the axes to fall again, separating the heads from the bodies, which after a few seconds became still and heavy. Steam rose from the blood as it ran out onto the ground.

The bodies of the horses were dragged to the boat and manhandled on board. One of the Ox-heads approached the two women with a sickle in his hand and cut the ropes by which they were bound. Another held one of the trough-like vessels to their mouths in turn, and they drank.

The women were led back into one of the tents, whereafter the Ox-heads went in one after another.

When again they were led out, they were lifted into the air three times, on each occasion uttering words in a language that was unknown to me, their voices wild and shrill.

None of those in whose midst I stood paid the slightest attention to any of this, and if their eyes happened to be directed towards it, they looked on only with indifference.

The women were bound again, and were given more to drink, and as the Ox-heads gathered in a semicircle around them, all now bearing swords and shields, an old woman emerged from one of the tents. The Ox-heads began to beat their swords against their shields, and the old woman now approached the two younger women. Pausing a moment, she then raised a knife high in the air, as if in triumph, before bringing it down and seamlessly slitting their throats as if they were fish. An Ox-head collected the gushing blood in a trough, smearing it over the now lifeless bodies.

Presently, they were placed on the raised litter, on either side of the figure that had lain there during the entire proceedings, and were carried on board the boat.

One of the Ox-heads then stepped up to the boat with a burning torch in his hand. He spoke, though again the language was strange to me.

> Því at hánum fylgja
> tvær ambáttir
> Því at hánum fylgja
> tveir hestar

With that, he boarded the boat and set it alight. When he stepped away from it again, the moorings were cut and the burning vessel launched into the darkness. Gradually, the flames caught, lighting up the gloom as the boat drifted from the shore. I stared at the scene and at the Ox-heads in turn as they continued to go in and out of the tents and to drink from their troughs.

I was dead.

Son was dead.

I was here to help him.

But he didn't want to be helped.

Why did Son not want to be helped?

An explosion came from the boat. The flames hissed and diminished as the vessel slowly keeled over and sank. It was as if the darkness intensified, as if a pitch-black wave rose up and extinguished the light, and I was there, in that darkness. And I was that darkness. And I was no one. And I was nowhere.

Yet suddenly, out of nowhere, I was somewhere.

And I was someone.

I was here.

Below me a room.

I was plummeting towards it.

Someone squeezed my hand, several times in succession.

I opened my eyes.

Light flooded in.

I blinked.

'He's waking up,' a voice said.

Her face, blurred and trembling, as if the air were unstable. Wife? I struggled to form the question.

'Wife?' I said, though not a sound emerged.

'Can you hear me?' a male voice said. 'Squeeze my hand if you can hear me.'

A rough hand, bigger, heavier than the first, took mine.

Everything I knew, everything I was, dislodged and was released from my brain.

'All right, no need to bloody hold hands,' I said. My voice was weak, but it was my voice.

And then I could see again.

A doctor was leaning over me, a nurse hovering behind him.

The room was small, a single. They'd had that much sense, at least.

I coughed and raised myself onto my elbows.

'Was it a heart attack?' I said.

The doctor smiled and straightened up. He actually looked like he was glad to see me awake.

'No,' he said. 'You've been in a coma. We don't know why. All we know is that it wasn't your heart.'

'How long have I been out?' I said.

'Thirteen days to the hour.'

'Where's Turid?' I said.

He glanced at the nurse.

Wimp.

'Where's Turid?' I said again.

'She's . . . with your son,' he said.

'Ole?'

Oh Christ. He'd shot himself, the idiot.

'Is he alive?'

'He's alive, yes. But not yet in a stable condition. It's touch and go, I'm afraid. We can't really say at the moment.'

'Can you fetch her?'

'Of course,' said the nurse, and went out.

'How are you feeling?' said the doctor.

'Fit as a fiddle,' I said. 'I've got to get back to work. This won't do.'

'We'd like to keep you in for another day, to be on the safe side. And to run some tests.'

'I'm a reporter,' I said. 'I'm the one who wrote about the three lads who were murdered out at Svartediket. It was my story. What's happened, do you know? Have they got whoever did it?'

'I don't know,' he said. 'I remember seeing something about it. One of those satanic rock bands, wasn't it?'

'That's right.'

He shook his head.

'So much has happened these last two weeks that I'm not sure anyone cares any more. I wouldn't worry about it. Another day here will do you the world of good.'

'What do you mean?' I said. 'What's happened that could possibly be bigger than that?'

ON DEATH AND THE DEAD

AN ESSAY BY EGIL STRAY

S trangely, I have never been afraid to die. Not because I am particularly brave, but because I have yet to fully comprehend that it will
in fact happen to me.

Intellectually, yes. Intellectually, I fully comprehend that one day
will be my last on this earth.

But I do not *believe* it, not *properly*.

At the end of the day, this is perhaps hardly surprising — existence
is of such unprecedented substance, and that substance, which is my
presence on earth, is experienced not simply as a material reality, is
perceived not merely as the result of chemical/electrical impulses in a
physical mass, but as having quite another nature altogether, and, perhaps most significantly, quite another duration.

Yes, I know that death will one day come to me. (Not from without,
but from within; for whatever form death takes, the result is always the
same: the body is starved of oxygen and breaks down.) It happens to
everyone. Not simultaneously, but one by one, as the pieces in a game
of chess are dismissed from the board. A classmate of mine from school,
Ernest, was taken at an early age, drowning while on holiday in France
when he was twelve years old. Another, Osvald, died in a car crash on
his way to work one morning, his skull crushed when his car ran into
a brick wall. My mother had a congenital heart defect that was discovered only after it was too late: she was spooning ground coffee beans
into the coffee maker one afternoon in winter when suddenly she lost
control of her movements, tossing the coffee into the air before falling
to the floor, and in hospital two days later she died. I saw her fall, it was
I who called the ambulance, and I saw her again an hour after death
had occurred. She was a stranger then, which is to say that what had

been *her* was there no more; only the body which had housed her remained.

These are the dead in my life. While I have been living, hundreds of thousands of others around me have died without me having seen or even thought about it. So yes, I know what awaits me — if not exactly the form in which it will come.

And yet.

Am I really to die?

My body will, yes. The sheath, the casing, the cocoon, yes.

But that inside of me which *is*?

Relating to death is a bit like relating to God, only the other way round: intellectually, I understand that God and the Divine do not exist, but I believe *nevertheless* that they do. In other words: I *believe* that I am not to die, and that God exists, at the same time as I *know* the opposite to be the case.

What does it mean to know?

What does it mean to believe?

I once asked God to deliver me a sign, and a raven came. It looked at me, squawked three times and then flew away.

This was in winter and I was walking in the forest during a storm; there were no other birds there.

It proves nothing, it was a chance occurrence.

I dreamt one night about my brother, he came into the room where I was sleeping, and bent over me. The next day, my father rang and told me my brother had been involved in a motorcycle accident in Vietnam, he had been close to death, but would survive.

I never dream about my brother otherwise, and am not close to him.

It proves nothing, it was a chance occurrence.

During the summer of my thirteenth birthday, I was staying with my maternal grandmother for a week. Her house was situated on high ground above a river. One day I helped her make a bonfire of some cardboard boxes. It started to rain and we went inside. When I came out again, I saw a figure standing by the fire. It was my grandfather. He had been dead for three years.

I missed him and had been thinking about him that day, which was why I saw him; he was conjured by my longing.

To entertain any other explanation is inadmissible. To entertain the notion that the dead live on is inadmissible. To entertain the notion that souls may inhabit our dreams is inadmissible.

The intelligent, reasonable, rational reader will no doubt already have put this essay aside, certain of its direction. Ghosts. The undead. Heaven and hell. Oh, the abomination of such conceptions, how they smack of blindness and dim-witted desperation. We *know* them to be folly. For the boundary between the rational and the irrational is almost as absolute as that between life and death. The rational perspective rejects all that is not rational, it is unable to absorb it, and thus in the rational perspective the irrational quite simply does not exist. Death is the cessation of life, and life is biological/material, so when the material heart ceases to beat and the material brain shuts down, life is over and only the body's biological decomposition in the grave or its destruction in the crematory oven remains.

A rational perspective can entertain *nothing else*, for then it would cease to be rational, which is to say true, and would become the opposite, irrational, which is to say untrue.

But since so many people view the world irrationally even so — believing for instance in God, a power that cannot be observed, measured or weighed, or believing that Jesus Christ rose from the dead, which of course by all known parameters is impossible — all that is irrational has been allocated its own designated sphere, a bit like a children's table at a family celebration, where belief rather than knowledge dictates the truth, which everyone else knows is not *true* at all, and this is the place of religion. It is where the children sit, with their children's food, indulging in their children's matters, while the grown-ups run the world.

Yet once, the opposite held. Then, what now is irrational — belief in God and the resurrection of Jesus Christ, and other miracles besides — was truth, whereas what now is rational was untruth.

By this I seek to say, not that truth is relative, but merely that reality is a complex phenomenon that never appears alone, in isolation, but always in interplay with the person who perceives and experiences it, and this is something that science has never been very good at taking into account. It is never the case that we know what we see, but rather the other way round: we see what we know. This explains, for example, how in the Middle Ages miracles were observed in abundance, whereas today none are observed at all. I recall reading a book containing accounts recorded at the actual time of such miracles and visions. One in particular was arresting: a woman on a donkey appeared in a church, floating in the air, not before a single person, but before a whole congregation, and not just for a brief moment, but for several minutes. People in those days knew that miracles were a part of life, and they saw them, whereas we today know that miracles are not a part of life, and we see them not.

But this of course says nothing about whether miracles occur or do not occur, only that we can never be certain that what we see in fact exists outside our minds, or exists in the way that we see it.

In Jakob von Uexküll's classic study of animal behaviour, an almost Copernican turn in biology, in which animals are viewed as subjects rather than objects, it becomes evident how differently reality appears to different species according to what aspects of the world their senses perceive. All that lies beyond the scope of the sensory apparatus does not exist to it, and therefore accordingly does not exist in the world. Little thought is required to understand that the same must apply to us and the world that is ours. That aspects of reality indeed exist beyond our scope, unseen and unperceived, remains, however, a thesis that cannot be substantiated, to the extent that if something exists beyond our scope, then of course it cannot ever, in any way, be captured.

I shall always remember my mother's final movements on earth, tossing ground coffee beans into the air in the kitchen that day in winter before slowly sinking to her knees and collapsing forward onto the floor. Nor shall I ever forget the compelling mood in the church on the day of Osvald's funeral. He was so young, just eighteen years old, and the grief that was felt, especially by the girls from our class, was so hysterical in its expression as to occasionally mutate into laughter. But although on both occasions death came close to me, and overwhelmingly so, in the first instance in its coldness, in the second in its detestable fullness, the feeling that I *cannot* die was not altered by it in the slightest. I know that my body will die, however hard that may be to believe — but equally I know that the part of me that *is* will never die.

Life after death cannot be proven — but neither can it be disproved. No scientist can with any certainty say that life after death *does not occur*. He may say that much would suggest it does not, and substantiate his claim with reference to the logic of matter and the physical world. But logical parameters will naturally capture only what is logical; the non-logical slips through its mesh.

Does the non-logical exist?

If we stand at the boundary of the logical, is there anything beyond? Anything we might sense or discern?

Let us proceed step by step.

What *is* death?

What *is* the body?

What *are* dreams?

As we know, death is not necessary. Thus Georges Bataille in 1949, and ever since I read that sentence for the first time, it has lived inside me. We are socialised into a world of circumstances we learn to accept: a ball kicked into the air will drop to the ground; water begins to bubble when it reaches a certain temperature; things happen and are consigned to the past, never to happen again; all that lives, dies. These circumstances are insurmountable; impervious to challenge, they are as invisible walls against which we collide, and we learn to live with them: that's life. We shall never know why the ball we kick into the air must drop to the ground, why water has its boiling point, why things that happen cannot happen again, or why death exists, for *such circumstances are determined in a place that is unknown to us, by means that shall forever be beyond our insight.* All we can relate to are the ways in which they manifest themselves to us, and the consequences they entail. We don't know why gravity exists, but we know what it is and how it impacts.

The same is true of death.

The best way of exploring the nature of death, or the way it works, is perhaps to imagine what life would be like if death did not occur. In such circumstances, life would be able to derive energy only from non-organic sources such as water and sunlight, and since there would be no death it would continue to spread until there was no more space left in the oceans in which it arose. Its expansion would then cease or continue on land. Before long, there would be no space on the land either and life would be compelled into the air — one can imagine great piles of primitive life in strange, fan-shaped formations extending stepwise into the skies — but eventually there would be no space left there either. Water and land would then be but a rather sticky, presumably green substance unable to develop in any direction, forever to remain in the same state, with no prospect of further reproduction.

But death does occur, and it clears space and makes room for new life, and besides perpetuating the processes of reproduction in this way, death also allows such life as becomes non-life to be consumed, which naturally further enhances the opportunities for life, and, together with the various climatic and geological circumstances that pertain, this creates a constant imbalance in life, which cannot stagnate, but only be propelled onwards in the manic slow-dance that is evolution.

Death patently makes room for more life, but the reasoning comes to a halt there, for a deeper rationale for its occurrence, other than ensuring that life does not merely pile up and stagnate, *is unavailable to us* — just as a rationale for life occurring at all is unavailable to us. If it were a random occurrence, something that happened simply because the conditions were right, why then does it not continue to occur? Why do new forms of life not continue to arise all around us, in their beginnings, evolving in their own directions, either more or less remote from the tree of life to which we ourselves belong? Is it the case that the prerequisites for life remain open and available only for a short period of time, then close again? Or is it the case that new life is continually arising, only to find no room because of the life that already exists? This may be so, and the theory that life's inception and evolution is haphazard, occurring without plan, which is a truth questioned by no one but a small number of religious fanatics in the USA, is of course by no means implausible. But the idea that death arose *quite as haphazardly* at the same time is something I have more difficulty believing. I can accept *one* random occurrence with consequences of that magnitude, but *two*? And at the same time? That smacks too much of a plan. And the doubt to which that suspicion gives rise gnaws at the very theory of evolution itself, which is unthinkable without death.

The problem with all thinking about death, as I see it, is that it takes death for granted. Death is an absolute circumstance to us, and there-fore we have great difficulty thinking, as Bataille did, that death may be unnecessary. But if that is so, the question then becomes one of what death adds to life, of what it is good for, and what it does. If the answer to that question is that death makes room for more life, the question then becomes one of what *that* might be good for. Certainly, *more* life opens up the possibility of *new* life, and *new* life alters the balance of existing conditions, creating challenges to which they must adapt, which is to say yet more change. Death is what makes evolution pos-sible. And evolution is what made us possible. We are just as unnecessary as death, and however odd it may sound, our presence here is more closely attached to death than to life.

Death created us.

The idea that death created us is made plain too in the biblical myth of the Fall of Man, albeit rather differently so. The narrative begins with the serpent asking the woman if it is true that God has told them not to eat of the fruit of any tree in the garden. The woman says that they may eat of the fruit of all the trees in the garden but for one. Of its fruit God has said: 'Ye shall not eat of it, neither shall ye touch it, lest ye die.' The serpent tells her they will surely not die, for God knows that the day they eat of the fruit their eyes will be opened and they will become as God, knowing good and evil. The woman eats of the fruit, as does the man. The first thing that happens is that they discover themselves to be naked, whereafter they hide themselves from God, who, on finding them and realising what has happened, banishes them from Paradise.

This of course concerns not the introduction of death into the world, but the introduction of awareness as to its existence. There, at the moment in which we are made aware of death, we become human. It is what sets us apart from the animals, and sets us apart from the moment. In God's eyes, this is a punishment. But to the serpent — who is often understood to be the Devil — the awareness of death is some-thing to be coveted, and knowledge a blessing. At least, this is the way he presents it. And strangely, of course, the serpent was right: they did not die, as God had told them they would. On the contrary, they became aware of who they were, and what kind of position they had in life.

This was an awakening, not death. Not many of us would consider knowledge to be an evil. So, did God lie to them? And if so, what kind of a God is that?

It is quite as hard to imagine existence without knowledge of death as it is to imagine existence without death itself. Animals are presumably unknowing of the fact that they must die, for although they may be gripped by the fear of death, as for instance occurs when cattle are taken to the slaughter and smell the blood of their fellows, or when the gazelle, with a pounding heart and drumming hooves, is chased by the leopard, there is little reason to believe that they know their life is about to end, much less what that might entail. Death belongs to the future — perhaps it even *establishes* the future — and can be perceived only as a future occurrence, for when death comes, the conscious mind, and its consciousness of death, ceases to exist. Death is our temporal horizon, unseen by the animals. They, on the other hand, are more closely bound to the moment, and in the Bible's account of the Creation that state is paradisiacal. Knowledge, including the knowledge of death, is considered a fall.

Could that be what God meant when He said they would die if they ate of the fruit from the tree of knowledge? That the paradisiacal would be lost to them? And that such a death was a punishment, the world into which they fell, the world we continue to inhabit, thereby almost to be perceived as hell itself?

Much would suggest it. Before God banishes them from the garden, He says to the woman: 'I will greatly multiply thy sorrow and thy conception; in sorrow thou shalt bring forth children; and thy desire shall be to thy husband, and he shall rule over thee.' And to the man: 'Because thou hast hearkened unto the voice of thy wife, and hast eaten of the tree, of which I commanded thee, saying, Thou shalt not eat of it: cursed is the ground for thy sake; in sorrow shalt thou eat of it all the days of thy life; Thorns also and thistles shall it bring forth to thee; and thou shalt eat the herb of the field; In the sweat of thy face shalt thou eat bread, till thou return unto the ground; for out of it wast thou taken: for dust thou art, and unto dust shalt thou return.'

It is a strange myth, for if the life into which man was thrust, in which we live still, is a punishment, it would seem to be the case that sin, the very reason we were ejected from Paradise, the acquisition of knowledge, at the same time proves to be our salvation. Certainly as far as the material aspect of that punishment is concerned. We were able to shape tools and implements, manufacture ploughs and carts, build houses and towns, thereby at first to loosen, then, at least ostensibly, to release ourselves from the bonds that bound us to the earth. We established a buffer zone between ourselves and the pressures of nature, as Peter Sloterdijk once put it. When it comes to the immaterial aspect, the awareness that we are to die, our acquisition of knowledge has spawned great philosophical and religious systems, of which science is one, which serve as it were to spin a net to cover over death's abyss, so that we see it not, being attentive only to the threads we follow. When death comes and someone we are close to is plunged into its darkness, the net, spun only from thought, comes apart and we despair without hope, racked with pain and grief, until it passes and the abyss is covered over once more.

This is how inauthenticity came into the world. The truth of death, delivered to us by the Fall, is so terrible that we must live as though it did not exist.

Yet God did not merely pronounce our punishment. He made coats of animal skins and clothed us in them, saying then: 'Behold, the man is become as one of us, to know good and evil: and now, lest he put forth his hand, and take also of the tree of life, and eat, and live forever.'

With that, he drove man from Paradise to till the ground from whence He was taken. And east of the garden of Eden He placed Cherubim, and a flaming sword that turned this way and that, to keep the way to the tree of life.

Was it to protect us that the way to eternal life was guarded thus? Or was eternal life a blessing our punishment was meant to deny us?

And why coats of animal skins? It seems almost like an ironic reminder of our origins, as animals with unconcerned animal lives, origins now long since departed. Inauthenticity again.

The myth of the Creation is ancient, and the figures that appear in it, including God, relate to a quite different reality from the one we inhabit today. But the yearning to live as one with nature, to be attached to it, rather than elevated above it, or removed from it, as the Paradise myth expresses to us, is still alive, and in rich measure. Søren Kierkegaard, that singular and inconceivably original Danish writer, sought God and the Divine in the moment, which to him was the very gateway into the kingdom of God. In one of his sermons, he takes as his point of departure a discourse given by Jesus concerning the birds of heaven and the lilies of the field, holding up their existence, so completely and so fully obtaining in the moment, as an ideal. Certainly, Kierkegaard's treatise is not without irony, yet it seems quite as clear to the reader that he is indeed in search of paradise, considering that it may be found only in the event that we relinquish awareness of the self and all that belongs to it — a matter that requires insight into both past and future in order to be sustained — and give ourselves blindly up to the moment. Our every worry, our every trouble, our every anxiety will then fall away — *what happens to the bird does not concern it*, he wrote. Our burdens are given up to God. Such innocence, which is the innocence still of the animals and the smallest children, was torn from us by the awareness of death, which made us and our godless world.

The biblical Creation narrative is a myth, but what it tells of happened in the real world too, for man did indeed appear in the animal, and although it happened unfathomably slowly, it nonetheless happened: we were animals, we inhabited a paradise, and we became humans who stepped from that paradise as we beheld the world and saw our place in it. The myth of the Creation, written down some three thousand years ago, though it undoubtedly existed much, much earlier than that in oral form, contains an insight into this, that we derive from the animals, or at least in some way must have lived as them, and that the revelation of death was a fall from that state, a fall that made us what we are now. Thus, the advances made by natural science in the mid-nineteenth century, with Darwin at the forefront, did not abandon the Bible, but picked it up anew. Tangible biological evidence was unearthed to substantiate what man had suspected since the dawn of time. We know little more about it today. We know approximately when it occurred — around three hundred thousand years ago — and we know that their numbers must have been small, perhaps only a few hundred.

Oh, the grey zone when a new species appears on earth; the changes take place so gradually as to make it impossible to draw a clear dividing line between what it has emerged from and what it has become. And, we now know, a myriad of other, similar creatures have existed at the same time, they too difficult to bring into focus. Nonetheless, the first humans were a local occurrence, if not two individuals, as in the Creation myth, then certainly no more than a small number. They could have known each other, all of them.

What did the world look like to them? Was it alien? Did they feel different, set apart from the life that surrounded them?

The German philosopher Hans Jonas believed that to the first humans *life* was the given, the natural default, while *death* was the mystery. To them *everything* was living — the wind, the water, the forest, the mountain — and the dead had accordingly also to be living, only in another way, or in another place. To us the opposite holds, Jonas wrote, for now death is the given, and is everywhere around us, whereas life is the mystery. Death, that is, in the sense of the lifeless, the dead matter, the stones, the sand, the water, the air, the planets, the stars, the emptiness of space. And in the same way as the first humans considered the dead to be alive in another way, we consider the living to be dead in another way: the body is but body, matter, the heart a mechanical apparatus, the brain electrochemistry, and death is a switch by which life is shut down.

The first humans came to Northern Europe some forty thousand years ago. While this may appear to be a huge span of time in view of the few decades over which our own lives extend, the span in culture is, if not negligible, then surely at least no greater than to allow us to understand each other. I once saw some of the objects they produced, and they were no more bewildering, in fact much less so, than many a work of contemporary art.

They spoke to me.

I happened upon them quite by chance, in a museum in Tübingen, where I had gone to see the tower where Hölderlin had lived the last forty years of his life, the time after he had gone mad, when he not only attributed his poems to 'Scardanelli' or some other made-up name, but also post-dated some of them far into the future. I was staying at a small and very old hotel at the top of a steep hill, just beside the wall behind which the castle rises. The hotel went back, I think, to the sixteenth century, as many other buildings in that modest town. On the morning of the day when I was due to return home, I had an hour or two to pass before my train departed and wandered for the sake of diversion into the castle grounds. It transpired that there was a small museum there, where a number of artefacts from that time were on display, all recovered from a cave not far away. The most striking of these was the Lion-man, a figurine with the face of a lion and the body of a man, carved from the ivory of a mammoth. It was discovered a week before the outbreak of World War II. In the same cave were furthermore found a voluptuously shaped female figure, assumed to be a fertility symbol or goddess, a small, meticulously carved horse, a web-footed bird, and a number of whistles.

They spoke to me, I wrote above — but of what?

Attachment.

The Lion-man ties the animal to the human, the web-footed bird connects the three elements of water, earth and air, while man by depicting them ties himself to them. And the whistles? What else would they be for but to bring together the humans?

No animal makes sculptures or musical instruments. Why did the first humans do so? What was it that prompted them after they had left the paradise of the animals?

The first thing that happened to Adam and Eve when they ate from the tree of knowledge was they became aware of each other. All animals think, of course, but what was new about humans was that they could think about thinking. It was as if a mirror had been held up before their thoughts. It is that mirror that makes awareness possible. Indeed, it is awareness itself. Prior to the mirror, attachment was not a thing, the animal was there and was what it was, bound to the context of its existence, doing whatever it did on that basis. The same applied to the amoeba as to the antelope. But the awareness of being, and of what one is, is meaningful only in relation to the other; on its own it is meaningless. The mirror, which is to say our human awareness, *is* the other. The fact is that we cannot think human thoughts alone, for to think human thoughts is merely a potential we possess, which cannot be realised anywhere else but within a culture. We think in our culture, and we think with our culture. That awareness brought us closer together, at the same time as it removed us from nature.

Attachment as a phenomenon can only arise when it's not a given, and this occurs when thoughts are not only thought but also mirrored. Naturally, basic attachment existed before this too — a baby elephant having wandered away from its mother will look for something that was there before, which it hadn't thought about then, but which now will be conspicuous in the form of longing: attachment. The apes already possessed considerable social skills long before man came along, establishing alliances and forging ties to one another, as they still do. But attachment to other animals? Attachment to the elements? Attachment to the world in itself? Such attachment came only with humans, because to them, as the first, due to the mirror, it was no longer a given.

This is what the Lion-man, the fertility goddess, the horse, the web-footed bird and the whistles said to me there in the castle museum at Tübingen. Not immediately, not as I stood there looking at them in their glass cases, for in those moments I was simply filled with a strong sense of excitement: something immeasurably distant and unclear had shifted close to me.

Emerging onto the castle forecourt, I decided to put off my return home for a day or two and see if I could make a trip to the cave where the discoveries had been made, the place those people had inhabited forty thousand years before.

This was late autumn, in the middle of a cold spell, the low November sun barely scraping the tops of the buildings, and in the tiny streets the cobblestones were ice-covered and consigned to shadow. I sat down at a table outside a cafe in the lower town, only a short distance from the church, wrapping a blanket around my legs to drink a cup of piping hot cocoa and have a smoke while I observed the people who passed through the narrow street, my inner being still quivering with excitement.

I had gone there because of Hölderlin, who had first studied theology at Tübingen along with Hegel and Schelling — a plaque on the wall of the pub just across from where I was seated said that Hegel used to drink there — and was later taken in by a carpenter after he went mad in middle age, lodging then for those forty years in the tower by the river. Much would indicate that he in fact simulated madness so as to escape life and other people, at least this is what I had held for some time, and seeing the tower and it surroundings to a certain extent only strengthened my view. Everything he needed was there. Behind him, the little town with its fond memories of his student days; in front of him the river — and Hölderlin loved rivers — the plains with their great deciduous trees beyond, and then the Swabian Alps rising up at the horizon. Hölderlin had written the most beautiful poems of all time, and was not the past in them, I had pondered as I stood in the tower looking out of the same window as he had done, quite as distant, quite as magnificent and impenetrable as the mountains I saw in the distance? With all their gods and heroes of mythology?

But the Greek past stretched no more than three thousand years back at most, I thought now. The objects I had seen at the museum were thirty-seven thousand years older. And they made the remote, hazy-blue mountain range of history appear vividly before me, as if a curtain had been lifted on a stage.

There they were!

I went inside and paid for my cocoa, then proceeded down the hill along one of the narrow side streets until I found a bookshop I had noticed the evening before. There I purchased a book of Hölderlin's poetry which I tucked into my shoulder bag before going back up to the hotel again to see if I could stay another night in my room. Regrettably, I could not, the receptionist informed me, for a chocolate festival was taking place and all the rooms had been booked for some time.

Eventually, I managed to find another, at a hotel across the river, in a more modern and shabbier part of town, among multi-storey parking facilities, shopping centres, businesses, supermarkets. I had a bath, for I was freezing cold, after which I lay down on the bed and began to read.

How wrong I had been.

There was no past in the poems, quite the contrary, everything was so very much the present, which the past suffused with its nearness, lending it fullness.

Are not many of the living known to you?
Does not your foot stride upon what is true, as upon carpets?
Therefore, my genius, only step
Naked into life, and have no care!

With these words about stepping boldly into the thick of life swirling in my mind, I fell asleep there in that hotel bed. The next morning, I hired a car and drove out across the plain in the direction of the forest, a hoary mist suspended above the fields. The sun was as yet but a suggestion, a faintly brighter glow in a grey-white sky. I pulled up in a car park of stamped earth covered in frost, and followed the path. The forest was different from what I was used to, less substantial in a way, more open. The cave was at the bottom of the path, in a small clearing, the entrance was low and would have been hard to find had it not been fenced off. But there was no one around, and the fence was easily surmounted, and a few moments later I lowered my head and went inside. After only a few steps it opened up into what can only be described as a hall.

Here, then, they had sat.

A fire would surely have burned round the clock in winter, certainly if it had been as cold as it was now. But perhaps it had not?

The entire continent lay empty around them, inhabited by barely a human soul. Germany, Poland, Russia, Scandinavia, nothing but forest and animals. Rivers and lakes. Plains and mountains.

They were here, and elsewhere were but a few scattered groups of their kind.

What was it like?

Did they tell stories about the past, of hardships and heroic deeds?

Yes, surely they did. Human beings cannot be envisaged without continuity, without a history.

And they knew death. They killed animals, and were themselves, from time to time, killed by animals.

How did they perceive it?

If everything was living and possessed a soul, even the water and the forest, the mountain and the sky, the dead too would be living, albeit in another place.

Life was everywhere. It was boundless. And presumably there were no boundaries within it either.

Perhaps the Lion-man was not about attachment, a connection they made, but was an expression of what life was actually *like* to them? That the lion and the man were the same? That the humans here had yet to distinguish between themselves and the animals?

The dead souls could be everywhere, including in the animals.

I put my hand against the ice-cold wall, wanting to touch what they had touched.

The cave was still, but its stillness was different from the stillness of the forest outside, which was open. The stillness of the cave was enclosed, kept in place.

They had sat as if in the womb, I thought. Protected from the external world into which now and then they would venture out on their small expeditions.

Children would have been born here, the space filled with groans and cries and howls, and then the sudden quiet when the child was expelled, a moment of silence before it gulped its first breath and began to wail. That joyous sound, of new life beginning. And here they would have died too, one after another, generation after generation. The expiration, the abruptly lifeless eyes, the body becoming motionless. The soul departing it.

Where did the soul come from that revealed itself when the child opened its eyes for the first time and looked at the one who lifted it up, its gaze mild and serene and ancient, not new and frightened and wild, as one might expect of a soul that is but a few minutes old? And where did it go when it no longer revealed itself in those same eyes?

The idea of the dead living on has accompanied man throughout human history; from the oldest times to the present day, it has existed in every culture, every religion known to us. None of us can know what conceptions were held by the first humans, but the artefacts they left behind give reason to believe they performed rituals we now call shamanistic and which exist to this day in cultures around the globe. In his seminal book on the phenomenon, the historian of religion Mircea Eliade makes clear that shamanistic practice has essentially been the same wherever it has been recorded, whether in the indigenous peoples of North America, the Amazon region or Australia, or in the cultures of the many different ethnic groups of Northern Asia. This would suggest that the phenomenon is ancient indeed, and if the figures of the Lion-man or the web-footed bird seem so seamlessly to accord with shamanistic practice, it becomes difficult to imagine that such practice did not take place even then. The shaman was a nominated or self-nominated figure apprenticed by a predecessor, ensuring thereby that the requisite skills were handed down through the generations, and besides functioning as a healer, a medicine man or woman, it was the shaman who bound together what were perceived as the various stages of life, he or she traversing the axis mundi to visit the underworld or the heavens, either while asleep or in a trance, usually under the influence of hallucinogenic substances.

The initiation of the shaman takes place almost invariably in the underworld, Eliade states, where dead shamans dismember the candidate's body, removing and replacing every bone, every organ; occasionally, this takes place with the head of the candidate looking on from a stake on which it has been placed. Roberto Calasso points to the likeness between such treatment of the shaman's body and that accorded to killed animals. The shaman thus connects with them too, not merely with the dead and the spirits.

Now, most people would be inclined to believe that the shaman's 'travelling' to other realities is an inward occurrence, in dreams or feverish fantasies, and that whatever the shaman claims to experience takes place nowhere but in his or her mind. So: no underworld, no heaven, no dead souls, only artificially provoked hallucinations.

This, however, presupposes not only a clear and conspicuous division between internal and external, but also that everything in a human being, which *is* the human being, exists internally. This internal world may — indeed will — be imbued with impressions, images, thoughts and conceptions hailing from its interface with the world without, and the individual may themselves infuse the external world with elements from within, though only by severing themselves from them, without leaving the internal world themselves.

I am thinking, as I write these words, about a great oak tree that stands in the woods behind the house in which I sit. A remarkable number of birds inhabit it, and I commit this thought to the typewriter. The thought has now left my inner being and become manifest on the sheet of paper in front of me, though I myself remain here: no part of me any longer exists in it. I am, and will always be, enclosed within my mind and body. When I dream, it *feels* as if I am removed to other places, but this is not the case, for I lie in my bed and the dream is merely a series of random images released by my brain without my conscious self — the mirror referred to above — being present to tell me that what I am seeing is not reality, but images dislodged from the bark of my mind.

But what if the human entity is not stable? What if there is no clear and conspicuous division between what is inside a person and what is outside? What if the two domains exist in constant flux? What if the bear is like us, and the wolf, the fox, the lynx, the owl? What if the soul can pass in and out of the body, in dreams, in ecstasies, in death? *Hamgjenga, hamhleypa, hamrammr* are the Old Norse words for shape-shifters capable of taking on animal form, figures such as Kveldulf or Odin, who, while their bodies stayed put, flew as a bird or swam as a fish in other places.

To us, for whom 'human' is such a definitive category and the boundaries of each individual are set so absolutely by the body, the container as it were of our personal existence, such a fluid conception and experience of reality can only be rejected. Any phenomenon that transcends the division between what is within a person and what is without — the *vardøger* of Scandinavian folklore, for instance, spirits delivering the sound or sight of a person before he or she actually arrives, or the glimpse we might have of a ghost, something that has left this life, but which yet remains in our world — is referred to under the heading of superstition. We see or hear something that is not found other than in the mind, and which, as the shaman, we confuse with some real phenomenon in the outside world.

That human beings have *always* seen ghosts, even in cultures and religions that reject such notions, does not of course mean that ghosts exist, only that belief in them exists, at least in folklore, and that such belief would seem to be unshakeable.

If we see what we know, and if what we know colours or even

determines what exists to us, then knowledge stands in our way, and, as the Fall narrative tells us, knowledge came into the world simultaneously with the awareness of death. If, further, knowledge must be dismissed in order for us to see death, then we must at the same time dismiss awareness of death, in which instance death is eliminated and there is no more to see.

This paradox is what occurs in the myth of Orpheus when he descends into the underworld to bring back Eurydice, and Hades tells him he may take her on one condition: that he should not look at her before coming out into the light of the overworld again. She is there only when he does not see her. If he sees her, she is not there.

In ancient Greece, death and sleep were related phenomena, in the mythology they were siblings, and in the *Iliad* even twins — Thanatos and Hypnos, charged with carrying the slain into the realm of the dead. Rationally, they are of course separated: sleep is the state into which we drift and drift out of again, whereas death is absolute. The question the Greek myths raise is whether the boundary between death and life too is fluid, a shifting state as between sleep and wakefulness, or whether it is, as we take it to be, absolute, a matter of either/or? Put differently: is the boundary between life and death a product of our limited senses, or is it real?

Another definitive category in our lives that raises the same question is time. Are the boundaries of *time* absolute? We live in the moment, and what we call the past and the future are found nowhere but in our minds, in the form of memories on the one hand and expectations on the other. The moment dissolves and is renewed with seeming constancy; we may sit quietly in a room and yet still be moving in time, in the sense that the moment at once is lost and replaced by another. Following Einstein, we know that time is relative, that it moves faster or slower according to where we are, and in what state, and that there is no such thing as simultaneity.

A British soldier, J. W. Dunne, who was also an outstanding aeronautical engineer, published in 1927 a book entitled *An Experiment with Time*, in which he proposed a theory to the effect that the past, the present and the future exist in parallel, but that limitations in our sensory apparatus and consciousness mean that we can exist only in the present. Linear time is an illusion. The source of Dunne's interest in such matters was his realisation, as a young man at the end of the nineteenth century, that he possessed precognitive abilities. On numerous occasions he dreamt things that later occurred. Dreams that took place in the future possessed the same characteristics as those that took place in the past, what happened in them was quite as distorted, and they were at once as clear as they were mysterious. Dunne's theory was that our dreaming consciousness was not bound to the moment in the same way as our wakeful consciousness, which filtered time as linear progression, but instead was open towards actual time. His book and the theory it contained created a stir in its day, and even the normally sober-minded Vladimir Nabokov repeated its experiment, writing down his dreams and comparing them to subsequent events.

Dreams belong to the sphere of the irrational, and any claim that *they* are what give us access to reality is of course inadmissible to the rational mind.

Oddly, though, our conception of time has also been challenged on the rational side of the fence; the further science has penetrated into its mysteries, the less apparent its divisions have become, a physicist such as Carlo Rovelli even ending up in the same place as Dunne — albeit on the basis of wildly different premises — positing that time does not exist and that we experience it only by virtue of constraints on our sensory apparatus.

Time and death are of course not the same. But they are related phenomena — the moment that seamlessly dissolves and is renewed resembles to no small degree the life that expires and at the same time goes on, and time passes quite as irretrievably as life comes to an end: the boundaries are in both cases absolute. In his belief that time was nullified in dreams, Dunne was merely repeating what Aristotle had written in the lost work of his youth, *On Philosophy*, that 'when the soul gets by itself in sleep, it then assumes its nature and foresees and foretells the future'. But where Dunne stopped at time, Aristotle continued towards death: 'The soul is also in such a condition when it is severed from the body at death.'

Aristotle is saying three things here: sleep nullifies time, sleep and death are related states, and the soul lives on after the body is dead.

But how? And where? For if the dead live on, if only as unembodied souls, they must exist somewhere?

In a society where the human is as yet unestablished and no boundaries exist to enclose the soul, death will accordingly be but provisionally defined, its nature too, alongside life and all its metamorphoses, fleeting and changeable. In the same way, when that which is human becomes established — and this happens presumably when humans become sedentary, settle into communities and develop written languages — death, and the dead too, become quite as fixed. All the great archaic civilisations, such as the Babylonian or the Egyptian, had richly developed conceptions as to the realm of the dead, its nature and geography.

The richest of these may undoubtedly be found in the ancient Egyptian culture, whose people thought more about death and exhibited greater solicitude for the dead than perhaps any other culture before or since, and this was so because to them the difference between the living and the dead was a matter of degree. Death did not entail the end of existence, but merely heralded another phase of life. An epitaph from the Fifth Dynasty contains the following phrase:

ba ár pet sat ár ta

where *ba* means soul, *pet* heaven, *sat* body, *ta* earth, thus: *soul to heaven, body to earth*. Straightforward enough, on the face of it, yet the relation between soul and body was infinitely complex in the Egyptian culture, and in ways quite mystifying to us, whose understanding of man is so grounded in the realms of biopsychology. Indeed, it may seem as if they were dealing with a completely different creature altogether. The physical body, referred to as *khat*, could attain new states subsequent to death, providing it underwent mummification so as to halt the processes of decomposition, at which stage it took on a physical/spiritual nature and was referred to as *sahu*. This was not the same as the soul, for the soul was termed *ba*, and *sahu* could communicate with *ba*. Both *sahu* and *ba* could ascend to heaven after death. Moreover, the physical/spiritual body and the soul were supplemented in each individual by a kind of abstract personality which existed freely and independently, able to move at will from place to place, removing itself from the body and rejoining it again

as it pleased. This personality — which seems to have been perceived as
a kind of doppelgänger — was referred to as *ka*, again distinct from the
soul itself, *ba*. *Ba* was non-physical, spiritual, its hieroglyph a stork. In
addition came an individual's shadow, *khaibit*, likewise independent,
though always in the vicinity of the soul. And then there was *khu*, which
was a person's spirit, *sekhem*, translatable as a person's form or power,
and finally *ren*, a person's name, which lived also in heaven.

This, then, was what constituted a human in ancient Egypt, a com-
posite of independent parts: a physical body, a spiritual body, a heart,
a doppelgänger, a soul, a shadow, a spirit, a form, a name.

Apart from the body, all these components lived on after death. The
living, the dead and the gods were closely connected, and the land of
the dead was to be found in the Eastern firmament, though in other
epochs (and we must remember that the culture stretched across several thousand years) the dead, like the sun, descended in the west, the
land of the dead being referred to accordingly as 'the West', the dead as
'Westerners'.

The ancient Egyptians did not fear death, but their souls were not
necessarily immortal, for in the land of the dead, where they lived on,
there existed something called 'the other death', which occurred when
a person died in that place, and *this* was indeed a death to be feared:
when it struck, existence was definitively brought to an end.

Although we have access to a large number of extant texts from the
Egyptian high culture, as well as many artefacts and construction
works, there remains something very alien about what they express,
something so remote that one can barely relate to it other than intellectually, which is to say in ways that are non-intimate, abstract,
non-emotional — it is as if their very dimensions are different from
ours, that what they express is so great and at the same time so very far
away from us as to appear almost un-human. Yet naturally they were
humans — naturally they fell in love, naturally they hugged their children, naturally they spat out the milk if it had soured, naturally they
enjoyed the hours when the sun had gone down after a hot day and
shadows filled the streets around them. A shout, a smile, a warm twin-
kle of an eye: someone they know, and they stop and chat.

But no such things are represented in the texts they left behind, which contain only the sun and the gods, and a mechanics of the afterlife so detailed it brings to mind an instruction manual for some strange and intricate machine no longer to be found. What it all *means* remains unclear, at least to me, as too does the bearing it all had on those ancient lives.

Against this vague and cloudy background we have the first extant works of literature of the ancient Greeks, from around the eighth century BC — the *Iliad*, the *Odyssey*, the *Theogony*, the *Works and Days* — a veritable revelation of human life. They come as if sailing out of the darkness, not unlike the way the first humans stepped from the darkness of the animals some hundreds of thousands of years earlier, we can imagine, though the darkness from which these Greek figures emerge so clearly belonged to culture, not to nature.

They came with emotion. The *Iliad* begins with the anger of Achilles and continues with an argument between Achilles and Agamemnon. They are heroes, sons of gods or kings, and yet they allow themselves to be offended, they sulk and are incendiary and domineering. The gamut of their emotions is run in the shadow of death — not an Egyptian sun-death, which was merely an extension in another place of life itself, but physical death, the death of slaughter in battle, the death of plagues. The *Iliad* is all about bodies and the emotions that stream through them, and it ends where it begins, with the anger of Achilles. Hector, the great Trojan warrior, kills Achilles' friend Patroclus, and in an act of vengeance Achilles kills Hector, though the deed is not enough for him: beside himself with grief and rage he drags Hector's body behind his chariot, three times around Patroclus' grave, and when he returns to his tent and lies down to sleep, he leaves the body in a heap on the ground. This he does every day for twelve days. The city to which Achilles' soldiers have laid seige, Troy, resounds with wailing and lamentation at the loss of Hector. Hector's father, King Priam, writhes with despair, we learn, filthy and unkempt. The impression we have is that the desecration of Hector's body is perhaps even more terrible than his death itself. In a magnificent closing scene, the ageing king, aided by the gods, sets out to the Achaean ships to retrieve the body of his son. Both Achilles and Priam weep, and Priam carries Hector's body back to Troy. Having mourned Hector for nine days under the agreement of a truce,

Priam cremates the body on the tenth day, and the fire is put out with wine. Hector's bones are gathered up and Priam places them in a golden chest which is committed to the ground and covered over with a barrow of stones, before a funeral feast is held in Hector's honour, and the epic poem thus concluded.

It is easy to think that with the Greeks everything was suddenly brought close to us, the Divine and the human, life and death, but this is so only because it was they who laid the foundation of the reality in which we live today. If the first humans left the animals gradually, turning their backs on them, then the Greeks established a space for the new human experience. Sciences and societal systems were founded, the physical world explored, and what lay between people was mapped. We can still identify with Achilles and with Priam; we can still follow the adventures of Odysseus and read our own times into the episodes involving Cyclopes or Sirens; we can peer into the depths of our own minds by viewing the Greek tragedies, which to this day continue to be staged by theatres across the globe, and if we wish to consider the nature of the world and our own circumstances in it, we begin with Plato or Aristotle, or perhaps even earlier, with the pre-Socratic philosophers. Even Christianity stems from the ancient Greek world, the old monotheistic Jewish religion first melding together with the extremely radical sect that had been established by Jesus, the resulting amalgamation subsequently being exploded into a system, first by neo-Platonism, then neo-Aristotelianism, to which large swathes of the world submitted.

But this Greek space with which we are so familiar has another side to it, one that has remained as if in shadow, closely connected with that age, though seen as irrelevant to our own, no longer referenced, barely mentioned at all other than as a curiosity, which is the relation between the classical world and death. To the ancient Greeks, life after death was not just an abstract fact, it was also a part of their physical reality. The literature of ancient Greece is full of encounters between the living and the dead, not only in the epic works, the poems and the dramas, but also in the histories, biographies and accounts of journeys. Common to all these instances is that the dead are awoken or summoned, normally at the grave to which the body was committed.

The most usual way of making contact with the dead was to offer something to the deceased at the site of his or her grave: honey, for instance, or wine, oil, milk or blood (in the latter case there was a name for it, *haimakouria*, or the moistening by blood). On a grave discovered at Mycenae there was an altar through which ran a duct, allowing blood to be poured directly into the mouth of the corpse. After the offering, it was customary to lie down to sleep on the grave, and the dead would then appear in dreams. The Greeks consulted the dead because they could see into the future, presumably on account of their existing beyond time.

Many accounts exist of the dead being unable to find peace for not having received a proper funeral — this occurs in particular after military battles such as the one that took place at Troy, where slain warriors were seen in the night on the plains outside the city, in the full armour of war, such sightings occurring as late as in the second century after the birth of Christ, according to Philostratus. By then, Homer's epic poem of that war, the *Iliad*, and his *Odyssey*, about the returning home of one of the Greek warriors, were already a thousand years old.

At the grave and on the battlefield, the dead came to meet the living. But the literature of the classical age is full also of descriptions of the reverse phenomenon, termed *catabasis*, in which the living descend into the realm of the dead. Such accounts belong to the myths, an example being the eleventh book of the *Odyssey* in which Odysseus travels to the land of the dead to consult Tiresias. They sail far to the south, to a land on the other side of the sea, barren and sunless, the sky there forever concealed by cloud and fog. On the shore, Odysseus digs a small trench in the ground, pouring into it first honey, then wine and water, and sprinkling white barley meal over the whole, before slaughtering a black sheep and letting the blood run down into the trench. At once, the dead come trooping up, wishing to drink of the blood. He holds them at bay, for the blood is for Tiresias. They pay him no heed, barely seeing him, their interest being only in the blood, and they are quite encapsulated in themselves. They are clad in the clothing they wore when they died. Odysseus sees teenagers, girls and boys, women who have perished in labour, warriors slain in battle. He sees also his mother, Anticlea, and realises she has died while he has been away. She does not recognise him. Only when the dead drink of the blood are they able to see him and talk to him. Tiresias does so, and Anticlea does so, and a number of women, daughters or wives of famous warriors, and eventually Agamemnon and Achilles.

In Hesiod, who was writing at the same time as Homer penned his *Odyssey*, the land of the dead is underground and is called Tartarus. He writes thus:

> *For a brazen anvil falling down from heaven nine nights and days would reach the earth upon the tenth; and again, a brazen anvil falling from earth nine nights and days would reach Tartarus upon the tenth.*

Tartarus is of course not an actual but a mythological place: down there, in a dungeon-like abyss in the underworld, behind an enormous wall of bronze, the first gods, the primordial Chaos deities, are held captive. There also, Night and Day cross each other's paths — when one goes in, the other goes out, and never are they home at the same time, Hesiod writes — and the children of Night, who are Sleep and Death, live there too.

The *Odyssey*, naturally, does not describe an actual place either, but the ritual Odysseus performs is realistic, it was how the dead were summoned, and the obscurity with which the journey to Hades is described — as if they sail into an eternal night — is supplanted by clarity when considered from a different angle: the encounter between the dead and the living takes place in a borderland, neither here nor there, in a kind of non-place, at the very periphery of existence.

But these mythological descents into the land of the dead could in fact be traced back to existing places in the actual geography of reality. Orpheus, depicted in Greek tradition as a factual historical figure, was said to have descended into the land of the dead through a cave close to what was then Taenarum, now Cape Matapan, the southernmost tip of mainland Greece. Anyone so inclined can go there today and see the cave for themselves. I have done so, though without feeling able to connect the glittering sea and the crystal-clear waters of the cave, shimmering now blue, now green beneath the little boat in which we tourists were sailed into the grotto, with the darkness and eternal night I associate with the land of the dead.

There are many such places that were connected with the underworld, usually caves and other subterranean areas, some of which even emitted poisonous vapours, though four in particular were central, these being, besides Cape Matapan, the Acheron in Thesprotia, Lake Avernus in Campania and Heraclea Pontica on the southern shore of the Black Sea. These were real places, not mythological, often with incumbent oracles, and the dead would be summoned there too. Since the caves did not in fact open out to the underworld, there is no reason to think that the Greeks believed descent into the land of the dead to be a physical journey: the cave *was* the land of the dead. The dead were also invoked in crypt-like chambers where the oracles went into states of trance.

The question to which all this leads concerns not so much where the dead existed, where Hades and Tartarus were actually sited and what they looked like, nor how the dead souls could appear in the bodily forms from which they hailed, at the moment of death, at the same time as their physical bodies in fact lay on the battlefield or in the grave. No, the question is why *we*, who have adopted so much of ancient Greece, and who continue to look towards it, have ceased to believe in life after death.

From where we stand, more than two thousand years on, it would seem that the world of the Greeks, illuminated by all its Apollonian sun, contained a remnant of something very ancient of which it never quite managed to divest itself. The Greeks constructed a space for rational thought, but were unable to rationalise death, which remained as ancient and mysterious as the forest, a place of unceasing metamorphosis, where the living became dead and the dead became living, animals became men and men became animals. Pan was the figure of this, the god with the human torso and the legs and horns of a goat, the man-animal, wild and unpredictable, but the mythology teems with other half-human, half-animal creatures, among them the Centaurs with their equine bodies and human heads, Medusa with her snake hair, the winged Erinyes, the Minotaur with the head of a bull and the body of a man, and above them all was Dionysus, the god of trangression. Homer referred to Dionysus as mad, and Walter Otto, who called him the god of 'ecstasy and terror', believed madness was Dionysus' very nature, while Nietzsche described him as follows: 'Dionysus is the frenzy which circles round wherever there is conception and birth and which in its wildness is always ready to thrust forward into destruction and death. It is life.'

In one of the Dionysian rituals, reminiscent of cult orgies in which wine would be poured from the heads of animals and all boundaries were upheaved, the maenads according to tradition set about Orpheus, tearing him apart, limb from limb, as if he were an animal, his head then being tossed into the river. Yet the head lived on, carried to the sea as it sang, to be washed ashore on an island where it was found and buried, though remained articulate, for as Philostratus writes, the head 'took up residence in a cleft in Lesbos and gave out oracles from a hollow in the earth'. The Orphic oracle continued its prophesying there until Apollo bade it stop.

Mircea Eliade places the myth of Orpheus in a shamanistic tradition on account of the descent into the underworld as well as the dismemberment and the singing head (as noted above, the head of the shaman was often placed on a stake during the initiation rituals in the underworld, from which vantage point it could look on as its own body was taken apart). But the head of Orpheus was not the only one to give out oracles in the classical age — the head of Trophonius too lay in a hole in the ground, delivering prophecies of its own, visitors climbing down a ladder to ask the head whatever they wished to know, while Cleomenes I of Sparta cut off the head of his friend Archonides, keeping it thereafter in a honey pot and regularly asking its advice. Aristotle writes that when a priest of Zeus Hoplosmios in Arcadia had been decapitated by a person unknown, the head would sing 'Cercidas killed man upon man' — a local man answering to the name was subsequently arrested and tried. And the Greek magical papyri cite several methods by which heads detached from their bodies may be made articulate.

Alongside the naissance of natural science and philosophy, then, we find severed heads predicting the future, corpses receiving fresh blood and coming to life again, dead souls unable to find rest, descending to the land of the dead, some (including one reported by Plato in his *Republic*) returning to tell of what they had seen there, oracles in caves, man-animals, animal-men, transformations, metamorphoses, transgression. There was something great and unfathomably ancient that could not be put to rest by the New. Or at least not at first, for they existed side by side, in the darkness of the cave and in the light outside it. But gradually, immeasurably slowly, albeit not as slowly as man had left the animals, it was indeed put to rest, and those ancient beliefs lie now inert and fossilised in our present day.

The animals were taken from the forest, some to industrial meat and milk factories to become producers of consumer goods, consigned to their designated places in the biological systems which define them, to be seen only in the highest definition and without ambiguity on the screens of our TVs, laptops and mobile devices, much as the lion and the web-footed bird, for instance. They may still be found in the wild (though the forest shrinks by the day) but what they have become to *us* are images, finally and totally disconnected from the human.

Death similarly was taken from the cave and out into the forest, out of the darkness and into the light, where it appears to us as it *is*: a slight fissure in a blood vessel in the brain, a few microscopic bacteria in the bloodstream, a tiny cell beginning to multiply in the pancreas.

What is happening here is death is becoming smaller and smaller, and so compelling has this development been that it is no longer inconceivable that death at some point will reach its nadir and vanish.

In this vision, science and religion strangely come together. Not only because medical science is now able to open our bodies, remove our inner organs — heart, lungs, kidneys — and replace them with new ones, the way shamans down the ages have described their initiation rites, but also because this, coupled with all our efforts in the field of genetics, where the cultivation of body parts and the manipulation of cells is no longer a Utopian notion but reality, allows our lives to be prolonged, and one might speculate, to the extent that ageing and all its processes are genetically determined, given to us at birth, that they might one day not only be delayed, but halted, and what we shall have then, eternal life, is, and always has been of course, principally a religious conception, as such connected with mysticism, transgression, transformation and the irrational — and until now accordingly deemed to be claptrap.

Christ emerged from the ancient world, and the story of his life contains a number of shamanistic elements, both his driving out of demons and his bringing the dead to life, but first and foremost his descending into the realm of the dead, like the shamans, like Hector, Orpheus, Odysseus and Aeneas, from where he returned and ascended into heaven. But oddly the sense of the irrational seems not to have stuck as strongly to the narrative of Jesus rousing the dead as it has to the myriad tales we know from classical antiquity that concern the same phenomenon. The madness and derangement surrounding Dionysus is completely absent when it comes to Jesus. And it is absent too in the case of the man who, from the depths of the ancient past and its reality of visions and prophecies from grottos and caves, wrote one of the most important books of the New Testament, the Revelation to John. In a grotto on the Greek island of Patmos he lay in a deep, hallucinatory sleep or trance, artificially induced or perhaps merely frothing forth from within him, and stared into the future.

John was one of many oracles of the time, but whereas the heathen visions of his peers have been lost, his own Christian ones remain: he saw the four horsemen of the Apocalypse, he saw the sea coloured red with blood, he saw the fire out of heaven — and he saw death be gone, writing: 'And in those days shall men seek death, and shall not find it; and shall desire to die, and death shall flee from them.'

This is not the same as the idea of eternal life, which came with Christianity and is related to Plato's theory of the soul; it is something different, concerning not a promised paradise, but reality. They shall seek death, he wrote, *and death shall flee from them.*

I believe 'those days' to be near. I believe 'them' to be us. But if it is the case that death one day will be gone, what then of the already dead?

*

Only a few weeks ago, I took the sleeper train across the country from Oslo. Excited about my impending journey, I arrived early at the station. There are few things I like better than travelling, and best of all is to go by train. The atmosphere of the station before the night train leaves, that childhood feeling of forbidden adventure that I always get from a late-evening departure. The passengers arriving late and scampering along the platform with their trolley suitcases trundling behind them, past those who came in good time and have already found their compartments, who are now making their farewells to people or who stand on their own and rather at a loss, heads bowed to gaze at their mobile phones. Old and young, men and women. The beautiful and the not-so-beautiful, the well dressed and the scruffy. Coarse hands ingrained with building dust, dainty unblemished hands that have only pattered the keyboard of a computer. A swish of hair and overcoat: a mother bends down to kiss the cheek of a child; next to them a man in a suit, his hands hanging awkwardly at his side as he watches. Three young men and two young women standing in a circle; one wears a backpack, a holdall clamped between her feet. A tall man with long white hair and a long nose, in a long coat, comes striding in a hurry; a musician, I think to myself, jazz, perhaps, or left-behind indie.

I had booked a double compartment and been allocated the top bunk. It was empty when I went in, and I turned on the light, put my suitcase down on the floor, took off my jacket and hung it on the hook behind the door. Although I don't usually care to install myself when I know someone else will be coming, especially a stranger, I nonetheless climbed the little ladder into my bunk and lay down to read as the sounds outside gradually seemed to converge towards departure.

Two minutes before the train was due to leave, my fellow passenger entered the compartment. He was holding his ticket in one hand, a small suitcase in the other, and stared, first at the ticket, then at the bunk number. Satisfied that they tallied, he looked up at me.

'Hello there,' he said.

'Hello,' I said.

His fleshy, suntanned face glistened in the ceiling light, while his frame was short and rather slight. He was formally dressed for the journey, I considered, in a dark suit and white shirt.

'Are you going all the way?'

'Yes,' I said. 'And you?'

He nodded and sat down on his bunk, bent forward and opened his suitcase.

'Beer?' he said.

'No, thanks,' I said. 'It's very kind of you, all the same.'

He produced a bottle from the suitcase. I did quite fancy one, but I didn't want to get too friendly with him and perhaps be compelled to talk for hours. I wanted to read for a bit, and then sleep.

'Are you scared of flying?' he said.

'No,' I said as he levered the top off with a bottle opener he apparently kept on his keyring. 'Why do you ask?'

'Not so many our age who take the sleeper across,' he said.

I turned onto my side to face the wall, making it plain that I perhaps wasn't that interested in chatting.

A whistle sounded outside and the train gradually pulled away, into the tunnel that would take us underground and lead us through the city.

He remained silent as he sat reading a magazine that lay open on his lap, taking a swig now and again from the bottle he held in his hand.

After a time, when we had left the city far behind and my book had begun slowly to slip from my hands, he spoke to me again.

'Academic, are you?' he said.

'Me? No,' I said. 'Not at all.'

'Perpetual student, then?' he said.

'I'm not sure about that,' I said.

'That book you're reading,' he said. 'It's not for the casual reader, more for people working in the field. Wouldn't you say?'

'Maybe,' I said.

'Come on!' he said. 'I'm trying to start a conversation here!'

Why hadn't I paid the extra few hundred for a single compartment?

I'd have preferred to ignore him completely, but something in me was averse to it, and I closed my book and sat up. I'd have to climb down to brush my teeth anyway.

'No need to stop reading on my account,' he said. 'Sorry to have bothered you. Go on with your book, by all means. It's late.'

'How come you know Lucius Accius?' I said.

He glanced up at me with a smile on his face.

'You sure you don't want that beer?'

'I suppose it won't do any harm,' I said.

He put his empty down on the floor, produced two more bottles, opened them and handed me one.

'I've read him,' he said. 'Only not in translation like you.'

'So you read Latin?' I said obligingly, before taking a good swig of the delicious golden-brown, bitter ale.

He nodded, clearly pleased with himself.

For some time, the only light outside had been the grey-white evening sky that was so typical of summer, the landscape occasionally opening out to accommodate a wide and gently flowing river, but now the lights of houses and buildings began flashing by.

'How come?' I said.

'My studies required so much Latin, I thought I might as well learn it properly. So I did a course in it at the same time. Has it been any use to me? No. Has it given me great pleasure? Yes.'

'So you're a doctor, then?' I said.

He nodded deliberately, scrutinising me like a teacher who had posed a difficult question and received a clever answer.

'And you are . . . ?'

'I make documentary films,' I said.

'Really,' he said. 'Any I might have seen?'

'I shouldn't think so,' I said.

'No need to be modest,' he said. 'Give me some titles.'

I'd oblige him as far as that went, I decided, then make my apologies, brush my teeth, turn the light off and sleep all the way across the fells.

'One's called *Friends for Life*,' I said.

'Oh?' he said. 'What's it about?'

'Have you heard of Smith's Friends?'

'The sect, you mean? Of course I have.'

He picked up his phone from where it lay on the bunk beside him. I realised he was googling. A moment later he looked up at me.

'Cheers, Egil,' he said, and raised his bottle. 'I'm Frank.'

The train slowed down and drew into a station. A few figures moved towards the door of our carriage. The sounds of railway travel — footsteps in the corridor, doors opening and banging shut, the rumble of the engine, muffled voices — amplified the stillness of impending night that had settled over the town and the fells that were visible beyond it.

'Are you a Christian?' he said.

I didn't reply. I didn't want to answer.

'I mean, since you made a documentary about them? They think Jesus was born human, don't they? That he didn't become divine until later. Through his deeds. Is that right?'

'Yes,' I said.

'What do you think, then?' he said.

'About what?'

'Was he born human, or was he born divine?'

'I wouldn't know,' I said.

He laughed.

'Of course not! But what do you think?'

I didn't reply. The train started moving again. Lights flicked by as we picked up speed. A car waited for green at a lonely junction. An empty room with all the lights on stood out in an office building, its furniture crying out in the glare. Then, almost abruptly, all that was to be seen were trees, pale beneath the balmy night sky.

'I'm an anaesthetist,' he said. 'For some years now, I've worked the air ambulance helicopter. It's one of the toughest jobs there is, inasmuch as we only fly out to the most serious incidents. Traffic accidents. Drownings. Strokes. Heart attacks. We go where normal ambulances can't reach. Remote villages and farms, islands far from the mainland. But I like it. It's a very special feeling, landing by a fjord in the middle of the night or early morning, descending into a drama of life and death. Because that's what it is, nearly every time.'

He fell silent.

After a moment, he looked up at me.

'How about another?'

'Go on, then. It'll have to be the last, though,' I said. 'I need to sleep before we get there.'

'Sleep's not that important,' he said.

The train was climbing, but so slowly that I only noticed when occasionally we reached a point where we could see into the valley below us.

'You mustn't think I'm mad,' he said. 'Because I'm not. But this spring just gone, some funny things started happening.'

'While you were on call?'

'That's right.'

'I'm not mad,' he said. 'But sometime during the winter I started seeing people who weren't there. Do you understand what I mean?'

'Not really,' I said.

'I was seeing more people at the scenes than the colleagues I was on
the job with could see,' he said. 'It was a while before I realised. But
when we talked about the calls we answered afterwards, I would suddenly refer to someone, an old man who'd been staring at us from the
sofa in the living room, for example, or the woman who'd been standing watching the helicopter when we landed, and my colleagues
wouldn't know what I was talking about. They hadn't noticed these
people. And when I realised this, I understood that it wasn't a matter of
them not having noticed, but that they simply couldn't see them. It was
as if they weren't there.'

'What was it you saw?' I said, though I knew the answer.

'The dead,' he said. 'I saw the dead who were there when the helicopter came.'

He paused.

'I've never told anyone before,' he said. 'I don't want to be the guy
who believes in ghosts. But you and I aren't likely to see each other
again.'

'What do you think they wanted?' I said.

'They didn't seem to want anything at all,' he said. 'They were just
there. A bit like animals, watching what was going on around them.
And in every case, it was people who had died only recently. At least,
that was the feeling I got.'

'And no one else could see them?'

'Not that I know of,' he said. 'And that's what I don't like about it.
How come I could see them and nobody else could? And why, all of a
sudden?'

He fell silent again.

I leaned back against the wall and looked at the pale, rocky landscape outside with its radiant white birch under a sky that seemed
oddly bright.

'But that's not all,' he said. 'One of them spoke to me. We were in
the parlour of a farmhouse. The man of the house, a big, old fellow,
had suffered a heart attack, and on the sofa opposite us this young lad

is sitting who no one else sees but me. Our eyes met. It's never happened before, they usually just go about in their own world. But this
lad he looked at me. And then he got up and pointed straight at me,
and said, *You are doomed*.'

'You are doomed?'

'That's right. Nothing else. We were just on our way out, but I noticed
there was a picture of him on the wall. A portrait from his confirmation. You know, taken in a studio.'

For a while, the noises of the train were all that was heard. The
wheels clacking along the tracks beneath us, the rattle and sigh of
the couplings, the faint whistle of the wind bearing down on the
carriages.

'You don't believe me,' he said.

'Of course I don't believe you,' I said. 'Or rather, I believe that you
saw what you saw. But I don't believe that what you saw was an accurate representation of reality.'

'An accurate representation of reality?' he said rather derisively.
'You'd have made a good academic. But what you're saying is that what
I saw existed only inside my head?'

'Something like that. I saw a dead person too once, my grandfather.
He was as plain to me as you are now. But he wasn't *there*. He was in my
mind.'

'What was he doing there?' said Frank, and laughed.

I smiled and lay back, and turned off the little night lamp next to my
pillow.

'Do you mind switching the ceiling light off?' I said.

He stood up without a word and did so, then lay down as I had done,
on top of his duvet.

'Would you believe me if I said the lad was right? That I *was* doomed?'

I didn't reply.

'My daughter died,' he said. 'She was six years old. Hit by a lorry on
the road outside our house. She'd just learned to ride a bike and had
only gone out to pedal about a bit in the drive. She wasn't wearing a
helmet.'

My eyes filled with tears.

He couldn't be making that up.

'Do you see now?' he said. 'It wasn't just inside my head. It really was the dead I saw.'

'I'm so sorry for your loss,' I said.

He laughed.

'I believe you!'

I couldn't go to sleep and leave him dangling like that. He was on the edge of an abyss.

But what could I say?

Nothing I said would be any help.

If I asked him about his daughter, it would allow him to talk about her, but then most likely he would break down. And if I didn't ask about her, any conversation that followed would feel inauthentic and wrong.

Someone opened the door between the carriages and the noise of the train rose abruptly, as if the door led out into a busy factory hall. When it closed again, voices were heard, passing along the corridor.

Frank got up from his bed and stepped towards the window.

'Do you mind if I open it just a crack?' he said.

'Not at all,' I said.

'It's the hottest summer on record, they say.'

'So I've heard,' I said.

He drew the top part of the window down a measure, and a draught came flapping in.

'Are you married?' he said, pressing his brow to the pane.

'Divorced,' I said.

'Why?'

None of your business, I thought. But I couldn't snub him now.

I drew myself up onto my elbows.

'I couldn't stick it.'

'Simple as that!' he said with a laugh, and then turned to face me. 'What was she like?'

'There were different sides to her.'

'Too much for you?'

'No, it wasn't that. At least, I don't think so. But she was always looking for an argument.'

'And you weren't?'

'No.'

'You'd rather sit in a chair and read Lucius Accius?'

He was mocking me, and a shadow fell over me. He must have realised, for his tone changed immediately.

'I'm divorced as well,' he said. 'Twice, actually. Officially because I spend too much time working. Unofficially because I couldn't keep my hands to myself.'

He sat down on his bunk again.

'But it goes deeper than that, of course.'

'Of course,' I said.

He was quiet for some time. I lay down again and closed my eyes. I heard him settle too.

'I've not been a particularly good person,' he said then. 'Not that I failed, because I never set out to be one either. Why should I? We're here for a while, then when we die it's all forgotten. Including what was good about us. Do you know what I'm saying? We might as well *live*. Go your own way, that's what I've always thought. Or perhaps not *thought* as such, but it's certainly how I've lived.'

'And now you've stopped?' I said.

He didn't reply at first, and I imagined him shaking his head down there in the dark.

'I no longer know what I think,' he said after a moment. 'I don't know anything any more.'

Another pause.

'How about you?' he said. 'Are you a good person?'

'I don't know,' I said. 'It depends on what you mean by good, I suppose.'

'What was your wife's name?'

'Camilla.'

'Like the girl in *When the Robbers Came to Cardamom Town*?'

'I think that was Camomilla,' I said.

'You're right,' he said, and laughed again. 'But were you good to her? Did you care about her? I mean genuinely *care*? Did you think about what it was like to be her? What she wanted? What she wanted you to do? Did you turn yourself towards her, fully and with all your heart? At least occasionally?'

'I don't know,' I said.

'You don't know? Well, I'll tell you. You didn't. Am I right?'

'Perhaps,' I said. 'But there are two in a relationship.'

'That's where you're wrong! A good person gives without expecting anything in return. You've got to be unselfish.'

'But that's cancelling yourself out,' I said.

'To you, yes. But not necessarily to her. Anyway, I'm speculating now. I never did myself. Care like that. Which is fair enough. But what gets me now is that I didn't care about Emma either. Not properly. I thought she was lovely and all that, and she gave me joy. But I didn't really *care*.'

'Emma? That was your daughter?'

'That's right. With emphasis on the *was*.'

Again, he paused.

'What do you think about that?' he said then.

'About how you related to her?'

'Yes.'

'I think it was enough that she gave you joy and that she knew that.'

'That's not what you think at all,' he said. 'You're just saying that because you think it suits me. But we don't know each other. And we're never going to see each other again. We might as well be honest.'

'But it is what I think,' I said.

'Have you got kids?'

'Yes. A boy aged ten. He lives with his mother.'

'Right, so you're most probably talking about yourself. Listen, I've got a bottle of cognac here too. How about we have some of that?'

We sat there and drank through the night, talking about our lives as we crossed the fells, their wild, faintly illuminated expanses, before descending into the valley, following a river that hurtled over its rapids and gleamed in the sun of morning below green hillsides. Gradually, I let go of myself completely, saying things I'd never said to anyone, he likewise, though the whole time I felt a nagging doubt as to whether what he was telling me was in fact true, or whether he was making things up, or at least embellishing the truth, wishing primarily to be distracted from his own thoughts. At one point I even wondered if his daughter

really was dead. At the same time, I found it so edifying to talk to someone in such a way, quite freely, that sometimes I was convinced he'd
been sent to me. That he brought with him a message, to me.

I was drunk by the time the train pulled into the station, though in
full control of myself and with the strong feeling that the alcohol had
lit a flame inside me that now burned brightly and would consume my
every problem. It was as if anything were possible all of a sudden.

I stood on the platform outside the carriage and waited for Frank.

'I suppose this is where we say our goodbyes?' I said when he
emerged.

'That would be a waste of good cognac,' he said, extending the handle of his trolley suitcase. 'Have you got any plans for the morning?
Meeting anyone?'

I shook my head and we went towards the exit. Sunlight flooded the
old station building, flashing in every surface of metal and glass.

'The funeral doesn't start until eleven,' he said without looking at
me. 'How about keeping me company until then?'

'The funeral?' I said. 'You mean your daughter's?'

He nodded.

My blood ran cold.

Wasn't she even buried yet?

Oh, no, no, no.

'Of course,' I said. 'Where do you want to go?'

'I'm booked into the Hotell Norge. We can have a drink there. You
don't have to stay that long. Only I don't feel like being on my own just
for the moment.'

'I quite understand,' I said. 'No problem.'

'Where are you staying?'

'A hotel on the Torgellmenningen. I can't remember what it's called.'

'The Norge will be posher, then,' he said. 'How come the son of a
wealthy man like your father doesn't stay at the best hotels?'

'It doesn't matter to me,' I said, and he glanced at me sceptically.

I bought some cigarettes at the Narvesen and smoked one as we
walked past the pond in the centre of town, another before we reached
the hotel.

I sat down in reception while he checked in.

'We can stay down here,' he said. 'It's a bit more adult than drinking in the room, don't you think?'

'Yes, fine,' I said. A wave of fatigue came over me, so if I was going to stay upright, I'd need something more to drink.

'I don't know about you, but I could do with some breakfast,' he said after popping up to the room to dump his suitcase.

The change of environment had altered everything, it was as if we had nothing left to talk about, didn't know each other at all, and were as different as two people could be, I thought in the silence as we ate.

Afterwards, we downed a few beers. I'd just started wondering how I was going to get away without him feeling offended, when he asked if I would go with him to the funeral.

'Would that be appropriate?' I said. 'I didn't know Emma.'

'You know me.'

'In a way,' I said.

'You know me better than anyone, I can assure you. Say you will, and I'll stop pestering you.'

'Of course I'll go with you,' I said. 'I haven't got any suitable clothes, though.'

'For crying out loud, man,' he said. 'It's a *funeral*. Everything's over. It's all darkness and misery. Who the hell cares about clothes?'

A few minutes before half past ten, we got into a taxi up at Teaterbakken. Frank was drunk, his face stiff and inscrutable, his movements as if incomplete. I was drunk too, though not as conspicuously as he was; a person would have to know me in order to tell.

There were a lot of people outside the church, women in black dresses, men in black suits, many wearing sunglasses, most relatively young, many in their thirties. The mood was restless and uncertain in the way that is characteristic of those moments that precede the security of the ritual. Nervous smiles, awkward glances. Someone crying.

'Give me a smoke,' said Frank, stopping at the gate.

I handed him the packet and my lighter.

He lit up and inhaled deeply.

'Do I look drunk?' he said.

'A bit,' I said.

'I'm drunk for her,' he said. 'Nothing means anything any more now that she's dead.'

'I understand,' I said.

'I'm honouring her memory,' he said, and peered at me with narrow eyes, swaying slightly on his feet.

The church bells began to ring.

'It's time,' he said, dropping his cigarette to the ground and stepping on it. I touched his shoulder.

'My deepest regrets,' I said.

He looked at me and laughed.

'Yes, it is certainly regretful. Come on, let's go inside!'

Everyone stared at us as we crossed the open area in front of the church. Frank did not return their looks, his eyes fixed ahead as he propelled himself forward in the stiff and measured manner of the inebriated. But people weren't just looking at us, they were looking at each other too, and whispers were heard.

'I'll just sit at the back here,' I said when we entered and I saw the white coffin in front of the altar, so very small. The coffin and the floor surrounding it were awash with floral tributes.

'No, come and sit with me at the front,' he said.

'I can't,' I said. 'That's only for the family.'

I slipped into the nearest row. He nodded to himself and carried on down the aisle to the front pews. No one seated there acknowledged him. They made room without a word.

What had he done?

What was his sin?

The church filled up in the silence of all funerals, heard in the rustle of clothing, the cautious whisper, the clacking heels of best shoes on the stone floor.

The priest appeared from the sacristy, and I was stunned. I'd known her once, we'd been in the same class at gymnasium school.

I had even loved her.

Kathrine, I said to myself. So this is where you are.

She halted in front of the coffin and lowered her head as the organist struck up the prelude of the first hymn. I picked up the hymn book from the back of the bench in front of me, opened it and followed the words without joining in, listening as she led the mourners in song, her voice confident and comforting, and rather splendid in an unadorned kind of way.

A flower so fine in the forest I see
'Neath the pines which tower so high
Lo, from the moss there and heather doth peep
A bloom so delicate and shy!

O, art thou afraid to be thus so concealed
Where shadows must darken thy light?
— No, for the Lord is my meadow and field
His sunshine from Heaven so bright!

But wouldst thou not in a garden grow tall
Where folk would come and behold thee?
— O, no, for I thrive with the little and small
A flower of the forest is me!

And though I am little the Lord holds me dear
He makes me so happy of heart
Each morning I pray to Heaven sincere
And with prayer to sleep I depart!

As flowers in winter I must wither and die
Yet death with but joy I shall meet
For my body at peace in God's earth shall lie
And my soul shall be God's to greet!

When the music faded away, sobbing broke out here and there. Even I, who had not known the girl whose funeral it was, had tears in my eyes. There was so much pain in the church that it was almost unbearable.

'Grace to you and peace from God our Father and the Lord Jesus Christ,' said Kathrine. Her voice was warm and relaxed. She directed her gaze at the first rows of benches, as if to make contact with some-one there. I liked the calmness of her manner, and her face was as beautiful as I remembered it, though with more of an edge about it now, a severity even, as if she had been sharpened by life.

'We are gathered here today to say a last farewell to Emma Johansen,' she said. 'Together, we will surrender her into God's hands and follow her to her final resting place. For God so loved the world that He gave His one and only Son, that whoever believes in him shall not perish but have eternal life. Let us pray.'

She bowed her head. I bowed mine, and folded my hands together.

'My God, my God, why have you forsaken me? Why are you so far from saving me, so far from my cries of anguish? My God, I cry out by day, but you do not answer, by night, but I find no rest. But you, Lord, do not be far from me. You are my strength; come quickly to help me!'

I looked up and saw Kathrine ascend to the pulpit, where she placed a hand on the rail on each side and looked out over the gathering of mourners. It was as if the air trembled, sniffles and sobs could be heard, and occasional whimpering.

'Emma is dead,' she said. 'Emma, so dearly cherished by so many, has been taken from us. And Emma was only six years old. There is no greater grief. There is no deeper despair. The death of a child is the night of life. Today, we shall say our farewell to Emma, and we shall share our memories of her — and those memories are bright. Emma was a tiny star. She was born on the sixth of October, two weeks overdue, her two brothers, Emil and Noa, having waited so patiently for her to arrive. She smiled for the first time when she was ten days old, began to walk at eleven months, and spoke her first word at the age of one. Emma was a happy, giddy little girl who loved animals, especially dogs, and there was nothing she liked better than to go for walks with her mummy Monica and Kasper the golden retriever. Emma was kind and considerate, she had a big heart for others, and filled the house with joy. Her laughter was infectious, she could make everyone laugh. Emma was a master of the jigsaw puzzle. She enjoyed drawing and painting, and loved to wear clothes with unicorn designs.'

It was insufferable to listen to. But I could hardly get up and leave, not during the memorial tributes, nor after them either.

I looked at the coffin as Kathrine held forth about the girl inside it.

A deluge of flowers.

This was God. A deluge of life. A deluge of death. White flowers with green leaves. It wasn't about our individual destinies and fates, but rather the inevitable lifeslide of which we all were a part.

No one was to blame for the child's death. No one to whom one's anger and grief could be directed.

No one was God.

'Emma was a tiny flower in the great forest,' said Kathrine. 'Now, Emma is a light in the darkness. Those who were closest to her will remember and miss her always.'

God was no one.

In the first row of benches, someone rose abruptly. It was Frank. He forged a path into the aisle on unsteady legs, his eyes fixed harshly on the floor in front of him.

A faint gasp went through the great space. His face was inscrutable, but as he looked up on his way down the aisle, I saw his eyes were filled with rage.

Kathrine was no longer speaking.

Frank paused at the row where I was seated.

'Are you coming?' he said, and smiled.

The rest of the day and evening were terrible. I couldn't leave him on his own in the state he was in, but I couldn't help him either, other than by staying with him and offering my company, which wasn't really worth much, as he and I both knew, since I was not a proper friend, but someone he had met on a train and was now hanging out with.

'Why did you get up and go?' I said, when half an hour later we sat drinking beer outside a cafe on the Bryggen quayside.

'I couldn't bear to share her with everyone,' he said, staring out across the harbour, Vågen, whose dark blue waters lay heavy and still against the quays.

'The priest was talking as if she knew her. She didn't. And hardly anyone else there did either.'

He looked at me.

'What do I do now, Egil? I've got maybe forty years left to live. And nothing to live for.'

I swallowed a mouthful of beer and wiped the froth from my lips.

I could say he had to accept his loss and live on with the memories, and that one day perhaps they would be less painful. But it would just be words, unfounded in experience, worthless.

'I don't know,' I said.

'No, I don't suppose you do,' he said. 'But do you at least believe what I told you on the train?'

'About the dead people you saw?'

'Yes. In particular the one who told me I was doomed.'

'Something in you saw them. I believe that.'

He stared at me for a long time. His gaze was like the ones you can encounter in clubs and bars late at night when someone has decided they're looking for trouble. But then he let it drop, leaned back in his chair and looked out across the water again.

High above us in the sky, some gulls circled. Their occasional cries were distant.

'I'm sorry I can't be more of a help,' I said.

'You've been a great help,' he said without looking at me. 'I just need to get through today, that's all. And tomorrow. My problem is that I don't know why. And don't tell me to get counselling, please!'

He laughed bleakly.

A gaggle of tourists straggled past, trailing a guide who was wearing shorts and holding a stick in the air with a little red pennant on top. He was in his mid-twenties, the tourists all pensioners, but it still looked like a nursery school outing.

'Are you having another?' I said.

'That's the cleverest thing you've said all day,' he said.

We drank another couple of beers there on the Bryggen before going into town and finding a restaurant for something to eat. I ordered a chateaubriand with fried potatoes, starving as always after a funeral. The first time was when my grandfather died and they had served soup in the community hall afterwards. The salty meat and the vegetables had tasted so good, and my hunger was so insatiable that three portions had been barely enough. Since then I've found it to be the case on every occasion, including the one I describe here, where I sat next to the wall in a French restaurant in the company of a man I didn't know, who had just buried his daughter.

I knew the situation required restraint, but he had himself over-stepped just about every imaginable boundary that day, so I considered a good meal to be admissible once the chance came round.

We hardly spoke, immersed in our own thoughts at the table — or rather, I don't suppose Frank had that many thoughts, for he was in thrall to his emotions, held captive in their darkness. Now and again, he would glance up at me, often smiling faintly.

'You're hungry, I see,' he said eventually.

My mouth was full of food, and all I could do was nod.

'Funerals do that to people,' he said. 'Give them appetite for life.'

'I'm sorry,' I said. 'It must seem incredibly insensitive of me. But all that drinking has made me ravenous.'

'Worse things have happened today,' he said. 'And a lining on your stomach helps with the booze.'

We enjoyed a few glasses of cognac after the meal, a 1973 vintage, its taste unruly and wild, which was only natural, for it had lived an entire life sealed from the world, only then to be released inside us.

'I know you want to go now,' he said as we waited for the bill. 'And I understand that. But I'd like you to hang around if possible, until this day's over. I'll be fine in the morning. But I can't cope today if I'm on my own. I know it's a big ask. Perhaps you could think of it as a good deed?'

'Thou art my neighbour,' I said. 'I'll see you all the way to the door.'

'You *are* a Christian!' he said. 'I knew you were!'

I said nothing. 'Christian' seemed so rigid; that wasn't what I was.

The sun was still high in the sky when we emerged onto the square and found it teeming with life. Again, I found myself thinking of del-uge: a deluge of people, a deluge of events, a deluge of movements great and small. Heads bending towards the ground, turning this way and that; hands waving in the air, gripping carrier bags, lifting glasses, tying shoelaces; glances here, glances there; loud voices, low voices; laughter, deep and rumbling, or shrill in the register's upper reaches.

All that appeared before the eyes disappeared again in the very next instant.

That too was a form of death, was it not?

But what then was fate? Fate, which connected the one with the other and allowed it to prevail?

Kathrine had not disappeared, she had come back.

Was that why Frank had been delivered to me?

Or was it to teach me about death and the dead?

'Where do you fancy going?' Frank said. 'Maybe you know of a good cafe somewhere?'

'I'm not sure,' I said. 'I haven't been here for years. Last time I was here, there was a kind of arts venue further along by the water. It was a good place to sit.'

'I know where it is,' he said. 'The walk will do us good, too.'

We stopped for a beer in a place down the hill from the theatre, it was packed with punters, and then we had another, with a Fernet-Branca chaser, even though we both agreed it wasn't a drink for hot weather. Frank seemed to have gained some equilibrium, but still barely spoke, so it was hard to tell what was going on inside him.

On our way along the Nordnes point, passing through an avenue of chestnut trees where there were no more shops or restaurants, he started talking again.

'Monica turned the kids against me. She was so angry about the divorce, you've no idea. And since this happened, the reason you're walking here with me now, she's shut me out completely. Won't let me see the boys, or the house we lived in together. She's taken my grief away from me too.'

He glanced at me with drunken eyes.

'Which is only to be expected, I suppose. I wasn't that bothered. They were all right, I was all right. It was an OK deal. Only now Emma's in the ground, and it's so terrible. It's so terrible.'

He shook his head in despair, and I put my hand on his shoulder. He looked at me as if I'd gone mad, and I withdrew it again.

'In the *ground*,' he said. 'She can't talk. Do you understand what I'm saying? She can't move. She can't even think! She's lying there completely still and alone. It's so terrible. And then that cunt of a priest with her hymn about the little flower in the forest. And what else did she say, that Emma was a star in the sky? She's nothing! Nothing! Nothing!'

He swiped the air in front of him, once for every 'nothing'.

And after that he looked at me and smiled.

'I'm really sorry to have dragged you into this. But there's a good chance you'll remember this day for a while. And that's something, I suppose.'

'Yes,' I said, not knowing what else to say.

He blew out some air.

'Let's find that place you were talking about and get drunk,' he said.

'Sounds like a good plan,' I said.

We followed the road along, but we must have made a wrong turn at some point because all of a sudden we found ourselves at the aquarium instead. The car park was packed with tourist buses and there was a long queue to get in.

'There's bound to be a restaurant inside where we can get a beer,' said Frank.

'We'll have to queue up though,' I said.

'True,' he said. 'Anyway, they've probably only got bottled. No time for that. Maybe if we go that way instead?'

He nodded towards a narrow road on the other side of the point. I lit a cigarette and smoked it as we went. The rush I'd felt from the alcohol was beginning to subside, an enormous fatigue taking its place.

The road we followed took us down towards the fjord. After a bit, an outdoor swimming baths appeared just below us. It had a white-painted pool with a diving tower and springboards, and beside it was a children's pool. The grassy areas surrounding it, leading up to where we stood, were brimful of people sitting around on rugs and towels with their picnic baskets and whatnot, children running about in trunks and bathing suits.

'We used to come here,' said Frank.

'You and . . . ?'

'Me and the kids, yes,' he said. 'You don't have to be so afraid of mentioning them, by the way.'

He put his hands on the railing and stood looking down on the life that abounded there. Against the great blue sky, the still blue of the fjord, with the green fells and hills in the background, the bathers with all their paraphernalia were a patchwork of colour.

Suddenly, he raised his arm and pointed. His mouth opened, though without a word escaping.

'What?' I said.

'Over there,' he said. 'Can you see her? Under that tree. By that yel-low mountain bike?'

I looked. A little girl was sitting with her arms folded around her knees.

'I can see a girl?' I said, immediately feeling the urge to move on before the situation escalated, realising straight away what he was thinking. That it was Emma.

'It's Emma,' he said. 'It's my little Emma.'

He started towards the entrance, breaking into a run.

'Frank,' I said. 'It's not her. It's just someone who looks like her.'

He wasn't listening. I hurried after him. I had to make sure he didn't make a scene in there.

I caught up with him as he reached the lawns. He moved as quickly as he could among the sunbathers, the towels that were spread out on the grass.

'Frank,' I said as gently as I could. 'You don't know what you're doing any more. Come with me instead. Leave her alone.'

He halted and looked at me. His eyes flashed.

'You shut it!' he hissed.

'All right, all right,' I said.

He walked towards her, slowing as he came closer. The girl did not look at us, but sat unmoving under the tree, gazing in the direction of the swimming pool. Frank crouched down in front of her. I pulled up a few paces behind him.

'Emma,' he said, 'I'm so sorry. I'm so terribly sorry. You're the most precious little girl in all the world. Do you know that?'

She gave no indication of even noticing he was there. All she did was stare into space.

A sliver of doubt crept into my mind as I noticed that her T-shirt was flecked with what appeared to be blood.

'Say something to me, Emma. Anything at all. I love you. I love you, my petal.'

She stood up, and a chill went through me. The right side of her head was crushed.

'Don't go,' said Frank. 'Not now that I've found you again.'

She walked up the slope towards the fence where there was some thick shrubbery, and then she was gone.

Frank put his head in his hands. I turned round. Everyone looked away abruptly, as people do when caught staring.

It couldn't be true.

It could only be a hallucination.

But we'd both seen her.

Was I now so completely on Frank's wavelength as to have been induced to see the same as him?

He straightened up and without looking at me began to walk back. I followed him. People had lost their inhibitions now and watched us as we wove our way between them.

Why had no one else seen the girl?

And why had *I* seen her?

Emerging onto the road again, Frank walked faster than before.

'Now do you believe me?' he said as I caught up. His face was wet with tears.

I nodded.

'I don't want to believe you, but I believe you,' I said.

'Now let's get drunk and forget all about it,' he said, and looked at me with what I understood was supposed to be a smile, but which in fact was a grimace, his upper lip twisted and trembling.

'Sounds good,' I said.

I left Frank at around nine that evening, at which point he was slumped on his hotel bed asleep, and have not seen him since. I have thought about him a great deal and have on a couple of occasions visited the library in the town closest to where I live to look him up on the internet, though he never told me his surname and all I have to go on is his daughter's surname, which I now assume was not his own. He knows my name though, so if he wished to make contact all he needed to do was phone.

The image of the girl in the shade beneath the tree is something I have seen every day since.

I saw her, and she was dead.

It could not be explained.

And yet it was the case.

The first thing I did when I returned to the summer house in which I live was to take from the shelf a three-volume work I have owned ever since I was a student, though without having read it, which is *The Realm of the Dead: A World History*. Its author is one Olav O. Aukrust, and the reason I bought it all those years ago was that I thought it to be by the great poet Olav Aukrust, which of course it is not — how could I ever have thought that he had written a major treatise on death without my having heard of it? — but all of a sudden my mistake stood me in good stead. I read about how the Babylonians, the Egyptians and the Greeks perceived death, as well as about various Gnostic conceptions, and how the death realm was imagined in the Viking Age, in the medieval period, in Indian, Tibetan and Chinese cultures, and of more modern takes such as are found in parapsychology and spiritism.

I travelled to London and visited my father, though not because I had read Swedenborg, who of course postulates a London beneath London, for his visions were, I believe, the result of pathological delusions combined with megalomania. No, I spent my time browsing the new and second-hand bookshops in search of books concerning the dead. There was no shortage of literature on the subject, for life after death has been a keen interest of all cultures. As far back as we can see, to the very origins of written language, man has concerned himself with what occurs following death. The written language forms the horizon of our cultures, as death forms the horizon of our lives, and that we should turn so immediately to address death in our writing may be as strange as it is understandable. But whereas the visible, tangible world has been explored and charted through centuries, meaning ostensibly that no mysteries remain to us, only facts that continue to slot into place in our constantly modified theories of reality, our insight into death has not changed. Einstein knew as little about death as did the first cave dwellers. In the slow process by which natural science over centuries has diminished the size of truth so considerably in its quest to discover the smallest possible entity, which is the particle of the atom, thereby to explain the world from *that* vantage point, death has been given no place. In earlier models of explanation such as those obtaining in classical antiquity or in the European Middle Ages, truth was sought in the antipole of the particle, which is to say in the world's very complexity, and from such a holistic perspective, however incorrect it may seem from our own vantage point, death was accorded an important place.

What do we do about what we can sense, but cannot know?

We close our eyes to it.

We are rather like the drunk standing under the lamp post late at night, staring at the illuminated ground at his feet when a passer-by stops to enquire if he is looking for something. He nods and says he is looking for his key. The passer-by helps him search, but the key is nowhere to be found. Is he sure he lost it just there? No, says the drunk, pointing away into the darkness, I lost it over there. But I'm never going to find it there, so I'm looking here in the light.

I returned from London with my suitcase filled with books, and more on their way in the post. I could not forget that I had seen a dead girl sitting by an outdoor swimming pool, silent and withdrawn, dressed in the clothes she had been wearing when she died, nor could I pretend not to have seen her. So I began to write about it, and about what it could mean. And as I wrote, it was as if something opened up inside me, I began to understand to what great extent our language constrains the world, arranging it and placing its various elements in logical systems that are of such nature that we see neither the system nor the logic, only the world it presents to us. I saw the gulls sailing high under the blue sky, I heard their cries and understood that they, as us, were living creatures, without name, boundless, free. Their soul was something that lifted in the world, opening wide to become a presence, and it was unthinkable, unthinkable to them that such presence could ever cease. I saw the oak trees in the woods behind the house, so ponderous and calm, and I saw that they too, as us, were living things, without name, boundless and free. In glimpses I saw the world behind language, a world of transformation and mystery, and one night I saw my mother, Torill, in a dream. Which is to say that I was asleep and images filled my mind, but the nature of those images seemed in no way random as is the case with most dreams, or at least mine. No, it was as if Torill had been waiting for me in that dream, and was already there when I came. I walked towards the jetty, the sea was grey and made choppy by the wind, the waves were topped with white, and I saw that someone was there, someone in a yellow waterproof, and as I stepped out onto the jetty, the figure turned and it was her.

'Egil,' she said. 'My child.'

I said nothing.

'I never understood who you were. I'm sorry if it made things difficult for you.'

'Not at all,' I said.

'I was not a good mother to you. To your brothers, yes, but not to you.'

'You were a fine mother, of course you were,' I said.

She stepped towards me and zipped up my anorak, as she always used to.

The next thing I knew, I was staring at the ceiling in my bedroom. I got up and pulled the curtains open. The sea was grey and choppy, the waves topped with white. The jetty slippy-looking with rain.

But there was no woman there in a yellow waterproof.

Foxes emerged, and deer in the fields beyond the road. The weather grew warmer. One morning, an enormous flock of black birds settled on the rocks at the shore. I have never seen anything quite like it, there must have been thousands. They remained there, huddled together for several hours, before taking off all at once, a gigantic black cloud rising into the sky, a shifting curtain of flesh, almost as one, to disappear over the trees across the inlet.

And last night a new star appeared in the sky.

It shines above me now.

The Morning Star.

I know what it means.

It means that it has begun.

Acknowledgements

Thanks to Henry Marsh, Pål-Dag Line, Cecilie Jørgensen Strømmen and Naomi and Yaron Shavit for invaluable help with things I know nothing about, and to Bjørn Arild and Kari Ersland, Yngve Knausgård, Monika Fagerholm, Birgit Bjerck and Kristine Næss for reading the manuscript as it progressed.

Credits

Quotes are from the following works.

Aristotle, *On Philosophy*, cited in a fragment by Sextus Empiricus found in *Aristotle: New Light on His Life and on Some of His Lost Works* (transl. A.-H. Chroust), Routledge & K. Paul, 1973

Johan Alfred Blomberg, 'A Flower So Fine in the Forest I See', 1890 (transl. Martin Aitken)

Hesiod, 'Theogony', *The Homeric Hymns and Homerica* (transl. Hugh G. Evelyn-White), Harvard University Press, 1914

Friedrich Hölderlin, 'Timidity' (transl. Stanley Corngold), found in 'Two Poems by Friedrich Hölderlin', *Walter Benjamin: Selected Writings*, Volume 1, 1913–1926, ed. by Marcus Bullock and Michael W. Jennings, 18–36, Harvard University Press, 2004

B.S. Ingemann, 'Deilig er jorden' (Danish: 'Dejlig er jorden'), found in *Fashioners of Faith: The Danish Hymn-Writers Kingo, Brorson, Grundtvig and Ingemann* (transl. John Irons), University of Southern Denmark Press, 2018

Søren Kierkegaard, *The Lily of the Field and the Bird of the Air: Three Godly Discourses* (transl. Bruce H. Kirmmse), Princeton University Press, 2016

Friedrich Nietzsche, cited in Carl Kerényi, *Dionysos: Archetypal Image of Indestructible Life* (transl. Ralph Manheim), Princeton University Press, 1996

Theodor V. Oldenburg, 'Deep and Glorious, Word Victorious' (transl. Carl Doving)

Philostratus, *Heroicus*, cited in Daniel Ogden, *Greek and Roman Necromancy*, Princeton University Press, 2001

Rainer Maria Rilke, 'The Book of Monastic Life', *The Book of Hours*, found in *Selected Poems of Rainer Maria Rilke* (transl. Robert Bly), Harper Perennial, 1981

Verses cited in the funeral service are from the Church of Norway's official order for a funeral (https://kirken.no/nb-NO/church-of-norway/worship-and-church-services/) and The Apostles' Creed is from the Order of the Principle Service (https://kirken.no/globalassets/kirken.no/om-troen/liturgier-oversatt/the-order-of-the-principal-service.pdf). Erlend's draft translation is an adapted version of Leviticus 3:12-17 from the New Revised Standard Version, Anglicised Edition. Other quotes are from the King James Version.

THE LEOPARD

The leopard is one of Harvill's historic colophons and an imprimatur of the highest quality literature from around the world.

When The Harvill Press was founded in 1946 by former Foreign Office colleagues Manya Harari and Marjorie Villiers (hence Har-vill), it was with the express intention of rebuilding cultural bridges after the Second World War. As their first catalogue set out: 'The editors believe that by producing translations of important books they are helping to overcome the barriers, which at present are still big, to close interchange of ideas between people who are divided by frontiers.' The press went on to publish from many different languages, with highlights including Giuseppe Tomasi di Lampedusa's *The Leopard*, Boris Pasternak's *Doctor Zhivago*, José Saramago's *Blindness*, W. G. Sebald's *The Rings of Saturn*, Henning Mankell's *Faceless Killers* and Haruki Murakami's *Norwegian Wood*.

In 2005 The Harvill Press joined with Secker & Warburg, a publisher with its own illustrious history of publishing international writers. In 2020, Harvill Secker reintroduced the leopard to launch a new translated series celebrating some of the finest and most exciting voices of the twenty-first century.

Laurent Binet: *Civilisations*
    trans. Sam Taylor
Paolo Cognetti: *Without Ever Reaching the Summit*
    trans. Stash Luczkiw
Pauline Delabroy-Allard: *All About Sarah*
    trans. Adriana Hunter
Urs Faes: *Twelve Nights*
    trans. Jamie Lee Searle

Ismail Kadare: *The Doll*
  trans. John Hodgson
Jonas Hassen Khemiri: *The Family Clause*
  trans. Alice Menzies
Karl Ove Knausgaard: *In the Land of the Cyclops: Essays*
  trans. Martin Aitken
Karl Ove Knausgaard: *The Morning Star*
  trans. Martin Aitken
Geert Mak: *The Dream of Europe*
  trans. Liz Waters
Haruki Murakami: *First Person Singular: Stories*
  trans. Philip Gabriel
Haruki Murakami: *Murakami T: The T-Shirts I Love*
  trans. Philip Gabriel
Ngũgĩ wa Thiong'o: *The Perfect Nine: The Epic of Gĩkũyũ and Mũmbi*
  trans. the author
Intan Paramaditha: *The Wandering*
  trans. Stephen J. Epstein
Per Petterson: *Men in My Situation*
  trans. Ingvild Burkey
Dima Wannous: *The Frightened Ones*
  trans. Elisabeth Jaquette